THE SWEDISH EMPIRE

DENMARK-NORWAY

CHRISTIANIA

STOCKHOLM

GOTLAND

ÖLAND

THE BALTIC SEA

BORNHOLM

COPENHAGEN

Goteborg

COURLAND

Mitau

Riga

KÖNIGSBERG

VILNIUS

PRUSSIA

HOLSTEIN

Rostock

POMERANIA

Gdańsk

MECKLENBURG

Lübeck

Stettin

Bremen

BRANDENBURG

Posen

Hanover

BERLIN

Magdeburg

Warsaw

THE POLISH-LITHUANIAN COMMONWEALTH

Cologne

SAXONY

Bel...

KINGDOM OF BOHEMIA

THE HOLY ROMAN EMPIRE

Teutenberg

PRAGUE

KRAKOW

Lwow

Kiev

Zhytomir

Schweinfurt

REGENSBURG

Nürnberg

Ammendorf

KINGDOM OF HUNGARY

PRESSBURG

WALDENSTEIN

VIENNA

Munich

MIRENBURG

Buda

PRINCIPALITY OF MOLDAVIA

Iasi

PRINCIPALITY OF TRANSYLVANIA

Basel

ARCHDUCHY OF AUSTRIA

Alba Iulia

Odessa

VENICE

MILAN

Verona

VENICE

ISTRIA

Brescia

Zadar

Belgrade

Targoviste

Tulcea

PRINCIPALITY OF WALLACHIA

Cremona

GENOA

Florence

THE BLACK SEA

TUSCANY

DALMATIA

Ragusa

Sofia

Varna

THE PAPAL STATES

CORSICA

ROME

ADRIATIC SEA

THE OTTOMAN EMPIRE

Edirne

CONSTANTINOPLE

NAPLES

SARDINIA

KINGDOM OF NAPLES

Salonica

TYRRHENIAN SEA

Cagliari

AEGEAN SEA

ANATOLIA

Smyrna

Ankara

Palermo

SICILY

Syracuse

Athens

MOREA

Tunis

MALTA

TUNIS

CRETE

Candia

THE MEDITERRANEAN SEA

Von Bek

Also by Michael Moorcock

A Cornelius Calendar
comprising—
The Adventures of Una Persson
and Catherine Cornelius in
the Twentieth Century
The Entropy Tango
The Great Rock 'n" Roll Swindle
The Alchemist's Question
Firing the Cathedral/Modem
Times 2.0

The Eternal Champion
comprising—
The Eternal Champion
Phoenix in Obsidian
The Dragon in the Sword

The Dancers at the
End of Time
comprising—
An Alien Heat
The Hollow Lands
The End of all Songs

Kane of Old Mars
comprising—
Warriors of Mars
Blades of Mars
Barbarians of Mars

Moorcock's Multiverse
comprising—
The Sundered Worlds
The Winds of Limbo
The Shores of Death

The Nomad of Time
comprising—
The Warlord of the Air
The Land Leviathan
The Steel Tsar

Travelling to Utopia
comprising—
The Wrecks of Time
The Ice Schooner
The Black Corridor

The War Amongst the Angels
comprising—
Blood: A Southern Fantasy
Fabulous Harbours
The War Amongst the Angels

Tales From the End of Time
comprising—
Legends from the End of Time
Constant Fire
Elric at the End of Time

Behold the Man

Gloriana; or, The Unfulfill'd Queen

Mother London

SHORT FICTION
My Experiences in the Third World
War and Other Stories: The Best
Short Fiction of Michael Moorcock
Volume 1

The Brothel in Rosenstrasse and
Other Stories: The Best Short Fiction
of Michael Moorcock Volume 2

Breakfast in the Ruins and Other
Stories: The Best Short Fiction of
Michael Moorcock Volume 3

Von Bek

The War Hound and the World's Pain
The City in the Autumn Stars

MICHAEL MOORCOCK

SAGA PRESS

LONDON SYDNEY **NEW YORK** TORONTO NEW DELHI

SAGA ✶ PRESS

AN IMPRINT OF SIMON & SCHUSTER, LLC

1230 AVENUE OF THE AMERICAS, NEW YORK, NEW YORK 10020

This Saga Press hardcover edition December 2024

SAGA PRESS and colophon are trademarks of Simon & Schuster, LLC

Simon & Schuster: Celebrating 100 Years of Publishing in 2024

For information about special discounts for bulk purchases, please contact Simon & Schuster Special Sales at 1-866-506-1949 or business@simonandschuster.com.

The Simon & Schuster Speakers Bureau can bring authors to your live event. For more information or to book an event, contact the Simon & Schuster Speakers Bureau at 1-866-248-3049 or visit our website at www.simonspeakers.com.

Manufactured in the United States of America

1   3   5   7   9   10   8   6   4   2

Library of Congress Control Number: 2024946769

ISBN 978-1-6680-6769-7
ISBN 978-1-6680-6771-0 (ebook)

Introduction to
The Michael Moorcock Collection
John Clute

HE IS NOW over 70, enough time for most careers to start and end in, enough time to fit in an occasional half-decade or so of silence to mark off the big years. Silence happens. I don't think I know an author who doesn't fear silence like the plague; most of us, if we live long enough, can remember a bad blank year or so, or more. Not Michael Moorcock. Except for some worrying surgery on his toes in recent years, he seems not to have taken time off to breathe the air of peace and panic. There has been no time to spare. The nearly 60 years of his active career seems to have been too short to fit everything in: the teenage comics; the editing jobs; the pulp fiction; the reinvented heroic fantasies; the Eternal Champion; the deep Jerry Cornelius riffs; NEW WORLDS; the 1970s/1980s flow of stories and novels, dozens upon dozens of them in every category of modern fantastika; the tales of the dying Earth and the possessing of Jesus; the exercises in postmodernism that turned the world inside out before most of us had begun to guess we were living on the wrong side of things; the invention (more or less) of steampunk; the alternate histories; the *Mitteleuropean* tales of sexual terror; the deep-city London riffs: the turns and changes and returns and reconfigurations to which he has subjected his oeuvre over the years (he expects this new Collected Edition will fix these transformations in place for good); the late tales where he has been remodelling the intersecting worlds he created in the 1960s in terms of twenty-first-century physics: for starters. If you can't take the heat, I guess, stay out of the multiverse.

His life has been full and complicated, a life he has exposed and hidden (like many other prolific authors) throughout his work. In *Mother London* (1988), though, a nonfantastic novel published at what is now something like the midpoint of his career, it may be possible to find the key to all the other selves who made the 100 books. There are three protagonists in the tale, which is set from about 1940 to about 1988 in the suburbs and inner runnels of the vast metropolis of Charles Dickens and Robert Louis Stevenson. The oldest of these protagonists is Joseph Kiss, a flamboyant self-advertising fin-de-siècle figure of substantial girth and a fantasticating relationship to the world: he is Michael Moorcock, seen with genial bite as a kind of G.K. Chesterton without the wearying punch-line paradoxes. The youngest of the three is David Mummery, a haunted introspective half-insane denizen of a secret London of trials and runes and codes and magic: he too is Michael Moorcock, seen through a glass, darkly. And there is Mary Gasalee, a kind of holy-innocent and survivor, blessed with a luminous clarity of insight, so that in all her apparent ignorance of the onrushing secular world she is more deeply wise than other folk: she is also Michael Moorcock, Moorcock when young as viewed from the wry middle years of 1988. When we read the book, we are reading a book of instructions for the assembly of a London writer. The Moorcock we put together from this choice of portraits is amused and bemused at the vision of himself; he is a phenomenon of flamboyance and introspection, a poseur and a solitary, a dreamer and a doer, a multitude and a singleton. But only the three Moorcocks in this book, working together, could have written all the other books.

It all began—as it does for David Mummery in *Mother London*—in South London, in a subtopian stretch of villas called Mitcham, in 1939. In early childhood, he experienced the Blitz, and never forgot the extraordinariness of being a participant—however minute—in the great drama; all around him, as though the world were being dismantled nightly, darkness and blackout would descend, bombs fall, buildings and streets disappear; and in the morning, as though a new universe had taken over from the old one and the world had become portals, the sun would rise on glinting rubble, abandoned tricycles, men and women going about their daily tasks as though nothing had happened, strange shards of ruin poking into altered air. From a very early age, Michael Moorcock's security reposed in a sense that everything might change, in the blinking of an eye, and be *rejourneyed* the next day (or the next book). Though as a writer he has certainly elucidated the fears and alarums of life in Aftermath Britain, it does seem that his very early years were marked by the epiphanies of war, rather than the inflictions of despair and beclouding amnesia most adults necessarily experienced. After the war ended, his parents separated, and the young Moorcock began to attend a pretty wide variety of schools, several of which he seems to have been expelled from, and as soon as he could legally do so he began to work full time, up north in London's heart, which he only left when he moved to Texas (with intervals in Paris) in the early 1990s, from where (to jump briefly up the decades) he continues to cast a Martian eye: as with most exiles, Moorcock's intensest anatomies of his homeland date from after his cunning departure.

But back again to the beginning (just as though we were rimming a multiverse). Starting in the 1950s there was the comics and pulp work for Fleetway Publications; there was the first book (*Caribbean Crisis*, 1962) as by Desmond Reid, co-written with his early friend the artist James Cawthorn (1929–2008); there was marriage, with the writer Hilary Bailey (they divorced in 1978), three children, a heated existence in the Ladbroke Grove / Notting Hill Gate region of London he was later to populate with Jerry Cornelius and his vast family; there was the editing of NEW WORLDS, which began in 1964 and became the heartbeat of the British New Wave two years later as writers like Brian W. Aldiss and J.G. Ballard, reaching their early prime, made it into a tympanum, as young American writers like Thomas M. Disch, John T. Sladek, Norman Spinrad and Pamela Zoline found a home in London for material they could not publish in America, and new British writers like M. John Harrison and Charles Platt began their careers in its pages; but before that there was Elric. With *The Stealer of Souls* (1963) and

Stormbringer (1965), the multiverse began to flicker into view, and the Eternal Champion (whom Elric parodied and embodied) began properly to ransack the worlds in his fight against a greater Chaos than the great dance could sustain. There was also the first SF novel, *The Sundered Worlds* (1965), but in the 1960s SF was a difficult nut to demolish for Moorcock: he would bide his time.

We come to the heart of the matter. Jerry Cornelius, who first appears in *The Final Programme* (1968)—which assembles and co-ordinates material first published a few years earlier in NEW WORLDS—is a deliberate solarisation of the albino Elric, who was himself a mocking solarisation of Robert E. Howard's Conan, or rather of the mighty-thew-headed Conan created for profit by Howard epigones: Moorcock rarely mocks the true quill. Cornelius, who reaches his first and most telling apotheosis in the four novels comprising *The Cornelius Quartet*, remains his most distinctive and perhaps most original single creation: a wide boy, an agent, a *flaneur*, a bad musician, a shopper, a shapechanger, a trans, a spy in the house of London: a toxic palimpsest on whom and through whom the *zeitgeist* inscribes surreal conjugations of "message." Jerry Cornelius gives head to Elric.

The life continued apace. By 1970, with NEW WORLDS on its last legs, multiverse fantasies and experimental novels poured forth; Moorcock and Hilary Bailey began to live separately, though he moved, in fact, only around the corner, where he set up house with Jill Riches, who would become his second wife; there was a second home in Yorkshire, but London remained his central base. *The Condition of Muzak* (1977), which is the fourth Cornelius novel, and *Gloriana; or, The Unfulfill'd Queen* (1978), which transfigures the first Elizabeth into a kinked Astraea, marked perhaps the high point of his career as a writer of fiction whose font lay in genre or its mutations—marked perhaps the furthest bournes he could transgress while remaining within the perimeters of fantasy (though *within* those bournes vast stretches of territory remained and would, continually, be explored). During these years he sometimes wore a leather jacket constructed out of numerous patches of varicoloured material, and it sometimes seemed perfectly fitting that he bore the semblance, as his jacket flickered and fuzzed from across a room or road, of an illustrated man, a map, a thing of shreds and patches, a student fleshed from dreams. Like the stories he told, he seemed to be more than one thing. To use a term frequently applied (by me at least) to twenty-first-century fiction, he seemed equipoisal: which is to say that, through all his genre-hopping and genre-mixing and genre-transcending and genre-loyal returnings to old pitches, *he was never still*, because "equipoise" is all about *making stories move*. As with his stories, he cannot be pinned down, because he is not in one place. In person and in his work, it has always been sink or swim: like a shark, or a dancer, or an equilibrist . . .

The marriage with Jill Riches came to an end. He married Linda Steele in 1983; they remain married. The Colonel Pyat books, *Byzantium Endures* (1981), *The Laughter of Carthage* (1984), *Jerusalem Commands* (1992) and *The Vengeance of Rome* (2006), dominated these years, along with *Mother London*. As these books, which are nonfantastic, are not included in the current *Michael Moorcock Collection*, it might be worth noting here that, in their insistence on the irreducible difficulty of gaining anything like true sight, they represent Moorcock's mature modernist take on what one might call the rag-and-bone shop of the world itself; and that the huge ornate postmodern edifice of his multiverse *loosens* us from that world, gives us room to breathe, to juggle our strategies for living—allows us ultimately to escape from prison (to use a phrase from a writer he does not respect, J.R.R. Tolkien, for whom the twentieth century was a prison train bound for hell). What Moorcock may best be remembered for in the end is the (perhaps unique) interplay between modernism and postmodernism in his work. (But a plethora of discordant understandings makes these terms hard to use; so enough of them.) In the end, one might just say that Moorcock's work as a whole represents an extraordinarily multifarious execution of the fantasist's main task: which is to *get us out of here*.

Recent decades saw a continuation of the multifarious, but with a more intensely applied methodology. The late volumes of the

long Elric saga, and the Second Ether sequence of meta-fantasies—
Blood: A Southern Fantasy (1995), *Fabulous Harbours* (1995) and *The War Amongst the Angels: An Autobiographical Story* (1996)—brood on the real world and the multiverse through the lens of Chaos Theory: the closer you get to the world, the less you describe it. *The Metatemporal Detective* (2007)—a narrative in the Steampunk mode Moorcock had previewed as long ago as *The Warlord of the Air* (1971) and *The Land Leviathan* (1974)—continues the process, sometimes dizzyingly: as though the reader inhabited the eye of a camera increasing its focus on a closely observed reality while its bogey simultaneously wheels it backwards from the desired rapport: an old Kurosawa trick here amplified into a tool of conspectus, fantasy eyed and (once again) rejourneyed, this time through the lens of SF.

We reach the second decade of the twenty-first century, time still to make things new, but also time to sort. There are dozens of titles in *The Michael Moorcock Collection* that have not been listed in this short space, much less trawled for tidbits. The various avatars of the Eternal Champion—Elric, Kane of Old Mars, Hawkmoon, Count Brass, Corum, Von Bek—differ vastly from one another. Hawkmoon is a bit of a berk; Corum is a steely solitary at the End of Time: the joys and doleurs of the interplays amongst them can only be experienced through immersion. And the Dancers at the End of Time books, and the Nomad of the Time Stream books, and the Karl Glogauer books, and all the others. They are here now, a 100 books that make up one book. They have been fixed for reading. It is time to enter the multiverse and see the world.

September 2012

Introduction to
The Michael Moorcock Collection
Michael Moorcock

B Y 1964, AFTER I had been editing NEW WORLDS for some
months and had published several science fiction and fantasy
novels, including *Stormbringer*, I realised that my run as a writer
was over. About the only new ideas I'd come up with were miniature computers, the multiverse and black holes, all very crudely
realised, in *The Sundered Worlds*. No doubt I would have to return
to journalism, writing features and editing. "My career," I told my
friend J.G. Ballard, "is finished." He sympathised and told me he
only had a few SF stories left in him, then he, too, wasn't sure
what he'd do.

In January 1965, living in Colville Terrace, Notting Hill, then an
infamous slum, best known for its race riots, I sat down at the
typewriter in our kitchen-cum-bathroom and began a locally
based book, designed to be accompanied by music and graphics.
The Final Programme featured a character based on a young man
I'd seen around the area and whom I named after a local green-
grocer, Jerry Cornelius, "Messiah to the Age of Science." Jerry was
as much a technique as a character. Not the "spy" some critics
described him as but an urban adventurer as interested in his
psychic environment as the contemporary physical world. My
influences were English and French absurdists, American noir
novels. My inspiration was William Burroughs with whom I'd
recently begun a correspondence. I also borrowed a few SF ideas,
though I was adamant that I was not writing in any established
genre. I felt I had at last found my own authentic voice.

I had already written a short novel, *The Golden Barge*, set in a
nowhere, no-time world very much influenced by Peake and the

surrealists, which I had not attempted to publish. An earlier auto-biographical novel, *The Hungry Dreamers*, set in Soho, was eaten by rats in a Ladbroke Grove basement. I remained unsatisfied with my style and my technique. *The Final Programme* took nine days to complete (by 20 January, 1965) with my baby daughters sometimes cradled with their bottles while I typed on. This, I should say, is my memory of events; my then wife scoffed at this story when I recounted it. Whatever the truth, the fact is I only believed I might be a serious writer after I had finished that novel, with all its flaws. But Jerry Cornelius, probably my most successful sustained attempt at unconventional fiction, was born then and ever since has remained a useful means of telling complex stories. Associated with the '60s and '70s, he has been equally at home in all the following decades. Through novels and novellas I developed a means of carrying several narratives and viewpoints on what appeared to be a very light (but tight) structure which dispensed with some of the earlier methods of fiction. In the sense that it took for granted the understanding that the novel is among other things an internal dialogue and I did not feel the need to repeat by now commonly understood modernist conventions, this fiction was post-modern.

Not all my fiction looked for new forms for the new century. Like many "revolutionaries" I looked back as well as forward. As George Meredith looked to the eighteenth century for inspiration for his experiments with narrative, I looked to Meredith, popular Edwardian realists like Pett Ridge and Zangwill and the writers of the *fin de siècle* for methods and inspiration. An almost obsessive interest in the Fabians, several of whom believed in the possibility of benign imperialism, ultimately led to my Bastable books which examined our enduring British notion that an empire could be essentially a force for good. The first was *The Warlord of the Air*.

I also wrote my *Dancers at the End of Time* stories and novels under the influence of Edwardian humourists and absurdists like Jerome or Firbank. Together with more conventional generic books like *The Ice Schooner* or *The Black Corridor*, most of that work was done in the 1960s and 70s when I wrote the Eternal Champion supernatural adventure novels which helped support my own and others' experiments via NEW WORLDS, allowing me also to keep a family while writing books in which action and fantastic invention were paramount. Though I did them quickly, I didn't write them cynically. I have always believed, somewhat puritanically, in giving the audience good value for money. I enjoyed writing them, tried to avoid repetition, and through each new one was able to develop a few more ideas. They also continued to teach me how to express myself through image and metaphor. My Everyman became the Eternal Champion, his dreams and ambitions represented by the multiverse. He could be an ordinary person struggling with familiar problems in a contemporary setting or he could be a swordsman fighting monsters on a far-away world.

Long before I wrote *Gloriana* (in four parts reflecting the seasons) I had learned to think in images and symbols through reading John Bunyan's *Pilgrim's Progress*, Milton and others, understanding early on that the visual could be the most important part of a book and was often in itself a story as, for instance, a famous personality could also, through everything associated with their name, function as narrative. I wanted to find ways of carrying as many stories as possible in one. From the cinema I also learned how to use images as connecting themes. Images, colours, music, and even popular magazine headlines can all add coherence to an apparently random story, underpinning it and giving the reader a sense of internal logic and a satisfactory resolution, dispensing with certain familiar literary conventions.

When the story required it, I also began writing neo-realist fiction exploring the interface of character and environment, especially the city, especially London. In some books I condensed, manipulated and randomised time to achieve what I wanted, but in others the sense of "real time" as we all generally perceive it was more suitable and could best be achieved by traditional nineteenth-century means. For the Pyat books I first looked back to the great German classic, Grimmelshausen's *Simplicissimus* and other early picaresques. I then examined the roots of a certain kind of moral fiction from Defoe through Thackeray and Meredith then to modern times where the picaresque (or rogue tale) can take the form of a road movie, for instance. While it's probably fair to say that Pyat and *Byzantium Endures* precipitated the end of my second marriage (echoed to a degree in *The Brothel in Rosenstrasse*), the late '70s and the '80s were exhilarating times for me, with *Mother London* being perhaps my own favourite novel of that period. I wanted to write something celebratory.

By the '90s I was again attempting to unite several kinds of fiction in one novel with my Second Ether trilogy. With Mandelbrot, Chaos Theory and String Theory I felt, as I said at the time, as if I were being offered a chart of my own brain. That chart made it easier for me to develop the notion of the multiverse as representing both the internal and the external, as a metaphor and as a means of structuring and rationalising an outrageously inventive and quasi-realistic narrative. The worlds of the multiverse move up and down scales or "planes" explained in terms of mass, allowing entire universes to exist in the "same" space. The result of developing this idea was the *War Amongst the Angels* sequence which added absurdist elements also functioning as a kind of mythology and folklore for a world beginning to understand itself in terms of new metaphysics and theoretical physics. As the cosmos becomes denser and almost infinite before our eyes, with black holes and dark matter affecting our own reality, we can explore them and observe them as our ancestors explored our planet and observed the heavens.

At the end of the '90s I'd returned to realism, sometimes with a dash of fantasy, with *King of the City* and the stories collected in *London Bone*. I also wrote a new Elric / Eternal Champion sequence, beginning with *Daughter of Dreams*, which brought the fantasy worlds of Hawkmoon, Bastable and Co. in line with my realistic and autobiographical stories, another attempt to unify all my fiction, and also offer a way in which disparate genres could be reunited, through notions developed from the multiverse and the Eternal Champion, as one giant novel. At the time I was finishing the Pyat sequence which attempted to look at the roots of the Nazi Holocaust in our European, Middle Eastern and American cultures and to ground my strange survival guilt while at the same time examining my own cultural roots in the light of an enduring anti-Semitism.

By the 2000s I was exploring various conventional ways of story-telling in the last parts of *The Metatemporal Detective* and through other homages, comics, parodies and games. I also looked back at my earliest influences. I had reached retirement age and felt like a rest. I wrote a "prequel" to the Elric series as a graphic novel with Walter Simonson, *The Making of a Sorcerer*, and did a little online editing with FANTASTIC METROPOLIS.

By 2010 I had written a novel featuring Doctor Who, *The Coming of the Terraphiles*, with a nod to P.G. Wodehouse (a boyhood favourite), continued to write short stories and novellas and to work on the beginning of a new sequence combining pure fantasy and straight autobiography called *The Whispering Swarm* while still writing more Cornelius stories trying to unite all the various genres and sub-genres into which contemporary fiction has fallen.

Throughout my career critics have announced that I'm "abandoning" fantasy and concentrating on literary fiction. The truth is, however, that all my life, since I became a professional writer and editor at the age of 16, I've written in whatever mode suits a story best and where necessary created a new form if an old one didn't work for me. Certain ideas are best carried on a Jerry Cornelius story, others work better as realism and others as fantasy or science fiction. Some work best as a combination. I'm sure I'll write whatever I like and will continue to experiment with all the ways there are of telling stories and carrying as many themes as possible. Whether I write about a widow coping with loneliness in her cottage or a massive, universe-size sentient spaceship searching for her children, I'll no doubt die trying to tell them all. I hope you'll find at least some of them to your taste.

One thing a reader can be sure of about these new editions is that they would not have been possible without the tremendous and indispensable help of my old friend and bibliographer John Davey. John has ensured that these Gollancz editions are definitive. I am indebted to John for many things, including his work at

Moorcock's Miscellany, my website, but his work on this edition has been outstanding. As well as being an accomplished novelist in his own right John is an astonishingly good editor who has worked with Gollancz and myself to point out every error and flaw in all previous editions, some of them not corrected since their first publication, and has enabled me to correct or revise them. I couldn't have completed this project without him. Together, I think, Gollancz, John Davey and myself have produced what will be the best editions possible and I am very grateful to him, to Malcolm Edwards, Darren Nash and Marcus Gipps for all the considerable hard work they have done to make this edition what it is.

Michael Moorcock

Contents

The War Hound and the World's Pain

A Fable

Being the true testimony of the Graf Ulrich von Bek, lately Commander of Infantry, written down in the Year of Our Lord 1680 by Brother Olivier of the Monastery at Renschel during the months of May and June as the said nobleman lay upon his sickbed.

(This manuscript had, until now, remained sealed within the wall of the monastery's crypt. It came to light during work being carried out to restore the structure, which had sustained considerable damage during the Second World War. It came into the hands of the present editor via family sources and appears here for the first time in a modern translation. Almost all the initial translating work was that of Prince Lobkowitz; this English text is largely the work of Michael Moorcock.)

For Jonathan Carroll

Chapter One

I T WAS IN that year when the fashion in cruelty demanded not only the crucifixion of peasant children, but a similar fate for their household animals, that I first met Lucifer and was transported into Hell; for the Prince of Darkness wished to strike a bargain with me.

Until May of 1631 I had commanded a troop of irregular infantry, mainly Poles, Swedes and Scots. We had taken part in the destruction and looting of the city of Magdeburg, having somehow found ourselves in the army of the Catholic forces under Count Johann Tzerclaes Tilly. Wind-borne gunpowder had turned the city into one huge keg and she had gone up all of a piece, driving us out with little booty to show for our hard work.

Disappointed and belligerent, wearied by the business of rapine and slaughter, quarrelling over what pathetic bits of goods they had managed to pull from the blazing houses, my men elected to split away from Tilly's forces. His had been a singularly ill-fed and badly equipped army, victim to the pride of bickering allies. It was a relief to leave it behind us.

We struck south into the foothills of the Hartz Mountains, intending to rest. However, it soon became evident to me that some of my men had contracted the Plague, and I deemed it wise, therefore, to saddle my horse quietly one night and, taking what food there was, continue my journey alone.

Having deserted my men, I was not free from the presence of death or desolation. The world was in agony and shrieked its pain.

By noon I had passed seven gallows on which men and women had been hanged and four wheels on which three men and one boy had been broken. I passed the remains of a stake at which some poor wretch (witch or heretic) had been burned: whitened bone peering through charred wood and flesh.

5

No field was untouched by fire; the very forests stank of decay. Soot lay deep upon the road, borne by the black smoke which spread from innumerable burning bodies, from sacked villages, from castles ruined by cannonade and siege; and at night my passage was often lit by fires from burning monasteries and abbeys. Day was black and grey, whether the sun shone or no; night was red as blood and white from a moon pale as a cadaver. All was dead or dying; all was despair.

Life was leaving Germany and perhaps the whole world; I saw nothing but corpses. Once I observed a ragged creature stirring on the road ahead of me, fluttering and flopping like a wounded crow, but the old woman had expired before I reached her.

Even the ravens of the battlegrounds had fallen dead upon the remains of their carrion, bits of rotting flesh still in their beaks, their bodies stiff, their eyes dull as they stared into the meaningless void, neither Heaven, Hell nor yet Limbo (where there is, after all, still a little hope).

I began to believe that my horse and myself were the only creatures allowed, by some whim of Our Lord, to remain as witnesses to the doom of His Creation.

If it were God's intention to destroy His world, as it seemed, then I had lent myself most willingly to His purpose.

I had trained myself to kill with ease, with skill, with a cunning efficiency and lack of ambiguity. My treacheries were always swift and decisive. I had learned the art of passionless torture in pursuit of wealth and information. I knew how to terrify in order to gain my ends, whether they be the needs of the flesh or in the cause of strategy.

I knew how to soothe a victim as gently as any butcher soothes a lamb. I had become a splendid thief of grain and cattle so that my soldiers should be fed and remain as loyal as possible to me.

I was the epitome of a good mercenary captain; a soldier of fortune envied and emulated; a survivor of every form of danger, be it battle, Plague or pox, for I had long since accepted things as they were and had ceased either to question or to complain.

I was Captain Ulrich von Bek and I was thought to be lucky.

The steel I wore, helmet, breastplate, greaves and gloves, was of the very best, as was the sweat-soaked silk of my shirt, the leather of my boots and breeches. My weapons had been selected from the richest of those I had killed and were all, pistols, sword, daggers and musket, by the finest smiths. My horse was large and hardy and excellently furnished.

I had no wounds upon my face, no marks of disease, and, if my bearing was a little stiff, it gave me, I was told, an air of dignified authority, even when I conducted the most hideous destruction.

Men found me a good commander and were glad to serve with me. I had grown to some fame and had a nickname, occasionally used: *Krieghund*.

They said I had been born for War. I found such opinions amusing.

My birthplace was in Bek. I was the son of a pious nobleman who was loved for his good works. My father had protected and cared for his tenants and his estates. He had respected God and his betters. He had been learned, after the standards of this time, if not after the standards of the Greeks and Romans, and had come to the Lutheran religion through inner debate, through intellectual investigation, through discourse with others. Even amongst the Catholics he was known for his kindness and had once been seen to save a Jew from stoning in the town square. He had a tolerance for almost every creature.

When my mother died, quite young, having given birth to the last of my sisters (I was the only son), he prayed for her soul and waited patiently until he should join her in Heaven. In the meantime he followed God's Purpose, as he saw it, and looked after the poor and weak, discouraged them in certain aspirations which could only lead the ignorant souls into the ways of the Devil, and made certain that I acquired the best possible education from both clergymen and lay tutors.

I learned music and dancing, fencing and riding, as well as Latin and Greek. I was knowledgeable in the Scriptures and their commentaries. I was considered handsome, manly, God-fearing, and was loved by all in Bek.

Until 1625 I had been an earnest scholar and a devout Protestant, taking little interest (save to pray for our cause) in the various wars and battles of the North.

Gradually, however, as the canvas grew larger and the issues seemed to become more crucial, I determined to obey God and my conscience as best I could.

In the pursuit of my Faith, I had raised a company of infantry and gone off to serve in the army of King Christian of Denmark, who proposed, in turn, to aid the Protestant Bohemians.

Since King Christian's defeat, I had served a variety of masters and causes, not all of them, by any means, Protestant and a good many of them in no wise Christian by even the broadest description. I had also seen a deal of France, Sweden, Bohemia, Austria, Poland, Muscovy, Moravia, the Low Countries, Spain and, of course, most of the German provinces.

I had learned a deep distrust of idealism, had developed a contempt for any kind of unthinking Faith, and had discovered a number of strong arguments for the inherent malice, deviousness and hypocrisy of my fellow men, whether they be Popes, princes, prophets or peasants.

I had been brought up to the belief that a word given meant an appropriate action taken. I had swiftly lost my innocence, for I am not a stupid man at all.

By 1626 I had learned to lie as fluently and as easily as any of the major participants of that War, who compounded deceit upon deceit in order to achieve ends which had begun to seem meaningless even to them; for those who compromise others also compromise themselves and are thus robbed of the capacity to place value on anything or anyone. For my own part I placed value upon my own life and trusted only myself to maintain it.

Magdeburg, if nothing else, would have proven those views of mine:

By the time we had left the city we had destroyed most of its thirty thousand inhabitants. The five thousand survivors had nearly all been women and their fate was the obvious one.

Tilly, indecisive, appalled by what he had in his desperation engineered, allowed Catholic priests to make some attempt to marry the women to the men who had taken them, but the priests were jeered at for their pains.

The food we had hoped to gain had been burned in the city. All that had been rescued had been wine, so our men poured the contents of the barrels into their empty bellies.

The work which they had begun sober, they completed drunk. Magdeburg became a tormented ghost to haunt those few, unlike myself, who still possessed a conscience.

A rumour amongst our troops was that the fanatical Protestant, Falkenburg, had deliberately fired the city rather than have it captured by Catholics, but it made no odds to those who died or suffered. In years to come Catholic troops who begged for quarter from Protestants would be offered "Magdeburg mercy" and would be killed on the spot. Those who believed Falkenburg the instigator of the fire often celebrated him, calling Magdeburg "the Protestant Lucretia," self-murdered to protect her honour. All this was madness to me and best forgotten.

Soon Magdeburg and my men were days behind me. The smell of smoke and the Plague remained in my nostrils, however, until well after I had turned out of the mountains and entered the oak groves of the northern fringes of the great Thuringian Forest.

Here, there was a certain peace. It was spring and the leaves were green and their scent gradually drove the stench of slaughter away.

The images of death and confusion remained in my mind, nonetheless. The tranquillity of the forest seemed to me artificial. I suspected traps.

I could not relax for thinking that the trees hid robbers or that the very ground could disguise a secret pit. Few birds sang here; I saw no animals.

The atmosphere suggested that God's Doom had been visited

9

on this place as freely as it had been visited elsewhere. Yet I was grateful for any kind of calm, and after two days without danger presenting itself I found that I could sleep quite easily for several hours and could eat with a degree of leisure, drinking from sweet brook water made strange to me because it did not taste of the corpses which clogged, for instance, the Elbe from bank to bank.

It was remarkable to me that the deeper into the forest I moved, the less life I discovered.

The stillness began to oppress me; I became grateful for the sound of my own movements, the tread of the horse's hoofs on the turf, the occasional breeze which swept the leaves of the trees, animating them and making them seem less like frozen giants observing my passage with a passionless sense of the danger lying ahead of me.

It was warm and I had an impulse more than once to remove my helmet and breastplate, but I kept them firmly on, sleeping in my armour as was my habit, a naked sword ready by my hand.

I came to believe that this was not, after all, a Paradise, but the borderland between Earth and Hell.

I was never a superstitious man, and shared the rational view of the universe with our modern alchemists, anatomists, physicians and astrologers; I did not explain my fears in terms of ghosts, demons, Jews or witches; but I could discover no explanation for this absence of life.

No army was nearby, to drive game before it. No large beasts stalked here. There were not even huntsmen. I had discovered not a single sign of human habitation.

The forest seemed unspoiled and untouched since the beginning of Time. Nothing was poisoned. I had eaten berries and drunk water. The undergrowth was lush and healthy, as were the trees and shrubs. I had eaten mushrooms and truffles; my horse flourished on the good grass.

Through the treetops I saw clear blue sky, and sunlight warmed the glades. But no insects danced in the beams; no bees crawled upon the leaves of the wild flowers; not even an earthworm twisted about the roots, though the soil was dark and smelled fertile.

It came to me that perhaps this was a part of the Globe as yet unpopulated by God, some forgotten corner which had been overlooked during the latter days of the Creation. Was I a wandering Adam come to find his Eve and start the race again? Had God, feeling hopeless at humanity's incapacity to maintain even a clear idea of His Purpose, decided to expunge His first attempts? But I could only conclude that some natural catastrophe had driven the animal kingdom away, be it through famine or disease, and that it had not yet returned.

You can imagine that this state of reason became more difficult to maintain when, breaking out of the forest proper one afternoon, I saw before me a green, flowery hill which was crowned by the most beautiful castle I had ever beheld: a thing of delicate stonework, of spires and ornamental battlements, all soft, pale browns, whites and yellows, and this castle seemed to me to be at the centre of the silence, casting its influence for miles around, protecting itself as a nun might protect herself, with cold purity and insouciant confidence. Yet it was mad to think such a thing, I knew.

How could a building demand calm, to the degree that not even a mosquito would dare disturb it?

It was my first impulse to avoid the castle, but my pride overcame me.

I refused to believe that there was anything genuinely mysterious.

A broad, stony path wound up the hillside between banks of flowers and sweet-smelling bushes which gradually became shaped into terraced gardens with balustrades, statuary and formally arranged flower beds.

This was a peaceful place, built for civilised tastes and reflecting nothing of the War. From time to time as I rode slowly up the path I called out a greeting, asking for shelter and stating my name, according to accepted tradition; but there was no reply. Windows filled with stained glass glittered like the eyes of benign lizards, but I saw no human eye, heard no voice.

Eventually I reached the open gates of the castle's outer wall and rode beneath a portcullis into a pleasant courtyard full of old trees, climbing plants and, at the centre, a well. Around this court-yard were the apartments and appointments of those who would normally reside here, but it was plain to me that not a soul occu-pied them.

I dismounted from my horse, drew a bucket from the well so that he might drink, tethered him lightly and walked up the steps to the main doors which I opened by means of a large iron handle.

Within, it was cool and sweet.

There was nothing sinister about the shadows as I climbed more steps and entered a room furnished with old chests and tap-estries. Beyond this were the usual living quarters of a wealthy nobleman of taste. I made a complete round of the rooms on all three storeys.

There was nothing in disorder. The books and manuscripts in the library were in perfect condition. There were preserved meats, fruits and vegetables in the pantries, barrels of beer and jars of wine in the cellars.

It seemed that the castle had been left with a view to its inhabit-ants' early return. There was no decay at all. But what was remarkable to me was that there were, as in the forest, no signs of the small animals, such as rats and mice, which might normally be discovered.

A little cautiously I sampled the castle's larder and found it excellent. I would wait, however, for a while before I made a meal, to see how my stomach behaved.

I glanced through the windows, which on this side were glazed with clear, green glass, and saw that my horse was content. He had not been poisoned by the well water.

I climbed to the top of one of the towers and pushed open a little wooden door to let myself onto the battlements.

Here, too, flowers and vegetables and herbs grew in tubs and added to the sweetness of the air.

Below me, the treetops were like the soft waves of a green and frozen sea. Able to observe the land for many miles distant and see no sign of danger, I became relieved.

I went to stable my horse and then explored some of the chests to see if I could discover the name of the castle's owner. Normally one would have come upon family histories, crests and the like. There was none.

The linen bore no mottoes or insignia, the clothing (of which quantities existed to dress most ages and both sexes) was of good quality, but anonymous. I returned to the kitchens, lit a fire and began to heat water so that I might bathe and avail myself of some of the softer apparel in the chests.

I had decided that this was probably the summer retreat of some rich Catholic prince who now did not wish to risk the journey from his capital, or who had no time for rest.

I congratulated myself on my good fortune. I toyed with the idea of audaciously making the castle my own, of finding servants for it, perhaps a woman or two to keep me company and share one of the large and comfortable beds I had already sampled. Yet how, short of robbery, would I maintain the place?

There were evidently no farms, no mills, no villages nearby; therefore no rents, no supplies. The age of the castle was difficult to judge, and I saw no clear roads leading to it.

Perhaps its owner had first discovered the tranquil wood and had had the castle built secretly. A very rich aristocrat who required considerable privacy might find it possible to achieve. I could imagine that I might myself consider such a plan. But I was not rich. The castle was therefore an excellent base from which to make raids. It could be defended, even if it were discovered.

It seemed to me that it could also have been built by some ancient brigandly baron in the days when almost all the German provinces were maintained by petty warlords preying upon one another and upon the surrounding populace.

That evening I lit many candles and sat in the library wearing fresh linen and drinking good wine while I read a treatise on astronomy by a student of Kepler's and reflected on my increasing disagreement with Luther, who had judged reason to be the chief enemy of Faith, of the purity of his beliefs. He had considered reason a harlot, willing to turn to anyone's needs, but this merely displayed his own suspicion of logic. I have come to believe him the madman Catholics described him as. Most mad people see logic as a threat to the dream in which they would rather live, a threat to their attempts to make the dream reality (usually through force, through threat, through manipulation and through bloodshed). It is why men of reason are so often the first to be killed or exiled by tyrants.

He who would analyse the world, rather than impose upon it a set of attributes, is always most in danger from his fellows, though he prove the most passive and tolerant of men. It has often seemed to me that if one wishes to find consolation in this world one must also be prepared to accept at least one or two large lies. A confessor requires considerable Faith before he will help you.

I went early to bed, having fed my horse with oats from the granary, and slept peacefully, for I had taken the precaution of lowering the portcullis, knowing that I should wake if anyone should try to enter the castle in the night.

My sleep was dreamless, and yet when I awoke in the morning I had an impression of gold and white, of lands without horizon, without sun or moon. It was another warm, clear day. All I wished for to complete my peace of mind was a little birdsong, but I whistled to myself as I descended to the kitchens to breakfast on preserved herring and cheese, washing this down with some watered beer.

I had decided to spend as much time as I could in the castle, to recollect myself, to rest and then continue my journey until I found some likely master who would employ me in the trade I had made my own. I had long since learned to be content with my own company and so did not feel the loneliness which others might experience.

It was in the evening, as I exercised upon the battlements, that I detected the signs of conflict some miles distant, close to the horizon. There, the forest was burning; or perhaps it was a settlement which burned. The fire spread even as I watched, but no wind carried the smoke towards me.

As the sun set I saw a faint red glow, but was able to go to bed and sleep soundly again, for no rider could have reached the castle by the morning.

I rose shortly after sunrise and went immediately to the battlements.

The fire was dying, it seemed. I ate and read until noon.

Another visit to the battlements showed me that the fire had grown again, indicating that a good-sized army was on the move towards me. It would take me less than an hour to be ready to leave, and I had learned the trick of responding to nothing but actual and immediate danger. There was always the chance that the army would turn away well before it sighted the castle.

For three days I watched as the army came nearer and nearer until it was possible to see it through a break in the trees created by a wide river.

It had settled on both banks, and I knew enough of such armies to note that it was constituted of the usual proportions: at least five camp-followers to every soldier.

Women and children and male servants of various sorts went about the business of administering to the warriors. These were people who, for one reason or another, had lost their own homes and found greater security with the army than they would find elsewhere, preferring to identify with the aggressor rather than be his victims.

There were about a hundred horses, but the majority of the men were infantry, clad in the costumes and uniforms of a score of countries and princes. It was impossible to say which cause, if any, it served, and would therefore be best avoided, particularly since it had an air of recent defeat about it.

The next day I saw outriders approach the castle and then almost immediately turn their horses back, without debate. Judging by their costume and their weapons, the riders were native Germans, and I formed the impression that they knew of the castle and were anxious to avoid it.

If some local superstition kept them away and thus preserved my peace, I would be more than content to let them indulge their fears. I planned to watch carefully, however, until I became certain that I would not be disturbed.

In the meanwhile I continued my explorations of the castle.

I had been made even more curious by the fearful response of those riders. Nonetheless, no effort of mine could reveal the castle's owner, nor even the name of the family which had built it. That they were wealthy was evident from the quantity of rich silk and woollen hangings everywhere, the pictures and the tapestries, the gold and the silver, the illuminated windows.

I sought out vaults where ancestors might be buried and discovered none.

I concluded that my original opinion was the most likely to be true: this was a rich prince's retreat. Possibly a private retreat, where he did not wish to be known by his given name. If the owner kept mysteries about him as to his identity, then it was also possible that his power was held to be great and possibly supernatural in these parts and that that was why the castle went untouched. I thought of the legend of Johannes Faust and other mythical maguses of the previous, uncertain, century.

In two days the army had gone on its slow way and I was alone again.

I was quickly growing bored, having read most of what interested me in the library and beginning to long for fresh meat and bread, as well as the company of some jolly peasant woman, such as those I had seen with the army. But I stayed there for the best part of another week, sleeping a good deal and restoring my strength of body, as well as my strength of judgement.

All I had to look forward to was a long journey, the business of recruiting another company and then seeking a fresh master for my services.

I considered the idea of returning to Bek, but I knew that I was no longer suited for the kind of life still lived there. I would be a disappointment to my father. I had sworn to myself long since that I should only return to Bek if I heard that he was dying or dead. I wished him to think of me as a noble Christian soldier serving the cause of the religion he loved.

On the night before I planned to leave I began to get some sense of stirring in the castle, as if the place itself were coming to life.

To quell my own slight terrors I took a lamp and explored the castle once more, from end to end, from top to bottom, and found nothing strange. However, I became even more determined to leave on the following morning.

As usual, I rose at sunrise and took my horse from the stable. He was in considerably better condition than when we had arrived. I had raised the portcullis and was packing food into my saddlebags when I heard a sound from outside, a kind of creaking and shuffling.

Going to the gates, I was astonished by the sight below. A procession was advancing up the hill towards me. At first I thought this was the castle's owner returning. It had not struck me before that he might not be a temporal prince at all, but a high-ranking churchman.

The procession had something of the nature of a monastery on the move.

First came six well-armed horsemen, with pikes at the slope in stirrup holsters, their faces hidden in helmets of black iron; then behind them were some two score monks in dark habits and cowls, hauling upon ropes attached to the kind of carriage which would normally be drawn by horses. About another dozen monks walked at the back of the coach, and these were followed by six more horsemen, identical in appearance to those at the front.

The coach was of cloudy, unpainted wood which glittered a little in the light. It had curtained windows, but bore no crest, not even a cross.

The regalia of the riders looked popish to me, so I knew I would have to be wary in my responses, if I were to avoid conflict.

I wasted no time. I mounted and rode down the hill towards them. I wished that the sides of the hill were not so steep here, or I should not have had to take the road at all. I could not, as it happened, make my departure without passing them but I felt happier being free of the castle, with a chance at least of escape should these warriors and monks prove belligerent.

As I came closer I began to smell them. They stank of corruption.

They carried the odour of rotting flesh with them. I thought that the coach contained perhaps some dead cardinal.

Then I realised that all these creatures were the same. The flesh appeared to be falling from their faces and limbs. Their eyes were the eyes of corpses. When they saw me they came to a sudden stop.

The horsemen prepared their pikes.

I made no movement towards my own weapons, for fear of exciting them. Nonetheless, I readied myself to charge through them if it should prove necessary.

One of the riders spoke sluggishly and yet with horrifying authority, as if he were Death Himself and that pike in his hand the Reaper's scythe:

"You trespass, fellow.

"You trespass.

"Understand you not that this land is forbidden to you?"

The words came as a series of clipped phrases, with a long pause between each, as if the speaker had to recall the notion of language.

"I saw no signs," said I. "I heard no word. How could I when your land is absolutely free of population?"

In all my experience of horror I had witnessed nothing to compare with this talking corpse. I felt unnerving fear and was hard put to control it.

He spoke again:

"It is understood—

"By all. It seems.

"Save you."

"I am a stranger," I declared, "and sought the hospitality of this castle's lord. I did not expect the place to be empty. I apologise for my ignorance. I have done no damage."

I made ready to spur my horse.

Another of the riders turned his iron head on me.

Cold eyes, full of old blood, stared into mine.

My stomach regretted that I had broken its fast so recently.

He said:

"How were you able to come and go?

"Have you made the bargain?"

I attempted to reply in a reasonable tone. "I came and went as you see, upon my horse. I have no bond, if that is what you mean, with the master of this castle."

I addressed the coach, believing that the castle's owner must sit within:

"But again I say that I apologise for my unwitting trespass. I have done no harm, save eat a little food, water my horse and read a book or two."

"No bargain," muttered one of the monks, as if puzzled.

"No bargain he is aware of," said a third horseman.

And they laughed amongst themselves. The sound was a disgusting one.

"I have never met your lord," said I. "It is unlikely that I know him."

"Doubtless he knows you."

Their mockery, their malicious enjoyment of some secret they believed they shared, was disturbing my composure and making me impatient.

I said:

"If I may be allowed to approach and present myself, you will discover that I am of noble birth . . ."

I had no real intention of talking with the occupant of the coach, but should I be able to advance a little farther I would gain time and distance—and with some luck I might break free of them without need of my sword.

"You may not approach," said the first rider.

"You must return with us."

I spoke with mock good manners:

"I have already sampled your hospitality too long. I'll impose upon it no further."

I smiled to myself. My spirits began to lift, as they always do when action is required of me. I began to experience that cool good humour common to many professional soldiers when killing becomes necessary.

"You have no choice," said the rider.

He lowered his pike: a threat.

I relaxed in my saddle, ensuring that my seat was firm.

"I make my own choices, sir," I said.

My spurs touched my horse and he began to trot rapidly towards them.

They had not expected this.

They were used to inducing terror. They were not, I suspected, used to fighting.

I had broken through them in a matter of seconds. Barely grazed by a pike, I now attempted to ride the monks down.

I hacked at the cowled men. They did not threaten me but were so anxious not to release their grasp on the carriage's ropes that they could not move from my path. They seemed perfectly willing to die under my sword rather than give up their charge.

I was forced to turn and face the riders once more.

They had no battle skill, these people, and were uncertain in their movements, for all their arrogance. Again I received an impression of hesitation, as if each individual action had to be momentarily remembered. So clumsy were they that their pikes were tangled by a few passages of my sword.

I used the bulk of my horse to back farther into the press of monks. They offered the heavy resistance of corpses.

I turned the steed again.

I let him rear and strike down two monks with his hoofs.

I jumped first one taut rope and then the other and was aiming for the grassy flanks of the steep hillside when the riders from the rear came galloping forward to cut me off.

I had a balustrade before me, some statues to my left, an almost sheer drop beyond these.

Again I was forced to pause. I tried to pull a pistol loose and fire in the hope it would startle their horses. I did not think I could delay their charge by wounding one.

My horse was moving too much beneath me, ready to gallop, yet not knowing where to go. I reined him tight, standing firm against that rocking nest of pikes which was now almost upon me.

A glance this way and that told me that my chances had improved. There was every possibility of escape. I no longer felt in terror of my attackers. At worst I could calculate on a few flesh wounds for myself and a sprained tendon or two for my horse.

The pikes drew closer as I reached for my pistols.

Then a clear, humorous voice sounded from the interior of the coach:

"There is no need for this. It wasn't planned. Stop at once, all of you. I demand that you stop!"

The riders drew in their own reins and began to raise their pikes to the slope.

I put my sword between my teeth, drew both pistols from the saddle-holsters, cocked the flints and fired.

One of the pistols discharged and flung a rider straight out of his seat. The other needed recocking, having failed to spark, but before I could see to it, I heard the voice again.

It was a woman. "Stop!"

I would let them debate her orders. In the meantime I had a little time in which to begin my descent. I sheathed my sword and looked down the hillside. I had planned to skirt this party and continue down the road if possible. It would mean driving directly through the pikes, but I believed I could do it fairly easily.

I prepared myself, while giving the impression that I was relaxing my guard.

The door of the coach opened.

A handsome woman of about thirty, with jet-black hair and wearing scarlet velvet, clambered swiftly onto the coachman's seat and raised her arms. She seemed distracted. I was impressed by her bearing and her beauty.

"Stop!" she cried to me. "We meant no harm to you."

I grinned at this. But since I now had something of an advantage and did not wish to risk either my life or my horse more than necessary, I paused. My loaded pistol was still in my gloved hand.

"Your men attacked me, madam."

"Not upon my orders." Her lips matched her costume. Her skin was as delicate and pale as the lace which trimmed her garments. She wore a matching broad-brimmed hat with a white ostrich feather trailing from it.

"You are welcome," she said. "I swear to you that it is so, sir. You came forward before I could present myself."

I was certain that all she was doing now was to change tactics. But I preferred these tactics. They were familiar enough.

I grinned at her. "You mean you had hoped that your servants would frighten me, eh, madam?"

She feigned puzzlement. She spoke with apparent sincerity, even urgency: "You must not think so. These creatures are not subtle. They are the only servants provided me." Her eyes were wonderful. I was astonished by them. She said: "I apologise to you, sir."

She lowered her arms, almost as if she appealed to me. She struck me as a woman of substance, yet there was an engaging touch of despair about her. Was she perhaps a prisoner of those men?

I was almost amused: a lady in distress, and myself a knight errant to whom the notion of chivalry was anathema. Yet I hesitated.

"Madam, your servants disturb me by their very appearance."

"They were not chosen by me."

"Indeed, I should hope that's so." I retained my pistol at the cock. "They were chosen by Death long since, by the look of 'em."

She sighed and made a small gesture with her right hand.

"Sir, I would be much obliged if you would consent to be my guest."

"Your men have already invited me. You'll recall that I refused."

"Will you refuse me? I ask," she said, "in all humility."

She was a clever woman and it had been some years since I had enjoyed such company. It was her eyes, however, which continued to draw me. They were wise, they were knowing, they contained in them a hint of deep terror and they were sympathetic, I thought, to me in particular.

I was lost to her. I knew it. I believe she knew it. I began to laugh. I bowed to her.

"It is true, madam," said I, "that I cannot refuse you. Boredom, curiosity and what is left of my good manners drive me to accept. But most of all, madam, it is yourself, for I'll swear I see a fellow spirit and one as intelligent as myself. A rare combination, you'd agree?"

"I take your meaning, sir. And I share your feeling, too." Those wonderful eyes shone with ironic pleasure. I thought that she, too, could be laughing, somewhere within her. With a delicate hand she brushed hair away from the left side of her face and tilted her head to look at me. A conscious gesture, I knew, and a flirtatious one. I grinned this time.

"Then you'll guest with me?" she said.

"On one condition," said I.

"Sir?"

"That you promise to explain some of the mysteries of your castle and its surrounds."

She raised her brows. "It is an ordinary castle. In ordinary grounds."

"You know that it is not."

She answered my grin with a smile. "Very well," she said. "I promise that you shall understand everything very soon."

"I note your promise," said I.

I sheathed my pistol and turned my horse towards the castle.

I had taken my first decisive step towards Hell.

Chapter Two

I GAVE THE lady my arm and escorted her through her court-yard, up the steps and into her castle, while her horrid servants took horse and coach to the stables. Curiosity had me trapped.

Lust, half-appreciated as yet, also had me trapped.

I thought to myself with a certain relish that I was, all in all, thoroughly snared. And at that moment I did not care.

"I am Ulrich von Bek, son of the Graf von Bek," I told her. "I am a Captain of Infantry in the present struggle."

Her perfume was as warm and lulling as summer roses. "On whose side?" she asked.

I shrugged. "Whichever is the better organised and less divided."

"You have no strong religious beliefs, then?"

"None."

I added: "Is that unusual for men of my kind in times like these?"

"Not at all. Not at all." She seemed quietly amused.

She took off her own cloak. She was almost as tall as I and won-derfully formed. For all that she gave the impression of possessing a strong and perhaps even eccentric will, there was yet a softness about her now which suggested to me that she was presently defeated by her circumstances.

"I am Sabrina," she said, and gave no title or family name.

"This is your castle, Lady Sabrina?"

"I often reside here." She was non-committal.

It could be that she was reluctant to discuss her family. Or per-haps she was the mistress of the powerful prince I had originally guessed as owner. Perhaps she had been exiled here for some appalling crime. Perhaps she had been sent here by her husband or some other relative to avoid the vicissitudes either of love or of war. From tact I could ask her no other questions on the matter.

She laid a fair hand upon my arm. "You will eat with me, Captain von Bek?"

"I do not relish eating in the presence of your servants, madam."

"No need. I'll prepare the food myself later. They are not permitted to enter these quarters. They have their own barracks in the far tower."

I had seen the barracks. They did not seem large enough for so many.

"How long have you been here?" She glanced about the hall as we entered it.

"A week or two."

"You kept it in good order."

"It was not my intention to loot the place, Lady Sabrina, but to use it as a temporary refuge. How long has your home been empty?"

She waved a vague hand. "Oh, some little while. Why do you ask?"

"Everything was so well-preserved. So free of vermin. Of dust, even."

"Ah. We do not have much trouble of that kind."

"No damp. No rot."

"None visible," she said. She seemed to become impatient with my remarks.

"I remain grateful for the shelter," I said, to end this theme.

"You are welcome." Her voice became a little distant. She frowned. "The soldiers delayed us."

"How so?"

"On the road." She gestured. "Back there."

"You were attacked?"

"Pursued for a while. Chased." Her finger sought dust on a chest and found none. She seemed to be considering my recent remarks. "They fear us, of course. But there were so many of them." She smiled, displaying white, even teeth. She spoke as if I would understand and sympathise. As if I were a comrade.

All I could do was nod.

"I cannot blame them," she continued. "I cannot blame any of them." She sighed. Her dark eyes clouded, became inturned, dreamy. "But you are here. And that is good."

I should have found her manner disturbing, but at the time I found it captivating. She spoke as if I had been expected, as if she were a poor hostess who, delayed abroad, returns to discover an unattended guest.

I offered some formal compliment to her beauty and grace. She smiled a little, accepting it as one who was very used to such remarks, who perhaps even regarded them as the opening feints in an emotional duel. I recognised her expression. It caused me to become just a little more remote, a little more guarded. She was a gameswoman, I thought, trained by one or more masters in the terrible, cold art of intellectual coquetry. I found the woman too interesting to wish to give her a match, so I changed the subject back to my original reason for accepting her invitation.

"You have promised to explain the castle's mysteries," I said. "And why there is no animal life in these parts."

"It is true," she said. "There is none."

"You have agreed with me, madam," I said gently, "but you have not explained anything to me."

Her tone became a shade brusque. "I promised you an explanation, did I not, sir?"

"Indeed, you did."

"And an explanation will be forthcoming."

I was not, in those days, a man to be brushed off with insubstantial reassurances. "I'm a soldier, madam. I had intended to be on my way south by now. You will recall that I returned here at your invitation—and because of your promise. Soldiers are an impatient breed."

She seemed just a fraction agitated by my remark, pushing at her long hair, touching her cheek. Her words were rapid and they stumbled. She said: "No soul—that is no free soul, however small—can exist here."

This was not good enough for me, although I was intrigued. "I do not follow you, madam," I said with deliberate firmness. "You are obscure. I am used to action and simple facts. From those simple facts I am able to determine what action I should take."

"I do not wish to confuse you, sir." She appealed to me, but I refused to respond to her.

I sighed. "What do you mean when you say that no soul can exist here?"

She hesitated. "Nothing which belongs," she said, "to God."

"Belongs? To God? The forest, surely . . . ?"

"The forest lies upon the"—she made a baffled gesture—"upon the borders."

"I still do not understand."

She controlled herself, returning my stare. "Neither should you," she said.

"I am not much impressed by metaphysics." I was becoming angry. Such abstract debate had caused our present woes. "Are you suggesting that some sort of plague once infested this land? Is that why both men and beasts avoid it?"

She made no reply.

I continued: "Your servants, after all, suffer from disease. Could they be suffering from an infection local to this area?"

"Their souls—" she began again.

I interrupted. "The same abstraction . . ."

"I do my best, sir," she said.

"Madam, you offer me no facts."

"I have offered you facts, as I understand them. It is hard . . ."

"You speak of a sickness, in truth. Do you not? You are afraid that if you name it, I shall become nervous, that you will drive me away."

"If you like," she said.

"I am afraid of very little, though I must admit to a certain caution where the Plague is concerned. On the other hand I have reason to believe that I am one of those lucky souls apparently immune to the Plague, so you must know that I shall not immediately run quaking from this place. Tell me. Is it a sickness of which you speak?"

"Aye," she said, as if tired, as if willing to agree to almost any definition I provided. "It could be as you say."

"But you are untouched." I moved a pace towards her. "And I."

She became silent. Was I to think, I wondered, that the signs of that horrible sickness which possessed her servants had not yet manifested themselves in us? I shuddered.

"How long have you lived at the castle?" I asked.

"I am here only from time to time."

This answer suggested to me that perhaps she was immune. If she were immune, then so, perhaps, was I. With that consideration I relaxed more.

She seated herself upon a couch. Sunlight poured through stained glass representing Diana at the hunt. It was only then that I realised not a single Christian scene existed here, no crucifix, no representations of Jesus or the saints. Tapestries, glass, statuary and decoration were all pagan in subject.

"How old is this castle?" I stood before the window, running my fingers over the lead.

"Very old, I think. Several centuries, at least."

"It has been well-maintained."

She knew that my questions were not innocent or casual. I was seeking further knowledge of the estate and the mysterious sickness which haunted it.

"True," she said.

I sensed a new kind of tension. I turned.

She went from that room into the next and came back with wine for us. As she handed me my cup I observed that she did not wear a marriage ring. "You have no lord, madam?"

"I have a lord," she said, and she stared back into my eyes as if I had challenged her. Then, seeing my question to be fairly innocent, she shrugged. "Yes, I have a lord, captain."

"But this is not your family property."

"Oh, well. Family?" She began to smile very strangely, then controlled her features. "The castle is my master's, and has been his for many years."

"Not always his, however?"

28

"No. He won it, I believe."

"Spoils of war?"

She shook her head. "A gambling debt."

"Your master is a gambler, eh? And plays for good-sized stakes. Does he participate in our War?"

"Oh, yes." Her manner changed again. She became brisk. "I'll not be cryptic with you, Captain von Bek." She smiled; a hint, once more, of helplessness. "On the other hand it does not suit me to pursue this conversation further at present."

"Please forgive my rudeness." I think that I sounded cold.

"You are direct, captain, but not rude." She spoke quietly. "For a man who has doubtless seen and done so much in the matter of war you seem to retain a fair share of grace."

I touched the cup to my lips—half a toast to her own good manners. "I am astonished that you should think so. Yet, in comparison with your servants, I suppose I must seem better than I am."

She laughed. Her skin appeared to glow. I smelled roses. I felt as if the heat of the sun were upon me in that room. I knew that I desired Sabrina as I had desired no-one or nothing else in all my life. Yet my caution maintained distance. For that moment I was content merely to experience those sensations (which I had not experienced in many years of soldiering) and not attempt fulfilment.

"How did you come by your servants?" I sipped my wine. It tasted better than any of the other vintages I had sampled here. It increased the impression that all my senses were coming alive again at once.

She pursed her lips before replying. Then: "They are pensioners, you might say, of my master."

"Your master? You mention him much. But you do not name him." I pointed this out most gently.

"It is true." She moved hair from her face.

"You do not wish to name him?"

"At this time? No."

"He sent you here?" I savoured the wine.

"Yes," she said.

"Because he fears for your safety?" I suggested.

"No." Sadness and desperate amusement showed for a second in the set of her lips.

"Then you have an errand here?" I asked. Again I moved closer.

"Yes." She took a couple of paces back from me. I guessed that she was as affected by me as I was by her, but it could have been merely that my questions cut too close to the bone and that I was unnerving her.

I paused.

"Could I ask you what that errand can be?"

She became gay, but plainly her mood was not altogether natural. "To entertain you"—a flirt of the hand—"captain."

"But you were not aware that I stayed here."

She dropped her gaze.

"Were you?" I continued. "Unless some unseen servant of your master reported me to you."

She raised her eyes. She ignored my last remark and said: "I have been looking for a brave man. A brave man and an intelligent one."

"On your master's instructions? Is that the implication?"

She offered me a challenging look now. "If you like."

The instinct which had helped me keep my life and health through all my exploits warned me now that this unusual woman could be bait for a trap. For once, however, I ignored the warning. She was willing, she suggested, to give herself to me. In return, I guessed, I would be called upon to pay a high price. At that moment I did not care what the price was. I was, anyway, I reminded myself, a resourceful man and could always, with reasonable odds, escape later. One can act too much in the cause of self-preservation and experience nothing fresh as a result.

"He gives you liberty to do what?" I asked her.

"To do almost anything I like." She shrugged.

"He is not jealous?"

"Not conventionally so, Captain von Bek." She drained her cup. I followed her example. She took both cups and filled them again. She sat herself beside me, now, upon a couch under the window. My flesh, my skin, every vein and sinew, sang. I, who had practised self-control for years, was barely able to hold on to a coherent thought as I took her hand and kissed it, murmuring: "He is an unusual master, your lord."

"That is also true."

I withdrew my lips and fell back a little, looking carefully at her wonderful face. "He indulges you? Is it because he loves you very much?"

Her breathing matched mine. Her eyes were bright, passionate gems. She said: "I am not sure that my master understands the nature of love. Not as you and I would understand it."

I laughed and let myself relax a little more. "You become cryptic again, Lady Sabrina, when you swore that you would not be."

"Forgive me." She rose, hesitating.

I watched her form. I had never known such beauty and such wit combined in any human individual before. "You will not tell me your history?"

"Not yet."

I interpreted this remark as a promise, yet I pressed her just a little further:

"You were born in these parts?"

"In Germany, yes."

"And not very long ago." This was partly to flatter her. It was unnecessary, that flattery, I knew, but I had learned pothouse habits as a soldier of fortune and could not in an instant lose them all.

Her answer was unexpected. She turned to me, taking a wine-cup in each hand. "It depends on your definition of Time," she said. She gave me my filled cup. "Now you probe and I mystify. Shall we talk of less personal matters? Or do you wish to speak of yourself?"

"You seem to have determined who and what I am already, my lady."

"Not in fine, captain."

"I've few secrets. Most of my recent life has been spent in soldiering. Before that it was spent in receiving an education. Life is not very brisk in Bek."

31

"But you have seen and done much, as a soldier?"

"The usual things." I frowned. I did not desire too much recollection. Magdeburg memories still lingered and were resisted with a certain amount of effort.

"You have killed frequently?"

"Of course." I displayed reluctance to expand upon this theme.

"And taken part in looting? In torture?"

"When necessary, aye." I grew close to anger again. I believed that she deliberately discomfited me.

"And rape?"

I peered directly at her. Had I misjudged her? Was she perhaps one of those bored, lascivious ladies of the kind I had once met at Court? They had delighted in such talk. It had excited them. They were eager for sensation, having forgotten or never experienced the subtle forms of human sensuality and emotion. In my cynicism I had given them all that they desired. It had been like bestowing lead on gold-greedy merchants who, in their anxiety to possess as much as possible, could not any longer recognise one metal from another. If the Lady Sabrina was of this caste, I should give her what she desired.

But her eyes remained candid and questioning, so I answered briefly: "Aye. Soldiers, as I said, become impatient. Weary . . ."

She was not interested in my explanation. She continued: "And have you punished heretics?"

"I have seen them destroyed."

"But have taken no part in their destruction?"

"By luck and my own distaste, I have not."

"Could you punish a heretic?"

"Madam, I do not really know what a heretic is. The word is made much of, these days. It seems to describe anyone you wish dead."

"Or witches? Have you executed witches?"

"I am a soldier, not a priest."

"Many soldiers take on the responsibilities of priests, do they not? And many priests become soldiers."

"I am not of that ilk. I have seen poor lunatics and old women named for witches and dealt with accordingly, madam. But I have witnessed no magic performances, no incantations, no summonings of demons or ghouls." I smiled. "Some of those crones were so familiar with Mephistopheles that they could almost pronounce the name when it was repeated to them . . ."

"Then witchcraft does not frighten you?"

"It does not. Or, I should say, what I have seen of witchcraft does not frighten me."

"You are a sane man, sir."

I supposed that she complimented me.

"Sane by the standards of our world, madam. But not, I think, by my own."

She seemed pleased by this. "An excellent answer. You are self-demanding, then?"

"I demand little of myself, save that I survive. I take what I need from the world."

"You are a thief, then?"

"I am a thief, if you like. I hope that I am not a hypocrite."

"Self-deceiving, all the same."

"How so?"

"You hide the largest part of yourself away in order to be the soldier you describe. And then you deny that that part exists."

"I do not follow you. I am what I am."

"And that is?"

"What the world has made me."

"Not what God created? God created the world, did He not?" she said.

"I have heard some theorise otherwise."

"Heretics?"

"Ah, well, madam. Desperate souls like the rest of us."

"You have an unusually open mind."

"For a soldier?"

"For anyone living at this time."

"I am not quite sure that my mind is open. It is probably careless, however. I do not give a fig for metaphysical debate, as I believe I have already indicated."

"You have no conscience, then?"

"Too expensive to maintain nowadays, madam."

"So it is unkempt, but it exists?"

"Is that what you would say I hide from myself? Have you a mind to convert me to whatever Faith it is you hold, my lady?"

"My Faith is not too dissimilar to yours."

"So I thought."

"Soul? Conscience? These words mean little, I'm sure you'd agree, without specification."

"I do most readily agree."

We continued to debate this subject only for a short while and then the discussion broadened.

She proved to be an educated woman with a fine range of experience and anecdote. The longer we were together, however, the more I desired her.

The noon meal was forgotten as we continued to talk and to drink. She quoted the Greeks and the Romans, she quoted poetry in several tongues. She was far more fluent in the languages of modern Europe and the Orient than was I.

It became obvious to me that Sabrina must be highly valued by her master and that she was probably something more than his mistress. A woman could travel the world with a little more danger but a little less suspicion than a male envoy. I formed the impression that she was familiar with a good many powerful Courts. Yet I wondered how her servants must be received if they accompanied her to such places.

Evening came. She and I retired to the kitchen where, from the same ingredients, she prepared a far better meal than anything I had been able to make for myself. We drank more wine and then, without thought, took ourselves up to one of the main bedrooms and disrobed.

Sheets, quilts, bed-curtains, were all creamy white in the late sunshine. Naked, Sabrina was perfect. Her pale body was flawless, her breasts small and firm. I had seen no woman like her, save in statues and certain paintings.

I had not believed in perfection before that night, and although

I retained a healthy suspicion of Sabrina's motives I was determined to offer no resistance to her charms.

We went quickly to bed. She became by turns tender, savage, passive and aggressive. I turned with her, whatever her mood, as she turned with mine. My senses, which had become almost as dead as those of Sabrina's servants, had come to life again.

I felt my imagination coming back to me, and with it a certain amount of hope, of the old optimism I had known as a youth in Bek.

Our union, it seemed to me, was preordained, for there was no doubt that she relished me as thoroughly as I relished her. I absorbed her scents, the touch of her skin.

Our passion seemed as endless as the tides; our lust conquered all weariness. If it had not been for that nagging memory that she was in some way pledged to another, I should have given myself up to her entirely. As it was, some small part of me held back. But it was a minuscule fraction. It need hardly have existed.

Eventually we fell asleep and woke in the morning, before light, to make love again. A week or two went by. I was more and more entranced by her.

Half-asleep as one grey dawn came, I murmured that I wanted her to come with me, to leave her ghastly servants behind, to find some other place which the War did not touch.

"Is there another place?" she asked me, with a tender smile.

"In the East, possibly. Or England. We could go to England. Or to the New World."

She became sad and she stroked my cheek. "That isn't possible," she said. "My master would not allow it."

I became fierce. "Your master would not find us."

"He would find me and take me from you, be assured of that."

"In the New World? Is he the Pope?"

She seemed startled and I wondered if, with my rhetorical question, I had struck upon the truth.

I continued: "I would fight him. I would raise an army against him if necessary."

"You would lose."

I asked her seriously: "Is he the Pope? Your master?"

35

"Oh, no," said she impulsively, "he is far greater than the Pope."

I frowned. "Perhaps in your eyes. But not the eyes of the world, surely."

She stirred in the bed and avoided looking directly at me, saying softly: "In the eyes of the whole world, and Heaven, too."

In spite of myself, I was disturbed by her reply. It took another week before I found the courage to make a further statement. I would rather not have pursued the subject:

"You have promised to answer my questions," I said to her, again in the morning. "Would it not be fair to tell me the name of your all-powerful lord? After all, I could be endangering myself by remaining here."

"You are in no particular danger."

"You must let me decide that. You must offer me the choice."

"I know . . ." Her voice died away. "Tomorrow."

"His name," I insisted the next day. I saw terror reflected and compounded, hers and mine.

Then from where she lay in bed she looked directly into my eyes. She shook her head.

"Who is your lord?" I said.

She moved her lips carefully. She raised her head as she spoke. Her mouth seemed dry, her expression strangely blank.

"His name," she said, "is Lucifer."

My self-control almost disappeared. She had shocked me in several ways at the same time, for I could not decide how to interpret this remark. I refused to let superstition attack my reason. I sat up in bed and forced myself to laugh.

"And you are a witch, is that it?"

"I have been called that," she said.

"A shape-changer!" I felt half-mad now. "You are in reality an ancient hag who has englamoured me!"

"I am who you see me to be," she said. "But, yes, I was a witch."

"And your powers come from your compact with the Prince of Darkness?"

"They did not. I was called a witch by the people who determined to kill me. But that was before I met Lucifer . . ."

"You implied some time ago that you shared my opinions of witches!"

"Aye—of those poor women so branded."

"Yet why call yourself one?"

"You used the word. I agreed that I had been called that."

"You are not a witch?"

"When I was young I had certain gifts which I put to the service of my town. I am not stupid. My advice was sought and used. I was well-educated by my father. I could read and write. I knew other women like myself. We met together, as much to enjoy each other's intelligence as to discuss matters of alchemy, herbalism and the like." She shrugged. "It was a small town. The people were small merchants, peasants, you know . . . Women are, by and large, denied the company of scholars, even if they resort to the nunnery. Christians do not permit Eve wisdom, do they? They can only suggest that she was influenced by a fallen angel." She was sardonic. Then she sighed, leaning on one bare arm as she looked at me.

"Scholarly men were suspect in my town. Women could not admit to scholarship at all. Men are afraid of two things in this world, it seems—women and knowledge. Both threaten their power, eh?"

"If you like," I said. "Were there not other women in the town afraid of such things?"

"Of course. Even more afraid in some ways. It was women who betrayed us, in the end."

"It is in the way of events," I said. "Many speak of freedom, of free thought, but few would want the responsibility of actually possessing them."

"Is that why you insist that you are a soldier?"

"I suppose so. I have no great hankering after real freedom. Is that why you let me call you a witch?"

Her smile was sad. "Possibly."

"And is that why you now tell me that Satan is your Master?"

"Not exactly," she replied. "Though I follow your reasoning."

"How did you come to be branded a witch in your town?"

"Perhaps through Pride," she said. "We began to see ourselves as a powerful force for good in the world. We practised magic, of sorts, and experimented sometimes. But our magic was all White. I admit that we studied the other kind. We knew how it could be worked. Particularly by the weak, who sought spurious strength through evil."

"You came to believe that you were strong enough to resist human prejudice? You grew incautious?"

"You could say so, yes."

"But how did you come, as you put it, to serve Satan?" Now I believed that she spoke metaphorically, or that at least she was exaggerating. I still could not believe that she was insane. Her confession, after all, was couched in the most rational terms.

"Our coven was discovered, betrayed. We were imprisoned. We were tortured, of course, and tried, and found guilty. Many confessed to pacts with the Devil." Her expression became bleak. "I could not, in those days, believe that so many evil people would pose as good while we, who had done no harm and had served our neighbours, were submitted to the most disgusting and brutal of attentions."

"But you escaped . . ."

"I became disillusioned as I lay wounded and humiliated in that dungeon. Desperate. I determined that if I was to be branded an evil witch I might as well behave as one. I knew the invocations necessary to summon a servant of the Devil."

She moved carefully, looking full into my face before she spoke next:

"In my cell one night, because I wished to save myself from death and further barbarism; because I had lost belief in the power of my sisters, upon which I had faithfully relied, I began the necessary ritual. It was at my moment of greatest weakness. And it is at that moment, you must know, when Lucifer's servants come calling."

"You summoned a demon?"

"And sold my soul."

"And were saved."

"After the pact was made, I appeared to contract the Plague and was thrown, living, into a pit on the outskirts of town. From that pit I escaped and the Plague went from me. Two days after that, as I lay in a barn, my Master appeared to me in person. He said that He had special need of me. He brought me here, where I was instructed in His service."

"You truly believe that it was Lucifer who brought you here? That this is Lucifer's castle?" I reached out to touch her face.

"I know that Lucifer is my Master. I know that this is His domain on Earth." She could tell that I did not believe her.

"But He is not in residence today?" I said.

"He is here now," she told me flatly.

"I discovered no sign of Him." I was insistent.

"Could you recognise the sign of Lucifer?" she asked me. She spoke as if to a child.

"I would expect at least a hint of brimstone," I told her.

She gestured about her. "This whole castle, the forest outside, is His sign. Could you not guess? Why do even the smallest insects avoid it? Why do whole armies fear it?"

"Then why did I feel only a hint of trepidation when I came here? How can you live here?"

Her expression approached pity.

"Only the souls He owns can exist here," she said.

I shuddered and became cold. I was almost convinced by her. Happily, my reason once again began to function. My ordinary sense of self-preservation. I stepped from the bed and began pulling on my linen. "Then I'll be leaving," I said. "I have no wish to make a pact with Lucifer or anyone who calls himself Lucifer. And I would suggest, Sabrina, that you accompany me. Unless you wish to remain enslaved by your illusion."

She became wistful.

"If only it were an illusion, and you truly could save me."

"I can. On the back of my very ordinary horse. Leave with me now."

"I cannot leave and neither can you. For that matter, because the horse has served you, neither can your horse."

I scoffed at this. "No man is wholly free and the same, madam, may be said for the beast he rides, but we are both free enough to go from here at once!"

"You must stay and meet my Master," she said.

"I am not about to sell my soul."

"You must stay." She reached a hand to me. It trembled. "For my sake."

"Madam, such pleas to my honour are pointless. I have no honour left. I thought that I had made that perfectly clear."

"I beg you," she said.

It was my desire, rather than my honour, which held me there. I hesitated. "You say that your Master is in the castle now?"

"He waits for us."

"Alone? Where? I'll take my sword and deal with your 'Lucifer,' your enchanter, in my own habitual fashion. He has deceived you. Good, sharp steel will enlighten Him and prove to you that He is mortal. You'll be free soon enough, I promise you."

"Bring your sword if you wish," she said.

She rose and began to dress herself in flowing white silk. I stood near her, watching impatiently as she took pains with her clothing. I even felt a pang of jealousy, as a cuckolded husband knows when he sees his wife dressing for her lover.

It was odd, indeed, that such a beautiful and intelligent woman could believe herself in thrall to Satan Himself. Our times were such that human despair took many forms of madness.

I buckled my sword belt about my shirted waist, pulled on my boots and stood before her, trying to determine the depth of her illusion. Her stare was direct and there was pain in it, as well as a strange sort of determination.

"If you are crazed," I said, "it is the subtlest form of insanity I've ever witnessed."

"The human imagination confers lunacy on everyone," she said, "dependent upon their condition. I am as sane as you, sir."

"Then you are, after all, only half-mad," I told her. I offered her my arm as I opened the bedroom door for her. The passage beyond was cold. "Where does this Lucifer of yours hold Court?"

"In Hell," she said.

We walked slowly along the passage and began to descend the broad stone steps towards the main hall.

"And His castle is in Hell?" I asked, looking about me in a somewhat theatrical fashion. I could see the trees through the windows. Everything was exactly as it had been during my stay there.

"It could be," she said.

I shook my head. It took much to threaten my rational view of the world, for my mind had been tempered in the fires of the War, by its terrors and its cruelties, and had survived the contemplation of considerable evil and delusion. "Then all the world is Hell? Do you propose that philosophy?"

"Ah," she said, almost gaily, "is that what we are left with, sir, when we have discarded every other hope?"

"It is a sign of Hope, is it, to believe our own world Hell?"

"Hell is better than nothing," she answered, "to many, at least."

"I refuse to believe such nonsense," I told her. "I have become grim and absolute, madam, in most of my opinions. We appear to be returning to the realm of speculation. I wish to see a concrete Devil and, if we are in Hell, concrete proof of that statement."

"You are over-economical, sir, in the use of your intelligence."

"I think not. I am a soldier, as I've told you more than once. It is a soldier's trait. Simple facts are his trade."

"We have already discussed your reasons for choosing to become a soldier, sir."

I was amused, once more, by the sharpness of her wit.

We were walking down the steps, alternately through sunlight and shadow. The shift of light gave her features a variety of casts, which had become familiar to me.

Such strength of mind or of body was not usually associated either with witchcraft or with Satan-worship. In my experience, as Sabrina had already hinted to me, those who sought the aid of demons were wretched, powerless creatures who had given up hope of all salvation, whether it be on Earth or in Heaven.

We were crossing the main floor now, towards the huge doors of the library.

41

"He is in there," she said.

I stopped, loosening my sword. I sniffed.

"Still no brimstone," I said. "Has He horns, your Master? A long tail? Cloven hoofs? Does fire come from His nostrils? Or is His enchantment of a subtler sort?"

"I would say that it was subtler," she told me softly. She seemed torn between proving herself and wishing to flee with me. Her expression was challenging and yet fearful as she looked up at me. She seemed even more beautiful. I touched her hair, stroking it. I kissed her upon her warm lips.

Then I strode forward and pushed the large doors open.

Sabrina put her hand on my arm and preceded me into the room. She curtseyed.

"Master, I have brought you Captain von Bek."

I followed immediately behind her, my sword ready, my mind prepared for any challenge, yet my resolve left me immediately.

Seated at the central table and apparently reading a book was the most wonderful being I had ever seen.

I became light-headed. My body refused any commands. I found myself bowing.

He was naked and His skin glowed as if with soft, quivering flames. His curling hair was silver and His eyes were molten copper. His body was huge and perfectly formed, and when His lips smiled upon me I felt that I had never loved before; I loved Him. He bore an aura about His person which I had never associated with the Devil; perhaps it was a kind of dignified humility combined with a sense of almost limitless power.

He spoke in a sweet, mature voice, putting down the book.

"Welcome, Captain von Bek. I am Lucifer."

I was speaking. I believed Him at that moment and I said as much.

Lucifer acknowledged this, standing to His full height and going to the shelves, where He replaced the book.

He moved with grace and offered the impression of exquisite sadness in His every gesture. It was possible to see how this being had been God's favourite and that He was surely the Fallen One, destroyed by Pride and now humbled but unable to achieve His place in Heaven.

I believe that I told Him I was at His service. I could not check the words, although I recovered myself sufficiently to deny, mentally, the implications of what I said. I was desperately attempting to secure my reason.

He seemed to know this and was sympathetic. His sympathy, of course, was also disarming and had to be ignored.

He answered my words as if I had offered them voluntarily:

"I wish to strike a bargain with you, Captain von Bek."

Lucifer smiled, as if in self-mockery:

"You are intelligent and brave and do not deny the truth of what you have become."

"The truth—" I began, with some difficulty, "is not—is not . . ."

He appeared not to hear. "That is why I told my servant Sabrina to bring you to me. I need the help of an adult human being. One without prejudice. One with considerable experience. One who is used to translating thought into determined action. One who is not given to habits of fearfulness and hesitation. Such people are scarce, always, in the world."

Now my tongue was not thickened. I was allowed to speak. I said: "It seems so to me, also, Prince Lucifer. But you do not describe me. I am but a poor specimen of mankind."

"Let us say you are the best available to the likes of me."

A little of my wit returned. "I believe you think you flatter me, Your Majesty."

"Not so. I see virtue everywhere. I see virtue in you, Captain von Bek."

I smiled. "You are supposed to recognise evil and wickedness and appeal to those qualities."

Lucifer shook His head. "That is what humankind detects in me: the desire to find examples for their own base instincts. Many believe that if they discover an example it somehow exonerates them from responsibility. I am invested with many terrible traits, captain. But I, too, possess many virtues. It is the secret of my power and, to a degree, your own. Did you know that?"

"I did not, Your Majesty."

"But you understand me?"

"I believe that I do."

"I am asking you to serve me."

"You must have far more powerful men and women than I at your command."

Lucifer reseated Himself behind the desk. He seemed to give His full attention to every word that I uttered now. And this in itself, of course, was flattering to me.

"Powerful," he replied, "certainly. Many of them. In the way in which power is measured upon the Earth. Most of the Holy Church is mine now; but that's a fact well-known to thinking people. A majority of princes belong to me. Scholars serve me. Poets serve me. The commanders of armies and navies serve me. You would think that I am satisfied, eh? There have rarely been so many in my service. But I have few such as you, von Bek."

"That I cannot believe, Your Majesty. Bloody-handed soldiers abound in these times."

"And always have. But few with your quality. Few who act with the full knowledge of what they are and what they do."

"Is it a virtue to know that you are a butcher, a thief? That you are ruthless and without altruism of any kind?"

"I believe so. But then I am Lucifer." Again the self-mockery.

Sabrina curtseyed again. "My Lord, shall I leave?"

"Aye," said Lucifer. "I think so, my dear. I will return the captain to you in due course, I promise."

The witch withdrew. I wondered if I had been abandoned for ever by Sabrina, now that she had served her purpose. I tried to stare back at the creature who called Himself Lucifer, but to look into those melancholy, terrible eyes was too much for me. I directed my attention to the window. Through it I could see the mass of trees that was the great forest. I attempted to focus on this sight, in order to preserve my reason and remember that in all likelihood I had been drugged by the accomplice of a man who was nothing more than a charlatan sorcerer of a very high order.

"Now," said the Prince of Darkness, "will you not accompany me to Hell, captain?"

"What?" said I. "Am I damned already? And dead?"

Lucifer smiled. "I give you my word that I shall bring you back to this room. If you are uninterested in my bargain, I will allow you to leave the castle unharmed, to go about whatever business you choose."

"Then why must I come with you to Hell? I have been taught to believe that Satan's word is in no way to be trusted. That He will use any means to win over an honest soul."

Lucifer laughed. "And perhaps you are right, captain. Is yours an honest soul?"

"It is not a clean one."

"But it is, by and large, honest. Yes?"

"You seem to place value on such honesty."

"Great value, captain. I admit to you freely that I have need of you. You do not prize yourself as highly as I prize you. Perhaps that is also one of your virtues. I am prepared to offer you good terms."

"But you will not tell me your terms."

"Not until you have visited Hell. Will you not satisfy your curiosity? Few are able to sample Hell before their time."

"And the few I have read of, Your Majesty, are usually tricked to return there soon enough."

"I give you my word, as an angel, that I am not about to trick you, Captain von Bek. I will be candid with you: I cannot afford to trick you. If I gained what I need from you by deception, then what I gained would be useless to me."

Lucifer offered me His hand.

"Will you descend, with me, to my domain?"

Still I hesitated, not entirely convinced that this was not a complicated and sophisticated enchantment wholly of human origin.

"Can you not bargain with me here?" I said.

"I could. But when the bargain was struck—if it was struck—and when we had parted, would you remain truly certain that you had negotiated with Lucifer?"

"I suppose that I would not. Even now I think that I could be in some kind of drugged glamour."

"You would not be the first to decide that an encounter with me had been nothing but a dream. As a rule it would be immaterial to me whether you decided you had experienced an illusion or were utterly sure that you had enjoyed a meeting with the Prince of Darkness. But I am anxious to prove myself to you, captain."

"Why should Lucifer care?"

A trembling of old Pride. Almost a glare of anger. Then it was gone. "Be assured, captain," replied Lucifer in deep, urgent tones, "that on this occasion I do care."

"You must be clearer with me, Your Majesty." It was all that I could do to utter even this simple phrase.

He exerted patience. "I cannot prove myself to you here. As you doubtless know, I am largely forced to use humankind for my purposes on Earth, being forbidden direct influence over God's Creations, unless they seek me out. I am anxious to do nothing further in defiance of God. I yearn for freedom, von Bek." His copper eyes showed a more intense version of the pain I had observed in Sabrina's. "I once thought I could achieve it. And yet I know now that I cannot have it. Therefore, I wish to be restored."

"To Heaven, Your Majesty?" I was astonished.

"To Heaven, Captain von Bek."

Lucifer applying for a return to Grace! And suggesting that somehow I could be His agent in effecting this! If this were indeed a spell, a trance, it was a most intriguing one.

I was able to say: "Would that not produce the abolition of Hell, the end of Pain in the world?"

"You have been taught to believe that."

"Is it not true?"

"Who knows, Captain von Bek? I am only Lucifer. I am not God."

His fingers touched mine.

Unconsciously, I had stretched my hand towards Him.

His voice was a throb of pleading, of persuasion. "Come, I beg thee. Come."

It was as if we swayed together in a dance, like snake and victim.

I shook my head. My mind was too full of conflict. I felt that I was losing both physical and mental balance at once.

He touched my hand again. I gasped.

"Come, von Bek. Come to Hell."

His flesh was hot but did not burn me. It was sensuous, that touch, though immensely strong.

"Your Majesty . . ." I was pleading, in turn.

"Will you not have pity, von Bek? Have pity on the Fallen One. Pity Lucifer."

The urgency, the pain, the need, the desperation, all conspired to win me, but I fought for a few seconds more. "I have no pity," I said. "I have scoured pity from my soul. I have scoured mercy. I feel only for myself!"

"*That is not so, von Bek.*"

"It is so! It is!"

"*A truly merciless creature would not even know what it was. You resist mercy in yourself. You resist pity. You are a victim of your reason. It has replaced your humanity. And that is truly what death is, though you walk and breathe. Help me restore myself to Heaven, and I shall help you to come to life again . . .*"

"Oh, Your Majesty," said I, "you are as clever as they say you are." For all that I was, at that moment, His, I still attempted to strike some temporary sort of bargain. "I'll come, on the understanding that I shall be back in this room before the hour's over. And that I shall see Sabrina again..."

"*Granted.*"

The flagstones of the library melted away before us. They turned to mercury and then to blue water. We began to float downwards, as if through a cold sky, towards a distant landscape, wide and white and without horizon.

Chapter Three

M Y SKIN NOW seemed to have turned almost as white as that featureless plain. I observed on my hands details of line, contours of vein and bone, which I had never before noticed.

My nails glittered like glass and appeared extraordinarily fragile.

I possessed virtually no weight at all. I thought that I might have been a crystal ghost.

"This is Hell?" said I to Lucifer.

The Prince of Darkness, too, was pale. Only His eyes, black as weathered iron, were alive.

"This is Hell," He said. "One part, I should say, of my domain. A domain which is, of course, infinite."

"And has infinite aspects?" I suggested.

"Of course not. You speak of Heaven. Hell is the Realm of Restraint and Bleak Singularity." His smile was almost hesitant, His glance sidelong, as if He was concerned that I should not miss His irony.

Lucifer seemed to exhibit a certain shyness with me. I could believe that He hoped for my good opinion. I was puzzled as to why this should be. He still gave off an aura of tremendous power and genius. I was still, against every effort of will, drawn to Him. I was certainly no match for Him in any conceivable terms. Yet it was my impression that He was nervous of me. What might I possess that He could not demand? Why should He be so desperate to own my soul?

But I saw no sense in trying to outguess Satan. Surely He could read every thought, anticipate every argument, forestall every action I chose to take.

It then occurred to me that perhaps He was refusing to do this. Perhaps His apparent delicacy was the result of His own reluctance to use the power that was His. The Prince of Darkness, who could manipulate kings and generals, Popes and cardinals, to whom such manipulation was second nature, was seeking somehow to be direct, was resisting in Himself the habits of an eternal lifetime.

This impression of mine could in itself have been created by means of careful deception.

There was plainly no point in attempting to understand Lucifer's motives or guess His character. Neither should I, I told myself, waste what few mental resources I still had in trying to anticipate either His actions or His needs.

I should merely trust that He would keep His word. I would let Him show me what He wished to show me of His Realm. And I would believe nothing to be wholly what it might seem to be.

"You are a pragmatist, captain," said Lucifer casually, "in your very bones. To your very soul, one might say."

My voice seemed fainter than was normal. There was a slight echo to it, I thought. "Do you see my soul, Your Majesty?"

He linked His arm in mine and we began to walk across the plain. "I am familiar with it, captain."

I knew no fear at this statement, whereas on Earth I should have shuddered at least a little. Although aware of Lucifer's presence, my body was now neither corporeal nor ethereal, but somewhere between the two. Emotions which should have been strong in me were presently only hinted at; my brain seemed clearer, but that in itself could have been an illusion; my movements were slow and deliberate, yet they followed my thoughts well enough.

This state of being was not uncongenial, and I wondered if it might be the usual condition of angels and the more powerful orders of supernatural entities.

It did not strike me as strange, as I strolled through Hell, side by side with Lucifer, that I had begun to think in terms of spiritual creatures, of Realms beyond my earthly world, when, for many years, I had refused to believe in anything but the most substantial and material of phenomena.

Flesh and blood—predominantly the preservation of my own—

had been my only reality since my early days of soldiering. My mind and my senses had become blunted, almost certainly, but blunted sensibilities were the only kind one could safely have in the life I led. And the life I led was the only sane one in the world in which I had found myself.

Now, of a sudden, I was not only discovering a return of all my subtlest sensibilities, but exploring sensations—illusory or not— normally denied the bulk of humanity.

It was no wonder that my judgement was confused. Even though I allowed for this, I could not help but be affected. I fought to remember that I must make no pact with Lucifer, that I must agree to nothing, that no matter how tempting any offer He made I must play for time. For not only my life could be at stake, my fate for all Eternity could be the issue.

Lucifer seemed to be trying to console me. "I have given my word to you," He reminded me, "and I shall keep it."

An archway of silvery flames appeared immediately before us. Lucifer drew me towards it.

This time I did not hesitate, but entered the archway and found myself in a city.

The city was of black obsidian stone. Every surface, every wall, every canopy and every flag were black and gleamed. The folk of the city wore clothes of rich, dark colours—of scarlet and deep blue, of bloody orange and moss green—and their skins were the colour of old, polished oak.

"This city exists in Hell?" I asked.

"It is one of the chief cities of Hell," replied Lucifer.

As we passed, the people knelt immediately to the ground and made obeisance to their Lord.

"They recognise you," I said.

"Oh, indeed."

The city seemed rich and the people seemed healthy.

"Hell is a punishment, surely?" I said. "Yet these people are not evidently suffering."

"They are suffering," said Lucifer. "It is their specific fate. You saw how swiftly they knelt to me."

"Aye."

"They are all my slaves. They are none of them free."

"Doubtless they were not free on Earth."

"True. But they know that they would be free in Heaven. Their chief misery is simply that they know they are in Hell for all Eternity. It is that knowledge, in itself, which is their punishment."

"What is freedom in Heaven?" I asked.

"In Hell you become what you fear yourself to be. In Heaven you may become what you hope yourself to be," said Lucifer.

I had expected a more profound reply, or at least a more complicated one.

"A mild enough punishment, compared to what Luther threatened," I observed.

"Apparently. And far less interesting than Luther's torments, as he would tell you himself. There is nothing very interesting in Hell."

I found that I was amused. "Would that be an epigram to sum Hell up?" I asked.

"I doubt if such an epigram exists. Perhaps Luther would believe that it was. Do you wish to ask him?"

"He is here?"

"In this very city. It is called the City of Humbled Princes. It might have been built for him."

I had no wish to encounter Martin Luther, either in Hell, in Heaven or on Earth. I must admit to a certain satisfaction at the knowledge that he had not gained his expected reward but doubtless shared territory in Hell with those churchmen he had most roundly condemned.

"I believe I understand what you mean," I said.

"Oh, I think we both understand Pride, Captain von Bek," said Lucifer almost cheerfully. "Shall I call Luther? He is very docile now."

I shook my head.

Lucifer drew me on through the black streets. I looked at the faces of the citizens, and I knew that I would do almost anything to avoid becoming one of them. This damnation was surely a subtle one. It was their eyes which chiefly impressed me: hard and hope-less. Then it was their whispering voices: cold and without dignity. And then it was the city itself: without any saving humanity.

"This visit to Hell will be brief," Lucifer reassured me. "But I believe it will convince you."

We entered a huge, square building and passed into deeper blackness.

"Are there no flames here?" I asked Him. "No demons? No screaming sinners?"

"Few sinners receive that sort of satisfaction here," said Lucifer.

We stood on the shores of a wide and shallow lake. The water was flat and livid. The light was grey and milky and there seemed no direct source for it. The sky was the same colour as the water.

Standing at intervals in the lake, for as far as I could see, naked men and women, waist-deep, were washing themselves.

The noise of the water was muffled and indistinct. The move-ments of the men and women were mechanical, as if they had been making the same gestures for aeons. All were of similar height. All had the same dull flesh, the same lack of expression upon their faces. Their lips were silent. They gathered the water in their hands and poured it over their heads and bodies, moving like clockwork figures. But again it was their eyes which displayed their agony. They moved, it appeared to me, against their will, and could do nothing to stop themselves.

"Is this guilt?" I asked Lucifer. "Do they know themselves to be guilty of something?"

He smiled. He seemed singularly satisfied with this particular torment. "I think it is an imitation of guilt, captain. This is called the Lake of the False Penitents."

"God is not tolerant," I said. "Or so it would seem."

"God is God," said Lucifer. He shrugged. "It is for me to inter-pret His Will and to devise a variety of punishments for those who are refused Heaven."

"So you continue to serve Him?"

"It could be." Lucifer again seemed uncertain. "Yet of late I have begun to wonder if I have not misinterpreted Him. It is left to me, after all, to discover appropriate cruelties. But what if I am not supposed to punish them? What if I am supposed to show mercy?" I noted something very nearly pathetic in His voice.

"Are you given no instructions?" I asked somewhat weakly. "Tens of millions of souls might have suffered for nothing because of your failure!" I was incredulous.

"I am denied any communion with God, captain." His tone sharpened. "Is that not obvious to you?"

"So you never know whether you please or displease Him? He sends you no sign?"

"For most of my time in Hell I never looked for one, captain. I am, as I have pointed out, forced to use human agents."

"And you receive no word through such agents?"

"How can I trust them? I am excommunicate, Captain von Bek. The souls sent to me are at my mercy. I do with them as I wish, largely to relieve my own dreadful boredom." He became gloomy. "And to take revenge on those who had the opportunity to seek God's grace and rejected it or were too stupid or greedy to recognise what they had lost." He gestured.

I saw a sweep of broad, pleasant fields, with green trees in them. An idyllic rural scene. Even the light was warmer and brighter here, although again there was no sense of that light emanating from any particular direction.

It could have been spring. Seated or standing in the fields, like small herds of cattle, dressed in shreds of fabric, were groups of people. Their skins were rough, scabrous, unclean. Their motion through the fields was sluggish, bovine. Yet these poor souls were by no means contented.

I realised that, although the shape of the bodies varied, every face was absolutely identical.

Every face was lined by the same inturned madness and greed, the same pouched expression of utter selfishness. The creatures mumbled at one another, each monologue the same, as they wandered round and round the fields.

The whined complaints began very quickly to fill me with immense irritation. I could feel no charity for them.

"Every single one of those souls is a universe of self-involvement," said Lucifer.

"And yet they are identical," I said.

"Just so. They are alike in the smallest detail. Yet not one of those men or women there can allow himself to recognise the fact. The closer they get to the core of the self, the more they become like the others." He turned to look sardonically down at me. "Is this more what you expected of Hell, captain?"

"Yes. I think so."

"Every one of these when on Earth spoke of Free Will, of loyalty to one's own needs. Of the importance of controlling one's own destiny. Every one believed himself to be master of his fate. And they had only one yardstick, of course: material well-being. It is all that is possible when one discounts one's involvement with the rest of humanity."

I looked hard at those identical faces. "Is this a specific warning to me?" I asked Lucifer. "I should have thought you would be attempting to make Hell seem more attractive to me."

"And why is that?"

I did not reply. I was too afraid to answer.

"Would you enjoy the prospect of being in my charge, Captain von Bek?" Lucifer asked me.

"I would not," I told him, "for on Earth, at least, one can pretend to Free Will. Here, of course, all choice is denied you."

"And in Heaven one can actually possess Free Will," said Lucifer.

"In spite of Heaven's ruler?" I said. "It would seem to me that He demands a great deal of His creatures."

"I am no priestly interpreter," said Lucifer, "but it has been argued God demands only that men and women should demand much of themselves."

The fields were behind us now. "I, on the other hand," continued the Prince of Darkness, "expect nothing of humanity, save confirmation that it is worthless. I am disposed to despise it, to use it, to exploit its weakness. Or so it was in the beginning of my reign."

"You speak as one who saw all humanity as His rival. I should not have believed an angel—albeit a fallen one—to admit to such pettiness."

"That rage, I still recall it. That rage did not seem petty to me, Captain von Bek."

"You have changed, Your Majesty?"

"I told you that I had, captain."

"You are frustrated, then, that you have failed to convince God of this?"

"Just so. Because God cannot hear me."

"Are you certain of that, Your Majesty?"

"I am certain of nothing. But I understand it to be the truth."

I felt almost sorry for this great being, this most defiant of all creatures, having come to a point where He was willing to admit to His defeat, and there being no-one to acknowledge or perhaps to believe His admission.

"I am weary of the Earth and still more weary of Hell, captain. I yearn for my position in Heaven."

"But if Your Majesty is truly repentant . . ."

"It must be proved. I must make amends."

Lucifer continued: "I placed high value on the power of the intellect to create a luxury of wonders upon the Earth. I sought to prove that my logic, my creativity, my mind, could all outshine anything which God made. Then I came to believe that Man was not worthy of me. Then I came to believe that perhaps I was not worthy, that what I had sought to make had no substance, no definition, no future. You have seen much of the world, captain."

"More than most are permitted to see," I agreed.

"Everything is in decay, is it not? Everything. The spirit decays as the flesh and the mind decay." Lucifer uttered a sigh. "I have failed."

His voice became hollow. I found that I was pitying Him, even more than I pitied the souls who were trapped in His domain.

"I wish to be taken back into the certainty, the tranquillity, I once knew," Lucifer continued.

We stood again upon the white plain.

"I sought to show that I could create a more beautiful world

55

than anything God could create. I still do not know what I did wrong. I have been thinking on that for many a century, captain. And I know that only a human soul can discover the secret which eludes me. I must make amends. I must make amends . . ."

"Have you decided how you can do that?" I asked quietly.

"I must discover the Cure for the World's Pain, Captain von Bek." He turned his dark eyes upon me and I felt my whole being shiver at the intensity.

"A Cure? Human folly, surely, is the cause of that Pain. The answer seems simple enough to me."

"No!" Lucifer's voice was almost a groan. "It is complex. God has bestowed on the world one object, one means of healing humanity's ills. If that object is discovered and the world set to rights again, then God will listen to me. Once God listens, I might be able to convince Him that I am truly repentant."

"But what has this to do with me, Your Majesty? Surely you cannot think that I possess a Cure for human folly."

Lucifer made an almost angry gesture with His right hand.

We were suddenly once more in the library of the castle. We faced one of the great windows. Through it I could see the green, silent forest and noted that very little time had passed. My body was now as solid as it had always been. I felt some relief. My ordinary senses were restored.

Lucifer said: "I asked you to help me, von Bek, because you are intelligent, resourceful and not easily manipulated. I am asking you to embark upon a Quest on my behalf. I want you to find me the Cure to the world's ills. Do you know of what I speak?"

"I have heard only of the Holy Grail, Your Majesty," I told Him. "And I believe that to be a myth. If I were shown such a cup I would believe in its powers as much as I would believe in the powers of a piece of the True Cross, or Saint Peter's fingernail."

He ignored these last remarks. His eyes flamed and became remote. "Ah, yes. It is called that. The Holy Grail. How would you describe it, von Bek?"

"A legendary cup."

"If it existed, what would you say it was?"

"A physical manifestation of God's mercy on Earth," I said.

"Exactly. Is that not the object I have described to you?"

I became incredulous. "Lucifer is commissioning a godless soldier of fortune to seek and secure the Holy Grail?"

"I am asking you to seek the Cure for the World's Pain, yes. Call it the Grail."

"The legend says that only the purest of knights is permitted to see it, let alone touch it!"

"Your journey will purify you, I'm sure."

"Your Majesty, what are you offering me, should I agree to this Quest?"

He smiled ironically at me. "Is it not an honour in itself, von Bek?"

I shook my head. "You must have better servants for such a monumental Quest."

Was Lucifer mad? Was He playing a game with me?

"I have told you," He said, "that I have not."

I hesitated. I felt bound to voice my feelings:

"I am suspicious, Your Majesty."

"Why so?"

"I cannot read your motive."

"My motive is simple."

"It defeats me."

His miserable, tortured eyes looked full on me again and He spoke in an urgent whisper: *"It is because you fail to understand how great is my need. How great is my need! Such souls as yours are scarce, von Bek."*

"Can I assume that you are trying to buy my soul at this moment, Your Majesty?"

"Buy it?" He seemed puzzled. "Buy your soul, von Bek? Did you not realise that I own your soul already? I am offering you the chance to reclaim it."

I knew at once that He spoke the truth. I had known, within me, for some while.

It was then that Lucifer smiled, and in that smile I saw simple confirmation of what we both knew. He did not lie.

A coldness came into me. That was why He had shown me Hell; not to lure me there, but to sample my eternal doom.

I drew away from my Master. "Then I am already forbidden Heaven. Is that what you are telling me, Your Majesty?"

"You are already forbidden Heaven."

"If that is so, I have no choice, surely?"

"If I rejected you, it would allow you a new chance to be restored in God's grace—just as I hope to be restored. We do indeed have much in common, von Bek."

I had never heard of such a bargain before. Yet by taking it I could only lose my life a little sooner than I had planned.

I said: "Then in reality I have little choice."

"Let us say that your character has already determined your choice."

"Yet you cannot promise me that God will accept me into Heaven."

"I can promise you only that I will release your soul from my custody. Such souls do not always enter Heaven. But they are said to live for ever, some of them."

"I have heard legends," I said, "such as that of the Wandering Jew. Am I to try to save myself from Hell merely so that I may wander the world for Eternity seeking redemption?"

It occurred to me of a sudden that I was not the first mortal soul to be offered this bargain by Lucifer.

"I cannot say," said the Prince of Darkness. "But if you are successful, it is likely, is it not, that God would look with mercy upon you?"

"You must know more of God's habits, Your Majesty, than I." A strange calm was creeping into me now. I felt a degree of amusement.

Lucifer saw what was happening to me and He grinned. "It is a challenge, is it not, von Bek?"

"Aye, Your Majesty." I was still debating what He had said. "But if I am already your servant, why did you go to such elaborate means to ensure this meeting? Why send Sabrina?"

"I have told you. I am forced to use human agents."

"Even though she and I are already your servants?"

"Sabrina elected to serve me. You have not yet agreed."

"So Sabrina cannot be saved?"

"All will be saved if you find the Grail."

"But could I not ask one thing of Your Majesty?"

Lucifer's beautiful head turned down towards me. "I think I follow you, von Bek."

"Would you release Sabrina from your power if I agreed to what you ask of me?"

Lucifer had anticipated this.

"Not if you agree. But if you are successful. Find the Cure for the World's Pain, and bring it to me, and I promise you I will release Sabrina under exactly the same terms as I release you."

"So if I am doomed to eternal life, I shall have a companion with me."

"Yes."

I considered this. "Very well, Your Majesty. Where shall I seek this Cure, this Grail?"

"All that I know is that it is hidden from me and from all those already dwelling in infernal regions. It is somewhere upon the Earth or in a supernatural Realm not far removed from the Earth."

"A Realm not of the Earth? How can I possibly go to such a place?"

Lucifer said: "This castle is such a place, von Bek. I can allow you the power to enter certain parts of the world forbidden to ordinary mortals. It is possible that the Cure lies in one of those Realms, or that it lies in a most ordinary place. But you will be enabled to travel more or less where you wish or need to go."

"Do you mean to make a sorcerer of me, Your Majesty?"

"Perhaps. I am able to offer you certain privileges to aid you in your Quest. But I know that you take pride in your own intelligence and skills and it is those which shall be most valuable to both of us. And you have courage, von Bek, of several kinds.

Although you are mortal, that is another quality we have in common. That is another reason I chose you."

"I am unsure if I am entirely complimented, Your Majesty. To be Satan's representative upon Earth, some Anti-Pope." I changed the subject. "And what if I should fail you?"

Lucifer turned away from me. "That would depend, let us say, on the nature of your failure. If you die, you travel instantly to Hell. But should you betray me, in any way at all, von Bek—well, there is no way in which I cannot claim you. You shall be mine soon enough. And I shall be able to debate my vengeance upon you for all Eternity."

"So if I am killed in pursuit of my Quest, I gain nothing, but am transported at once to Hell?"

"Just so. But you have seen that Hell can take many forms. And I am able, after a fashion, to resurrect the dead . . ."

"I have seen your resurrections, Your Majesty, and I would rather be wholly dead. But I suppose I must agree to your bargain, because I have so little to lose."

"Very little, captain."

How radically had my life been turned about in the past twenty-four hours! I had over the years managed successfully to rid myself of all thoughts of damnation or salvation, of God or the Devil, during my career as a soldier. I had served many masters, but felt loyal to none of them, had never let them control my fate. I had believed myself my own man, through and through, for good or ill.

Now, suddenly, I had been informed by Lucifer Himself that I was damned and that I was to be offered at the same time a chance of salvation. My feelings, needless to say, were mixed. From a pragmatic agnostic I had been changed not only into a believer, but into a believer called upon to take part in that most fundamental of all spiritual concerns, the struggle between Heaven and Hell. And I had become an apparently important piece in the game. It was hard for me to accept so much at once.

I understood what Sabrina had meant when she had told me,

also, that only souls already owned by Lucifer could exist in the castle and its environs.

I had originally refused to accept that knowledge, but it was no longer possible for me to resist it. The evidence had been presented to me. I was damned. And I had already begun (more than I would have admitted then, I think) to hope for salvation. As a result, I had committed myself, against all former habit, to a cause.

I bowed to Lucifer. "Then I am ready to embark upon this Quest, Your Majesty, whenever you wish."

It was ironic, I thought, that Hope had been revived in me by the Fallen One and not, as should be traditional, by a vision of the Madonna or a meeting with some goodly priest.

"I would like you to begin almost immediately," said the Prince of Darkness.

I looked outside. It was not yet noon.

"Today?" I asked Him.

"Tomorrow. Sabrina will spend some time with you."

At this hint of manipulation of my private emotions I bridled. "Perhaps I have no further desire to spend time with her, Your Majesty."

Lucifer clapped his hands lightly and Sabrina entered the library and curtseyed.

"Captain von Bek has agreed to my bargain," Lucifer told her. "You must now do as I instructed you, Sabrina." His voice had become gentle, almost kindly.

She curtseyed again. "Yes, Your Majesty."

I looked upon her beauty and I marvelled all the more. My feelings for her had not changed. At once I became almost grateful to Lucifer for sending her to me.

Lucifer returned to the central table, taking another book with Him, for all the world like a rural nobleman preparing himself for a little solitude before lunch.

"And Captain von Bek has involved you in this bargain, my dear. He has news for you which you might find palatable."

She frowned as she rose. She looked enquiringly from her

Master to myself. There was nothing I was prepared to say to her at that moment.

He was plainly dismissing us both. Yet I hesitated.

"I had expected a somewhat more dramatic symbol of our bargain, Your Majesty."

Lucifer smiled again. His wonderful eyes were, temporarily at least, free of pain.

"I know few mortals who would feel that a visit to Hell was undramatic, captain."

I bowed again, accepting this.

"Should you be successful in your Quest," Lucifer added, "you will return to this castle with what I have asked you to find. Sabrina will await you."

I could not resist one last question: "And if Your Majesty is displeased with what I bring Him?" I said.

Lucifer put down His book. The eyes had become hard again as they looked into mine. I knew, then, that He must surely own my soul, He understood it so well.

"Then we shall all go back to Hell together," He said.

Sabrina touched my arm. I bowed to my Master for the third and last time. Lucifer returned to His reading.

As she led me from the room, Sabrina said: "I already know the nature of your Quest. There are maps I must give you. And other things."

She curtseyed. She closed the library doors on the Prince of Darkness. Then she took my hand and led me through the castle to a small chamber in one of the north-western towers. I could not remember having explored this particular region of the castle.

Here, on a small desk, was a case of maps, two small leather-bound books, a ring of plain silver, a roll of parchment and a brass flask of the ordinary kind which soldiers often carried.

These objects had been arranged, I thought, in some sort of pattern. Perhaps Sabrina's habits of witchcraft, with their emphasis on shapes and symbols, influenced her without her being aware of it.

By way of experiment, I stretched a hand towards the flask. I moved it slightly. She made no objection.

That action of mine, however, gave me pause. I realised that I had already begun to think in terms which a day or two earlier would have been ridiculous. My world was no longer what it had seemed to be. It was not the world I had trained myself to see. It was a world, in some ways, which threatened action. Imposed upon my world was another, a world in which the smallest detail possessed an extra significance. I attempted to dismiss this unwelcome awareness, at least from my conscious mind. It would not do, I thought, to observe potential danger in the way a bird flew across the sky, or see importance in the manner in which two tree branches intersected. This was the madness of those who thought themselves seers or artists, and I should always remind myself that I was a soldier. My concerns were with the physical world, with the reading of another man's eyes to see if he meant to kill me or not, with the signs of groups of infantry on the move, with the detection of a peasant's secret storehouse.

I turned to Sabrina. It was almost a plea for help.

"I am afraid," I said.

She stroked my arm. "You regret your bargain with our Master?"

I was unable to reply directly. "I regret the circumstances which have put us both in His power," I said. "But if it is so, I have little choice but to do what He asks of me."

"He suggested that something you had agreed with Him would be of significance to me." She spoke carelessly, but I think she was eager to hear what had been agreed. "The bargain you struck?"

"I am attempting to regain your soul as well as my own," I said. "If I find this—this Grail, we are both free."

At first she looked at me with hope and then, almost immediately, with despair. "My soul is sold, Ulrich."

"He has promised to restore it to you. If I am successful in my Quest."

"I am moved," she said, "that you should think of me."

"I believe that I love you," I said.

She nodded. I understood from her expression that she also

loved me. She said: "He has commissioned you, has He not, to seek the Cure for the World's Pain?"

"Just so."

"And the chances of your success are poor. Perhaps that Cure does not exist. Perhaps Lucifer is as desperate as we are." She paused, almost whispering: "Could Lucifer be mad?"

"Possibly," I said. "But mad or not, He owns our souls. And if there is even a little hope, I must follow it."

"I shall forget hope, for my own part." She came towards me. "I cannot afford to hope, Ulrich."

I took her in my arms. "I cannot afford not to hope," I told her. "I must take action. It is in my nature."

She accepted this.

I kissed her. My love for her was growing by the moment. I had become increasingly reluctant to leave. Yet Lucifer, sane or insane, had convinced me that our only chance to be truly together lay in my fulfilling the terms of our bargain.

I drew away from her. I contained my emotions. I looked down at the desk.

"Show me what these things are," I said to her.

She could hardly speak. Her hand trembled as she picked up the map-case and gave it to me.

"The maps are of the world, both known and unknown. There are certain areas marked on them which are not marked on ordinary maps. These are the lands which exist between Earth and Heaven, between Heaven and Hell.

"This"—she picked up a box from the desk—"is a compass, as you can see. It will lead you through the natural world as surely as any good compass can. And it will point towards the entrances and exits of those supernatural lands."

She put down the compass and pointed to the brass flask. "That contains a liquid which will restore you to energy and help heal any wounds you might sustain. The books are grimoires, so that you may summon aid if you need it. They are to be used judiciously."

"And the ring?" I asked.

She took it from the desk and placed it carefully on the second finger of my right hand.

"That is my gift to you," she said. Then she kissed the hand.

I was moved. "I have no gift for you, Sabrina."

"You must bring yourself safely back," she said. "For surely if you are dutiful in your Quest, even if you fail, our Master will allow us some time together in Hell."

She was afraid of hope. I understood her.

There were tears in her eyes. I realised that I, too, was weeping. I forced control on myself again and said unsteadily:

"The parchment? You have not told me what it is."

"The parchment is to be opened if you succeed." Her voice, too, was trembling. "It informs you how you may return to the castle. But you must not open it before you find the Cure for the World's Pain."

She leaned down and picked up a pouch from the floor. "There are provisions in this," she said, "as well as money for your journey. Your horse will carry more provisions and will await you in the courtyard when you are ready to leave."

She began to pack the maps and the other objects into the pouch. She buckled it carefully and gave it into my hands.

"What next?" I asked her.

Her smile was no longer bold, no longer challenging. It was almost shy. I smelled roses again. I touched her hair, the soft skin of her cheek.

"We have until the morning," she said.

Chapter Four

M Y MOOD, UPON awakening the next morning, was peculiar. All kinds of conflicting feelings stirred within me. My love for Sabrina was coloured by the knowledge that she had helped to trap me, though I knew, too, that I had not really been trapped. Lucifer had, after all, offered me the opportunity of redeeming my immortal soul. My impressions of my brief visit to Hell were if anything stronger, and I believed almost without question that I had indeed encountered the Prince of Darkness and had accompanied Him to His domain. I had always claimed to welcome the truth; yet now, in common with most of us, I was resentful of the truth because it called upon me to take an unwelcome course of action. I longed for the grim innocence I had so recently lost.

Sabrina was still sleeping. Outside, a mist of light rain obscured the forest. I brooded upon the conversations which had taken place between myself and Sabrina, between myself and Lucifer. I sought for some saving logic, some means of questioning the import of what I had heard, and could find none. This castle, alone, convinced me. The previous night Sabrina had said: "You see the surface translated by your mortal eye. Your mortal mind could not, in normality, accept the truth. There is nothing to do in Hell: no fulfilment, no future, no hope at all. No faith in anything. Those souls who dwell there also had faith only in their own survival. And now they have lost that, also."

I had not answered her, after this. I had become absorbed in my feelings which were impossible to put into thoughts, let alone words. At one time I had been flooded with anger and had said: "Sabrina, if all this is a deception, an enchantment in which you have conspired, I will surely return to kill you."

But my anger had disappeared even as I spoke. I knew that she did not wish me ill. My threat had been made from a habit of attitude and action which was virtually meaningless now.

I knew for certain that she loved me. And I knew that I loved her. We were like-minded in so many ways; we were equals. I could not tolerate the notion that I might lose her.

I returned to draw back the curtains and sit on the edge of the bed, looking down on Sabrina's sleeping face. She started suddenly, crying out, reaching her hand to where I had lain. I touched her cheek. "I am here."

She turned and smiled at me. Then her eyes clouded. "You are leaving?"

"I suppose that I must. Soon."

"Yes," she said, "for it is morning." She began to sit up. She sighed. "When I made my bargain with Lucifer I thought that I was resisting circumstance, taking my fate into my own hands. But circumstance continues to affect us. Can it even affect who we are? Is there any proof beyond ourselves that we are unique?"

"We feel ourselves to be unique," I said. "But a cynic sees only familiarity and similarity and would say that we are all pretty much the same."

"Is it because a cynic does not possess the imagination to distinguish those subtle differences in which you and I believe?"

"I am a cynic," I said to her. "A cynic refuses to allow distinctions of motive or of temperament."

"Oh, but you are not!" She came into my arms. "Or you would not be here."

I held her closely. "I am what I have to be at this moment," I said. "For my own sake."

"And for mine," she reminded me.

I felt a terrible sadness well within me. I suppressed it. "And for yours," I agreed.

We kissed. The pain continued to grow. I pulled away from her. I went to the corner of the room and began to wash myself. I noticed that my hands were shaking and that my breathing had become unusually deep. I had a wish, at that moment, to return to

Hell, to summon up an army of all those poor damned souls and set them in rebellion against Lucifer, as Lucifer had set Himself against God. I felt that we were in the hands of foolish, insane beings, whose motives were more petty even than Man's. I wanted to be rid of all of them. It was unjust, I thought, that such creatures should have power over us. Even if they had created us, could they not, in turn, be destroyed?

But these ideas were pointless. I had neither the means, the knowledge nor the power to challenge them. I could only accept that my destiny was, in part at least, in their charge. I would have to agree to play out my role in Lucifer's terms, or play no role at all.

I drew on fresh linen. Sabrina sat with the curtain drawn back, watching me. I put on my breastplate, my greaves, my spurs. I buckled my sword and daggers about me. I picked up my helmet. I was ready, once again, for War.

"You say the horse will be ready?" I said.

"In the courtyard."

I stooped to pick up the pouch she had given me the previous day. I had regulated my breathing and my hands did not shake as much.

"I will stay here," she said.

I accepted this. I knew why she would not wish to accompany me to the courtyard.

"I intend to do my best in this matter," I said to her. "With you, I think that there is little chance of discovering any Grail, but I shall maintain my resolve if I know that you believe in me. Will you remember to trust me to return to you?"

"I will remember," she replied. "It is all that I will have to sustain me. Yes, Ulrich, I will trust you."

We were both desperate for certainty, and in that uncertain world we were attempting to make concrete that most amorphous and changeable of emotions, as people often will when they have no other sense of the future.

"Then we are pledged," I said. "And it is a more welcome bargain than any I have made in recent hours." I moved towards her, touched her naked shoulder with the tips of my fingers, kissed her lightly upon the lips.

"Farewell," I said.

"Farewell." She spoke softly. And then: "You must travel first towards Ammendorf, where you will seek out the Wildgrave."

"What can he tell me?"

She shook her head. "I know no more."

I left the room.

Outside her door I found that my legs were weak and that I could hardly make my way down the spiralling flights of stone steps to the main hall. I had never experienced such emotion before. I had hardly any means of coping with it.

In the main hall, upon the table, a breakfast had been prepared for me. I paused only to take a deep draught of wine, then continued to stride for the doors with long, faltering steps.

The courtyard was silent, save for the sound of my horse's breathing and the dripping of the drizzle upon the leafy trees. I sniffed the air. Apart from the warm smell of the horse there were no scents at all in it.

My horse stood near the central wall. He looked freshly groomed. There were large panniers on either side of his saddle. My pistols shone in their holsters. Every piece of harness had been polished, every piece of metal and leather was bright. There was a new cloth under the saddle. The horse turned his head to regard me with wide, impatient eyes. His bit clattered in his jaws.

With an effort, I mounted. The wine gave me enough strength and enough resolve to touch my heels to the steed's flanks. He moved smartly forward, glad to be on his way.

The portcullis was up. There were no signs of Sabrina's half-dead servants, no sign of our Master. The castle looked exactly as it had when I had first arrived.

It might have been an elaborate illusion. With that thought in mind, I did not look back: partly from fear that I would see Sabrina herself at a window, partly because I thought I might see nothing at all.

I rode out under the archway towards the path which wound

down through ornamental gardens. The rain washed the statues and the bright, lifeless flowers; it obscured the outlines of the forest below. My horse began to gather speed. Soon we were cantering and I made no attempt to check him. Water poured from my helmet. As I rode I dragged my leather cloak from one of the panniers and wound it round me. The water washed from my face any trace of tears.

I rode down through the cold rain and into that deep, barren forest. It was only a little later that I looked back, briefly, to see the tall stones, the towers and the battlements, to confirm that they were, indeed, realities.

I did not look back again. The forest was dark and grey now and some part of me welcomed its embrace. We rode steadily until nightfall.

My journey to the outskirts of the forest took the better part of two days, and it was not until the morning of the third day that I awoke to birdsong and faint sunshine, to the smells of damp earth and oak and pine. The sense of joyful relief I felt upon hearing the whistling of finches and thrushes reminded me of the strangeness I was leaving behind me, and I wondered again at the reality of it all.

I never once believed that I had dreamed my experience, but it remained a very slight possibility that I had been victim to a sophisticated hallucination. Naturally, part of me desired that this be so. I could not, however, afford to indulge that hope.

I breakfasted lightly of the food provided and drew the maps from my case. I had determined not to consult them until Lucifer's wood was at my back. Ammendorf was not even a familiar name to me and it took me some while to discover it marked.

I as yet had no bearings, but at least I was again in the lands of mortal creatures, and sooner or later I would discover a village, or a charcoal burner, or a woodsman—someone to tell me where I was. Once I knew, I could head for Ammendorf, which appeared to be a relatively small town about fifty miles from Nuremberg.

My horse was eating the sweet-smelling grass with some relish. The grass we had left behind was nourishing enough, but presumably it had had no taste. He looked like a prisoner who had dined too long on bread and water and is suddenly offered a rich repast. I let him eat his fill, then saddled him and, mounted once again, continued on my way until I came, very soon, upon a reasonably wide track through the forest. This I began to follow.

By mid-morning I was riding across gentle hills towards a rich valley. Mist lay upon the tops of the hills and through it broke strong rays of sunshine which struck the deep greens of fields and hedgerows and illuminated them. There was a faint smell of wood-smoke on the spring air and I was warmed, as the rain lifted, by a south-westerly wind.

I made out old cottages and farmsteads, all apparently untouched by the War. I saw cattle and sheep grazing. I breathed in rich scents of the farmyard, of flowers and wet grass, and my skin felt cleaner than it had felt in months. So peaceful was the scene that I wondered if it might be another illusion, that it was designed to snare me somehow, but thankfully my rational, pragmatic mind refused such speculation. I had embarked upon an insane Quest, prompted by a being who could, Himself, be insane; I had need to maintain my sanity in small matters, at least.

As I approached the nearest cottage I smelled baking and my mouth began to water, for I had eaten no hot food since before my encounter with Lucifer. I stopped outside the cottage door and cried a "halloo." At first I thought that, in the manner of wary peasants, no-one would answer me. I took a step or two towards the time-darkened oak of the door just as it opened. A small, plump woman of about forty-five stood there. Seeing my warlike finery, she automatically bobbed her head and said, in a thick accent which I did not recognise: "Good morrow, Your Honour."

"Good morning to you, sister," I returned. "Is it possible for an honest man to purchase some hot food from you?"

She laughed heartily at this. "Sir, if you were a thief and prepared to pay, you would receive the same fare. We have little coin, these days, and a pfennig or two would not go amiss when the time comes to go to town and buy ribbon for a new frock. My daughter is marrying two months from now."

She ushered me into the dark warmth of the cottage. As was typical of such places it was simple and neat, with rushes on the flagstones and a few holy pictures upon the walls. I noted from the pictures that these people were still loyal to Rome.

She took my helmet and cloak and put them carefully upon a chest in the far corner. She told me that she was about to bring a meat pie and an apple pie from her oven, if I could wait but a quarter of an hour, and that she could offer me some good, strong beer of her own brewing, should I partake of such drink. I said that I would greatly welcome a sample of everything on her list and she retired to the kitchen to fetch the beer, chatting about the uncertainty of the weather and the chances of the various crops.

When she brought the beer I remarked that I was surprised the War had not touched them. Her little round face became serious and she nodded. "We believe that God hears our prayers." She shook her head. "But I suppose that we are luckier than most. There is only one road into the valley and it goes nowhere, after our village, save the forest. You must have travelled a very great distance, sir."

"I have indeed."

She frowned as she considered this. "You came through the Silent Marches?"

My ordinary caution made me lie. "I circled them," I said, "if you mean the lifeless forest."

The woman crossed herself. "Only Satan's followers can inhabit those marches."

I knew that she had tested me. For if I had admitted to having travelled through the Silent Marches she would have known that my soul was Lucifer's, and I doubt if I should have been able to have enjoyed her hospitality as much as I did. Both pies were soon forthcoming and they were both delicious.

As I ate I told her that I was an envoy for a prince and that I could not divulge his name. My mission was to attempt to bring peace to Germany, I said.

At this the good frau looked pessimistic. She picked up my empty plate. "I fear that there will be no peace for the world until the Day of Judgement, Your Honour. We can merely pray that it comes soon."

I agreed with her wholeheartedly, for, after all, if my Quest were successful, Judgement Day must surely follow rapidly upon Lucifer's repentance.

"We live," said she, "in the century in which the world is bound to end."

"That is what many believe," I agreed.

"You suggest that you do not, sir."

"I might hope for that event," said I, "but I am not convinced that it will occur."

She cleared away the dishes. She refilled my stein. I was offered a pipe of tobacco from her husband's jar, but I told her that I did not take it. Her husband was at work in the fields, she told me, and would not be back until that evening. Her daughter was with her husband-to-be, helping with the spring planting.

All this wonderful ordinariness had begun to lull me and I thought that perhaps I might stay with these people for a while. But I knew if I did so I should not be fulfilling my pledge to Lucifer and might bring His vengeance not only upon myself but upon these people, also. It comforted me to know that there was one small corner of Germany where War and Plague were unfamiliar.

I finished my beer and asked directions for Nuremberg. The woman was vague, for she had never travelled very far from her village. But she gave me directions for Schweinfurt, which I decided to follow until I came to a large settlement and more sophisticated people.

I left the woman with a piece of silver, which, had she known its origin, she would not have taken with such joy or such gratitude, and was soon upon my way.

The track wound through the valley, climbing gradually to the hills on the far side. I rode through the widely spaced pines, over loamy, reddish soil, and looked back frequently at the cottages and farms with their heavy, peaceful smoke and their sense of dreamy security.

The track led me to a wider road and a signpost for Teufenberg, the nearest town. It was almost sunset when I embarked upon this road, and I hoped that I might come upon an inn or at least a farm where I could beg a bale of hay in a barn for the night, but I was unlucky. I slept again in my cloak, in a ditch by the side of the road, but was undisturbed.

I rose in the morning to warm sunshine and birdsong. Butterflies flew through the clumps of poppies and daisies at the edge of the track and the scents of those flowers were delicious to my nose. I regretted that I had not purchased a little more beer for my journey, but I had expected to be in Teufenberg by now. I promised myself that I would at least break my fast at the nearest inn, and when, by noon, I turned a bend and saw the carved gables of a substantial-looking hostelry, with outhouses, stables, and a little cluster of cottages at the back, I was glad of having made that promise.

The inn was called The Black Friar and it stood upon the banks of a broad but shallow river. A good-sized stone bridge spanned the river (although it seemed possible to ford it without wetting the thighs) and farther up on the far bank I saw a mill, its wheel working slowly as it ground corn. I guessed that both mill and inn were, as was quite common, owned by the same family.

I almost cantered into the courtyard, looking up at the wooden gallery, which went the entire circumference of the place, and crying out for the landlord as I dismounted.

A black-browed fellow, very heavily built and with red arms to match his nose, came through a downstairs door and took the bridle.

"I am Wilhelm Hippel and this is my tavern. You are welcome, Your Honour."

"It looks a well-kept place, landlord," I said, handing him my cloak as an ostler appeared to take my horse.

"We think so, Your Honour."

"And well-stocked, I hope."

I noticed a familiar peasant craftiness as he hesitated. "As best it can be in these times, sir."

I laughed at this. "Have no fear, landlord, I am not about to requisition your food and wine in the name of some warlike prince. I am on a mission of peace. I hope to be instrumental in putting an end to strife."

"Then you are doubly welcome, Your Honour."

I was taken into the main taproom and here enjoyed a mug of beer even better than that which I had had from the woman in the village. Venison and game were presented to me and I made my choice, feasting well and chatting with Herr Hippel about his trials and tribulations. These appeared extremely minor in comparison with those of men and women who had been directly touched by the War, but of course to him they were large enough.

There were robbers on this road, he warned me, and although they did not give him much trouble, some of his guests had been robbed and badly beaten (one even killed) during the previous autumn. The winter had not been so bad, but now he heard that the robbers were returning, "like swallows in spring," he said. I reassured him that I would journey warily. He said that he was expecting two or three more guests shortly and that it might be wise if we all travelled together to Teufenberg. I said that I would consider the idea, although privately I determined to continue alone, for I did not want the company of merchants or clerics on their slow, reliable horses.

In the shadows of the far corner, half-asleep with his tankard in his hand, I noted a surly red-headed youth dressed in a stained blue silk shirt with cuffs and collar of tattered lace; red silk breeches, baggy and loose after the Turkish fashion, tucked into high folded-over riding boots. He had on an unbuttoned leather waistcoat of heavy hide, of a sort which swordsmen often wear in preference to a breastplate. There was a long, curved sabre propped near him on his bench, and round his waist I detected a long knife and a pistol, both in black and silver, looking almost Oriental in design.

I had the youth for a Muscovite, since he was evidently no Turk. I raised a comradely tankard to him but he avoided my eye. The landlord whispered that he was well-behaved enough, but spoke poor German and seemed suspicious of even the friendliest action. He had been there since the day before and was apparently waiting for some soldier-priest who had agreed to meet him at the inn. The soldier-priest, said the landlord, had some sort of Latin name which the youth had misheard or else could not pronounce properly. It was a little like Josephus Kreutzerling, he said. He seemed to hope that I might recognise it, but I shook my head. I had a wariness and dislike for those soldier-priests who, in my view, were capable of worse depredations, fouler cruelties, than almost anyone else I had ever encountered.

Having discovered that I could reach Teufenberg by nightfall, I decided to be on my way, and was just rising when the doors of the taproom opened and in came a tall, thin individual with hard grey eyes in a cadaverous face, a black wide-brimmed hat upon his head, collar and cuffs of plain linen, coat and breeches of black wool, black buckled shoes and gaiters which, as he sat down upon a stool, he proceeded to remove, revealing white stockings. He had a plain, straight blade at his side and he wore gauntlets, carrying one in his left hand. The only fancy thing he wore was a purple plume in his hat, and even this gave the impression that he was in mourning for someone.

He looked first at me and then at the landlord. Herr Hippel stood up.

"Can I be of service, Your Honour?"

"Some wine and a jug of water," said the newcomer. He turned his head and looked back at the young Muscovite who had grown more alert. "You are Grigory Sedenko."

"I am Grigory Petrovitch Sedenko," said the youth in his strange, rumbling accent, stressing vowels and consonants in a way which made me certain of his origin. He stood up. "Who knows me?"

"I am he who promised to meet you here."

I had, as I thought, recognised the face and manner of a soldier-priest. The man was typical of his kind; all human feeling had been turned into pride and cruelty in the name of his Crusade. "I am Johannes Klosterheim, Knight of Christ."

The young Muscovite crossed himself dutifully, but looked with boldness into the austere face of the fighting monk. "You have a commission for me, Brother Johannes, in Teufenberg."

"I have. I know the house. I have all the evidence. The case has been judged. It is left for you to execute it."

The boy frowned. "You are certain?"

"There is no question."

I wondered if I was listening to a witch-hunter. But if Klosterheim were an ordinary witch-finder, he would not be here at this time, talking to the youth. Witch-finders travelled with an entourage, with all the paraphernalia of their calling. If they did not travel, they stayed in one town or one area. Few of them were soldiers.

Grigory Sedenko reached for his scabbarded sabre and made to tuck it into his belt, but Klosterheim raised his naked hand and shook his head. "Not yet. There is time."

The landlord and myself listened in silence, for it seemed evident that Klosterheim had commissioned the boy to do murder, albeit murder in God's name. Both of us were uncomfortable in the presence of the pair. The landlord wished to leave. My instinct was to take the boy aside and warn him not to involve himself in whatever disgusting venture the soldier-priest must surely be initiating. But I had made a virtue of silence and inactivity in recent years. It did not do to speak one's mind in those days.

The boy sat down again. "I would rather have it done," he said, "as soon as possible."

"There are things I must tell you in private," said Klosterheim. "This is no ordinary work."

At this Sedenko laughed. "Ordinary enough in Kieff," he said. "It is how we spend our winters."

Klosterheim disapproved of his levity, even of his enthusiasm. "We must pray together first," he said.

"And pay?" said the youth.

"Prayer first, pay second," replied the soldier-priest. He looked at us as if to warn us not to interfere and preferably not to listen. The landlord went from the room, leaving only me as witness to what took place between the strange pair.

77

I decided to speak:

"I have not heard of the Knights of Christ, brother," said I. "Is that an order from these parts?"

"It is not an order, as such, at all," said Klosterheim. "It is a society."

"Forgive me. I am not entirely conversant with Church lore."

"Then you should make it your task to become conversant, sir," he said. His grey eyes were angry. "And you should consider your manners, also. You should think of making their improvement another goal."

"I'm much obliged for the advice, brother," I said. "I shall consider it."

"Best do so, sir."

Against my saner judgement I remained where I was, even though the older man wished me to leave. Eventually he rose and went to sit beside Sedenko, speaking in a voice too low for me to overhear. I continued to drink my beer, however, and to give them my attention. The youth was undisturbed, but the soldier-priest remained uncomfortable, which, out of sheer devilment, I wished him to be.

At last, with a curse ill-befitting a celibate man of God, he got up from the bench and drew the youth with him to the door. They went outside into the yard.

I had amused myself long enough. I drained my tankard, shouted for the landlord, paid him and asked that my horse be fetched for me.

In a little while I peered through the window to see that the ostler had returned with my steed. I donned my helmet, folded my cloak under my arm and opened the door.

Klosterheim and the Muscovite were deep in conversation on the far side of the yard. As I emerged, Klosterheim turned his back on me.

The sun was shining strong and hot as I mounted. I cried: "Farewell, brother. Farewell, Herr Sedenko." And I urged the beast out of the courtyard toward the open road.

The sun had gone down by the time I sighted, in the twilit mist, the spires and rooftops of Teufenberg. It was a pleasant enough little town with a population that was only reasonably suspicious of a man like myself, on a good horse and in armour, and I had hardly any difficulty finding a hostelry with room for me and my horse. Again, to relieve my host's perturbation, I told the story of being an envoy commissioned to try to bring peace to the warring factions and, naturally enough, was given a much-improved welcome.

In the morning I was directed onto the road for Schweinfurt and wished Godspeed in my mission by the landlord, his wife, his son-in-law and his three daughters. I had almost begun to believe that I was the hero I presented myself as being!

On the outskirts of the town I passed a house which had a crowd surrounding it. Men, women and children stood packed together, watching wide-eyed as a group of people in black began to emerge from the house. The women were wailing and the boys and girls were pale and stunned. They were carrying three corpses from the house.

I wondered if this had anything to do with the pair I had encountered on the previous day.

I asked one fat townsman what had happened.

"It's the Jews," he said. "All the men were struck down in the night by the Sword of God. It is His vengeance upon them for their crimes.

I was disgusted. Their fate was familiar enough, but I had not expected to witness such an event in the pleasant town of Teufenberg.

I did not wait to hear the catalogue of crimes, for it would be the same wretched list one heard from the Baltic to the Black Sea.

Grimly, I spurred my horse and was more than glad when I reached the highway. The air seemed purer. I galloped a few miles until Teufenberg was completely out of sight, then I let my horse walk for a while.

In one sense I was grateful for what I had seen that morning in Teufenberg. I had been reminded of the realities of the world which lay ahead of me.

Chapter Five

THE WEATHER GREW warmer and warmer as the miles between Teufenberg and Schweinfurt narrowed. It was almost like summer and I was tempted, against my ordinary caution, to divest myself of some of my armour. But I kept it on, pouring a dram of water into my shirt occasionally to cool me. The roads were fairly good, there having been little rain in recent days and few armies to churn them up, and I was lucky in that, every night, I found reasonably pleasant accommodation. Signs of the War began to increase, however. I passed the occasional gallows and more frequently came upon burnt-out ruins of farmsteads and churches.

I had reached a mountainous region, of pines and glittering limestone, one day and was emerging from a small gorge, when I saw before me a broad meadow in which, quite recently, some gory fight had taken place. There were bodies strewn everywhere, most of them stripped or at least partially shorn of their best clothing. Crows and ravens flapped and hopped, squabbling over the red, stinking flesh of the slain. There was absolutely no means of telling the loyalties of the combatants, and there was little point in trying to find out. It would probably emerge, as always, that their motives for fighting had been confused, to say the least.

Normally I should have skirted the battlefield, but my path took me directly through it and there were boulders on either side of the meadow. I was forced to let my horse pick his way between the corpses, while flies rose in clouds to attack me, presumably finding something more attractive about warm blood than cold.

I was halfway across the meadow, holding a cloth to my nostrils to try to block out the sickening smell of death, when I heard a noise from the rocks on my right and, looking up, saw a small boulder come tumbling down towards me. I detected a flash, as of metal, a hint of blue cloth, and immediately my old instincts came to my service.

The reins were wound around my pommel and both pistols were in my gloved hands. I cocked them carefully just as the men began to reveal themselves. They were all on foot, dressed in a motley of armour, carrying a variety of weaponry, from rusty axes and pikes to glittering Toledo swords and daggers. The ruffians belonged to no particular army, that was certain. They were old-fashioned brigands, with sweating red faces, unshaven chins, and all manner of minor diseases written on their skins.

I levelled my pistols as they began to scramble down the hillside towards me.

"Stand back," I cried, "or I shall discharge!"

Their leader, almost a dwarf, wearing a stained black cloak and hat and a torn linen shirt, produced one of the largest pistols I had ever seen and grinned at me. Most of his teeth were missing. He squinted along the gun and said in a wheedling voice:

"Fire away, Your Honour. And we'll have the pleasure of doing the same."

I shot him in the chest. With a groan he flung up his arms and fell backwards, twitching for a second or two before he died. His pistol slithered towards his feet and none of his men was prepared to pick it up.

I reholstered the pistol I had used and drew my sword. "You'll not find me easy game, my friends," I said. "I would advise you that the cost of robbing me will prove far too dear."

One of the ruffians at the back raised a crossbow and loosed his bolt. The thing went just past my shoulder and I betrayed no sign that I had noticed it. My horse, well-trained, held his ground as well as did I.

"No more of that," said I, "or this other pistol will do its work. You have seen that I am a good shot."

I noted an arquebus lowered and a musket lifted from its aiming rod.

A creature with a squint and a Prussian accent said: "We are hungry, Your Worship. We have not eaten for days. We are honest soldiers, all of us, forced to live off the land when our officer deserted us."

I smiled. "I would hesitate to guess who had deserted whom. I have no food to spare. If you wish to eat, why don't you seek out an army and attach yourselves to it?"

Another began: "For the love of God . . ."

"I do not love God and neither does He love me," I said, with some certainty. "You cannot beg charity from a man you had hoped to murder."

They were creeping closer. I raised my pistol as a warning. They stopped, but then one of them, from the middle, brought up a pistol and fired it. The ball grazed the neck of my horse and he jumped, losing his composure for a moment. I fired back and missed my man, wounding another behind him.

Then they were upon me.

I had left it too late to run from them. They had quickly surrounded me, clutching at the horse's bridle, feinting at me with their pikes. I defended myself with my sword, loosening one foot from its stirrup to kick and shoving my pistol back into its holster so that I could tug a long poignard from its sheath at my belt. I took the lives of three and wounded several more, but they had lost their fear of me now and I knew that I must soon be borne under.

I received two small wounds, one in my thigh and one in my forearm, but they did not stop me from using either the leg or the arm. The brigands had begun to try to bring down the horse—a desperate action since he was probably the most valuable thing I owned—when I heard the sound of more hoofs behind me and a wild, terrible yell cut through the general din. Some of the thieves detached themselves from me to deal with this new antagonist.

I recognised him at once. It was the young Muscovite from the inn. His sabre swirled this way and that as he rode low on his pony, slicing living flesh as a surgeon might dissect corpses. And he continued with his blood-curdling yells until all the thieves were on the run. Then he flung back his head, dragged off his sheepskin cap and laughed, hurling insults after those few robbers left alive.

It was only then that I saw another rider some distance behind us. He was positioned at the mouth of the gorge, sitting almost motionless upon his chestnut cob and looking at both Grigory Sedenko and myself with pursed lips and a disapproving eye.

Sedenko wheeled his pony, still laughing. "That was good fighting," he said to me.

"I am grateful to you," I said.

He shrugged. "This journey was becoming boring. I was only too glad to relieve the boredom."

"You risked your life for a fool and an agnostic," said Klosterheim, pushing his wide-brimmed hat back from his face. "I am disappointed in you, Sedenko."

"He's a fellow soldier, which is more than you are, Klosterheim, for all your protestations."

I was pleased that the youth had grown impatient with the soldier-priest. But then I recalled the Jews at Teufenberg and I looked with a slightly wary eye upon the Muscovite, for I was almost convinced that he had slain the three Jews in their sleep.

Klosterheim's lips twisted in distaste. "You should have let him die," he told Sedenko. "You disobeyed me."

"And would again in similar circumstances," said the boy. "I am tired of your sermons and your quiet deaths, brother priest. If I'm to continue on to Schweinfurt, let this gentleman accompany us, for my sake if not for his."

Klosterheim shook his head. "This man is cursed. Can you not see it written on him?"

"I can only see a healthy soldier, like myself."

Klosterheim spurred his horse forward. His hatred of me seemed entirely reasonless. He rode on past me, through that meadow of fresh and not-so-fresh corpses.

"I'll travel alone," he said. "You have lost my friendship, Sedenko. And my gold."

"And good riddance to both," cried the red-haired youth. Then, turning to me: "Where do you journey, sir, and would you tolerate my company?"

I smiled. The boy had charm. "I go to Schweinfurt and beyond. I'll happily ride with such an excellent swordsman. What's your destination?"

"I have none in mind. Schweinfurt's as good as any." He spat after the retreating Klosterheim. "That man is mad," he said.

I looked to my wounds. They were not serious. A little balm was smeared on each. Soon we were riding along together, side by side.

"How were you employed by Klosterheim?" I asked casually. "As a bodyguard?"

"Partly. But he knows that I have no love for Jews, Turks or any other form of infidel. Originally he wanted me to help him in the execution of some Jews in Teufenberg. He said he had evidence of their having sacrificed Christian babies. Well, everyone knows that Jews do that and they must be punished. I was quite prepared to help him."

I said nothing to this. The fierceness with which the southern Muscovite hated his Oriental, Mussulman neighbours was well-known. The boy seemed no worse than most in this.

"You killed those Jews?" I asked.

He scoffed. "Of course I did not. One was too old and the others were too young. But the main reason was that Klosterheim had deceived me. There was no evidence at all that they had done what he said."

"And yet they were killed."

"Naturally. I told Klosterheim to do his own work. In the end that is what he did, though reluctantly. Then he told me that there were more infidels to kill and that I would be well-paid for my trouble. Gradually I began to realise that it was murder, not fighting, he wanted me to perform. And whatever else I am, sir, I am not a murderer. I kill cleanly, in fair fighting. Or, at least, I make sure the odds are fair, in the matter of Jews and Turks. I have never struck one of them from behind."

He seemed proud of this last fact. I laughed tolerantly enough and told him that I had known a few decent Jews in my time and at least one noble Turk. He politely ignored this remark which, I am sure, he judged to be in extremely poor taste.

Sedenko's company had the effect of shortening the journey to Schweinfurt. Every so often, along the road, we saw ahead of us the purple plume and the black garb of Klosterheim, but he was travelling at speed now and was soon at least a day ahead of us. Sedenko's story was familiar enough:

He was a son of those hardy pioneers, the Kazaks, who had expanded Muscovite territory against the Tatars (thus his traditional hatred of Orientals) and had grown up in a village near the southern capital of Kieff. His people were famous riders and swordsmen and he had, according to his own boasts, excelled in every Kazak skill until he had become embroiled in a feud between rival clans over whether or not to rise against the Poles, and had killed a chief (or *hetman*). For this crime he had been banished, so had decided to strike westward and enlist in the army of some Balkan prince. For a while he had served with a Carpathian king in a war which, as far as I could tell, was no more than a quarrel between two gangs of robber-knights. Being of a fanatically religious bent, like most of his kind, he had heard of a "Holy War" in Germany and had decided that this was more to his taste. He had been disappointed to discover that he could find no particular sympathy with either side, for his religion recognised a Patriarch in Constantinople, not a Pope, yet in other respects was even more elaborate in its forms of worship than the Roman faith.

"I had thought I would be fighting infidels," he said in a disappointed voice. "Tatars, Jews or Turks. But this is a squabble between Christians and they do not appear to know the essentials of their arguments. They are all faithless fools, in my opinion. I decided I could fight for none of them. I enlisted as a personal bodyguard with a couple of noblemen, but they found me too wild, I think, for their taste, and I was close to starvation when I met Klosterheim."

"Where did you meet him first?"

"Where you saw us. I had had word through a third party—a monk in Allerheim—that this soldier-priest had employment for a defender of Christ's people. Well, I decided to see what it was, particularly since I had received a silver florin in advance. That was what paid my way to Teufenberg. Now we all know that a good Christian is worth twenty Jews, in any circumstance, and that twenty-to-one constitutes fair odds if one is attacking a village. I had expected a shtetl-full, at least. I had the impression that it was a veritable army threatening Teufenberg. But three! The only male Jews in the whole town! I felt insulted, sir, I can tell you. I have rarely tolerated such condescending behaviour as that which I tolerated in Klosterheim. Everyone is an infidel to him. He sought to convert me from the religion of my fathers to his own grey faith!"

I found his open naïveté, his unjustified and somewhat innocent prejudices, his enthusiasm, at once disarming and amusing. His prattle took little of my attention, but it served to keep my brain from morbidly dwelling on my own problems.

Schweinfurt was soon reached: a moderate-sized city which bore the usual traces of the War. Our presence was unremarked and I asked directions for the best road to Nuremberg. Sedenko and I put up at an inn on the outskirts of Schweinfurt and the following morning I prepared to say farewell to him, but he grinned at me and said: "If you've no objection, Captain von Bek, I'll stick with you for a while. I've nothing better to do and you have the air of someone who has embarked upon an adventure. You've said little of yourself or your mission, and I respect your silence. But I enjoy the comradeship of a fellow swordsman and, who knows, something might happen to me in your company which will lead to my finding decent employment with a company of professional soldiers."

"I'll not attempt to dissuade you now, Master Sedenko," said I, "for I'll admit that your company is as enjoyable as you claim mine to be. I head for Nuremberg, and from there go to a small town called Ammendorf."

"I have never heard of it."

"Neither had I. But I have instructions to go there and go there I must. It's possible that you would not wish to continue with me, once we reach Nuremberg, where there will be plenty of opportunities for you to find employment. And it is possible that, once I find Ammendorf, you will not be able to accompany me farther. You know that I have no wish to describe my true mission to you, but you are right in recognising its importance. You must agree, for your own sake as well as mine, to accept orders where they relate to my Quest."

"I am a soldier and accept a soldier's discipline, captain. Besides, this is your country and you know it a good deal better than I. I shall be proud to accompany you for as long as it suits you."

Sedenko pushed back his sheepskin cap on his head and grinned again. "I am a simple Kazak. All I need is a little food, a worthy master, my faith in God and a chance to ride and use this"—he drew his sabre and kissed the hilt—"and I am completely satisfied."

"I can promise you food, at least," I said. We mounted again together. I felt that I would come to miss Sedenko's companionship when the time came for our ways to part, but was selfish enough to allow him to stay with me until then.

A little later, as we took the highway to Nuremberg, he spoke more of Klosterheim. His distaste for his former employer was profound.

"He told me of the witches he's killed—some of them children. Christian folk, by the sound of them. I draw the line at children. What do you say, Captain von Bek?"

"I have a great deal of blood on my hands," I said. "Too much to let it grieve me immoderately, young Muscovite."

"But in War—the blood was spilled in War."

"Oh, indeed, in War. Or in the name of War. How many children do you think have died because of me, Sedenko?"

"You are a commander of men. There are always casualties which one regrets."

I sighed. "I regret nothing," I said. "But should I have regrets, I would regret that I ever left Bek. It is far too late for that now. I was not always a soldier, you see. You come from a race of warriors. Mine is a race of scholars and rural noblemen. We had no great tradition of warlike exploits." I shrugged. "There have been peasant children killed by my men, one way or another. And I was at Magdeburg."

"Ah," said Sedenko, "Magdeburg." He was silent for a while, almost, I thought, from a sense of respect. Nearly half an hour later he said to me: "It was an unholy shambles, Magdeburg, was it not?"

"Aye, it was that."

"Any true soldier would wish not to have been there."

"I'd agree," I told him.

It was the last we were to speak of Magdeburg.

Soon we began to detect the signs of large movements of armies upon the road and we took to travelling along tracks which, according to my maps (which were the most accurate I had ever used), roughly paralleled the main highway. Even then we occasionally encountered small parties and once or twice were challenged. As had become my habit I cried: "Envoy!" and we were permitted to pass without much in the way of questioning.

I determined that it would be unwise to go directly into Nuremberg. Rumour had it that a number of Saxony's greatest nobles were gathering there, perhaps to plan peace but more likely to consider fresh strategies and alliances. I had no wish to become involved in this and it would be harder, under sophisticated questioning, to maintain my deception. In those days one was the object of suspicion if one did not declare a loyalty or a master. It scarcely mattered what the cause might be, so long as one swore fealty to it.

About five miles beyond Nuremberg, in a glade where we had set up our camp, I asked Sedenko if he did not consider it time to part company. "They would welcome you in Nuremberg," I said. "And I can guarantee you that it would not be long before you saw an action."

He shook his head. "I can always go back," he said.

"There are lands ahead," I told him, "where you could not travel."

"Beyond Ammendorf, captain?"

"I'm not sure. I receive fresh orders there."

"Then let us determine what I do when you discover the nature of those orders."

I laughed. "You're as tenacious as a terrier, Grigory Petrovitch."

"We of the Kazak hosts are famous for our tenacity, captain. We are a free people and value our freedom."

"Yet you have picked me as a master?"

"One must serve something," he said simply, "or someone. Is that not so, captain?"

"Oh, I think I would agree," I said. But what would he think, I wondered, if he knew I served the cause of Satan?

Privately, I had another cause. I was maintained in my Quest by the thought that sooner or later I must be reunited with the Lady Sabrina. Witch or no, she was the first woman I had loved as I had always expected to be able to love. It was more than enough. If I dwelled too long on the implications of my Quest I would lose my ordinary judgement. Lucifer might speak of the fate of the world, of Heaven and Hell, but I preferred to think simply in terms of human love. I understood that imperfectly enough, but I understood it better than anything else.

The following morning we passed a long gallows-tree on which six bodies swung. The bodies were clothed in black habits and blood was encrusted on the limbs, showing that the men had been tortured and broken before being hanged. At the foot of one I saw a wooden crucifix. It was impossible to determine to what order the monks had belonged. It scarcely mattered, as I knew. What was certain was that they would have been robbed of anything of value they had possessed. It was no wonder that so many orders were these days renewing their vows of poverty. There was no value in amassing wealth when it could be taken from you on almost any excuse.

A mile or two farther along the road we came upon an abbey. Parts of it were still burning and, for some reason, the bodies of monks and nuns had been folded over the walls at regular intervals, in the way a farmer might hang the corpses of vermin to warn off others. I had seen many an example of such dark humour in my years of War. I had been guilty of similar acts myself. It was as if one wished to defy one's conscience, to defy the very eye of God which, one sometimes felt, was looking down on all the horror and noting the participants.

If Lucifer were to be believed, God had indeed looked down upon me and judged me unfit for Heaven.

I was glad when, the next day, I consulted my map and discovered that Ammendorf was only a few hours' ride away.

I had no notion of how I was to find the Wildgrave, the Lord of the Hunt, but I would be relieved to have completed the first stage of my Quest, come what may.

The road took us through a thick forest whose floor was covered with mossy rocks and a tangle of vines which threatened the footing of our horses. The smell of that undergrowth, of the damp earth and the leaves, was so thick that it seemed at times to cover my nostrils. The path rose until we were riding a steep hill, still in the wood. Then we had reached the crest but, because of the foliage, could see little of what lay ahead of us. We rode down the other side.

Sedenko had become excited. He seemed to be gaining more from my adventure than was I. He was evidently having trouble in not asking me further questions and, since I could in no way answer him, I encouraged his discretion.

When I judged Ammendorf to be little more than a mile from us I reined in my horse and reminded my companion of our earlier conversation. "You do know, Sedenko, that you might not be able to follow me beyond Ammendorf?"

"Of course, captain." He offered me a frank stare. "It is what you said before."

Satisfied with this, I continued to ride along the narrow trail which now twisted to follow the natural contours of the valley floor.

The trees began to thin and the valley to widen until at last we came to Ammendorf.

It lay beneath a huge, grey cliff streaked with moss and ivy. It was built all of dark, ancient stone which seemed to blend with the rock of the cliff itself.

No smoke lifted from Ammendorf's chimneys. No beasts stood in the walled yards, no children played in the streets; no townsfolk stood at Ammendorf's doors or windows.

Sedenko was the first to bring his horse to a halt. He leaned on his saddle-bow, staring in surprise at the strange, black town ahead of us.

"But it's dead," he said. "Nobody has lived here in a hundred years!"

Chapter Six

A MMENDORF AT CLOSE quarters gave off an odour of rot and
decrepit age. Slates had fallen from roofs; thatch and wooden
shingles were broken and tattered; only the heavy stones of the
buildings were in one piece and they were covered in damp foliage
and mildew.

The whole village had been abandoned suddenly, it seemed to
me, and the green cast of the light through the gloom of the overhanging crag, the distinct and regular drip-drip of water, the soft
yielding of the ground underfoot when we dismounted, all contributed to an impression of desolation.

Sedenko sniffed at the air and put his hand to the hilt of his
sabre. "The place stinks of evil."

We peered upwards. I thought I detected more man-cut stone
at the top of the crag, but a tangle of ivy and hawthorn obscured
everything.

Could Lucifer, I wondered to myself, be losing His memory to
send me to a place deserted for so long? There was none here to
direct me to a Wildgrave doubtless long since dead.

Sedenko's look was questioning. Plainly he did not wish to say
what he was thinking: that I had been, at the very least, badly
misdirected.

The day was closing in. I said to Sedenko: "I must camp here.
But if you wish to travel on now I would suggest that you do not
hesitate."

The Muscovite grunted, fingering his face as he considered the
prospect. Then he looked up at me and uttered a small laugh.
"This could be the adventure I have been expecting," he said.

"But not one you would relish."

"It's in the nature of adventure, is it not, to risk that possibility?"

I clapped him on the back. "You are a companion after my own

92

heart, Kazak. Would that you had been with me in some of my former engagements."

"I have it in mind, captain, to be with you in some of your future engagements."

The future for me was so mysterious, so numinous, that I could not answer him. We began to explore the houses, one by one. We found flagstones cracked and pushed apart by plants. In some, small trees were growing. Everything was damp. Pieces of furniture were rotting; fabric fell to shreds at a touch.

"Even the rats have gone." Sedenko returned from a cellar with a wine jar. He broke the seal and sniffed. "Sour."

He dropped it into an empty fireplace.

"Well," he said, "which of these comfortable houses shall we make our own?"

We decided in the end upon the building which had evidently been the town's meeting-place. This was larger and airier than the others and we could light a fire in the big grate.

By dusk, with our horses billeted in one corner of the room and the fire providing us with sufficient heat and some light, we were ready to sleep.

Outside, in the deserted streets of Ammendorf, there was little movement. A few birds hunted for insects and occasionally we heard the bark of a fox. Soon Sedenko was snoring, but it was harder for me to lose consciousness. I continued to speculate on Lucifer's reasons for sending me to this place. I thought about Sabrina and despaired of ever seeing her again. I even considered retracing my steps part-way and seeking service with the Swedish King whose army was just now marching at some speed through Germany. Then Magdeburg came back to me, as well as Lucifer's threats of what should happen if I betrayed Him, and I lapsed into despondency. Two or three hours must have passed in this useless state of mind before I nodded off, whereupon I was immediately aroused by what I was sure was the sound of hoofbeats.

I was on my feet almost with relief, picking up my scabbarded sword as I ran towards the window and looked out into the murk. A thin drizzle had begun to fall and clouds obscured moon and stars. I thought I saw the glow of an oddly coloured lantern moving between the buildings. The light began to grow brighter and brighter until it seemed to be flickering over half of Ammendorf. And the hoofbeats grew louder, filling my ears with their din— yet still I could see no rider.

Sedenko was beside me now, his sabre ready in his fist. He rubbed at his face. "In the name of God, captain, what is it?"

I shook my head. "I've no idea, lad."

Even the meeting hall was shaking and our own mounts were stamping and whinnying, trying to break free of their halters.

"A storm," Sedenko said. "Some kind of storm, eh, captain?"

"It's like none I've ever witnessed," I told him. "But you could be right."

He was convinced that he was wrong. Every gesture, every movement of his eyes, betrayed his superstition.

"It is Satan's coming," he whispered.

I did not tell him why I thought that explanation unlikely.

All at once, from around a bend in the street, a horseman appeared. As he came into sight the hounds which surrounded his beast's feet, an undulation of savagery, began to bay. There were other riders behind him, but the leader was gigantic, dwarfing all. He wore a monstrous winged helmet framing a bearded face from which the eyes glowed with the same green-blue light which flooded the village. His great chest was encased in a mail shirt half-covered by the bearskin cloak which hung from his shoulders. In his left hand was a long hunting spear of a type not used in at least a hundred years. His legs were also mail-clad and the feet stuck into heavy stirrups. He lifted his head and laughed up at the sky, his voice joining in the note his hounds made until all seemed to be baying together, while his companions, shadows still behind him, began one by one to give forth the same dreadful noise.

"Mother of God," said Sedenko. "I'll fight any man fairly, but not this. Let's go, captain. They are warning us. They are driving us away."

I held my ground. "Drive us they might," I said, "and it would be a good sport for them, no doubt, for they would drive us like game, Sedenko. Those are hunters and I would say that their prey is Man."

"But they are not human!"

"Human once, I'd guess. But far from mortal now."

I saw white faces in the wake of the bearded horseman. The lips grinned and the eyes were bright (though not as bright as their leader's). But they were dead men, all of them. I had come to recognise the dead. And, too, I could recognise the damned.

"Sedenko," I said, "if you would leave me now, I would suggest you go at once."

"I'll fight with you, captain, whatever the nature of the enemy."

"These could be your enemies, Sedenko, but not mine. Go."

He refused. "If these are your friends, then I will stay. They would be powerful friends, eh?"

I had no further patience for the discussion, so I shrugged. I walked towards the door, strapping on my sword. The door creaked open.

The huntsmen were already gathering in Ammendorf's ruined square. I felt the heat of the hounds' breath on my face, the stink of their bodies. They flattened their ears as they began to lie down round the feet of their master's horse.

The chief huntsman stared at me from out of those terrifying eyes. White faces moved in the gloom. Horses pawed the weed-grown cobbles.

"You have come for me?" I said.

The lips parted. The giant spoke in a deep, sorrowing voice, far more melodious than I might have expected. "You are von Bek?"

"I am."

"You stand before the Wildgrave."

I bowed. "I am honoured."

"You are a living man?" he asked, almost puzzled. "An ordinary mortal?"

"Just so," I said.

He raised a bushy eyebrow and turned his head to look back at his white-faced followers, as if sharing a small joke with them. His reply was given in a tone that was almost amused:

"We have been dead these two hundred and fifty years or more. Dead as we once reckoned death, in common with most of mankind."

"But not truly dead." I spoke our High Tongue and this gave Sedenko some puzzlement. But it was the speech in which I had been addressed and I therefore deemed it politic to continue in it.

"Our Master will not let us die in that sense," said the Wildgrave of Ammendorf. He evidently saw me as a comrade in damnation. "Will you guest with me now, sir, at my castle yonder?" He pointed up the cliff.

"Thank you, great Wildgrave."

He turned his glowing eyes upon Sedenko. "And your servant? Shall you bring him?"

I said to Sedenko: "We are invited to dinner, lad. I would suggest you refuse the invitation."

Sedenko nodded.

"He will await me here until morning," I said.

The Wildgrave accepted this. "He will not be harmed. Will you be good enough to mount behind me, sir?"

He loosened his booted foot and offered me a stirrup. Deciding that it would be neither diplomatic nor expedient to hesitate, I walked up to his horse, accepted the stirrup and swung onto the huge beast's stinking back, taking a firm hold of the saddle.

Sedenko watched with wide eyes and dropped jaw, not understanding at all what was happening.

I smiled at him and saluted. "I'll return in the morning," I said. "In the meantime I can assure you that you will sleep safely."

The Wildgrave of Ammendorf grunted a command to his horse and the whole Hunt, hounds and all, turned out of the square. We began to race at appalling speed through the streets and onto an overgrown path which climbed through low-hanging foliage and outcrops of mossy rock to the top of the cliff, where it was now possible for me to see that my eyes had not earlier deceived me. I had thought that I had detected masonry from the village, and here it was—a horrible old castle, part fallen into ruin, with a massive keep squatting black against the near-black of the sky.

We all dismounted at once and the Wildgrave, who stood more than a head taller than myself, put a cold arm about my shoulders and led me through an archway directly into the keep. Here, too, staircases and flagstones were cracked and broken. The hall was lit by a single guttering brand stuck into a rusting bracket above a long table. Over the fire a deer's carcass was turning. The white-faced huntsmen moved with agility towards the fire where they warmed themselves, paying no heed to two shaking servants, a boy and a girl, who were evidently neither part of this clan nor among the living dead, but could have been as damned as the rest of us.

The Wildgrave's eyes seemed to cool as he placed himself at the head of the table and made me sit at his right. With his mailed hand he poured me brandy and bade me drink deep "against the weather" (which in fact was relatively mild). To him, perhaps, the world was permanently chill.

"I was warned of your coming," he told me. "There is a rumour, too, amongst the likes of us, that you are entrusted with a mission which could redeem us all."

I sighed. "I do not know, Lord Wildgrave. Our Master has greater faith in my capabilities than have I. I shall do my best, of course, for should I succeed, I, too, might be redeemed."

"Just so." The Wildgrave nodded. "But you must be aware that not all of us support you in your Quest."

I was surprised. "I cannot follow you," I said.

"Some fear that should our Master come to terms with God, they will be worse doomed than ever before, with no protector, with no further means of preserving their personalities against the Emptiness."

"Emptiness is not a term I am familiar with, Lord Wildgrave."

"Limbo, if you prefer. The Void, my good captain. That which refuses to tolerate even the faintest trace of identity."

"I understand you now. But surely, if Lucifer is successful, we shall all be saved."

The Wildgrave's smile was bitter. "What logic provides you with that hope, von Bek? If God is merciful, He provides us with little evidence."

I drank my brandy down.

"Some of us came to this pass," continued the Wildgrave, "through just such an understanding of God's nature. I am not amongst them, of course. But they believed God to be vengeful and unrelenting. And some, I would guess, will try to stop you in your mission."

"It is difficult and numinous enough as it is," I said as, with a clatter, the boy placed a plate of venison before me. The meat smelled good. "Your news is scarcely encouraging."

"But it is well-intentioned." The Wildgrave accepted his own plate. With the manners of a former time he courteously handed me a dish containing ground salt. I sprinkled a little on my meat and returned it to him.

He picked up his venison and began to munch. I noted that his breath steamed as it contacted the heat. I copied him. The food was good and was welcome to me.

"We have still to hunt tonight," said the Wildgrave, "for we continue to exist in our own world only so far as we can provide fresh souls for our Master. And we have caught nothing for almost a month."

I chose not to ask him to elaborate upon this, and he seemed grateful for my tact.

"I have been instructed to take you through into the Mittel-march," he said. As he spoke, others of the Hunt brought their plates to table. They ate in silence, apparently without interest in our conversation. It seemed to me that they had an air of slight nervousness, perhaps because they resented this interruption to their nightly activities.

"I have not heard of the Mittelmarch," I told him frankly.

"But you know there are lands upon this Earth of ours which are forbidden to most mortals?"

"So I was told, aye."

"Those lands are known by some of us as the Middle Marches."

"Because they lie on the borderlands between Earth and Hell?"

He smiled and wiped his mouth on his mailed sleeve. "Not exactly. You could say they lie between Hope and Desolation. I do not understand much about them. But I am able to come and go between them. You and your companion shall be taken through tomorrow evening."

"My companion is not of our kind," I said. "He is a simple, innocent soldier. I shall tell him to return to a world he will better understand."

The Wildgrave nodded. "Only the damned are permitted to pass into Mittelmarch," he told me. "Though not all who dwell in Mittelmarch are damned."

"Who rules there?" I asked.

"Many." He shrugged his gigantic shoulders. "For Mittelmarch, like our own world, like Hell itself, has multitudinous aspects."

"And the land I go to tomorrow. It will be marked on my maps?"

"Of course. In Mittelmarch you will seek out a certain hermit who is known as Philander Groot. I had occasion to pass the time of day with him once."

"And what am I to ask of him? The location of the Grail?"

The Wildgrave put down his venison, almost laughing. "No. You will tell him your story."

"And what will he do?"

The Wildgrave spread a mailed hand. "Who knows? He has no loyalty to our Master and refuses to have any truck with me. I can only say that I have heard he might be curious to talk to you."

"He knows of me?"

"The news of your Quest is rumoured, as I said."

"But how could such news spread so quickly?"

"My friend"—the Wildgrave became almost avuncular as he put a hand upon my arm—"can you not understand that you have enemies in Hell as well as in Heaven? It is those you should fear worse than any earthly foe."

"Can you give me no further clue," I asked, "as to the identity of these enemies?"

"Naturally I cannot. As it is I have been kinder to you than is sensible for a creature in my position. I am feared in the region of Ammendorf, of course. But as with all our Master's servants, I have no real power. Your enemies could one day, therefore, be my friends."

I became distressed at this. "Have you no courage to take your own decisions?"

The Wildgrave's great face became sad for a moment. "Once I had courage of that sort," he said. "But had I had the courage to be self-determining in my own mortal life I would not now be a servant of Lucifer." He paused, looking out from eyes which, moment by moment, had begun to glow again. "And the same must be true of you, too, eh, von Bek?"

"I suppose so."

"At least you have a chance, however small, of reclaiming yourself, captain. And oh"—his voice became at once bleak and heartfelt—"how I envy you that."

"Yet if I am successful and God grants Lucifer His wish, we shall all be given the chance again," I said, innocently enough.

"And that is what so many of us fear," said the Wildgrave.

Chapter Seven

S EDENKO, HE SAID, had slept well all night. When I returned at
dawn he had been snoring, certainly, as if he was still a little
boy in his mother's tent.

As he breakfasted he asked eagerly of my encounter with "the
Devil."

"That was not the Devil, Sedenko. Merely a creature serving
Him."

"So you did not sell your soul to him."

"No. He is helping me, that's all. I now know the next stage of
my journey."

Sedenko was awed. "What great power must you possess to
order such as the Wildgrave!"

I shrugged. "I have no power, save what you see. It is the same
as yours—good wits and a quick sword."

"Then why should he help you?"

"We have certain interests in common."

Sedenko looked at me with some trepidation.

"And you must go back to Nuremberg," I said, "or wherever
you think. You cannot go where I go tonight."

"Where is that?"

"A land unknown."

He became interested. "You travel by sea? To the New World?
To Africa?"

"No."

"I would serve you well if you would permit me to go with
you . . ."

"I know you would. But you are not permitted to follow where
I travel now."

He continued to argue with me, but I rejected all his proposals
until I was weary and begged him to leave, for I wished to sleep.

He refused. "I will guard you," he said.

I accepted his offer and eventually was able to sleep, waking in the late afternoon to smell Sedenko's cooking. He had found a pot, suspended it over the fire and was boiling some sort of stew.

"Rabbit," he told me.

"Sedenko," I said, "you must go. You *cannot* follow me. It is not physically possible."

He frowned. "I have a good horse, as you know. I am not prone to the seasickness, as far as I have been able to tell. I am healthy."

I again fell into silence. Only the damned could travel to Mittelmarch. Follow me as he would, he could not enter that Realm. I determined to waste no energy on the matter, contenting myself with advice to the young Kazak to go back to Nuremberg and find himself a good captain or, if he thought it a better idea, to leave the conflict altogether and begin to travel homeward, where he could direct his energies, if he wished, against his Polish overlords.

He became obstinate, almost surly. I shrugged. "The Wildgrave comes for me tonight," I said, "and I must ready myself for that journey. The stew is good. Thank you." I got up and began to see to my horse.

Sedenko sat cross-legged beside the fire, watching me. He hardly moved as I donned my battledress, strapping my steel breastplate tightly about my body, adjusting the set of my greaves. I thought it wise to enter the Realm of Mittelmarch with as much of the odds in my favour as possible.

Night fell. Sedenko continued to watch me, saying nothing. I refused even to look at him. I fed my horse. I oiled my leather. I polished my pistols and checked their locks. I cleaned my sword and my poignard. Then I gave close attention to my helmet. I whistled. Sedenko watched on.

By midnight I was beginning to grow a little nervous, but refused to show my state of mind to my silent companion. I looked through the windows at Ammendorf which, tonight, was lit faintly by the moon.

Even as I began to turn back I heard the echoing yell of a great horn. It sounded like the Last Judgement. It was a cold, desolate noise—a single, prolonged note. Then there came quiet again.

The building shook to hoofbeats. The green-blue glow flickered through the buildings outside. I heard the baying of the hounds.

I took my horse by his reins and led him through the hall and out down the steps into the square. I longed to say farewell to Sedenko but I knew I must discourage him at all costs from following me.

The Hunt came sweeping in. Red mouths gaped and tongues lolled. The Wildgrave's eyes seemed the single source of the hideous light. His men howled in unison with the dogs until all at once they were still as statues on frozen horses. Only the Wildgrave moved, his winged head turning towards me.

"You are ready, I see, mortal."

"I am ready, my lord."

"Then come. To the Mittelmarch."

I mounted my horse. The Wildgrave made a sign and the Hunt began to move again, with me riding beside him, my horse snorting and complaining in fear of the dogs. We did not ride back towards the castle, but out of Ammendorf and through a wood. The chill of the Wildgrave's monstrous body seemed to draw my own heat and I was shivering within half an hour. We rode beside a lake and I imagined that the lake shone with ice, an impossibility at that time of year. We rode until we saw the lights of a town ahead of us, and here the Wildgrave drew rein on the hill some miles above the town and wished me well in my Quest.

"But how shall I find Mittelmarch?" I was baffled.

"I have brought you to Mittelmarch," said the Wildgrave.

I noted that snow was falling on my sleeve.

"There was no transition," I said. "Or no sense of one, at any rate."

"Why should there be, for our sort? You merely follow certain trails."

"You could not have shown me the trail?"

"There is a way of looking," said the Wildgrave. "Do not fear. You are not trapped here."

"It snows late, in Mittelmarch," I said. I saw that the snow had settled. It was quite deep in some places. It weighted the trees. My breath was white.

The Wildgrave shook his head. "No later than in your own Realm, captain."

"Then I do not understand this," I told him.

"The seasons are reversed here, that is all. You will know when you have left Mittelmarch only by that sign."

His men glared anxiously at him. They wished to continue with their Hunt. For all the terror they must inspire, they were themselves more terrified than their victims—for they knew for certain what their fate must be should they fail Lucifer.

That cold, strangely friendly hand was placed again upon my arm. "Seek out Philander Groot. That is my best thought for you. And go wisely in this Realm as in your own, captain. I hope you find the Cure for the World's Pain."

He lifted his horn to his lips and blew that long, single note. Trees shook the snow from their branches. The dogs lifted their heads and bayed. In the forest behind me I thought that I heard beasts in flight.

The Wildgrave laughed: a sound even more hideous than his horn's cry.

"Farewell, von Bek. Discover for all of us, if you can, if there is such a thing as Freedom."

The ground trembled as the Hunt retreated, and then it was still, of a sudden, and I was alone. I drew my cloak about me and pushed my horse on towards the town below, guiding him carefully through the snow.

Overhead the sky fluttered and light appeared, first from a large yellow moon, then from the stars. There seemed something odd about the constellations, but I was no astrologer so could not tell what, if anything, was different. In the far distance were towering, jagged peaks. This land seemed somehow larger, more monumental, than the land I had left. It seemed wilder and was mysterious, yet it also contained in it an atmosphere if not of peace then at least of familiarity, and this sense in itself was comforting to me. It was almost as if I were back in Bek. As if I had gone into the past.

I knew that I must go warily in Mittelmarch and that I could be in even greater danger here than in my own land. Nonetheless it was with lifting spirits that I continued on my way, and when I heard the sound of a rider behind me I became cautious, but was not unduly perturbed.

I turned my head, crying out a "halloo" to warn the rider that there was someone ahead of him.

No reply came back, so I drew my sword slowly and halted my horse before coming about to face whoever it might be.

The rider himself had slowed and now stopped. I could only dimly see him in the moonlight, stopped on the trail beside a great, snow-covered rock.

"Who are you, sir?" said I.

No reply again.

"I must warn you that I am armed," I said.

A movement of the figure, a slight stirring of the horse's feet, but no more. I began to approach at a walk. It was then that the rider decided to reveal himself.

He came out into the moonlight. He looked apologetic and defiant at the same time. He gestured with one gloved hand and he shrugged. "I am used to snow, master. Is that what you feared would distress me?"

"Oh, Sedenko," I said, without anything but sadness filling me.

"Master?"

"Oh, Sedenko, my friend." I rode forward and embraced him.

He had not expected anything but my anger and was surprised. But he returned the embrace with some vigour.

He did not know what I knew: that if he had been permitted to follow us into Mittelmarch it could mean only one thing. Poor Sedenko was already damned.

At that moment I railed against a God who could condemn such an innocent soul to Purgatory. What had Sedenko done that was not the result of his upbringing or his religion, which encouraged him to kill in the name of Christ? It came to me that perhaps

God had become senile, that He had lost His memory and no longer remembered the purpose of placing Man on Earth. He had become petulant, He had become whimsical. He retained His power over us, but could no longer be appealed to. And where was His Son, who had been sent to redeem us? Was God's Plan not so much mysterious as impossible for us to accept: because it was a malevolent one? Were we all, no matter what we were or how we lived, automatically damned? Was Life without point? Did my Quest have any meaning? All these things were questions in my mind as I looked upon the Kazak youth and wondered what crime he could have committed that was evil enough to send him so young to Hell. Surely, I thought to myself, Lucifer is a more consistent and intelligent Master than the Lord Himself.

"Well, captain," said Sedenko with a grin. "Have I proved myself to you? Can I come another step of your journey with you?"

"Oh, by all means Sedenko. You can, if it is only my decision, travel with me all the way to my ultimate destination."

Here was another soul whom I hoped Lucifer might spare in his gratitude were I successful.

Sedenko began to whistle some wild and rousing tune of his own people. He slipped sideways in his saddle and scooped up the fresh snow with his free hand, throwing it into the air and cheering. "This is more the kind of place for me, captain. I was born in the open snow, you know. I am a child of the winter!" His whistling turned into a song in his own language. He was like a happy boy. I did my best to smile at his antics, but my heart was heavy.

By morning we were in sight of a village which somewhat resembled the one we had left. A castle stood upon a crag, but this castle was in excellent repair. And the village was far from deserted. We saw smoke lifting and heard voices, sharp in the cold air. We rode down, through white trees, and plodded on our horses through the street until we came to the square where a market had already been set up.

I dismounted beside a stall which was selling slices of cooked meat and pickled fish and asked the red-faced woman in charge of it what the name of the town might be.

Her answer was one I had half-expected.

"Why, master," said she, "this is Ammendorf."

Sedenko had overheard me. "Ammendorf? Are there two, so close together?"

"There is only one Ammendorf," said the woman proudly. "There is nowhere else like it."

I looked beyond the town and the forest to the huge spikes of the mountains. I had not seen those mountains before. They seemed taller than the Alps. They might have stretched all the way to Heaven.

"Do you have a priest?" I asked her.

"Father Christoffel? You will find him at the church." She pointed to the other side of the village. "Up the little lane beyond the well."

Leading my horse, with a mystified Sedenko muttering behind us, I made for the lane. If anyone knew of the hermit Philander Groot it would surely be the priest. I found the lane. There were cart tracks in the snow, between tall hedges.

Sedenko continued to sing behind me. I think he was pleased with himself for being able to track me. I could hardly bear the sound of his voice, it was so sweet, so happy.

I turned a corner in the lane and there was the stone church with its spire and its graveyard. I tethered my horse to the fence which surrounded the graveyard and opened the wicket gate, bidding Sedenko to stay where he was and watch our mounts.

The doors of the church opened easily and I found myself in an unpretentious building, evidently Catholic but by no means reeking of incense and Mary-worship. The priest was at his altar, arranging the furniture there.

"Father Christoffel?"

He was fat and bore the scars of some earlier disease. His mouth was self-indulgent, like the mouth of a lazy, expensive whore, but his eyes were steady. Here was a man likely to commit sins of the flesh in abundance, but sins of the intellect would be few.

"I am Captain Ulrich von Bek," I said, doffing my helmet and pulling off my gloves. "I am upon a mission which is secret, but there are religious aspects to it."

He looked hard at me, cocking his little fat head to one side. "Yes?"

"I am looking for a man whom I heard to be dwelling in these parts."

"Hm?"

"A certain hermit. Perhaps you know him?"

"His name, captain?"

"Philander Groot."

"Groot? Yes?"

"I wish to speak to him. I hoped you would know of his whereabouts."

"Groot hides from himself and from God," said the priest. "And so he also hides from us."

"But you know his whereabouts?"

The priest lifted heavy brows. "You could say so. Why is a soldier looking for him?"

"I seek something."

"Something he possesses?"

"Probably not."

"Of military importance?"

"No, Father."

"You are interested in his philosophy?"

"I am not familiar with it. I have little curiosity where philosophy is concerned."

"Then what do you want from Groot?"

"I have a story for him, I think. I've been led to understand that he would wish to listen to me."

"Who told you of Groot?"

This was not a man to whom I wished to lie.

"The Wildgrave."

"Our Wildgrave," said the priest in some surprise. Then his face began to frown. "Oh, no. Of course. The other one."

"I suspect so," I replied.

"Do you serve Lucifer, too? Groot, for all his failings, is adamant. He will speak to none who does."

"I could be said to serve the world," I told the priest. "My Quest, some have suggested, is for the Grail."

The priest showed some surprise. His lips silently repeated my last two words. He peered into my face with those bright, intelligent eyes.

"You are sinless, then?"

I shook my head. "There are few sins unknown to me. I am a murderer, a thief, a despoiler of women."

"An ordinary soldier."

"Just so."

"So you have no hope of ever finding the Grail."

"I have every hope."

The priest rubbed at the stubble on his jowls. He became thoughtful, glancing at me from time to time as he considered what had passed between us. Then he shook his head and turned his back on me, attending to the altar-furniture again.

I heard him murmur: "An ordinary soldier." He even seemed amused, though there was no mockery in him. Eventually he looked back at me.

"If you possessed the Grail, what would you hope from it?"

"A Cure," said I, "for the World's Pain."

"You care so much for the World?"

"I care for myself, Father."

He smiled at this. "Fear is a disease few of us know how to fight."

"It is also a drug," I said, "to which many are addicted."

"The World is in a sorry state, Sir Warrior."

"Aye."

"And any man who continues to hope that it can still be helped has my good will, my blessing even. Yet Philander Groot . . ."

"You think him evil?"

"There is no evil at all, I would say, in Philander Groot. That is why I am so angry with him. He refuses to accept God."

"He is an atheist?"

"Worse. He believes. But he refuses to accept his Creator."

I found this description sympathetic.

"And so," continued the priest, "he shall be refused Heaven and unjustly be swallowed up by Hell. I despair of him. He is a fool."

"But an honest fool, by the sound of him."

"There is none I know more honest, Captain von Bek, than Philander Groot. Many seek him, for he is said to have magical powers. He lives under the protection of a mountain kingdom which in its turn is also protected by powerful forces. To reach that kingdom you must journey to the far peaks and find the Hermit Pass, which leads into the valley where Groot dwells."

"The pass is named for him?"

"Not at all. It was always fashionable with hermits." There was a sardonic note to the priest's remark. "But Groot is no ordinary hermit. It is said that he spent his boyhood as the apprentice to a Speculator. Perhaps they are unknown in your part of the world. Speculators professionally spend their time watching for signs of the Coming of the Anti-Christ and Armageddon. The living can be good, particularly in troublesome times. But Groot, from what he has told me, became tired of the Future and for a while studied the Past. Now, he says, he cares only for an Eternal Present."

"Would that I could reject Past and Future," said I with some feeling.

"Oh, and then we should be able to reject Conscience and Consequence, eh?" said the priest. "But I have had this argument with my friend Groot and I will not bore you with it. Should you meet him, he will be able to present his position far more fluently than I."

I took the map-case from my pouch and drew forth several of the maps. "Is Hermit Pass marked here?" After much opening and closing I was able to withdraw the appropriate map (it showed both Ammendorfs) and display it to the priest. With a fat finger he indicated a road which led into the great mountains I had already seen. "North-west," he said. "And may God, or whoever rules in Mittelmarch, go with you."

I left the church and rejoined Sedenko. "We will provision here," I told him, "and continue our journey in the afternoon."

"I saw what seems a good inn as we came through the town," he said.

"We'll dine there before we set off."

I had been at once cheered and disturbed by my encounter

with Father Christoffel. I wanted to leave Ammendorf behind me as soon as possible and be upon my journey.

"Was your confession heard, captain?" innocently asked the young Kazak as I got into my saddle.

I shrugged.

Sedenko continued: "Perhaps I should also seek the priest's blessing. After all, it is some time . . ."

I became angry with him, knowing what I knew. I almost hated him at that moment for his ignorance of his own unfair fate. "That priest is next to an agnostic," I said. "He cannot unburden himself, let alone you or me. Come, Sedenko, we must be on our way." I paused, deciding that it was as well if I told him a little more of my story.

"I seek nothing less than the Holy Grail," I said.

"What's that, captain?"

Whistling, his breath clouding the sharp air, he fell in behind me.

I explained to him as much as I could. He listened to me with half an ear, as if I told a fabulous story which had not much to do with either of us. His very carelessness made me all the more gloomy.

Chapter Eight

A s WE RODE out of Ammendorf my bitterness against a Deity who could consign such as Sedenko so easily to Hell continued to grow. There seemed no justice in the world at all, no possibility of creating justice, no being to whom one could appeal. Why should I be concerned about redemption in such a world? What would I escape, if I escaped Hell?

Sedenko had earlier attempted to interrupt my broodings, but for some while had said hardly a word, cheerfully accepting my silence and respecting my reluctance to answer his very ordinary questions. The day grew colder as night came nearer, yet I made no preparations for camp. I was tired. Ammendorf's good wine and food were sustaining me against weather and lack of sleep, and I told myself that Sedenko was young enough to lose another night's rest. Only the condition of the horses concerned me, but they seemed fresh enough, for we did not push them hard. Movement was all that I desired. We passed through rocky hills and over snowy moorland, through woods and across streams, heading steadily towards the high peaks and Hermit Pass.

As night fell, I dismounted, leading my horse. Sedenko did not question me, but followed my example.

It had been some years since I had lost my Faith, save in my own capacity to survive a world at War, but evidently in the back of my mind there had always been some sense that through God one might find salvation. Now, as I journeyed in quest of the Holy Grail (or something identified as the Holy Grail), I not only questioned the possibility that salvation existed; I questioned whether God's salvation was worth the earning. Again I began to see the struggle between God and Lucifer as nothing more than a squabble between petty princelings over who should possess power in a tiny, unimportant territory. The fate of the tenants of that territory did not much seem to matter to them; and even the rewards of those tenants' loyalty seemed thin enough to me. For my own part, I believed that I deserved any fate, no matter how cruel, for I had used my intelligence in the service of my self-deceit. The same could not be said of Sedenko, who was merely a child of his times and his circumstances. I had received positive proof of the existence of God and the Devil and my Faith in them was weaker now than it had ever been.

My cloak would not keep out the bite of winter's night. I heard my teeth chattering in my skull. My heart seemed as if it were turning to ice. Even Sedenko was shivering, and he was used to far worse cold than this.

We were climbing higher into the foothills of the mountains. Their peaks were now tall enough to block off half the sky and the snow became deeper and deeper until it threatened to spill over into our boots. Towards dawn I began to realise that if we did not have heat and food soon we should probably perish, whereupon we should both go straight to Hell. The prospect reminded me of the reason I had accepted Lucifer's bargain.

Although it was difficult to see through the murk, I selected a place where an outcrop of rock had left the ground relatively clear of deep snow and told Sedenko to prepare a fire.

As he gathered wood, the dawn began to come up, red and cold. I watched him while he moved about in the nearby spinney below, bending and straightening, shaking snow from the sticks he found, and for some reason was reminded of the parable of Abraham and his son. Why should one serve a God who demanded such insane loyalty, who demanded that one deny the very humanity He was said to have created?

I watched as Sedenko prepared the fire for us and selected food from our bag of provisions. He seemed cheerful merely to be in my company. He was excited, expecting great and interesting adventures. If he died on the morrow, he would probably look wonderingly at Hell itself and find it interesting.

And then it came to me that perhaps Lucifer had lied to me, that He had lied to all who served Him. Perhaps none of us were damned at all, but could somehow wrest our destinies free of His influence as He had attempted to wrest His own destiny free of God's. Why should we be controlled by such beings?

And the answer came to me, as it always did when I followed that logic: because they can destroy us at will.

I could almost sympathise with those the Wildgrave had warned me against; those who saw me as aiding in Lucifer's betrayal of His own creatures. They had seen Lucifer as representing if nothing else a defiance of an unjust God. A pact between God and Lucifer would find them without protection, sacrificed because Lucifer had found it expedient to change His mind.

But would God let Lucifer change His mind? Even Lucifer had no clue to that. And I, if I succeeded in discovering the Cure for the World's Pain, might not be finding a remedy at all. What if, when it was put to the lips of mankind, the Holy Grail was discovered to contain a deadly poison? Perhaps, after all, the only Cure for pain was the absolute oblivion of death, without Heaven or Hell.

My heavy sighs caused Sedenko to look up from where he was warming his hands against the fire. "What did the priest tell you, master? You have been distressed ever since you met him."

I shook my head. It had not been the priest, of course, who had disturbed me. And I could not explain to Sedenko that I knew him destined for Hell, that the God he claimed to serve had rejected him and had not even given him a sign of that rejection.

"Did he refuse you grace?" Sedenko continued.

"My state of mind has little to do with my encounter in the church," I said. "I received information from the priest. He has told me where I might look for a certain hermit, that is all."

"And you still do not know the purpose of your journey?"

"I know it, I think, as well as I ever shall. Make us our breakfast, young Kazak. And sing us one of those sonorous songs of yours, if you can."

I was asleep before he had begun to cook anything and it was noon before I woke up again. Simmering on the well-made fire was some soup. Sedenko himself had taken the opportunity to rest and was wrapped in his blankets a short distance from me. I ate the soup and cleaned the pan before waking him.

The mountains were taller than anything I had ever seen before. They were jagged and steep and the snow had frozen on them so that they glittered like crystal in the heavy winter sun. Everywhere was whiteness: the purity of Fimbulwinter, of the Death of the World. A few streams continued to run through the snow, which proved to me that it could not be as cold as it seemed. I had grown used to the warmth of spring, I suppose, and it was taking my body time to adjust. Sedenko seemed much easier with the elements than was I.

"A man can understand snow," he said. He told me that in his language there were a considerable number of words for different kinds of snow. "Snow can kill," he continued, as he packed our things back onto our horses, "but you also learn how to stop it from killing you. Or at least how to improve your chances. It is not so, captain, with men."

I smiled at this piece of philosophy. "True."

"Men will tell you what to do to avoid their killing you. You do it. They kill you anyway, eh?"

"Oh, very true, Sedenko." I consoled myself that this innocent would at least be good company in Hell, were we permitted to remain together. And I did not add that what he observed in Man, I observed the more sharply in God and His Fallen Angel. He would not have wanted to believe me. I did not wish to believe myself.

The smell of the snow was good in my nostrils now and I began to sense that peculiar elation which comes when you have lost all Hope of anything, save another hour or two of life. At one point, displaying considerable risk to my horse, I galloped for a short distance through the snow, sending it flying about me. Sedenko yelled and cheered and let his pony race, swinging his body from side to side of the beast with extraordinary agility, at one point leaping, apparently with a single movement, to stand on his saddle and balance there like an acrobat, arms outstretched.

He had boasted that the Kazak was the finest rider in the world and I must say that I could not dispute the fact, if his fellows rode as he rode. His ebullience infected me. I tried to push from my mind all thoughts of Good and Evil, of the War in Heaven, and did my best to sense again the pleasures of the scenery, while Sedenko gradually subsided, like a happy puppy, and eventually drew up beside me, panting and grinning.

That evening Sedenko again built a fire while I checked the map. We were high into the hills now and the mountains seemed to press in on us. There was the plain far behind us, but even this was obscured by the hills. Hermit Pass was not more than five miles to the north-west. We should be there, if we met no obstacles, by the middle of the next morning.

I wondered how this pass might be defended and what kind of danger, from what source, lay ahead of us. But I said nothing to Sedenko.

We reached the first range of mountains just before noon and the entrance to the pass was easily discovered. We had tied rags around our horses' feet. The rocky ground was patched with ice, so that it was better to walk our mounts whenever we could. The peaks of the mountains were invisible now. It seemed that we approached an infinitely tall wall of glittering crystal, white and pale blue, or grey where the rock was exposed. I continued to marvel at the height and shape of them; they were characteristic of nothing I had seen before.

The pass was a dark gash, seemingly in the side of a cliff. It was only as we drew nearer to it that we saw it lay between the mountains, turning sharply inwards so that it was not possible to see very far ahead. The snow was thinner here, but the ice thicker. We should have to move very carefully.

Without ado we stepped forward. The winter sun no longer fell on us and so the temperature dropped immediately, and we wrapped ourselves more thickly in our cloaks. The sound of our footfalls echoed in the canyon and we heard the rushing of water somewhere to one side of us, the drip of half-melted ice, the creaking and shifting noise of uncertain snow. Even as we moved some snow fell from overhanging rock and struck our heads and shoulders.

Sedenko looked upwards towards the crack of light far above

us. "It's almost a cave," he said in some awe. "A monstrous huge tunnel, captain. Will it lead us into Hell?"

"I sincerely hope that it will not," I replied. I had a better idea of the implication of his words than did he.

We spoke quietly, as if we knew that too much noise could dislodge rock, ice and snow which would bury us within seconds. We turned the bend into deeper darkness. Every tiny noise from around us had significance, for it could herald a landslide. I realised that I was scarcely breathing and that I could hear my heartbeats in my ears.

Gradually the pass widened a little until the gap above admitted more light. The snow was deeper and wetter, but the ground was not so icy where the rays of the sun had fallen and we were able to relax into a more normal form of procedure. A few more bends and it had widened again until it was almost a narrow valley. Some bushes and small trees grew here and every so often I detected a patch of green. The noise of the ice and snow grew fainter and assumed less significance to us. After an hour or so into the pass, feeling somewhat more relaxed, we decided to rest and eat some of the bread and pickled herring we had purchased in Ammendorf.

It was as we cleared snow from a flat rock that I heard a scuffling sound and then what I was certain was a human gasp. I paused and listened, but heard nothing else like it. However, I removed my pistols from their holsters and placed them beside me on the rock as I ate.

Sedenko had not heard the sound, but he knew that something was alerting me and he watched my face, listening as he ate.

Another sound. Loose rock and snow fell towards us from our right. I put down my bread and picked up both pistols, levelling them in the general direction of the disturbance.

"Be warned!" I called. "And display yourself, so that we may parley."

A girl of about fifteen, thin-faced, freezing, wrapped in a miscellany of rags, shuffled from the other side of a rock. Her eyes were wide with fear, hunger and curiosity.

I did not lower my pistol. I had become wary of children in my profession. I levelled one of the barrels all the more firmly at her face.

"Are there more of you?"

She shook her head.

"Is your village near here?"

Again a shake of the head.

"Then what in the name of God and Saint Sophia are you doing here?" asked Sedenko of a sudden, slamming his sabre back into its scabbard and marching towards her. I felt he was incautious, but I did not warn him. He went up to her and looked at her face, taking it in his big hands. "You're quite pretty. What's your story, girl? Was your party waylaid by brigands? Are you the sole survivor? Are you lost?"

A sudden thought. He took a step backwards.

"Or are you a witch? A shape-changer?" He looked up at the far rocks. He looked behind him. He spoke over his shoulder to me. "What do you think, captain? Could she be tricking us?"

"Easily," I said. "But then I have assumed that since we saw her."

Another pace backwards. And another, until he was almost presenting his spine to my left-hand pistol. He was staring hard at her. He spoke very quietly to me now. "A witch, then?"

"A wretched girl, most likely, who has been abandoned in these mountains. No more and no less."

She pointed behind her. "My master . . ."

"There!" said Sedenko triumphantly. "A wizard she serves."

"Who is your master, girl?" said I.

"A holy man, excellency." She dipped a curtsey of sorts.

"A magus!" said Sedenko in an urgent whisper to me.

"One of the hermits who dwell in this pass, is he?" I asked.

"He is, Your Honour."

"She's no more than a hermit's companion," I told Sedenko. "You've seen such children before, surely?"

Sedenko rubbed at his lower lip with the joint of his thumb. He looked sideways at the girl. But he was almost convinced by my reasoning.

"And where's your master?" I asked her.

"Above, sir. And dying. We have had no food. He has been injured for many, many days. Since before the snow." She pointed.

Now I could see the shadow of a cave in the rock. There were several such caves here and there, which was no doubt why they were favoured by hermits. As well as providing the kind of living accommodation hermits seemed to find most satisfactory, they were close to the pass and travellers could be prevailed upon to offer food, money or any other form of aid.

"How long have you been with your hermit?" I asked her. I decided to replace the pistols in their holsters. It was obvious to me that she was not lying. Sedenko, however, was not so certain now.

"Since I was a little girl, sir. He has looked after me from the time when my brother, my mother and my father were all killed. By the eagles, sir."

"Well, then," I said, "lead us to the dying hermit."

Sedenko had a thought: "Could this be your Groot, captain?"

"I think not. But he could know of Groot. Most of these hermits tend to be rivals, in my experience."

We clambered up the snowy rocks in the wake of the girl until the cave was reached. A dreadful stench came out of it, but again I was familiar with the kind of stink surrounding such holy creatures and braved it readily, with a hand over my mouth.

The girl pointed into a corner. Something stirred there.

Sedenko remained outside, complaining. I made no attempt to force him to follow me.

A gaunt face raised itself a little and dark eyes stared into mine. If the smell and the sight were sickening, the worst was the smile I was offered by the hermit. It was radiant with insane piety. It offered itself as an example, it accused, it forgave all at once. I had seen such smiles before. More than once I had killed the ones who had presented them to me. I had once argued that a smile of that kind upon the lips was worth a second smile in the throat.

"Greetings, holy hermit," I said. "Your servant tells us that you are ailing."

"She exaggerates, sir. I have a wound or two, that is all. But what are my wounds compared to the wounds of our own dear

Christ, whom we all wish to follow and to imitate? Those wounds take me closer to Heaven, in more than one sense."

"Ah, and they smell of Heaven already, do they not?" I replied. "I am Ulrich von Bek and I am upon a Quest for the Holy Grail."

I knew that would have an effect. He fell back, almost resentfully. "The Grail? The Grail? Ah, sir, but the Grail would cure me!"

"And all others who are dying or lie sick," I said. "However, I have not yet found it."

"Are you close to your Quest's end?" he asked.

"I do not know." I stepped closer. "I will get you something to eat. Sedenko!" I called back to my companion. "Food for this pair."

Sedenko with a certain reluctance scrambled back the way we had come.

"I am honoured to be in the company of one so holy," said the hermit.

"But you are quite as holy as I," I said.

"No, sir, you are far holier than myself. It stands to reason. How you must have suffered to have attained your present state of grace!"

"Oh, no, Sir Hermit, I am sure that your sufferings outstrip mine a hundredfold."

"I cannot believe that. But look!" He held up an arm. There was movement in the arm which was not muscle or bone. I peered hard at it.

"What must I see?" I asked.

"My friends, Sir Knight. The creatures I love more than I love myself."

The main stink, I now realised, was coming from the arm he displayed. And as my eyes grew accustomed to the gloom I could see that his limb writhed with maggots. They were feeding off him. He smiled at them, much as he had smiled at me. He doubtless regarded them with more affection than he felt for any human being. After all, these were actively aiding him in his martyrdom.

I am a man used to disguising my disgust, but it took a considerable effort of will not to turn away from that madman there and then.

"Such pious suffering is outstanding," I said. I straightened and looked towards the cave mouth, yearning for the clean air and the snow.

"You are very kind, Sir Knight." With a sigh he fell back into the general filth.

The thought of putting food into the mouth of this wretch so that he might feed his maggots was obnoxious to me, but the unwitting child deserved to eat. Sedenko reappeared and I went towards him, taking the bread he gave me and handing it to the girl. She immediately broke off the largest piece and took it to her master. As she crumbled the bread and placed it between his lips he chewed with a kind of eager control, the saliva running down his grimy chin and into his beard.

For a moment or two I stepped outside, barely able to quell my nausea.

Sedenko murmured: "That girl is wasted here. The old beast will be dead in a few more days at the most."

I agreed with him. "When he has finished eating I'll ask him what he knows of Groot, then we'll be on our way."

"There are holy men of his kind in many parts of my country," Sedenko said, "thinking that dirt and humiliation of the flesh bring them closer to God. But what can God want with them?"

"Perhaps He desires that we should all follow this hermit's example. Perhaps it satisfies God to see His Creations denying all the virtues they believe He has instilled?"

Sedenko muttered at me: "Heresy, captain. Or close enough." He did not like my tone, which I am sure contained more than a little mockery. I was in a darkly embittered mood.

I moved back into the cave. "Tell me, Sir Hermit, if you have heard of one of your kind. A certain Philander Groot."

"Of course I have heard of Groot. He dwells in the Valley of the Golden Cloud on the other side of these mountains. But he is not a holy man, though he may claim to be. Why, I have heard that he even denies God. He does not mortify his flesh. He is said to bathe very frequently, at least ten times in the year. His clothing . . ." The creature began to cough. "Well, suffice to say that he is not of our persuasion, though I am sure," added the hermit with some effort, "that he has his reasons for choosing his particular path and it is not for us to say who is wrong or who is right." Again that smile of exquisite and self-congratulatory piety.

"He has no maggots, I take it," said I.

"Not one," said the hermit. "So far as I know, Sir Knight. But I could be condemning him without cause. I have only heard of Philander Groot. There were once many other hermits living in these caves. I am the last. But they used to tell me of Groot."

"Thank you," I said with as much courtesy as I could muster. I looked from the hermit to the girl. "And what will become of your protégée when you finally attain Heaven, Sir Hermit?"

He smiled upon her. "She will be rewarded."

"You think she will survive this winter?"

The hermit frowned. "Probably not, of course, if I do not. She will rise up to Heaven with me, perhaps. She is, after all, yet a virgin."

"Her virginity will be sufficient passport?"

"That and the fact that she has served me so loyally all these years. I have taught her everything I know. When she came to me she was ignorant. But I have taught her of Sin and of Paradise. I have taught her of the Fall of Lucifer and how our parents were driven out of Eden. I have taught her of the Ten Commandments. I have told her of Christ's birth, suffering, death and resurrection and I have taught her of the Day of Judgement. For a woman, she has been blessed with more than is usual, you will agree."

"Indeed," I said, "she is a singularly fortunate young person. What else do you think she will inherit from you?"

"I have nothing," he said proudly, "but what you see."

"Shall you leave her your maggots?"

For the first time, now, he caught my irony. He frowned, lost for an answer.

I grew impatient with him. "Well, Sir Hermit, what's your answer?"

"You jest with me," he said. "I cannot believe . . ."

"I think it is time you received your reward," I told him, and I drew my sword. "It is not just that you should wait any longer."

The girl gasped. She ran forward, guessing my intention. I pushed her back with my free hand, shouting out for Sedenko's assistance. I advanced upon the hermit.

Sedenko appeared beside me, grinning. Plainly, he approved of my intention. He seized the girl in both arms and bore her from the cave as I raised my blade.

"Go with my friend, girl. There is no need for you to witness this."

"Kill me, too," she said.

"That would be unseemly," said I. "Should you die, too, it would be a veritable surfeit of sacrifice. I doubt if God Himself could contemplate so much at once. But if you wish to sacrifice something, do not make it your soul. I am sure that Sedenko here can think of some pleasurable alternative."

She had begun to sob as I turned my back on them and looked down on the holy man. He showed no fear.

He said: "You must do what you have to, brother. It is God's work."

"What?" I said. "Shall you and I take no responsibility at all for your murder?"

"It is God's work," he repeated.

I smiled. "Lucifer's my Master." I found his heart with my steel and began to push slowly. "And I suspect that He is yours, also."

The hermit died with only the smallest groan. I walked out of the cave. Sedenko was already carrying the girl down. He was grinning at her and saying something in his own language.

That night, while I tried to sleep, Sedenko took his pleasure with the girl. She became noisy at one point, but then grew quiet. In the morning she was gone.

"I think she will try to get to Ammendorf," he said.

I was not in a talkative mood.

For the next few days we travelled through the mountains while Sedenko sang all his songs several times over and I contemplated the mysteries of an existence I had come increasingly to consider arbitrary at best.

Chapter Nine

I HAD FALLEN into the habit of deriving a kind of joy from the irony of my position, from the paradoxes and contrasts of my Quest. It led me to contemplate the most horrible crimes which could be committed by me in the name of the Grail Search. Was I strong enough, I wondered, to commit them? What kind of self-discipline was involved in forcing oneself, against one's own nature, towards vice? My inner debates became increasingly complex and unreal, but perhaps they served to take my mind off unwelcome actualities.

A hard week saw us through the heart of the mountains. We had experienced landslides, a couple of poorly organised attacks from local brigands, two or three near-falls on the higher passes and, of course, the ordinary vicissitudes of the climate. Sedenko's spirits had not declined a jot and my own gloom had begun to lift when we halted our horses on a high promontory and looked down into what we assumed must be our destination.

All we could see was glowing, golden mist, filling the wide basin of a valley, whose cliffs were snow-capped and whose sides were almost sheer.

"There's where Philander Groot dwells, captain," said Sedenko, leaning on his pommel, "but how do we reach it?"

"We must keep looking," I said, "until we find the way in. It must surely exist, if Groot has come and gone from there."

We began, by means of a narrow trail, to descend. There would be about four hours left until twilight, when we should of necessity camp. These mountains were too dangerous for night travelling.

The first intimation we had of the valley's guardians was a whistling in the air. When we looked back and up towards the clear blue of the sky we saw two of them, sharply outlined. Their intentions were clear. They meant to kill us.

I had never seen eagles so huge or so resplendent. Their bodies were pretty near as big as those of a small pony and their wings were, each one, about twice the length of their main bulk. They were predominantly white and gold and scarlet, with a certain amount of deep blue around the heads. The beaks shone like grey steel and were matched in appearance by their wide-stretched claws. As they came down on us, they shrieked their intention, celebrating their anticipated triumph.

Our horses began to rear and cry out. I pulled one pistol free, cocked it, aimed and fired. The ball struck the first eagle in the shoulder and it veered off silently, blood streaming from the wound. Sedenko's sabre cut at the second and caused it to stay its attack, fluttering over his head and making such a wind as to threaten to blow us down into the valley. My other pistol was produced and fired. This was a better shot, to the head. With a terrible wail the eagle tried to regain height, failed and fell heavily into the chasm. I watched its body pass through the mist and vanish. Its companion (perhaps its mate) sailed over the spot for some little while before its attention returned to us and, glaring and screaming, it resumed its attack. I had no time to reload. We had only our swords, now, for defence. The creature dived and snatched and, had not Sedenko ducked his head, the young Kazak would have been carried off for certain. As it was his sabre sliced several tailfeathers from the gigantic bird. These Sedenko grabbed from the air and brandished with a grin as a prize.

The bird came to me next. Those claws could easily impale me as readily as any pike. My horse was bucking and trying to flee and half my attention was on him, but I struck back with my sword and drew blood, though nothing worth the trouble.

The eagle was flying erratically, thanks to its wounded shoulder and lack of tailfeathers. Sedenko got in another blow which removed the better part of one claw and now the bird was weakening, though it had no thought of giving up its attack.

With every fresh dive it was driven off, having sustained another small wound or two.

And that was how we fought it. Slowly but surely we cut the

great creature to pieces until all of its lower body and limbs, its neck and head, were a mass of blood and ruined feathers.

On the bird's final attack, Sedenko leapt onto his saddle and, standing on tiptoe, sliced so that a wing-joint was severed. The eagle fell to one side in the air, desperately trying to regain its balance, then smashed down into the snow, which immediately became flecked with blood and feathers of white, gold and scarlet. It screamed in outrage at what we had done to it and neither of us had the stomach to watch it die or the courage to descend the slope and put it out of its misery. We looked at it in silence for a few minutes before sheathing our blades and riding on. Neither of us believed that we had won any kind of honourable victory.

Slowly the trail led down through the glowing, golden mist, until we could hardly see a couple of feet on any side. Again we dismounted and went with considerable caution, until night fell and we were forced to find a relatively flat stretch of ground where we might tether our horses and camp until morning.

Before he slept, Sedenko said: "Those birds were supernatural creatures, eh, captain?"

"I have never heard of natural creatures like them," I said. "I am certain of that, Sedenko.

"They were the servants of this magus we seek," he said. "Which means that we have offended him by killing his servants . . ."

"We do not know that they serve him or that he will be angry at our saving our own lives by killing them."

"I am afraid of this magus, captain," said Sedenko simply. "For it is well-known that the greatest sorcerer is the one who can command the spirits of the air. And what were those eagles but air-spirits?"

"They were large," I said, "and they were dangerous. But for all we know they saw us merely as prey. As food for their young. There can be few travellers in these parts, particularly during the winter months. And little large game, either, I would guess. Do not speculate, Sedenko, on things for which no evidence exists. You will waste your time. Particularly, I would guess, in Mittelmarch."

Sedenko took this to mean that he should be silent. He closed his lips, but it was obvious he had not ceased to consider the matter of the eagles.

We continued our journey in the morning and noted that the air grew gradually warmer, while the golden mist became thinner, until at last we emerged onto a broad mountain trail which wound down into a valley of astonishing beauty and which was completely without snow. Indeed, it might have been early summer in that valley. We saw crops growing in fields; we saw well-ordered villages and, to the east, a large-sized town built on two sides of a wide and pleasant river. It was almost impossible for either Sedenko or myself to realise that all around us lay stark crags and thick snow.

"We have gone from spring into winter in a single stride," said Sedenko wonderingly, "and now we are in summer. Are we sleeping, like the old man of the legend, through whole parts of the year, captain? Are we entranced without realising it? Or is this valley the product of sorcery?"

"If it be sorcery, it's of an exceedingly pleasing kind," I told my friend. I took off my cloak and rolled it up behind me.

"No wonder they guard this place with gigantic eagles." Sedenko peered down. He saw herds of sheep and cattle: a land of plenty. "This would be a place to settle, eh, captain? From here it would be possible to ride up into the snow when one wished, to sally out on raids . . ." He paused as he contemplated his own version of Paradise.

"What would we steal on the raids?" I asked him good humouredly, "when all that we should need is here already?"

"Well"—he shrugged—"a man has to raid. Or do something."

I looked up. The golden mist stretched from end to end of the valley, giving it its name. I could not understand what caused this phenomenon, but I believed it to be natural. Somehow the cold, the snow, did not touch the valley. I had known well-protected places in my time, which were harmed less by the seasons than most, but I had never witnessed the likes of this.

We rode down slowly and it took us well over an hour before

we had neared the bottom. Here, on the trail ahead of us, we saw a great gate, impossible to pass, and before the gate a mounted sentinel, standing four-square on a giant charger, dressed in all the warlike regalia of two or three centuries since, with plate armour and crests and plumes and polished iron and oiled leather, in colours predominantly gold, white and scarlet, bearing a device of just such an eagle as we had fought above.

From within the closed helm a voice called out:

"Stop, strangers!"

We drew rein. Sedenko had become cautious again and I knew he was wondering if this being, too, were of supernatural origin.

"I am Ulrich von Bek," I said. "I am on the Grail Quest and I seek a wise man who dwells in this valley."

The guardian seemed to laugh at this. "You are in need of a wise man, stranger. For if you seek the Grail you are a fool."

"You know of the Grail?" Sedenko was suddenly curious.

"Who does not? We know of many things in the Valley of the Golden Cloud, for this is a land which is sought by those who dream of Eden. We are used to legends here, stranger, since we are ourselves a legend."

"A legend and you exist. So might the Grail exist," I said.

"One does not prove the other." The guardian shifted a little in his saddle. "You are the men who killed our eagle, are you not?"

"We were attacked!" Sedenko became defensive. "We protected our own lives . . ."

"It is not a crime to kill an eagle," said the guardian evenly. "We of the Valley of the Golden Cloud do not impose our own laws on strangers. We merely ask that strangers do not bring their specific ideas of justice to us. But once you have passed this gateway, you must agree to obey our laws until you leave again."

"Naturally, we would agree," I said.

"Our laws are simple: Steal Nothing, whether it be an abstract idea or another life. Examine Everything. Pay a Fair Price. And, remember, to lie is to steal another soul's freedom of action, or some fragment of it. Here a liar and a thief are the same thing."

"Your laws sound excellent," I said. "Indeed, they sound ideal."

"And simple," said Sedenko feelingly.

"They are simple," said the guardian, "but they sometimes require complex interpretation."

"And what are the penalties for breaking your laws?" asked Sedenko.

The guardian said: "We have only two punishments here: Expulsion and Death. To some, they are the same."

"We will remember all you have said," I told him. "We seek Philander Groot, the hermit. Do you know where we might find him?"

"I do not know. Only the Queen knows."

"She is the ruler of this land?" asked Sedenko.

"She is its embodiment," said the guardian. "She dwells in the city. Go there now."

He moved his horse aside and made a sign so that the iron portcullis might be lifted by unseen hands within the towers.

As we passed through, I thanked him for his courtesy, but such was my state of mind that I determined to look carefully about me. It had been many years since I had been able to believe in absolute justice, and some weeks since I had been able to believe that there existed in the world (or beyond it) justice of any kind.

The air was sweet as we followed a road of well-trodden yellow earth through fields of green wheat towards the distant city, whose towers and turrets were predominantly white, reflecting the gold of the mist above us.

"A noble creature, that guard," said Sedenko, in some admiration, looking about him.

"Or a self-righteous one," I said.

"One must at least believe in Perfection"—he had become serious—"or one cannot believe in the promise of Heaven."

"True," said I to that poor damned youth.

Chapter Ten

THE GUARDS AT the city gates were clad in the same anti-quated regalia as the first guard we had encountered. They did not challenge us as we entered the wide streets to discover a well-ordered collection of houses and public buildings, a cheerful and dignified population and an active market. Since we had been ordered to present ourselves to the Queen of this land, we continued on our way until we reached the palace: a relatively low building of extreme beauty, with sweeping curves and pinnacles, bright stained glass and a general air of tranquillity.

Trumpets announced our coming as we passed under the arch-way into a wide courtyard decorated with all manner of shrubs and flowers. The unpretentiousness of the palace, its atmosphere, reminded me somehow of my boyhood in Bek. My father's manor had possessed just such a mood.

Ostlers came forward to take our horses and a woman in skirt and wimple of olden times emerged from the doorway to beckon us. She was an exceptionally lovely young female, with large blue eyes and an open, healthy face. She looked like the better type of nun.

"Greetings to you," she said. "The Queen expects you. Would you wish to refresh yourselves, to bathe, perhaps, before you are presented?"

I looked at Sedenko. If I was half as filthy and as unshaven as he, I felt I would be happier for a bath and a chance to change my clothes.

Sedenko said: "We have been travelling through snow, lady. We hardly need to wash ourselves. See? Nature's done that for us."

I bowed to the young woman. "We are grateful to you," I said. "I, for one, would like some hot water."

"It will be provided." She beckoned and led the way into the palace's cool interior. The ceilings were low and decorated with murals, as were the walls. We passed through a kind of cloisters and here were apartments evidently prepared for guests. The young woman showed us into one of these. Heated water had already been poured into two large wooden tubs in the centre of the main room.

Sedenko sniffed the air, as if he saw sorcery in the steam.

I thanked the young woman, who smiled at me and said: "I will return in an hour to escort you to the Queen."

Refreshed, I was ready and dressed in my change of clothes when she came back. Sedenko had no change of clothes and had scarcely let the water touch his skin, but even he had deigned to shave his face, save for his moustache. He looked considerably more personable than when he had arrived.

Again we followed the young woman through a variety of corridors, cloisters and gardens, until we were led into a large-sized room with a high ceiling on which was painted a representation of the sun, the stars and the moon, what is sometimes called, I believe, a Solar Atlas.

There on a throne of green glass and carved mahogany sat a girl of perhaps fifteen years. Since she wore a crystal-and-diamond crown upon her dark red hair we naturally bowed and murmured what we hoped were the appropriate greetings.

The girl smiled sweetly. She had large brown eyes and red lips. "You are welcome to our land, strangers. I am Queen Xiombarg the Twenty-fifth and I am curious to know why you braved the eagles to visit us. You were not drawn here, as are some adventurers, by legends of gold and magic, I am sure."

Sedenko became alert. "Treasure?" he said, before he thought. Then he blushed. "Oh, no, madam."

"I am upon the Grail Search," I told the young Queen. "I seek a hermit by the name of Philander Groot and believe that Your Majesty knows where I could find him."

"I am trusted with that knowledge," she said. "But I am sworn never to reveal it. What help can Herr Groot provide?"

"I do not know. I was told to seek him out and tell him my story."

131

"Is your story an unusual one?"

"Many would believe it more than unusual, Your Majesty."

"And you will not tell it to me?"

"I have told it to no-one. I will tell it to Philander Groot because he might be able to help me."

She nodded. "You'll trade him secret for secret, eh?"

"It seems so."

"He will be amused by that."

I inclined my head.

Sedenko burst out: "It's God's work he's on, Your Majesty. If he finds the Grail . . ."

I tried to interrupt him, but she raised her hand. "We are not to be persuaded or dissuaded, sir. Here we believe neither in Heaven nor in Hell. We worship no gods or devils. We believe only in moderation."

I could not disguise my scepticism and she was quick to notice.

She smiled. "We are satisfied with this state of things. Reason is not subsumed by sentiment here. The two are balanced."

"I have always found balance a nostalgic dream, Your Majesty. In reality it can be very dull."

She was not dismayed. "Oh, we amuse ourselves adequately, captain. We have music, painting, plays . . ."

"Surely such ideas of moderation require no true struggle. Thus they defeat human aspiration. What greatness have these arts of yours? How noble are they? What heights of feeling and intellect do they reach?"

"We live in the world," she replied quietly. "We do not ignore how it is. We send our young people out of the valley when they are eighteen. There they learn of human misery, of pain and of those who triumph over them. They bring their experience back. Here, in tranquillity, it is considered and forms the basis of our philosophy."

"You are fortunate," I said with some bitterness.

"We are."

"So justice requires good luck before it can exist?"

"Probably, captain."

"Yet you seek out experience. You tell your young people to search for danger. That is not the same as being subjected to it, willy-nilly."

"No, indeed. But it is better than not searching for it at all."

"It seems to me, madam, that you yet possess the complacency of the privileged. What if your land were to be attacked?"

"No army can reach us without our knowing of it."

"No army can march by land, perhaps. But what, for instance, if your enemies trained those eagles to come through the Golden Cloud carrying soldiers?"

"That is inconceivable," she said with a laugh.

"To those who live with danger and have no choice," I said, "nothing is inconceivable."

She shrugged. "Well, we are satisfied."

"And I am glad that you are, madam."

"You are a stimulating guest, captain. Will you stay at our Court for a few days?"

"I regret that I must find Philander Groot if I can, as soon as I can. My commission has some urgency to it."

"Very well. Take the West Road from the city. It will lead you to a wood. In the wood is a wide glade, with a dead oak in it. Philander Groot, if he pleases, will find you there."

"At what time?"

"He will choose the time. You will have to be patient. Now, captain, at least you will eat with us and tell us something of your adventures."

Sedenko and I accepted the invitation. The dinner was superb. We filled ourselves to capacity, spent the night in good beds and in the morning went by the West Road from the young Queen's town.

The wood was easily reached and the glade found without difficulty. We made a camp there and settled down to wait for Groot. The air was warm and lazy and the flowers softened our tempers with their beauty and their scents. "This is a place to come home to when you are old," said Sedenko as he stretched himself on the ground and stared around at the great trees. "But I'd guess it's no place to be young in. No fighting, precious little hunting . . ."

"The lack of conflict could bore anyone under forty," I agreed. "I cannot quite get to the root of my irritation with this place. Perhaps there is a touch too much sanity here. If it is sanity, of course. My instincts tell me that this kind of life is in itself insane in some ways."

"Too profound for me, captain," said Sedenko. "They're rich. They're safe. They're happy. Isn't that what we all want for ourselves in the end?"

"A healthy animal," I said, "needs to exercise its body and its wits to the full."

"But not all the time, captain." Sedenko looked alarmed, as if I was about to expect some action from him.

I laughed. "Not all the time, young Kazak."

After three days of waiting in the glade neither of us was so willing to rest. We had explored every part of the surrounding country, its rivers, its meadows, its woods. We had picked flowers and plaited them. We had groomed our horses. We had swum. Sedenko had climbed every tree which could be climbed and I had studied, without much understanding, the grimoires Sabrina had given me. I had also studied all the maps and had seen that Mittelmarch territories seemed to exist in gaps between lands where, in my own world, no gaps were.

By the time the fifth morning dawned I was ready to mount my horse and leave the Valley of the Golden Cloud. "I'll find my way to the Grail without Groot's help," I said.

And these words, almost magically, seemed to conjure up the dandy who sauntered into our camp, looking around him a little fastidiously but with the good humour of self-mockery. He was all festooned lace and velvet, gold and silver buckles and embroidery. He walked with the aid of a monstrous decorated pole and he stank of Hungary Water. His hat had a huge brim weighted down with white and silver feathers and his little beard and moustache were trimmed to the perfection demanded of the most foppish French courtier. His sword, of delicate workmanship, seemed of no use to him at all as he stared at me with a quizzical eye and then made one of those elaborate bows which I have never been able to imitate.

"Good morrow to thee, gentlemen," lisped the dandy. "I am enchanted to make your acquaintance."

"We're not here to pass the time of day with men dressed as women," said Sedenko, scowling. "We await the coming of a great sage, a hermit of the wisest disposition."

"Aha, forgive me. I will not keep you long, in that case. Pray, what are your names, sirs?"

"I am Ulrich von Bek, Captain of Infantry, and this is my companion Grigory Petrovitch Sedenko, swordsman. And yours, sir?"

"My name, sir, is Philander Groot."

"The hermit?" cried Sedenko in astonishment.

"I am a hermit, sir, yes."

"You don't look like a hermit." Sedenko put his hand on the hilt of his sabre and strode forward to inspect the apparition.

"Sir, I assure you that I am, indeed, a hermit." Groot became polite. He was distant.

"We heard you were a holy man," Sedenko continued.

"I cannot be held responsible for what others hear or say, sir." Groot drew himself up. He was somewhat shorter than Sedenko, who was no giant. "I am the same Philander Groot for whom you were looking. Take me or leave me, sir. This is all there is."

"We had not thought to find a dandy," said I, by way of apologising for Sedenko's frankness. "We imagined someone in homespun cloth. The usual sort of garb."

"It is not my way to fulfil the expectation of my fellow creatures. I am Groot. Groot is who I am."

"But why a dandy?" Sedenko sighed and turned away from us.

"There are many ways of keeping one's distance from the world," said Groot to me.

"And many others to keep the world at a distance from oneself," I added.

"You appreciate my drift, Sir Knight. Self-knowledge, however, is not self-salvation. You and I have a fair way to go in that direction,

I think. You through action and I, coward that I am, through contemplation."

"I believe that I lack the courage for profound self-examination, Master Groot," said I.

He was amused. "Well, what a fine man we should be, if we were combined into one! And how self-important, then, we could become!"

"I was told, Master Groot, that you might wish to hear my story and, that once you had heard it, you might wish to give me a clue or two to the solution of my problem."

"I am curious," admitted this gamecock philosopher, "and will be glad to pay for entertainment with information. You must rely on me, however, to set the price. Does that go against your wishes?"

"Not at all."

"Then, come, we shall take a walk together in the forest."

Sedenko looked back. "Careful, captain. It could be a trap."

"Grigory Petrovitch," I said, "if Master Groot had wished to ambush us, he could have done so at any time, surely."

Sedenko pushed his sheepskin cap high on his head and grumbled something before kicking violently at a clump of flowers.

Philander Groot linked his elegant arm in mine and we began to walk until we reached the stream. At its banks we paused.

"You must begin, sir," he said.

I told him where I was born and how I had come to be a warrior. I told him of Magdeburg and what followed. I told him of Sabrina. I told him of my meeting with Lucifer and of my journey to Hell. I told him of the bargain, of Lucifer's expectations. I told him what it was I sought—or rather what I thought it was.

We walked along the bank of the stream as I spoke and he nodded, murmured his understanding and very occasionally asked for clarification. He seemed delighted by what I had to say, and when I had finished he tugged at my arm and we stopped again. He removed his plumed hat and stroked at his carefully made curls. He fingered his little beard. He smiled and looked at the water. He brought his attention back to me.

"The Grail exists," he said. "And you are sensible to call it that because it frequently takes the form of a cup."

"You have seen it?" I asked.

"I believe I have seen it, on my travels, sir. When I travelled."

"So the legend of the Pure Knight deceives us?"

"It depends somewhat upon your definition of purity, I think," said Groot. "But suffice to say the thing is useless in the hands of one who would do evil with it. And as to the definition of evil, we can accept the crude, commonplace definition well enough here, I think. A certain amount of altruism exists in all of us and if properly maintained and mixed with appropriate self-interest, it can produce a happy man who gives offence neither to Heaven nor to Hell."

"I have heard that you refuse loyalty to either God or the Devil," I said.

"That's true. I doubt if I shall ever choose sides. My investigations and my philosophy do not lead me in their direction at all." He shrugged. "But who knows? I am yet a relatively young man . . ."

"You accept their existence, however?"

"Why, sir, you confirm it!"

"You believe that I have been the guest of Lucifer, that I am now His servant?"

"I must accept it, sir."

"And you will help me?"

"As much as I can. The Grail can be found, I believe, in a place known as the Forest at the Edge of Heaven. You will discover it, I am sure, marked on your charts. It lies on the farthest border of Mittelmarch. You must find it in the west."

"And are there any rituals I must follow?" I asked Philander Groot. "I seem to recall . . ."

"Ritual is the truth made into a child's game, at best. You will know what is for the best, I am sure."

"You can give me no more advice?"

"It would be against all I believe should I do so. No, Sir Knight, I have told you enough. The Grail exists. You will find it, almost certainly, where I said it can be found. What more could you need?"

I smiled in self-mockery. "Reassurance, I suppose."

"That must come from your own judgement, from your own testing of your conscience. It is the only kind of reassurance worth having, as I am sure you would agree."

"I agree, of course."

We were now walking back towards the glade. Groot mused. "I wonder if any object can cure the World of its Pain. It must be more than that. Would you say that your Master is desperate, captain?"

"His layers of defiance and rationalisation seem to fall away," I told the hermit, "to reveal little else but desperation. But can an angel fall so low in spirit?"

"There are entire monasteries, vast schools, debating such issues." Groot laughed. "I would not dare to speculate, Sir Knight. The Nature of Angels is not a branch of philosophy which captures my imagination much. Lucifer, I would say, cannot actually deceive an omniscient God, so therefore God must already know that the Grail is sought. If Lucifer has another purpose than the one He has told you, then God already knows it and continues, to some degree at least, to permit your Quest. This is the sort of talk which idle scholars prefer. But it is not for me."

"Nor for me," I said. "If I find the Grail and redeem my soul, that will be enough. I can only pray that Lucifer keeps His bargain."

"To whom do you pray?" asked Groot, with another smile. The question was rhetorical. He shook his hand to show that he was not serious.

"You seem an unusual subject of Queen Xiombarg," I said. "Or perhaps I misjudge her and this land."

"You probably misjudge the Queen and her country," he said, "but whether you do or you don't I can assure you that in all of Mittelmarch there is no more tranquil a valley, and tranquillity, at present, is what I seek above anything else, at this stage of my life."

"And do you understand the nature of Mittelmarch?" I asked him.

He shrugged. "I do not. All I know is that Mittelmarch could not survive without the rest of the world—but the rest of the world can survive without Mittelmarch. And that, I suspect, is what its denizens fear in you, if they fear anything at all."

"You are not, then, from Mittelmarch originally?"

"I am from Alsatia. Few who dwell here were born here. This valley and one or two other places are exceptions. Some exist here as shadows. Some exist as shadows in your world. It is very puzzling, captain. I am not brave enough to look at the problem with a steady eye. Not as yet. I have a feeling that if I did, I should die. Now, you will be wanting to be gone from the Valley of the Golden Cloud, eh? And on your way. I will escort you to the Western Gate. A trail will lead you through the mountains and onto a good road out of Mittelmarch."

"How shall I know which road it is?"

"There are not many roads in these parts, captain."

We had returned to the glade where a frowning Sedenko awaited us. "I believed you murdered or kidnapped, Captain von Bek."

I felt almost light-hearted. "Nonsense, Grigory Petrovitch! Master Groot has been of considerable help to me."

Sedenko sniffed at the strong odour of Hungary Water. "You trust him?"

"As much as I can trust myself."

Groot beckoned. "Pack your goods, gentlemen. I will walk with you to the Western Gate."

When we were ready to ride, the little dandy removed a lacy kerchief from his sleeve and mopped his brow beneath his hat. "The day grows warm," he said. With his tall cane held at a graceful angle, he began to stroll back to the road. "Come, my friends. You'll be out of here by nightfall if we hurry."

We walked our horses in Groot's wake as he moved rapidly along, more like a dancing master than anything else, humming to himself and commenting on the beauties of the fields and cottages we passed on our way, until at length we reached the far side of the valley and a gatehouse very similar to that by which we had entered. Here, Groot hailed the guard.

"Friends are leaving," he said. "Let them pass."

The guard, in the same livery as we had seen before, moved his horse aside and the portcullis was raised. At the gate Philander Groot paused, looking out at the trail, which wound up and up until it reached the golden mist. His expression was hard to read. I thought for a moment his eyes were those of a prisoner or an exile yearning to go home, but when he turned his face to me he had the same controlled, amused expression. "Here we are, captain. I will wish you good luck and good judgement on your Quest. It would be pleasing if we could meet again, in the fullness of time. I shall follow your adventure, as best I can, from here. And I shall follow it with interest."

"Why not come with us?" I said impulsively. "We should be encouraged by your company and I for one would be glad of your conversation."

"It is tempting, captain. I say that with all sincerity. But it is my decision to remain here for a while and so remain I shall. But know that I go with you in spirit."

A final elaborate bow, a wave, and Philander Groot was stepping backwards to let us ride through the gate. The portcullis closed behind us. A scented kerchief fluttered.

Soon we were engulfed again in golden mist and once more resorted to our cloaks as the weather grew colder.

By the time we were out of the mist, night had come and we camped upon the trail, there being no other suitable place. By morning we were able to look down at the far foothills of the mountains and know that very soon we should be on level ground again. We had not gone more than half an hour along our way before we heard the pounding of hoofs and, looking back, observed some twenty armoured men coming up at a gallop.

Their leader was not armoured. I saw black and white. I saw a purple plume. I recognised Sedenko's former master, the warrior-priest Klosterheim.

We spurred our horses forward, hoping to outrun the armoured pack. There was something mysterious about them. Their armour glowed. Indeed, it seemed to burn, though only with black fire. Wisps of mist escaped the helms, and the mist was a terrible grey colour, as if the lungs which breathed it were in some way polluted.

"What can the Knight of Christ be doing with that company?" Sedenko gasped to me. "If ever creatures bore the stamp of Hell it is they. How can they be serving God's Purpose?"

I wanted to retort that if I served the Devil's then perhaps they could serve God's, but I bit back the comment and concentrated on doing my best to control my horse's descent of the trail. His hoofs were slipping and twice he almost went over—once where a chasm loomed.

"We shall perish if we maintain this speed!" I said. "Yet Klosterheim means us harm for certain. And we cannot hope to defeat armoured knights."

We sought escape. There was none. We could go forward, or we could stand and wait for Klosterheim's devilish troop. As the trail widened I spied ahead that it entered a cleft in the rock, hardly space enough for one man to pass. It would be there, if anywhere, we could defend ourselves. I pointed, pulling at my reins. My horse reared. Sedenko saw my meaning and nodded. He dashed past me into the cleft, then turned his horse cautiously, inch by inch. I threw him one of my pistols and a pouch of shot and powder, backing my own horse round. With the cleft on both sides of us we could command our front without risk of attack from any other quarter.

Klosterheim scarcely realised what we had done as he raced forward. I aimed my pistol at him, drew back the hammer and then discharged. The shot went wide of him, but it served to halt him of a sudden. He shouted, glared, shortened his rein and held up a stilling hand to his pack. They stopped with unnatural discipline.

"Klosterheim," I called, "what do you want with us?"

"I want nothing from Sedenko, who can continue on his way

without fear," said the thin-faced priest. "But it is your life I want, von Bek, and nothing less."

"Can I have given you so much offence?"

It was then that I realised we were still in Mittelmarch. I began to chuckle. "Oh, Klosterheim, what terrible things you have done in God's name! Were our Master still the creature He was, He would be more than pleased with you. You are as damned as the rest of us! And you are one of those who fears that my Quest shall bring an end to everything, that you will have no home, no master, no future, no identity. Is that why you fear me so, Klosterheim?"

Johannes Klosterheim almost growled in reply. His eyes darted from side to side of the trail. He looked upwards. He was seeking a means of outflanking us. There was none. "You reckon without my power," he said. "That has not been taken from me. Arioch!"

He cried the name of one of Lucifer's Dukes, perhaps his patron. He moved his hand as if he flung an invisible ball at the cliff. Something cracked high overhead. It might have been lightning. A disgusting smell came into my nostrils.

"Try the pistol, Sedenko," I murmured.

The gun boomed from behind me and I felt its flash. The ball went wide of Klosterheim, and I heard it strike a glowing black breastplate and then bounce against a rock.

"Arioch!"

Again the lightning and I glimpsed a huge piece of rock as it fell away from the outer wall of the crevice and dropped hundreds of feet into the chasm on the other side.

"You are a powerful magus, Klosterheim," said I. "And one wonders why you posed for so long as a holy priest."

"I am holy," said Klosterheim through his teeth. "My cause is the noblest there has ever been. I leagued myself with Lucifer to destroy God! I have been about the world showing, in the name of God, what horrors can exist. There was no cause nobler than Lucifer's—and now He seeks to capitulate, to abandon us, to let Hell and all it stands for be swept away. As Lucifer defied God, so it is my right to defy Lucifer. We are threatened with betrayal. He is my Master, von Bek, as well as yours. And I have served Him well!"

"But you do not serve Him now. He will be angered with you."

"What of it? He has no allies worth the name. His own Dukes are against Him. What will happen to them if God takes Him back?"

"Is Hell in rebellion?" I said in surprise.

"So it could be said. Lucifer loses authority by the hour. Your Master is weaker now, von Bek, than even the simpering Christ who first betrayed humanity! And I will not tolerate weakness! Arioch!"

Another crack of lightning. The burning black helms looked up as if in appreciation. Fragments of rock began to fall down on Sedenko and myself. "Ride fast, Sedenko," I cried. "Away from here. It is our only hope."

Sedenko hesitated. I insisted. "Ride! It is a command!"

From overhead the slabs of granite began to groan, and snow poured down the sides of the crevice until I thought I would be buried.

"Now you are alone, von Bek," said Klosterheim with relish. "I owe you much and would like to repay it slowly. But I'll be satisfied with taking your life and returning your failed soul to our Master."

"You deny that He is your Master," I reminded the warrior-priest. "And yet you know that He is. He will punish you, surely, Johannes Klosterheim. You cannot escape Him."

"Then why should Lord Arioch lend me twenty of his knights?" said Klosterheim with a sneer. "There is Civil War in Hell, Captain von Bek. You shall be a victim of that War, not I."

He cried out the name of his patron again. Again lightning cracked.

I did not wait, but turned my horse about and galloped along the crevice in Sedenko's wake, as rock tumbled down from above. I recalled something I had read in one of the grimoires and as I rode I leaned into my saddlebag to find the book. I came out onto a clear part of the trail. The foothills were less than half an hour's ride ahead. There we should have more of a chance of escaping Klosterheim's hellish force.

I looked back.

The knights in their fiery black armour were riding their black horses over the rubble. I glimpsed a purple plume. I sensed that my own horse was weakening, that before long he must turn a leg and throw me. I reined him in and shortened his stride. He was panting. I could feel his heart thumping against my leg. I found the grimoire, took my reins in my teeth and sought the page I remembered. Here, in cramped letters, I discovered what I needed: *Words of Power Against the Servants of Duke Arioch.* Had Lucifer anticipated the treachery of his Dukes? The words themselves were meaningless to me but I brought my horse about, knowing I possessed no other weapon against the knights.

I cried out: *"Rehoim Farach Nyadah!"* in as loud a voice as I could muster.

I saw the knights begin to slow their pace, only to be urged on by a yelling Klosterheim.

"Rehoim Farach Nyadah! Gushnyet Maradai Karag!"

The knights drew up suddenly. Klosterheim emerged from the press, still galloping. He was glaring at me, his blade in his hand, and I dropped the grimoire back into the saddlebag as I drew my own sword, just in time to meet a fierce and accurate blow which, had it landed, would have removed my arm.

I thrust, was parried and blocked Klosterheim's retaliation. I saw that the knights were beginning to stir. They seemed confused.

Klosterheim was snarling like a beast as he fought. His very hatred might have been enough to destroy me. He struck and struck again. I defended myself. Then I heard hoofbeats behind me and Sedenko was riding up to my aid. A pistol exploded. Klosterheim's horse shouted and went down. The knights were beginning to move forward. Klosterheim struggled to his feet, his sword still in his hand. He ran at me, mindless with fury.

"Best leave now, captain," called Sedenko.

I took his advice. Even as we fled down the trail I saw Klosterheim stumbling towards Arioch's soldiers and pushing one of them from his steed so that he collapsed in a heap of blazing black metal.

We reached relatively flat ground at about the same time the sun came out and made the snow glitter. We heard Klosterheim and his men behind us. The sun grew warmer and warmer, threatening to melt the snow, by the time we dared to look back and see that they were almost upon us. I tried to recall the exact words I had used from the grimoire and I shouted them. But our pursuers did not this time stop.

Even as they gained on us the riders in black armour spread out in a widening semicircle to surround us.

The sun was uncomfortably hot. The road was dusty and so disturbed that it impaired my vision. I could see Sedenko ahead of me but I could only hear our enemies.

I was drenched in sweat as I caught up the young Muscovite and cried that we had no choice but to fight, though it was almost certain we were doomed. I fished for the grimoire and found the words of power again.

We set our horses back to back, peering through the dust and trying to see the riders as they closed in. *"Rehoim Farach Nyadah!"* I shouted with desperate authority.

The dust began to settle. Our pursuers were upon us. I saw Klosterheim's purple plume. I saw dark shapes advancing.

A long blade darted at me and I blocked it. I struck back, expecting to connect with plate armour. Instead my sword point entered flesh and I heard a grunt of pain.

I saw the face of my attacker. It was swarthy, unshaven, cross-eyed.

It had become the face of a common brigand.

Chapter Eleven

THE SUN WAS improbably hot. Out of the dust came a press of mounted ruffians clad in all manner of crude finery. Klosterheim still directed them. I almost lost my guard in my astonishment, wondering how the knights of Arioch had turned into these far less impressive creatures. But there were yet a good many more of them than could be easily dealt with. I coughed as the dust found my throat and nostrils. Sedenko and I were surrounded by what seemed a veritable forest of steel, and our horses and ourselves were cut with a myriad of minor wounds. Yet we had killed five or six within almost as many minutes and this caused the rest to proceed more warily. Behind them I could hear Klosterheim's voice, high with temper and eager bloodlust, urging them on.

I had a strong sense that my grimoires would be of no use here and that we had passed out of the Middle Marches and into our own world. Overhead the sun was strong and I glimpsed small trees and dry grass which reminded me of my journeys through Spain.

The rogues were pressing us hard. I saw Klosterheim's face now. He was relishing our defeat. We were being forced slowly off the road towards a precipice with a drop of some fifteen feet— quite enough to break our bones and those of our horses.

Sedenko shouted something to me but I did not catch it. The next moment he had vanished and I was fighting on my own. I could not believe he had abandoned me in order to save himself and yet it was the only sensible conclusion.

The snapguzzlers closed in tighter and I was moments from death when I heard Klosterheim's strangled tones from behind me. Suddenly my enemies had fallen away.

"Stop!"

Sedenko had Klosterheim by the throat. The witch-seeker's face writhed with anger and frustration.

"Stop, you oafs!"

The Kazak's steel was against Klosterheim's adam's-apple and had already drawn a thin line of blood. "Oh, Sedenko," he swore, "you might have been spared. But not now. Not if I can come back from Hell to destroy you."

I was laughing. I am not sure that I knew my reasons for mirth. "What? Is Duke Arioch not here to save you?" said I. "Why are his men all vanished?"

I kept my sword out as I rode up to Sedenko. Klosterheim's eyes had that mad, inturned look I had seen on more than a few denizens of Hell.

"Kill one of us," I said, "and we kill your master. If he dies, as you well know, you are doomed, every one. Go back up the road until you are out of sight."

The survivors became shifty, but another touch of the Kazak sabre had Klosterheim raving at them to obey. He knew what death meant for him. It was worse than anything he had threatened for me. He would hold on to life while there was the faintest chance. Pride and honour must be discarded, but anything was better than giving up his black soul to Him who owned it.

"Obey them!" called Klosterheim.

The survivors began to drag themselves away. I saw mountains behind them, but they were not the high peaks of the Mittelmarch. These were grassy and low.

Limping, leading their mounts, swearing at us, nursing wounds, the bewildered rogues retreated. We watched. When they were a good distance from us we saw that their breath began to steam and they showed signs of cold, shivering and stamping their feet, looking about them in some surprise. They had gone into the Mittelmarch. Then they vanished.

"Duke Arioch's warriors could not follow us," I suggested. "And you had those men waiting if we succeeded in returning to this world. The damned can no more enter the Earth than the innocent can enter the Mittelmarch."

Klosterheim was shaking. "Are you going to kill me, von Bek?"

"I would be wise to kill you," I said. "And all my better judgement tells me to do so. But I am aware of what killing you means, and unless I am fighting you I cannot easily bring myself to kill you, Klosterheim."

He found my charity disgusting, it was plain, but he accepted it. He feared death more than anyone I had ever seen.

"Where are we now?" I asked him.

"Why should I tell you?"

"Because I could still summon enough anger, perhaps, to do what I know should really be done to cleanse the world of an obscenity."

"You are in Italy," he said. "On the road to Venice."

"So those mountains behind us would be the Venetian Alps?"

"What else?"

"We must go west," I said to Sedenko. "Towards Milan. Groot said that our goal lies in the west."

Klosterheim's pale features became tense as Sedenko wrenched the sword from his fingers and threw it away.

"Dismount," I said. "Your horses are fresher than ours."

We tied Klosterheim to a tree by the side of the road and transferred our saddles to his beast and another which had belonged to a dead ruffian. We kept our own horses and packed the remainder of our gear on them.

"We should not leave him alive," said Sedenko. "Shall I cut his throat, captain?"

I shook my head. "I have told you that I cannot easily consign any soul to the fate which inevitably awaits Klosterheim."

"You are a fool not to kill me," said the soldier-priest. "I am your greatest enemy. And I can conquer yet, von Bek. I have powerful allies in Hell."

"Not as powerful, surely, as mine," I said. Again I spoke in High German, which Sedenko could not understand.

Klosterheim replied in the same tongue. "Indeed they could now be more powerful. Lucifer has lost Himself. Most of His Dukes do not want Reconciliation with Heaven."

"There is no certainty that it will come about, Johannes Klosterheim. Lucifer's plans are mysterious. God's Will is equally mysterious. How can any of us judge what is actually taking place?"

"Lucifer plans to betray His own," said Klosterheim. "That is all I know. It is all that is necessary to know."

"You have simplified yourself," I said. "But perhaps that is how one must be if one follows your vocation."

"We are betrayed by God and Lucifer both," said Klosterheim. "You should understand that, von Bek. We are abandoned. We have nothing we can trust—even damnation! We can only play a game and hope to win."

"But we do not know the rules."

"We must invent them. Join me, von Bek. Let Lucifer find His own Grail!"

We got up onto our horses.

"I have given my word," I said. "It is all I have. I hardly understand this talk of games, of loyalties, of betrayals. I have promised to find the Cure for the World's Pain if I can. And that is what I hope to achieve. It is your world, Klosterheim, which is a world of moves and counter-moves. But such gamesmanship robs life of its savour and destroys the intellect. I'll have as little part of it as I can."

As we rode away Klosterheim shouted fiercely at me:

"Be warned, war hound! All that is fantastic leagues against you!"

It was a chilling threat. Even Sedenko, who did not understand the words, shuddered.

Chapter Twelve

W E RODE NOW across comparatively flat country which was broken by the low white buildings of farms and vineyards, yellow and light green under the heavy sun.

At the first good-sized town we came to I sought a doctor for our wounds. I had Satan's elixir, but preferred to keep it for more urgent purposes. By dint, however, of a little of Satan's silver we were able to get the doctor to tend to our horses as well. The man made a fuss but I argued that he had probably killed more men than horses in his career and that here was his opportunity to try to even up his score. He saw no humour in my jest, but he did his work skilfully enough.

We took the road to Milan, falling in with a mixed group of pilgrims, most of whom were returning to France and some to England. These men and women had visited the Holy City, bought all sorts of benefices, observed all the wonders, both ancient and modern, and seemed thoroughly satisfied that they had gained much from the hardships of travel. They had stories of maguses, of miracle-working priests, of visions and revelations. Many displayed the usual sorts of gimcrackery still sold as the bones of this or that saint, the feather of an angel, pieces of the True Cross and so on. At least three separate people I met had the real Holy Grail but considered themselves too sinful, still, either to perceive its actual beauty (these things were pewter got up to look like silver, mostly) or to be allowed to witness its magical properties. Naturally, I neither informed them of my Quest nor attempted to persuade them that the artefacts they had purchased were false.

When we got to that lovely city of Verona, we found the place in a bustle. Some Catholic knight, doubtless tired of the War in Germany and believing the cause without much worth anyway, had aroused a group of zealous young men to join him in a Crusade. The object of the Crusade, it seemed, was to attack Constantinople and free it from the Turks. This idea appealed greatly to Sedenko, whose people lived to take the city they called "Tsargrad" out of Islam's chains. When he saw the leader of the Crusaders, however, a near-senile baron evidently eaten with syphilis, and the tiny force he had gathered, Sedenko decided to wait "until all the Kazak hosts can ride at once to Saint Sophia and destroy the crescent which profanes her altar."

Near Brescia we witnessed the trial and burning of a self-professed Anti-Christ: a gigantic man with wild black hair and a black beard, wearing a red robe and a crown of roses. He called upon the people to give up their false pride, their presumption that they were the children of Christ, and admit that as sinners they were followers of his. The Final War must come, he preached, and those who were with him would be triumphant. The Bible, he said, lied. It was plain that he believed every word he spoke and that his concern for others was sincere. He died at the stake, pleading with them to save themselves by following him. During his burning a thunderstorm began some miles away. The priests chose to see this as a sign of God's pleasure. The people, however, plainly expected the beginning of Armageddon and knelt to pray. In the main they prayed to Christ, though I believe I heard several praying to the charred bones of the Anti-Christ. And in Crema I was taken to meet another mad creature, some hermaphroditic monster, who claimed that it was an angel, fallen to Earth and, having lost its wings, unable to return to Heaven. The angel lived on what it could beg from the people of Crema. They were kind to it. Some of them half-believed it. However, I had met an Angel, albeit a Dark One, and I knew what they were like. But when this angel of Crema begged me, as a holy traveller and a Goodly Knight, to confirm that he had truly plummeted from Heaven, I told all those who would listen that, to the best of my limited knowledge, this was what an angel looked like and that it was quite possible that this one had lost its wings. I suggested it be given all possible comfort during its stay on Earth.

Five miles past Crema we saw an entire village destroyed by brigands clad in the hoods of the Holy Inquisition of Spain. They went off with the contents of the church, with all goods of value, with women and with children whom they plainly intended to sell as slaves. And those who survived believed, many of them, that they had been visited by Christ's servants and that what had been given up by them had been given up in support of Christ's cause.

I met few good men on that road. I met many whose honour had turned to pride yet who were contemptuous of me for what they saw as my cynical pragmatism. Bit by bit I had told Sedenko most of my story, for I thought it fair to let him know whom he served. He had shrugged. After what he had witnessed of late, he said, he did not think it mattered a great deal. At least the Quest was holy, even if the men upon it were not.

Beyond Crema we passed again into the Mittelmarch. Save that the seasons were, of course, reversed, the landscape was not greatly different. We were in a kingdom, we discovered, which was the vestige of a Carthaginian Empire which had beaten Rome during Hannibal's famous campaign, conquered all of Europe and parts of Asia and had converted to the Jewish religion, so that the whole world had been ruled by Rabbinical Knights. It was a land so horrifying to Sedenko that he believed he was being punished for his sins and was already in Hell. We were treated hospitably and my engineering experience was called into play when the Chief Judge of this Carthaginian land pronounced a sentence of death upon a Titan. A gallows had to be built for him. In return for aid and some extra gold, I was able to design a suitable scaffold. The Titan was hanged and I received the gratitude of those people for ever.

Shortly after this we entered a great, complicated city maintained by an infinite series of balances and relationships whose acute harmony was such that I could not then tolerate it. It was a place of divine abstractions and the citizens were scarcely aware of us at all. Sedenko was not as badly affected as was I, but we were both glad to leave and find ourselves soon in a familiar France near Saint-Étienne where, for some weeks, we were imprisoned as suspected murderers and heretics, released only through the intercession of a priest who had discovered several eyewitnesses. The priest was paid with the Carthaginian gold and we went on our way gladly. Both our own world and the world of the Mittelmarch seemed to have increased in peril, but we moved steadily westward through both, crossing the sea, at last, to England, where we did not fare particularly well.

In England we were regarded by almost everyone with deep suspicion. The nation was full of discontent and any stranger was considered either a Puritan traitor or a Catholic agitator, so we were pleased to leave that country and set sail for Ireland, where there were various small wars afoot. We found ourselves drawn into two such campaigns, once on the side of the Irish and once on the side of the English; Sedenko fell in love and killed the woman's husband when discovered. Thus we left Ireland in some haste and from there set foot, once more, in the Mittelmarch.

We had been on the Quest for almost a year and seemed no closer to the blue-green Forest at the Edge of Heaven, while I had seen much of the world but learned little, I thought, that I had not known already. I longed for my Lady Sabrina, whom I had in no way forgotten. My love for her was as strong as it had ever been.

Sometimes I believed I had caught sight of Klosterheim or that he had revealed his hand in several attacks on our persons, but I could not be sure. It did seem that his warning had been accurate. Fewer and fewer of the lands we visited would welcome us. We began to feel like criminals. The hospitality of even common folk declined. The struggle between Heaven and Hell, the struggle which was taking place in Hell alone, the wars which shook the lands of the Mittelmarch, were all reflected in the strife which tore Europe. There was no end to it. Death and Plague continued to spread. We wondered, should we continue our way west and come at last to the New World, if we should discover any better there. Young Sedenko had taken on a haggard look and seemed ten years older than when we had met. I, apparently, had not much changed in my appearance. I had become familiar with many of the spells in the grimoires and had on occasions used them. Of late, their use had become more frequent. And of late, also, they seemed to have become less effective. I wondered if Hell's Dukes were massing and gaining strength over their Master. In which case, I thought, my Quest and all my efforts were absolutely without meaning.

It was raining in the Mittelmarch, one spring day, at noon. Sedenko and I were drenched and our horses were beginning to steam. We were crossing a wide plain of cracked earth. At intervals on the plain we saw tall pyres burning, sending black smoke low into the sky. The rain pattered on our cloaks and made puddles in the mud. We had encountered and defeated four or five misshapen men who I suspected were Klosterheim's, and I was following my compass which directed us to the way out of Mittelmarch. I was beginning to know a deeper despair than any I had known before, for I suspected my journey had no ending, that a terrible trick had been played upon me.

The pyres were closer together. No mourners stood near them, but upon each one was a heavily wrapped corpse. I wondered if the occupants of those pyres had died of disease. Then I saw a moving figure which was obscured by the smoke and I pointed it out to Sedenko, but the Muscovite could see nothing.

So long had it been since our last encounter with Klosterheim that we had begun to think him gone directly from our sphere, but now I was almost certain that the shadow in the smoke was the witch-seeker himself. I drew up, raising a cautionary hand to Sedenko, who followed my example. The rain and the smoke continued to make it all but impossible to see any distance.

Eventually we decided to ride on as the rain began to lift and the sun emerged, dark red and huge in the eastern sky.

The smoke gave way to mist rising from the broken earth and we left the pyres behind us, though the plain continued to stretch for miles in all directions.

Sedenko saw the village first. He gestured. Distant metal glittered in the heavy evening light. The houses seemed to be rounded, topped by little spires. Coming closer, I saw that they were in actuality leather tents mounted on wheels and decorated with all manner of symbols. The glitter came from their roof-spikes, of gold, bronze and silver inlay.

Sedenko drew in his breath. "Those yurts are a familiar sight!" His hand went to the hilt of his sabre.

"What?" said I. "Are they Tatars?"

"By all the signs, aye."

"Then perhaps we should skirt that camp?" I suggested.

"And lose the chance of killing some of them!" he said, as if I were insane.

"There are likely to be rather more of them, friend Sedenko, than there are of us. I do not think my Master would be pleased if I diverted my time to the cause of genocide . . ."

Sedenko scowled and muttered. He was like a hound restrained from hunting its natural game.

"Besides," I added, "they are showing a keen interest in ourselves."

A score of horsemen were riding towards us. I spurred my steed into a trot, but Sedenko did not follow me. "I cannot run from a Tatar," he wailed.

I went about and got hold of his reins, dragging him and his horse after me. But the Tatars were moving with astonishing speed and within minutes we were surrounded, staring at their mounts, which were not creatures of flesh at all, but were fashioned from brass. They had dead, staring eyes and creaked a little as they moved. The Tatars, however, were evidently flesh and blood.

"Those horses are mechanical," I said. "I have never heard of such a wonder!"

One of the Asiatics pulled at his long moustache and stared at me for several moments before speaking. "Yours is the tongue of Philander Groot."

"It is German," I said. "What do you know of Groot?"

"Our friend." The Tatar chief looked suspiciously at the glaring Sedenko. "Why is your companion so angry?"

"Because you chased us, I suppose," I told him. "He is also a friend of Philander Groot. We saw him less than a year hence, in the Valley of the Golden Cloud."

"It was said that he would go there." The Tatar made a sign to his men. Pressing on either side of us, they began to steer us towards their village. "It was Groot who made our horses for us, when the Plague came, which destroyed all mares and lost us our herds."

"Is that what burns yonder?" I asked him, pointing back at the pyres.

He shook his head. "Those are not ours." He would say no more on the subject.

My opinion of Groot was even higher now that I had seen an example of his skill. I found it difficult to understand why the dandy had chosen to live the life of a hermit when he was capable of so much.

The mechanical horses clattered as we moved. Sedenko said to me: "They are not true Tatars, of course, but are creatures of the Mittelmarch, and so I suppose are not necessarily my natural blood-enemies."

"I think it would be politic, if nothing else, Sedenko," said I, "if you held to that line of reasoning. At least for the next little while."

He looked suspiciously at me, but then nodded, as if to say he would bide his time for my sake.

The village was full of dogs, goats, women and children and it stank. The Tatars brought their mechanical mounts to a halt and the creatures stopped, still as statues, where they stood. Fires and cooking pots, half-cured skins, wizened elders: all at odds with the sophistication of Groot's inventions.

We were led into one of the larger yurts and here the stench was more intense than anything we had experienced outside. I was almost driven out by it, but Sedenko took it for granted. I gathered that his own people had borrowed many Tatar customs and that, to a stranger, Kazaks would not be easily distinguishable from their ancient enemies.

"We are the Guardians of the Genie," said the Tatar chief as he bade us sit upon piles of exotic but unclean cushions. "You must eat with us, if you are Groot's friends. We shall kill a dog and a goat."

"Please," said I, "your hospitality is too much. A simple bowl of rice is all we need to eat."

"You must eat meat." The chief was firm. "We have few guests and would hear your news."

I was amused, wondering what he would make of our real story. I had learned in such circumstances to be a little vague, since oftentimes we had not even journeyed from any neighbouring kingdom, and thus could be unfamiliar with geography, customs and politics which might be the only experience of our hosts. We had become used to saying that we were upon a pilgrimage, in quest of a holy thing; that we were vowed not to mention it, nor the name of the Deity we worshipped. This way I, at least, was able to identify this fictitious god of mine with the gods of those we met. Sedenko, being still somewhat more pious than myself, preferred to say nothing.

As best I could, I described some of my adventures in the Mittelmarch and some of our experiences in our journey across Europe. There was quite enough for the Tatar chief to hear, and by the time we were setting to about the dog and the goat (both of which were stewed in the same pot, with a few vegetables) I think we had paid more than amply for our food and it was time for me to ask the chief:

"And what is this Genie which you guard?"

"A powerful creature," he said soberly, "which resides in a jar. It has been imprisoned there for aeons. Philander Groot gave it to us. In return for the gift of horses, we guard the Genie."

"And what did you do before you became Guardians of the Genie?" I asked.

"We made war on other tribes. We conquered them and took away their horses, their livestock, their women."

"You no longer make war on them?"

The Tatar shook his head. "We cannot. Even by the time Philander Groot came to us we had destroyed everyone but ourselves."

"You wiped out every other tribe?"

"The Plague weakened them. We considered attacking Bakinax, but we are too few. Philander Groot said that with the power of the Genie we should not have to fear the Plague. And this seems to be so."

"And what is Bakinax?" asked Sedenko.

"The City of the Plague," said the Tatar chief. "It is where the Plague came from in the first place. It is created by a demon the citizens have with them. I have heard that they try to destroy the demon but that it feeds on the souls of men and beasts and that is why it sends the Plague to them. It sits in a sphere at the centre of Bakinax, eating its fill."

"Yet your souls are untouched."

"Quite. We have the Genie."

"Of course."

After we had eaten, the Tatar chief caused a brand to be lit and he took us to the outskirts of the camp where a little wooden scaffolding had been erected. From it, hanging by plaited horsehair, was a decorated jar of dark yellow glass. The Tatar held the brand close and I thought I saw something stirring within, but it might have been nothing more than reflected light.

"If the jar is broken," said the chief, "and the Genie is released, it will grow to immense proportions and wreak a horrible destruction throughout Mittelmarch. The demon knows this and the folk of Bakinax know this and that is why we are left untroubled."

He took a woven blanket and with some reverence draped it over the scaffolding, hiding the jar from our sight. "We cover it at night," he said. "Now I will show you to our guest yurt. Do you require women?"

I shook my head. I had known no other woman since I had taken the Lady Sabrina's ring. Sedenko considered the offer a little longer than did I. But then he also decided not to accept. As he murmured to me: "To sleep with a Tatar woman would be tantamount to heresy amongst the Kazak people."

The yurt in which we were to sleep was relatively clean and had sweet straw upon the floor. We stretched out on mats and were soon asleep, although not before Sedenko had grumbled that he had lost considerable pride by missing the opportunity to kill a Tatar or two. "At very least I should have stolen something from them."

When I awoke at dawn Sedenko had already been out, to relieve himself, he said. "It's stopped raining, captain. One of the children said that it is only about a day's ride to Bakinax, due west. It lies directly on our way. What do you think? We're low on provisions."

"Are you anxious to visit a place known as the City of the Plague?"

"I am anxious to eat something other than dog or goat," he said feelingly.

I laughed at this. "Very well. We shall take the risk."

I arose and washed myself in the bowl of water provided us, breakfasted off the rice brought by a shy Tatar maiden and stepped out of the yurt. The camp was only just beginning to wake. I strode through it to the yurt of the chieftain. He greeted me civilly.

"Should you come upon our friend Philander Groot," he said, "tell him that we long to see him again, to do him honour for the honour he does us."

"It is unlikely," said I, "but I will remember your message."

We departed on good terms. Sedenko seemed overeager to reach Bakinax and I suggested, after about half an hour, that he slow his pace. "Do the fleshpots become so attractive to you, my friend?"

"I would feel more comfortable with a city wall between myself and the Tatars," he admitted.

"They plainly mean us no harm."

"They might wish us harm now," he said. He looked back in the direction of the camp. It was no longer visible. Then he reached behind him into a saddlebag and withdrew something which he displayed in his gloved hand.

It was the jar containing the Tatars' Genie.

"You are a fool, Sedenko," I said grimly. "That was a treacherous action to perform upon those who treated us so kindly. You must return it."

"Return it!" He was amazed. "It is a question of honour, captain. No Kazak could leave a Tatar village without something they value!"

"Our friend Philander Groot gave that to them, and they gave us their hospitality in the name of Groot. You must take it back!" I drew rein and reached out for the jar.

Sedenko cursed me and pulled on his horse's head to move out of range. "It is mine!"

I sprang from my horse and ran towards him. "Take it back or let me!"

"No!"

I jumped for the jar. His horse reared. He tried to control it and the jar slipped from his hand. I flew forward in an effort to save the thing, but it had already fallen to the hard earth. Sedenko was yelling something at me in his own barbaric tongue. I stopped to pick the jar up, noticing that the stopper had come loose, and then Sedenko had struck me from behind with the flat of his sword and I momentarily lost my senses, waking to see him clasping the jar to his chest as he ran back for his horse.

"Sedenko! You have gone mad!"

He turned, glaring at me. "They were Tatars!" he cried, as if reasoning with a fool. "They were Tatars, captain!"

"Take the jar back to them!" I clambered to my feet.

He stood his ground defiantly. Then he shouted wildly, as I came up: "They can have their damned jar, but they shall not have their Genie!" He dragged forth the stopper of the jar.

I stopped in horror, expecting the creature to emerge.

Sedenko began to laugh. He tossed the jar at me. "It's empty! It was all a deception. Groot tricked them!"

This seemed to please him. "Let them have it, if you wish, captain." He laughed harder. "What a splendid joke. I knew Philander Groot was a fellow after my own heart."

Now, as I held the jar, I saw tiny, pale hands clutching at the rim. I looked down into it. There was a small, helpless, fading thing. As the air reached it, it was evidently dying. It was manlike in form, but naked and thin. A tiny, mewling noise escaped its wizened lips and I thought I detected a word or two. Then the miniature hands slipped from the rim and the creature fell to the bottom of the jar where it began to shiver.

There was nothing for it but to replace the stopper. I looked at Sedenko in disgust.

"Empty!" He guffawed. "Empty, captain. Oh, let me take it back to them. I threatened to ruin Groot's joke."

I forced the stopper down into the jar and held the thing out to Sedenko. "Empty," said I. "Take it back then, Kazak."

He dropped the jar into his saddlebag, mounted his horse and rode away at that breakneck pace he and his kind preferred.

I waited for some forty minutes, then I continued on westward, towards Bakinax, not much caring at that moment if Sedenko survived or not. I had consulted my maps. Bakinax lay not much more than a week's ride from the Forest at the Edge of Heaven.

My foreboding grew, however, as I came closer to the city.

Sedenko, grinning all over his face, soon caught me up.

"They had not noticed its disappearance," he said. "Is not Philander Groot a wily fellow, captain?"

"Oh, indeed," said I. It seemed to me that Groot had had his own reasons for deceiving the Tatars. By means of that Genie, alive or dead, they survived and the people of Bakinax dared not attack them. Groot had given the Tatars life and a reason, of sorts, for living. My admiration for the dandy, as well as my curiosity about him, continued to increase.

The vast plain was behind us at long last when we came to a land of dry grass and hillocks and thousands of tiny streams. It had begun to rain again.

I reflected that the Mittelmarch appeared to have become bleaker in the year of our journey. It was as if less could grow here, as if the soul of the Realm were being sucked from it. I told myself that all I witnessed was a difference of geography, but I was not in my bones content with that at all.

In the evening we saw a city ahead of us and knew that it must be Bakinax.

We rode through the streets in the moonlight. The place

seemed very still. We stopped a man who, with a burning torch in each hand, went drunkenly homeward. He spoke a language we could not understand, but by means of signs we got directions from him and found for ourselves a lodging for the night: a small, ill-smelling inn.

In the morning, as we breakfasted from strange cheeses and mysterious meats, we were interrupted by the entrance of five or six men in identical surcoats, bearing halberds, with morion helmets decorated by feathers, their hands and feet both mailed. They made it plain that we were to go with them.

Sedenko was for fighting, but I saw no point. Our horses had been stabled while we slept and we had no knowledge of their exact whereabouts. Moreover, this whole country was alien to us. I had, as had become my habit, all Lucifer's gifts about my person and my sword was at my side, so that I did not feel entirely vulnerable as I rose, wiped my lips and bowed to the soldiers as an indication that we were ready to accompany them.

The streets of Bakinax, seen in daylight, were narrow and none too clean. Ragged children with thin, hungry faces stopped to look at us as we passed and old people, in rags for the most part, gaped. It was not an unusually despondent place, this city, compared to many I had seen in Europe, but neither did it seem a cheerful one. There was an atmosphere of gloom hanging over it and I thought it well-named the City of the Plague.

We were escorted through the main square where, upon a great wooden dais, stood a huge globe of dull, unpleasant metal, guarded by soldiers in the same uniform as those who now surrounded us. The square was otherwise empty of citizens.

"That must be the house of the devil the Tatar mentioned," whispered Sedenko to me. "Do you really think it lives on the souls of the people hereabouts, captain?"

"I do not know," said I, "but I would cheerfully feed it yours, Sedenko." I was not yet prepared to forgive him for his foolishness concerning the stolen jar. He, for his part, was absolutely unrepentant. He took my remark, as he had taken others, as a joke, craning his head to look again at the sphere as we were marched up stone steps and through the portal of what was evidently some important public building.

We were taken into a room lined on both sides with pews. Not one of the pews, however, was occupied. At the far end of the room was a lectern and behind the lectern, where a priest might stand, was a tall, thin man with a bright red wig, dressed in a gown of black and gold.

Said he in the Latin language: "Speak you Latin, men?"

"I speak a little," I told him. "Why have we been brought here so roughly, Your Honour? We are honest travellers."

"Not so honest. You seek to avoid the tolls. You have ridden through our sacred Burning Grounds and desecrated them. You have entered Bakinax by the East Gate and placed no gold in the plate. And those are only your main crimes. Do not offer me your hypocrisy, sir, as well as your offences! I am the Great Magistrate of Bakinax and it was I who ordered you arrested. Will you speak?"

"We cannot know your laws," I said, "for we are strangers here. If we had been aware that your Burning Grounds were sacred we should have ridden clear of them, I assure you. As for the gold which must be placed in the plate, we will willingly pay it now. None challenged us as we entered."

"Too late to pay in gold," said the Great Magistrate. He cleared his nose and glared at us. "You cannot claim that nobody told you of Bakinax as you journeyed here, for it is a famous place, this City of the Plague. Did no-one mention our demon?"

"A demon was mentioned, aye." I shrugged. "But nothing was said of tolls, Your Honour."

"Why come here?"

"For fresh supplies."

"To the City of the Plague?" He sneered. "To this awful City of the Demon? No! You came to cause us distress!"

"But, sir, how can we two cause a whole city distress?" I asked. The man was mad. I believed, reluctantly, that probably all Bakinax was mad. I regretted my decision to come here and felt in agreement with the Great Magistrate when he suggested that only a fool would seek out Bakinax.

"By being what you are. By seeing what you see!" replied the Magistrate. "We shall not be mocked, travellers! We shall not be mocked."

"We do not mock," I told him. "We promise that we shall not ever mention Bakinax again. Only, good sir, let us continue on our way, for we have a holy mission to perform."

"Aye, indeed you have," said the old man with some relish. "You must pay for your stupidity and your contempt for us with your souls. You will be given to our demon. Two of us shall thus be saved for a little longer and you will receive fitting punishment for your crimes. Your souls will go to Hell."

At this I laughed. Sedenko had no idea what had passed between us. I told him roughly what had been said.

He was not as amused as I. Perhaps he did not really believe that his soul was already destined for Lucifer's Realm.

Chapter Thirteen

"Y OU, SIR," SAID the Great Magistrate, addressing me, "shall be the first to fight our demon. None has ever beaten him. Should you, however, manage to kill him, the door of the sphere shall be released and you will be free. If you have not emerged in an hour, your friend will be sent to join you."

"I am to be allowed to carry my sword?" said I.

"All you possess you may take with you," he told me.

"Then I am ready," I said.

The Great Magistrate spoke to his soldiers in their own tongue. One stood guard over Sedenko, while the rest escorted me from the Court and back into the square where the rain had again begun to fall.

We mounted steps onto the platform. The sphere had set in it a small round door which one of the guards approached. He was nervous. He put his palm against the handle and hesitated.

I saw a figure enter the square.

If anything, Klosterheim was even more gaunt than when last I saw him. He was grinning at me now. He was almost trembling with pleasurable anticipation. His black garments were stained and neglected; the purple feathers in his hat were matted and stringy and he had developed a peculiar, almost undetectable stoop. His eyes had that same inturned insanity. He removed his hat in a mock salute as the door groaned open and the soldiers pushed me forward.

"Was this your doing, Klosterheim?" I asked.

The witch-seeker shrugged. "I am a friend," he said, "to Bakinax."

"Is this demon your gift to the city?"

He ignored me, signing casually to the guards.

With a wave to him I bent and entered the foul-smelling darkness, salty and damp, of the sphere. Crouching there, I blinked, peered, but saw nothing. The round door clanked shut behind me. Gradually I began to see. The light came from a peculiar substance washing the floor of the sphere. It was white and it was viscous and it was obviously, too, the source of the smell. Something emerged from it at the farthest point from me. The fluid at the bottom of the sphere made sucking sounds. There was no colour here. All seemed grey, black and white. The thing which moved through the liquid was larger than I. It had scales. It had a great, sad, misshapen head which had fallen to one side and almost rested on its left shoulder. Its long teeth were broken and its lips were ragged, as if they had been chewed to destruction. From one large nostril came a little vapour. The monster squeaked at me, almost a question.

"Art thou the Demon of the Sphere?" I asked him.

The head lifted a fraction. Then, after some while, a voice came from the back of its throat.

"I am."

"Thou must know," said I, "that my soul is not for eating. It already belongs to our Master, Lucifer."

"Lucifer." The word was distorted. "Lucifer?"

"He owns it. I can offer you no sustenance, therefore, Sir Demon. I can only offer you death."

"Death?" It licked its torn lips with a ruined tongue. A smile seemed to appear on his features. "Lucifer? I wish to be free. I want to eat nothing more. Why do they feed me so much? All they have to do is release me from the pact and I will fly straight back to Hell."

"You do not want to be here?"

"I have never wanted to be here. I was tricked. Through my own greed I was tricked. I know your soul is not for me, mortal. I could smell it if it were mine. I cannot smell your soul."

"Yet you will still kill me, eh?"

The demon sat down in the fluid. He splashed at it with his taloned fingers. "Children and youths. This stuff is all that remains. There is not one soul in Bakinax—not one adult soul, that is—

which is not already claimed. I will not kill you, mortal, unless you grow bored and want to fight. You are one of the few who has wished to talk. Most of them scream. The children, the youths and the maidens, I eat. It silences them. It entertains me. It feeds me for a little while. But I have more than enough. More than enough."

"But you will not release me from your lair?"

"How can I? I am trapped here myself. A pact. It seemed worthwhile all that time ago."

"Who was the magus who trapped you?"

"He was called Philander Groot. A cunning man. I roamed free before, across this whole kingdom. Now I am limited to Bakinax and this cage. Oh, I am so tired of the flavourless souls of the young." He took some of the fluid up on his finger and sucked. He sighed.

"But they fear you," I said. "It is why they keep you here. They believe you will escape if they do not placate you."

The demon said: "Is that not always the way with Men? What must I represent to them, I wonder?"

I leaned, as best I could, against the wall of the sphere. I was growing used to the smell. "Well, they will not release you and they will not release me unless I kill you. You have food. I have not. I must starve to death, it seems, or destroy you."

The demon looked up at me. "I have no desire to kill you, mortal. It would give offence to our Master, would it not? Your time is not yet arrived."

"I believe that," I said. "For I am upon a mission directly instructed by Lucifer."

"Then we have a dilemma," said the demon.

I thought for a moment. "I could attempt to exorcise you," I told him. "That would at least release you from the sphere. Where would you go?"

"Directly back to Hell."

"Where you would wish to be."

"I never want to leave Hell again," said the demon feelingly.

"I am no expert at exorcism."

167

"They have attempted to exorcise me, but those already pledged to Hell, whether they know it or not, cannot bid me leave."

"Therefore I cannot exorcise you either."

"It would seem so."

"We have reached impasse again," I said.

The demon lowered his head and sighed a deeper sigh than the first. "Aye."

"What if I killed you?" I said. "Where would your own soul go?"

"Oblivion. I would rather not die, Sir Knight."

"Yet I was told the door will open only after I have slain you."

"Since nobody has slain me, how are they to know that?"

"Perhaps Philander Groot told them."

I brooded on the problem for a while. "The door must be opened eventually, to admit my companion, who is to be your next victim. Why cannot we escape when his turn comes?"

"It might be possible for you to escape," said the demon. "But I am trapped by more than metal. There is the pact, you see, with the magus. Were I to break it, I would be destroyed instantly."

"Therefore only Philander Groot can release you."

"That is so."

"And Philander Groot has become a hermit, dwelling in a far kingdom."

"I have heard as much."

"Inevitably I am led to the logic," I said, "that my only means of escape is by killing you. And I know that my chances of doing so are virtually nothing."

"I am very strong," said the demon, by way of confirmation, "and also extremely fierce."

"I think that my only hope," I told him, "is to wait until the hour is up and, when my friend is sent to join us, attempt to leave by the door."

"It would seem so," agreed the demon. "But they would kill you anyway, would they not?"

"That is a strong likelihood."

The demon brooded for a moment. "I am trying to think of another solution, one which would benefit us both."

"Not to mention the remaining children and virgins of Baki-nax," I said.

"Of course," said the demon. He became nostalgic. "Are there any Tatars left, do you know?"

"A few. They are protected against you by a Genie they have."

"The one in the jar?"

"That's the one."

"Aha." He frowned. "I was fond of Tatars."

It was beginning to seem to me that the supernatural creatures of this land were somewhat ineffectual beings. I wondered if not only the Mittelmarch but the whole of Hell was in decline. Or perhaps the powers had been marshalled to cope with the Civil War which Klosterheim had said was raging between Lucifer and His Dukes.

I thought I detected a movement overhead. I stretched out my hand to the demon. He placed his own scaly fingers in mine. "Would you oblige me," I asked him, "by allowing me to stand upon your shoulders so that when the door is opened I will be able to escape?"

"By all means," said the demon, "if you will agree one thing: should you escape and find Philander Groot again, tell him that I guarantee that if he will break the bond I will go home immediately and never venture into the regions of the Earth again."

"The likelihood," I said honestly, "of my seeing Groot is slender. However, I give my word that if I should meet him again, or be in a position to get a message to him, I will tell him what you have told me."

"Then I wish you Lucifer's luck," said the demon, bending so that I might climb upon his back. "And I hope that you kill that Great Magistrate who has caused me so much boredom."

The door was opening. I heard guards laughing. I heard Sedenko cursing.

His face appeared above me. I put my finger to my lips. His eyes widened in amazement. I whispered: "Draw your sword now. We are going to try to fight our way clear . . ."

"But—" began Sedenko.

"Do not question me," I said.

The Kazak shrugged and called back. "Wait, fellows, while I free my blade!"

The sabre was in his hand. I drew my own sword as the demon began to lift me higher towards the door. I took hold of the sill and jumped through, past Sedenko, lunging at the nearest guard and taking him in the heart. Two more fell to me before they realised what had happened. The remaining three set upon me and Sedenko and would have been finished easily, had I not been distracted by Sedenko's agitated gesturing. I turned to glance in the direction he pointed.

Klosterheim was there, mounted on a heavy black charger. At his back were twenty mounted suits of armour, glowing with eery black fire. Here were the demons-at-arms of Arioch, Duke of Hell.

For a moment I was tempted to scramble back into the sphere.

Klosterheim was laughing at me as he waited for the fight to end.

I killed one more guard and Sedenko sliced apart the other two.

Behind us, out of the open sphere, came the stench of rotting souls. Before us was the face of a triumphant Klosterheim and his impassive minions.

"We are certainly doomed," murmured Sedenko.

I had by now memorised the spell which held back these riders. I dismissed Sedenko's fears. I raised my hand:

"*Rehoim Farach Nyadah!*"

Klosterheim continued to laugh. Then he stopped and raised his own hand: "*Niever Oahr Shuk Arnjoija!*" His expression was challenging. "I have neutralised your spell, von Bek. Do you think I have wasted the past year in wondering how you stopped my men the last time?"

"So you have us," I said.

"I have you. I knew your destination. I knew you must come through this land, for you are seeking the Holy Grail in the Forest at the Edge of Heaven. You will never see that forest now, von Bek."

"How goes the War in Hell?" I said.

Klosterheim sat back in his saddle. "Well enough," he told me. "Lucifer is weakening. He retires. He will not fight. Our allies increase. You were a fool not to join me when I offered you the chance."

"I accepted a task," I said. "I knew that I had little hope of achieving it. But a bargain is a bargain. And Lucifer holds my soul, not you, Klosterheim."

A shadow fell suddenly across the whole town. I looked up and saw the strangest sight I had yet met in Hell or the Mittelmarch. A huge black cat was looking down on us. If he had moved one paw or flicked his tail, he could have destroyed the entire city. I thought at first that this was another of Klosterheim's allies, but it became plain that the witch-seeker was as surprised as were we.

"What have you conjured now, von Bek?" he said. He was disconcerted. Then he cursed at something he had seen behind us.

Sedenko turned first, yelling in astonishment. There was a great twittering: the kind of sound starlings make in the evening. I looked back.

A chariot, of bronze and silver, was drifting down through the sky towards us, drawn by thousands of small golden birds.

"Attack them!" cried Klosterheim. He drove his horse towards the platform, the black riders a mass of glowing metal in his wake.

As the chariot settled onto the platform, Klosterheim leapt his horse onto it and came riding directly at me. I parried his first blow. The armoured minions of Duke Arioch were dismounting, lumbering up the steps towards us. We were driven back rapidly.

I heard a voice from the chariot. It was a gentle, chiding, half-mocking voice. It said:

"Demon of the Sphere, I release thee from thy bondage on the condition thou hast made and on the further condition that you fight these enemies of your Master's, for they conspire against Lucifer."

In spite of the danger I turned my head. The little man in the chariot tugged at his beard and bowed to me. I caught the odour of Hungary Water. I saw lace and velvet. It was Philander Groot himself. "Will you join me, gentlemen?" he asked politely. "I think that Bakinax is about to become a battlefield and it will be no sight for sensitive men."

Sedenko needed no further invitation. He was running hell-bent-for-leather towards the chariot. I followed him.

From out of the sphere, blinking and snarling, came the demon. He screamed his exultation. His scales clashed and began to glow. He laughed in hideous joy. And I saw a snarling Kloster-heim still riding at us, still determined to kill me, even as we climbed into Groot's chariot.

Now the Demon of the Sphere and the knights of Duke Arioch were joined in battle. It seemed to me an unequal match, but the demon was accounting well for himself.

Klosterheim's horse reared beneath us as we rose into the air, pulled by the little birds. His teeth were bared. He cried out almost as a child might cry out when it has been deprived of some favour-ite food.

The last I saw of the witch-seeker, he had leapt his horse from the platform and was riding away from the terrifying carnage tak-ing place on the platform. I saw two armoured knights flung so far that they crashed into the Court. Bricks and stone collapsed. A horrible fire began to flicker wherever Duke Arioch's knights fell.

Then, beneath the tranquil stare of that great black cat, we passed beyond Bakinax and over the red plain.

"I planned none of this," said Philander Groot, as if he apologised to us. "But I knew that the state of balance which I had achieved could not last. I am glad to see that you are well, gentlemen."

I was speechless. The dandy raised an eyebrow. "You are doubt-less wondering why I am here. Well, I spent some time contemplating your story, Captain von Bek, and contemplating my old decision to remove myself from the affairs of Men, Gods and Demons. Then I considered the nature of your Quest and, you must forgive me this, I decided that I would like a part in it. It seemed momentous."

"I had no idea that you were so great a magus," I told him.

"You are very kind. I have had the sense, of late, that important events are taking place everywhere. Vain creature that I am, and growing a little bored, I must admit, with the Valley of the Golden Cloud and its decent moderation, I thought I might once again see if I could make use of my old powers, though I regard them, as I am sure do you, as childish and vulgar."

"I regard them as Heaven-sent," I told him.

He was amused. "Well, they are not that, Captain von Bek. They are not that."

The dandy was silent for a little while as we continued on our journey through the upper air. Then he spoke more seriously than was his wont. "At present," he said, "no soldier of the Dukes of Hell can pass into the ordinary Realm of Earth. But should Lucifer be defeated, there will be a wild carelessness come upon Creation and it will be the end of the world, indeed. There will be no single Anti-Christ, though Klosterheim could be said to represent them all. There will be open warfare, in every region, between Heaven and Hell. It will be Armageddon, gentlemen, as has been predicted. Mankind will perish. And I believe, no matter what the Christian Bible predicts, that the outcome will be uncertain."

"But Lucifer does not wish to make war on God," I said.

"The decision could be Lucifer's no longer. Nor God's. Perhaps both have lost their authority."

"And the Grail?" said I. "What part can the Grail play in all this?"

"Perhaps none at all," said Groot. "Perhaps it is no more than a diversion."

Chapter Fourteen

P HILANDER GROOT'S CHARIOT came to earth eventually on a quiet hillside overlooking a valley which reminded me very much of my own lost Bek.

In the valley a village was burning and I could see black smoke rising from farmsteads and mills. Dark figures with brands marched across the landscape, setting fire to anything which would ignite. It was familiar enough to me. I had ordered such destruction many times myself.

"Are we still in the Mittelmarch?" I asked the dandy. "Or have we returned to our own Realm?"

"It is the Mittelmarch," he said, "but it could as easily be the ordinary Earth, you know. There is very little now which is not destroyed or threatened."

"And all this," I said, "because Lucifer sent me upon a Quest for the Grail!"

"Not quite." Groot motioned with his hand and the chariot ascended again into the air. He said as an aside: "That will be the last we shall see of that, I fear. Mostly such things are leased by the Powers of Darkness, even if not used in their work. Did you know that, Captain von Bek?"

"I did not."

"Now that I am no longer of the Grey Lords, as those of us who are neutral are named by Hell, I do not expect to conjure things so easily." He paused, smoothing back his little moustache. "You are an unusual man, captain, but your Quest has not brought all this about. Lucifer's decision to attempt peace with His Creator is what has exacerbated a crisis which has been in the making since at least the Birth of Christ. The lines have become confused, you see. The pagan faiths are all but destroyed. Buddha, Christ and Mahomet have seen to that. To many the death of paganism heralded the coming decay of the world (and I will not elaborate, for it is a sophisticated theme, though it does not sound it). We have given up responsibility, either to God or to Lucifer. I am not sure that God demands that of us, nor am I sure that He wishes it. Nothing is certain in the universe, captain."

"Nothing will be gained if I discover the Cure for the World's Pain?"

"I do not know. Perhaps the Grail is no more than a bartering tool in a game so mysterious that not even the two main partici- . pants understand its rules. But there again, I could be utterly wrong. Know this, however: Klosterheim is now more powerful than you begin to realise. Do not think, because his pride made him bring the same twenty knights who lost you before, that he can command only twenty. He is now one of the main generals of rebellious Hell. Your Quest, you will recall, is the ostensible cause of that rebellion. They will stop you if they can, Captain von Bek. Or they will take the Grail from you if you find it."

"But with you to help, magus," said Sedenko, "we stand a better chance."

Groot smiled at him. "Do not underestimate Klosterheim, gentlemen. And do not overestimate me. What little I know has been worked for. It has been wrested away from others, the power itself. They can claim much back, whenever they wish. My conjuring tricks with genies and demons are small things. They are pathetic in the eyes of Hell. Now I have not much left. But I will travel with you, if I may, for my curiosity is great and I would know what befalls you. We are a day or two farther on in the journey towards the Forest at the Edge of Heaven, and I fancy we shall see little of Klosterheim for a while. He must have lost some valuable knights in that brawl at Bakinax. But when he comes again into our ken he will come with far more power than he has ever possessed in the past."

"Everything that is fantastic leagues against me," I said, repeating Klosterheim's warning.

"Aye. Everything that is fantastic is threatened. Some believe all these marvels you have witnessed to be productions of the World's

Pain. Without that Pain, some say, they would not be necessary. They would not exist."

"You suggest that mankind's needs create them?"

"Man is a rationalising beast, if not a rational one," said Philander Groot. "Come, there are horses waiting for us in yonder spinney."

We followed him down the hill a little way, and sure enough the horses were there. As we mounted, Groot chatted urbanely, telling anecdotes of people he had known and places he had visited, for all the world as if we went on a merry holiday. We rode along the crown of the hills, avoiding the soldiers in the valley below, and continued through the night until we were well past it. Only then did we think of resting. We came to a crossroads in the moonlight. Philander Groot considered the signs. "There," he said at last. He pointed to the post which said: *To Wolfshaben, 3 miles.*

"Do you know Wolfshaben, captain? Herr Sedenko?"

We both told him that we did not.

"An excellent town. If you take pleasure in women you will want to visit the harlotry they have there. I will entertain myself at the harlotry, where the beds are anyway more comfortable."

"I'll gladly join you," said Sedenko with some eagerness.

"If I can have a good bed and no harlot," said I, "I'll cheerfully keep you company."

My friends were entertained royally at Wolfshaben's wonderful harlotry (which is quite famous, I gather, amongst the travellers in the Mittelmarch) and I slept like a dead man until morning.

The spring morning was fresh as we rode away from Wolfshaben, and there was dew on the light-green grass and a touch of rain upon the leaves of the trees so that everything smelled sweet.

Philander Groot, riding ahead of myself and Sedenko, sniffed at the air, for all the world like one of Versailles's courtiers on a frolic, and cried: "A beautiful day, gentlemen. Is it not wonderful to be living?"

The road descended to another valley, as green as the last, and this was deserted of soldiery, apparently completely untouched by War of any kind. But as we took a turn we came upon a great procession of men, women and children, on horseback, in carts, with bundles on their backs and a look of terror about their eyes. They were from all walks of life. Philander Groot hailed them merrily, as if unaware of what they signified. "What's this? Pilgrims seeking Rome?"

A man in half-armour, which had been hastily strapped about his person, rode up urgently. "We are fleeing an army, sir. You would be warned not to go any farther in this direction."

"I'm grateful for the warning, sir. Whose army is it?"

"We do not know," said a wretched woman with a cut across her brow. "They came upon us suddenly. They killed everything. They stole everything. They did not speak a word."

"Nothing justified. No threats. No chivalry," said the man in half-armour.

"I think, sir," said Groot, glancing at us for confirmation, which we readily gave, "that we will travel with you for a while."

"You would be wise, sir."

And so it was in the company of more than a thousand people that we took another road than the one we had originally hoped to follow, though we did not go back the way we had come. We were with them for almost two days. For the most part they were educated men and women: priests and nuns, astronomers, mathematicians, surgeons, lords and ladies, scholars, actors. And not one of them could understand why they had been attacked or who had attacked them, though there were many theories, some of them exceedingly far-fetched. We could only conclude that these were mortal soldiers serving the Dukes of Hell, but even that was by no means certain, particularly since a few of the clerics had come to the familiar conclusion that their community had committed some dreadful sin against God and that God had sent the soldiers to punish them.

We departed from this concourse eventually and found upon our maps a fresh road to take us westward. But armies were galloping everywhere. We hid frequently, being too faint-hearted to offer battle to anyone who might be a minion of a Duke of Hell.

Yet now all the world seemed to be afire. Whole forests burst into flame; whole towns burnt as fiercely as ever Magdeburg had burnt.

"Ah," said Philander Groot, "it could be the End, after all, my friends."

"And good riddance to it," I said. "It is a poor world, a bad world, a decadent world. It expects love without sacrifice. It expects immediate gratification of its desires, as a child might, as a beast might. And if it does not receive gratification it becomes pettish and destroys in a tantrum. What's the use of seeking a Cure for its Pain, Philander Groot? What's the use of attempting, by any means, to divert it from its well-earned doom?"

"Because we are alive, I suppose, Captain von Bek. Because we have no choice but to hope to make it better, through our own designs." Philander Groot seemed amused by me.

"The world is the world," said Sedenko. "We cannot change it. That is for God to do."

"Perhaps He thinks it is for us to do," said Groot quietly. But he did not press this point. "Oh, look ahead! Look ahead! Is that not beautiful, gentlemen?"

It was a tall structure which reached to the sky, all curves and angles of crystal. A great building of glass and quartz such as I had never seen before.

"It's gigantic," said Sedenko. "Look inside. There are trees growing there. It is like a jungle."

Philander Groot put fingers to lips and drew his brows together. Then his face cleared. "Why, it is the famous aviary of Count Otto of Gerantz-Holffein. Shall we go through it, gentlemen? You will see that the road passes directly into the aviary and out the other side. I did not realise it was so close. I have heard of it, but never seen it before. Count Otto is dead now. His obsession was with exotic birds. He had the aviary built by a friend of mine many, many years ago. That is why it is full of trees, you see. Trees for the birds. And it still stands! It was a miracle of architecture. Or are you nervous? Should we skirt the place?"

"We'll go through," said Sedenko.

"I should like to see it," I agreed. I felt that I would be glad of any relaxation, however temporary.

"Count Otto was so proud of his aviary and his collection of birds that he insisted on all travellers visiting it," said Philander Groot, "which is why he had the road going through it." He seemed genuinely delighted.

As we came closer I saw that the entrance to the vast aviary was overgrown and neglected; it seemed to have been abandoned for years. I listened for birdsong. I heard a noise, a kind of chattering and murmuring, like the inner musings of a disconsolate giant.

"Count Otto had at least one example of every known bird," said Philander Groot as he led the way into the miniature jungle. Branches tangled over our heads, but the road was fairly clear. "When he died his nephew would have nothing to do with the aviary. That is why it is now as it is."

There was a strong odour of mould and ancient undergrowth and far ahead of us, through soft, diffused, greenish sunlight, I saw the glitter, I thought, of bright feathers.

"It's a large enough bird," said Sedenko. He glanced about him. "A perfect place for Klosterheim to set an ambush . . ."

"He's behind us," I reminded the Muscovite.

"He has hellish aid," said Philander Groot. "He is now one of Arioch's chief generals. He is not constrained by the considerations of mortals; not at present. But no one place is any more dangerous to us than another, given the powers Klosterheim commands."

"Is that why you seem so insouciant, Philander Groot?" I asked the dandy-magus.

He turned to me with a smile and was about to speak when it came crashing out of the foliage.

It was at least four times the size of a horse and limping on three of its legs. The other, the right foreleg, was lifted above the ground and had plainly been wounded a long while. Its scales were what I had seen and mistaken for feathers: primarily glowing reds and yellows. Its gaping jaws were full of silvery teeth, and its heavy tail thrashed behind it like the tail of an angry cat.

It came at us with incredible speed. Groot went one way, Sedenko the other, and I had drawn my sword and was left facing the lame dragon.

I had no experience of dragon fighting. Until now I had not believed that such creatures existed. This one did not breathe fire, but its breath stank mightily. And it meant us harm. There was no doubt of that.

My horse was shrieking with terror and trying to escape, but I knew that I could not flee and live. I struck at the beast's snout with the point of my sword and drew blood. It roared and snapped, but it slowed its progress. I struck again. It half-reared on its hind legs, unable to strike with its single front leg without toppling forward. I rode past it, leaping over the thrashing tail and forcing it to turn, its passage hampered by the heavy tree trunks. Silver teeth snapped at my sleeve and caught some flesh. I cried out, but I was not seriously hurt. I glimpsed Philander Groot and Sedenko riding up behind the dragon, striking at it with their own swords.

I was being forced farther and farther back into the undergrowth until I came to a great wall of glass and was trapped. Again the dragon's head darted down and the teeth narrowly missed me, fastening on the neck of my horse which screamed. I fell backwards out of the saddle as the horse was lifted clear of the ground. I landed heavily, amongst branches, and began to get to my feet at once.

The horse was dead, hanging twitching in the dragon's jaws. It sniffed at the air for a moment before dropping the beast, which crashed down a few yards from me. The dragon plainly had me for its prey and would be satisfied with nothing else. I had only my sword for protection. I tried to crawl into the cover of a large tree trunk, but I knew there was nowhere I could find safety in that ruined aviary.

Glass cracked as the dragon's tail struck it. From the roof came a strange chiming and then, as if awakened, a flock of varicoloured birds went flapping upwards, twittering and crying. Then they began to descend upon the corpse of the horse. They ignored the fight and the dragon ignored them. They began to feed.

The long snout sniffed at the air again and found my scent. Hobbling, the dragon continued in pursuit of me, while behind it Philander Groot and Grigory Petrovitch Sedenko yelled and struck, to no effect. My strength was fast going. Shards of crystal began to fall all around me, one of them almost impaling me.

Again the teeth found me and I felt my left arm raked. It was as if the dragon had shredded the whole limb in a single movement. I became faint, but continued to flee.

Philander Groot was calling to me, but I could not distinguish the words. I struck again at the dragon's mouth, driving my sword up into its palate. It grunted and lifted its head, taking my sword with it, then spitting it out. I was totally without defence now.

I fell. I began to drag myself along the ground, hoping to find some temporary sanctuary. A claw found my right leg and pain sang up to my spine and suffused my whole body. Yet I continued to move, grasping low branches to pull myself along.

Then my hand fell upon something smooth and cool. Through fading eyes I looked and saw that it was one of the shards from the broken roof. It was like a long icicle. I saw that it tapered to a sharp point. With one hand I attempted to lift it, using my good leg as a lever, until it was braced on the ground between two roots, the thin, jagged edge jutting towards the dragon.

The beast reared again and tottered forward on its hind legs. Saliva ran from the jaws. The silver teeth snapped. I rolled behind the huge shard of crystal even as the dragon dropped down upon me.

The point caught it in the chest, just below the throat, and went straight through. The dragon roared and bellowed, glaring down at me as if it recognised me as the source of its pain.

Black blood burst from the body as the dragon struck with its good leg at the shard, and every blow had the effect of forcing the wound wider so that more blood came. I was covered from head to foot with the horrible liquid, but I fancy I was grinning, too.

Philander Groot and Sedenko had dismounted. They came running towards me, ducking under the branches. Groot had another spear of crystal in his arms. He drove this with all the strength of his tiny body into the side of the dragon.

The beast groaned and turned towards this new source of pain. A terrible coughing began to sound in its throat.

Then it had heeled over against one of the walls, already cracked, and smashed through. For a moment it seemed that it would try to rise as it lay amongst leaves, bits of broken tree, the fallen fragments of glass and crystal. It snorted and blew blood through its nostrils for several feet. The birds were rising from the body of my horse. They had picked its bones completely clean. Again the awful, almost pathetic coughing began to sound from the dying dragon.

One last, long sigh and it had expired.

The bright birds began to settle on the scales until the dragon was completely buried under a wave of bustling feathers and bloody beaks.

Philander Groot and Grigory Sedenko came to my aid. Their faces were full of concern. I turned my head and looked at my arm. It was torn to the bone. My leg had fared scarcely any better.

I gestured towards the skeleton of my horse. My saddlebags were untouched. "The little bottle." I gasped as the pain began to manifest itself.

Sedenko knew the bottle I meant. He ran to the saddlebags and found it. It was dented and buckled, but still in one piece. It took him some while to tear the cork free and put it to my lips. I drank sparingly. The pain gave way to something akin to a kind of cold ecstasy and then there was oblivion. I dreamt that I was a youth again in Bek and that this adventure had, itself, been nothing more than a nightmare.

When I awoke, my friends had cleaned my body and changed my clothes. I wondered, for a moment, if, like Siegfried, I would be made immune by dragon's blood. My left arm was a mass of scars, but I could move it and there was only a soreness and a stiffness to it. Similarly, my leg had healed.

Philander Groot was smiling at me, tugging at his little beard. He appeared as composed as ever. His dress was perfect, as was his poise. "Now you are a true Knight of Chivalry, Captain von Bek," he said. "You have slain a dragon in pursuit of the Holy Grail!"

From his sash he withdrew his scabbarded sword. He offered the beautifully wrought hilt to me. "Here," he said, "you cannot be a knight without a blade."

I did not hesitate in accepting his gift. I am still unsure why he made the gesture or why I so readily responded to it.

"I am grateful to you," I said.

I was sitting upright in a corner of the great aviary. Through the foliage I could see the shattered wall and the bones of the dragon beyond it. There was no longer any sign of those birds. It was as if they awoke only when they smelled death.

I climbed to my feet.

"You have been insensible for a full day," Philander Groot told me as I strapped his sword to my belt.

"Precious hours," said I, "lost to Klosterheim."

"Perhaps," said the magus.

Sedenko came forward, leading the two remaining horses. "I have ridden ahead," he said. "There is a great plain beyond us. And beyond that is a blue-green forest which reaches to the sky. I think we have found the edge of the world, captain."

Chapter Fifteen

"I T IS JUST like my homeland," said Grigory Petrovitch Sedenko with considerable joy, "just like the steppes of Ukrainia."

Beyond this rolling grassland the world seemed to curve upwards so that it was possible to see the hazy blue-green of a great, tranquil forest.

We were crossing a small stone bridge which appeared to have been built for a town no longer in existence. "Count Otto loved to live here, by all accounts," said Philander Groot. "It is said that he built his castle within sight of Heaven and that when he died not only did he rise up to Heaven, but that the castle was taken with him. Certainly there is no sign of it in these parts."

"Well," I said, "it should be only a little while now before I am at the end of my Quest."

"The Grail really lies yonder?" said Sedenko.

"I shall know soon." I hesitated. "I shall know if all these adventurings, all these ordeals, have been meaningless or not. Man struggles in the belief that he can, by dint of perseverance, affect his own destiny. And all those efforts, I think, lead to nothing but ruin."

"You remain a fatalist, then," said Philander Groot quietly.

"I know that Man is mortal," I said. "That famine and disease are not his to control. I sought to become a man of action in response to what I experienced. And all I brought to the world was further Pain."

"But now you could be in reach of its Cure." Philander Groot's tones were kindly. "It might be possible to free Man from his captivity, his dependency on either God or Lucifer. We could see the dawning of a New Age. An Age of Reason."

"But what if Man's Reason is as imperfect as the rest of him?" I

184

said. "Why should we praise his poor logic, his penchant for creating laws which only further complicate his lot?"

"Ah, well," said Philander Groot. "It is all we have, perhaps. And we must learn, must we not, through trial and error."

"At the expense of our natural humanity?"

"Sometimes, perhaps." Philander Groot shrugged. "You must take my horse now, Sir Knight. I shall follow on foot as best I can."

"You have no further magic to aid you in your journey?" I asked.

"It is all used up, as I said. The Dukes of Hell are recalling every scrap of power they have leased to the likes of me. Let them have the fantastic and the sensational. I had rejected it once and now reject it again. Though I do not believe I have the choice, as I once had. However, since when I had the choice I made the same decision, I have no great sense of loss. And my need for it disappeared many years ago."

Sedenko cried out suddenly: "Look! Look back!"

We turned our heads.

Beyond the bridge, beyond the hills, a great, dark cloud had gathered and was moving.

"It is Klosterheim and the Forces of Hell," said Philander Groot simply. "You must make haste now, Captain von Bek. They pursue you."

"So many?" I said.

He smiled quietly. "Are you not flattered?"

"They will kill you, Philander Groot," said Sedenko. "I insist that you ride pillion with me."

"I love life," said the magus. "I will accept your offer, Muscovite."

And so we continued our journey, with Philander Groot clinging to Sedenko's back. We travelled far more slowly than our urgent hearts demanded, with the black cloud looming larger, it seemed, with every step. And soon we felt the ground trembling beneath us, as though an earthquake had begun, yet we ignored it as the far horizon became filled with blue-green haze.

Soon it seemed that half the world was dark and half was light.

Behind us were the Forces of Hell and Klosterheim; ahead lay Heaven, which we could not enter. We were in a kind of timeless Limbo, the last three mortals caught between adversaries in a mysterious and meaningless War which threatened to destroy all the Realms of Earth.

We were still several miles from the forest when we heard shouts in our rear and saw about a dozen riders bearing down on us. Outriders from Klosterheim's main army.

These were fearfully hideous-looking warriors with distorted, disease-racked faces—some with half the flesh missing from their bones. All of them grinned the familiar grins of the decomposing dead.

Out came our swords and we were at once in battle, our effectiveness impaired by the fact that Groot not only was a passenger but was now unarmed. Neither were our spirits improved by the awful giggling noises which escaped the lips of our attackers whenever our swords struck them.

Round and round us they galloped, making it impossible for us to progress, while I racked my memory for a spell to hamper them. Groot it was who succeeded, with:

"Brothers! Why do you not pursue von Bek? He will destroy you if he succeeds. See—there he is now, almost at the forest!"

As they turned lustreless eyes in the direction he pointed, he murmured to me: "I find that the dead are in the main a dull-witted breed."

The riders ceased their giggling and began to confer amongst themselves, whereupon we were again spurring our horses towards the blue-green haze. Behind us we could see an army stretching the length of the horizon and above them the blackness which now crept towards the sun. Soon it would be blotted from view.

A coldness came from the east now, like a wind yet with no power. It was more reminiscent, I thought, of a vacuum which threatened to suck us in. We shivered as we laboured on, the Hell-creatures once more in pursuit.

"Duke Arioch spreads his wings," said Groot of the black cloud. "He has put his entire army at Klosterheim's disposal."

Dead flesh stank in our nostrils; dead hands reached out for us. And more came up behind the first riders: running things, half-ape, half-man, in knotted leather with spears and hardwood clubs, their teeth like tusks. And behind them came thin-faced, long-bodied warriors with waving grey hair, in green-and-white livery and no armour. These carried great two-handed blades and guided their thick-bodied mounts with their thighs. And to one side of them were demons, all horns and warts, on demon-horses, and there were women with filed teeth, and women with the snouts of pigs, and apparitions whose flesh ran liquid on their bodies, and there were lizards bearing monkey-riders, and ostriches carrying lepers in arms, and hooded things which cawed at us—and still we galloped, barely in front of them, while Sedenko set up a wailing and a crying out to God, the Tsar and Saint Sophia for their aid and Groot was pale, exhausted, no longer able to maintain his poise.

The gabbling, squeaking and giggling din filled our ears. It alone might have driven us mad, just as the smell brought us close to fainting. Our horses were tiring. I saw Sedenko's stumble once and almost dislodge the magus. It seemed to me that Philander Groot was as frightened as I was, that he had spent all his resources. Yet now he had no option but to run with us in the faint hope that the forest might offer at least some temporary sanctuary.

We were not far enough ahead of our pursuers. Little by little they caught up with us again and began to surround us.

"O God, have mercy on me. I repent! I repent!" shouted Sedenko, even as he slashed with his sword at a demon and took off its head. "I confess I am a sinner and a rogue!" Another head went clear of a body. Blood spattered the Kazak's face. He was weeping, pale with fear, scarcely conscious, I guessed, that he prayed even as he killed. "Mother of God, take me to thy bosom!"

The stinking press grew tighter and tighter. Yet not a single sword had cut at us. Not one blow had landed on us. I realised that Klosterheim had ordered that we be taken alive. His nature was such that he would be gratified only if he could supervise our deaths.

"The grimoire!" cried Sedenko to me. "There must be something in the grimoire!"

I drew out first one and then another. I called out words of power. I chanted the spell which had previously commanded Duke Arioch's forces. But nothing affected those Hell-creatures now. It spoke much for Arioch's growing strength and for Lucifer's waning authority. I flung the grimoires at laughing, hideous faces. I flung my maps at Klosterheim even as his horse parted the ranks and he rode slowly, stiff-backed, towards us, a little smile upon his thin lips, a slight swagger to his shoulders. He reached out a hand and caught the map-case, emptying it onto the ground. He shrugged. "Now you are mine, von Bek," he said.

It was then that Philander Groot quietly dismounted and placed himself between me and my old enemy.

"Klosterheim," he said in a quiet, small voice which nonetheless carried enormous weight, "thou art the personification of intellectual poverty."

Klosterheim sneered. "Yet here I am, Philander Groot, in the ascendant, while all you can hope for is a merciful death. Perhaps you would argue that there is no justice. I would argue that the strong make their own justice, through action and through the gathering of power to themselves."

"You have been granted power, Johannes Klosterheim, because Duke Arioch finds it worth his while to grant it. But when you have no further use, Johannes Klosterheim, you will be discarded."

"I command all this!" Klosterheim swept his hand to indicate the endless ranks of the damned. "Lucifer Himself trembles. See! We have reached the borders of Heaven itself. When we have done with you, we shall march upon the Holy City, if we so decide. We lay siege to the feeble, decadent old God residing there. We lay siege to His idiot Son. Duke Arioch uses me, it is true, but he uses me as Lucifer uses von Bek. For my courage. For my mortal courage!"

"In von Bek it is courage," said Philander Groot. "In you, Johannes Klosterheim, it is madness."

"Madness? To seek power and to hold it? No!"

"Despair leads to many forms of thought," said the magus, "and many kinds of action. Despair drives some to greater sanity, towards an analysis of the world as it is and what it might be. Others it drives to deep and dangerous insanity, towards an imposition of their own desires upon reality. I sympathise with your despair, Johannes Klosterheim, because it has no solace, in the end. Your despair is the worst there is to know. And yet men often look upon the likes of you and envy you, as you doubtless envy Duke Arioch, as Duke Arioch doubtless envies his master Lucifer, whom he would betray, and perhaps as Lucifer envied God. And what does God envy, I wonder? Perhaps he envies the simple mortal who is content with his lot and envies nobody."

"I'll not listen to this drivel," said Klosterheim. "You become boring, Philander Groot. I shall kill you all the sooner if you bore me!"

Philander Groot had straightened his back. He seemed far more relaxed now. He struck one of his old poses and tweaked for a moment at his moustache. "Fa! This is crude, even for you, Johannes Klosterheim. If you demand entertainment in others, you should at least be prepared to offer some yourself."

All around us the Forces of Hell were snuffling and snorting, growling and drooling. They were so hungry for our deaths.

"Is this—" Groot continued, waving a fastidious hand at the demons and the misshapen living dead, "is this all you can offer? Mere sensation? Terror is the easiest of all human passions to arouse. Did you know?"

Klosterheim was not cowed by the magus. He shrugged. "But you will admit that terror is most effective in winning one's goals. By far the most economical of emotions, eh, philosopher?"

"I suppose that we are temperamentally opposed," said Philander Groot, for all the world as if he played host to a guest at dinner, "and that we shall never quite understand the other's motives or ambitions."

He reached up into the air and appeared to pull on something, an invisible cord. Then in his hand there was a ball of blazing gold. The gold flared brighter and brighter until his whole body seemed to burn with it. His calm, somewhat bored face continued to look out at us as the hordes of Hell fell back, muttering and dismayed. He moved one of his hands and a swathe of fire spread across the nearest group of demons. Instantly they began to burn, howling and stamping and beating at their bodies. Another movement and several score more monsters were afire.

Klosterheim staggered backwards, shielding his face from the heat. "What? You have tricked me. Kill him!"

Philander Groot spoke to me in a conversational tone. "I shall be dead within moments, I think. I would advise both of you to flee while you can."

"Come with us!" I said.

"No. I am content."

I looked westward and there was the blue-green haze, my goal.

"Here!" I threw him the flask containing the last of Lucifer's elixir. He took it with a nod of gratitude and put the rim to his lips.

"Sedenko!" I shouted to my companion. Then I lashed at my horse and was away.

"Oh, you must kill them now!" I heard Klosterheim shout.

We broke out onto the grass again. I looked back. Everything was shadow save for the golden fire which seared through the ranks of the damned. Sedenko was white. He was clutching at his back, even as he rode. He seemed to be weeping.

I saw Philander Groot move. I saw fire spring between us and the Hell-horde. The stink of that army gave way to purer air and there was softness ahead of us.

As we reached the forest and entered the first clumps of trees, Sedenko fell forward on his horse's neck. His breathing was ragged. Small sounds came from his lips.

I saw that he had a gash in his back which stretched from his shoulders to his hip. He continued to weep. "They have killed me. Oh, by all that is holy, they have killed me, captain."

The golden fire was out now. The black army was on the move again. Then it stopped.

I knew that it would not come into the Forest at the Edge of

Heaven, but that it would be waiting for me should I ever emerge again.

I jumped from my weary horse and went to tend to Sedenko. I supported his body as it slid from its saddle. Blood flowed over my arms and my chest. He looked up at me and his face was now innocent and pleading. "Am I truly damned, captain? Am I bound for Hell?"

I could not reply.

When he was dead I raised myself to my feet and I looked about me. Everything was still. A loneliness had come upon my soul.

There was darkness everywhere now but in the forest. And even here there were wisps of grey, as if evil crept in.

I lifted my head to the sky and I shook my fist. "Oh, I reject you. I reject your Heaven and I reject your Hell. Do as you wish with me, but know that your desires are petty and your ambitions have no meaning!"

I addressed no-one. I addressed the universe. I addressed a void.

Chapter Sixteen

A SILENCE HAD fallen over the world.

The plain now seemed filled from end to end by Klosterheim's army, a frozen, waiting gathering. The forest itself was like the forest I had first entered when I discovered Lucifer's castle. No animals, no birds, nothing moving; only the sweet scent of the flowers and the grass.

I gathered leaves and wild tulips and covered Sedenko's body with them. I did not have the strength to bury him. I left his horse to guard him and mounted my own beast, striking due west into the depths of the blue-green forest. My mind and my body both were consumed by a curious numbness. Perhaps they were incapable of accepting any more terror or grief.

I knew, too, that I had changed as much since I had left Lucifer's castle as I had since I had left Bek on the road to Magdeburg. The changes were subtle. There had been no strong sense of revelation. My bitterness was of a different order. I blamed nobody, not even God, for the woes of the world. Neither did I blame myself too hard for past crimes. However, I was determined to follow a path that was entirely my own. Should I ever return to the world I had left, I would not serve Protestant or Catholic. I would use my soldier's skills to protect myself and mine, if need be, but I would not volunteer to go a-warring. I mourned for Sedenko and for Philander Groot and I told myself that should I have the chance to avenge their deaths, I would probably take it, though I felt no special anger, now, towards the wretched Johannes Klosterheim, who daily increased his own terror as he increased his power.

The ground began to rise upwards, almost following the curve I thought I had detected from a distance. And now, away from the influence of Klosterheim's forces, I heard a wren's voice, then the sound of blackbirds and magpies. Small animals moved in the undergrowth. All was natural again.

I rode for many hours before I realised that night did not fall in this forest. The sky was cloudless and still and the sun was benign. And eventually I heard the sound of children laughing as I breasted a rise and looked down into a little glade, with a thatched cottage and a few outbuildings, a cow and a plough-horse. Three little boys were playing in the yard and at the door stood a grey-haired woman with a straight back and clear, youthful skin. Even from that distance I saw her eyes. They were as blue-green as the forest and they were steady. She smiled and gestured.

I rode down slowly, savouring this scene of peace.

"I must warn you," said I, "that a great army out of Hell besieges your forest."

"I know," said the woman. "What are you called, man?"

"I am called Ulrich von Bek and I am upon a Quest. I seek the Holy Grail so that the World's Pain might be cured and Lucifer taken back into the Kingdom of Heaven."

"Ah," said she, "at last you are here, Ulrich von Bek. I have it for you."

I dismounted. I was astonished. "You have what, lady?"

"I have what you would call the Grail. It is a cup. It is what you seek, I think."

"Lady, I cannot believe you. I think that up to now I never did truly believe that I would find the Grail, and never so easily as to be offered it by one such as you."

"Oh, the Grail is a simple thing. And it has a simple function, really, Ulrich von Bek."

My legs were weak. I felt faint. I had not realised how exhausted I had become.

The woman signed to one of the boys to take my horse. She put her arm about my waist. She was extremely strong.

She led me into the cool peace of her parlour and sat me down upon a bench. She brought me milk. She gave me bread with honey on it. She took off my helmet and she stroked my head and murmured soothingly to me so that I wept.

I wept for an hour. And when I had finished I looked up at the lady and said: "All that I love is threatened or is lost for ever."

"So it must seem," she said.

"My friends are dead. My true love is in Satan's thrall, as am I. And I cannot trust my Master to keep His bond."

"Lucifer cannot be trusted," she agreed.

"He offered to return my soul," I told her.

"Aye. It is the only thing He can offer, Ulrich von Bek, which has any value to a mortal. He can offer power and knowledge, but they are worthless if the price is one's soul. Many have come to me, at the Forest at the Edge of Heaven. Many soldiers and many philosophers."

"Seeking the Grail?"

"Aye."

"And you have shown it to them?"

"To some, yes, I have shown it."

"And they have taken it forth into the world?"

"One or two have taken it forth, aye."

"So it is all a trick. There is no special power to the Grail."

"I did not tell you that, Ulrich von Bek." She was almost chiding. She poured me more milk from a pitcher. She spread honey on the good bread. "But most of them expected magic. Most expected at very least some heavenly music. Most were so pure, Ulrich von Bek, and so innocent, that they could not bear the truth."

"What? The Grail, surely, is not a deception of Satan's. If so, the implications of what I have been doing . . ."

She laughed. "You expect worse, for your experience has led you to expect worse. Oh, I have seen great-hearted men and women kneeling in worship of the cup. I have seen them pray for days, awaiting its message, some sign. I have seen them ride from here in disappointment, claiming that they have been offered a false Grail. I have even been threatened with death, by that same Klosterheim who now commands Hell's armies."

"Klosterheim has been here? When?"

"Many years since. I treated him no differently. But he expected

194

too much. So he got nothing. And he went away. He stabbed me here"—she indicated her left breast—"with his sword."

"And yet he did not kill you, plainly."

"Of course not. He was not strong enough."

"He has strength with him now."

"That he has! But he has refused to learn," she said, "and it is a great shame. He had character, Johannes Klosterheim, and I liked him, for all that he was naïve. He refused to learn what Lucifer refused to learn. Yet I believe you have learned it, Ulrich von Bek."

"All I have learned, lady, is to accept the world's attributes as they are. I have learned, I suppose, an acceptance of my own self, an acceptance of Man's ability to create not sensations and marvels but cities and farms which order the world, which bring us justice and sanity."

"Aha," she said. "Is that all you have learned, then, young man? Is that all?"

"I think so," I said. "The marvellous is of necessity a lie, a distortion. At best it is a metaphor which leads to the truth. I think that I know what causes the World's Pain, lady. Or at least I think I know what contributes to that Pain."

"And what would that be, Ulrich von Bek?"

"By telling a single lie to oneself or to another, by denying a single fact of the world as it has been created, one adds to the World's Pain. And pain, lady, creates pain. And one must not seek to become saint or sinner, God or Devil. One must seek to become human and to love the fact of one's humanity."

I became embarrassed. "That is all I have learned, lady."

"It is all that Heaven demands," she said.

I looked out through her window. "Is there such a place as Heaven?"

"I think so," she said. "Come, we shall walk together, Ulrich von Bek."

I was much refreshed. She took my hand and led me from the cottage and through the forest behind it until we stood upon a precipice, whence issued the blue-green haze. I felt a sudden soaring of the mind and senses, such as I had never before experienced.

I felt a joy and a peace, previously unknown. I wanted to plunge from that place and into the cool haze, to give myself up to whatever it was I felt. But the woman tugged at my hand and I had to turn my back on Heaven.

Even now I cannot be sure if I experienced a hint of what Heaven might be. It seemed a kind of clarity, a kind of understanding. Can Hell and Heaven be merely the difference between ignorance and knowledge?

I turned my back on Heaven.

I turned my back on Heaven and walked with the lady to her cottage. The children had disappeared and only the cow and the horse were there, placid.

I sat at the table and she poured me milk from her pitcher.

"Where is this?" I asked her. "Where does Heaven lie?"

"That must be obvious to you by now." She went to the wooden dresser behind her and she opened a drawer. From the drawer she took a small clay pot and she placed it on the table before me.

"Here. Take this back to your Master. Tell Him you have found the Grail. And tell Him that it was fashioned by the hands of an ordinary woman."

"This?" I could not touch it. "This is the Holy Grail?"

"This is a production of that which you believe inhabits the Grail," she said. "And it is holy, I think. And it was made by me. And all it brings is Harmony. It makes those who are in its presence whole. Yet, ironically, it can be handled only by one who is already whole."

"I, whose soul is in Lucifer's charge, can be called whole, lady?"

"You are a man," she said. "A mortal. And you are not innocent. Neither are you destroyed. Yes, von Bek, you are whole enough."

I reached fingers towards the little clay pot. "My Master will not believe in this."

She shrugged. "Your Master is a fool," she said. "Your Master is a fool."

"Well," I said, "I will take it to Him. And I will tell Him what you have told me. That I bring the Cure for the World's Pain."

"You bring Him Harmony," she said. "That is the Cure. And the Cure is within every one of us."

"Has this cup no other power, lady?"

"The Power of Harmony is power enough," said she quietly.

"But difficult to demonstrate," said I in some amusement.

She smiled. Then she shrugged and would say no more on the subject.

"Well," I told her, "I thank you for your hospitality, lady. And for this gift of the Holy Grail. Must I believe in it?"

"Believe what you like. The cup is what the cup is," she said. "And it is yours to take."

I picked up the cup at last. It was warm in my hand. I felt a little of what I had experienced as she and I looked into the abyss beyond her house. "I thank you for your gift," I said.

"It is no gift," she told me. "It is truly earned, Ulrich von Bek. Be sure of that."

"I have a scroll," I said, "which I must open if I am to return to my Master."

"You cannot open it here," she said. "And even if you did open it, you could not return to Hell from here, nor any part which Hell commands. It is the rule."

"Ah, but madam, I have come so far! Am I to be cheated now?"

"You are not cheated," she said kindly, "but it is the rule. Use your scroll once you are out of the forest again. It will serve you then."

"Klosterheim and Duke Arioch's horde await me there."

"That is true," she said. "I know."

"So I am to be doomed just as it seems I achieve my goal?"

"If you think so."

"You must tell me!" I was close to weeping. "Oh, madam, you must tell me!"

"Take the Grail," she said. "And take your scroll. They will both serve you well. Show Klosterheim the Grail and remember that he has seen it before."

"He will mock me."

"Of course Klosterheim will mock you if he has any chance at

all. Of course he will, Ulrich von Bek. He is all armour, that
Klosterheim."

"And then he will kill me," I said.

"Then you must have courage."

She rose from the table and I knew she meant me to leave.

One of the little boys was holding my horse for me as I went
out into the yard. Another sat on the pump, watching me. The
third was unconcerned. He was studying the chickens.

I sat down upon my horse and set my feet in my stirrups. I felt
the clay pot in my purse, together with Lucifer's scroll.

"There will be no legend told of you," said the grey-haired
woman, "yet you are my favourite amongst all those who have
come to me."

"Mother," I said, "will you tell me your name?"

"Oh," she said, "I am just an ordinary woman who made a clay
pot and who dwells in a cottage in the Forest at the Edge of
Heaven."

"But a name?"

"Call me what you will," she said. She smiled and her smile was
warm. She put a hand upon mine. "Call me Lilith, for some do."

Then she had struck my horse upon his flank and I was riding
east again. Back to where Klosterheim and all his horrid army
awaited me.

Chapter Seventeen

I KNEW THAT it was a foolish hope, yet I deliberately went to where I had left Sedenko's body. I recalled a legend concerning one of the properties of the Grail, that it could bring the dead back to life. I held out the little clay pot over the corpse of my poor damned friend, but his eyes did not flicker and his wounds did not magically heal, though his face seemed more at peace than when I had covered him with flowers and leaves.

This dream, I thought, has no meaning. This clay pot is nothing more than a clay pot. I have learned nothing and I have gained nothing. Yet I rode on, out of the blue-green Forest at the Edge of Heaven, and I stood alone against all the ranks of rebellious Hell, reaching for my parchment even as Klosterheim rode out from the infinite black cloud and came slowly towards me.

"I give you the opportunity to join in this adventure," he said. He was frowning. He pursed his lips. "You and I have great courage, von Bek, and together we could storm Heaven and take it. Think what would be ours!"

"You are mad, Johannes Klosterheim," I said. "Philander Groot has already told you that. He was right. How can Heaven's gifts be taken by storm?"

"The way I take Hell's, fool!"

"I have found the Grail," I said, "and would ask you to let me pass, for I am on my way to my Master. I have been successful in my Quest."

"You have been deceived. You are not the first to be so deceived."

"I know that you have looked upon the Grail and have rejected it," I said, "but I have not rejected it, Klosterheim. Do not ask me why, for I could not tell you, though I am sure you have many reasons as to why you would not accept it."

"I would not accept it," he said, "because it was a trick. There

199

were no miracles. Either God deceived us or He had no power. It was then that I decided to serve Lucifer. And now I serve myself against even Lucifer."

"You serve nothing," I said, "save the Cause of Dissension."

"My cause has far more meaning! Von Bek, I offer you all that you desire."

"You offer me more than ever Lucifer offered," I said. "Do you believe that His power is already yours?"

"It shall be!"

He signalled and the black weight of Hell came moving in on me. I smelled the stink. I heard the gibbering and the other noises. I saw the hideous, malformed faces. Rank upon rank upon rank of them. "This is what rules now," said Klosterheim. "Death and terror are the means by which all power is maintained. I make my justice for myself. A just world is a world in which Johannes Klosterheim has everything he desires!"

I took the little clay pot from my purse. "Is this what you rejected?"

The ground began to tremble again. It seemed the whole Earth swayed. From the ranks of Hell came a monstrous ululation.

Klosterheim looked hard at it. "Aye. It's the same. And you've been deceived by the same trick, von Bek, as I told you."

"Then look upon it," I said. "Let all your forces look upon it. Look upon it!"

I hardly know why I spoke thus. I held the Grail up high. No shining came out of it. No music came out of it. No great event took place. It remained what it was: a small clay pot.

Yet, here and there in the ranks of Hell, pairs of eyes became transfixed. They looked. And a certain sort of peace came upon the faces of those who looked.

"It is a Cure," I cried, following my instincts, "a Cure for your Pain. It is a Cure for your Despair. It is a Cure."

The poor damned wretches who had known nothing but fear throughout their existence, who had faced no future but one of terror or oblivion, began to crane to see the clay pot. Weapons were lowered. The gruntings and the gigglings ceased.

Klosterheim was stunned. He made no protest as I moved towards his army.

"It is a Cure," I said again. "Look upon it. Look upon it."

They were falling to their knees. They were dismounting from their beasts. Even the most grotesque of them was transfixed by that clay pot. And still no special radiance came out of it. Still no miracle occurred, save the miracle of their salvation.

And thus it was, with Klosterheim coming beside me, that I rode through the ranks of Hell and was unharmed. Klosterheim was the only one who was not affected by the Grail. His face writhed with a terrible torment. He was fascinated by what happened, but did not wish to believe it. He coughed. He began to groan. "No," he said.

We passed together through his entire army. And that army lay upon the ground. It lay upon the ground and it seemed to be sleeping, though it might also have been dead; I did not know.

And Klosterheim and I were now the only two who were conscious, just then.

Klosterheim was shaking. He moved his head from side to side and he bit at his lip and he glared at me and the little clay pot. And he could not speak. And he had tears in his tormented eyes.

"No," said Klosterheim.

"It is true," I told him. "You might have had the Grail. But you rejected it. You rejected your own salvation as well as the salvation of your fellow men. You might have had this Grail, Johannes Klosterheim."

And he put fingers to his wretched lips. And now tears ran down his gaunt, pale cheeks. And he said again: "No."

He said: "No."

"It is true, Klosterheim. Yes, it is true."

"It cannot be." This last was a terrified shout. He stretched gloved hands towards the Grail, as if he still believed he might be saved.

Then he fell forward from his horse. His soul had been taken out of him. Duke Arioch had claimed him.

I dismounted. Klosterheim was quite dead.

Duke Arioch's forces either continued to sleep on or were beginning to rise and disperse. Those who had awakened wandered off, perfectly at peace with themselves. Not only was the Forest at the Edge of Heaven no longer threatened, but Lucifer would be victorious in Hell.

I wondered at the significance of my Quest and of the cup itself. Somehow it had served both God and the Devil. And then I remembered the woman's words. She had spoken of Harmony.

From out of my purse I took the scroll and opened it. I read the words that had been written there, and even as I read them I found myself in the library of the castle where I had last seen my Master, Lucifer.

The library was empty, save for its books and its furniture. Morning light came in through the great windows. Outside, the trees were moving in a breeze. Birds perched in them. Birds sang in them.

I realised that this place was no longer within the domain of Hell.

Chapter Eighteen

I wondered now if Lucifer had been defeated and if, in His defeat, He had taken Sabrina's soul with Him and would continue to claim mine.

For some time I stood by the window, looking out on that ordinary and comforting beauty. I placed the little clay pot upon the table at which Lucifer had been sitting. Then I left the library and I went into the cool hall and climbed the staircase to Sabrina's room. I did not expect her to be there.

I opened the door.

She was lying in her bed. Her expression was so full of peace that momentarily I believed her to be dead. Her face was as lovely as ever and her wonderful hair flooded the pillows. She was breathing softly as I stooped to kiss her brow. Her eyes opened. She looked at me without surprise. She smiled and she opened her arms to me. I bent to embrace her.

"You have brought the Grail with you," she said.

"You know?" I sat beside her. I stroked her shoulder.

"Of course I know." She kissed me. "We are free."

"I thought I had lost everything," I said. "Everyone."

"No," she said. "You have gained much and you have gained it for all. Lucifer is grateful. You achieved your goal and in so doing you defeated His worst enemy."

"And He is no longer our Master."

"No longer." She looked at me with intelligent eyes. "He has gone back to Hell. He claims no part of Earth for His Realm."

"We shall never see Him again?"

"We shall see Him. In the library. At noon." She rose from the sheets and sought her gown. I handed it to her. It was white, like a wedding dress.

"And God?" I asked. "Does He still parley with God?"

"I do not know." She glanced out the window. "It is almost noon. Lucifer asked us to come together."

We embraced again, more passionately now. Then we left the room and walked down the staircase to the library.

Once more, as I had done a year before, I opened the huge doors of the library. And once more Lucifer sat at the table. But He was not reading. He was holding the clay cup in His hands. He turned beautiful eyes upon us. Some of the terror, I thought, had gone out of Him, some of the defiance.

"Good morrow to thee, Captain von Bek," He said.

"Good morrow, Prince Lucifer." I bowed.

"You would wish to know," He said, "that your friends do not reside in Hell. I have released their souls as I have released yours."

"Then Hell still exists," I said.

He laughed His old, melodious laugh. "Indeed it does. The antidote for the World's Pain cannot abolish Hell, any more than it can bring immediate surcease to all that ails Man."

He replaced the cup gently upon the table and He got to His feet. His naked skin glowed like silver fire and His fiery copper eyes still contained that element of melancholy I had seen before. "I had sought to have no more to do with your Earth," He told us. Gracefully He moved towards us and looked down on us. There seemed to be love in His eyes, too, or at least a kind of affection. I still did not know if He lied. I still do not know. He reached out His marvellous hands and touched us. I shivered, sensing that strange ecstasy which, to many, could be a compelling drug. I gasped. He withdrew his hands. "I have spoken with God," said Lucifer.

"And He has refused you, Your Majesty?" Sabrina spoke softly.

His sweet, vibrant voice was almost as low as hers when He replied. "I do not think it is a refusal. But I hoped for more." The Prince of Darkness sighed and then He smiled. It was a bitter and it was a very sad smile.

"I am not accepted into Heaven," Lucifer continued. "Instead, Heaven has put the world into my sole charge. I am commissioned to redeem it, in the fullness of time. If I help mankind to accept its own humanity, then I, Lucifer, shall be all that I was before I was cast down from Heaven."

"Then you are now the Lord of this Earth, Your Majesty?" I said. "God no longer rules here?"

"I do not rule, as such. I am charged to bring Reason and Humanity into the world and thus discover a Cure for the World's Pain. I am charged to understand the nature of this cup. When I understand its nature and when all mankind understands its nature, we shall both be redeemed!"

Lucifer raised His head and He laughed. The sound was musical and full of irony as well as humour.

"How things turn, von Bek! How things turn!"

"So you are still our Master," said Sabrina. She was frowning. She had come to be afraid again.

"Not so!" Lucifer turned, almost in rage. "You are your own masters. Your destiny is yours. Your lives are your own. Do you not see that this means an end to the miraculous? You are at the beginning of a new age for Man, an age of investigation and analysis."

"The Age of Lucifer," I said, echoing some of His own irony.

He saw the joke in it. He smiled.

"Man, whether he be Christian or pagan, must learn to rule himself, to understand himself, to take responsibility for himself. There can be no Armageddon now. If Man is destroyed, he shall have destroyed himself."

"So we are to live without aid," said Sabrina. Her face was clearing.

"And without hindrance," said Lucifer. "It will be your fellows, your children and their children who will find the Cure for the World's Pain."

"Or perish in the attempt," said I.

"It is a fair risk," said Lucifer. "And you must remember, von Bek, that it is in my interest that you succeed. I have wisdom and knowledge at your disposal. I always had that gift for Man. And now that I may give it freely I choose not to do so. Each fragment of wisdom shall be earned. And it shall be hard-earned, captain."

This time Lucifer bowed to us. His glowing body seemed to flare with brighter fire and the library was suddenly empty.

He had taken the clay cup with Him.

I reached out for Sabrina's hand.

"Are you still afraid?" I asked her.

"No," she said, "I am thankful. The world has been threatened too long by the extraordinary, the supernatural and the monstrous. I shall be happy enough to smell the pines and hear the song of the thrush. And to be with you, Captain von Bek."

"The world is still threatened," I said to her, "but perhaps not by Lucifer." I held her hand tightly.

"Now we can go home to Bek," I said.

Sabrina and I were married in the old chapel in Bek. My father died soon after we returned and he was pleased that I was there, to maintain the estates as he would have wished. He said that I had "grown up" and he loved Sabrina, I think, as much as did I. She bore us two girls and a boy, all of whom lived and all of whom are now well. We continued with our studies and came to entertain many great men, who were impressed with Sabrina's grasp of Natural Philosophy in particular, though I think they sometimes found my own speculations a trifle obscure.

I was not to meet Lucifer again and perhaps I never shall.

I continue to remain unclear, sometimes, as to whether my soul is my own. It is still possible that Lucifer lied to us, that God did not hear Him, that God did not speak to Him. Has Lucifer claimed the whole Earth as His domain in defiance of God? Or did God ever exist at all?

These are not thoughts I express to anyone, of course, save now, when I believe myself to be dying. The world is unsafe for a man who utters such heresies. I see little evidence that Reason is triumphant or that it ever shall be triumphant. But if I have Faith, it is in the faint hope that mankind will save itself, that Lucifer did not, after all, lie.

I have entered into Hell and know that I should not like to

spend Eternity there. And I believe that I have been permitted a taste of Heaven.

We came to be happy in Bek. We sought Harmony, but not at the expense of muscular thought and passionate argument, and I believe that we achieved it in a small measure. Harmony is hard-won, it seems.

The War eventually subsided and did not touch us much. And as for the War which had threatened the supernatural Realms, we heard no more of it. The Plague never visited Bek. Without deliberately pursuing commerce we became well-to-do. Musicians and poets sought our patronage and returned it with the productions of their talents, so that we were consistently and most marvellously entertained.

In the year 1648, through no particular effort of good will and chiefly on account of their weariness and growing poverty, both of money and of men, the adversaries in our War agreed a peace. For several years afterwards we were to receive men and women at our estates who had known nothing but War, who had been born into War and who had lived by War all their lives. We did not turn them away from Bek. Many of them continue to live amongst us, and because they have known so much of War, they are anxious to maintain a positive Peace.

In 1678 my wife Sabrina died of natural causes and was buried in our family crypt, mourned by all. As for myself, I am alone at present. Our children are abroad; our son teaches Medicine and Natural Philosophy at the University of Prague, where he is greatly honoured; my elder daughter is in London as an ambassadress (there, I gather, her Salon is famous and she enjoys the friendship of the Queen) and my younger daughter is married to a successful physician in Lübeck.

To my subjective eye, the Pain of the World is a degree less terrible than it was some thirty years ago, when our Germany was left in ruins. If Lucifer did not lie to me, I pray to Him with all my heart and soul that He can lead mankind to Reason and Humanity and towards that Harmony which might, with great efforts, one day be ours.

I pray, in short, that God exists, that Lucifer brings about His own Redemption and that mankind therefore shall in time be free of them both for ever: for until Man makes his own justice according to his own experience, he will never know what true peace can be.

With this, my testament, I consign my soul to Eternity, offering it neither to God nor to Lucifer but to Humanity, to use or to discard as it will. And I urgently beg any man or woman who reads this and who believes it to continue that which my wife and myself began:

Do you the Devil's work.

And I suspect that you will see Heaven sooner than ever shall your Master.

> *Signed by my own hand in*
> *this Year of Our Lord*
> *Sixteen Hundred and Eighty:*
> *BEK*

The City in the
Autumn Stars

*Being a continuation of the story of the von Bek family
and its association with Lucifer, Prince of Darkness,
and the cure for the world's pain*

The second chronicle, in which is recorded the
Confession of Manfred von Bek, sometime Cpt. of
Cavalry in Washington's Revolutionary Forces; Deputy
of the French Commune; also Former Secretary to the
Saxon Embassy at the Court of the Empress Catherine
of Russia; said Confession chiefly Relating to
Certain Strange Events in the City of Mirenburg
during the Winter Months of the Year 1794.

For Colin Greenland

THE DIRECTION OF this new force, liberated by the love, vanity and inspiration of a sharp little shop assistant, was through the spirit of the times to a personal power that both were content to wish as large as possible, without any limitation or detailed idea. This spirit, since it was the Age of Reason, was love of Mystery. For it cannot be disguised that the prime effect of knowledge of the universe in which we are shipwrecked is a feeling of despair and disgust, often developing into an energetic desire to escape reality altogether. The age of Voltaire is also the age of fairy tales; the vast *Cabinet des Fées*, some volumes of which Marie Antoinette took into her cell to console her, it is said, stood alongside the Encyclopédie . . . This impression of disgust, and this impulse to escape were naturally very strong in the eighteenth century, which had come to a singularly lucid view of the truth of the laws that govern our existence, the nature of mankind, its passions and instincts, its societies, customs, and possibilities, its scope and cosmical setting and the probable length and breadth of its destinies. This escape, since from Truth, can only be into Illusion, the sublime comfort and refuge of that pragmatic fiction we have already praised. There is the usual human poverty of its possible varieties . . . there are all the drugs, from subtle, all-conquering opium to cheating, cozening cocaine. There is religion, of course, and music, and gambling; these are the major euphorias. But the queerest and oldest is the sidepath of Magic . . . At its deepest, this Magic is concerned with the creative powers of the will; at lowest it is but a barbarous rationalism, the first of all our attempts to force the heavens to be reasonable.

—William Bolitho, "Cagliostro (and Seraphina),"
Twelve Against the Gods, 1929

Preface

THIS ACCOUNT, FIRST published in Heidelberg in about 1840, was printed and written anonymously. Only recently, through the records of the Vernon family, has the authorship been traced to Manfred von Bek who was born in Bek in 1755 and died in Mirenburg in 1824, having in his youth been involved in a number of scandals and dubious adventures throughout Russia, Asia Minor, America and most of Europe.

The narrative (mentioned in passing in Carlyle's *German Romance*, 1827) does not seem to have had much public distribution and today's Count von Bek, to whom I am indebted for much more help than is evident here, points out that his ancestor issued instructions for it to be printed only after his death. This accords with his references in the text.

The account is in the nature of a Confession and if read as fiction might well qualify as a romance; though it does bear resemblances both to the classic picaresque and to the Gothic novels then fashionable. The Grail itself of course has been part of the family's coat of arms for over three hundred years and their name is inextricably bound up with the German versions of the myth. There is, for instance, a legend (mentioned in many sources) that the von Bek family is fated to keep and protect the Grail, to seek it out if it ever becomes lost.

Manfred von Bek's reputation as a young man—he was frowned upon by many—might suggest this story was a hoax, either written by himself or someone who had known him well. The reader must judge that. However, before making a final assessment it might be worth consulting the records of the present Count which have not yet been made available to the public, either in Germany or elsewhere. These records are currently in preparation.

This somewhat modernised version of Manfred von Bek's "Confession" is adapted from an English edition published in London by D. Omer Smith of St. Paul's Churchyard, 1856, revised and expanded by Michael Moorcock, who acknowledges, as always, his enormous debt to Prince Lobkowitz and, of course, to the von Bek family itself which has entrusted him with many documents covering the last four centuries of its history.

The Publishers

Chapter One

In which I take my leave of Paris, Romance,
and the Radical Cause

WERE IT NOT for that Terror which captured France in 1793, and which at length caused me to flee Paris, I might never have discovered an exquisite love, nor ventured to the City in the Autumn Stars, where, with wits, sword and the remnants of Faith, I fought again for the world's future, and lost my own.

The day Tom Paine was jailed on Robespierre's specific order, I determined at last to put revolutionary ideals behind me. Even as I pleasured sweet Madame F— (whose bad news was incidental to her visit) I planned my impending flight. Tom imprisoned meant I had lost my final ally in the Assembly. My own name would now inevitably appear on a warrant issued by the Committee of Public Safety. Indeed, a boisterous mob of enragés could already be on its way to my lodgings with the intention of offering me its familiar choice: tumbril to the guillotine or rotten hulk to the Seine's bottom. Clearly it would be prudent for me to spend the New Year of '94 abroad.

As soon as was seemly I dressed in the disguise held ready for that moment, packed all I owned into two old leather saddlebags, made hasty courtesies to my mistress and hurried through Paris's dawn alleys to a certain mews in the rue de l'Ancienne Comédie. There, for 2fr., I redeemed my feckless manservant's nag from a sleepy ostler. More silver got me a saddle and harness, which had seen far better days, and this I settled on the poor beast as she shivered and fumed in the stableyard's chill.

I fancied I now looked the image of some medium-rank revolutionary officer. My customary silks and lace were abandoned (or hidden). I was engulfed in an old black coaching cloak, while a crushed Kevenküller bicorne rested on my uncombed hair. To this I had added a coarse muffler of greyish wool, greasy dun-coloured breeches, cheaply finished Jack-leather boots, and I had pinned a tri-colour cockade to my hat. An antique cavalry scabbard sheathed my own good Samarkand sabre and this was tucked into a blue, white and red sash of doubtful cleanliness. I must surely pass as a typical servant of the Committee and I intended to claim that identity if anyone stopped and questioned me. Should disguise and argument fail to persuade my suspicious zealot, then I would resort to two large Georgian flintlocks settled in my greatcoat's gunpockets.

I could not help but despair the progress of my career and the collapse of our political dreams. In the previous year France had executed her King and proclaimed a true Republic. But now the Mob's passing whim had become the only law, as Robespierre himself would soon discover. I felt cruelly betrayed: by the Revolution, by men I had embraced as brothers, by Circumstance, and, as always, by God.

Being no admirer of despotism or privilege, I had first cele-brated then served the Revolution, becoming at last a deputy in the parliamentary assembly. When, however, the bloodletting grew unjust and excessive I, like Paine, lifted my voice against that nightmare of hypocrisy and falsehood, that degenerate orgy of revenge and animal savagery! But, like Paine, I was a foreigner and next encountered sudden antagonism from the very comrades whose own rights and liberty I had lately championed.

They claimed the Mob performed identical crimes as the aris-tocrats, yet not so prettily disguised. To me, this justified nothing. Their argument was in itself illustrative of their impoverished and perverted souls.

Such was the substance of my statements to my fellow depu-ties when my doubts grew to a new kind of certainty after I witnessed their "September Days,' those days when the Beast in all his horrid barbarity stalked our streets wearing Liberty's cap and wiping his bloody chops on Liberty's flag.

The first I saw of it was beneath a brilliant late Summer sky when six coaches full of captured priests were set upon in the rue

Dauphine. The rabble sliced off hands stretching from windows in search of Mercy, then hacked the occupants to pieces. The same day a Carmelite Convent near rue de Vaugirard was likewise attacked, its inhabitants murdered and thrown into a well. Prisons were invaded and their defenceless charges slaughtered. The murder of innocents continued. Drunken Septembristers dragged young and old, mad and sane, into the jails' courtyards and impaled them on pikes. When not stabbing prisoners to death in their very cells where they awaited trial, those frightful savages split their victims' heads with hatchets. I grew used to seeing heaps of horrid, mutilated corpses. Other bodies were displayed in the streets for public amusement. Crones dragged to the pavements the still limp cadavers of young boys, jerking these lifeless partners in a further parody of human illusion, the figures of a hideous, erotic dance. At La Petite Force prison the Princesse de Lamballe was stripped, humiliated before the crowd, then repeatedly raped. Her breasts were cut off and while she still lived she was again subjected to indecencies of every description, her tormentors constantly sponging blood from her skin so the Mob should note its aristocratic whiteness. When the lady at last expired, her private organs were amputated, impaled on a pike by the same gallant who ripped out her heart, roasted it on the stove of a nearby wineshop, and ate it.

Everywhere in Paris similar barbarities were practised, distracting me almost to madness. My wretched brain could not encompass all that horror; the cruel destruction of my idealism. That month alone fifteen hundred persons were tortured and killed by wine-swilling rogues and harlots who in coming weeks proudly exhibited swords, spears and axes crusted with innocent blood. Even that, perhaps, I might have ignored, had the Tribunal voiced its outrage. Instead, the Mob was praised. Marat and Billaud-Varenne encouraged it: it performed a public duty in slaying the nation's enemies. By force of will I yet remained in the Assembly, passionately arguing a return to our Cause's original virtues, but even born Frenchmen were howled down if they offered such pleading!

A native of Saxony, I had been invited to join the Revolution by Anarcharsis Cloots and my Jacobin friends. With Cloots I had renounced lands, title and family loyalty, following him to Paris where we were welcomed as brothers and immediately made citizens. Elsewhere in Europe of course my enthusiasm was not so well received. Having cried out for the Rights of Man and shown my wholehearted support of that most violent upheaval in the body politic there was now every chance, should I travel beyond France's boundaries, I would be immediately arrested.

I had so thoroughly committed myself to the Revolution that even when I came to understand the evil we had created with our miserably naïve philosophies I continued to deceive myself of Robespierre's humanistic claims. I appealed for the abolition of the death penalty: let it not punish either the weakest peasant or Marie Antoinette Capet, the Queen. Those who had never before known power, I reasoned, were the first to fear the loss of it and suspect all of trying to steal it. Given the moral superiority of our Cause, we should not descend to the methods of our predecessors but must show the world we returned to our stated moral purpose. (This plea was resisted by the self-same gentlemen who very soon would impose fresh tyrannies upon the people in the name of that corrupt Directorate!) Thus my departure was no hasty dash from danger. I saw no joy in martyrdom, nor satisfaction in last speeches from the scaffold. My plan for escape had been exactly drawn.

Mirenburg was to be my final destination. In that tolerant city I had money and old friends. There was no lovelier city in which to weather out a social storm. Like Venice in her singularity, Mirenburg moreover had an enlightened Prince; but to reach her I would have to cross half the rest of belligerent Europe. I had no other reasonable choice. I was unwelcome in Saxony, wanted for treason in Russia, had bad debts in Vienna, was branded libertine in Genoa and excommunicated in Rome (as a Protestant born I was not unduly alarmed by this), and as a known Jacobin, an intimate of Robespierre, I could not expect to enjoy a leisurely and uninterrupted journey.

Thus I rode with many a wary glance and at what I prayed was an unremarkable pace, into streets which were now rife with random violence.

Ghastly fog gave Paris an appearance of spectral unreality, as if she herself had become a bloodless cadaver, greatest and final victim of the Terror.

In time, cold morning sunshine dispersed the fog and sharpened the texture of the stones, revealing the filth and verminous rubble which Égalité left untreated and which Fraternité ignored. I was glad to find the iron gates standing open, my way unchallenged by three drunken National Guardsmen who wished me a cheerful *"Bonjour, citoyen!"* with a hiccup and a yawn. Without pausing, I waved passport and travelling documents (none fully ordered and some bearing only poor facsimiles of the proper seals) and entered the ill-tended highway with its thin snow and black, etiolated trees.

As Parisian cobbles gave way to the Dijon Road's frost-hardened ruts, I could at last spur to a smarter trot, more in keeping with my heart's rhythm. I had known terror and danger before (most notably when the Empress Catherine exiled me to Siberia whence I escaped, spending two years with wild Tatars, learning their martial skills and daily forced to prove me as good a savage as themselves), yet that bloodthirsty democracy was the cruellest sport that ever Christians performed.

I had lost all hope for the perfectibility of our world. My time in America, where I served with von Stauben, Lafayette and Wayne, had shown me how soon the fire-eaters become the fire-men: as quick to dampen the Spirit of Liberty when it threatened their interests as they were to ignite it when it served them best. Since my departure, events in that first great modern Republic had proven more melancholy still, with half the leading spirits dead, in jail or exiled. I heard they planned to choose a monarch and General Washington was proposed! Were they bent merely upon replacing one King George with another? If so, the Tyranny of Autocracy would at least be given an honest name!

My horse, an old country hunter, sniffed at the air and grew almost lively as we left the city's stink, but I enjoyed only the mildest sense of release. Louis himself had reached the Belgian border before being caught and brought back. The King, moreover, had the advantage of aid from my acquaintance, the Baron de Korff, Russian ambassador to France, whereas I remained a wanted criminal by the Muscovites, on their suspicion of my involvement in a murder plot against Catherine. With every friend in France either dead, emigrated, imprisoned or too prudent to associate with a suspected Royalist (I had begged, with Paine and a few others, that the Queen be exiled rather than beheaded) I had only my own poor wits for an ally.

The Parisian fashion for wholesale slaughter had spread by now to the provinces so I could not count myself safe from Democracy until I had at least a country or two at my back. I began to regret my earlier decision to wear beneath homespun and tarred leather my fine shirt, silk breeches and (within my boots) elegant shoes. Born into an age which regarded it as no minor heresy to go about improperly adorned, I was deuced uncomfortable. I had dressed well and presented a good figure throughout the turmoil and shared this quality (if no other) with Robespierre whose coat was always impeccably cut even as he lifted a lace wrist to urge on his tide of barefoot arsonists and whores-turned-harpy.

Paris faded into mist. My few fragments of illusion faded with her.

Rousseau, Voltaire, Descartes, even Paine himself, by now seemed little more than foolish, over-hopeful prattlers, whose notions bore no relation to the world as she really was.

All I retained of Rousseau was his warning that blind following of his theories must inevitably lead to the substitution of the tyranny of dictators for a tyranny of kings.

Louis had ruled merely by the Will of God. Robespierre chose to believe he ruled by the Will of the People. This moral conviction allowed him to condone, participate in and initiate deeds for which no Biblical justification existed. Like a good many fierce revolutionaries who failed to influence reality as thoroughly as they had dreamed, he had a knack for calling old pots by new names and proclaiming the result a triumph of the Enlightenment.

To abolish God, I thought, was one thing—but to replace Him with oneself was quite another! I could only guess at the heresies, blasphemies and distortions of nature yet to come. No longer did I see the decline of the Romans merely as the result of ancient ignorance. That decline now seemed proof of a lasting human desire for slavery.

To shape, therefore, my new direction, my discarding of a moral wardrobe gone rotten, I fostered a determination to follow our old von Bek family motto to *Do you the Devil's Work*, handed down from father to son through generations of our people.

At last I had the interpretation which in the past had always baffled me. Now I knew it meant I should indulge myself in all those impulses which hitherto I had dismissed as base or ignoble. If Rome must be the model of our modern world, then I would turn from that narrow Stoic philosophy which had brought me to my present pass.

I had my well-developed taste for fine clothing, and had always enjoyed good food and wine, as well as lechery. But to my hedonism I would marry a new loyalty—to my own person alone.

Renouncing my quest for justice and human dignity, I would seek instead the comfort of Riches: gold was both a reliable mistress and a tangible friend.

A few years in Mirenburg, I reasoned, enjoying her various delights while increasing my fortune by fair means or foul, and I would return to my own Saxon estates, purchase my respectability and retrieve from my father my birthright. I would not go cap in hand to Bek. I would buy her back, enrich her, installing model farms and dwellings so that at least my own people should be happy.

Once rich, moreover, I should again travel easily about Europe, for while in the public eye a poor radical is a dangerous rogue, a rich radical is merely an eccentric gentleman!

The loyalty I had given to liberty would now be set to work in the cultivation of Mammon. I had a little money with my friend, the Helvetian philosopher Frederic-Caesar de La Harpe of Vaud, whom I had met in St. Petersburg while performing my office as secretary to the Saxon ambassador. Lausanne was therefore my first destination, but to reach that city I must navigate wild mountainous country whose brigands were reputedly so poor they would murder a traveller for the hair on his head. However, even before I began that stage of my journey I must pass through the village of Sainte-Croix where there was usually a strong garrison of the National Guard, primed to expect the likes of me.

As the miles passed I found my disguise to have been well chosen; the only close attention it drew was fearful or respectful. I had learned during my sojourn in Muscovy and Tatary that the art of achieving congruity with one's surroundings lies not in dressing exactly as the common man, nor yet as one of his superiors; 'tis best to be one who communes between the two.

An unimaginative, carping Civil Servant, a scribe, courier or what have you?—all would be in the mould of those for whom the vulgar people go in awe but which the aristocracy treats as invisible or as a despised necessity. If one swims towards the middle of the human stream one may fairly be expected to be carried on a current of preconception and insensible habit. Thus with my inferiors I showed impatience and a condescending self-importance, while to any superior met on the high road (military commander, important provincial communard and so forth) I saluted with servile cheer and obedient respect, earning their immediate contempt which was always to my advantage: one never looks closely at that which one neither fears nor admires.

So I crossed France.

At inns remote from any town I was most easily able to wave my sheaf of forgeries and requisition my needs from folk who blushed to hear my accusatory snarls of "Royalist!" and who served me their inadequate best with trembling hands.

My name was "Citizen Didot" and my business, I instructed them, was Secret or Important: enough to impress them without informing them. Should I share a table with a priest I glared, while a lieutenant would receive my camaraderie and dislike me for it. A captain, it need scarcely be said, received my cringing admiration.

Winter made bad roads worse and the going was slow, but the seeming absence of pursuit consoled me. Perhaps France was so taken up with her foreign wars and fears of invasion she showed little concern for one Saxon traitor running for freedom. I now regretted deeply my decision to accept French citizenship during those early euphoric days. Agents of the revolution were in every country, furthering Cloots's avowed ambition to take Liberty abroad in the form of a conquering French army which would free all from their chains. Cloots himself would soon be guillotined with the other Hébertist radicals, but his logic of international liberation would provide the impetus for an Imperial France to embark upon the rape of Europe. (Thus one generation's idealist provides useful rhetoric for the next generation's greedy pragmatist!) I shall not say I foresaw the rise of Napoleon while I rode for Switzerland but my family's reputation for second sight is famous throughout Germany and my own gloom was enough to impart a certain accuracy to my prophecies.

Switzerland drew near. Villages came fewer and lodgings were scarce.

Close to Sainte-Croix I found shelter at last in a noxious farmhouse-turned-hostelry on a truckle bed set over boards through which I observed and heard the constant movement and noisy outpourings of three thin cows, my own horse, two dray mares and a pig, as well as a stable lad with a woman of uncertain age who set upon him halfway through the night and enjoyed him while he groaned and she grunted. It soon became impossible to determine if they retained their duet or if the pig had joined them.

The mingled stench of all these beasts became so overwhelming I believe it was this which at last set me off to sleep.

The next morning was blowing cold rain. My innkeeper, picking lice from beneath his belt, guessed the nearby river must surely flood by noon. He suggested I go by another road than that which led directly through Sainte-Croix. I, however, grew steadily troubled at the prospect of another day in France and did not wish to risk suspicion by avoiding the garrison. I told him I would take my chances with the ford.

He shrugged. There was heavy ice in it, he said, and if the current ran hard I stood a fair chance of being knocked from my horse.

Ignoring him, I signed a paper in the name of the Committee, assured him the State would settle as soon as he presented himself with the paper in Paris, and set off, head down, into the stinging wind which, carrying frozen rain, threatened to lacerate both nag and self.

The wind increased. The branches of bare elms waved like the limbs of drowning starvelings.

I searched the sky in hope of an interlude; but the grey clouds raced on to be replaced by others.

I shivered in my greatcoat and tried to spur the reluctant beast to greater speed. If her circulation stopped I feared she would freeze, a statue, in her tracks. We went by a creaking windmill of ancient black wood and whitewashed stones. The sails complained and shrieked as they slowly turned, though they ground no corn.

By about eleven o'clock we passed through Sainte-Croix, a pretty little village of stone and slate and carved wood where, to my surprise, the garrison consisted of two or three dozing soldiers. I guessed the rest had been called upon other errands and I congratulated myself on my good fortune. I showed my papers and explained how I was on government business, keeping a rendezvous with a Swiss agent of ours. They innocently accepted all I told them and wished me luck in my work. The Swiss border was only a mile or two on the other side of the river.

Now snowy alpine foothills with their evergreens offered a modicum of shelter from the weather until I came at last to the ford.

As foretold, slabs of ice tumbled and clapped, rushing in a foaming torrent all but obscuring the narrow causeway I must cross.

With considerable cursing and some hesitation, I urged my poor steed knee-deep into the chilly tide.

Water clawed my boots like the fingers of some furious Arctic troll and I was halfway across, using scabbarded sword to push away larger slabs of ice, before I heard a cry from the bank ahead.

Peering through spray, rain and mist, I made out a group of mounted men amongst the pines. My attention was distracted long enough for a block of glowing ice to rake against my horse's chest, causing her to whinny and skitter in the water and almost lose her footing on the causeway.

"Hold, gentlemen, I pray you!" cried I above the wailing rain. I feared they would begin to cross before I had reached their side and thus risk all our lives. "I shall soon have reached your bank, then you can ford. But if you startle my horse or your own, likely none of us will get to our destination!"

Either they heard me and fell silent or they had no more to communicate. They did, however, seem content to wait for me.

My horse remained in her agitated condition and I was soon obliged to dismount, lest we both fall. Though the foam threatened to drown me I nonetheless plunged into the deeps, then eventually found shallower waters which came only to my breast.

With relief I struggled at last into the calmer reaches and stood, gasping and quaking, beside the muddy, root-knotted bank.

I felt sure my breath must freeze in the air or turn solid in my lungs. Both my horse and I were shivering. It was a minute or two before I could give an eye to the dark figures who, seated upon the backs of big horses, regarded me with impassive concentration.

They were soldiers by the look of them. Renegades were frequently found between borders when countries disputed by lifting the Law against Murder and dignifying its commission as a necessity of War.

I put hand to pocket and clasped the damp butt of a barker. The pistol was useless.

If these horsemen were indeed thieves, my sword was my only defence.

They continued to be patient. Several more minutes went by as if they waited for me to catch my breath and straighten my back.

I, naturally, became watchful, yet tried to seem unwary and not a bit concerned by them, speaking aloud to myself and to them, commenting on the foulness of the weather and the need of a bridge over the river. Still they did not reply.

It was only when I made to remount my horse that one of the riders broke away from the rest and advanced down the bank, keeping his huge horse to a calculated walk.

This man had handsome aquiline features, pale under a broad forehead and thick, black brows. His long hair hung in pigtails about his face and he wore a large bicorne on the back of his head, brim pinned so it would not lose its shape in the rain. From the gulleys so formed water poured upon the shoulders of his leathern cape wrapping his body to the knees. From the cape protruded a dark sleeve and a white gauntlet gripping reins and pommel. His boots, too, were black, the tops turned over to reveal soft brown inner leather.

The rider's thin lips pursed as he drew his horse in before me and looked me up and down.

"Good morning, citizen," I called with false good cheer. "D'ye plan to ford here? 'Tis, as you have seen, just possible."

"We've already crossed, Sir," said the pale one, "and proceed towards Nyon. Yourself?"

"On State business, citizen." I gave him my habitual reply.

"Then we share an honour," he said. He appeared to be quietly amused.

Meanwhile, as this exchange took place, his men moved forward, positioning their horses so that they formed a barrier across the muddy road.

I listened to the pines creaking and dripping. The air was full of their scent mingled with the lushness of the forest mould, the warm stink of damp horseflesh.

"Citizen," said I, ignoring all these alarming signs, "I thank ye for your courtesy in waiting to see that I crossed safely." I was reaching the conclusion that I had found Sainte-Croix's garrison. Reins in hand I trudged up the bank, my nag snorting as she tried to shake her mane free of water. The river crashed and howled behind me. As I approached him, the pale man dismounted. He came stalking to offer me a hand for my final step up to the road.

His eyes were black as the devil's and full of that secret amusement either denoting superior intelligence or chronic short-sightedness. "Your name, citizen?" His tone was friendly enough.

"Didot," said I. "Carrying orders from the Committee."

"Indeed? Then we're comrades. My name is Montsorbier."

Now I placed him! We had met thrice before—once in Metz during some benighted Clootsian conference designed to bring revolution to Prussia and Belgium, then most recently in Paris when Danton had arranged for deputies to question officers of the National Guard. He was famous for his zeal at sniffing out royalists. But our earliest meeting he was less likely to recall for it had not taken place in France. It had been in Munich, before either of us was a declared servant of the people. Both incognito, members of the same secret metaphysical brotherhood, we had been dedicated to scientific enquiry, the evolution of Man's natural equality, rather than to the unpleasant practicalities of turning the world upside-down. His name had been the Vicomte Robert de Montsorbier then. Mine had been Manfred, Ritter von Bek.

For all his rather elegant sans-culottism, de Montsorbier was as natural a son of the People as myself. Blood flowed in his veins blue as my own, though like me he had renounced privilege. Originally a follower of Laclos, he was now under the spell of Cloots and other extreme Hébertists. To him Robespierre was a lily-livered conservative and Marat a feeble, weak-stomached revolutionist-manqué.

I prayed the grime of travel and the stubble of my lower face would offer sufficient disguise. When next my fellow ex-Illuminatus addressed me I changed my voice to a wheedling whine.

"From whom are your orders, citizen?" he asked.

"From the Commune, citizen. I'm commissioned by Citizen Hébert himself." This, of course, to impress Montsorbier.

"You have your documents?" He stretched out a gauntleted hand. Silver drops of rain fell on the black leather of his cloak. "Citizen," he moved his fingers, "I must see your documents."

"By what Authority?" said I.

"By the People's!" said he, all full of righteous pomp.

I held hard to my role. "By which of their representatives are

your own orders signed, citizen? I believe I must ask to see yours
before I can reveal mine. They are secret."

"Mine also."

"We are close to the border. Our enemies surround us on
almost every side. You might be a Prussian, citizen, for all I know."
I could only attempt to carry him in a rush, an attack of my own.

"It is you, citizen, has the accent, not I." His reply was calm,
still containing amusement. "I'm true-born French. But you, Citizen 'Secret Orders,' have both the voice and the demeanour of a
German!"

"I'll not be insulted. Is Lorraine Germany? I'm a loyal republican. A revolutionist before ever you aristos pulled off your calfskin
boots to play at peasants as you played Arcadians under Louis."
Aggression was my only remaining rhetorical weapon.

Montsorbier frowned. "Why so insulting of a sudden? Is it fear
makes you snap like an otter in a trap, citizen? Why are you
afraid?" A finger crooked and his five men dismounted, pulling
muskets from their backs and readying them. Whereupon I
swung up into my saddle, drove spurs deep into my poor mare's
flanks and rode straight through them. The nag's hoofs slipped in
the mud, her nostrils blubbered, her mane flew, and muskets shot
off in every direction, their balls whistling about us. All missed.
Pretty soon I had left the road and was galloping over deep leafy
moss in the hope of evasion, of crossing into Switzerland without
troubling the borderguards.

Montsorbier's voice was still too close as he yelled to his men
to stop reloading and follow me, but their confusion had given me
a minute's start and I meant to use the old hunter to my advantage. One thing she was used to was a chase over rough ground.
Thus I had the smallest chance of escape and even should I be
cornered I'd be able to choose territory more easily defended.
With that in mind I had my sword unscabbarded, though its
unique Tatar workmanship would identify me at once to anyone
who knew aught of me.

Suddenly I was out of the forest and riding uphill between
snowdrifts, rocks and brush, blundering into depths which near

drowned the horse, breaking through; galloping over virgin, rain-spotted tracts of white, while behind came a floundering halloo; like drunk English huntsmen, all ways in the saddle, legs sliding, bridles hauling up resistant heads, muskets going off— only Montsorbier himself rode at full gallop after me, his face against his horse's neck, his hair flying and tangling with the stallion's mane, his hat askew, a great pistol in his left hand, the harness in his right: a true rider with a horse to match his skill.

My own skill was equal if not better. My nag, to my misfortune, was not. A pistol sounded in the frozen air and I heard the ball hiss, saw snow start up and flint shiver immediately ahead. I felt relief that with his pistol discharged Montsorbier and I came closer to parity. If he drew far enough ahead of his own men it would be worth fighting him in the hope of gaining a better horse as my prize.

I heard him shout: "Von Bek, I know you!" This from a yard or two away. I wondered how far it was to the border.

"Stop, traitor! Stop, you damned royalist. You'll be tried fair!" He was near to pleading with me, even offering me terms. He knew as well as I, however, that death was the only consequence of arrest in those days; so on I chased, risking all, driving my poor nag far too quick, hoping for some sign we were on Helvetian soil where Montsorbier would follow only so far. We vaulted a frozen stream, careered through copses, came close to falling on a dozen hidden outcrops, both mindless of the danger; while I panted and prayed the rush of air would dry my pistols or that Montsorbier, now half a mile from his nearest soldier, would fall at the next jump—leaving his mount unhurt.

"Von Bek, you need not die!" shouted my thin-lipped hounder-of-Dukes and off went his second barker with a bang loud enough to stop my heart and I'm demmed if powder didn't singe the sleeve of my miserable greatcoat.

"Zeus!" thought I. "It will be the worst end any man ever had to face—to meet his Maker in a third-hand artois and a dirty neck-cloth."

This consideration alone was enough to power the heels which rammed the rowels into my poor beast's bleeding flanks and she was over a hedge so neatly trimmed I would swear it belonged to some Swiss Landsdorf; though the rest of the fields seemed too rich for that notoriously impoverished mountain folk, whose main industry was the export of mercenary soldiers to various Courts abroad, especially to Rome. The Pope trusted them to guard him because, like hireling brigands everywhere, their firmest loyalty was to a full purse. Fanatic purpose is a mystery few Swiss can comprehend. They are not as a rule subject to fits of Idealism. Their lives have been too hard for long centuries so that, rich or poor, their main desire is for a warm hearth and a full belly. Only my friend La Harpe ever had any imagination amongst those mountaineers and his was essentially a practical quality, not much coloured by excess.

Next I was sliding. With ears flat, back legs bent as if to squat, my horse bore us down towards a shallow valley brimming with unbroken snow. Some distance off, through the sleet, I detected a single low, thatched house, from which gusted piney smoke. Another shot made me look up. At the crest of the hill stood Montsorbier, reloading his second thunderer and calling after me "Fool!" as if somehow I'd betrayed good taste and common sense by evading capture.

My mare reached the valley floor, tried to stand in six foot of yielding snow, then keeled over with a groan and lay panting. She looked at the grey sky with unseeing, rolling eyes and enough steam issuing from her to power one of Trevithick's monstrous road-engines. I disentangled my foot from the stirrup and peered back at Montsorbier, who now waved white and cried "Parley." But the scarf was not easily visible amidst the general whiteness so I felt free to assume I had seen nothing and dragged out one of my own pistols. The lock sparked but the powder in the pan refused ignition, so I lost my best opportunity to rid myself of that troublesome foe.

"Truce!" he yelled. "We've something to discuss, brother." He was referring to older loyalties, but I was never much convinced of Illuminati advertisement and was contemptuous of his ploy.

"Henceforth the world transforms herself without my help," I called back. "Let me go, Montsorbier. I'm no traitor, as you of all people must accept."

"I have read the Document of Arrest!" His breath poured in clouds and I expected to see in it the captions of a political cartoon. He was hoping to keep me fixed until his men arrived. Yet argument is one of my great temptations. Though I risked death for remaining where I was, I found myself replying.

"A mere restatement of the original tune, Montsorbier. Choose what you wish to believe. My reason for leaving France is that Truth's become altogether too malleable. I'll not revise my life and experience to accord with Theory. Robespierre imposes only his disappointment upon a broken dream. I refuse to be a victim of his dementia. Shall we guillotine the whole world if she refuses to accord with our original optimism?"

"You leave France in her moment of greatest need, like all the fine-talking fashion-plates who thought Revolution must come with the passing of a few hours, the changing of a few names."

I felt no pang of guilt. "I leave, Sir, because Robespierre wishes to lay blame everywhere but upon himself and his crazed delusions. Those delusions, Sir, would lose me my head. My motive therefore is singular. More to the point, I'd assay, than your own. Is this Switzerland, by the by?"

"The border's a league or more to the north."

I began inspecting my saddlebags. "I'll be upon my way, I think."

"You have made an enemy of me, von Bek."

"An honest enemy's preferable to a perfidious friend, Citizen Montsorbier. Good afternoon to ye." I made to revive my horse, but she had died as we talked. Montsorbier's dark brows were drawn together in a triumphant frown. I unstrapped my bags, considered the saddle and chose to leave it, for it was in even worse condition now than when I had bought it at the ostler's. I began to wade out of the ditch, hearing Montsorbier yelling from the horizon above (he had retired and was at that moment invisible).

231

Ten paces later another pistol belched at my back but I ignored it. "Lecher!" cried my miserable ex-fraternalist. "Libertine! Turncoat! You'll not escape your punishment."

Pretty soon I heard a scrabbling and confused shouting from the hillside. All the horsemen were cautiously descending. Montsorbier led them.

Perhaps, after all, I was still on French soil? I began to experience a dull expectation of death. I was helpless to evade so many mounted men. However, I maintained my direction and waded at last onto stonier ground, a track which appeared to pass the cottage ahead. I turned to see how far behind me they were.

Their horses were tired and encumbered by the deeper drifts, yet it would not be long before I was caught. I drew my Tatar scimitar and dropped my saddlebags, running for the shelter of a nearby copse. Then I stopped in fresh apathy.

Along the road before me came another detachment of some half a dozen well-equipped horsemen. All had muskets on their shoulders, giving them the appearance of regular soldiery.

It was plain, then, that Montsorbier had driven me into a trap.

Chapter Two

*In which I encounter young Revolutionists, old soldiers,
fresh friends and foes. I also fall in love.*

A S THEY UNLIMBERED carbines from their sturdy young backs,
the martial party also moved their horses, to form a wall
across my road. At this, I considered throwing myself on their
.mercy—of surrendering in the hope they were regular soldiery,
famously more merciful than the People's peace-keepers. I instantly
experienced self-disgust: since I was to die anyway, I determined to
do so with a degree of dignity. Thus disposed, I put the point of my
sabre to the frozen ground and my wrist upon my hip, in the attitude of a duellist awaiting his "en garde." However, when six
Brown Besses bellowed in unison I was astonished (for the accuracy of the English gun was famous) first that I was not struck and
secondly that I was not the target at all. I turned my head.

Four of the National Guard were down. One horse kicked on
the ground with red foam starting from his mouth. Two men
gasped over cracked leg-bones, while two more, with arms flung
back against the snow, were stone dead. Montsorbier himself was in
momentary retreat, riding hard for the security of what remained
of his squadron and yelling of "demmed Swiss gentlemen-bandits!"

Of a certainty his description could have been truth. The young
men shooting from the saddle were all decently dressed, used to
hunting customs, and were armed in uniform, even to the swords
at their belts (though the fashion they adopted was a year or two
past). I was reminded of youthful German landowners taking the
opportunity of a holiday jaunt to Munich or Nuremberg. But
their sashes, I would swear, contained the red, white and blue of
Revolution.

I decided we must surely be in Switzerland. Montsorbier knew, as well as I, the French government's policy of respecting Helvetian territory. Angering the Swiss Confederation could hamper France's policies elsewhere. If Montsorbier took my mysterious allies for Swiss, then Swiss they must surely be.

My adversary was wounded. Even as he rode he clutched his shoulder, swaying badly. Reaching his own ranks, he lost his balance in the saddle then fell directly into the arms of a comrade whose own leg was damp with blood. The great black Spanish courser drew up her knees, snorting her bafflement at being suddenly riderless. Fate offered a favoured second. Sword in hand I demanded all of my legs and ran towards my pursuers, met the first head on, cut him down, and with a final thrust of my calves mounted Montsorbier's Spaniard, turning her round once more towards Switzerland and the unknown landsmen.

These elegant youths were casually repriming their muskets as I galloped up. They were laughing and talking amongst themselves like lordlings at the pigshoot, careless or unexpectant of retaliation.

"I'm much obliged, gentlemen," said I with a finger to my hat.

One of their number, a boy with red cheeks and yellow hair, bowed in his saddle. "Always ready to serve a citizen of the Republic." His French was uninspired, his accent German by its gutturals. "Those Swiss dogs have no nerve for an honest fight, eh, brother?"

"Just so," said I, baffled by his logic but grateful for the mistake. "Just so, citizen." I was close to laughter as I realised how Montsorbier, by choosing to travel incognito, without flags or cockades, had defrauded himself of my skin!

The Germans again levelled their muskets on their shoulders, but this time they fired high, in impressive unison. At which Montsorbier and his remaining men made their way with unseemly haste to the terraces and bushes of the valley walls. For a moment my Hébertist pursuer stood upright, scowling and shaking his healthy arm at me. "Ye've not escaped me for long," cried he like a brigand in some Ritter-und-Räuber tale. "I'll find thee, von Bek!"

But I was laughing hard behind my hand, realising I was the

only one of us to be wearing the full sash and favour of the Revolution. He hesitated, then turned his back sharply, stamping up the hillside until he was gone from sight.

"See them scamper!" One of these merry youths rocked in his saddle and joined me in my laughter. "Is this France, monsieur?"

I used my amusement to disguise my further surprise and managed to utter a muffled "I thought this Vaud, in Switzerland!"

Their red-cheeked spokesman holstered his musket and rode closer to me. "In confidence, Sir, we're lost. We were seeking the border when we came upon you."

"I'm mighty pleased ye did, Sir. Pray, why d'ye travel to France in these times?"

He was proud of his moral nobility. I saw in him my own self of only a few years since. "We go to offer our services to the Revolution in the name of the Universal Republic."

I retained some fragments of my old conscience and believed I owed it to them to reveal at least an outline of what they must find now in France.

"The Revolution will welcome you as she welcomed me," said I. I began to mop sweat from my forehead. "Where do you come from, gentlemen?"

The answer to this simple question was also of some pride to them. A swarthy little cockerel in a red-edged tricorne on a slightly yellowed wig walked his horse past me. "Two from Poland, two from Bohemia, one from Venice and one from Wäldenstein," he informed me. He reached my fallen saddlebags and leaned down to pluck them up. He rode back as slowly as he had gone. "We're part of a club, monsieur, dedicated to Republicanism and the Rights of Man. We were chosen by our fraternity to ride to France and offer our services to the Cause. We are only six, but we are the representation of more than a hundred others. Their subscription equipped us!"

"Gold well-spent," murmured I with considerable sincerity and gratitude, since they had saved my life.

"I'm named Alexis Krasny," said the leader. He pointed out his comrades, one by one: "Stefanik" (moon-faced, bashful), "Poliakoff" (assured but a little dim-witted by the look of him), "Staszekovski" (gloomy, sardonic, dark), "Ferrari" (the swarthy cockerel, who now handed me my bags), "and von Lutzov" (pale, Slavic, grinning). "We saw your colours and bethought the Swiss sought to stop you reaching the safety of your homeland."

"Indeed, Citizen Krasny, that's a good guess at the facts." I was getting the feel of my Spanish thoroughbred, believing it might soon be necessary to choose swift flight once more. "My name's von Bek."

"Mary's teeth, Sir!" Stefanik was admiring and joyful. "Not the same who went to France with Cloots?"

I saw further advantage, so acknowledged him gracefully. A modest bow.

"This is an honour," said Ferrari, suddenly less of a bravo, and the others joined in the flattering chorus. In truth I had no notion of my fame and unfortunately became still more conscientious in the light of this new responsibility. "I'd advise you," says I to the whole party, "that I'm no hero to the Republic. Paine is jailed, so could Cloots himself be by now. Half the people who came with us to Paris are either dead, in prison or fled. Robespierre rules France as a King, and Terror attacks innocent and guilty alike."

"Yet the tricolour remains in your hat, Sir," said Krasny in boy-ish innocence.

"So it does, Sir." I was in two minds. Would these young ideal-ists, if told my whole circumstance, the mistake they had just committed, promptly turn upon me and arrest me?

"Thus, Sir, you show yourself not completely disillusioned," said Stefanik, his round face glowing in the cold air. "If all men of good will employed their energies in our Cause, the injustices can surely be corrected? We have travelled a great distance, Sir, to assist in your struggle. We met with suspicion and ostracism all the way from Austria and even here, in Switzerland." He put a thumb upon his discreet sash.

I feared that, in giving him the negative view, I pulled the very bread of life from a baby's hand. "You'll meet with great suspi-cion in modern France, gentlemen. Foreigners are almost all assumed natural traitors by the Mob. And the Mob has no taste for fine argument. You'd be dead and stripped before you could cry 'Jacobin.'"

Krasny fought for his bit of spiritual sustenance. "I fear that's mighty hard to believe, Sir. Schiller, Beethoven, Wilberforce, Pestalozzi, de Pauw—George Washington himself—are all honorary citizens of France. As you are, Sir. It is a brotherhood extending beyond nations—"

"No longer!" I raised my hand, bored and even afeared of these familiar phrases. "Believe me, I beg you, gentlemen. Turn your attentions to some other moral purpose. That of Poland's liberty, for instance. Her plight is more easily comprehended."

"Poland wants nothing but a king and bishops free to exploit what Russia and Prussia already claim for themselves," said Staszekovski. "Cloots preaches International liberation of the common people. So we concluded, in conversation amongst ourselves, that Poland's freedom begins in France."

"Cloots's freedom ends in France." I swore at myself for my foolishness in pressing this point. "And mark me, my young brothers, so shall your own!"

Krasny avoided my snatch at his heart's food and was firm in his reply. "We shall try our luck, at any rate, citizen, though we respect your opinions. Can we escort you part-way on your journey, Sir? Do you head for Dijon?"

I stretched a hand behind me. The last of Montsorbier's men could be observed labouring up to the crest of the steep hillside. "France lies yonder—where those guardsmen flee." I hesitated for a moment. "Myself, I journey to Lausanne. My revolutionary years ended with the last days of this past December. And why, Monsieur Krasny, should you ever wish to leave the sanity and justice of Wäldenstein? By repute she's the most contented nation on Earth!"

"Contented burghers make poor insurgents," he said soberly. "It's dull, my homeland, with self-importance and piety."

"Then, Sir," said I, "it is plain to me it's the Romance and Adventure of revolution you're hungry for. You'll find plenty of the latter in France just now, probably to your cost, but your romantic notions will scarcely survive, I think." •

Up piped the young Slav, von Lutzov. "Surely, Sir, if France's situation is as you describe, our ideals are unfounded and the world is ruled by the Seven Vices, by the Devil Himself!"

"Your hopes are not unfounded, Sir," I replied. "Neither shall I presume to question your generosity, your optimism, your faith— even your capacity to impose a little justice here and there upon our world. It is your sense of the horrid realities of life which is faulty, what we may truly term the 'common' sense. It was lack of this sense, of a proper education in the motives of the vulgar people, which brought me to this pass."

At the sound of what they might reasonably believe to be familiar pomposity they became impatient and showed their mood by many little gestures—arranging their harness, straightening their backs in their saddles, adjusting their spurs, pulling their hats forward on their heads. These signs I took as indications that persuasion was impossible, so I saluted them. "I bid you *bon voyage* and *bonne chance*, gentlemen. I thank ye for my rescue. I trust, in turn, you keep your heads." Whereupon I rode my fine new horse, replete with a sabre and pistols holstered on an excellent Castillian saddle, towards the cottage where now two women, one young, one middle-aged, stared from their gate.

"Then if you flee France, Sir," came Krasny's puzzled complaint, "who were the soldiers?"

"Members of the national army, Sir. That which serves the Committee of Public Safety."

I plucked the cockade from my hat and threw it back to Krasny. Then I was off at a smart trot, bowing to the ladies and complimenting them on the prettiness of their valley. "The loveliest in Vaud." They grinned and did not contradict me. I was in Switzerland! The mountains ahead of me were clear of political sanctities and hypocrisies; all I need fear in them were the usual natural dangers and the attacks of brigands who, if they cut my throat, would do it not for a cause but for a crust or two of bread. The air had a wholesome freshness to it of a sudden.

The road again grew steeper and the snow heavier as I ascended into the Alps proper. Peaks were soon in view as the sky cleared to a vivid blue. I, like Nature, was suddenly tranquil; she revealed herself, noble and monumental, in white and green, with black veins of rock and snow-covered pastures. Here, from time to time, little cottages, their thatched roofs stretching almost to the ground, crouched in sheltered ridges. Rooks and crows sprang up into the air at the vibrations of my trotting Spaniard. Those enormous pinnacles were one of the most uplifting sights on Earth, outstripping even the Appalachian grandeur of America, the only others I have witnessed to compare (lately I have seen engravings of the Rocky Mountains which seem, if the artist has not exaggerated, an equal to the Alps).

This vast pile of natural beauty, those crags and fir trees and hovering hawks, those echoing ravines and vast tumblings of snow and earth, brought me swiftly to the understanding of my own insignificance and, indeed, the insignificance of all human struggle. Thus absorbed in philosophic generalities, I scarcely noticed the growing twilight in my admiration of a scarlet sunset staining every detail with its bloody light. As luck would have it I was once again upon a fair-sized "toby" as my old friends of vagabond days used to call the high road. Twice I was passed by coaches whose drivers informed me of a reasonably clean and cheaply priced inn some five miles distant.

As the sun faded I entered a kind of corridor of trees whose interwoven branches blocked almost all the remaining light and whose sweetness of scent came close to overwhelming me so it seemed I entered another World, a World where Winter had turned to Spring and peace triumphed universally. Soon after, I heard the rattle of a four-horse coach ahead, travelling at fair speed. As I approached, the driver whipped his horses recklessly, almost as if he feared pursuit. The thought came to me that perhaps this road had a reputation for attracting rogues and highwaymen. I passed him with a friendly halloo, so as to assure him of my own pacific intent, but he did not answer, save to crack his long whip over his team. He had a lantern on a post by his head and it cast shadows into his cape:

all I could detect were eyes reflecting the yellow light. Was it my fancy made those eyes appear to glare at me with unwarranted ferocity? Whether this was true or no, I changed my mind about requesting his permission to ride beside his lantern. The darkness, indeed, became attractive by comparison. I left his cold yet fiery gaze in the tunnel as I broke out onto a grey landscape now considerably colder and with the mountains forming a black wall on every side. My clothing was still damp. I was like to freeze on my newly stolen saddle if I did not reach the inn soon after dark. If the air had not been dry, in keeping with the altitude, I might well have perished there and then.

At last I perceived a glimmering on the curve of the road and this soon became the cheering diffused glow of several fires, lamps and candles on the other side of thick green glass panes, while a sign on a gallows-post proclaimed the building as *Le Coq D'Or* (almost every hostelry in Switzerland was named so in those days, the Swiss prizing conformity above all else) while beyond this was an archway leading to a large courtyard. The inn was of good size and thoroughly appointed. I was approving as, very soon after my entry into the yard, ostlers with candle-boxes were immediately on hand to take the bridle and lead my horse to a well-earned grooming and a meal of oats.

Saddlebags shouldered and cloak dusted off as best it could be, I made my way through passages of old oak and older stone to the public room. Here I stood beside the fire, steaming away like a coster's brazier and causing chagrin to two priests, an Yverdon farmer and a couple of heavily armed freelance warriors on their way, they said cautiously, to enlist with the Prussians and save France. I had unwound my sash and stripped off my jackboots and greatcoat for the one-eyed innkeeper to take to his wife for her attention, but doubtless I remained the picture of the Communard, with my lank hair, unshaved face and ungentlemanly apparel. "It will take more than a pair of Switzer bravos to do that," said I. "But you might as well try. For my own part I've failed in the attempt, which is why I am presently taking myself as far from France as possible. Let 'em rot, is my view!"

"You're just come out of France then, Sir," said the elder priest in the eager accents of Provence. "What news for us?"

I was no friend of his class, but yet was in little mood for judging or lecturing. I told him simply that priests were no longer being murdered piecemeal, which was true. "But Guillotin's machine remains at work night and day, in capital and departments alike," I added. "Many believe this will only end if Robespierre himself is killed. My opinion is that he's too cautious to expose himself to a Mademoiselle Corday."

"So he remains the people's darling," said the old priest in a sour tone.

"Let the Mob stay on his side," I said, putting mulled wine of poor sweetness to my lips, "and he'll rule France for ever. If the Mob turns—and 'tis ever a fickle creature—he'll fall."

"Yet that event's unlikely, eh?" The priest was anxious for my denial. I could not give it.

"Sir," said I cruelly, "it is impossible." (Which speaks poorly for our family's famous "second sight.")

At this, the priest's novice chimed in with a peal or two of his own. He was an angular, spiderish creature, prominently pale, with a tendency to blubber his lips when he spoke. "Truly the devil's come to Earth. This Robespierre is the Anti-Christ so many have predicted. He will rise to his greatest power next year."

"Demme, Sir," I retorted, "if the Anti-Christ has not been predicted every other month since Anno Domini One! How many can there be? If there were as many about as the oracles predict, we'd be knee-deep in 'em. There would be more Anti-Christs on Earth than ordinary folk." I found myself grinning at my own jest and I looked about the room. "The odds are that seven out of every eight people at this inn are Anti-Christs!"

This set the martials to guffawing but it merely made the young priest bluster. Before he could reply to me, however, a clerkish fellow spoke up from the back. I had seen him slip in a few moments before. He wore the weeds of a bookman and he ran his gloved fingers up and down his beaker with that distant air of private mirth so common to many of his calling—the kind who have much borrowed wisdom but little original wit. "Is not the French mob as you describe, Sir? Could you not argue for the congregation of a mass of Anti-Christs as opposed to one? Would that congregation not be more effective than a single individual? Could Robespierre be no more than the crest upon the cockerel, the cockerel comprised in turn of a million peasants (or what have you?)?"

"Perhaps, Sir, perhaps," said I, scenting a tame bore, as it were, wandered in from the barren forest of unearned Learning. But this was not enough to stop him. One could tell how pleased he was with his humour:

"And might not that cockerel be in reality a cockatrice, his claws the claws of Hellish revenge upon Christ's followers—his breath the breath of Damnation, to set afire the whole world as a beacon summoning all our souls to judgement?"

This aroused curiosity only in the wretched, blubbering novice, who must come in eagerly with: "You ask these questions, Sir, as if the answers are already known to you."

The older priest turned to his Latin chapbook and his cup of ale, clearly no more willing than myself to maintain this deadly flow.

"I merely converse, brother," said the bookman piously. "I offer speculation, never opinion."

I was determined not to be trapped between this pair, so yawned loudly and spoke crudely, with the impatience of a dedicated revolutionary official. "Well, Master Schoolman, the majority here are uninterested in your fancies. Speaking for myself, my feet are planted four-square on this hearth-stone. My brain's weary and capable of handling only the simplest of facts, connected with my body's necessities. Imagination brings only bad luck, believe me. Mine at least had a little originality in its day. Yours, Sir, is all on hire from a library. By God, Sir, it gives off a dust which even now irritates my nose! Let me not sneeze, Sir, all over your fine weeds."

At my snub he retired into his demi-octavo, but I was still threatened by his blushing co-philosopher, the novice priest. I turned on

him with the habits of one who has been both a professional fighting man and a professional politician. "As for Robespierre," said I,
remarking to my surprise how the novice became unnaturally coloured, as if blood slowly filled up a parsnip from within, "he's the
very model of fallible mankind." The novice was taking as a personal matter my slighting of the clerk. "I know him well enough,"
I continued. "He's vain. His vanity's hurt by the world's refusal to
accept his remedies and become immediately Enlightened. And
what does a vain man do when insulted, Sir?"

The novice was now red as a boiled-over cooking pot. He
hissed a little at me; it seemed all his liquors were evaporating.

"He lashes out, Sir," says I. "He seeks to portion blame. He
fumes, Sir. He attacks. In the case before us, such is his despotic
power, he kills. He kills, Sir. He wars on other nations. Mary's
blood, Sir, but this poor sphere of ours suffers more from the
single, frustrated egoist than from any natural—or supernatural—
misery. Your own Church's history, Sir, illustrates my point well
enough, eh? We are too frequently in the power of mad children,
who rage and stamp and break Kingdoms as they break toys. They
order thousands of deaths a day as if they were spoiled brats kicking at their dolls!" I had overstretched my statement and, foolishly,
through my weariness, invited further reply.

"Those who respect God do not behave thus," said our Proven-
çal priest very primly.

I uttered a laugh. "The Pope cannot respect God in that case,
Sir. I'll not attack your Faith, father, but all your Church provides
for is a superior excuse for the same behaviour as Robespierre's,
sometimes expressed quite as dramatically, and executed with
much the same apparent self-control as the dictator's. Was Riche-
lieu any less guilty than Robespierre? The Huguenots did not
think so. And the Cardinal also acted, he said, for the good of
France."

The priest shook his head at this. "You have witnessed much
distress, my son."

I bridled. "Sir, I am not your son. Your choice of words assumes
an authority over me you do not possess." My radicalism, I

thought to myself, was going to be less easily suppressed than I had supposed.

His miserable wheedling having failed to gain him his expected effect upon me, he became at once offended. "Your experience has taught you nothing, Sir." He raised himself to his feet and, with a fuss or two at his cassock, herded self and novice off to bed, disappointed in his hopes for a grateful penitent, a comfortable ally, in me.

The two mercenaries were amused and offered to stand me a further flagon. Since they were the only company I found at all congenial I accepted their proffered jugs and warmed my bones with the contents. The youthful soldier, who was called Bamboche, had a pronounced limp, which he used for self-mocking comedy; his merry face was of the kind, as we used to say, to charm its owner out of a noose. He was joining the Prussians to avenge his brother, he informed me. Bamboche major had been executed by the Revolution; he had been a member of Louis's own Swiss Guard. The older warrior was thick-set, matter-of-fact, a rogue with a cropped head, scars visible on every inch of his exposed skin. He told me that while he found French peasants obnoxious, their women were attractive enough; so fighting was better for him than staying at home where both women and men were unsightly. He had tried farming up beyond Geneva and had become bored. The work was no different in the effort expended, he said, but it took longer; one's free hours were far too few and the choice of one's company severely limited. His name was Olrik van Altdorf. He was a musketeer. He pointed to three swaddled guns in the corner. All good English pieces, he said, from Baker in London and rifled for greater range, though the "twist" was not as exaggerated as in some of Baker's other guns. You could lose in accuracy what you gained in distance. "But they make a good musketeer and his loader the equal to a platoon in battle at long range."

He was content to dismiss Politics and lecture me on weaponry. I was weary enough to listen with half an ear while his hobby-horse was ridden through half the countries of the world, the quality of their steel and their skills at gunsmithery fully discussed. At length, drunk, I was ready for bed. My two companions readily helped me up a flight or two of stairs to the garret with its row of truckles. Onto these, one by one, we fell, having made only the poorest effort to disrobe. Happily, they were no more fastidious and smelled no worse than I. My dreams were of pursuit, of ancient monsters growling and furious as they sought to break free of the earth's deepest caverns, of an astonishing sweetness of atmosphere which filled my whole being with happiness, of hellfire and Satan Himself, in a sea-green coat and a perfect cravat, hooking innocents by their pleading mouths and swinging them with busy aplomb into the furnaces. I awoke briefly in a sweat, put my nightmares down to bad company and worse wine, and returned to sleep, whereupon I dreamed I searched through rocky tunnels for the source of that sweetness I had earlier experienced.

In the morning, as we shared a jug of water and a basin, I asked the musketeers, since I must soon pass through that country, what they knew about Bohemia at the present time. They had little to offer. Austria, Herr Olrik informed me, was by all accounts an easy-going master. As a result, Bohemia was effectively self-ruling. "If you're unwelcome in all these empires, Sir," he suggested, "you should go to Venetia." He was adamant in his recommendation. The Republic of Venice, though somewhat severe in certain of her laws, would not penalise a properly contrite ex-revolutionist. With a smile of gratitude I told him that my Italian was poor and my Latin not much better. I was anxious that they should not learn my true destination, lest they inadvertently release the information to my pursuers. "I have a mind to make myself rich," I told Olrik. "I've been a poor fighting man all my life. I had thought to set up business in Prague where, in the main, persons of consequence speak my native German."

"Well," said Olrik with consideration, "I've been in service in Venice and I've seen service in Prague, too. The only two advantages of the latter is that she's closer to Berlin and has dryer streets." This simple joke heartily amused Bamboche who, in his response, nigh spilled water over us all. "But the whores are better-natured in Prague," added Herr Olrik as an afterthought, "if not so pretty. And cheaper, by my recollection, though I'm not a man as often had to part with silver for a woman's favours."

Holding back the remark that, since all men claimed the same thing, it was a wonder how the poor whores managed to keep body and soul together (moreover I preferred courtlier references to the fair sex) I withdrew from the conversation while I shaved off my whiskers with a dry razor, and then clad me in what had become my best: red Nankeen frock-coat, with waistcoat of a slightly paler shade, both held by amethyst buttons, sleek white buckhide breeches which clarified every muscle they covered, fine doeskin riding boots, and atop this a fair peruke in need of dusting but still with a trace of the old-fashioned violet powder I favoured. My linen was crisper than might reasonably be hoped, after its hasty cramming into my bags, and my neck-cloth came to my chin in a fairly decent ruffle.

I was again a dandy to rival Robespierre and with my sword buckled in its undisguised scabbard of royal blue gilded leather, I felt immediately more confident than upon the previous day. The soldiers, however, became less candid and friendly as my dress improved. I quickly mollified them with a wink, that they might guess me a rogue in gentleman's tailorings and, despite contrary appearances, still one of themselves. I made a sardonic leg which had the older man grinning and the lame boy howling again.

"One must dress rich to get rich," I observed. "And a widow who's not impressed by a rich man's fortune will frequently have her head turned by a poor man's breeches."

"Aha!" said Olrik approvingly. "So you have a plan to marry for your money?"

"For my initial capital only."

Olrik put one red butcher's hand upon my silken shoulder. "Then Prague is, after all, your best choice, brother." He stepped back from me, as if I were a painting in a gallery. "Those Venetian families are mighty clannish and careful what or whom their fortunes wed. The Bohemians, on the other hand, are always grateful for any attention!"

Gravely I thanked him for his advice and refused offence even when he added in a thoughtful tone: "Ye'd have to be able to use that odd-looking blade in Venice, whereas the Praguers are impressed merely by a flash of steel."

It was on my tongue's tip to take exception to this and boast of my Tatar training, but it would have shown poor taste other than to bow again, thank him graciously and find some token compliment in return. This latter proved unnecessary, for just then his attention was distracted by noises from outside and below us.

Olrik cocked an ear. It was the sound of booted feet and the jangling of a great many harnesses. I knew the signature of regular cavalry and could guess its identity. I picked up my saddlebags and descended the narrow stair to the first landing. Through a window I looked down into the innyard. The coach I had passed that night was being prepared for the road. I saw a pretty little lady's maid step in, her quick smile unreturned by the dour coachman who did not look quite such a sinister monster as he had in the gloom. On the coach's door I could now distinguish a discreet coat-of-arms which looked vaguely Oriental and was not at all familiar. I guessed the coach's occupants to have reached the inn soon after me and gone immediately to their chambers. I now hoped I had been wrong in my opinion I had heard hussars. Several sturdy fellows standing near the coach wore dark coats and were heavily armed. All had a French appearance but it was easily possible they were royalists turned brigand. However, I was swiftly informed of the truth when their leader emerged from the doorway below my feet. I saw only his back at first. He was tall and slender, his left arm bandaged inside his half-buttoned military coat. His tone was arrogant and impatient and I recognised it. Robert de Montsorbier had divested himself of his tricolour sash and, I guessed, was making no claims to represent the French government. He turned to speak to an ostler coming up behind him. Montsorbier's face was pale and set in harsh lines. "Prove it? Prove that my own horse belongs to me? Bah!" He had evidently found his stolen Spaniard.

Without a horse, I was afraid I should find escape impossible.

Nonetheless I crept down the remaining flight of stairs, entered the kitchen, found it deserted, picked up some cold pork and cheese, then returned to the stair to find a window where I could gain intelligence of Montsorbier's position. I had reached a higher landing when I was alarmed by a sweet voice speaking with great merriment from above.

"What, Sir? Can't pay the tally?"

I turned with thudding heart, barely remembering to hold the food away from my Nankeen coat. Half in shadow, half in a beam of Winter sunlight, stood a figure of the most striking good looks I had ever beheld. I could not initially be sure if it were youth or maiden, until she moved further into the light and I realised she wore skirts. Her head was large and almost negroid, though her complexion was fair; her dark eyes were huge and her wonderful face was framed by brown curls. It was her broad shoulders and slim waist which gave her a slightly masculine look. Here was a woman with whom I could immediately fall in love! She embodied, in flesh and blood, the ideal of whom I still occasionally dreamed.

I paused, chewing slowly on a bit of tough pork crackling, and stared at her. Then I recovered my good manners enough to bend my body like a gallant of old and (a Tatar gesture which stood me well in the West) salaamed to indicate that I was at her service.

I hoped she might be enchanted and it was true she seemed pleased by me, but she lost none of her clear-eyed assessment of my person. "Must I pay your reckoning for you, Sir? You are clearly a gentleman and I would not see you so demeaned as this!"

The crackling secreted in my hand, I shook my head. "You misunderstand, Madam. I'm pursued by enemies—king-slayers who'll kill me if I do not immediately escape them. I could fight half their number, but these are too many."

"You're a scallawag then, Sir? And those dutiful bully-boys who peer with such rudeness into my private carriage, are they policemen?"

"No, Marm. They serve the Public Safety Committee of France and I'm wanted as a royalist."

She absorbed this information, nodding to herself. She began to button up her coat, which was cut like a man's hunting jerkin, and to pull on long gloves as if she prepared for a day's hunting. "What's their leader named?"

"Robert de Montsorbier, Marm. But no threat can frighten him, no gold can pay him. He puts duty first and mercy a poor second."

"I know his kind. I, by the by, Sir, am called Libussa, Duchess of Crete."

The house was unknown to me, but it should have my loyalty for ever! Her bones seemed delicate but were strong and large. Her skin looked soft as fine silk and glowed with health, a kind of wholesome fieriness which spoke of great strength of soul and of purpose. Her face, so serious in repose, so bright when lit by a witty retort, was exquisite. She truly could have been the Goddess of Reason come down to Earth. So struck was I by her beauty and character that I checked my usual responses, the kind I would normally make to a pretty woman. Where otherwise I might have played amusing fop and plotted conquest, I could conceive of no game in which this fair madonna would not easily best me. I wished to have her respect more than I wished for anything in the world, so I merely presented myself, giving name and title, then stating my business and intentions.

"You'll require a friend to distract 'em while you escape, eh, Sir?" says she.

"Aye, Madam, 'twould be of great help."

"Then get you as close as you can to the stables, Sir."

I obeyed. I could have done nought else. I was mesmerised by her. Republican feet stamped upon the landlord's gravy-stained boards. I fled to the back cloakroom, becoming lost in a collection of clothing which stank of every animal under the sun (but chiefly of man), yet could still hear my benefactress addressing the Frenchers with haughty impatience.

Montsorbier's retort was swift:

"We seek a common horse thief, Marm, 'tis all. Should you come upon a little, blown-up gamecock of a fellow, either wearing a coat two sizes too big or breeches one size too small, I'd thank you for giving us word of him."

It was all I could do to stop myself from springing from my hiding place there and then and tearing his throat out with my own teeth. It was no comfort to me that his insults were the result of my having bested him so thoroughly the day before!

My Libussa's tone was now placatory and charming. "Indeed, Sir? Might his name have been von Bek?"

"So he styles himself, aye."

"Why, I saw him off last night. So that horse was not his own! Lud, Sir, and such a fine dapple. A half-Arab, I'd swear."

"Fresh horse," said Montsorbier, taking her red herring. "Which way, Marm, did the villain ride?"

"I cannot recall, Sir. My impression was that he travelled in our direction, however. Aye, I'd swear it. He said something of risking the danger alone. Well, Sir, that's the Lausanne road, of course. Since you'll be going in that direction, I take it you'll be kind enough to give us escort. At least part-way, Sir? The pass is famous for its brigands, is it not?"

"We chase von Bek." Montsorbier then addressed one who was evidently the innkeeper. "You dog—why did you not say he'd taken another mount?"

"I saw none missing, Sir." The innkeeper's voice quavered. "A dapple, you say, Madam? Perhaps, then, 'tis the property of one of the priests?" I heard them all tramp out of the inn and enter the front yard. Creeping from the closet I peered through a shutter onto the yard itself just as the two Helvetian Knights-at-Arms swaggered in view, all jutted scabbards and pistolled cross-belts, bits of leather and metal here and there almost at random upon their persons. Olrik sniffed and glanced challengingly at Montsorbier. "The dapple, Captain, was my beast."

The innkeeper was taken aback. "Yours was a roan, surely? I took her in myself!"

"The dapple, too, fool!" Olrik should have been a mummer in a pantomime, with his exaggerated gestures. "With the packs! The boy, here, was leading her. Bamboche. Now you remember, eh?"

In baffled defeat, the landlord acquiesced.

Olrik next strode up to Montsorbier, glaring directly into the angry Frenchman's face. Olrik spoke with measured insolence. "What company d'ye serve? Not cavalry by your rig and not infantry by your boots and arsenal. Ye've the smell of Frenchies to me. But what sort of Frenchy? Aristo? Or regicide? 'Tis plain ye ain't Confederation fellows."

I realised Olrik performed this charade in order to benefit me, to confuse the pursuer.

"I'm Swiss as you, Sir," muttered Montsorbier, sensing a ploy but uncertain as to its nature. "Now, Sir, you say this rogue took your dapple? A mare, was it?"

"Liar!" Olrik puffed himself up, rattling gorget and creaking harness. "Liar, I say, Sir! Ye're no Switzer!"

"From Berne," said Montsorbier in a small, terrible voice.

Olrik looked the enraged Montsorbier up and down, took a bend to one side, then to the other, arms akimbo. These were all the familiar tricks of a belligerent professional duellist and to be sure Montsorbier recognised them as well as I. But he refused the bait. He held his ground, face and neck bright red on his thin dark body, like a bloodied spear topped by a black shield. He hated Olrik but could not be sure how many comrades the mercenary could call upon, and he wanted no extra trouble since he was illegally in Switzerland.

"Where's your papers, Frenchy?" demanded the Swiss bravo.

"I'm on a private mission, Sir, and have no wish to fight a fellow soldier." Montsorbier gritted fine white teeth so hard I thought I'd hear them crumble to powder. "We hunt the man who stole your horse. He's sought in France for treason. Posted in Russia for an assassin. A rogue, through and through, Sir."

"Of which there are none in all the Helvetian republics, as you'd know if you were true Swiss. What's this fellow really stolen, Sir?" Olrik put his sinister, amiable face on one side.

"Your damned horse, Sir, for a beginning!" Montsorbier's temper released itself in a sound like steel leaving leather.

"What, the roan?"

Montsorbier turned to look at his uncertain followers. They seemed embarrassed, yet were hiding some amusement.

Young Bamboche limped back into my picture. Evidently he had returned from the stableyard. "Someone's taken the dapple!" His loud exclamation was so melodramatic he might have been another actor in the Italian Comedy. What was plain to me, however, was not plain to Montsorbier who had never served in the ranks nor got himself drunk with those who did. Bamboche was performing a ritual, old soldier style, which in itself was the normal preparation for a brawl.

"Why'd the German take your horse, comrade?" Bamboche looked this way and that, then fixed a glare upon Montsorbier. "Is this gentleman involved?"

"He's a French notary, apparently," said Olrik with feigned patience. "He claims my dapple's stolen by von Bek, who is like a brother to us!"

Bamboche turned round eyes upwards, questioning Montsorbier. "You say, Sir, you saw Captain von Bek riding my comrade's horse? When was this, Sir?"

"That was not my exact accusation." Montsorbier was cold now.

Bamboche looked at Olrik. "When did you find the horse gone?"

"I did not. The Frenchy says the roan's gone, too! Go to the stable and see." Olrik fixed Montsorbier with a stern glare. For my part, I'd fear for the Swiss if he and the other were matched in different circumstances. But the farce continued to be played through and My Lady Libussa and her maid looking on as if in a box at the Opera.

Montsorbier was hating being made to seem such a fool. He breathed slowly and looked hard at his turned-back cuffs, plucked at frogging, put the heel of his boot in slushy dirt and ground it as if crushing vermin. But all this while every individual in the yard understood that the tension could snap and bloody swordplay become the order of the day.

Raising a fresh-trimmed brow, my lady pouted to display a patch and this gesture filled me with shivering lust such as I had not known since Catherine used me in her game with Prince Pushkin, when I was young enough to thrill at any promise, being barely seventeen summers. But this excelled all previous sensation, even the episode with the Delaware woman I alluded to in my previous memoir. Blood! If this witch could move me with a smile, what ecstasies could her touch command? I was already Cupid's most abject slave. I dared not let myself speculate upon my chances of winning this lady's favours for I was already threatened by the madness of Eros, as if a love-potion and a remedy for failing ardour had been fed to me both at once. I was a man of Reason, said I to myself: a Cynic (though not the libertine of repute) who planned to marry a plain, rich woman and so found a great fortune. Yet I hoped that I had intrigued the lady, at very least. I had an undeserved reputation little short of Casanova's and sometimes this attracted women, particularly those who felt secure in their circumstances. The fact was that I knew little of the Empress's charms. I had been a pawn in some plot which doubtless had little point. Had I indeed been everything my legend credited me as being, I might doubtless be dead. Catherine rewarded discarded lovers, it was said, with icy death under her balcony. She was famous for her Pomeranian thrift.

Back came Olrik's loader. His tone was baffled and accusatory. "The roan's in her stable! Not even saddled!"

"So she can't be stolen," said Olrik reasonably. "You call a man Thief unjustly, Sir." Now he blossomed in his role, almost grinning at the furious Montsorbier. "No Swiss, no Swiss man of honour that is, no Swiss of any character at all, no Swiss person, however mean his station, would wish to be guilty of breaking the fifth (or is it the eighth?) Commandment. Are you satisfied, therefore, that the matter's settled, Sir? Shall you skulk back to your Democracy, Sir, and inform Monsieur Robespierre that you've accused a man wrongly?"

"He stole my horse," said Montsorbier. Accustomed always to having his way, to winning all arguments, to riding through all defences, he had not the sense to drop the debate there and then. "He stole my horse not twenty miles from here. At carbine-point.

I was shot by him and his company, Sir. Now play no more with me. I see you're a well-meaning fellow and you think you do right, but be assured, von Bek's a thief and a ruffian who wants a smart hanging."

"The black hunter was stolen?" asked Bamboche, his blue eyes still wider, in fine imitation of bumpkin simplicity. He should not be a soldier, thought I: he should be performing Molière. "The black horse, Sir? Big Spaniard, Sir? Saddle of fine Moorish-work? Madrid-style? Brass irons?"

Montsorbier saw what was planned. "Very well. I'll accept your verdict. I know my horse is here."

"A true Democrat, Sir. But look you, these priests may have a vote. What do you vote, brothers? Is von Bek a thief?"

The old, tonsured, dried-up Father Sebastian mumbled as he lurked back in the shadows of the gables.

"What's that?" Bamboche cupped his hand to his ear. The priest complained about "that scallawag's godlessness" and was convinced without any doubt I was all Montsorbier said me to be. "Is he a wanted outlaw?"

"Aye, Father," said Montsorbier politely to one of those whom he had cheerfully sent to the gallows in dozens only a few weeks earlier. "He has left a black trail across half the world. In Russia, through most of Europe, even in the Americas. A traitor to Saxony, assassin of crowns, he is Vice personified!" Montsorbier spoke with unseemly relish. I began to fear that my lady, my new light of existence, should believe him and was close to flinging myself through the shutters and, sword in hand, defending my honour to the death.

Master Olrik, however, was himself by way of defending my name as he moved on his insteps, a little closer to his prey. "You say, Sir, he's wanted in France? For what? For plots against the King, Sir? For betraying your enemies, the Saxons? I'm only a dim musketeer, Sir, and fail to understand these paradoxes. I'd be obliged, Sir, if ye'd enlighten me."

Montsorbier, so used to power and the obedience of others, was again locked into rageful inactivity. His anger did not best him, but he was white-hot by now and his fingers were lost in his fists. "I'm bored with this, Sir." His words were only audible for a yard or two and I should not have caught them had I not been familiar with his voice. "I'll drop all charges, and continue about my business."

"Charges? You've authority, Sir, here in Vaud?"

Montsorbier made a movement, little more than a twitch of his arm, and I feared for Master Olrik's life. As it happened, just then one of Montsorbier's disguised National Guard led into the yard the Spaniard I had borrowed. Montsorbier was all solicitous attention suddenly. He studied his saddle as if for scratches, noted that his pistols were still holstered and the sabre in place. He looked at his horse's eyes and teeth, felt her at her joints, reassured himself, in what seemed genuine anxiety, that she was unharmed. Then he put boot to stirrup, seated himself, and stared securely down at Olrik who stood leaning on the shoulder of Bamboche, the pseudo-simpleton. Montsorbier's eye was colder than all the snows of Switzerland. "I greatly hope you gentlemen shall soon find yourself in my part of the world, so that I may return your hospitality."

Another figure entered the picture and helped again to break that violent ambiance. Out came the schoolman in his Quaker hat and grey, inky cloak, with strapped, oilskinned books in a thong on his arm. His voice was blurred as if he had overslept. His skin, I noted, was almost as coarse and dirty a grey as his garments. "Is that the Lausanne coach?" says he, indicating my lady's carriage.

"'Tis the coach of the Duchess of Crete." Montsorbier offered a nod and a small smile to his only other potential ally in the gathering.

The clerkish fellow blinked, saw Milady, removed his hat to display greasy hair dressed in a kind of half-hung plait. He seemed to recognise her, or at least her title. "I'm Meister Carl Plattz, your ladyship." He was momentarily disturbed by what he understood to be a serious *faux pas* and stood fidgeting in the mud of the yard.

Montsorbier was easy-mannered, almost unctuous in his courtesies, as he, too, lifted his heavy bicorne. "We'll gladly ride escort to ye, Marm, until the pass is forwarded." He had found a graceful means of extricating himself from his embarrassment.

To disguise his own confusion, the schoolman shouted rudely at the innkeeper. "Not the Lausanne coach! Odd's fish, why are you all so late? I've waited an hour or more in my chamber, packed and ready. Snow will be falling by noon. Look!"

It was true that white armies of cloud appeared behind the eastern mountains.

Meister Plattz sighed. "What shall I do?" He readied himself for the plod back to his apartment. But then Milady, who had been speaking quietly to Olrik, called out from her window. "How far do you travel, Sir?"

O, how I wished she had addressed those words to me! My body was consumed with a fresh wave of flame.

"To Lausanne. My post is in Lausanne." Plattz was pettish and surly.

"My destination, too. And Yverdon. Come in, Sir." She flung open the coach door, but Plattz hesitated, the fool! "You're welcome," said she. "The more we are, the snugger we'll be." I understood now that my wonderful ally was striving to draw off every possible enemy. "And you, reverend sirs?" She spoke most sweetly to those silly priests.

The young novice started forward but old Sebastian held him back. "Thank you, my lady. We have our own horses." He stared into the blue-and-cream upholstery with considerable regret. "However, we'll ride along with your party, if you'll agree. For safety."

"Best check the stables, Father," said Olrik, striding off in that direction. "The Gallic general here thinks some Dutchy's stolen an entire herd, as far as I can tell. Why he even claims the horse he rides is taken on the road to Fribourg. Maybe 'tis a magic horse, eh, Sir? That can split itself in twain whenever it's needed to go in more than one direction?" He clearly had decided that he had had the best of the encounter with Montsorbier. With a mocking conqueror's laugh he was gone from the stage before me. I knew I should go soon to meet him, that he was in league with my lady, but I wanted one last look at my vision of perfect womanhood.

Montsorbier, having lost any habits of common badinage he might once have possessed, could only shout at his men to mount in good order, straighten their hats (which now conspicuously lacked their red, white and blue cockades) and prepare themselves to leave. Yet he wondered, I could tell, as the old musketeer had meant him to wonder, if perhaps I was in truth galloping on a borrowed half-Arab for Fribourg while he (Montsorbier) had committed himself to escorting a pretty gentlewoman to Lausanne: the same blue-blooded, fastidious woman of wit and education whom he would, on his home territory, have thrown into a cart to be summarily beheaded by the merciful machine of sweet natured Dr. Joseph-Ignace Guillotin.

"You'll not desert us, Sir, I hope!" called out my benefactress, turning those huge, wonderful eyes upon him. I almost swooned. "Without your generosity, Sir, we should be in grave danger of encountering brigands. Think what would happen to my maid and I, not to mention this learned gentleman and two of Christ's servants! Oh, it chills my blood, Sir!"

I admired her wit and my impulse was still to follow her immediately. The mélange of passions within my breast was near unbearable! When the coachman cracked his long whip and the horses hauled upon their harness I was taken by surprise and all but fell backwards into Olrik's arms as the coach went off. I was elated with love, with laughter at Montsorbier's predicament. Ah, how I should have liked to have been within her coach, my head resting upon the bosom of that remarkable and resourceful creature who could not be much past one and twenty, yet bore the maturity and power to command; she had the quick habits of mind, the intelligence of any veteran General. To see Montsorbier dragooned into ensuring the safety of a fair sampling of the very people he regarded as his natural enemies was worth more to me than gold and was ample compensation for the risk of exposure. Olrik shook me, cursing, as I continued to look at the departing party. Montsorbier, to his credit, had accepted the situation with reasonable grace—his sans-culottism was younger than his breeding—betraying neither stupid fawning on the lady nor yet a frown of impatience. And, of course, as I am sure my lady designed it, he was so busy controlling his warring impulses that he did not for a second suspect I might still be at the inn. Olrik and Bamboche had proved themselves good friends. Now the Swiss musketeer was growing vociferously urgent. With one final look at the coach as it took the road for Lausanne, I allowed Olrik to lead me into the yard, where a good chestnut filly stood ready.

"She's all settled for, my friend. Off you go to wherever you please—but there's a short road on a higher pass, should you wish to risk it on horseback."

"To Lausanne?"

"It'll have ye there in half the time. 'Tis hard in parts, given to unstable snow and there are sometimes robbers."

"I'll cheerfully risk all of that." I was determined to get to Lausanne, collect my money from my friend La Harpe and present myself as soon as I could before that inspiration of all poetry, that divine goddess, my guardian angel, the Duchess of Crete.

Olrik laughed easily. "Ye've a spirit to ye, little captain, I'll grant ye!"

I ignored his insult, affirmed from him the directions to the high pass, and was off at once, thinking of nothing but reunion with my muse, my feminine ideal.

She had doubtless slipped some gold to Olrik, for my horse was thoroughly equipped and my own saddlebags were at my back. Upon my saddle was a scabbarded Bavarian hunting gun almost as good as Olrik's English muskets. My own Georgian flintlocks were also holstered there, together with a pouch of shot, a horn of powder, gun cotton—everything I should need upon my journey. I began to suspect my lady a sorceress—or at very least a seeress, invested with a most convenient second sight.

The tall mountains rose before me on the narrow trail and I drew my old coaching coat about me, glad of its protection against the threatening snow. Yet within I was warm and knew great happiness. Soon I must see my heart's desire once more!

Chapter Three

*In which brigands are encountered and skills at musketry
are tested. Nature, disturbed, responds dramatically to our
sport. As a result I meet with a traveller whose skills,
history and name are all equally unlikely.*

A S THE AIR grew colder and the landscape wilder I had little to
do but reflect on my fortune, good and bad. Was all to be put
down to coincidence? It seemed odd to me that Montsorbier
should pursue me with such dedicated vigour and that an
unknown lady should take such pains to help me. I wondered if,
somehow, Montsorbier believed I had betrayed him in betraying
his Cause. I did not consider myself a traitor. On the contrary I
had remained true to my own ideals. I wondered if Montsorbier
recalled me from the old gatherings of novice Illuminati? I had
sampled several such brotherhoods, including the Rosey Cross
and the Orange Lodge, during the period in which I examined the
Supernatural and found it not merely uninstructive but damnably
dull, its members possessing nothing in the way of individual
imagination and a great need to seek confirmation in numbers for
the merits of miserable little madnesses. Most clubs, even the Jacobins, had their share of spineless creatures looking for reflections
of their now morbid souls in the crazed faces of like-minded lunatics. But surely this was not Montsorbier? Such people as a rule
were lonely, confounded misfits, attempting to alter the surrounding evidence of Nature by inventing abstractions to explain why
common facts were false and ordinary reality a poor illusion.

It was impossible to guess what monstrous dreams lingered in
the skull of that dedicated Revolutionist. Perhaps he saw the Revolution as a practical means to a spiritual end? There was no more
dangerous kind of madman than one who devoted a good brain

and a courageous heart to unhealthy ambitions. Prejudice took the place of study and what might have begun as an investigation or debate, a genuine search for knowledge through an experimental scientific society, could soon become a coven of wretched fear-alls, too shy, too unhappy and too cowardly to question its own creed. An unquestioned creed is a noose about the throat of Reason, said Cloots to me once. And now he's dead because he insisted on clinging to a useless and discredited cause. Perhaps, by refusing that noose, I refused, in Montsorbier's eyes, to recognise the validity of the dream for which he had sold his own soul?

My horse climbed through massive corridors of pine and monstrous snow-clad rocks, through gorges winding between sheer cliffs, and sometimes I heard the hardened snow overhead creak and shift, threatening to fall and engulf me. I was careless of potential danger: increasingly Montsorbier was forgotten and I thought only of Libussa, Duchess of Crete. Her name was unusual while her title had the ring of something notional, such as the Pope or the Holy Roman Emperor were used to dispensing. Crete itself, I was fairly certain, lay now under the domination of the Ottomans. Yet the title could be rightfully inherited, for certain families (particularly those with roots in the Balkan kingdoms) went back to a time before Christ when their ancestors had been lords of half-barbaric tribes, the priests of dark and loveless religions. Perhaps she bore African blood, even? The blood of those forgotten and mysterious civilisations which had risen and fallen in the years preceding and during the age of the Egyptian Empire. . . That would explain, I thought, any gift for second sight she might possess.

Because of the might of Nature all around me, the solitariness of my situation, my mind grew fanciful until I was forced to take control of myself and remember the realities which presently affected me. Yet this exercise proved harder than the reader might suppose. For some great while, as the road had wound into wooded hills, I had been unconscious of the wildness of the weather, since the unsettled gathering of clouds mirrored so accurately that tumult within me: that mighty and unruly tide of emotions which, conflicting, drowned all logic with their din and offered to re-create me as a creature daemonically possessed. By the time the sky had darkened so as to seem almost nocturnal and the sleet transformed into whistling snow (making me blind even while I remained uncaring of my chilly bones) I was hard-pressed to keep my horse moving forward, let alone able to mark the way!

Soon I was forced to swing down off my saddle, grip my reins in one hand and use the other to brush back the snow which formed little drifts upon my face. Keeping thus to the Lausanne trail by instinct rather than observation, I pressed on. I had come to the idea that my lady was putting me to a test: that I must not only play her game through, I must also guess at the game's nature. Truthfully, I became alarmed at my own obsession, sensing something unwholesome in it. I had no great taste for abstractions of any kind, yet here was I apparently in the grip of an insensible dream. Even when I was forced to pause and shelter for a while, in a ruined hut beside the path, I took my travelling ink and quill from their case in my saddlebag and began to write, in bad light, attempting to organise my thoughts. But, now I look at what remains of those pages, I see that I was already departed from Sanity. I was bent on equipping myself with logic to explain the madness which had overtaken me, willing to drag in any old, unkempt speculation as evidence: *Man fühlt tief, hier ist nichts Willkürliches, alles ist langsam bewegendes, ewiges Gesetz.* (Goethe's ever useful in such exercises. My journal's surviving fragments do not give me *Befriedige deine natürlichen Begierden und geniesse so viel Vergnügen, als du kannst*, but doubtless it was there once.) Much I neither recall nor properly recorded, for the pages have a tendency to run like tangled roots; the ciphers meaningless. However, as I grew more weary and colder, all seemed of the deepest, not to say most painful, significance.

What dreadful form of idealism, erotomania, curiosity, fascination had filled me up so swiftly after I had called upon cynicism to armour me against the anguish of Lost Hope? It was not enough to claim this for the work of Cupid alone. I must suppose the horrors of the enragés, the fear of capture, the decline of my beliefs, all helped contribute to my state of mind. Rather than protect myself, it seemed I had made myself more vulnerable than ever! I was close to that state of insanity whereby I was fully conscious of the folly, the perversion, the danger of my actions, could catalogue it all (the journal proves it) and make the most perceptive and lucid commentaries, yet still drive on towards the brink above the gulf of uncontrollable lunacy.

Why was I so possessed? I asked myself. In those freezing mountains everything became sinister. I began to think that demons truly prowled the ancient woods where my own ancestors carved idols from the living trees and worshipped them with horrid, pagan ritual, pouring sacrificial blood into the dark earth so that they might commission or placate some grinning godling! And were those of us who thought ourselves most shielded from such ancient sorceries actually the easiest prey of all? Reason checked this questioning of mine and murmured "metaphor"; though a metaphor could sometimes be a map, recognised yet not understood.

The snow passed and I was able, with some difficulty, to continue. Sunshine came suddenly as I waded around a slab of ice-adorned granite, but still I could not easily ride. The snow was now glittering, threatening to blind me. As the shadows lengthened against the white and the green, I detected the tracks of a heavy vehicle. I was astonished to discover such a sign in this apparently uninhabited country. Could it, I thought, be Milady's own coach, taking an ill-considered shortcut? I dismissed this with what little reason remained to me, shrugged and refused further speculation.

The deep cart-tracks through the snow continued to mark my way ahead. Now the covering was sparser, melting in the heat of an afternoon sun. Ahead of me the Alpine peaks were sharp against the blue sky. I was thankful no further clouds gathered and became more cheerful in my disposition as I mounted, my steed's hoofs took steadier purchase and our speed increased. Around me the trees sparkled with moisture. My breath was a ragged plume floating across my shoulder. Ahead of me were massive spurs of rock, marking the pass. I ascended still higher. Here the snow was crisp and long since fallen. There appeared to be few signs of a storm. The tracks were sharper. I detected only two horses and possibly one driver, for there were signs where a man had climbed down in order to coax the beasts upwards.

I had begun to feel the pangs of hunger and a search in my saddlebags revealed some slices of beef, a piece of roasted pork, some mutton, black bread and those little sweetcakes the Swiss have a fondness for. Eating as I rode, my spirits soon lifted (thanks, too, to the flask of wine provided by the same mysterious hand) and I began to plan my lady's courtship. I was whistling by the time the pass loomed and the track narrowed, winding high above a rushing river on one side and with a great wall of lichen-covered granite on the other. Again I thought it prudent to dismount, so replaced my provisions in the pouch and clambered down.

I had gone only a few paces and turned a sharp corner on the path when I discovered to my despair that the way ahead was blocked by some six or seven armed men while a rattling and scrabbling from behind told me that more of their kind were now at my back. I knew that I might wait passively to be robbed or captured (for ransom) or I might try to make a fight of it. I decided that I could lose nothing by the latter choice. At which, I remounted, defying their threatening glares and pretending that I could understand nothing of their patois.

These men wore the short jackets and breeches, the broad hats and wide belts of mountaineers, but they were not honest Swiss peasants. They were plainly brigands, for they sported a variety of weapons, including two crossbows, an old blunderbuss, a couple of matchlock pistols, a variety of knives, flenching tools, cutlasses and swords, most of which were either rusty or encrusted with the blood of former victims.

Failing to make me listen to their argot, they tried me in Italian:

"O la borsa, o la vita!" they growled. Their faces were covered in matted hair and their stink was not dissipated by the mountain air. This choice of money or life was familiar enough, but since I had little money and could not trust them to spare my life, I answered by drawing my Bavarian gun from its scabbard and, pulling back the hammer, pointed it directly at the breast of the one who appeared to be the leader.

"Let me pass, gentlemen," said I in English (a language I could be sure they would not know), "or I shall be forced to blow your wretched bodies to kingdom come!"

I was rewarded by the fellow removing his greasy green hat from his head to offer me a mocking bow. He spoke in the old Swiss tongue (which I believe they call Romany), then attempted some French. I shrugged and shook my head, gesturing with the gun for him to clear the path.

Next he threw back his horrible head and laughed loudly. *"No, signor! Scusi, per favore. Buona sera."*

I suspected his Italian to be little better than my own and moreover saw no point in attempting further communication. It would merely waste time. Again I gestured with the gun, conscious of feet creeping slowly up behind me. This caused me to tuck the gun against my ribs and withdraw one of my pistols, aiming it back over my shoulder, an action which stopped their shuffling. We now appeared to have reached some form of stalemate. I could only rely upon their cowardice and there was every chance, though they be uncouth, godless murderers to a man, they were not short of courage. I urged my horse a pace or two further.

At this the crossbow bolt hummed and crashed into the rock just above my head. Another, made inaccurate I would guess by the warping of the stock, whistled past my left leg and killed a brigand who cursed, cried out, lost his footing and went hurtling towards the river far below. I seized my moment, discharging the Bavarian gun so that it roared loud enough to wake all the world's corpses, and driving a bloody hole through the leader's chest. I rode at them, brandishing the pistol, using the gun to club them away from me, while more powder flared and shots went off right and left. I thought we should all be dragged down to the river, for my horse was having difficulty keeping her balance, and then we were through.

They still ran at my heels, however, yelling for revenge, pelting me with knives, stones and useless firearms, lusting for my blood like hungered wolves, and it was quarter of an hour before I could put a little distance between us and ride out onto open ground while dusk rose up to engulf all.

The mare's hoofs sent a dry powder of snow into the air with every beat, but we were galloping now and the brigands were soon lost, screaming their disappointment and hatred amongst the pines. Eventually I slowed to a walk. It was growing darker by the moment. Rooks croaked and shouted, wheeling overhead. The walls of their rocky colonies echoed to their harsh cries, but the air smelled of clean conifers, the threat of murder was past and I knew I must be halfway to Lausanne, less than another day's ride before I should again see my lady. Within the hour I was readying myself to make camp for the night, not daring any further to risk the winding narrows, the deep chasms and lively rivers which everywhere foamed, rushing to feed the greater torrent lying at the valley's floor. Sunset coloured the snow a rosy pink and I paused to wonder at Nature's marvellous creation, the dramatic wildness of these mountains. Then a white hare ran suddenly across a drift of snow above me. I thought I was to be thwarted of a tasty dinner, for I had not yet had time to reload my Bavarian gun; nonetheless, I tried my last pistol, letting off a ball at the hare as she dashed for cover in a clump of rowans.

The shot sent echo upon echo through the distant valleys. When it had died, so had the hare. It was almost dark. I would have to play the part of game-dog next, sniffing out my prize. As I plodded through the snow and spied the dead animal, a splash of bright blood on its side just below the shoulder, I became aware of a muffled, distant rushing noise which I could not at once identify. It sounded rather like a rising wind or a river in flood. Then, as I picked up the limp body of Mademoiselle Scarum, the noise was suddenly over. I returned to where I planned to make camp and lit a pinecone fire, quickly skinning and cleaning my hare and wishing I had some means of preserving her lovely fleece. Her flesh, when cooked, was sweet and tender.

There fell upon the night a silence, a tranquillity I had not experienced so profoundly for many a year. In the sheer blackness overhead the stars were prominent, glittering and twinkling, with each astral configuration clearly defined. I entered my little tent yawning deeply, felt tiredness come to me and welcomed it as a friend; then I was immediately asleep.

Next morning, with dawn shining through the walls of the canvas room, I woke instantly, cheerfully certain that this day I should be reunited with my Duchess. I rose, breakfasted on the remains of last night's feast, watered, fed and saddled my horse, cleaned myself as best I could and was ready to continue. By evening, if not sooner, I should be riding through the streets of Lausanne, with plenty of time to visit my friend, receive some money, and then (if Montsorbier had gone on, as I was sure would be so) make a properly civil call upon my lady to discover, I hoped, why she had decided to help me and to find out, if I could, what service she required of me in return.

I was whistling as I mounted my mare. It even seemed to me there was a trace in the air of Spring's imminence. This gaiety appreciated with every forward step and Nature in all her aspects offered proof of my optimism. I had not enjoyed such a feeling of health and light spirits since before the Revolution. For about an hour my mood persisted until I turned a sharp bend in the serpentine track and my heart sank all of a sudden as I at once perceived what had created last night's great rushing noise.

It had surely been my own shot disturbing the snow above the pass and so starting the avalanche which, this morning, completely blocked it. Snow, boulders, even a small tree or two rose high above me. I opened my mouth and uttered my despair aloud, careless that another traveller was already present.

He was sitting in some dejection upon the thick wooden tongue of a large covered wagon; the sort generally used by itinerants: tinkers, gypsies or strolling players. That he was no common knife-and-organ grinder was plain. He wore a long ermine coat (not unlike the hare's I'd killed last night), a fur "three-eared" cap to match, and his hands were buried in a muff (also white fur). When he saw me, his glance went immediately to my holstered gun, yet without anger or malice he removed one slender hand to salute me. "Well, my noble Forester, I hope your aim was successful last night and ye ate well. Why are ye wailing? D'ye think Fate brought our mountain down?" He spoke French, sardonically, in an accent I could not place.

"We cannot go on?" I was stupefied.

"The chances of this wall of débris being cleared within a month are slight, I'll grant, though 'tis hard to judge the extent of it. Could be there's nothing for us to do, however—nothing to eat, nothing to pass the time—until Spring." He added amiably: "Perhaps you should try to accept your destiny cheerfully, since doubtless your shot was the cause of all this."

I studied the massive heap. I was sure the man in ermine was right and that my road was completely impassable. Carefully I reined in and dismounted; my passions in tight check.

The man on the wagon tongue had the style of a gentleman: tall, thin, exquisite. He looked up again at me and smiled with red, sensual lips (which turned at the corners in an expression of permanent irony). "Well, Sir?"

"I regret I've inconvenienced you, Sir, by my folly," said I. "'Tis some while since I hunted in mountains and being famished, having come recently out of combat with brigands, I did not think clearly. Pray forgive me. I am Manfred, Ritter von Bek, and need not tell you I'm at your service. Could one man on a horse try to ride over and fetch help?"

"Aye," said the tall man. "He could try. But I believe it would be quicker to fly." He laughed. His German was as excellent as his French, but his accent remained a mystery. As he rose, dusting snow from knees and bottom, I walked towards him. His van's two mules seemed at ease with their lot and content to nuzzle through snow to find grass on the fringes of that high gorge.

I shook hands. "I'm Orkie of Lochorkie, Sir," he told me. "Christened Colin James Charles."

The man was a North Briton. I had never heard his breed speak such good vernacular German. I took him for one of those soldiers of fortune originally attracted to Frederick's Prussian colour guard.

Since Prussia now fought Revolutionary France perhaps he had left his master's employ, having, like many others, no wish to join in an assault upon the young republic. There was most certainly a military air to him, as well as a dandified way of standing and talking. He seemed universally amused.

"I am also sometimes known as the Chevalier de St. Odhran. I should add, since I could so easily give an erroneous impression, I'm laird in name only. The few acres of land which remain to my estate are so inferior, Sir, as to have the remarkable distinction of maintaining neither plant nor beast. Nothing can live on it, Sir, not even myself."

"You are from Scotland, I gather."

"Aye, Sir. My father took old Charlie's route to the fleshpots and the more obscure European Courts. After the 'Forty Five there was precious little joy in remaining on Scottish soil. One was prey to the most uncivilised mobs of lowlanders and brute English ye've ever seen, Sir. Most of my life has been spent abroad—by which I mean twelve countries and a plethora of principalities, many of which could be prevailed upon to support me in some comfort. In return I displayed my wonders. Wonders learned, Sir, from those heroes of the air, my sometime masters and employers, the Montgolfiers!"

I looked at his wagon with new interest. "An Aviationist!"

He tapped the side of his wagon. "Here she is, Sir. My ship. My pride. My family and my honour, Sir. My destiny and I hope the destiny of all. Aye, Sir, as you've guessed I'm an aerial adventurer, currently touring the highways and byways of this continent to raise money for an expedition so bold, Sir, so monstrous well-rewarded, Sir, that the Treasure of London's Tower could not for an instant match the value. My maps are accurate and I read the compass reasonably well, so I see no difficulties."

"What, Sir, are you just a treasure-seeker?"

"Sir, I sell the *key* to treasure. The certain means of finding gold in the more remote quarters of our Globe. I know where one may discover lost races of mankind whose skins are of no colour we have ever known, or ancient jungle-buried cities where the inhabitants place value only on the leaves of the common plane tree and yet live surrounded by gold as their commonest material. They are willing to exchange a pound of 24-carat metal for a few fronds and possibly a piece or two of bark. There are countries, Sir, not on any modern map, countries known to the Ancients but forgotten by us, where the women are breathtakingly fair and the few men they have possess the faces of dogs, so that any ordinary, homely Bavarian, say, will seem devilish handsome to them. Plato mentions Atlantis and Socrates Polaris. Those are two of the many lands we may soon explore. Countries, sir, which are free of vice and upheaval, where mankind may live in peace, escaping from the horrid realities which presently alarm us all."

I believe I must have been weary, distracted by my disappointments, for I found myself saying dully: "Socrates doesn't mention Polaris, Sir."

The Chevalier de St. Odhran frowned as if he had caught me in an exhibition of bad manners. "He does, Sir."

"Not once, Sir. Not at all."

"Ye've not read the Secret Books, I take it?"

"Secret, Sir?"

"Those in London? Found by the Royal Society's explorers several years ago. Rescued from the dusty library of some Mussulman pasha. You recollect them now, Sir?"

"I do not, sir."

"At the British Museum, Sir. Yes. Six books of Socrates, all the genuine article, in the original Greek, the philosopher's own penmanship. I've seen 'em, Sir, and read 'em myself."

It was then that I believed I had taken the Chevalier's measure as he had meant me to take it. He was not bent on deceiving me at all, but rather demonstrating his profession. And the demonstration was for my amusement. I found myself smiling. "And sold 'em more than once, I dare say."

He laughed easily and relaxed. "More than once, I must admit. But the balloon is real and she can be flown."

"What, over this avalanche?"

"We should need more room than is available to us here. The

canopy must be laid out on the ground and a huge fire built. If we had it, we could use a gas which scientists term Combustible Air; but it's rare and very expensive. If we build a bonfire, we should build it against that cliff and attempt to melt it down!"

"I am on urgent business, Sir. Is there any other road to Lausanne?"

He pointed. "Over that way, I believe. To the West. But it is many miles. I would offer you a map, but mine are all of lands as yet undiscovered." He winked. "Some, indeed, are hardly yet invented." Again his healthy, fresh and wholesome face broke in a great smile. He had a long head to go with his long body and it was most handsome when he displayed amusement.

"You're a very open trickster, Sir," said I. "May I ask why you're so willing to lampoon the usual deceptions of your trade?"

"I hardly lampooned 'em at all, Sir. You *perceived* 'em, which is altogether different." He drew from the depths of the wagon a large magnum. "Will ye drink some good Claret wine with me, Sir?"

Holding the bottle between his knees he began awkwardly to apply the corkscrew. "I'll be frank, Sir. I took ye for a soldier of fortune who'd easily recognise my trade. However, I can assure you of one thing—I'm an amateur ballonnier of considerable experience. I studied under the Montgolfiers. I know all the tricks of the Charlier method. Blanchard and Lunardi, amongst others, have acknowledged me an equal. 'Tis even possible, with a proper study of wind-currents and such, to navigate a little. I am presently working on my system for making the balloon fully steerable. But one finds no demand, as yet, for the genuinely beneficial services of the machine. The public insists on treating the science of flying as a mere novelty. Yet the balloon I have in my wagon could be used for the observation of battles. It could study a piece of land upon which an architect planned to build. It could transport people and mail between cities and nations more rapidly than any coach or ship. It could be used for genuine exploration of all kinds. Yet, without the *flim-flams* I provide for a public forever demanding new sensations and marvels, there would not be a sou for the furtherance of our knowledge. Princes or peasants, they're the same in this—they'll put their entire fortune into a fanciful scheme promising to enrich 'em overnight, but they'll refuse with fury the opportunity to invest in a practical plan which has only common sense to sell it!"

He shrugged and pulled the cork. "Ha! This'll warm us! So, Sir, you see before you one who began as a serious engineer and has through necessity become a comedian, a showman. I have gone from being a man of science to a honey-tongued charlatan." He laughed in considerable amusement at this irony. "I would not do it, I suppose, if I did not enjoy it. Yet I began life, on the Continent at least, as an honest enough soldier."

I found his company stimulating and it helped take my mind off the miserable knowledge that by my own folly I had created a massive wall between myself and the object of my desire. What was more, his matter-of-fact manner, his ordinary good humour, aided me to regain my grasp on reality, to achieve at least a temporary mental balance. He was a stylish, charming rogue, able to amuse me even as part of my soul wailed in frustration, impulsively urging me to dash into the drift and with bare hands tear a tunnel through. As my attention wavered off after that wild goose, I reminded myself of my good manners and reflected that the Chevalier de St. Odhran had, after all, taken my responsibility for this disaster in excellent part. There was no saying how badly I had inconvenienced him, yet he had not uttered a word of complaint.

In spite of all this reasoning, I was, after my first pull on the magnum, unthinkingly upon my feet and running towards the tumble of filthy snow and earthy rock, burrowing like a badger, careless of the cold; shouting out the name of she who had enslaved my heart! It had come to me in horror that if indeed she had changed course and come this way she could be buried beneath the avalanche!

"I swear I heard a cry, St. Odhran! Help me dig, for God's sake!"

With a huge sigh, half-reconciled, half-critical, and a look of weary dismay upon his aristocratic features, the tall Chevalier returned to his wagon and fetched out two short spades, one of which he handed me. "The effects of a young prospector, Sir. He lost 'em in a game of cards even before he left for the Cornish silver-fields (just as well, since I'd sold him the map). I consoled myself I'd saved him a wasted journey."

I drove the shovel into the soft body of the landslide. It was a bright morning and the sun was shafting through the gorge while a variety of birds sang cheerful accompaniment to my own desperate running litany concerning my beloved's virtues. Meanwhile, the Chevalier listened with impassive good manners, removed his ermine coat, neatly folded it and set it aside, pushed back the lace of his shirt, and set to with a will, chanting obscure, rhythmical Scottish shanties and pausing only to wipe away sweat with a large yellow silk kerchief, occasionally muttering, "Is that so, Sir?" and taking another pull or two from the bottle.

As I subsided, he proceeded to describe for me the story of his own life from poverty (he was no Scottish lordling, after all) in the filthy slums of Edinburgh to his earliest escape from prison at the age of seven (after he had been sentenced to transportation in the matter of a bolt of cloth—a hanging crime in someone older) and his journey to London. There he had found himself swiftly in Newgate, but with a far better class, he said, of rufflers, upright men and wild rogues. Recruited in prison for the East India Company's army, he had gone to Asia and fought in a number of campaigns. Rising through the ranks, he meantime won the good graces of a certain native ruler to whom he deserted, helping this Khan to drive the Company back from his borders. He was made a Prince of Powjindra for his trouble, but aroused (in his view unreasonable) ire in the hearts of his former colleagues who put a high price on his head. This last, he told me, he found flattering, almost a reference to a future employer. Crossing through Afghanistan, trading various commodities, he eventually reached Russia in time to enlist with that nation's army and destroy a variety of Cossack rebellions in the Don and Dnieper regions, also making expeditions into Georgia and, as a freebooter, even into Turkey, where he had helped arm and prepare Christian Armenians against their

Ottoman masters in the hope this would provide Muscovy with sufficient excuse to declare War upon the Turks and annex as much of the Mussulman Empire as possible, in the name of a High Crusade!

The bottle was drained by the time he got to Turkey and I was now fairly certain my love did not lie crushed beneath the land-slide, so gave him increased attention. Here was my peer indeed! I felt as though I had found a true brother.

The Mussulman sultans, he said, were familiar with his manoeuvre and countered it simply by setting fire to six entire Armenian towns one night and burning the communities in their beds. He knew St. Petersburg well, and Moscow better than I, though he had never been so close to the Court. We compared memories here and he was overjoyed to learn of my time in Tatary. But I pressed him to continue:

"After a spell in Klinsky's 11th Light Infantry, as a major, I was taken up by the Duc de Mosset, who was part of a French diplomatic mission to Muscovy, and I returned with that gentleman to France where I became a darling of the Salons." He found ways, he said, of laying the foundations of a fortune, which he eventually spent in a couple of months, though not before being asked to suggest a new Financial Policy for the nation herself. "The Froggies seemed to conclude I was a financial Wizard since I had a fair idea how to balance a set of books and a decent instinct for buying and selling Investment Bonds. You'll recall they were by that time in the habit of stopping any passing stranger on the street and begging him to become Minister of Finance." This period lasted only a few months before he found himself in the service of the Duchy of Luxembourg as an administrator organising the Military College. He had been given his title in that country, choosing for himself the name of an obscure saint ("he was, I believe, St. Patrick's charioteer! From the misty Isle of Man"). It was perfectly genuine, he assured me, and had been bestowed for his many favours to the State; indeed he was a naturalised citizen of Luxembourg. By ill luck, he continued, he had gone back to France at the very moment the Bastille was stormed and, having no sympathy with Revolution, stayed only briefly, where he took up with the Montgolfiers before they were arrested. He and several other ballonniers moved quickly to Belgium, to carry on their work uninterrupted. Here his true career as an Aviationist, demonstrating the Montgolfier and Charles types of balloon, had begun. He had experimented with his own designs and dreamed of finding a means of steering the vessels accurately through the air.

Now he busied himself with a fire, dragging pots and pans from his wagon, preparing a luncheon such as one might easily have eaten in Paris before it was considered an act of Treason to enjoy one's meals in public. "My attempt to float capital for a new type of aerial boat, which possessed greater safety for passengers and more sophisticated accommodation than any before it, was at first successful. However, I spent the funds unwisely, forgetting they were not my own. The result—flight into Germany pursued by scandal. But in Germany, Sir! Ah, what a healthy and enlightened attitude towards Science, what a willingness to trust the New Mechanics!" He had displayed his balloon all over Prussia, Saxony, Hanover, Westphalia and Bavaria and was frequently asked if he planned larger ships and longer expeditions. He had begun to draw up plans for both, going so far as to design vessels which could carry whole platoons of Infantry, together with cannon to fire broadsides down upon the enemy. The latter were particularly popular with Frederick II, who ordered the Chevalier to build such a ship, whereupon my new friend deemed it prudent to repair to Austria. In Vienna and Prague he attempted to sell the plans for his fanciful Air-ships, together with maps and images of hitherto undiscovered lands. But such trade, he told me, though safe was petty. He had a far more interesting scheme which he hoped to launch in Mirenburg, whose populace, he had heard, was more open-minded than elsewhere.

At the mention of Mirenburg I came alert, wondering at the coincidence. St. Odhran's destination was identical to mine! However, I was not fool enough to trust him with every confidence. I said nothing of this to him.

Seeing that I had grown more relaxed with the wine he ventured to ask of me a personal question. The name von Bek, he said, was familiar to him. Was I related, perhaps, to a famous general in Old Fritz's army? I informed him that mine was a very respectable Saxon family. Members of our clan were inclined to worthy, frequently obscure, public office.

"You are too modest, Sir. I would swear I recall a tale, some sort of legend, attached to your family. Did you not have an ancestor in King Arthur's time? Or was it Charlemagne?"

I was embarrassed. "Ah, Sir, you speak of the Grail tales. There's scarcely an old German family which hasn't similar legends in it." I remembered the misery, as a boy, of being nicknamed Sir Parsifal and constantly asked where I was hiding Christ's blood. "We certainly don't credit 'em."

St. Odhran was grinning with delight, however. He snapped his fingers. "I once had a taste for such stuff. Your great-grandfather—possibly your great-great—was himself the subject of his own Romance. Was he not the knight in the story? Who went down to Hell to wage war against Satan? Who used magical charts to find an entrance into a new world and there discover the Grail?"

"The villain who published that tale was taken to Law by my grandfather, Sir. The book was destroyed by order of the Emperor himself!"

"Yet copies exist. The story's a favourite in Saxony."

"Sir," said I, leaning on my shovel, "I've no wish to discuss that vulgar tale."

St. Odhran acknowledged my discomfort and began digging again.

Perhaps the conversation, or at least the nature of it, had worked some magic upon us, however, for, as the Chevalier began to go into details regarding the good sense of opening a pork-shop in a street already full of butchers, we found the landslide was not near as bad as it had seemed. Suddenly, we were looking upon the trail beyond it! Part of the track had gone down with the fall, but there was enough remaining to allow the wagon to pass if we dug a little to one side. Moreover, of course, no other carriage had been buried.

We had been at work for some seven hours, but only now noticed our fatigue. The Chevalier put down his shovel to look back at the channel we had dug. He was proud of it. "By God, Sir, I am proved a demmed pessimist!" His face glowing, he shook my hand. "Shall you be immediately upon your way or will you celebrate with another bottle and the remains of our lunch? I have a mind to discuss a business partnership with you."

But I was anxious to continue my journey. Only politeness made me pause, offering to help clear the way for his wagon. He shook his head with a grin. "I can do that in my own time, Sir, for I'm in no great hurry and will camp here a further night."

As we stumbled back towards his wagon, I bluntly wondered why, with all his accomplishments, the Chevalier was not again wealthy. He laughed loudly at this. He thought his own restlessness was to blame. "I am easily bored. Taking the odd risk, throwing myself, as it were, into the arms of Fate, maintains my interest in life. Well, Sir, I'll not delay you. But should we meet again, I'll put that proposal to you!"

I went immediately to my horse. "I shall look forward to it, Monsieur le Chevalier, when my circumstances permit. Are you sure you need no aid to dig the last few feet?"

"It is less than an hour's work." He stood in his shirtsleeves, smiling up at me as I mounted. I leaned down to shake him, once more, by his hand.

"I am certain our paths shall cross again in time, Sir," said I.

"Should you journey to Wäldenstein, no doubt you shall find me in Mirenburg," said the Chevalier. "I always lodge as a rule at The Martyred Priest in Mladota Square."

"I know both inn and keeper very well, Sir. I thank you most truly for the pleasure of your company, and your aid."

I left him in an attitude of complete weariness, collapsing back onto the wagon tongue in the position he had assumed when I first encountered him. Yet there was a smile on his face and he seemed greatly satisfied with the day's adventure.

As I rode again towards Lausanne, I reflected how pleasant the encounter had been. If I ever reached Mirenburg (still many days' journey hence) I would surely seek him out.

But now, alone with my imagination once more, thoughts of Milady were paramount. I determined to ride as fast as I dared and pray the Duchess of Crete would still be in Lausanne when I arrived there.

Chapter Four

In Lausanne I am hugely disappointed. There begins a
chase across Europe. Loss of the majority of my reason.
Rumours of quarry, signs of pursuit. The most beautiful
city on Earth. My further frustration. The Martyred Priest.
Acquaintances renewed. The comforts of the past.
Dreams within dreams.

L AUSANNE, CONTRARY TO my expectations, was not a crowded
metropolis but rather a pretty country town, with a few
buildings of special note but none which was especially ugly. The
place smelled sweet enough (compared, say, to Paris or Venice)
and was as sedately ordered as any Swiss settlement where law
prevailed. Enquiries with gatekeepers and gendarmes led me to a
hostelry maintained by a monkish order (the Deniseans) as an
appendix to their abbey. Here I learned to my dismay that the
Duchess of Crete had left that morning, apparently for Vienna.
Montsorbier, it seemed, had ridden back, hell-for-leather, for Fribourg. This was my solitary consolation. Both my horse and I
were too tired for further travel, so I sought out my friend La
Harpe (who demanded all my intelligence, for he had grown pessimistic of the Revolution's progress) and was most hospitably
treated.

In return for my information, La Harpe told me all he knew of
the Cretan dukes and duchesses. It was an intriguing story. La
Harpe, folding his fine, almost transparent, fingers before him and
looking through his great windows at the moonlit waters of the
lake, admitted his own curiosity about the family.

"They're Spanish-French with Hungarian and Greek branches,
associated in past centuries with lechery and wanton cruelties.
The family name is Cartagena y Mendoza-Chilperic. According to

legend they were sorcerers and a good many seem to have entered Hell by way of the Inquisition! Others were priests, providing Rome with several Cardinals and almost a Pope (he was poisoned). There's suicide in the blood, too. Yet their patronage of the Arts and Sciences shows a genuine passion for creativity and natural philosophy. In modern times Prague is where they've chiefly left their mark. The Academy there could only exist thanks to the family's endowments. Other gymnasia in Prague and elsewhere were founded by discrete grants from cadet branches of Mendozas and Chilperics . . ."

"What of the present Duchess?" I asked eagerly.

He was puzzled. "I've heard only of the present Duke. Lucian he's called and he's wintered in Prague for five years past, travelling abroad only in the Summer months. They speak well of him. He is an enthusiastic patron of musicians and painters, I hear, and of natural philosophers in particular . . ."

"Alchemists, too?"

My friend shook his head. "I believe the young man is anxious that his family name no longer be associated with such pursuits. He has bestowed so much gold on convents, monasteries and lay schools it must be assumed he is a devout and conventional Christian!"

"And the Duchess? You've heard nothing at all about her?" I insisted.

"Unless he married secretly . . ."

"The lady I met was no matron, I'd swear. Could it be a sister— a cousin? This woman is a wit. A beauty!"

A look of mild irony and curiosity crossed La Harpe's features. "All this brings to mind is a scandalous whisper I heard a year or more since. I dismissed it. The gossips said the Duke had taken to dressing as a woman and venturing into quarters reserved for low, vicious creatures. Well . . ." He shrugged.

I laughed outright. "Friend, this was no male in doxy's garb!"

La Harpe appeared to humour me. "Just so. The Duke's regarded as a most eligible bachelor. And he's the last of his line. The Mendozas, you know, were *conversos* in Spain, of both Moorish and Jewish extraction. Those ancestors took up residence abroad during the unfortunate *limpieza de sangre* investigations which came to a head under Torquemada. They married into the Chilperics in France during the fifteenth century and so could be the only inheritors of that particular strain of Merovingian blood. Prague, as you know, has several families boasting similar antiquity. You say this woman introduced herself as Duchess of Crete?"

"Clearly. I'd never heard the name until then."

La Harpe sighed. "I've no other clues for you, my boy. But I would suggest you look for an answer to your mystery in Prague. There, I'd guess, you have the best chance of finding the person of your Duchess. Did she claim to be an alchemist?"

"Did I say so? She could be a witch or a ghost, the way she's vanished."

La Harpe was embarrassed by this fanciful remark. "All I can say is that in Prague there's said to be gathering a number of the more enlightened alchemists, called by Cornelius Groot, whom some believe a mere market-place trickster while others insist he has supernatural powers. You know my distaste for such stuff. Groot's a resident of Brno. I met him once. I must admit he impressed upon me a sense of great dignity and learning. But the alchemical brotherhood is a secret one, so I have no real knowledge of its affairs."

"No notion of this convention's purpose?"

"Only a rumour or two. Some churchmen have attempted to outlaw Groot and his comrades, declaring the meeting heretical, blasphemous, even illegal, but so many of their own kind now belong to Masonic and Mystical orders that very little's been done to dissuade Groot. The alchemists claim themselves men of learning, doing no harm to Austria. Plainly Austria believes them or we'd have seen a different story. Most of these alchemists appear to hold decidedly orthodox political opinions and are as pleased to maintain the Right of Kings as any Hapsburg. I gather it's some momentous date in the alchemical almanac. What would you guess?" He smiled quietly. "The imminence of the Second Coming?"

"An old-fashioned notion." I shared his amusement.

"Aye. I saw your brother's friend Lobkowitz just before the New Year. Lobkowitz has astrologers amongst his acquaintances. You know his huge curiosity! He told me that the astrologers were speaking of a specific conjunction of our own star with several others." La Harpe shrugged. "How strange if Prague were to provide the stable and the manger! A city most closely identified with Reason, containing more agnostics per acre than Paris or London! Only Mirenburg harbours greater doubters!"

"It surprises me they did not hold their conference there, where they would surely be doubly welcome."

"Mirenburg's Prince favours less supernaturally influenced bodies than the alchemical adepts. He's presently bent on passing laws to make all secret societies illegal."

"He fears a potential Jacobin Club?"

"Less, I would hazard, than most hereditary rulers. His stated principle is that all knowledge should be at the public disposal. He argues against the hoarding of scientific discoveries, believing that the miserly act of secretion is in itself bound to produce fear and unnecessary caution in the mind of the citizen. Superstitious destruction of the unfamiliar is its most common expression. Prince Badehoff-Fischer argues that in such matters a secret is parallel, if not identical, to a lie. Both occur because one body seeks power over another."

"So soon there will be no secret societies in Mirenburg?"

"Well," again La Harpe smiled, "the *least* secret of 'em will be outlawed, at any rate. But 'tis in the nature of such bodies to burrow deeper and grow unwilling to admit new members, for fear of betrayal."

"Then they must eventually wither up," I said.

"Your logic isn't perfect, my dear von Bek. Some are like fleas— apparently dead, then suddenly awake and more alive than ever, hungry for blood! I wonder what attracts men and women to join such things."

We debated this for another hour or two until both of us were completely tired and more than ready for our beds. Next morning early I bade goodbye to the kindly philosopher and set out in bright, cold dawn light, first for Vienna and then, should I fail to find my madonna there, for Prague. Yet in the back of my mind I believe I hoped I should see her sooner, somewhere on the road. I argued to myself that a lone man on horseback must surely overtake a carriage, as I had overtaken hers once already.

But my logic was not confirmed by actuality. I rode for many days, sometimes scarcely sleeping, from one town to another, from city to city, constantly enquiring after her, only to find I had missed her by hours. It was as if she, herself, were possessed by some peculiar will-o'-the-wisp supernatural quality. In my light-headed sleeplessness I would occasionally wonder if she was a kind of glamorous lure, a fly artfully manufactured to draw me further and further on into the middle of Europe. But for what reason? Why should anyone wish to trap me? Not Montsorbier, who still, I believed, pursued me (or if not Montsorbier then some of his agents—I learned to recognise the breed). Did she play a game for her mere amusement? That, too, I could not credit.

Reaching Vienna (and going incognito for obvious reasons), I again began my enquiries in that populous and confusing city. I had it on the best authority that the Duke of Crete was most certainly staying with his friend Eulenberg at an estate on the outskirts. But it was impossible for me to gain an invitation and I was informed, at the gates, that callers were not being received. Unwilling to give my true name, and thus embarrass Eulenberg who was a close friend of my uncle and a distant kinsman, I was doubly thwarted. For a time I kicked my heels in Vienna, hoping that either Eulenberg or the Duke, or both, would appear. They did not. The rumour was that they were engaged in some important scientific experiment. All my enquiries regarding the Duchess were equally fruitless. It was as if she had suddenly disappeared at the very gates of the city. I must conclude that she had not stopped in Vienna, but was by now several days' ride ahead of me, perhaps already in Prague.

In a daze of speculation and uncertainty, I took horse for Prague. My nights grew increasingly disturbed. Now I was plagued by peculiar nightmares in which I dreamed of myself naked, armed only with a sword, seeking through a series of underground tunnels a huge and stinking beast, half man but enormously powerful, which lived only for my destruction. Sometimes, too, Libussa entered these dreams, smiling at me, mocking me perhaps. I could never be certain whether she loved me or merely used me for some terrible entertainment of her own devising. And sometimes she was not a woman at all, but a creature of fantasy. Sometimes she appeared in male attire, claiming to be her own brother. Thus my poor weary brain attempted to make logic from all the conflicting stories I heard while in pursuit of a woman I had met briefly only once.

I reasoned this obsession was folly. I sought a solution to a mystery which would prove to be no mystery at all. But I could not rid myself of its burden. I came to believe that, once I confronted Libussa, I should understand why I pursued her. She had become an aspect of my own identity.

Was Libussa, therefore, a simple reflection of my own urgent desire to love? When at last we met would the ghost which plagued me be exorcised? Perhaps I hunted her not because she represented my perfect mate, but because I wanted to see her face to face and learn that, after all, she bore no relation to the creature I had invented!

What was more I could not separate my thoughts of her from the notion of alchemy. Earlier I had rejected that rude blend of mysticality and scientific experiment in favour of a more modern and enlightened school of investigation, yet my attraction to alchemy's romantic marvellousness remained somewhere within my breast. Might Libussa represent my past—a time when I had more readily embraced the irrational, the terrible and the miraculous?

In this miserably irrational state of mind I fled out of Vienna on the earliest diligence for Prague. There, I convinced myself, I should at last be able to seek her out and prove whether it was she I loved or whether I loved nothing but an invention of my own imagination. Yet with every mile I covered it seemed I lost a further fragment of my reason. From the way ordinary folk addressed me—warily, fearfully—I came to realise that my appearance now displayed my mind's turmoil. I made an effort to improve my costume, to ensure I was as elegant as in former times. I attempted to control my excesses of emotion, educating myself to speak with quiet, measured politeness to all I met. Even this, however, frequently had the effect of terrifying people!

Libussa, of course, was not my only source of distress; I was still unrecovered from the great blows sustained by my soul at the corruption of my noblest dreams.

To have swallowed my pride and gone straight home to Bek would probably have cured me. As it was, I had achieved no respite since the beginning of the Terror.

By the time Prague's spires and battlements came in sight my mind had settled a little better and I assured myself that should I miss Libussa there, I would rest for a while before making a leisurely journey to Mirenburg. Since that city had been my original goal and since she would certainly be resident there when I arrived, I would quell my anxieties and replenish both mind and body in the certainty that we must soon come together again.

In Prague—a close rival to Mirenburg in her beauty and complexity—I made my way directly to the house of Baron Karsovin, my kinsman and a friend from happier times. The house was a good, well-ordered solid place in the baroque style and was situated close to the St. Cyrillus Park. Anticipating a pleasant meeting, I rode with improved spirits through the streets. It was a fine day. The sunshine was bright on the sparkling roofs, upon the dancing waters of the river, on turrets and bridges. Prague is an ancient seat of learning, combining a sleepy, peaceful atmosphere with an excellent history of moral and intellectual investigation. Dressed in fresh-cut black and white (after the new English pattern—I'd had it done in Vienna) I crossed the park and entered my friend's gates, knocking at last upon his magnificent door. I deemed it safe enough to give my correct name and within moments Karsovin himself came down to greet me.

I was mightily relieved to see him. That amiable dissolute grinned broadly when he clasped my hand and asked immediately after a half-dozen Parisian courtesans, one or two of whom I knew and all of whom had not been one whit affected by the progress of the Revolution. Karsovin was showing his age somewhat more gracefully than at other times (he was my senior by almost two decades). His wig was unostentatious, his paint restrained and his clothing, while yet elegant, relied upon lace rather than on padding, sitting more loosely and more becomingly on his figure.

Karsovin had assumed the air of a respectable diplomat. His voice was quieter than formerly and his manner almost modest. In sober dark green, with only his coat displaying any attention to the mode, he escorted me through polished halls to a small dining room where he intended to break his fast. I asked him if there had been a letter delivered there for me. There had been none, he said. I enquired after my mother and my father. They were both, said Karsovin, in Bek health (a term then in common employment). Karsovin asked after my elder brother (with whom he had fought a thoughtless duel when Ulrich decided some harlot was insulted— neither in the end firing anywhere but at the ground) and I said Ulrich seemed reasonably unsickly, given the circumstances. He would doubtless go soon to the mountains for a rest at Lobkowitz's estate. Karsovin's heavy, tawny features once seemed to bear the lines of dissipation, but now they merely told of statesmanly cares. I asked if he continued to sport in Prague, since the city's women were what first brought him there.

He offered me the small, unenthusiastic smile of a reformed rake. He planned to marry, he said. A young Moravian princess. And with that in mind—her fortune was a comfortable one—he had put Scandal at his back, though he still went twice a year to Mirenburg, whose Corinthian cloisters were deservedly famous. "I have spent almost my whole inheritance and must now pay the price, old friend, if I'm to gain another and ensure myself of an heir or two beside. What's more, I'm demmed weary of the doings of women, whether they be bob-tail bold or the honest article, and I've had too much of 'em en masse, so it's my humour to try to get to know one well! A matter of curiosity, I suppose, which will maintain my interest when passion wanes and babies begin a-shrieking!"

At his suggestion we drank a toast to the whores and fine ladies we had known (though I had to feign enthusiasm), then another to his new-caught Slav, Princess Ulrica-Irmentrude of Buchweiss. A miniature was taken from its cabinet. Then I must admire her handsome, though somewhat stolid, physiognomy, her auburn hair—he produced a locket of the stuff—her learning (a poem was waved in the air but not read). Since Karsovin seemed almost serious I praised these treasures conscientiously and enquired upon the marriage date, which he said would be before Christmas of '94. There were contracts in preparation. But it was my own news he most craved, particularly of France, and I duly told him that all the horrid tales were true.

"But it must end soon," said Karsovin, "or France herself will perish."

I allowed my disdain to be seen upon my face. "Her army's healthy enough. It could be the best in the world."

Karsovin showed stern interest. "Not better than Austria's."

"Yes," I insisted, "and perhaps Prussia's, too."

"All the old soothsayers and oracles in the market place say there's a great change coming to the world," said Karsovin thoughtfully. "But I can't believe that France will be the cause. Unless she intends to do it by the pox!" He was back to laughing good spirits again. "Let them try their luck against our Uhlans." He spoke with a confident air. He winked and rang the bell as we sat down to table. "My little Slav tells me that if I'm marrying for wealth, she's marrying me for my cook, Frau Schtick."

The cuisine was excellent and the wine remarkable, considering its relative youth. We talked of old days and the future, of our current politics and religion and the like. He had already heard of my flight and presumed disaffection and wanted a conference on issues which I would rather have avoided. To him, a supporter of Enlightenment, but no democrat, these were of consuming interest. At last I was forced to reveal my wishes and, gentlemanly as ever, even at the height of his wildness, he moved to what for me were less explored territories. He spoke of the coming conference of alchemists, wondering, as La Harpe had done, what moved people to take up such ideas.

My own guess was that they retreated into ancient philosophies out of fear of the new ones. "So the Rosicrucians, for instance, are dedicated not to discovery at all, but to preserving what is familiar and which therefore offers them no threat. Romance goes hand in glove with the *effects* of Reason's triumphs. We move towards an age of revolution, of steam-engines, flying ships, spinning jennys and underwater boats. They fear the manufactories, the steel-mills, the rail-roads, the canals. They are baffled, yet they retain a human need for balance and symmetry. They find it only by embracing the Abstract. So in England they build Gothick ruins and erect iron bridges with the aim of racing along their highways at enormous speeds upon the backs of clockwork horses!"

"You alarm me, my friend," said Karsovin with a wink. "But I bow to your superior knowledge. Perhaps I should have spent more time studying steam-boilers and less in pursuit of chick-a-biddy buntlings. Perhaps, in old age, when my estate at Buchweiss is established, I'll become an eccentric inventor and build a flying machine with which to explore the world." He became more animated. "By the by, I saw the great Montgolfier device go over the town last week. Before your arrival, of course."

"A balloon?"

"With a basket of men dangling beneath. The basket was shaped like a cockatrice or perhaps a dragon. All gold and scarlet. It shocked me I must admit. Should men fly, d'ye think, von Bek? Or seek to whirl along the ground at excessive speeds?"

"It's never 'should' with engineers, my old friend, but 'how'? Have you not learned that much?"

He leaned back from the table as a footman cleared his plate away. Again he suppressed amusement. "Oh, just so! What a provincial I must seem. Yet I don't greatly care. My interest in the Millennium dwindles almost daily and is replaced by the comforting notion that the only thing of real value is land. By the simple expedient of putting an old, familiar friend into a damp little hole for an hour or so each night, I'll soon be assured, as any man can be in these days, of a great many hectares of security and capital. And how have I earned this for myself? By leading a Christian life? By risking my all for a Revolution? Not a bit of it. I've done it by virtue of my carnal appetites, by virtue of my vanity and self-love!"

I was smiling, though his coarseness gave me a certain amount of offence. Curiously, I asked: "Did ye perhaps hear the name of the aeronaut who flew by the other day?"

"If I did, it escaped me." He was apologetic. "I assumed him to be one of the alchemists congregating here."

"Too modish a means of transport for one of that ilk," said I. "They prefer more supernatural forms of travel."

He enjoyed my joke. "I had forgotten what a pleasure your company is. I trust you'll stay with me while you're in Prague."

I accepted his invitation. Next I asked after the Duchess of Crete. I was casual enough, but he readily understood my interest. He shook his head. "Again I must disappoint you. The young Duke of Crete, you know—Mendoza-Chilperic as he's called here—is still in Vienna, by all accounts. He will be in Prague within the week, I gather."

"And you've not heard of a Duchess?"

"I know only that the Duke's said to favour the occasional jaunt to Town in female attire. But that's trivial gossip and without any truth to my knowledge."

"You would know if there were."

"I think so, aye. As for a Duchess—I suspect you've met with an impersonator, my friend. Some strumpet posing as a blue-blooded lady—with a title at once familiar enough and obscure enough to deceive almost anyone."

"I am beginning to believe that's the truth," I agreed. "Yet she was a creature of astonishing beauty."

"She has captured your heart, eh?"

"Worse," said I, "she appears to have captured my mind. I cannot rid myself of her."

"Well, seek her under some other name, that's my advice.

She'll not have the temerity to call herself Crete in Crete's own adopted city."

Glumly I also accepted this verdict. "I have reason to believe, however, that she'll make for Mirenburg."

"A female rogue, eh? A swindler of some description? I appreciate the fascination you must feel. There's something about such women—an independence of spirit, perhaps—that's fatal to men like ourselves. Take further advice—find yourself a good placid creature like my Slav."

I pretended to consider his suggestion, but I was more intrigued than ever. My darling was an imposter! Now her tendency to appear and disappear so swiftly was explained. It was not surprising I had been unable to find her in all the cities I had searched.

"By the by," said Karsovin, "I'm reminded that your name came up only a day or so past, when I visited Holzhammer in the country. For the shooting."

"I'm unacquainted with Holzhammer. Is he not one of the Prince's ministers in Mirenburg?"

"That's his nephew. This one hasn't the brains to point his own gun, but must have a servant position it for him! An amiable fellow, however. He had just returned from Vienna. He knew that you were an old friend. I gather some Frenchy was at Court, seeking to obtain a special warrant for your arrest as a Jacobin spy."

"A Frenchman?"

"A viscount, as I recall."

"Robert de Montsorbier?"

"Aha! The same!"

"He serves the Committee of Public Safety. He's Robespierre's man."

"No, no. Holzhammer said he was a true royalist."

"Then he's posing as such to capture me. Be warned against him, Karsovin. Thousands have been murdered because of Montsorbier's zealotry."

"I'll tell Holzhammer, at least. And he can send a message to the Court. However, the Emperor, when last heard, was giving serious consideration to that warrant. So be careful, I beg you. It could be that you're already a wanted spy here."

"Then I suppose I should make haste to Mirenburg, so as not to embarrass you, old friend."

"Pshaw to that!"

I smiled and put my hand on Karsovin's shoulder. "Neither would I wish to spoil your marriage opportunity!"

He uttered a noisy laugh. "As for that, I'm in two minds. Could be you'd be saving me from my own folly!"

Nonetheless I determined to leave for Mirenburg the next morning. I had no liking to hurt Karsovin and even less care to find myself a prisoner in the old fort, awaiting trial for my life.

The weather was unusually mild when I left Prague. The road to Mirenburg was a good one, winding through the shallow valleys of the Carpathians, well policed by regular detachments of soldiery and with several excellent inns along the route. It was to be the easiest part of my journey before I arrived, at long last, in that most lovely of all the habitations of Man, the ancient city of Mirenburg.

Mirenburg lies on both sides of the winding River Rätt. Approaching from the north-east one descends a range of low hills from where the whole city can be observed, a silvery map upon the floor of the wide valley. Her walls are of white granite flecked with tiny deposits of iron and quartz so that in almost any light at all she glitters. In the early morning, under a clear blue Winter sky, with a haze rising from the river, it was as if I rode towards a vision of Heaven.

For all her steeples, her baroque towers and romanesque cupolas, her noble Gothick churches and antique meeting halls, the fanciful mansions of her great families, the gingerbread gables and asymmetrical half-timbers, moulded into natural contours by the passage of time and the weather, Mirenburg contained much that was pleasing to the human spirit's more prosaic requirements. She had little crowded streets of houses with high-peaked eaves and long chimneys, undulating roofs of grey tile, whitewashed lanes of old black beams and bottleglass panes, their top-heavy upper storeys leaning out almost to form archways sheltering the brown cobbles below. At the centre of all this, on a kind of mound near the Rätt's left bank, was the astonishing perpendicular flamboyance of her castle, residence of a Prince whose dynasty was old before the Hapsburg's began. The Krasnaya were chiefs of the Svitavian Slavs who drove out the original occupants of the valley long before Rome ever marched westward and who held the valley long after Rome had gone.

By an intricacy of marriages and alliances carefully made over the centuries, Wäldenstein retained her peaceful independence and Mirenburg had never known anything more than the threat of violence, had been allowed to grow, layer by layer, undisturbed so that every age of our civilisation was recorded in the cracks of her stones, the line of her mortar and the set of her timbers. In addition, under the liberal rule of her Princes many great men had sought her sanctuary, from Chrétien de Troyes to Mozart and Fragonard. Scarce an alley had not been inhabited at one time by a philosopher, a sculptor or a playwright of renown.

So magical was the city's appearance, so luxuriant her culture, some writers would have it that Mirenburg remained free of strife not by the will of her Princes or the accidents of History, but because she represented an ideal which not even the most brutal or depraved of kings and generals could bring themselves to attack.

Whatever the reason, the city had a mythological ambiance. As always when I had ridden through her gates I was possessed of that particular emotion experienced nowhere else. I thought to myself: *I am entering a Legend; it's as if I ride into Camelot.*

Yet here was a Camelot whose Court consisted of natural philosophers, astrologers, historians, theologians, dramaturgs and mathematicians, the majority of whom in some way received the city's patronage. Alone in the world for this, she possessed no less than four clearly separate universities, the oldest of which was founded in AD 592 by the great Bishop Cornelius Herulianus who encouraged the study of all philosophies and was the first to invite laymen to work with churchmen in their investigation of the natural world.

So steeped was Mirenburg in learning and the arts that it was of some astonishment to the stranger, impressed with the city's reputation, to encounter the noise, the crowded traffic, the hulla-baloo of her markets and barge-wharves, for above all she was a trading city, rich in every way, and with embassies from the Far East, the New World, as well as from the Osmanli nations with whom she had dealt for some three hundred years. Her absence of religious zealotry had always enabled her to treat with dignity and respect the representatives of pagan lands. While Prague, Kiev or Pesht were busy with displays of egocentric pride and unseemly condescension (and a consequent loss of business) Mirenburg, without cunning motive, made friends.

I had not visited Mirenburg since I attended the Royal Gymna-sium in my youth and I experienced considerable, if unanticipated, pleasure at finding the city exactly as I remembered. The progres-sion of change and disillusion which displayed itself physically on the face of Paris made me familiar with the notion that all must inevitably move towards destruction and decay and the corrup-tion of every form of nobility—but here was the denial of that. Here was affirmation and hope.

Yet, in a way, Mirenburg remained a dream and was the setting for another dream; my private compulsion, for I grew steadily confident the Duchess (or the imposter, I cared not a whit) would be there and readily found. There was scarcely a street I could not easily name from memory. Mirenburg was as familiar as my own body. Indeed I was filled with the notion that body, brain and architecture merged and were all part of the same thing. I experi-enced this humour nowhere else, not even in Bek. I was returning home, not to the placid security of my birthplace, but to the city where my brain first began to formulate its ideas.

In a gay mood I went directly to Schmidt's coffee house, which lay at the junction of Falfnersallee and Hangengasse near the Jew-ish Quarter. The place was vast, occupying several floors of a great, square building which originally had been a Convent hospi-tal. It was crowded as always, with tables and benches packed in every possible space. The ground floor was, according to tradition, frequented by men of business, those who dealt in the near-abstractions of finance; but it was also the centre of gossip. There I sought out familiar faces: German brokers, chiefly, and some French and Russians.

I made my enquiries swiftly but was disappointed. A Moravian assurer called Menkowicz accepted my offer of a glass of tea and paused in his babbling and paper-waving to excuse himself from his banker friends. He wore an old-fashioned periwig and dark coat of what we used to call "Quaker cut." This, he insisted, gave him an air of authority and stability, even when he was taking the wildest risks. He had heard the Duke of Crete was due back in the city, might even be there now, but he had no news of a Duchess. He it was, however, who displayed a different aspect of the story for me. "The Cartagena y Mendoza-Chilperics, for all their chief residence was once here and for all their good works, have never been much liked in Mirenburg, von Bek. Mysterious scandals— witchcraft, sorcery, torture, rapine and so forth—led several of them to be banished by the Prince little more than a hundred years ago. They have purchased their way back into the present Prince's favour, but many remain suspicious of them. Something odd about the Duke, though he's good-looking enough. All I can tell you for certain, however, is that Letters of Credit have been issued in favour of the Duke (but not of a Duchess) and they have not been presented."

"Which suggests he's yet to arrive?"

"He could yet be in his castle. He has one, you know, in the Carpathians. Half a mile from the border. It's about a day's ride, so he could appear at any time."

"And he has a residence here?"

The babble around us almost drowned his reply. A frantic wave of Exchanges followed by relieved laughter. Wigs bobbed and another year's cargoes were accounted for. He shook his head. "He owns a house in Rosenstrasse but as often as not prefers to be guest of some intimate amongst the local landowners, choosing to stay outside the city."

I told Menkowicz he could find me at The Martyred Priest

should he learn anything further. This was the inn St. Odhran had mentioned and I had fond memories of it. I was a trifle down-hearted at my broker friend's lack of news. He advised me to look through the columns of the *Mirenburg Social Journal* where I might find some snippet concerning the Duke's activities.

I made my way to Mladota Square, which was crowded with churches, lodging houses and taverns, all seeming to lean in towards the centre where an old, green fountain, representing some ancient Svitavian hero battling a sea-monster from horse-back, splashed. There were two or three plain trees, some benches, the inevitable beggar, groups of street arabs and hawkers selling ribbons, gewgaws and knick-knacks. The Martyred Priest (named, I believe, for Huss) was one of the most prominent buildings, with a wide archway leading to an expansive stableyard around which, on the first storey, ran a continuous balcony. The whitewash was peeling, some of the stucco had fallen away, the plaster faces of (I presume) Huss and his followers were worn, unrecognisable, though the sign was fresh-painted (a cassocked friar holding face to Heaven, hands bound to a stake, faggots flickering at his san-dalled feet). It hung on an iron bracket sticking from one of the massive, blackened beams. My horse was given to an ostler whom I also commissioned to guard my luggage while I went inside.

It was a familiar few feet to the inn's main public room. Since it was noon by now they were selling luncheons downstairs and the smell of the roasting was delicious. The low-ceilinged smoky interior was packed with the liveries of students and apprentices (most of them of medieval pattern, so it seemed one stepped from century back to century). As I pressed through the crowd, sniffing the soups and baked fowl which made the place so popu-lar, I cast an eye towards the long counter. This bar was illuminated, even at that hour, by several candelabra. Behind it a grim-faced man in a red leather apron, a huge periwig of the kind fashiona-ble fifty or sixty years earlier, and with shirtsleeves rolled above the elbows, displaying the whorls and primitive designs of South Sea tattooists, dispensed grog and ale at two pfennigs the pint to sweating maids who brought up their trays to be filled, then returned with practised grace to their customers. The man looked up and his thin lips formed something of a smile when he saw me.

"Captain von Bek!" His face burst from shadowy lines into beaming sunshine. "My Captain!"

I had been almost certain I should find him still behind his counter. "Sergeant Schuster! You told me you were buying land near Offenbau." He had been my servant, my companion in most of my American soldiering, and was himself the veteran of a hundred campaigns. I had lodged at the inn years before, when his father kept it. "You swore you would be a farmer and put city life behind you!"

He lifted up the flap of the bar and came to meet me. We embraced. "I'd heard you jailed in France, Captain."

"Almost," said I, "but they were outguessed by a matter of hours. I skulked from Paris like a cur with a stolen chop. Why aren't you behind a plough? You said you'd had enough of your father's trade!"

"My father retired while I was still abroad. When I came home I found he'd bought himself a farm! And leased the inn, moreover, to a useless dullard of a gentleman taverner from Hungary who upset all the customers, drank all the cellars dry and lost his wife to a passing ape of a Lancer on his way home to Hess! What ignominy, eh, Captain? So my father begged me to take up the management of the inn, at least until trade and good will were restored. Gradually I came to like it. A couple of years back my father gave me the whole thing, lock, stock and barrel, so here I am."

Sergeant Schuster insisted we have a stein of his best beer there and then. He called over his counter for assistance. A pretty girl of about fourteen, in local costume and with her blonde hair plaited atop her head, came into his vacated place. "This is Ulrica," he said. He was proud of her. "My eldest daughter. The other's two years younger, but Marya's a lazy kitten and falls asleep the moment she's called. Ulrica, my girl, it's my honour to present Captain Manfred von Bek, hereditary knight of Saxony, hero of

Saratoga and Yorktown, Deputy of the French Republic. You've heard me mention him, eh? He has as many decorations as he has scars and may yet become a Marshal in somebody's army. He's one of the world's last real soldiers."

"Your father's that," said I, "as witness his Münchhausen exaggerations. Schuster, Fräulein Ulrica's not interested in my military career, but I'm delighted to make your acquaintance, madam." I bowed to kiss her little hand and she blushed.

"Honoured, Sir," said she, and curtseyed.

I complimented them both on her manners, then asked Schuster if he had rooms to spare.

"I'll build 'em if I haven't, Captain." And he led me up the black wood of uneven stairs which had on their whitewashed walls a score of his own mementoes, symbols of his warlike career. Here was a captured Turkish banner, there Prussian epaulettes—a Dutch drum and the old French flag, a Yazoo warrior's battleshirt, together with portraits of Washington and Lafayette, and an English captain's spontoon. Here, too, were the spurs I myself saw him take from the half-Indian renegade Mingava, whose savages had ambushed us four or five miles from Georgetown. Schuster was all babbling reminiscence and pride in our prowess and I sank easily into the pool of his recollection, glad to speak of what was, for me, a simpler and a nobler time.

He told me word for word what General Steuben said to us when we captured Yorktown and how I had wept, so tired were we, when General Washington made a special detour through the ranks to congratulate us. "He knew our names, remember, Captain? And said the cause of Liberty went beyond any immediate concerns of Self-interest; that while he and his friends fought for the right to rule their own land, the likes of us were there solely because we believed in just republicanism and the Rights of Man. It was to us he felt most responsibility, to ensure the Six Colonies would be the foundation for a new kind of government which gave Free Speech to all and Law based upon every soul's undeniable right to justice." And Schuster stood before the portrait of Lafayette and saluted. "There's one who remained true to himself and the Revolution, Captain. A great man. Did you see much of him in Paris?"

"For most of the time our paths did not cross. He had many duties."

Another pause, before a silver-mounted scabbard with English markings at the hilt. I grinned, linking my arm in his. "And d'ye remember, Schuster, who that belonged to?"

"I do indeed, Sir! To Captain Muldoon of His Majesty's Muskets. The most honourable prize of all!"

We laughed heartily at this, for Schuster had won Muldoon's scabbard at a game of playing-cards the day after Saratoga.

"But are all those things we fought for truly lost?" he asked me as we proceeded along the dark landing to a door at the very end of the passage. "These are my best rooms. It's where my married sister and other relatives stay when they visit us." The door was opened onto fresh-waxed furniture smelling of bee-roses and linseed. "The bed must be prepared and so forth. My wife will see to it." He opened carved shutters which creaked as he folded them back and in came the silver light of a misty Mirenburg winter's afternoon.

I looked down at the cluttered little square with its time-worn buildings. On the left side some traders were setting up market stalls with pretty, decorated awnings. By some old agreement with their fellows they were not allowed to begin before noon. Dogs and children ran through the cold on their usual intense, mysterious business. Old men, clad in long gowns and bearing gongs, struck their instruments from time to time, crying the hour. "Thursday afternoon and the wind's freshening from the east!" When not banging and calling, they were employed by the town to give information to whomever enquired, so they could be seen pointing this way and that into the spokes of the wheel which were alleys leading out of Mladota Square to all other parts of Mirenburg. The square was said to be at the exact centre of the city.

"Now, Captain," said Schuster, cutting himself short, "what have you eaten today? Nothing? We'll give you our special jugged hare and some rotkraut. A Gospel-custard to follow. Where's your horse?"

"Already in one of your stables."

"Your bags?"

"With the horse."

"I'll send a boy to see to all that. There's another mews we hire in Korkziehiergasse which has slightly better accommodations. Would you like to use it?"

"I'll leave it to you, Sergeant. My one concern's for my panniers and musket, as well as my other et ceteras."

"The boy will bring them to you. Will you eat downstairs with us?"

"Gladly."

"You must tell me what brings you to Mirenburg." We descended again into cheerful tumult, for which he apologised. "This will subside in a few minutes, when the Cathedral sounds her one o'clock bell."

And sure enough, as I sat myself at Schuster's long kitchen table where several nearby fires heated an assortment of pots and cauldrons, where various meats turned on spits, all of which steamed with delicious scents bringing saliva to my mouth, the noise was suddenly drowned by the tolling of an enormous bell which shook the entire building. A single stroke, but it reverberated. When the echoes died there was a sudden upsurge of benches scraping, feet running, coins rattling, then, quite suddenly, the inn returned to a tranquillity better suited to its age. Next appeared an army of maids and pot-men, already preparing the Ordinary for that evening's business.

At the table, Schuster joined me with a plate of cold chops for himself. As I ate my own delicious hare and dumplings I gave him part of my tale. His little unsmiling face was bent forward in interest as he listened to me. "And you say this Duchess (who might not really be a duchess at all) travels here to Mirenburg? You think she's related to the Duke?"

"That's a guess, but I have only guesses. Their business here remains a mystery."

"Alchemy," said Schuster firmly. "Without question."

I was surprised by his certainty. "Why so?"

"The Duke's mightily interested in the art. Besides, gold-makers from across the Globe congregate in Mirenburg this week. Half the inns are full of 'em. Ask any taverner. I won't have that kind of trade. Not with young daughters in the place. Most are respectable enough, but some are not. The great part of them recently arrived from Prague, where they originally gathered."

"And they're not banned from Mirenburg?"

"You mean the law against secret societies? They've circum-navigated that. They're not in actuality a society, but a convention of individuals. There's no law says they must open their debates to the public. However, it's at short notice, this shift of locale, and nobody knows why they uprooted themselves so suddenly from Prague. Not an innkeeper in the city was forewarned of this until a few days past. They'll get no prejudice here, at least." He smiled. "Save from the likes of me."

"I fail to see why you've taken so hard against the profession."

"Because half of it's made up of charlatans, Captain. Fair-ground piss-gabblers who'll use their tongues instead of their swords to steal whate'er they can. And use their pricks if all else fails 'em. I'll not take the chance on 'em. No more than I would with tinkers." He was easy with me, peppering his language with canting words, for we were both familiar with the language of rogues.

"But why," mused I, "would they not have come here to begin with? Nothing drove them from Prague."

"I know nothing of their lore, but it would seem the most obvi-ous reason was astrological circumstance," said Schuster. "At first they might have judged their proper destination Prague, then dis-covered fresh auguries."

"It's true there seems to be astrology figuring large in this, from my own intelligence," I agreed. "Both La Harpe and Karso-vin had heard such. Some rare configuration in the heavens."

"Well, Sir," said Schuster, licking his fingers and setting aside his chop bones, "it's no business of mine. I'll leave them be if they'll leave me be. I'm surprised, mind you, at your taking an interest in such stuff."

"Unfortunately those I seek seem to be embroiled in it and I can only guess where to find 'em by getting some idea of what they're here for. I doubt if the Duchess herself is an alchemist, but her friends may well be. Should she be an imposter, seeking perhaps to cheat the cheaters, she could have heard of this congregation and dashed for it like a bee to a field of flowers."

"You describe her excellently, Captain. I'll pass the word amongst my fellow tradesmen to tell me if she guests with one of them. If she's here they'll soon have her flushed for you. In the meanwhile you must stay here for as long as you wish."

We raised our steins in a toast to friendship as through the doors came the daughters and the maids with dirty crockery piled high. At bowls, two boys carefully poured hot water from gigantic kettles, filling the kitchen so full of vapour it was almost impossible to see Sergeant Schuster a foot or two away. He added: "What's more, if she's not staying at an inn, but privately, we'll know that too. We all have friends and relatives who are servants at the great houses. Twenty-four hours should get you the news you need, once she's arrived. Now, Captain, drink another pot of this ale with me, for old times' sake, and if you've no other business, get you to bed for an hour or two, for ye're looking mighty weary."

"I'll take your advice gladly, Sergeant. Meanwhile, you're expecting, I gather, a gentleman named St. Odhran. He helped me on the road and I think he must recently have gone through Prague. Can you make sure he has a good room?"

"We've had his letter. From Prague, as you say. Aye, we'll treat him well, never fear. He shall have the chambers next to yours."

"You've a good heart, Sergeant." I clapped him on the arm.

"Captain, this is friendship. We're old comrades and you were always true to me. Equality under the Law and the Rights of Man—you taught me what that properly meant. You transformed my understanding."

I laughed, raising a hand to stop this gush. "You'll swell my head, Sergeant. We always were equals. You were a Captain your-self when we met!"

"Acting. A day later I lost my commission." The little thin lips which so belied his generous disposition broke once again in a shadow of a smile. "For duelling, remember, with that peacock of a Frenchman. At least I had the pleasure of pinking him before we were nabbed."

I had not witnessed the duel, but knew its details. I had forgot-ten the incident until now. "That peacock's now my pursuer," I said. "Montsorbier's an important man in France. I'd swear he still means to have my life."

"He's following you?"

"Through Austria at least. He might have given up the chase. He's older-looking now, though still a handsome dandy, even in his Revolutionary costume."

"I'll recognise him if he comes through my doors. Now, Sir, look you! You nod off as you sit there! Here's Martha." A woman who seemed scarcely older than her girls, with ruddy complexion, dark brown hair and smiling features, returned with a curtsey my kiss upon her hand. She made a dry joke about her husband's tall stories being reduced to truth at last and begged me, laughing, not to give details of every drunken brawl which he now retailed as a duel or an historic battle.

Assuring her of my discretion I went soon up to soft, sweet sheets, having washed away grime inside and out. As I lay naked in the linen, enjoying the sensation, my head gradually filled with unwelcome thoughts. Would I ever find Libussa? Would she agree to acknowledge me if I did find her? Would she reject me out of hand? Did she have an amour? Now jealousy made itself mon-strous fat on my uncertainties, no matter how I reminded myself the lady had given me no assurances, and merely helped me escape one who wished to kill me. Drifting into sleep I conceived the crazed notion that I must discover who my rival was. The Duke of Crete himself, perhaps? But even this fresh discomfort could not keep my eyes open for long. Soon I heard a snort or two from my own nose as I drifted into exhausted slumber, utterly dreamless at first. I recall waking and noting that it was dusk. My window revealed a darkening sky. Then I had returned to sleep, but now I began to experience the most barbarous dreams I had ever known. The awful emotion of terror which filled me was unlike any previous fear—and the images which beset me were also unlike anything in any previous dream I could recall. I was besieged by malevolent creatures of unsurpassed ugliness, menaced by something creeping, insidious and completely evil which alternately chuckled and snarled and had me in its power . . .

The supernatural pack waits only to choose its moment before sucking my soul and the marrow of my bones into their foetid, misshapen mouths. I walk through tunnels with no beginning or end. Somewhere a Beast is panting. Somewhere he stamps with cloven feet upon the ground and pounds at the walls with massive fists. Is it Satan Himself? Now he wields a great stone club. It is a Bull. It is the Bull and he rages against me alone. I am naked and helpless. I am a child. I am a girl. I can obey the Bull or I can perish. But surely I shall perish in obeying him?

I awoke, shivering with a chill but also perspiring so badly I had soaked the bed linen clean through. Before I could think clearly I had tugged on the bell rope. But it was no servant who came. It was Ulrica. She was alarmed when she observed my face, my shaking body, as, with sheet about my waist, I leaned against a tall chest. There were still voices in my head. The creatures spoke in the tones of cultured old men; old men jealous of my vitality, greedy for my youth. *Look, I hear one say, as if at my shoulder, I told you he would behave like this. I warned you. I turn and there's nought but the shuttered window.* Ulrica had closed it. The yellow light of candles spread from the taper in her pretty little hand. She had lit them to ease my mind but they cast shadows, alarming me... I took a grip on myself, for the frightened girl's sake as well as my own.

"What is it, Captain von Bek? Do you have the Malaria? Another friend of Father's, who was in India, suffers from it."

"A nightmare, child, I'm healthy enough. But I'm not much prone to bad dreams, so it came on me with some surprise!" I made some attempt to laugh it away. She was not impressed by my poor play-acting.

"You've nothing threatening you, Sir, in Mirenburg, surely?"

"Not at all." I smiled. I bowed. "Thank you for coming so swiftly, Fräulein Ulrica. I apologise for my stupidity."

Her little face was grave. "You are safe with us, Sir."

"That I believe! But the reassurance is welcome. And so's your company. Pray stay here a minute while I get my bearings on reality." I attempted to laugh but it was impossible as she continued to look at me with honest concern. I let a minute pass. The nightmares gradually faded from my mind and the shadows became merely shadows; the flickering movements were candlelight and candlelight alone. When next I smiled I met her eye and she smiled back.

"Recovered," said I with a nod, and I thanked her again. "A passing fever. Exhaustion of the journey, I suppose."

"Then I'll return to my duties, Sir."

I had been selfish. "Of course. Again, I apologise."

The anxieties and questions of my recent days had bitten deeper than I had realised and come out, I was sure, like a bursting boil—all at once, in a horrid rush given bizarre shape by my imagination. I have discovered, in the course of my adventures, that fear is an emotion which will seize upon any image and make of it its own. The more one refuses to acknowledge the true sources of one's terrors, the more one becomes prone to reasonless panic, until finally madness ensues. Yet I was intrigued by the image of that horrible beast, the Bull. It could only be the Minotaur, and myself some Theseus in the Labyrinth. I made an association in my mind with Crete, no doubt!

When Ulrica had gone with a message that I would be down soon to join the family at its supper, I washed with the water in the bowl and sat upon the edge of my bed to track the nightmare to its source if I could. It was plain I feared the power Libussa exercised over me. I feared the vulnerability of my condition. Was I becoming addicted, as some grow reliant upon laudanum? A further thought came into my head: *A drug can never become its own antidote.* Common sense told us so. Was I doing wrong in pursuing Libussa in that way? Was I like the drunkard who says he intends to give up wine but for a while must frequent the grog shop in order to know what kind of wine it is that harms him? I made up my mind to curb my pursuit of a woman who clearly had little interest in me or would have sought me out before now.

As I completed my toilet I was determined to forget her and return to my original purpose in the city. If I craved sensual adventure, I could find it readily enough in Mirenburg's whorehouses. Yet I knew I was in love, though the nature of my love was unfamiliar. Then I must reconcile myself to sadness in the matter. I should re-embrace comfortable cynicism as swiftly as could be. I must find something to engage my mind and, if possible, my emotions. A business enterprise. I must plot a fresh course, then lash my rudder and keep on. I would borrow funds from Schuster so that I could go that night to a brothel I knew nearby and there purge Eros from my body and my soul.

The money was willingly loaned, the address confirmed, and after supper I slipped off to taste the pleasures which Mrs. Sliney's inventive whores provided. Yet here came another coincidence, shortly after I had exhausted my lechery and was emerging, carrying half my clothes and tucking in the rest, from an upstairs room. The house was tall but somewhat narrow and the stairs curved tightly so I must step back hard against the wall to make room for another gentleman ascending.

He offered me an elaborate bow and grinned up at me. For a second I did not recognise him in that discreet light, then I found myself returning his grin and his bow, for it was the Chevalier St. Odhran, magnificent in golden silk and black linen, his hair lightly powdered and tied, his long, aristocratic features assuming a haughty, yet amiable expression and his eyes languidly hooded. He was a fine rival to Casanova!

"Sir," says he.

"Sir," says I.

"We are lodging, I believe, Sir, at the same Establishment. I arrived tonight, just after you had left."

"The landlord told you of my destination?" I was surprised at Schuster's lack of tact.

"Not at all, Sir. This is a regular resting place for me."

"I commend your taste, Sir."

"Thank you, Sir. Well," he paused with his left hand upon the banister, the other raised to his chin. "I'll be going up."

"And I'm off down, Sir."

"I trust ye'll consider my suggestion we combine our resources, Sir," said he as we passed. "One carriage or one horse is all we need between us, since it's plain our orbits become virtually identical!"

I smiled at this apposite jest, acknowledging it with a gesture of my head.

"Think upon it, Sir, I pray you." He passed into the upstairs room and the door closed to hide his golden figure. I was greatly delighted by the coincidence. St. Odhran might prove to be the Devil Himself, but he promised to be excellent company. I felt that the very best way of taking my mind off its unwelcome obsession might be to form the partnership he suggested.

In a hired diligence I returned whistling to my rooms at The Martyred Priest.

Chapter Five

*I embark upon a business career. The prospect of a
flying navy. The coming of the New Age and
how we plan to exploit it to our advantage.
We begin to raise Capital.*

NEXT MORNING AS I sat at my breakfast, into the taproom
came St. Odhran. He wore a blue Nankeen housecoat to his
ankles, a Chinese brocade cap and Oriental slippers making him
look for all the world like some successful Mogul returned home
with his fortune and bearing not a scrap of similarity to the mercenary rogue of his own description. His demeanour was that of an
amiable English buck, some overbred but not undereducated fre-
quenter of White's or Goosetree's, a crony of the Prince Regent. I
had met this type (and its Colonial imitators) before and had
learned not to underestimate the English dandy. That dandyism at
its best pretended a bored and foolish foppery which disguised
sharp wit and resolute courage. While I was in America I had
heard them dubbed Macaronis, on account of their taste for exaggerated foreign fashions, and even Washington had had a touch of
the same style.

So here he came, with a hint of lavender and rosewater, into
the taproom where Frau Schuster served hot chocolate, cheese,
ham, sausages, boiled eggs, gingerbread and anything else one
desired. St. Odhran had the good manners to refrain from asking
for one of those dishes with which the English ensure the bad
temper of their fighting men, in much the same way as Berserker
Northmen were given strong mead, or certain Polynesian tribes-
men are said to be insulted and humiliated by their wives on the
eve and morning of an important battle. The English, I now know,
eat mashed fish and devilled sheep's hearts to guarantee a bad

digestion (and consequent irritability). It is their abominable cooking which has given them half the world as their Empire.

My friend was a veritable Encyclopaedia of little bows, graces and gestures: a smile here, a brace of nods to myself and Schuster, a few legs made in the general direction of a skirt or a mobcap, and then seated across from me on my right, he praised Herr Schuster's militaria, expressing interest in the Copperplate (which Ulrica, it emerged, had water-colour'd) upon the panelled walls and asking if the landscapes were, like the trophies, of specific memories. He listened carefully with half-bent head as my old Sergeant listed the scenes and his own recollections of them.

St. Odhran was impressed, he said, by the wide extent of this veteran's travels. He smiled gently. "Most Wäldensteiners seem to feel little imperative to go beyond their own borders, perhaps because they know already that the rest of the world is unquestionably less perfect."

"One thing perfection brings, Herr Chevalier," said Schuster readily, "and that's boredom. To grow up in the certain knowledge one shall never know serious threat, nor yet much discomfort, has its own enervating influence. We Mirenburgers send our sons abroad as often and as soon as we can. Similarly, our daughters are generally given the better education. We're proud of our traditions, but there's danger in complacency and we seek to avoid decadence as best we can. Happily, since our population's constantly replenished from abroad, we keep our stock pretty healthy, while many Mirenburgers remain in the service of foreign nations. Then there's our standing army, which is of considerable strength and resources. While it's kept entirely for our defence, it's made up of men like myself, who've experienced War in all his evil forms and would not have him foul our own homes. Yet we never involve ourselves in the struggles of others. Thus no potential enemy ever considers it economical to attack us: at the same time they know they need fear nothing from us, so long as we're left in peace."

"Truly the triumph of Reason," said I, half-jesting.

"A state run upon such rational principles shows an example to the whole world," said our Chevalier. "Yet one wonders why her example's not followed. By England, say."

"I believe it's a question of acreage, Sir," I proposed. "Wälden-stein's an ideal state because she's an ideal size. Once a nation grows, say, to the size of my native Saxony her proportions dictate not merely the use of her resources but also her method of admin-istration and so forth. Kings and governments look upon expansive conquest as a means of increasing both wealth and security, but the larger their domain the more problematical are their deci-sions, for this item must be balanced against that, one party's interests against another's, and all this involves a plethora of promises and compromises. The small state need hardly consider compromise at all and debate is therefore more welcome, while solutions are sooner arrived upon."

"So you would recommend a breaking of the large states into several smaller ones? A general reduction of empires!" St. Odhran shook his head as his chocolate cup went down to his saucer with a rattle. "It would mean the end of our civilisation."

"It could mean the end of these bloody struggles for territory," said Schuster.

"But it will never happen," said I. "There's no suitable rhetoric, no vainglorious posture, no material justification, for the back-ward step. And since progress, the quest for Justice and Reason, is identified in all minds with the steady gaining of territory, we shall forever be in the position of knowing the solution and aware that while our race follows its present logical methods it can never solve its problems. Therefore, half at least of its hideous injustices will continue to be perpetuated, while Colonial conquest is cele-brated and we vie with one another to paint as much of the map in our own colours. Look what happens in America. Having rid themselves of imperial rule, the republicans already spread the rule of might by gun and sword throughout the Indian nations. A children's parlour-game in which each decision results somewhere in the death of thousands and the enslavement of millions! And, moreover, while we continue to judge ourselves in terms of our power, the lot of Woman will remain as miserable as ever."

"Ha!" cried St. Odhran in delight. "Wollstonecraftism!" Then his face clouded and he was no doubt thinking of his native heaths. "Not only could you convince no-one in England of the virtue of your argument, Sir," he said with a sigh, rising from his chair, "but if you attempt to put it into action, as they did in Scotland fifty years ago, you're called Traitor, Rebel and worse. Your people are tortured and executed. At best they're driven into exile. While as for the women, Sir, they're worse treated than ever. Women and children are hounded like game by brutal soldiery; raped and muti- lated, killed, allowed to starve, and your very houses are burned to the ground. I hold no brief for the Stuart cause and Charles Edward's name will forever be linked in my mind with Northum- berland's. Fine words cannot fight a battle. A mere wish for kingship is not an ideal. They were piled, those corpses, one upon the other, at Culloden, and still they ran—unarmed little boys—towards the English guns. Prince Charlie's as much to blame for their deaths as anyone." During this passion, his drawling manner fled him com- pletely and instead he pronounced his German with the fierce, rolling accents of Hibernia. Then he sank back in apology, fanned his face with one elongated Mandarin sleeve, flourished his hand and smiled. "Pray forgive me." A self-deprecating gesture to the ladies, an inclination of his head towards us. Then the familiar expression was resumed and he was saying: "Blood! But the large shall ever feed upon the small, the strong upon the weak, and we must not quarrel with our Lord's will, nor indeed with His mercy." There was a trace of a sing-song in his tone, as if he mocked some childhood guide. He smiled suddenly and put a piece of cheese into his mouth. "'Tis a pretty day," said he.

"And what of your aerial ship, Herr Chevalier? Shall you fly her this afternoon?" I was eager for a taste of the upper atmosphere, for it would distract me, possibly help maintain the objectiveness I hoped for (and which was already threatened by images of her beauty coming unbidden to my mind's eye). All the whorehouse had done, as I might have realised had I not still floundered between the dictates of mind and senses, was to alert my body to the possibility of real pleasure, of the profound satisfaction which

I had known in just those few minutes of Libussa's company. I still believed it would be more wonderful to spend an hour with her than to be all night amongst the artful whores of Mrs. Sliney's. And there I had already begun to logic myself back into a trap when St. Odhran said:

"This morning I'll ensure the Civic Authority has no objection. By two o'clock this afternoon I shall have my Montgolfier on the Little Field—you know it? the public garden outside the West Wall, by the Mirozhny Gate?—and be ready to make a demonstration by means of a tether'd ascent."

And thus he rescued me from morbid self-absorption.

"Mirenburg shall see our craft rise into the air," said St. Odhran with an elegant sweep of his long hand, "and so shall we establish our credentials as aerial navigators in the popular mind. If our reception seems generally favourable, then we shall surely find it an easy matter to interest the wealthier citizen in the prospect of a Society formed to build a larger vessel."

"Herr Chevalier," said I, in some amusement, "aren't you assuming some manner of agreement between us which has not yet been made?"

He looked surprised, rocked back in his chair and fingered his jaw. "Blood, Sir! I'd thought us partners, and that your wish to try out the ship was demonstration of the fact!"

"No hand's been shaken on it. No terms debated."

"True, Sir. Well, you know my proposals, I think."

"I recall what you told me of your own schemes. At the Hackmesser Pass."

"And on the stairs last night?"

"A couple of words, Sir."

"I proposed an alliance."

"True, you did."

"So, naturally, assumed . . ."

I laughed openly. "By God, St. Odhran, I can see the machinery of your tricks, yet still they succeed. And I admit I'd considered throwing in with you before last night. So let's shake a hand on it, hard and fast."

This ritual was completed and he beamed. "Your literary skills are required first, Captain. We need a hand-bill to distribute from the air. New territories. Gold. Wealth of all sorts to be easily gathered." He frowned. "But whether we should make reference to your secret charts as yet, I'm not sure. And would it be deemed heresy to mention the Grail?"

"Hold your horses, Sir," I cried. "What's this? It's all news to me."

"The von Bek family legend, Sir. Money in one's purse where this sort of venture's attempted. And the respectability of the von Bek name, of course—well-known in Mirenburg as you're aware. A sober name, Sir, and a pious one. Upright to a fault, you might say!"

"Sir?" said I.

He grinned frankly at me. "Well, Sir?"

"Do I understand you wish me to exploit my family name? St. Odhran, you ask too much. And as for that demmed legend . . ."

"Being damned, no honour's lost if you make use of it."

"True." I hesitated.

"No need at all to consider that part of the business now," he said generously. "Why not simply add a poetic flourish to the hand-bills and we'll see how we fare?"

There was nothing to lose from that suggestion, so I agreed.

St. Odhran was on his way about the town as soon as he was properly and perfectly attired and I remained at The Martyred Priest drafting our Advertisements which we should, in good time, scatter as messages from the sky. I was not required to be specific. Choosing between Zeus and Jupiter as titular drivers of our Flying Chariot took up more than an hour and finally I rejected both and decided upon *DONAN* as most apt for Nordic climes, though I believe Svitavian gods were of a still grimmer, Slavic persuasion and had names like *Graak* or *Kog*. Sergeant Schuster took an interest. He asked if I'd ever witnessed the Parisian balloon-flights and I was bound to admit I had missed them all, though of course other balloons had been used strategically during the conflict. He himself had seen a vessel in flight only once, he said. It was meant to go from Salzburg to Basel, but the wind had changed. He heard the Aeronauts were eventually found in the Bulgar Mountains, though every scrap of the balloon's bright silk had been stolen by brigands and the Aeronauts themselves were shivering, mother-naked in their basket. "An abnormal knowledge of the paths of the wind, greater than any sea-borne navigator's, must be something of a necessity," he said.

I agreed that it seemed likely. But St. Odhran apparently had methods of steering as yet untried. I held up his notes. "The large ship he plans will have appropriate mechanisms."

I realised I was doubtless already acting as a megaphone for the British swindler. I had no means of telling how much the Chevalier drew the long bow and would have to bide my time before I found out. Moreover, I could not say much abroad of St. Odhran's schemes, lest I betray his confidence. So I held my tongue. Sergeant Schuster, however, had plainly noticed nothing odd in my manner and went on to talk about the fears expressed in a Viennese journal that a French flying army might at any time attack the city.

In those days, of course, the French were thought to be Masters of the Air and nobody had any clear notion of how such a fleet could be built and, if built, how it might be resisted. It occurred to me that St. Odhran and I would do well to play upon that misconception. What else would make immortal Mirenburg stronger still but the construction of a flotilla of aerial men-o'-war?

St. Odhran, returning from the Staatshaus in some elation, displayed his licence, a mixture of printing, ornamental script, decoration (in five colours, including gold) and several seals and ribbons. It was our permission to hold our demonstration.

Now, he said, we would have to canvass prominent burghers and drum up a popular crowd besides. The time seemed too short, I said. "No," said St. Odhran, "we have brushes and ink. A brief notice is always best on a wall. Paint this, von Bek, if you will"—and he writes with a flourish in large letters: *LITTLE*

FIELD TODAY! AIR-SHIP ASCENT. 3PM—"as many times as you can!"

Within an hour I'd a stiff wrist and a hundred posters. St. Odhran was long since gone to make all his arrangements. It was noon. Sergeant Schuster's Martha had boiled us up a huge pot of paste. Armed with this and the bills, we attacked every blank wall we could find in Mirenburg. Church, school and public building—none was safe from us. Then it was thirty minutes past one o'clock and urchins followed us here and there while large crowds were assembling in our wake. I was mightily pleased at the attention. St. Odhran was already at the Little Field and as soon as our work was finished we raced to meet him. The day was passing in a whirl. If only, I thought, the same pace could be maintained for a month or so, then I would be more confident of Libussa ceasing to tempt my thoughts. This pining was repugnant to me. It was demeaning. I was like a schoolgirl panting after the first man to kiss her lips, ready to give up honour, dignity, ambition in furtherance of a senseless passion. It should not be so.

Then we were off up the wide Mladota Steps and into Grünegasse, Schuster and me, running like boys on holiday, taking the shortest route through covered alleys, lanes and passages, to reach the West Gate, the Bull's Gate of Alaric III, the Mirozhny Gate, and out through evergreens, down a long grassy slope under a wonderful, hazy Winter sun, misty with melting snow, to where a monstrous brazier burned, copper and iron, red as rubies, giving forth a blast of smoke and flame like the voice of Siegfried's dragon. Two lads in wool coats and sheepskin hats, with mittens on their hands, held the wide brass hoop of the balloon's neck close to the hot air while the silk rippled and bubbled and slowly filled. Up behind us the walls were already crowded with every class of townsfolk. (Some few had spyglasses and these were passed swiftly from eye to eye.)

Used to addressing such gatherings, but not used to being observed like an ape at a fair, I became embarrassed, and wondered if I should make a speech or at very least salute the crowd. But this, I supposed, would have been in poor taste, for the balloon

313

was the chief performer and St. Odhran her keeper, her trainer. The Scotchman's full attention was upon the filling up of his vessel with hot air. Distant cries issued from the crowd—doubtless expressing its curiosity, asking questions. A few little boys and their dogs dared come closer but were sternly waved back by a dignified St. Odhran. On the far side of the growing canopy, and attached by stout bell ropes, was an ornamental wooden and wicker car, gilded, tasselled, a trifle on the threadbare side, with a head, wings and tail of some fabulous creature. This was the cockatrice, no doubt, which my friend saw flying over Prague. To me it resembled a Gryphon more. It was brightly painted (if chipped here and there) and resembled the kind of thing Indian Princes used to decorate their shrines or place upon the backs of their ceremonial elephants.

As the balloon took shape St. Odhran gestured for Schuster and myself to join him. "I'm much impressed, gentlemen, by your crowd-gathering skills," he said cheerfully as he took a hefty pair of bellows to the brazier and made it roar with an intensity which seemed to me unnecessary but which pleased the audience. They clapped and whistled, sending little clouds of steamy breath into the cold air. The sky remained sharp blue and with no hint of snow. Nearby was St. Odhran's emptied cart. His mules cropped the lawn. Two members of Mirenburg's militia stood by, guarding the cart, fingering their muskets and asking bored, unsophisticated questions.

One of these guards, a confirmed and noisy atheist, discoursed on how the wind, which progressed at different speeds according to the height one achieved, must eventually be charted so that we should be able to move along its courses much as we presently moved on highways. His main theme, however, was on the subject of Heaven and how the Air-ship would not find it, thus revealing as balderdash the religious tyranny to which our race had been subjected for nigh twenty centuries. "That's why the Church wishes to abolish such vessels," he confided.

The canopy bulged and was restless as the hot air slowly filled it. The "Charlier," St. Odhran said, was easier to fill and to fly, but the "inflammable air," the hydrogen gas, which lifted her was also very dangerous and liable to ignite at a spark. The canopy lurched upright and ropes tightened on the Gryphon. The crowd, amongst it scientists and bureaucrats, which stood upon the wall gave a great cheer whenever it seemed the silk filled another significant inch or two. All we were missing was a municipal orchestra and a few words from the Mayor! Meanwhile the wall continued to be crammed, at its top and at its feet, with all manner of folk, from well-to-do ladies in bonnets and crinolines to barge-captains in their oilskins.

All the rivermen had arrived together, drunk and pretending they were taking an official holiday, each with at least one stone bottle of gin or aquavit upon his person. The militia stared coolly at the bargees as if challenging them to do anything even mildly destructive. The rivermen all removed their hats at once and leaned dutifully towards the growing balloon, pursing their lips and widening their eyes in so comical a display that even St. Odhran was forced to laugh at them. He looked up at his balloon, cocked his head on one side, squinted, ran his hand across the tightening silk and meanwhile pumped furiously with his remaining arm at his bellows, forcing the hot air into the envelope until his long face cleared in relief. Either a leak he suspected was not there or it was too small to be of much significance.

Still the crowd grew bigger. I began to think entertainment must be hard to come by in Mirenburg. I recognised half the whores from Mrs. Sliney's, looking more like gentlewomen of the *beau-monde*, in beaver hats and fine shawls, and not generally seen for what they were, save by certain embarrassed gentlemen who shook their heads when their wives enquired after this unusually large group of single women. Then with a lurch the canopy was up to full height, rising swiftly to halt suddenly and strain on her tethering rope with the green, gold, red, blue and white gondola swaying below like a captured beast from mythology.

St. Odhran was quick with his ropes, testing each one to ensure it was securely anchored, bowing to the good-humoured spectators like some circus lion-tamer who had accomplished a particularly daring trick. The canopy rose high above my head and I, like the people on the walls, gasped in awe. I had never realised the thing could be so huge. It was the size of a building and it shone green and gold and scarlet in the bright Winter light.

I felt I was witnessing an authentic miracle. Suddenly I had a profound respect for St. Odhran, who no longer seemed a charming rogue but an engineer of genius, since few had ever learned the techniques of the unfortunate Montgolfiers (one of whom was now dead, while the other continued to enjoy the disfavour of a Revolutionary government identifying him with the king who had patronised him). Secondly I knew some measure of pride in my native land and its contribution to this miracle. The Montgolfiers always acknowledged the writings of Albert of Saxony, the fourteenth-century monk whose treatise on flight inspired them to begin their own experiments. Albert, so family legend ran, was an ancestor to the von Beks.

Now St. Odhran was on the move, lifting his tall hat in recognition of the crowd's applause, bowing this way and that, checking his machine in all its details, testing the pegs to which a single thick coil of rope was attached, then he signed to me.

There was room for at least four in the gondola, but Schuster would not be tempted. He hung back, a look of pale terror on his little face. So I smiled, clapped him on the shoulder and joined St. Odhran at the rope ladder we must climb. The Scotchman was chuckling and full of himself. I shook his hand enthusiastically. Overhead the silk blazed and strained: Donan's Chariot must fly to greet Tomorrow's Dawn!

St. Odhran went up first, moving rapidly as the ladder swayed. I imitated him, more self-consciously, attempting to keep at least a semblance of dignified balance as I followed him into the car (which within resembled a large rowing boat). The vessel itself, once boarded, was surprisingly steady. One might hardly have been airborne at all! There was a large picnic hamper fixed under a seat, books in a glass box, scientific instruments and all manner of blankets, quilts, clothing, weapons—indeed what was probably the entire contents of his wagon, all carefully stowed. St. Odhran leaned out as I walked to the far side to help balance the car. The stern was equipped with a large oar and there were monstrous bellows, too, also a ship's anchor, giving the whole contraption a parodically nautical appearance.

St. Odhran cried "Let go!" to the lads below and I sensed a tiny jerk, but no sensation of flying, so I assumed we were not yet ascending. It was only when I stepped to peer over the side and saw the ground rushing away below at terrific speed that I realised we were leaving Earth behind! I could not hold back my exclamation. My stomach spun like a treadmill and I was close to vomiting. Then I recovered enough to watch.

Within a minute or two, when the balloon was some three hundred feet into the air, I could look down upon the walls and palaces of Mirenburg and see little white faces all staring upwards. It was possible to imagine the power one would feel should one be in command of the large vessel St. Odhran imagined. With mounted cannon and a brave crew one could achieve more than any Army. I began to think in terms of aerial piracy. An entire city might be taken, as the bandits of the High Seas once took single galleons!

Base though the emotion was, there was no denying I felt at least a demigod as we listened to the tiny voices of the crowd cheering while we were borne upward, standing as it were upon a balcony in a Palace of the Skies. One moment I was Mercury, the next I was Blackbeard! There could be no defence at all against a navy able to anchor overhead and rain grenades or whole barrels of gunpowder upon the rooftops. Under the leadership of some new Attila, some purifying Scourge which came not from the East but from the regions of Heaven itself, a world revolution might indeed be possible! Here was an instrument of relentless justice and infinite destruction!

(My recollection suggests that my ascent—upon 300 foot of tethering bell rope—by aerial ship was the first moment I truly realised the world had embarked upon a radical new course in which mankind's theories and dreams could now be made reality. Not by philosophical persuasion or example, but by mechanical means! We were at the threshold of a Millennium, whereby we would steadily increase our mastery of the natural world. Weather and all the elements would eventually come under our control. So, too, should we master our own sensibilities. By the power of Vulcanic mesmerism, if not by the power of our wills.)

Near drunk with all this, I waved again to the little upturned heads. St. Odhran began to unfurl flags here and there, like a side-show conjuror. A reader might reflect upon the irony of my situation at that moment. There was I, a veritable king of the air, admired by a crowd which would not be so impressed had Frederick of Prussia himself risen from death and come a-visiting; borne up (it seemed) by distant cheers from below, and swelling with unearned pride (in spite of being nought but a passenger); supported upon a platform hanging from no more than a few yards of silk, a little hot air and (of most significance) the application of a scientific theory some four hundred years old, preening and strutting and symbolising (for myself at any rate) prospective conquest not of other nations but of the world of intellect and spirit, while at the same moment looking into the immediate future I foresaw a treasure in gold and silver coin which must surely be the tribute paid to us, the prophets (and profiteers!) of this quintessential monument to a dawning age of science—yet planning a *flim-flam*, a confidence trick, a Share Bubble, of the lowest mediocrity! At last it seemed I'd discovered the secret of financial success, of retaining authentic idealism while, without apparent contradiction, turning a handsome gain. The future was not to be Rousseau's Natural Kingdom nor yet Paine's Utopia, after all. It was to be the creation of men who'd labour in iron-foundries to give flesh to the dreams of Arkwright, Smeaton, Watts, Trevithick and other engineers who'd become to the nineteenth century what Voltaire, Burke and Kant had been to our eighteenth. It was at this point I thought to ask my elated companion when we might expect to return to Earth.

The Chevalier scratched his head, looked to the horizon, wet a finger and held it to the wind, crossing rapidly to the side of the gondola, swayed suddenly and set the whole vessel to rocking, apologised as I clung to a rope to stay upright, stared at the darkening sky, studied the western mountains, stroked at his chin, frowned upon his watch, patted his neck-cloth, tapped a foot on the boards of the vessel's bouncing floor and shrugged. "It depends, Captain, upon the weather."

It seemed we would have to wait for the air to cool. Then we should slowly descend. The Chevalier explained in some embarrassment that there were perfectly accurate means of controlling the ship but for this exhibition he did not have time to install every piece of equipment normally utilised. He would explain, he promised, as soon as we were on the Globe's surface once again.

Thus I witnessed from that gondola a magnificent sunset. The stars grew bright and clear in the darkening sky. The cold wind brought the sharp scents of snow; and inch by inch, it seemed, our vessel gradually dropped earthward. At last we clambered from our basket to be greeted by Sergeant Schuster, together with two shivering boys of about ten years, their mangey poodle, the resentful militia men, an old woman wanting to sell us a charm against, she said, vultures, and a thin, long-nosed clerk from the partnership, he said, of Hoehenheim, Plessner and Palaski.

"We're dem' near frozen, Sir," said the Chevalier, rubbing at his hands. "Is your business so urgent?"

"We're advocates, Sir," said the clerk. And when the Chevalier offered him a blank look: "A legal practise, Sir. The law, you know. We are lawyers!"

"Aha!" With an aggressive movement, St. Odhran accepted a card and squinted at it hard in the light from the brazier (which, for their own comfort, the militia had maintained). "Too dark to read. Bailiffs, eh? Leave it with us."

"Ten o'clock tomorrow morning, Sir," said the puzzled clerk. "Something to your advantage, I believe."

"Advantage, hm?" The tall Chevalier's manner changed suddenly and he put one arm around my shoulders, the other around Schuster, and stared up at Mirenburg's exquisite silhouette. The moon was by this time quite high. He murmured to me: "A bite, I'm certain. Say nothing." Then more loudly he added: "Come, friends, we'll celebrate our success with wine."

From the darkness the clerk wailed his bafflement. "Shall you be there, sir?"

The Chevalier paused. He was grand; he was haughty. "Very well, tomorrow. But it must be eleven." He spoke as if to an ill-bred child.

"Eleven, Sir. Yes, Sir."

Behind us the aerial ship, guarded now only by the boys, swayed and creaked and sighed, its canopy forming bumps, distortions, ripples as the air slowly escaped. "'Tis a question of weights and counter-balances," said St. Odhran, "of simple ballast, too. In the larger vessel, or one with a metal gondola, for instance, a brazier's carried which is damped until the need for hot air arises—to keep one aloft, you understand. But it did not seem wise to introduce such an instrument today. One goes up heavy, using ballast to lighten, and comes down cold. What d'you think, von Bek? Did you enjoy the adventure? Are you with me?"

"I've already given you my hand, Sir. But I'm still curious as to how you believe I'll be handy to your enterprise."

"Handy? Demme, man, you're essential. Who would give a Scottish soldier cash before the job's completed? But a Saxon, a von Bek, is a different tale."

We returned to the warmth of The Martyred Priest and when Sergeant Schuster had gone off to explain his long and inconvenient absence to his wife, we sat together in the inglenook, smoking good, cool churchwardens and toasting our boots against the fire-dog, knowing something close to contentment as we continued to discuss the coming of the New Age and how best we might enrich ourselves by it.

Then we went to our suppers and immediately thereafter to our beds. For the first few hours I slept undisturbed, only waking just before dawn, hearing a noise from Mladota Square outside my window. I rose and turned down the lamp I had left burning, so that I might clearly look through the glass upon deserted flagging, cobbles and statuary. Waning moonlight presented yet another aspect of Mirenburg. Two figures stepped rapidly from the eastern corner to the western. Both men wore swords and held scabbards against their thighs as they walked, in the manner of soldiers. The pair doubtless went to duel, almost certainly near the Mladota Bridge which spanned the Rätt. It was the traditional meeting-ground for such encounters. I envied them the simplicity of their conflict which would be concluded in an hour or two without appeal. A little snow danced against my window and thin light came swaggering up the sky from behind a black line of steeples and eccentric roofs. A cold wind entered the room and I hastened back to bed to lie for a while in a reverie of melancholy and dramatic rhetoric, the consequences of my own vanity. How I longed to see my Libussa again!

At last, impatient with this, I was up to the water bowl and splashing hastily before dragging on my clothing and homing like a cat for the warmth of the kitchen stove below. Disconcerting the maids and Frau Schuster, who would not usually expect to see me for another two hours, I retreated to a quiet corner with a cup of warm milk and brandy, claiming it was a headache which affected me.

Watching those hardworking people go about their business, preparing stoves, food, beverages; cleaning all that must be cleaned in a thriving hostelry, drawing up inventories, planning what must be bought, and doing all with fair grace, even cheerfully, I felt divorced from ordinary life and jealous of their apparent tranquillity. I had spent my youth and manhood largely in the service of enlightened causes (save for my Russian years), and this devotion to politics, to campaigns and strategies, to the "general welfare," had left me in some ways ill-prepared, even naïve, when it came to viewing the concerns which these women, for instance, took for granted. There was an attraction in grand designs, for they frequently allowed us to ignore the daily matters of domestic drama which surrounded us. I imagined myself Ulrica Schuster, that friendly, good-hearted girl. If I were she, would I not by her age already have felt half my current disappointments and be expressing almost none of the resentment which I, by sex and position brought up to take power for granted, currently suffered? This observation, while improving my moral state, did very little for my pain.

When St. Odhran came down he was dressed like a Forester or a country gentleman, in hunting green, with a brown waistcoat and top-turned riding boots. A costume my father might have worn to visit the pastor on a weekday. And indeed the Chevalier wore his outfit, he said, in order to create an impression of himself as an unostentatious aristocrat, someone with land-wealth. He had the actor's gift of responding accurately to whatever disguise he adopted. He smiled at my lifted eyebrow. "I've a carpenter, and a smith, who must be induced to allow me credit. They would supply a landsman what they'd refuse point black to a popinjay in dandy's threads."

"So the von Bek name shan't be used yet?"

"Used," he said, "but not abused." And he winked.

"I presume you shall not take me with you."

He shook his head. "You're needed, my friend, for the Prospectus. It must be written in a properly educated manner." He drew some folded documents from his tail pocket. "Here are all the saliencies of my aerial man-o'-war. Make her a merchant craft instead. Put a literary and fanciful touch to her particulars while I'm out. Then meet me at the lawyers' in Königstrasse at eleven."

"You require the whole Prospectus by then?"

"I'd be obliged, aye." He drank a rapid tot of hot grog to prepare him for the weather outside then stood up, plucking his heavy cloak and his stick, his gloves and wide-brimmed hat from the bench beside him. "I'll take it to the printer this afternoon. By tomorrow we'll be ready to begin. Wear whatever you fancy for yourself. You have an old name, which can always carry the newest fashion. Those of us with shop-new names must endeavour by our waistcoats to suggest antiquity!" And with a wink he was gone out into the awakening street.

Having paid my respects to Sergeant Schuster I returned up the stairs, passing Ulrica coming down. She greeted me pleasantly and asked if I intended to stay in my rooms that morning. When I told her I'd be writing there, she said she would light the stove in my little parlour. It was too cold, she said, for thinking and shivering at the same time. I was touched by her thoughtfulness. I wondered how I should have fared in Mirenburg had I arrived there without friends and my obsession still upon me.

Soon, in the easy warmth of my parlour, I had composed the following:

AN AERIAL EXPEDITION

The Latest Intelligence of a Modern Columbus

But recently reported in the English Press, the return of a remarkable aeronautical navigator, **Le Chevalier Colin James Charles Gordon Cowie Lochorkie St. Odhran**, nobleman of **Scotland** and **Luxembourg**, lately in the service of the **Emperor Frederick of Prussia**, was celebrated with great Rejoicing in London and Edinburgh after the Chevalier's absence of nearly a year aboard his Aerial Schooner, the *DONAN*. In his Address to the Royal Exploration Society at Greenwich, the Chevalier spoke of new Lands discovered beyond the Antarctic Continent and of the Astonishing variety of Creatures and Peoples he had found there. At the end of his Address he displayed Gems of unique size and purity. These were subsequently loaned to the Crown Agents who are yet attempting to Assess their monetary Value, since nothing of their like has been seen before.

The Chevalier de St. Odhran, who is both a Hero of the East Indian Campaigns and a Knight of St. Leopold, informed the Society of his intention to Found an Aerial Navigation Society which would equip a larger vessel to journey by Air to the Newly Discovered Regions and return with Examples of both Flora and Fauna together with further Examples of those Precious Minerals which he himself saw in considerable Quantities.

Venality of The English Parliament

This Noble Scheme has been Threatened, however, due to the English Government insisting, in Spite of Considerable Publick

Outcry, that the Crown receive half of any Cargo so Discovered. Subsequently the Chevalier de St. Odhran Departed in his Vessel from England and it is Rumoured that he journeyed to his Estates in Africa, which may only be reached from the Air.

INTENTION OF HIS VISIT TO MIRENBURG

On the Eve of his Departure the Chevalier expressed his Hope of meeting more Confidence and less Greed amongst the Continental Nations. He Expressed the Intention of visiting the Enlightened City of Mirenburg, which is the Capital of Wäldenstein whose People are Famous for their Generosity and Positive Curiosity. There, he would Solicit Interest in his Newly formed Para-Antarctical

AERIAL NAVIGATION SOCIETY

I will admit I was singularly proud of my literary invention. For the past few years I had written nothing but speeches, and their high-toned Rhetoric, it now seemed to me, was better suited for the form of commercial advertisements. In this time of Revolution and Discord, I went on to say, it was wise for men of property to invest their capital in more distant lands, not yet settled by civilised peoples with Radical notions. The Chevalier St. Odhran possessed charts, made by himself and other explorers, of lands as yet unmarked upon the familiar Globe. It was his intention to have built a great Aerial Frigate, armed with the latest in weaponry and with a complement of seasoned veterans of good character, and, thus equipped, embark for these lands, claiming them in the name of the Society or any nation which should commission him. Any commissioning body or individual should have the honour of assuring one of the noblest ventures in modern times and, moreover, be enriched by a profit many degrees greater than the original investment.

I went on in this vein for a while, making reference to the drawings (which were excellently done) of the projected frigate itself, which would consist of an oval-shaped canopy and a wooden hull.

Upon this would be mounted an assemblage of sails and Wind Oars, as well as various forms of ballast. The present Director of the Society was none other than the Ritter Manfred von Bek of that great and noble Saxon family whose name had been associated for many centuries with ventures of only the most reliable stability and provenance. The Ritter's experiences in France, where he stood against Robespierre and defied the Mob in his valiant defence of the King and his family, were now common currency, I wrote. These events impressed upon the Ritter von Bek an urgent need for fresh Colonies abroad where the mistakes of the past could not be repeated. To ascertain himself of the Chevalier St. Odhran's absolute integrity, he himself accompanied the Explorer on his most recent voyage to the idyllic territory, free of disease and discord of any kind, which St. Odhran had named *QUASI-AFRICA*. The drawings in the Figures were the work of the Ritter's own hand and displayed the wonderful Tropical world, its riches and its fruits, together with its natives who were gentle and friendly and whose simple costume included headdress and harness of emeralds, sapphires and diamonds, which they dug from the floor of a certain valley not two miles from their Capital Town. As for vegetation and beasts, these consisted of many edible fruits and vegetables and varieties of animals, most of which were not dangerous. The largest was a kind of Ostrich, with multicoloured plumage, used for ploughing and for pulling carriages by the natives, as well as a kind of Ocelot, whose coat resembled that of an Ermine, though was of a pinker cast.

In danger of carrying myself away by these flights of fancy, I forced myself to stop and, hearing the Cathedral clock strike ten, rolled up my best copies, tied them with a ribbon, drew on my topcoat and was off to the Lawyers, via Radoskya Avenue, where I made enquiries at a Tailor's after a new suit of clothes, so impressed had I become by the promises of my own Prospectus.

Early at Messrs Hoehenheim, Plessner and Palaski, I was shown into a Waiting Room lit by a large bay window with a view of the Falfnersallee, busy and wide: below and beyond it the river was so crammed with the morning's traffic, the water was hardly visible. The room was sparsely furnished, containing a set of high-backed uncomfortable chairs, a map of Mirenburg on the wall, a long, brightly polished bench, an ornamental stove in black and blue tiles, giving off a parsimonious warmth, and a framed testimonial that in the year 1732 Isaac Hoehenheim passed with honours the High Examination of the Royal Wäldenstein Legal Council. The room smelled of beeswax and old parchment. The firm was a rich one, doubtless with aristocratic clients. There was a Turkish carpet on the floor. The uniformed Beadle asked if there was anything I required while I waited. I told him there was nothing. I was content to breathe this wealthy dust for a while.

Soon the Beadle was back, ushering my partner into the room. St. Odhran was very much the busy owner of estates come reluctantly into town on business. He displayed the suggestion of a wink to me as he handed his outer garments to the servant hovering in the shadow of the Beadle's worsted and braid. Another minute while he went through my handiwork, praising, grunting, considering a phrase, then the Beadle was back and we were on the move again, through panelled passages, past libraries of mysterious books and offices where perched Clerks at high stools and desks, like so many captive flamingoes, quills squeaking on vellum, until we came to a great cabin, a Throne Room of a Prince of Law, which had a circular window set near the roof. Through this window a massive sunbeam entered, piercing the ever-present dust and falling at last upon a bust of some seventeenth-century Lawmaker in a fluted wig and a gown so trimmed with stonework-lace I thought it must surely crack at a touch. His white, unsmiling face was at odds with all this frippery, making it seem someone had played a practical joke upon him and dressed him in his costume while he slept. He seemed, however, sublimely unconscious of the deception.

From the room's far shadows now stalked a figure whose face not only bore a striking resemblance to the elaborate bust, but was almost as pale. He was in cream-coloured silk. Only the bright eyes, clear and without expression, had colour. The thick lips moved ponderously to utter a "Good morning, gentlemen," then to introduce himself as Herr Doctor-Lawyer Hoehenheim-Plessner, the Junior Partner (sixty if a day!) and to ask our names. We bowed, announced our titles, and took his proffered chairs in front of his desk as he moved to a seat which had doubtless shaped his body over most of his life.

"I am, gentlemen, representing a Client and the matter requires your assurance of complete discretion before we continue." He fluffed and patted at his cravat while he spoke, but when he folded his hands to listen, he fixed the speaker with unblinking turquoise eyes which, on their own merit, must have won him the majority of his cases.

We gave him our word on our silence. Satisfied, he picked up a folder to consult while he continued his deliberate discourse. "My Client's a person of quality, a resident of this city. For reasons which cannot as yet be divulged my Client wishes to commission your aerial ship."

"Wholly commission her, do you mean, Sir?" St. Odhran spoke in some surprise. "The existing ship?"

"The existing ship, Sir."

"Sir, we plan to build a better, more sophisticated vessel."

"I shall inform my Client, Sir. Thank you."

"Then"—St. Odhran frowned—"which ship do we discuss?"

"Either, Sir. I believe that to be immaterial in this particular case."

"A great deal of money is required to equip her," said St. Odhran.

"I am able to inform you that money shall be forthcoming. As much as is appropriate."

I could tell that the lawyer was anxious not to make large promises to us, but it was also clear that his Client was not troubled by any shortage of gold. Both of us could scarcely contain our greed! Our scheme was progressing more swiftly and smoother than we had dared to hope!

"Are we to know nothing else of your Client, Sir?" asked St. Odhran carefully. "As I am sure you are aware, we are ourselves men of principle and—"

"Nothing underhand, Sir, is proposed." The lawyer pursed his pale lips.

"Of course not, Sir."

"My Client proposes to underwrite your entire expenses and to place only one condition upon your Society."

"Sir?"

"That my Client have first choice of the ship's destination and purpose—for the maiden voyage only. Thereafter, it is your own affair where you sail her."

St. Odhran, who had no intention whatsoever of completing the proposed ship, pretended to consider this carefully. Then he said: "And we are not to know of this destination and purpose?"

"Not until you are ready to depart."

"A single voyage? Then the ship is wholly ours?"

"Wholly."

"It's an attractive offer, Sir. With an element of mystery and risk which whets my appetite, I must say. Yet, according to the vessel's destination, there will be things we shall have to know. The climate must be prepared for and so on."

"My Client understands as much. Now, gentlemen, do you wish to accept the commission or shall we simply shake hands and go our separate ways?"

"I'm tempted to accept, Sir, but here's a problem for you—we are in the process of talks with investors interested in shares of the larger ship. Indeed, a Prospectus is in preparation. Would it not be wiser for your Client to wait until the Prospectus is ready? To read it, to make suggestions even? There is a problem of shareholders already committed and so on. Money has already been spent in certain quarters . . ."

"We can reach financial agreement, I am sure, easily enough. All my Client wishes is that the first voyage be determined by them. Shall I tell my Client that you are planning this new ship and that you'll send me a Prospectus as soon as you have one?"

"If you would, Sir."

"And where are you lodging, Sir?"

Lawyer Hoehenheim-Plessner made a note of our address. "I shall send a message as soon as possible."

"Perfection, Sir!" said St. Odhran. "Much obliged."

"I hope we shall meet again, Sir," said I.

Hoehenheim-Plessner paused as he made to rise from his desk. He seemed a trifle embarrassed. "Excuse me, Sir, but the name von Bek's more than familiar to me. The Beks I know are from across the border in Saxony. I had the honour to represent the Graf Rickhard von Bek in a business matter some years ago."

"My grandfather, Sir."

Hoehenheim-Plessner was suddenly ten times more affable, which was to say that a fraction of him relaxed. He was as close as could be to Enthusiasm. Now my hand was shaken, almost warmly, amid the Doctor-Lawyer's murmuring courtesies. I was highly impressed, once again, by St. Odhran's judgement. The family name was worth cash, after all.

"I told my Client that I thought you a Saxon von Bek. I foresee few difficulties, my dear Sir!"

The lawyer's offices vacated, we walked up the Vlescstrasse in the cold air of imminent snow as cloud formed from the east. St. Odhran was cheerful. All necessary business had been accomplished in the matter of Smithery and Joinery and he was optimistic about attracting wealth from all quarters. "Hoehenheim-Plessner, a most cautious old gaffer, is won over, that's obvious. If we can impress a man like him, the rest of our task will be all oil and Billy Griffin!" (He had a tendency to use the obscure catch-phrases of Glasgow and Newgate when ebullient.)

But I was suffering qualms. My family name was a trust. One day I would be head of our clan. Bek and honesty have been synonyms for generations. I was involved, I feared, in too many lies already. Yet why should a name alone have meaning? Better to betray it, I insisted to myself, and show the world how innocent and foolish it could be. I had learned, after all, to trust neither religion nor politics and to put my faith in the realities of metal, wood and steam, in practical engineering, whose rules could neither be changed nor made the subject of morality, so why should I show reverence for mere antiquity?

These fears were to a degree put to rest by St. Odhran's insistence that he take me to a large chophouse near the Mladota Bridge from where we could watch the hurly-burly of the city. The bridge was crowded with horses, oxen, tumbrils, carriages, cabs, diligences, donkey carts and all manner of men and women from every walk of life. "Dem' near as crowded outside as in," said I. We were jostled by waiters as they danced between the tables with smoking trays of Kalbshaxe and Eisbein and a variety of cutlets, half-cabbages, bowls of potato soup, hunks of black bread. St. Odhran was familiar with the place and soon had service for us. We toasted our future in strong Mirenburg Stout and after downing one full stein I remarked upon my uncertainties regarding use of my family's name.

St. Odhran was dismissive, dabbing delicately at his mouth with his sleeve and leaning over the table towards me. "Wealth's always a fair substitute for Virtue, von Bek. I mentioned your name to an acquaintance this very morning, a clever old fellow called Protz, who's dabbled in supernatural studies but earns his livelihood by producing lineage charts for the *nouveaux riches*. He says your family's reputed not merely to have sought the Holy Grail, but to be its hereditary guardians!"

"What, the Beks are Fisher Kings?" I laughed heartily and spontaneously. "We've no connection with that myth at all! Half my ancestors were this side of being Atheists and the other half were practical Lutherans. We've a tradition of intellectual rather than religious enquiry. Why, there's more evidence of us being devil-worshippers than grail-keepers!"

"Well, it's generally thought here that your ancestors came from or were intimately acquainted with certain mysterious lands bordering on our own, yet invisible to most of us. The Middle Marches some call 'em. Protz says that there are fifty accounts in his reading alone which suggest the von Beks were more than a little familiar with supernatural beings!"

I was uncomfortable with this. "The old romances attached

any name to their tales, as you must know, St. Odhran. Doubtless by chance a 'von Bek' appeared in one of those. And from that beginning—well, the Romancier did the rest, eh? If you were to believe all the old, degenerate German legends, there's a Grail in every castle, a Charlemagne or an Arthur under every mound! There's not a noble house without at least one werewolf offspring or a younger son who's made a pact with the Devil, an uncle practising the profane arts of alchemy, a vampirical grandfather, a mad monk, a ruined abbey in the grounds where witches meet, an incarcerated lunatic (or heiress—or both), an infanticide or two (and a patricide), and, of course, a family ghost. I grew up with such stuff—though my own father always dismissed it.

"St. Odhran, I'd be happy enough to see the end of all such superstitious gibble-gabble in Germany. It's the bane of reformers, even if it's presently fashionable amongst young Romantics who celebrate the Teutonic past, thanks I suppose to the reborn popularity of *Fortunatus*, the *Nibelungensage*, the extravagances of Goethe, Schiller and all the other *Sturmers* and *Drangers* who've followed 'em, now seeking out Occult experiences! Not only do I lack interest in such things, my dear Sir, I possess a positive instinct for Reason, a distaste for myth, legend and the German reverence for antiquity. I am old-fashioned enough to be a supporter of Nicolai, in literary matters. This fascination for mouldering tapestries and rotting tombs is one of the chief reasons for my leaving Saxony in the first place—and Saxony's far more Enlightened than many other provinces!"

St. Odhran was disappointed by my scepticism. "You sound like a Canting Methodist," he said, and sniffed. "There's no harm in a little Fancy, surely, to give colour to dull lives. Your family legends are famous enough in Mirenburg to be of considerable use to us. My maps shall now be partly taken from your ancestral collection. To certain people—and this city's full of those young aristocrats you so despise, ever ready to join some new coven or discover a receipt for the Elixir of Life—they'll be of greatest importance. And a touch or two of Romance in our scheme will mean the sale of many more shares."

I sat back as my meat arrived. I was silent. A great cloud of melancholy engulfed me suddenly and I stared out at the bridge wondering how I could have strayed so far from the course I set for myself when I put Castle Bek behind me and rode east. My radicalism in those days had not been sophisticated. It had been little more than a faith in Reason, a belief in somewhat abstract notions of Justice and an honest understanding that by appeal and some small demonstration, everyone could be made to realise how self-interest was synonymous with a rational altruism. My experience of Catherine's Court, where many men of intellect gathered to debate these very issues, had served more to baffle than to illuminate and my two years with the Tatars had given me little opportunity for philosophical enquiry. It had been in America I'd begun to develop my sense of the complexities which go to organise the modern State and in France I had attempted to balance those complexities in a practical experiment. At least, I thought glumly, my actions and words were then united. Now I was discovering I could be an accomplished liar when I chose. The understanding gave me no sense of pride.

"Moping again, von Bek?" said St. Odhran. "Is it that woman you told me about? The Cretan? She'll come chasing you when you're the toast of Mirenburg—as you shall be soon, at this rate." In his own way I believe he honestly tried to ease my pain. He ordered more stout and encouraged me to eat as he babbled of his plans, the eminent people he hoped to attract to our scheme, the possible identity of our would-be backer.

He asked for the draft Prospectus I had made and pored over it while he uncharacteristically consumed an entire beef pudding, nodding and exclaiming. "You're a literary genius, von Bek. This is excellent stuff. It has just the right ring to it. Have you written for publication before?"

I denied it, though in truth I was already the author of a handful of broadsheets, a couple of treatises against Slavery in America (which I'd hoped to abolish, but while Washington offered a patron's argument for the institution I supposed it would be some years before the Rights of Man were judged to extend to those whose freedom was not of economical benefit to the nabobs and landowners who only a few years before had cried "Freedom for All"; it now emerged they'd wanted freedom only to improve their profits and not pay English taxes). I had also written a volume of Radical poetry, a verse Romance (long since vanished in its only edition and called *Chickenawpoo; or, The Pastoral Utopians*; it had been suppressed in America) and, of course, continued to keep my journal (since partially published as a Memoir). I would never again be so foolish as to draw my sword or wield my pen in what proved to be a rich man's cause. As the friendly stout softened moral argument, I informed St. Odhran that I was tired of being deceived by others. For a change, I would be the deceiver. Thus I quelled my conscience, and maintained my progress as a capitalist.

Soon, by this drawing forth of anger and attaching it to past resentments, I was able to grin suddenly at St. Odhran, give wild acquiescence to all his proposals and, with horrid savagery, set upon my cooling chop.

Chapter Six

Bargains are struck and work, of sorts, is begun. My
Young Radicals Again. A Further Mysterious Endowment.
A Challenge Accepted. Callers in the Night.
Discomforts of a Charnel-house wagon.

MY BEAUTIFUL DUCHESS had still failed to arrive in Mirenburg
and while the Duke of Crete was said to be abroad from time
to time, dealing with the visiting alchemists, even going so far as to
let several guest at his house, I had been unable to gain any further
knowledge either of her movements or of his. Meanwhile the Lawyer Hoehenheim-Plessner had received our elaborate Prospectus,
passed it to his anonymous Client, and requested a further interview. News of our mysterious backer (rumoured to be none other
than the Prince himself) inspired many Mirenburger worthies to
press us into accepting their gold and soon we had a box full of the
stuff hidden in the gondola of St. Odhran's balloon, in case (he said)
we needed to depart suddenly from the city. St. Odhran became so
euphoric he said he was almost tempted to try to build the flying
frigate he had described. It was I who was forced to remind him that
we had designed a Swindle, not a genuine expedition, and that even
if we built the ship we could certainly never find the fabulous lands
we claimed to be familiar with! Our shareholders were either greedy
or foolishly romantic. One woman of middle-years, the Landgräfin
Theresa-Wilhelmina Krasnaya-Badehoff-Mirozhnitski, cousin by
marriage to the Prince, hoped that by investing in our ship we might
sail it into the Mittelmarch and find her missing husband. We
accepted her fortune, though we knew what she did not, that her
husband, though given to dabbling in sensational melodramas
involving the Black Arts, had actually died in the arms of one of
Mrs. Sliney's whores. To avoid scandal, the Landgräfin's nephew, it

was said, had seen to the body's disposal in the Rätt. Since he was due to inherit his aunt's wealth he was also said to be furiously resentful of her bestowing money on a quest for her missing husband, yet ironically was no longer in a position to reveal that his uncle was dead! In the main, however, our investors were of the usual greedy merchant sort.

Back in the lawyer's office, gloomy now that no sun shone into it (for the sky was full of seasonal snow), we were quizzed with a list of questions prepared by Hoehenheim-Plessner's Client. Since we had no great need of further backing we cheerfully answered, knowing that we could only double the fortune we should take with us from Mirenburg when our balloon sailed. About halfway through this interrogation (which was perfectly friendly) the pale advocate held up an old book in a tattered binding. "Van Brod confirms all you say and I have discovered other evidence in support of your claims which, frankly gentlemen, I thought a little fanciful myself, though of course I am not the principal here."

"What's the book, Sir?" asked St. Odhran. It was passed over the desk to us. I read the title-page: *A Treatise Upon The Discovery & Occupation Of Occult Worlds.* My guess was that the lawyer had been loaned it by his Client.

"In there, gentlemen, is Van Brod's description of the world he called the Middle Place, which lies, he thought, between our own and Heaven. I also have a sheet from an old journal acquired by one of our agents, which gives instructions for entering those worlds; while here's another description, from the fourteenth-century monk Augustus of Nierstein, where he has interviewed a warlock and a witch who visited what the monk names 'The World Between.'"

I was amused by all this. It was as if he assembled evidence for a trial and, satisfied that there was a case to prove, was now prepared to believe every lie we invented! He even seemed excited. I knew a pang of guilt.

"A few leaves," he continued, "from the records of Henry Alaminus of Danzig, a famous alchemist of the fifteenth century, again upon the identical subject; a fragment from a letter written by an unknown husband to his wife, describing an expedition into what he termed the 'Geistwelt.'"

I listened patiently with a mixture of boredom and discomfort. Having never encountered such stuff before, the old man did not know how easily such evidence could always be accumulated. It was a question of the specific selection one made from the vast whole of the world's information. But now he paused and his enthusiasm for our scheme came clearer.

"And here's something, Captain von Bek, of interest to yourself. Perhaps you've heard of it before? It is a letter written by Brother Wilhelm of the Monastery at Renschel to a fellow monk at Olmitz. It is dated June 1680. Do I make familiar reference?"

I shook my head, whereupon he handed over the following modern copy of a parchment which he said was still in the hands of his Client (and the chief reason, I was led to believe, for the said Client's interest in our enterprise). I reproduce the thing here, as I acquired it later:

I am presently embarked upon the strangest of tasks, which is the copying of a Confession made by our Patron Lord, the Graf von Bek, whose good works are well known. I cannot, of course, describe the Confession itself, but he has already caused considerable astonishment and consternation amongst our Fraternity and speaks of exploring lands which lie somewhere beyond our Earthly perceptions, being neither Heaven nor Hell, but in somewise of this world and which he calls The Mittelmarch. Brother Olivier takes the Confession direct and it is only my task to Transcribe it. Yet my pen shakes in my hand sometimes as I record his story and I must pause frequently to bless myself. Sometimes I pray the Graf raves in a fever or lies to us, or is mad. But he seems as sane as always and in full command of himself, though weak from his illness. He describes lands wherein the most fantastic beasts and races dwell, more strange than anything found in the old Romances and which seem in no wise unusual to him. However, it is the import of his tale which chiefly distresses us. Pray for us all, dear Brother, and I beg you pray additionally for me that I may not go mad from this Task.

This was the second unwelcome reference to my family's legend in recent days and when the lawyer looked significantly at me I was forced to pretend an intelligence I did not feel, for by now, of course, I was committed to the role St. Odhran had imposed on me.

"You will know, of course, which ancestor is referred to," said the lawyer respectfully, folding the paper when I had handed it back to him.

"My paternal ancestor. My grandfather's great-great-grandfather, I believe, Sir." I felt a fool and a rogue.

"Well, Sir, and you know well enough where he travelled. You have been to those regions yourself. With your partner."

"Of course, Sir," said St. Odhran. "You have seen the maps and such."

"Which convinced my Client. These other questions, you will appreciate, are merely those drawn up by myself, in my capacity as a lawyer. We're a cautious breed—more cautious than adventurers such as yourselves." And I believe he attempted to utter a laugh.

The deception was growing less and less to my taste and I was divided between making my own confession and so betraying St. Odhran or keeping silent. Needless to say, I kept silent, and felt myself a worse coward. Some silly nobleman no doubt had collected a great many old books and cobbled from them a theory which could be disproved by rational argument in a flash. Who was I to destroy their dream? I argued. They would learn their own folly when I disappeared with their gold!

"Aha, Aha!" St. Odhran chimes like a Cathedral steeple. "The Mittelmarch. Just so. And that's why the expedition shall require the building of a new ship. Our old vessel, the aerial boat we flew the other week, is neither large enough nor strong enough for the journey!"

"I understand that, Sir. I was about to come to the question of capital. First I must know how long the ship would take to build."

"It depends, Sir, upon the craftsmen employed. For the hull, the best are in Bremen. The canopy should be made in Lyons. The rest could be constructed here in Mirenburg. But it will take, as you'll understand, a matter of months."

"You would be ready, say, by September of this year?"

"Very likely, Herr Doctor-Lawyer. But the craftsmen of Bremen and Lyons will require money in advance as proof of our good faith."

"I understand. How would the money best be sent abroad? By draft? By note?"

"I have not enquired, Sir, but could have that information for you within a few days."

"They are the best, these Bremen people?"

"As good as my native Scottish shipbuilders, aye. And it would not be practical to deal with those at present. Hitherto, of course, the Bremeners have only built for the sea, but the lines of their ships are ideal for aerial voyaging. The air must flow"—a mysterious gesture with both hands—"so. The oars must pull, thus"—a kind of paddling movement—"and the sails have to be rigged on leaning masts at an angle of at least forty-five degrees, so—" a geometrical representation, palm to palm, "and then there are all the subtler engineering problems, though we're fortunate in having the services of an ideal architect who has worked in his time for both British and Dutch navies. He's at present on the way home from America where he has been advising the government there on the most suitable designs of ships for their needs." And so St. Odhran pealed on in this by now familiar mode, a musical invention which built upon the simplest of melodies to provide dazzling complexities stimulating the listener's imagination. In other words, the listener's own picture was painted in the shining colours St. Odhran provided. By seeing what they wished, they also saw what he wished them to see. "They are the Orchestra," he had told me earlier, "and I am merely the Conductor."

When he had completed his performance I was almost as

impressed as the sober-faced lawyer across the desk. St. Odhran assured the Lawyer-Doctor that our ship would not only sail into the Mittelmarch, crossing barriers impossible to negotiate by land or sea, but would be ideally equipped for any eventuality. He made sly references to "the illustrious gentleman" and "your noble Client," as convinced as I that Mirenburg's ruler was the person giving us this backing. Why the Prince should outlaw Secret Societies dedicated to similar claptrap as we were selling and yet be impressed by our claims I did not bother to question on the basis that frequently it was possible for an enthusiast to embrace one ludicrous notion while vehemently attacking another which was quite as ludicrous. Human nature explained everything for me in my mood of cynicism.

As we returned to Mladota Square in our new-hired carriage, St. Odhran had the weary air of a great actor who had satisfactorily given a difficult part to an appreciative audience. "The launching of our Society is to be easier than I'd guessed," he said.

For my part I had grown anxious. It was one thing to cheat a burgher or two, but quite another to cheat an illustrious Prince. I believe that it was from then that I began to experience a recurrence of my nightmares.

Thus my nights were once again spent in the dream company of my Duchess, with a bull-man snorting his heat into my face and the Labyrinth growing more complicated and the whispering voices threatening, while daily St. Odhran was producing more and more fine forgeries—Letters of reputation, together with a whole variety of other testimonials and documents ostensibly emanating from the shipbuilding firm of Linder & Linder in Bremen, offering to construct a hull for the Aerial Navigation Society at a cost of some 27,000 Talers, with T9,000 down, T9,000 to be paid on completion of the main frame and T9,000 on completion of the whole. For 10,000 Talers Messrs Vingleur of Piedmont would weave and make airtight a silk envelope to the specifications given (they had worked for the Montgolfiers) but required half the price in advance. They would charge extra for any insignia, flag or coat of arms which must be incorporated before the final varnishing of the fabric. Mr. Markess, the Naval Architect, enclosed plans and looked forward eagerly to beginning detailed work upon his return from America, and so on. The more elaborate St. Odhran's swindle became, the queasier I grew and the worse my dreams. If discovered, we should be exiled at best—probably executed. There would be nowhere in the civilised world we should be able to travel. I had planned to make my fortune with smaller deceptions, more traditional strategies, yet now I was in too deep to escape without betraying St. Odhran and revealing the extent of my own roguery.

Oblivious to all morality, to all consequence, my friend continued to sink deeper into this morass of illusion. In further conversations with the lawyer he regrets the lack of "inflammable air" for the powering of our new ship and wonders if this, too, might be purchased. The lawyer makes notes. Contracts are drawn up and at last I must put my signature to them. I feel I am selling my soul to Satan. I can scarcely believe St. Odhran's light and easy attitude to the whole thing. The money we stand to accumulate is too much. I had no ambition to attract the wealth of a nation, merely the fortune of a widow!

And so the time fled by, as unreal to me by day as it was by night. I took to drinking more than was wise and to stalking the streets in the faint hope I should come upon my Duchess. The Winter grew colder. I felt that my spirit was dying within me. I had never experienced such a bleak unhappiness as I knew then. Frequently I thought of taking my horse from the stable and merely riding away from Mirenburg, as much a pauper as I had been when I arrived. I longed for Bek, for peaceful Bek and the security of my family. Yet stubborn, pointless, destructive Pride kept me in Wäldenstein's capital—that and my misplaced friendship for the Scotch rogue.

On paper, our great vessel began to take shape. St. Odhran even went so far as to draw elaborately coloured sketches of the ship's progress and this contented the more nervous shareholders. I did not dare estimate the amount of money we now stored in our box and only reluctantly, at my partner's insistence, went out to the Little Field when he visited the shed which had been erected to shelter the old balloon. There, laughing to himself, he deposited the latest bag of Talers, seemingly oblivious of my misery's origins.

"This cold weather depresses you, eh?" he said. "No matter. Warm your hands against that gold!"

We made to return to the city. He sang out a cheery word to the guards. "Protect my ship, gentlemen, as if it were the treasure of El Dorado!"

The Little Field lay deep in snow and snow was piled thick on evergreens, on the ornamental shrubs and trees, on the marble statues, on our wooden shed. The sun was thin ivory.

Mirenburg was before us, her white walls and towers shading imperceptibly into the general whiteness of land and sky. St. Odhran wore a red cloak and hat but I was in the black I had grown to favour. As we trudged back towards the gates a carriage came rolling through and from the window we saw the fur-swathed figure of one of our patrons, the Landgräfin Theresa-Wilhelmina, all lurid paint and wild, despairing blue eyes, waving to us and calling for us to be careful of the ice underfoot. We had learned that she was moved by whims connected with the predictions of her astrologers and clairvoyants. The whole family was touched by the same disease. Her husband, when not a devoted whoremonger, had dabbled in the Mysteries; his mother had been, scandal said, a full witch and her sister a bestialist, while her nephew was known to run with a set, mostly younger Austrian bloods, who affected to practise Satanism. But our Landgräfin had no interest in the wilder reaches of the superstitious ocean. We bowed and lifted our hats as she went by. Much of the gold in our coffer was hers.

As we turned to watch her carriage go by I saw to my surprise four riders approaching. They looked as if they had been on their horses all night. I recognised them almost at once as the young Radicals who had saved me in my flight from Montsorbier. I was delighted to see them and wondered what had befallen the rest of their party.

"Good morrow, gentlemen! Do you remember me?"

The four were scarcely able to lift their heads, so weary were they. Stefanik looked at me from the depths of a haggard face. "Aye, Sir. Of course I know you." His voice was almost a whisper. A flight of crows spread themselves, croaking and complaining, into the sky and scattered, their noise all but drowning his words. This was no time for conversation. I directed them to The Martyred Priest with the suggestion we dine there together. They were glad of this and promised to do as I proposed. Their Company was now two short and their clothes and weapons no longer so neat. Indeed, only one of the Poles—Stefanik himself—still had his Brown Bess. It had taken only a matter of weeks for him to be robbed of his air of innocent enthusiasm, his youthful superiority. Doubtless they had gone to Paris and found all I warned them of to be true. They rode on ahead of us, St. Odhran looking a little disturbed, wondering aloud if perhaps it was good that we should be seen in the company of radicals, now that all the sheep of Mirenburg's Bourse were beginning to bleat for their chance of acquiring grazing rights on our Bubble. I dismissed his fears.

With each successful fraud St. Odhran grew more cheerful, more sure of himself, for he estimated his worth according to his ability to deceive the world. For my part, I was merely astonished at how men and women would throw off all sense when confronted with an appeal to their inner-selves: the prospect, no matter how unlikely, of their dreams being made concrete. Promise a man a cheap interest in a timber mill and he shows instant suspicion; but promise him immortality, eternal fidelity from his mistress, a glimpse of El Dorado, and treacherous hope will always trap him. Thus old men are turned into fools by clever doxies and widows into wet-eyed girls by handsome rogues: yet these are the same who count their change in the button shop and study a servant's accounts to the last fraction of a pfennig, who are sceptical of the existence of the next valley, let alone the next world, and doubt the need of the blind beggar in the street. Indeed, it's fair to say that the more cautious and miserly the person, the more easily they're lured to a greater folly.

Pausing at the Chevalier's breezy insistence to celebrate our successes with a glass or two of gin and water in a riverside Ordinary, we made our way finally to our headquarters. In the large taproom of The Martyred Priest my four young friends were warmer and less travel-stained than earlier and I cried "Halloo" (for I was slightly drunk) and brought forward St. Odhran to be introduced. They were rueful and a little shy, for they had lost more than two of their company; they had also lost some of their enthusiasm for the Commune and had to say that my warnings of Paris had substance: but they were otherwise remarkably undaunted. They'd find their Utopia yet, they said. "Where?" asked I. "South America," replied Krasny, the native Mirenburger.

"Peru?" St. Odhran wanted to know. "Colombia? What do you hope to find there?"

"We mean to begin a new civilisation, Sir, based on fair principles."

"All you'll find, boys, is disease. And dying Indians. She's short of gold, moreover, that sub-Continent. Not what she's cracked up to be at all." He said this most feelingly, as if the entire land once conspired to betray him.

"We're disinterested in gold, Sir," said pale-haired von Lutzov, grown gaunt since his adventure began.

"You'll not be after a year," promised the Chevalier, munching a trotter. "What Sylvania, what Golden Paradise, shall bloom amongst the deadly vines and monstrous snakes, the swamps and unnavigable torrents, the strangling forests and gigantic birds of prey, where Indians lurk in the shadows of your stockade, ready to kill you for the colour in your kerchief, with little poisoned darts you neither hear nor see—nor yet even feel, until you're threshing!"

"You're rhetorical, Sir, but unspecific." Von Lutzov was offended.

"Specific enough," muttered St. Odhran, and fell silent.

"By what means shall you travel to South America?" I asked.

"By ship, Sir, probably from Venice or Genoa. We'd charter your vessel and go by Air, but I doubt we could afford it." Young Stefanik spoke.

343

"You've heard of that?"

"In Prague. And here, of course, where the whole town has the news."

I feared that the more the world heard the sooner it would understand our fraud. The road back to Bek was narrowing. Soon it would close for me altogether. I attempted to cauterise the pain in my heart. I was like a surgeon who must open up his own body, trying to retain objectiveness as he took a scalpel to his infection. What continues to push me in this direction? Surely it must be more than it seems; or is it just a fascination for the unexplained permutations of my own character, as if I'm carried along by the plot of a sensational tale, mesmerised by the progress of my own destruction.

Sergeant Schuster had joined us halfway through this exchange. He made a motion with his hand, wanting my attention alone. I excused myself and crossed to his counter. He had a sealed letter addressed jointly to St. Odhran and myself. I asked him who brought it. "A street boy," he said. "My wife received it."

The hand was educated, foreign, a little familiar. Perhaps it was from the Landgräfin. I broke the seal. The note inside was simple enough and was not signed:

> The inflammable air you require for your ship is now available
> in this city and shall be supplied to you whenever you wish. No
> price is asked save that you agree to provide a short passage to
> the donor and the donor's servant at a time of their choosing.
> A messenger will call for your reply tomorrow.

St. Odhran came up, still expressing impatience with the young idealists. "What's this?"

When he read the letter he frowned. "Hydrogen! What excellent fortune, von Bek." He meant, of course, that we should be able to make off with our stolen money in even swifter time, for the gas was as easily used to inflate our existing ship as it was to fill the one as yet unbuilt. I knew the outlines of his plans but not the details. At some time we should make a "practise ascent" and become "lost." "We must accept this offer," he said. "Who proposes it, I wonder?

Mirenburg's presently as full of alchemists as fleas on a dog. It could be any one of them." He turned the letter this way and that. "Only a Master would have both the equipment to manufacture that volume of the gas as well as a means of storing it. He's probably easily identified. Johannes Carithianus most likely, who is also very rich and has his own estate ten miles upriver. Or Marcus van der Geet, who came here twenty years ago from the Low Countries. Like many, he chose Wäldenstein because of her traditional encouragement of Scientific enquiry. Or it could be one of those who visits the city for this mysterious conjunction of theirs."

"Whoever he is," said I, "you had best write our answer. I'll abide by it. But I dislike the idea of making vague bargains with anonymous alchemists."

"The bargain suits me, since the gas shall be delivered before we're called to keep our side. It's all to our advantage, von Bek."

I shrugged. The Scot was the steersman on this voyage into deception and damnation. My will had been left behind somewhere between Paris and Prague. What remained of my resolve was used to keep me sane when the nightmares assailed me. I feared that uncontrollable chaos might result from St. Odhran's euphoric decisions. I was fearful, while at the same time in some wise elated with myself, as if I welcomed the inevitable consequences, the vengeance which Fate must bring.

Meanwhile our quartet of idealists continued to discuss the immorality of war, the natural goodness which the invention of money and private ownership of land stunted or corrupted in us all. I felt near jealous of them, regretting the loss of my own innocence while wishing I had possessed some measure of St. Odhran's pragmaticism when I had been their age: then perhaps I should not have swung so easily from one pole to the other and found myself in my present moral predicament. Suddenly I realised that I was trembling, close to swooning. I felt as if I had been poisoned, but more likely I was merely the victim of sleeplessness and disturbed conscience. I decided that I must try to rest and was about to bid goodnight to my young friends when I looked towards the door and saw something which made me fear that

I was, indeed, going mad, making phantasms from my own imagination.

Framed momentarily in the white glare, surrounded by grey smoke which rushed to escape from the taproom, banging snow from cape and hat and stamping mightily upon the floor, was the tall, slender figure of my Nemesis!

Had Montsorbier followed my quartet of Romantics all the way from Paris? Had he read reports of the balloon enterprise in the foreign press? Or was he now, like me, a fugitive from the treacherous tyranny he had helped create?

I came up straight, alert as a wary Mohock, and stared directly at him while he advanced slowly, with his usual elegant and attractive stride (almost a wolf's lope) through the crowd, glancing here and there about the tables as he re-creased his huge bicorne hat. Swinging his cloak off his shoulders and over his arm, he revealed a sword and a single long-handled pistol in his sash. Thin, well-formed lips were curved as usual in the suggestion of a smile and the piercing eyes had a veiled, deceptively amiable expression. His hair was tied back and fell to his shoulder blades; his frock-coat was perfectly cut, his boots and breeches as exquisite as ever. He remained the Revolutionary dignitary in all aspects, whether he had renounced his politics or not. I found that in a strange way I was strengthened by that familiar danger. I inclined my head in his direction, enquiring after his health.

"Improving, thank you, citizen. And yours?" His voice was sardonic.

"These winters bring a little fever, you know, but otherwise I'm in capital condition. You're too far from Paris, Sir. Do you not find the weather here inclement?"

"It's devilish cold and sharp, but that's always suited me, citizen, in season or in steel."

"Yet sustenance is hard to come by, eh?"

"Not so hard, citizen. My needs are spare. And I'm amply satisfied at present."

"Then I'm mistaken, Sir. I thought you survived by sucking on a he-wolf."

At this reference to Robespierre his eyes became angry for a split second, like a sudden squall at sea, then they returned to a deceptive tranquillity.

"How did you learn I was in Mirenburg?"

"I did not. I have other business, you see. I am an invited guest, part of a mission. I'm an envoy representing France. But, of course, I welcomed the opportunity to renew our old association. I have been in Mirenburg for two days. How is your friend, the woman who styles herself Duchess of some remote rock in the Adriatic?"

"You speak in code, Sir. You'd oblige me if you could be more direct. Are you here to arrest me?"

"I've no authority here, von Bek. What can you mean?" He lifted his dark brows. I could not believe him suddenly free of hatred for me. Even now there was some suggestion that he coiled to strike. And sure enough his next words clarified the matter: "It's a personal dispute which must be settled now," he said. "I trust you've kept a trace or two of honour since you became a man of business. You take my meaning?"

"Perfectly, Sir."

"I shall leave the choice of weapons to you."

I shrugged. "And the place?"

"I'm told it's traditional to use the Wool Yard at Mladota Quay. By the bridge there."

"I'll say swords," I said in a murmur, not wishing to be overheard by my friends.

"Sabres?"

"Your choice."

"Sabres, since we're both so equipped. What time, Sir?"

"I'm easy on that, Sir. But dawn's traditional. That would bring us to the bridge by about seven. Tomorrow, being a Sunday, we should be undisturbed." Duelling was frowned upon in Mirenburg and sometimes there were heavy penalties inflicted on those who resorted to the practise.

"It should not take us long, I think," said Montsorbier signalling to Sergeant Schuster who was busy at the far end of his counter.

"I hope not, Sir. I've much to do."

He was almost grinning with pleasure, anticipating his Satisfaction. I had had little experience at swordplay in recent months, but I believed that we were evenly matched. Neither of us could have stood against a master for more than five minutes, but we were both fair steelmen nonetheless. This would not be his first duel, nor mine.

Somehow this challenge had come at a perfect moment for me. I felt relieved by its simplicity, by the promise of resolution. Sergeant Schuster came up at Montsorbier's signal. The Frenchman's eyes narrowed as he recognised Schuster but could not place him. Schuster, on the other hand, began to frown. Montsorbier became uncomfortable. Suddenly he turned away from Schuster and bowed to me, then he began to stride rapidly towards the door. "Tomorrow, Sir!"

I would need St. Odhran and Schuster as seconds, so I informed them that I had accepted my pursuer's challenge. St. Odhran at once began to scheme a method of besting Montsorbier by a trick, remembering a duel he won by such means in Prussia, while Schuster offered me the use of himself as an exercise partner, for which I was grateful. "I recall the Frenchie's style," said my Sergeant, "having fought him before, as you know. All I lost then was a commission, but you stand to lose your life, Captain."

"But what shall I do for a partner if you're killed?" demanded St. Odhran in genuine alarm. Reality had provided an unwelcome break in the brightly coloured clouds which had come to shroud the terrain of his thoughts.

I smiled. "Perhaps Montsorbier will join you, should he kill me?"

"I need the name," said St. Odhran reasonably. "Your name, not his."

"Before I go to keep my appointment, I'll draft a letter to my brother, outlining your proposals."

St. Odhran then betrayed a sudden genuine sympathy. "I am serious, dear friend."

"I shall not be, if I'm extinguished tomorrow. However, I expect to win. I've had more direct experience at defending my life than I suspect has Montsorbier. Why do you not write an answer to the mysterious donor of inflammable air?"

He hesitated, glanced at Schuster, then, with parchment in hand, climbed the stairs to his rooms. For my part I had welcomed Montsorbier's challenge, though I now grew cold with that category of fear which provided me with what had often proved a false sense of objectiveness yet which nonetheless successfully lifted my spirits.

That evening the taproom was emptied early. My four young friends were weary and went to Krasny's family home to sleep. Sergeant Schuster saw that benches were cleared back, then with our sleeves rolled up and our knees bent, we addressed each other's sabres, while St. Odhran, returned from above, bit his nails in a corner and Ulrica and her mother watched with troubled eyes from the gallery above. I was pleased just to be active. Very rapidly my skills came again to me as we fenced back and forth over the sawdust, with Schuster grinning his pleasure at the sport.

But this single day was to be the pivot on which all our future fortunes would depend. There were many further events ahead of us. Even when we were through with all our feints and gambits there came a tapping on the door. Sergeant Schuster signed for Frau Schuster to respond. "It cannot be the Watch," said he. But for caution's sake we set our swords behind his counter and snatched tankards in their place.

Frau Schuster took her comfortable bulk to the entrance, lifted up the bar and then staggered backwards as the door was driven violently inward and a dozen men, their faces masked by scarves, pushed brutally into The Martyred Priest. I thought first they were Montsorbier and his party, but they were dressed wrongly for Frenchmen. These bully-boys now pulled out great pistols from beneath their dark greatcoats, levelling some at Frau Schuster, the rest at Ulrica (who was fierce with anger).

"The women die if you resist," said the muffled leader. He had the coarse, impatient tone of one who was a professional at this work and had, moreover, a vocation for terror and torture. Had Montsorbier turned coward and hired a parcel of footpads to save himself the trouble of rising early? I was unable to believe it of him. Then who had sent them? What other enemies had we in Mirenburg?

"You're St. Odhran?" asked the leader of me, gesturing with his barker. I made no reply. He looked towards my partner, who was feigning carelessness, still in his corner.

"Oh, aye," he drawled. "What can I do for ye, gentlemen?" He stood up and looked down his long nose at them. "Gad, ye're big, healthy fellows. Are we off to a prize fight?"

"Then this will be the other," said the leader of me. He sucked in air and blew it out suddenly through his muffler. "Good."

We were surrounded. My only handy weapon was the sword I had hidden behind the counter. Sergeant Schuster and his family were helpless. The Sergeant looked towards our secreted weapons but I shook my head slightly. We could not risk the lives of the women. He contented himself with a snarl. "What is it you want? Money? It is already gone from the premises. The Watch will be passing here within ten minutes and if I do not respond to its signal you'll find yourselves fighting half a score of trained militia! You'll leave now if you've sense!"

But the leader of these invaders was unimpressed. He motioned with his pistol. "We've come for these gentlemen. You're safe enough if you don't interrupt us in our commission." His voice remained coarse and sinister. "And you'll say nothing to the Watch, innkeeper, or you'll find this pair skinned and gutted before morning, with apples in their mouths, trussed for the oven." Not one of his crew laughed or otherwise acknowledged his morbid jest. Silence dropped like a winding sheet upon us all.

For a moment the scene was completely still; then the leader signalled again and St. Odhran and myself were roughly shoved, made to stumble towards the door where, in the snowy darkness, a box-wagon stood waiting, its doors open. It was the kind of covered cart used for transporting cows to market, or bringing butchers' meat from the charnel house. It stank of just such recent use.

"Do not jeopardise your family, Sergeant," I said. "We'll send news to you if we can."

"Get inside," ordered the chief rogue.

St. Odhran hesitated, his manner theatrical. "Demme," he said in drawling English. "I do believe the fellow's not joking. Old friend, we're captured for no special merit of our own! The butcher's run short of pork! We're to become the contents of a pie!"

He led the way into the stinking, blood-spotted hold, crying out for all the world like an impatient aristo: "Drive on, man! Drive on! 'Tis a cold night and we've no topcoats!"

Chapter Seven

In which we discover a little of what lies beneath
Mirenburg's surface. A dangerous Farce. Lucifer's name
taken in vain. Conversation regarding the Anti-Christ.
A supposed acquaintance of my family.
An invitation to dine in Hell. I accept.

W ITH SO FEW clothes upon our backs we were, indeed, near
to freezing by the time the van passed into what, by the
echo, was a courtyard. A gate was locked shut behind us and we
heard whispers in the darkness outside.

"This stink is dreadful," complained St. Odhran. "Do they
mean to stifle us to death?"

Almost as if we had been overheard, the doors of the charnel-
wagon were opened and we gasped gratefully at the purer air.
Three men entered the van. Two held pistols at our temples while
the third tied our hands behind our backs and blindfolded us, for
all the world as if we were prisoners on the way to execution.

Perhaps, thought I, Montsorbier had prepared this death. Did
he possess his own guillotine? Might he not, in his fury, believe
that I must not cheat the machine? But why manifest his vengeance on poor St. Odhran, who had given him no offence, save in
the bearing of a title and an aristocratic lisp, albeit both recently
acquired.

Now we stumbled, boots upon rough paving, from van to
doorway and into somewhat warmer air (though damp), down
steps on which we slipped, grunting and falling, shoulder against
shoulder, no longer caring to protest since we had no answers as
yet—and would possibly never have any until we were finally in
Hell. Down still further—echoed drops of water from high vault
to flooded floor—and further—natural rock, stalactites and fun-

gus, the sound of viscous liquid and a stink as if a sewer emptied nearby.

"Cover my nose and not my eyes, I beg thee, gentlemen," said St. Odhran desperately, perhaps by way of a joke. The rufflers pushed us on, sliding and staggering, down another level at least. Could there be anything below the very sewers? Were these Svitavian catacombs where Christians hid from Pagans and then vice versa? Where Ritter Igor von Miroff slept to wake if his name-city were ever subjected to the rule of tyranny? I'd once thought these caverns fanciful legend, borrowed from Rome or Constantinople. But here they were for certain and I told myself that no-one could mean to kill us out of hand or we should have been dead by now. Such White Thuggees as these are too lazy for overmuch caution or for considered finesse. It had become almost hot. I felt, in fact, a fire's heat on my face, sensed a flickering brand. Footsteps retreated. A door was closed.

There was a smell of sulphur in the air. A stink more reminiscent of chemicals and retorts. Could it be he who had written us the note about the inflammable gas? A benefactor with a savage's sense of humour. We were pushed by invisible, insistent hands back until we reached a wall. The stones were smooth. Something snapped around my ankle and chain was slithering now. We were manacled.

The blindfolds were taken away from our eyes, but the bonds remained. I could see only glaring flame, then red baskets of coals swinging from the roof, then a huge, bloated face—and the whole charade was suddenly explained!

We were surrounded by the banalities of a theatrical stage; the kind of scene one finds everywhere in the modern Playhouse, where a multiplicity of mechanical devices is used to affect the Public sensibility, to make folk swoon with terror for want of being moved by poetry of honest drama. Here was a setting for a Satanist coven if ever I'd seen one! And sure enough the men and women who stood in the shadows of this grotto were clad in monastic habits, cowled and masked. I was convinced now that this was not of Montsorbier's engineering. From behind the great Goat-faced screen came a diminutive red-robed Abbot with splayed feet. He spoke in that sing-song all such people prefer to substitute for ordinary speech: archaic and somewhat immoderate in its use of adjectives. Out it rushed as if from a suddenly unblocked Privy:

"Wretched, reckless, rebellious rogues! You dared reject the warnings of our Malevolent King. Now you must suffer our ruthless revenge! Horrid wriggling worms, your heresies make you hateful in the eyes of Hell and her Unholy Host!" All this affected by the speaker's difficulty in pronouncing the letter "R" and substituting for it the familiar "W." "How plead you in your perversity? Can you reasonably claim your crimes have not made you ripe for Lucifer's righteous revenge?"

"Gad!" said St. Odhran, still in English, "a worse fate than this is impossible to imagine, eh, von Bek? We've fallen into the clutches of a demented juvenile with a penchant for poor alliteration. You and I shall discover no wit here, I fear."

"You'll speak a civilised tongue, Sir," squeaked our captor, "or suffer to have it removed completely!"

Now I recognised the speaker. I had met him once before, at our Landgräfin's. It was her devil-dabbling nephew who had so resented the largesse she had thrown our way. Doubtless he was already counting his inheritance.

"My dear Baron," said I, "'tis easy to tell you're piqued because your aunt favours our enterprise over your expectations. Yet don't you think even your friends here would agree your reaction's a touch exaggerated . . ."

"Mock not this terrible tribunal, lest ye be judged instantly and condemned with neither indictment nor defence. We have gathered, miserable man, to try you in the matter of your disobedience to the dictates of our sinister Master, Lord of the Infernal Realms, Ruler of Rulers, Commander of the Infinite Legions of the Damned, His Most Satanic Majesty, Prince Lucifer! You defy the dictates of Hell by intruding into that disputed territory of the upper air—the Realm already claimed by our master and to which Man is forbidden. That the Arch-usurper Jehovah already claims this region as his own is well known, but that men should interject their prideful designs into that dispute is unacceptable either to Hell or to Heaven. For the War is soon to be fought that shall decide the Struggle. The Stars Conjoin!"

St. Odhran raised a well-trimmed eyebrow. "I must congratulate you, Herr Baron, on your most splendidly elaborate disguise." He spoke bravely enough. "But I must say I find your speech a trifle confusing." His words came out a touch blurred, with a tremble to them. He knew as well as I that we were in the hands of a small-minded degenerate. This Baron sought only the mildest excuse to commit the most hideous acts of torture and murder. There was no appeal to such as him (as I'd already found in France): one's only appeal would be to God, and God had long since been abolished from my Universe. St. Odhran, however, would call on any aid, whether he believed in its existence or not. He there and then flung back his head to shout:

"O, my Patron! O, Lucifer, Prince of the Morning, make these ignorant people aware of whom they Persecute!"

The Baron was baffled for a second by that. He hesitated. He cleared his throat. There came a murmuring from the congregation. How many used their Satanism to release their carnal lusts, how many at least partially believed in the power of Lucifer? How many were faithful converts to His cause? I did not know. But St. Odhran had found our only argument and again I was impressed by the facility (if not the morality) of his wits.

"Lucifer! Hear me!" bellowed the clever Scot. "Your name is used in vain, Master, and turned upon your Son!"

The red robe made an agitated, flat-footed swirl, to address the throng. "He lies! He's no adept!"

"Adept?" says St. Odhran, gathering momentum and pushing forward his small gain. "True, I'm no 'adept.' I am Thog-Mogoch, Count of the Fiery Pit, and Lucifer is my father! I am His emissary upon Earth. The sole vessel of His power and wisdom! I shall be called the Beast!"

He had his audience captured, whispering amongst themselves while our Baron is trapped midway, a rogue sphere between Sun and Earth.

"Now do ye know me, foolish dabblers!" St. Odhran bellowed. *"NOW DO YE KNOW ME!"* The echoes of the catacombs amplified his voice. He had their properties finely judged. His skills of play-acting were being fully utilised. Even I might have believed him the Son of Lucifer! *"RELEASE ME!"*

"Aye, release him," cried one of the cowled fraternity.

"Charlatan!" shouted St. Odhran. "Villain! 'Tis you, Sir, who's the heretic! I am come here to reveal the truth to you all! This body is sacred. If you slay it, you release me in all my vengeful glory! Hell shall visit Earth in all its howling horror! You rob yourselves of privilege and bring upon yourselves my father's wrath!"

The little Baron (von Bresnvorts is his name) attempted to hold them back, squeaking at them, most undignified. "He is not the Beast! I assure you, he is not the Beast!"

"I am the Beast! I am the Lord of the City of the World! I am the Avenger. I am the Fire that shall lay waste all that Man treasures! I am the Sword which shall execute my fated task. I am the Scythe—"

"You are an imposter!" shrieked the Baron. "You deceived my aunt and now you seek to deceive my followers. You shall be doubly punished!"

"No, Sir—'tis you who'll be doomed!" I broke in now, with the voice one used to rally frightened troops. "Hear me, people. This is Thog-Mogoch, I swear upon my soul. He allowed himself to be brought here so that he might address you. Kill him and you shall forever be damned, for he is the one destined to be the Anti-Christ!" I babbled such nonsense, seeing no harm in taking our claims a step or two further.

"You lie, Sir!" said the furious miniature Baron. "This is the Chevalier St. Odhran, charlatan and trickster. A thief who is condemned to death in England, exiled from Berlin, wanted as an outlaw in Vienna. And you, Sir, are the son of the Graf von Bek, who renounced your title and inheritance to follow the king-slayers of France!"

At this, a thin man stepped into the firelight. He was tall, gaunt, his face more nearly a fleshless skull than any I had ever seen. He was dressed in black, like a Quaker, and had a Quaker's wide-brimmed hat upon his grey locks. He had no age, this man, but he had burning, tormented eyes which had witnessed everything, from the world's creation, perhaps to its end. The white lace at collar and wrist, at knee and ankle, was emphasis for his bloodless face. "You cannot be the Anti-Christ," he said reasonably to St. Odhran, "for the Anti-Christ is already chosen and shall soon begin to reign."

I was inclined to believe that sonorous skeleton. He had more authority than any I had heard in all my life before. His voice was as old as Time and though empty of all feeling it was weighted with a terrible wisdom. He wore no masquerader's weeds. His clothes were his own, severe and familiar to him; he and they were of a single piece. And all the while I regarded him there was some kind of recognition stirring in me, as if he was a creature of my deepest dreams taking flesh before my eyes. "You claim knowledge of us, sir," I said. "But we do not know you."

"Ah, I know you, von Bek. I know all your ancestors. First there was Ulrich, the cause of my great distress more than a hundred years past. I knew him very well. Surely your family's archives take note of me."

The Baron was defeated and lost. This man was his superior and was acknowledged as such by all present.

"You must tell me a name, Sir, before I can answer that. Who are you, Sir?"

"I was once what St. Odhran claims to be. Do your histories record me?" He seemed almost anxious on that matter. "I am Klosterheim, who turned against his powerful master. Do they speak of Klosterheim, who almost held the Grail? That is who I am, Sir. Do they recall me as evil personified, von Bek? Do they make a story of me to frighten children around the fireside? I am Klosterheim and now I'm opposed to God and Satan both. Now I serve Mankind. I am known as the ambassador of the stolen future and the unremembered past. Did the tales of Klosterheim chill your boyhood nights, von Bek?" With every question he took another pace towards me. St. Odhran, pale and puzzled, looked from his face to mine, from mine to his.

I was not facetious when I replied, for my legs were weak and I was sweating. "I have never heard of you, Sir. Read nothing of a Klosterheim."

"Is there no book which calls me Satan's steward? Nothing at all in the libraries of Bek?"

"Nothing, Sir, that I know."

His eyes grew almost sad. "So my name is gone, too, from that world," he said. "Too much is fading." He looked at me with a momentary expression of agony. "I've much hatred for the name of von Bek. It cannot be satisfied by killing you. Moreover our destinies are too tangled, even now. What's more, I lack courage for it. Do you know what damnation can be, Sir? It can be a state of permanent caution, making one chronically unable to risk anything, even a risk which might save one from extinction. Not that extinction would be unwelcome, I suppose." He spread his white hands before him and stared at them. "I hate you, von Bek." Musingly, and to my utter horror, he reached to stroke my cheek with his dead, thin fingers. "Yet I suppose I must love you, too. At least you have meaning for me. I wonder now if your ancestor and I were not unconscious allies. Part of the same design. Would you be my ally, von Bek? Would you love me?"

I turned my head. "Sir," said I through clenched teeth, "you terrify me and I dislike the sensation. What do you want of me?"

He seemed puzzled and dropped his hand. "Nothing, as yet. Von Bresnvorts is a dolt. I lodge in these catacombs. I have lived in them for more than fifty years. Do you believe me?"

"You're mighty well-preserved, Sir. The air down here must be conducive to Immortality."

"It is." He answered without humour, choosing his next words with slow care. "The Graf Ulrich von Bek robbed me of my birthright. He accepted a commission in Lucifer's service."

It came to me that this poor creature was mad. "Sir, I've heard nothing of any of this."

He was disbelieving. "Nor of the Grail which Ulrich brought to Satan?"

"I beg you, Herr Klosterheim, to let us go. We offer you no harm."

"I serve Mankind," he said. "There'll be no wanton murder because a little popinjay of a Baron feels out of sorts. He has misused his power." Klosterheim's voice was a frozen whisper. "I serve Mankind now," he said again. "Do you believe that?"

"Sir, I believe," said I, humouring him any way he wished. "But as for the rest, concerning my ancestor . . ."

"I regret I did not see him die. Do you know, young man, how von Bek's soul sought its reward?"

Once more I was urgently sincere. "I know nothing of any of that. My ancestor died a natural death I believe."

He nodded slowly. Klosterheim was mad, but in a far grander and more impressive way than anyone else in those vaults. "Will you dine with me?" he whispered, then, without waiting for my answer, he turned and glared at the others. "Bring a key, you vermin. My master tolerates stupidity only in the humble. You are too proud, all of you. Kneel—every one save he who has the key!" And they fell at once to the rocky floor, as though a single creature. Thus Klosterheim demonstrated his power to me, while a female in a white robe which split to show scabrous, naked flesh, turned open first one padlock, then the next, and a knife parted our bonds. "Well, von Bek? Will you dine?" Did I imagine a hint of some terrible yearning? Did he trick me towards my death or some worse enslavement?

"What of my friend?" I asked. "What of St. Odhran?"

"He can go free. At once." He raised his voice to address his kneeling servants. "See that the Chevalier is taken back to his lodgings." He put a cold hand on my arm. "Dine with me before you leave."

I was devilish afraid of the man, yet I was curious, I know not why, and I almost felt sympathy for him. I hesitated. "Sir, I must rest tonight, for I have a duel to fight at dawn . . ."

He turned away with such a hopeless sigh I found my mouth moving before my brain. "Very well, Herr Klosterheim. I accept your invitation."

"I am obliged." He strode to where the red robe made obeisance. He lifted up the trembling chin with the sharp toe of his boot. "You shall never act again without my express instructions. You are vain and you are foolish. You do not deserve the power I allow you. One more transgression, Sir, and I shall take you"—he points with his thumb—"down there."

Von Bresnvorts attempted to beg forgiveness but he was gagging on his own bile.

Klosterheim dropped the chin. "Farewell, Monsieur le Chevalier. Be assured, the Ritter von Bek shall follow in due course."

St. Odhran made to resist this plan, but I raised my hand to show that I was satisfied of my safety. With a murmured farewell I followed Klosterheim past the Goat-head screen and into a narrow passage illuminated by brands giving off unusual, silvery light.

"Those men and women wait the coming of the Anti-Christ," said Klosterheim without looking back. "They know the Birth, the Place, the Time. They believe they will be chosen for positions of power when the Anti-Christ's rule begins. They're a large and common herd. Each carries the mark of a Pagan godling branded upon its rump and believes it's thus especially favoured. They're of use to the Anti-Christ, I suppose, but they are ignorant and poor company. No more than field beasts, do you see?" His confidences were unwelcome to me.

We turned down a short flight of steps and into a large stone chamber, lit by more of the silvery flambeaux. Here was a Spartan room furnished with desk, two chairs, a table and a few old volumes and parchments, together with a steel Globe. A chest of drawers stood against one wall, near a truckle bed. There was no heat. Klosterheim crossed to the chest and from it removed a dish containing some white bread and two good-sized cheeses. On the dish he placed a knife. He poured water into two glass goblets and his meal was ready. As he drew the chairs to the table he removed his hat, gesturing for me to sit.

He looked curiously at my face, pushing cheese and bread towards me in an awkward movement. He seemed to think me an animal whose behaviour he could not fathom. I cut a piece of cheese, took a goblet of water, and waited until he had served his own miserly portion. He was looking beyond me as he chewed. His eyes appeared to follow the movements of invisible armies and I was tempted to glance over my shoulder in case I should see what he saw. As he watched this illusory panorama he said to me: "Some hundred and fifty years ago, you and I sought the same thing."

I cleared my mouth. "Not I, Sir."

It was as if I split unnecessary hairs. "Your ancestor, then. The same blood. Same name. We sought the Holy Grail. Are you aware the Anti-Christ awaits only possession of the Grail before beginning to rule?"

The man was crazier than I had originally suspected! "No, Sir," said I. "I thought the Anti-Christ a faded fashion."

"The Grail was once given into the hands of my master, as He then was, by your ancestor. Thus was I condemned to this existence. It came, the Grail, from the Forest at the Edge of Heaven. In the Middle Marches. However, as you must know, the geography of the Mittelmarch is ever unstable. Now the Forest can no longer be found. My master sought to placate God and offer the Grail to Mankind as the sign of His good faith. But the Grail is—it is *itself*. It vanished, once the gesture was made by the master. It is lost to us. But you could find it again, von Bek."

I did not intend to deny anything or make any gesture which might anger that madman. I let silence be my agreement. "You think the Grail's still in the Mittelmarch, Herr Klosterheim? Surely that's a place of Damned Souls, not Holy Cups?"

Klosterheim frowned. "So it was. But now, because of the truce between God and Satan, there are no damned souls. We live in an age, Sir, where sin has no consequence. Do you find that heartening news, you who sought to create Paradise in Paris?"

"I do not."

"Well, we're agreed on that." He cut carefully at his morsel of cheese but did not eat it.

"So you serve the Anti-Christ, eh, Herr Klosterheim? Thus I must take it that Lucifer's your master still."

"I did not say so, Sir. The Anti-Christ is neither God nor Satan.

The Anti-Christ would rule the territory they've renounced. As would I. Our interests are therefore the same. Is there a record in your family concerning the Grail's present location?"

"I have some vague idea of that, aye." I wished to learn more and so did not want him to think me ignorant or inclined to contradict his fantasies.

"Vague? It is common knowledge in Occult circles that the chief purpose of your aerial expedition is to retrieve the Grail!"

I was greatly surprised to be told so certainly of my plans. Yet again I held my tongue. "How did they guess?" I asked.

"Your name, Sir, of course!"

"Is it so famous?"

"The family legend. Those who concern themselves with things mystical and supernatural say you also possess the Paracelsian sword."

"Indeed, Sir?"

"Whoever had possession of those two objects of power, both the Cup and the Blade, would rule Earth and challenge the authority of Heaven!" Klosterheim pushed away his goblet. "My hatred for you is profound, von Bek, though you offer me no direct harm. But you exist because my enemy Ulrich von Bek succeeded over me." He looked beyond my shoulder again. I shivered and refused to follow his cold glare. "But perhaps you're not so casually acquainted with a hatred as constant and intense as mine? Eh, Sir?"

"I think not, Sir."

He frowned, returning his gaze to the table. He spoke almost to himself. "I am divorced from so much." He drew a deeper breath and looked at me directly again. "Well, Sir?"

"Well what, Sir?" I did not know what he expected of me.

"Will you join the quest, Sir? Or rather will you allow me to accompany you on your own expedition?"

"And have you kill me at the end?" I would not otherwise dissuade him from his misunderstanding. We could lose nothing by it, I reasoned. It seemed everyone but myself and St. Odhran had absolute faith in the reality of our fraud.

Klosterheim was astonished. "Why kill you, Sir?"

"Your hatred, Sir. The hatred you recently mentioned."

He shrugged, close to amusement (or whatever resembled the emotion in his cold, miserable heart). "What use would be served by killing you? Death is nothing. That which follows death is of some importance, however. Do you take me for a petty revenger?" He spoke distantly, his voice fading like ice turning to vapour. Again his eyes followed invisible dramas. "Well, Sir, will you make a bargain with Klosterheim? I'll guide you through the Mittelmarch and can rally aid of several kinds. Then we take an equal share of all that's gained . . ."

"I'm a little unsure of what you're offering me, Sir."

"Wisdom. Guidance. You have not journeyed there before, I know. All manner of intelligence. And, of course, ultimately true power. Greater power than any before. A territory upon our Earth wherein you may work any experiment you wish. Your disappointments in France could be rectified, if that was what you still dreamed of."

"It's an attractive prospect, Sir," said I, becoming somewhat light-hearted as the fantasy grew out of all sane proportions. "But I fear I lack the other object of power mentioned. What's this sword?"

"The Sword of Paracelsus? I respect your discretion." He shook his head. "It's safest wherever you keep it now. The great danger will be in the subsequent struggle and that could as easily be fought in this Realm."

I gave up any attempt to follow his reasoning. "You know a deal of secrets, Herr Klosterheim."

He was almost apologetic. "I am no longer omniscient." His eyes seemed to look back at a time when he had command of millions. He began to speak of a life which perhaps he had dreamed, when he was Hell's captain and led an army against Satan Himself: a great rebellion. An attempt to achieve a further revolution. Now he was condemned, he said, to perpetual exile and eternal doubt. He, like Lucifer before him, had failed and been cast out. But his punishment had never properly been revealed to him. He had devoted himself to what he termed "the Triumph of Man" and waited for the day when he might again challenge both God and Lucifer.

The man's ravings were so grandiose and his tone so matter-of-fact that I could do nothing but listen in silence. The alliance he proposed would (had I believed in such things) commit my soul to immediate damnation. He was mighty convincing, however, for a madman. I agreed with whatever seemed politic and set my lips closed on anything which might alarm him. At length he subsided. "I have kept you late, Sir. But the meeting has proved rewarding to me. I'll guide you to the surface."

He led me back through the catacombs to the outer world, still speaking somewhat repetitiously, in the manner of a man who has received a great blow to his spirits, in the death, for instance, of some beloved relative. His voice soon blended with the other noises in the tunnels. Then he stood with me in a narrow doorway and looked in apparent bemusement at the white dawn sky. I yawned.

"You're tired, Sir?" said he.

"A little, Sir."

He nodded his head slowly, his brow slightly furrowed, as if he understood intellectually but had no memory of a time when he himself needed sleep. "I'll send a message when I hear your ship is ready," he said. Then, with the air of a wondering child, he pointed at a tiny swirl of snow which blew from a nearby roof. He held out his finger and with an introspective narrowing of his eyes waited until a flake settled at last on the tip. He sighed, but his breath did not materialise as mine did. I first thought he intended to make some remark; then I realised he merely wanted me to look at what seemed strange to him: the snowflake.

"It is Winter," he said dreamily, "of course." But the snowflake did not melt.

Coatless and shivering, I bid him farewell. I ran through the streets until at last I found the Mladota Bridge. I looked for Montsorbier down on the old Wool Quay. He was not there. It was only an hour past sunrise and it was conventional for one adversary to await another for at least that long.

The paving stones of the Wool Quay had a light covering of snow. No-one had been there since the previous night. Puzzled, I ran on until I was at last banging gratefully upon the tradesman's door of The Martyred Priest.

I was admitted by Frau Schuster, who gave a mighty gulp of relief and took me immediately into her plump and comforting arms!

Chapter Eight

An unkept appointment. Further dreams. St. Odhran's
solution to our promised embarrassment. News of our
inflammable air. A Cretan nightmare. My bafflement.
More horrid discoveries. A cowardly decision.

A S I ENTERED the taproom, I heard a great galloping noise on the stairs and then St. Odhran, all thigh-booted military man with pistols in his pockets and powder at his belt, led our four young friends, also armed like Pickaroons, down to the main floor, giving orders as he went until he fetched up in comical surprise a nose-length from me: "Deuce! You're rescued already!" He was almost aggrieved.

"Released," I said. "Herr Klosterheim's madness is at once more elaborate and subtler than that of the Landgräfin's nephew." I went to sit in the nook by the old iron stove. I was still shivering. "He's been talking at me all night. You've had word from Montsorbier?"

"God's blood! I'd forgotten. He'll be waiting."

"He is not. He never was."

St. Odhran's long face clouded. "Montsorbier's no coward. He must be dead or down with a fever at least." The four Radicals stood awkwardly at his back, as disappointed as my partner in their expectations of adventure. "Someone should be sent to his address." He frowned. "But as I recall he gave none."

"Doubtless he'll find us." I accepted spiced wine from Frau Schuster's hand. "Did the Baron himself escort you home?"

"He sent two of the ruffians who originally captured us. But before I left he'd recovered his spirits a little. He let me know that tragedy would result if we continued to drain his inheritance from his aunt."

"He'd disobey Klosterheim? He's bolder than I guessed."

"Or more stupid. He's the kind who'll take his master's literal meaning but will count himself a cunning villain if he conceives a plot avoiding the exact letter of Klosterheim's law. He'll be shocked, too, if accused of it."

"He still plans to murder us, you think?"

"He'll try to arrange our deaths, more likely. Clumsily." St. Odhran smiled, loosening his sword belt. "I'm more curious about Klosterheim. Why should he save us? Did he say? He seemed familiar with your name."

"My friend, he's another who demands a passage on our aerial frigate. He, like the Landgräfin, believes the Mittelmarch exists!"

St. Odhran sat himself down on a bench and began to untie his jabot. "Perhaps we should after all build the thing. We stand to make as large a fortune, at least, from selling berths aboard her!"

"And follow one of your fanciful maps, too?" I began to laugh louder than the joke deserved. "Where should we go, St. Odhran? Into Klosterheim's imagined worlds? Into the Mittelmarch to look for the Landgräfin's husband? And what of our mysterious backer? Does the Prince wish to create an empire in the netherworld? And he who gives us the Hydrogen gas—where does he wish to fly— the land of Cockaigne?" Breakfast was beginning to accumulate on the nearest table and at Frau Schuster's urgent gesturing I rose to put my legs under the board.

Then I'd fainted on St. Odhran before I knew it, swooning with what was probably no more than fatigue, yet dreaming of Kloster-heim's bleak presence, of a sword with a bird trapped in a glowing pommel, of a radiant cup. And I dreamed of the mistress of my heart. Libussa stroked my breast and breathed into my ear, mak-ing me helpless as a snake in a swami's basket, and I woke in the familiar swamp of my own perspiration. Where was Montsor-bier? Had the duel been fought and was I wounded? I could not tell where the dream and the actuality divided. Moonlight ran into the room as the clouds broke above Mirenburg's delicate tow-ers. I sat upright, pulling off my wet nightshirt, washing my body in the cold water which was silver in the china bowl, and I remembered that Klosterheim talked at me all night and Montsorbier failed to meet me for his satisfaction and sent no seconds to apologise. Some alchemist or natural philosopher had promised us Hydrogen gas for our aerial barque. All in one day. Yesterday? My instinct shouted "Conspiracy" but my head reasoned "Coincidence." When such conflict occurred I heeded neither but stayed on a middle course, if that were possible. Yet when I drew on shirt and breeches and went to visit St. Odhran in his rooms, the Britisher also thought some conspiracy against us was afoot. His rooms were bright with lamps and candles, littered with diagrams and charts. Some of these were unfamiliar to me.

"I suspect all our enemies conjoin to achieve our ruin," he said. "Though we planned to winter here, my friend, I think it would be wise if we met with an accident very soon."

"St. Odhran," said I grimly, "you've mentioned no accident before."

"I keep so many possibilities in mind, dear friend, I cannot always express 'em in words. Our method of escape has been forming in my thoughts for the past few days. Shall I enlarge?"

"I'd be grateful if you would, Sir."

"Then here's what I foresee—we announce a further demonstration of our existing ship, using, if possible, the proffered gas. The balloon shall slip her tether—a frayed rope! We'll shout for help! We'll agitate the Gondola! We'll make a great hullabaloo of despair—and the wind'll do the rest. With Hydrogen to lift us we can go higher and faster than ever. We'll be a hundred miles away in less than five hours. With the right wind we'll be in Arabia before we need to land. With gold and our ship we'll find dusky patronage amongst the Eastern Ottomans, the independent Sultans or even the Chinese, changing our names to whatever takes our fancy. Then, in a couple of years, we return to Europe with a good tale which serves to explain our absence and our wealth. None shall condemn us and only a few shall mourn!"

I was willing enough to accept escape on almost any terms at that juncture. Klosterheim had frightened me to my bones. But as for the gold, I said, how shall that be explained away?

"Robbery," he said. "Those villains who kidnapped us will do. A plot against us. We'll broadcast something of that in the next day or two. Other money's banked in Germany, by the by. I'll go to the Landgräfin this morning and tell her of her nephew's bid to crush our venture and murder us. He'll be suspected of any foul play. As for the French silk-weavers, their perfidy can be explained by Revolution. Meanwhile I'm writing to our mysterious bestower of inflammable air asking for enough of the gas to test the handling of our present craft, so that we may redesign our steering mechanism and enlarge the size of our gondola. We'll know tomorrow if that's granted. Then we'll announce our intention of testing the gas. We'll choose a time when the breeze is blowing its best. After that 'tis merely a question of deciding which Continent we wish to land upon!" All this was given in English so that we should not be understood if overheard.

In the same language I said: "The balloon cannot be steered."

"True, but wind can be gauged and we can control our drift with simple sails. I'll admit we'll be somewhat at the wind's mercy, but not completely helpless. There are no complexities in this, you'll note. It shall be a simple plan, simply realised."

I was beyond moral scruples at that stage. I wished only to be free of nightmares and nightmarish events, of a man who claimed to have lived for more than one hundred and fifty years and a female will-o'-the-wisp who haunted every hour of my days.

"This gives you gold—and Bek, too, if you want it," said St. Odhran.

Bek regained with a lie, I thought, could not be Bek at all. The consequences of habitual deception and lies, Goethe tells us, are the loss of self-trust, the loss of true love and the loss of the good will of one's fellows. (But the balloon escape, though cowardly, might lift me from Libussa's lure and allow me perspective, release from my madness.) Thus my panic easily conquered my conscience. My only concern was that we should not come down in some land where I was already outlawed! The image of our craft entangled upon a Kremlin onion gave me an ironic pleasure which the reality would certainly lack. St. Odhran reassured me.

He was already, he said, anticipating our voyage—the adventures we should have in Arabia, India, China and some unknown islands in the South Seas.

"You surely cannot steer so clear a course?" said I.

"No, indeed, but I can gauge the taste of a public which presently finds any sensation preferable to reality. The fictions with which we ease our daily burdens, you know. I'm planning how we'll retail these adventures (which explain our absence). Our recruitment, for instance, to the wild Bedouin; our discovery of the Elephant's Graveyard; our witnessing of the Dance of the Dead (in Cook's Land); our capture and subsequent escape from the hands of white devil-worshippers in a hidden valley deep within the Saharan vastness. We shall never know poverty, von Bek, do you see?" And St. Odhran winked, disarming all my arguments. There is only one thing less resistible than a charming and subtle Rogue and that is his reminder to you that he knows better than anyone what his rhetoric is worth and does not for a moment deceive himself.

Later that evening I bundled up in a huge four-caped coachman's coat, muffler and woollen gloves, and went down to the river to walk to the middle of the Mladota Bridge, the Bridge of Kings with all its great monarchs set in stone at intervals along both balustrades, to achieve the solitude I felt I required while I reviewed my thoughts and considered my experiences of the past thirty-six hours.

Klosterheim remained the most memorable. I wondered at his undoubted familiarity with my great ancestor. His insane tale of revenge and magic spoke of a poet's imagination, for it turned all accepted Theology upside-down. Yet he was surely mad if he actually believed I could find the Holy Grail or possessed a magic sword or could wander at will into shadowy worlds which he described as a mirror to our own. He spoke of marvellous peoples and beasts reported by travellers down the centuries and entering the general consciousness through the medium of legend and fairy-tale. The more likely logic was that the lands of his description were no more than a reflection of his own profound need to believe the truth of simple, Romantic tales. In simple lands are found simple solutions to mankind's ills. So what was Klosterheim but a poor lunatic in retreat from ambiguity and baffling subtlety? I shrugged as I looked down into the dark, fast water of the Rätt. I answered myself aloud:

"He's more than that."

He was, I was certain, far more than a common madman in quest of common resolutions. Yet he could not, surely, be speaking in anything other than elaborate metaphor? I looked up at my surroundings. Mirenburg was a dreaming city now. Pale clouds, moonlit, appeared in her sky, like a malleable geography, as yet unfixed by a Creator's command. Was all the Earth but agitated gas and molten stone before she was born? And was she founded all of a sudden by some galvanic thought which itself existed only for a split second? Did God truly build and populate a small planet for His own purposes; perhaps merely to relieve His boredom? Could God and Lucifer, as Klosterheim suggested, truly be locked in permanent debate as they attempted to decide the terms of their truce and eventual reunion?

I had no talent for abstract Theology. My chances of learning an answer to the last question were as good as my convincing Baron von Bresnvorts of the wisdom of buying shares in an Aerial Navigation Society or giving away his inheritance to the closest Almshouse.

I walked back towards the Right Bank. Looking down I saw the Wool Quay again, still silent and the snow now frozen on the flagstones, near as unblemished as when I went that morning to meet Montsorbier. Against the demands of all reason I had the growing conviction that indeed there were forces presently at work which were larger and more powerful than anything I had previously experienced. Logic continued to lead me towards the supposition that these forces could be, at least in part, supernatural.

It was time, I decided, to return to the inn for a glass or two of grog before retiring. I prayed I should sleep more soundly than of late, but I had little hope my prayers would be answered.

In bed that night my thoughts returned often to Klosterheim

and his references to our mutual destiny, my family's special gifts. I had always thought of us as a modest and respectable line of Saxon landowners, diverse in most interests, rarely in agreement on any subject but the most fundamental. It struck me that perhaps my Duchess of Crete had also seen me in the role of some Parsifal or other and had consequently saved me from my enemy. At this, she returned to me, as I crossed the border from waking to sleeping. I imagined that her lithe, pink body was soft against mine while she told me what my character was and how our destiny was shared. Had my own faith in my imagination become so weakened I could be prey to other, fanatical minds? Detecting the enervated condition of my spirit, did they seek to impose their own dreams upon mine, hoping that thus I would become what they desired me to be, some kind of questing hero?

I must, I thought, escape from all of it. The prospect of our flight grew more attractive to me by the moment. "I am von Bek," said I defiantly, lying naked on my bed and touching chest and head and thighs, those familiar contours and textures. Then: "But I must know. I must know, Libussa. *I must know you . . . Why do I have it in my mind there's a revelation to be discovered in your Greek blood? That somewhere within your name lies the secret, the foundation of all your other actions." I pant as if in the first blaze of a new passion. My whole body's mobile, though I make every attempt to lie quiet. At night I cannot deceive or distract myself, I am enchanted still. The Minotaur rages in the Labyrinth, furious at Gods who made him neither Beast nor Man, and Daedalus flies free of this island while Icarus, elated in his first experiment, lifts himself too close to the Sun and is destroyed.*

On Crete a blue sea sends white breakers upon a yellow beach. The rocks are worn to shards, resembling the ruins, almost as ancient, built upon them. A black sail on the horizon disappears. Now beautiful Theseus stands upon the shore, looking towards the City of the Bull. Time has not yet begun to be recorded. This is a scene painted in unclouded primaries. From somewhere a Bull's voice rages, its thickened speech complaining and challenging as if it utters the poetry of distress.

Theseus brandishes a hard, polished club. There is a green cloak upon his wonderful shoulders, a helmet with a great crest of purple horsehair upon his perfect head; painted sandals upon his perfect legs. Yet he has the breasts of a woman and the genitals of a man. Hermaphrodite challenges the old, mad beast, the raging monster whose uncontrolled passions and appetites shall threaten his existence, our own future. He must be slain.

The youth-woman begins to stride with easy, athletic steps up the beach towards the City of the Beast, the City of the Labyrinth, in a time before History, when Man first came to value Reason over Sensibility and gave combat to the hairy halflings which ruled Him. The cloven hoofs dance upon the pavements of the maze, a great spiked club is beaten upon the earth, again and again. The Beast snorts and fumes in the darkness, its anger and its pride demanding sacrifice, the tasting of blood. Theseus pauses at the entrance, her chest rising and falling in conscious rhythms, half-willing, even now, to kneel worshipping before the enormous vitality of the mindless Bull.

Theseus grits his teeth and rubs the head of his club against his leg, letting his jealousy and his fears build themselves into bloodlust. The rich stink of the Minotaur is in his nostrils and he must call upon his own warlike skills and courage. She summons a spirit of determination few have ever needed. This Theseus, my Theseus, advances. The sword of his youth had a bird beating inside the crystal pommel. A hawk, flinging itself again and again in inaudible fury against its glassy prison.

In Byzantium the art of alchemy became European. Here lived Maria the Jewess and Zosimos the Egyptian, who sought to understand the bonds making mankind one with the universe; for surely each was mirrored in the other. Each was contained within the other? The alchemists reduced the elements to a single tincture into which all was concentrated; all matter, all human aspiration, all Time, all knowledge. A pill the size of a pea brought the gift of transmutation (for it was one and therefore the same) and a means of perpetual restoration, both physical and mental. The great glass beakers, the stone retorts, the brass pans and tubes, the smoking elemental potions, had all led towards that end, the creation of a human being: Hermaphrodite, self-reproducing, possessing the sum of all knowledge and virtue; an harmonious and immortal creature neither master nor slave; both male and female; the being described in Genesis. This self-contained creature springs light-footed across the landscapes of my dreams and I see it from without; yet sometimes I myself am that creature, joyous in my power and freedom. In me is Eve and Adam combined. My mind is clear, my senses alert, as I breathe the new-minted air of an Earthly paradise.

Then Klosterheim is speaking and his voice is like a wind from Limbo, singing of death, cold ashes and a nostalgic ambition to reawaken those hopeless, envious legions of Hell, so that he might again command something, even though it be an army of wretches only capable of cruel destruction and the reduction of human aspiration. They quest for a reawakening of Sensibility, the likes of von Bresnvorts, yet it is true Sensibility which shall, by definition, forever be denied those who desire power over others more than they desire the delights of their own human sensuality.

Hermaphrodite sniffs the dangerous breeze. Should she fight or should he flee?

Again I was awakened in a midnight flood as my own juices sprang from every pore. I was godlike. I was afraid. Could so much truly be at stake? The very future of mankind? Until morning my Reason was locked in a struggle with what I must describe as my Instinct; but without resolution. I felt as if some version of the past and some potential tomorrow battled within me for my present loyalty. I feared to resort to the laudanum bottle at my bedside (placed there in all kindness by St. Odhran) but at length I sipped a drop or two and fell back into dreams where my actions, I felt, at least had no effect upon my ordinary existence. I was awakened by my friend hammering upon a door I had inadvertently locked (perhaps during the course of my Cretan nightmare). He told me that he had heard our inflammable air was to be delivered that morning and he went to supervise its arrival at the Little Field. In my dazed condition I scarcely understood him. He was also, I gathered, off on some half-described business with the Landgräfin. I fell back into my stupor and it was midway through the morning before I found the strength to rise, perform my toilet, and enter the world of common reality below.

St. Odhran returned to The Martyred Priest with snow on his hat and more than a little concern in his eyes. He found me in the kitchen, where I listened to Ulrica reciting her dissertation which she was due to present on her return to the Gymnasium the following week. He was impatient to speak to me but did not interrupt. She concluded (sentimental, youthful stuff echoing the rhetoric of our young Utopians who would leave soon for Venice) and I applauded.

Ulrica darted a look at the Chevalier, who bent a knee in empty recognition (for he had not heard a word), and she rolled up her pages. "You'll move the whole school to high-minded aspiration," I told her. But she desired criticism, so I mentioned a clumsy phrase here, a muddy notion there, and all the while St. Odhran tensed his fingers and did everything but pace or cough. At last she was satisfied and I turned in some impatience to chide my partner for his unusually poor display of etiquette when he said, low and horrified: "The Landgräfin is murdered!"

I led him from the kitchen to the public room, which had only a few rural travellers in it, here to buy ploughs and weaving machines (they had been drunk since last night so were unaware of their own boots, let alone we two). "You've just come from there?"

"Questioned by a Beadle for two hours; held by militia, then questioned by a major. First she was stabbed, then her room was fired but servants extinguished the flames before they took firm hold. She was naked and had been tortured. Money stolen and, the servants say, some books, but many of her papers were burned or charred beyond recognition. The servants vouched for me, finally, and I had no reason for wanting her dead. I was released, but both of us are required for a further interview and shall be called as witnesses at the inquest. Von Bresnvorts is whom they suspect. He claims to have been at a country estate while the crime was committed. Their description of the corpse was unsparing of my feelings. Two or three symbols had been cut in the flesh, suggesting black magic."

"Why torture her?" I had been fond of that good-hearted widow. "Von Bresnvorts inherits anyway. Had she changed her will or dictated an appendix? Why kill her in a Satanist rite which would make him suspect? His dabbling's famous!"

"They believe they derive power from such rituals. And doubtless, stupid as he is, he expected the house to burn down. The likes of him believe that the violence of the sacrificial death is directly in proportion to the strength gained. These are mad people, von Bek. Their reasoning is rarely penetrable."

"I pray the monster's hanged."

"He could escape. The major and advocate investigating the crime must prove him directly responsible or capture accomplices who'll give evidence against him. His devil-loving friends, clearly, were tools or aides. The Prince has ordered the whole city alerted for his cousin's murderers. There's a fair chance they'll be caught."

"They could escape into the catacombs."

"Major Wochstmuth has every detail of them I could recall. He seeks Klosterheim, too."

"So thwarted of our blood, he takes his aunt's! Klosterheim will not be over-pleased by his minion's folly. Von Bresnvorts was drooling to slaughter someone. Perhaps he planned to accuse us of the murder and so solve all his problems at once? Or are there more depths to the matter, do you think?"

St. Odhran answered with slow sobriety. "I'd say there were extra complexities, aye. But I have no trust in my judgement at present, for I'm still horrified by the bloody nature of the crime. 'Tis hard to credit the evidence of such perverse evil. And can it all be for the sake of a few hundred Talers donated to us, when his aunt possessed millions?"

"Maybe he does not wish our ship to sail? Or visit the Mittelmarch (which he believes in, if we don't)? What if he did not truly see us as a pair of charlatans but thinks we actually possess supernatural secrets, maybe even the key to immortality? Did he feel threatened by the prospect of his aunt's eternal life? We're reckoning, I think, without his credulity!"

St. Odhran accepted this theory, but lifted his hand to stop me speaking further. "I'll be frank, von Bek. I've discussed such things for half the day and no amount of debate pushes away the image of her corpse or improves my spirits. She's dead. We cannot resurrect her. The sooner we're gone from Mirenburg the better. Too many lunatics focus their dreams through us. Had I known this city contained so many morbid seekers after arcane lore, I would not have suggested this swindle at all."

I became aware, suddenly, that St. Odhran was profoundly terrified. At least we now had fear in common, I thought. "I would suggest," said I, "that we try by conventional means to free ourselves from our contracts, return most of the monies at least and then be on our way."

"I'd arrived at the same conclusion." I could read from his eyes that he had never been closer to despair. "But we have contracts and, as far as the Law's concerned, von Bresnvorts is a primary shareholder. I've read those papers every way and we're committed (mainly because of that damned lawyer) to all kinds of penalties. We've promised passages. Will Klosterheim be pleased when we announce the venture cancelled? Our lives are at stake, my friend. In brief, we're back to putting our trust in high winds, frayed ropes and the gullibility of our backers, both anonymous and all too famous."

St. Odhran was badly affected by our Landgräfin's fate. He drank more brandy than he would normally allow himself. He displayed more emotion that he had ever shown, even when it had seemed we were to be filleted at the Devil's pleasure. Yet I understood that he could not easily voice sentiment in the matter, for it would be a sort of hypocrisy since he had planned to steal from the murdered woman. St. Odhran was the kind of man who tested his wits upon the world, like a gambler at the card-table, and was moved as much by love of his game as by the prospect of profit. He lifted his bumper in a toast, he said, to the memory of a worthy player, the Landgräfin.

I would gladly have joined him in this excursion into maudlin escape, but some instinct kept me wary, so I sat with him and suffered his mourning as a friend must. Then, as the taproom filled with its evening trade, I helped him and his bottle to his rooms where he loosened his neck-cloth and the buttons of his breeches, eased off his stockings and pumps, and continued his ritual litany. He revealed all his fears and courage that night, his love for the human race, his wounds, his amours, the origins of his stylish foppery, of his taste for disguise; a duellist's conscious guard rather than the entrapping armour of the mounted knight. Words were used to hold back and contain the attacks of the world, for he had a hatred and a horror of violence which I could comprehend without fully understanding. "And mysteries," he told me, "I'm afraid of all these shadowy people who give us money and materials. Why, von Bek? We're in too deep, man!"

Then he fell sweetly to sleep, a seraphic child. I kissed his unwrinkled brow and drew a blanket around his body, but did not at once leave the room. I was possessed of an enervating melancholy and had no desire to return to my own bed and my unsettling dreams. Most of my life had been spent in my own company. I had rarely maintained a regular mistress, let alone a wife, and had never envied those who did. Presently I had a dim sense of being incomplete, of being only part of a divided soul. I had a yearning for what I could only describe as Unity. What had I lost that was mine? Were we all, in some way, like poor Klosterheim?

"Satan," murmured St. Odhran in his untroubled sleep. I watched the lines of terror gradually return. His lips moved rapidly. Beneath their lids his eyes were agitated. "Dead."

I leaned forward, as if he was an oracle whose words would unlock all my own mysteries at once. He took short, panting breaths. He struggled in the blankets and his right arm came free. "Brandy," he said, then sank again into peace.

I sat in a ladder-backed chair reading through his neatly drawn maps. Some showed continents which did not exist; unfamiliar groups of islands, a familiar map of France with additional territories named and marked, or Germany magnified to three times her proper area, yet having on her borders the same countries. Here for instance were Grünewald, Halbenstein and Alfersheim, all bordering Saxony. St. Odhran claimed he had all the maps (some of which were ancient, kept together on oiled rag or varnished onto wood) from one collection. A drunken monk had sold them to him at a Bavarian fair, begging a gold mark for them and saying they were beyond price. Certainly they were the work of different hands, or else done by a master forger. I rolled those not damaged into his leather tube. The case was worn and frayed and the brass fittings were pitted, dull. The others I placed carefully one upon the other.

St. Odhran began to snore loudly. My vigil had run its time. I extinguished the lamps and both candles and trudged up the passage to my bed. The room around me seemed to sway, I was so fatigued. The candlelight added shadows in the corners of my eyes and I could almost smell the presence of a woman. She was not there, but it would take more than a careless dismissal of my fancies to free me. I desire no other. I still burn for her. It is with Libussa of Crete I must be reunited!

I checked myself from further folly and instead offered up a prayer to a God I did not believe in for the survival of my own non-existent soul and that of the poor murdered woman. Major Wochstmuth had my blessing in his search for evidence to convict von Bresnvorts. If jailed the Satanist would have his effects frozen by the State. He would find it hard to command his horrid flock without money to pay them.

I looked out again into the Mladota Square, which gleamed black with rain. Two men hated me enough to want my life, another hated me but disdained to kill me. A woman remained hidden from me, yet had saved my life. Were these people in any way connected with one another? My only allies in this city were a veteran sergeant and a foreign trickster. I decided I must do as St. Odhran suggested and leave, wind or no wind, balloon or horse. I felt in greater danger than any I had known in Paris. I felt that my body's very essence was threatened.

Fearing sleep I found myself writing letters: one to my mother (waxing sentimental and nostalgic), another to Robespierre (begging him be moderate), to Talleyrand asking to encourage policies, not mere stage-trappings masking the procedures of the old régime; to Tom Paine, in jail, advising him to accept any humiliation if it meant his release and passage to America. *You were my mentor, dear Tom, as was Cloots. For all the madness of his anarchy and world rebellion (a most marvellous fancy but a hopeless practicality) I yet retain great affection for him. But you must recall your own Common Sense and, seeing the world as she is, and how she may be improved, do nothing else which might result in your own prolonged imprisonment, or even death, for this age needs a cool eye upon it, now more than ever, and there are precious few of those currently to hand.*

Another letter was written to Libussa Urganda Cressida Cartagena y Mendoza-Chilperic, Duchess of Crete, in which I proclaimed my love and offered a complaint. She had shown me too much of paradise to deny me at least the hope of earning a key. *"I yearn to fling myself into Infinity,"* says Goethe, *"and float above the awful Abyss." O, madam, I would be at your mercy, trusting you with the care of my entire being. I would be your servant.* And so forth. The letters were sanded, folded, addressed, sealed with my von Bek crest, the Sign of the Cup. Was that cup actually the Grail? Or was it, as I suspected, the cup which gave rise to legends of our connection with the Grail?

The last letter I would leave with Sergeant Schuster, not knowing my lady's whereabouts. I became eager for the dawn, when I intended to sleep. I feared the dark and my dreams. I wrote a further letter to Montsorbier, whom I presumed returned to Paris, informing him of my respect and offering him satisfaction should we ever meet again. It was at this stage that I realised I was writing as if certain of my imminent death. However, I wrote a note to Schuster, enclosing a few Talers, thanking him for his kindness, hospitality, the good will of his family and asking him not to think ill of me should my departure be sudden. Another note was addressed to my young Utopians, telling them that their hearts were purer than the world they beat in. They must remember South America could not be tamed by Reason; Reason could only tame the Beast within us. Even a letter to St. Odhran was written, containing what was not far short of my own memorial: *I aspired to Roguery but was thwarted by circumstance.*

When we think ourselves close to death, how desperately do we aim a little of our substance towards the living, as if they are spars and boats from a wreck, to carry something of us on towards the shore. Another letter, to Mirenburg's Prince, describing in detail the circumstances of our capture by the Baron and begging him to abolish (in Law and Deed) the folly of Satanism and occultism which is nought but infantile, witless, ignorant, dangerous, inhumane, cruel and deleterious to the well-being of his great city. I wrote to my brother, Rickhardt, telling him something of my enslavement to lies and romantic lust, but assuring him I could yet judge right from wrong, though my choice be dubious, *for I have become as uncertain of my past Virtue as I am of my present Vice.*

It was dawn at last. The rain was all gone but a thin white line upon the horizon crept like distant cavalry, in a flurry of wispy gases, up the sky and over our rooftops, bringing snow. I put my final letter upon the pile then took to my bed and a dreamless sleep from whence I awoke, a newborn optimist, with St. Odhran's slurred voice in my ears crying: "See them for a moment! Your young Utopians. Your seekers of the Grail."

They left for Venice, I remembered, that morning. I sat up. "Enter, dear friends." I was glad to see their stern, embarrassed faces, scrubbed and ready for a further stage in their explorations. I hoped, in private, they would find a diversion before they reached Peru. I handed them their letter from the heap.

"Our ship puts us down at New York or maybe Baltimore," Krasny said. "From there we make our way south, either by ship or land."

"Go by land," was my advice, "so that you may see for yourselves what the Millennium has offered others before you."

He was puzzled. "Sir, I do not follow you."

"See Washington's rebellious nation," I said. "The first in modern times to build her constitution upon a genuine faith in the power and the virtue of Law. A gentleman's country. You will like it. And it will not disappoint you as badly as France." I sensed I was speaking inappropriately. "Whatever you decide, young masters, I wish you good luck."

"Well, Sir," said Krasny, "we are honoured to have met you."

"Honoured, also, my friends. I wish you a satisfactory journey through the New World."

St. Odhran interrupted with mock gravity. "Your money would be better spent on an aeronautical voyage, but folly's the privilege of youth as it's the punishment of age."

Then they were gone; four sons it seemed to me. Four princes from an Arabian tale, riding across our world in search of the non-existent cure for all human woe. I made St. Odhran sit down on my bed. "We must leave tomorrow," I told him. "Or 'tis my guess we'll be dead."

"The hydrogen's delivered to the Little Field. Its donor expects a passage, as does Klosterheim, but if we follow our plan and describe the ascent as a mere preliminary experiment, to test the gas's power, we should be able to give them the slip easily enough. However, my friend, I'll warn you now that if there is indeed a plot to kill us, you must understand that inflammable air burns quicker and faster than anything known to man's science. Should we catch fire on board, we'd be charred before we touched ground again. But ain't ye bein' a mite too fretful, von Bek? Are you still not sleeping well?"

"Could be I've gone mad, St. Odhran. But if you will not take me from Mirenburg, I'll go by any other route. Our enemies converge, on that we're both agreed, eh? But if we escape 'em now, we'll surprise 'em. They'd not anticipate such an immediate departure, I'm sure. Announce the demonstration, as you proposed. Say it's to be in two days. But we'll leave in one."

St. Odhran shrugged. "I share your wish to be gone from here. Very well, I'll do as you say." At my request he took another pile of papers from me. It was a kind of confession and must, I said, be given into safe-keeping. He would send it, he assured me, to Mr. Magagold, an English lawyer who for some years had represented his interests.

When my friend had gone I took all the other letters I had written, crammed them into my stove and burned them. I began to prepare. Our journey must not look premeditated. I used changes of clothes as packing for my few other possessions. Most of St. Odhran's goods were already gone ahead to the Little Field. He had repacked the gold, he said, into ballast sacks, distinguished by their green colour. Our sword and pistols were hidden in sea-chart cases and leather tubes. The gas was with our ship outside the walls; seven large jeroboams which, said St. Odhran, had to be handled with extraordinary care. Special hoses accompanied them. Through these the element must be introduced to the envelope by means of an already existing valve. St. Odhran was grinning as he told me this. "We shall never know, I suppose, from whom most of our gold came, or who sent us the gas, but I wish him good luck for the rest of his life!"

For once I had no inclination to question my conscience. I was too eager to escape. Admitted it was a coward's panic. I was in a mood to say anything or do anything to be gone from that just and kindly Mirenburg. For Mirenburg's foundations, it seemed to me then, harboured maggots which depended for their existence upon a steady progress of corruption.

I grew disinclined to leave my room yet remained too fearful for sleep; and when the time came to venture into the streets to make the journey from The Martyred Priest to the *Donan* I was almost afraid to go from the confines of the inn to the carriage. Sergeant Schuster and his family bid us farewell, expecting to see us at supper that night. I knew further pangs of self-disgust at this.

It was left to St. Odhran to coax me, with patient sympathy, into the carriage which took us, all too speedily, through Mirenburg's great walls and out upon the Little Field.

Chapter Nine

In which everything's escaped—and everything
escaped is fresh encountered!

IN A CONDITION of near delirium, I allowed myself to be borne
to where, in muddy snow, our balloon was already swelling.
Our escape, however, was not to be made in secret for word was
already out. Our vessel had been detected by the folk of Mirenburg before she was half inflated and the wall beside the Mirozhny
Gate was so crowded with spectators the top was invisible. At the
base of the wall people stood upon the roofs of their carriages,
the backs of their mules, the seats of their wagons. The street-
sellers had joined us. Red braziers glowed everywhere, both to
warm the crowd and to cook chestnuts and potatoes. There
were sweetmeat vendors, ginger-beer sellers, broadsheetmen
(their standard rhymes and tunes suitably adapted for the occasion), gypsy women selling charms and hot apples. And all in the
space of the hour it had taken to connect our balloon to the
hydrogen!

The *beau-monde* had made itself a kind of enclosure from
red-and-white-striped canvas and now talked, as always, as if the
object of its visit was not there. St. Odhran's amused dismay,
whispering to me as he waved in full fashion at my side, was
somewhat cheering to me. "Was ever an escape so well-attended?"

I grew at once less nervous and yet more wary of sly attack.
The sky was blue and so cold it might have been a single sheet of
ice. A steady but only moderate breeze blew towards the south.
Our balloon slowly took shape as the last of the hydrogen was
pumped through one valve and into another. A barrel organ
played the same banalities over and over and the mechanical monkey its proprietor substituted for the reality had more life than the

tune. Red-faced women leaned against the weight of their food-baskets. Militiamen, their uniforms hastily tidied, stood on guard, muskets at the slope. They had more gold buttons and braid than any private outside the Turkish Sultan's janissaries, and monstrous fine helmets: helmets which engulfed their heads and were moulded or engraved with an elaborate relish for classical motifs, topped with red and yellow plumes.

Major Wochstmuth of the militia was there, eyes narrowed as he peered up at that huge, wobbling sphere of green-and-blue silk, at the undulating hose which hissed like a cobra as it passed gas from jar to ship. Elsewhere half Mirenburg's aristocracy, many of her men and women of learning, wandered across the Little Field, their attention focused on the vast bulk of our vessel.

The gondola was a proud and stern-eyed (if battered) bird. Most of our boxes now lay under a trap door, between the double layers of the gondola's bottom, originally designed to carry the travelling galley required by King Louis's pastoral enthusiasts, when shepherd-boy and shepherd-lass (in honour of Rousseau, they said) picnicked in the arbours and grottoes of Versailles's new-fashioned Arcadia. There was room for us to sleep and food for more than a week. Once free of Mirenburg we would merely drift until some suitable landing place was sighted. We waved again as we walked towards the gondola. St. Odhran had announced that we intended to ascend, tethered, to a height of five-hundred feet in order to test and demonstrate the properties of the inflammable air. The crowd grew noisy on the walls, cheering and calling out to us. The balloon thumped and tugged: she was almost filled to capacity. She lifted our gilded Gryphon about a foot off the ground, but he was still held captive by anchors, ropes and ballast. Nearby was the capstan which would as a rule wind us down to earth (and on that winch—borrowed from a barge owner at the docks—a section of rope had been designed to snap. St. Odhran had rubbed at it in darkness for over two hours during the previous night).

My partner opened the little gate allowing us to step into the gondola. He winked at me as I closed the gate behind us. The

Gryphon swayed. The canopy was caught by the wind and boomed like a flaccid drum. St. Odhran and I hauled in the first small anchor. The crowd cheered us again. Again, we waved.

We were pulling in the second anchor when a carriage came in sight, drawn by four dappled mares. I guessed it was the convey-ance of the Prince himself. He wished to get some measure, I supposed, of his investment. Had it been he who had given us the gas? The coach stopped nearby, only a few feet from us, the horses blowing and skittish in the shadow of the great Air-ship, and from it emerged the figures of two slender men, both swathed in fash-ionable black travelling cloaks and hats: unrecognisable. Then to my faint surprise, the man signalled for the coach to leave. The couple (surely the Prince and his brother, incognito) walked slowly towards our gondola, for all the world as if they were expected by us. I looked to St. Odhran, he to me. Together we shrugged our mystification. Were we to be blessed? Were titles to be bestowed? Was some other ritual planned?

Again the crowd began its wild cheering. I thought they had recognised their rulers. We were helpless. St. Odhran murmurs to me: "Let 'em inspect us. Let 'em make any request of us. Then we'll warn 'em of the danger of ascending with untested gas."

The taller man handed up the shorter, who steadied himself with a gloved palm against the side of the basket, offering me a faint bow by way of acknowledgement. Then the other jumped in, panting a little. His face was revealed as he turned towards me: "You can proceed, Captain von Bek. We are ready to rise."

"I'm obliged to you, Sir." I continued to haul in rope while below St. Odhran's hirelings untied tethering cords. But my heart was on the thump and my head was swimming, for our visitor was not the Prince of Mirenburg! It was Klosterheim and I knew he was there to hold me to my bargain. He went to lean with his back against wicker and carved wood, one hand upon a taut can-opy rope, his features as expressionless as always. The other man's face remained completely hidden. He was too tall for von Bresn-vorts, perhaps a little short for Montsorbier. I could not be entirely sure of the latter idea.

"What's this, Herr Klosterheim?" hissed St. Odhran under his breath. "Don't ye know, Sir, this is no more than an experiment to try the lifting power of our gas?"

Klosterheim was joined by his companion, who wore some kind of domino mask. They stood together like two huge carrion birds, swathed in their black, and watched as we worked. Now all the ropes and anchors were free, save for the tether attached to the capstan. My heart was sinking. We had no choice but to continue and know that Klosterheim and his companion (a hired swordsman?) must be our passengers wherever we sailed. There was no chance of turning back.

We rose with steady majesty above the Little Field, above Mirenburg, above the whole white world, and while the great crowd huzzahed and hallooed, our breath threatened to turn to ice in our mouths. The audience grew to the size of dolls, then insects, its cheering and applause a tiny sound. I remained aware of my miserable cowardice, no longer feeling godlike as I had done during my initial ascent. Everywhere was the great silence of the sky. Then the balloon had yawed and the gondola made a crazy, dangerous swing, as if suddenly pushed from the side, and we heard a vibrating, musical noise. The rope reached its maximum stretch.

St. Odhran's stance suggested he would gladly push Klosterheim overboard at some appropriate moment. He took a step towards the gaunt intruder, then the gondola had rocked wildly again and we were all flung down. The rope had snapped, as it had been meant to snap. We were drifting free.

I had no sense at all of exhilaration. Now we were forced to give an even more elaborate theatrical pretence than we had planned. St. Odhran and I regained our footing, rushed to the side, made a pantomime of distress for the benefit of the innocents below. We pretended to shout. We displayed panic. The ship was still swinging too much for my taste and I was flung to the floor again. Klosterheim, steadying himself by the rope and the velvet tassels (designed for this purpose) running along the top edge of the gondola, looked down at me. "Flying," he said.

I turned my head to stare at his earnest skull. His lips moved as if seeking to frame unspeakable thoughts. He said no more on the subject. And the other man, too, was silent. He had a lithe, athletic way of keeping his balance, scarcely moving at all. It was not, I thought, Montsorbier. St. Odhran was forgetful of both at that moment. He was laughing like an ape and hurling ballast down, bag after bag, at an immoderate rate, his neck-cloth whipping in the wind and his hair in wild disarray about his long face. He was careless of everything; he scarcely seemed aware any longer of the baffled Klosterheim and his close-mouthed companion. "Oh, von Bek, my dear! The plan's succeeded!"

Remindful of our company, he turned, straightening his clothing as he hung by one hand to the edge and made a quick, unbalanced bow. "Servant, gentlemen." He looked towards me. "Get up, man. What's wrong?"

I felt unwell. Slowly, after several false starts, I climbed to my feet and drew in deeper breaths. The air was a razor to my lungs. I opened a hamper and dragged out an old sea-cloak Schuster had given me and I wrapped it around my shivering body. St. Odhran was oblivious of the cold. He was shouting at the Sun; shouting at the pale gold and silver of the infinite sky. There was nothing else to be seen, save the contours of white clouds in the distance and mist above like a milky lake.

The clouds were all that remained of the malleable landscape, of the unstable past. St. Odhran yelled in pleasure at the glittering canopy of our ship. A rainbow flashed across it every few seconds as the coloured silk gyrated in the sun's light. He was taking us too high and at last realised it when the air grew distinctly thinner and even he saw that his own skin was turning blue.

So now he reached up to his valve-wire and let out a little gas to drop us lower. "I've sighted Africa!" He was smiling, for he joked. "Over there!" Only Klosterheim looked.

The wind had an odd relentlessness to it, neither strengthening nor weakening, neither whirling nor gusting. I had never known it so consistent, on land or sea. It might have been generated by a machine. I went to our compass. Something confused it, for the needle could not be steadied. Light struck the glass, half-blinding me. When I looked back into the gondola everyone was an unfocused shadow. Another turn of the Gryphon and the clarity was restored. Everything sharpened and the two black-clad passengers seemed a solid silhouette against the gilded wickerwork. St. Odhran now squatted nearby. He was like an overbred wolf as he stared at the pair. He addressed me: "Has Klosterheim made introductions?"

I shook my head. The gondola swayed regularly now: the gradual pendulum of some enormous clock.

"Shall you make introductions, Herr Klosterheim?" asked St. Odhran sardonically.

Klosterheim considered this without any hint that he had understood the implication. Then: "Not yet," he said.

"Was it you, Sir, who sent us the gas?"

The gaunt immortal shook his head and looked out at the sky. St. Odhran shrugged. He reached for his map-case, smoothing the chart on the floor and trying to calculate our progress. We were travelling at a speed of some twenty miles an hour; the gauge showed it as a steady 19.7. We were heading due south and must soon, he thought, be over Italy, then the Mediterranean, then— with a wild, excited look to me—the African continent.

Plainly he had decided to ignore our unwelcome passengers. Both of us spoke quietly together, wondering at their motive for joining us. I wondered if they might be the Landgräfin's murderers, after all, escaping Major Wochstmuth. At this I decided to make a small test of my own. "Klosterheim," said I, "did you hear that von Bresnvorts had murdered his aunt?"

The pale lips formed careful words. "I did not. But 'twould explain his anxiety to leave when last I saw him. And, of course, Montsorbier's already gone with the others. Is that the reason so many soldiers searched my catacombs? Yes, I suppose so."

"You know Montsorbier?" I was on a fresh tack already.

"His brotherhood had dealings with von Bresnvorts. There was talk of co-operation. Their methods and goals are dissimilar, however. Montsorbier was lodging with Bresnvorts."

Now the Republican's absence was explained! He had known

me captured, guessed me dead, and so made no attempt to rise before dawn to keep his appointment at the Wool Quay. But, unless my reading of his character was utterly topsy-turvy, Montsorbier would have had no part in our kidnapping, nor in the Landgräfin's murder. Had he despaired of von Bresnvorts as an ally (in what?) and returned to France? "How were they in league?" I asked Klosterheim. I pulled on heavy gauntlets to protect myself from the cold, but his hands, though clearly as frozen as my own, were naked on the rope he held. He replied in his monotone. "They merely debated alliance."

"Why consider one in the first place?"

"On account of the predicted Conjoining." He was mildly surprised. "Every brotherhood so confers. We must gather forces, share knowledge, abolish rivalries. It is necessary."

"Scientists, occultists, alchemists? The Church? The Jews? The Mussulmans? Who conjoins for what?"

"But you must know." He put a tongue to his lower lip. He looked towards his feet, then looked up again. His eyes were searching. He looked momentarily at his partner, but he did not respond. "For many centuries the various occult brotherhoods have understood that on rare occasions the stars appear in such an order in the heavens that the invisible universe intersects with the visible. Thus it becomes possible for adepts—even those who are not adepts—to cross the geometry separating one plane from another. This momentous event comes infrequently. Sometimes a thousand years must pass. Sometimes two thousand. Coincident with these concurrences are certain events in the histories of all worlds, when a watershed is reached and new realities established—sometimes because one world, normally hidden from another, influences its neighbour."

"And that's why alchemists congregate, eh?" said St. Odhran. "The Baron mentioned some astral event, I recall."

"The future of our Globe can be determined," continued Klosterheim, almost in excitement, "for the next Millennium at least. Shall the machine be dominant? Or shall we have a planet where Man's reconciled with his own Nature?"

"You take an old-fashioned view, then?" said I.

"I'm neutral on that," said he.

"The alchemists in the main are against the mechanistic philosophies of Newton, Arkwright and Tom Paine," said St. Odhran.
"Which makes it all the more mysterious why one should supply
us"—he pointed above—"with that!"

Klosterheim turned his head away.

"It's said to be a period for the gathering of power," I recalled.
"Much is decided during the time of an astral concordance: which
tendency shall rule, for instance. Is that what you promised me,
Klosterheim, when you promised me my own Realm?"

"You shall have it still," he said. "My word was given. Even if
you plotted to break yours."

"So now mankind stands between Reason and Faith, is that it?"
I was openly contemptuous. "Between mechanical flight and the
magic carpet?"

"You think you speak rationally, von Bek, but what if the supernatural regained control of the world? What if the Anti-Christ
were to emerge? Would God and Satan set aside their discussion
and go to War? Would Man lift his sword against both Heaven and
Hell, making a reality of *Revelations*?"

"It's nonsense-talk, Klosterheim. The world slowly embraces
Enlightenment. The age of superstition has gone the way of religious wars. The future belongs to Newton and his followers."

"There's a battle already taking place," said Klosterheim firmly.
"Armies are being drawn up. Great forces are at work everywhere.
You must know this! You, of all people, have seen the evidence."

"I know only what you've told me. Warlocks and witches
debate to determine how to make their broomsticks fly again. But
how shall they ever come together in strength? Even if your ideas
had any truth, they're so frequently, by their very character, at
odds. Each claims to hold the key to the only wisdom. That's
where natural philosophers, who do not *impose* what they need to
believe (or at least not so readily!) upon the world, but *analyse*
what they see, have the strong advantage."

From the corner of my eye I saw the other man make a

movement with his hand, but he restrained the gesture. Klosterheim could not rise to my bait, however. He was incapable of
ordinary anger. Perhaps a deeper, hungrier anger burned like a
volcanic stone at the core of his being. "There have ever been
momentary advantages and disadvantages to those viewpoints,"
he agreed placidly. "But the Astral Concordance will decide the
matter, at least for a while. Why, I wonder, are you such a spokesman for Reason with a family history, a family destiny indeed,
more rooted in supernatural experience than most?"

"Perhaps because I abhor the fictions which shape those histories, as they shape nations. A myth to me, Herr Klosterheim, is no
more than a fanciful lie, allowing men and women to deceive
themselves and others with all manner of fine-sounding rhetoric.
A legend, if called upon to justify action, is an excuse for murder,
theft, rape, genocide—any crime, so long as it's committed in the
name of a dead hero or some dignified pagan devil to whom, for
political reasons doubtless, you give the title 'Saint.' There may be
less truth in the world than there are glamorous lies, Klosterheim,
but I'll take the few scraps we have in preference to a basketful of
your Romance."

Klosterheim had no interest in the discussion. He seemed both
bored and mystified by my attitude. His deep-set eyes were fixed
on matters singular to himself. The other man drew back his cloak
a little to reveal garb resembling that of a Turk. He made a small
sound. What was he? I wondered. Some Oriental Magus requiring a swift passage home?

St. Odhran began to smile. "Is it not time, von Bek, to manhan-
dle these two over the side and see if their magic helps 'em fly?"

I laughed, but I was battling uncertainty and fear again.

St. Odhran dragged food and wine from our hold. The black-clad
pair refused it, so the Scotchman and myself sat us down
cross-legged to dine in that swaying platform, close to a mile
above the world. As we completed our meal with some soft
Wäldensteiner *flenser*, St. Odhran took one of the two matched
pocket watches he carried and studied it. "We must soon be over
Vienna," he said. "At this rate we'll be looking down on the Adri-

atic by nightfall. I've never known a more regular flight." He was delighted by the wonder of his own machine. He took slate and charcoal from amongst his jumble of possessions and began to calculate again, every so often getting up to peer over the side.

"By Heaven, von Bek, there's no reason why, with a study of wind-tides and air-streams, we shouldn't be able to send any number of aerial craft about the world's business! I'm beginning to suspect there are different currents at different levels, as that guard suggested. Thus we're upon the main Southern stream. By careful ascents each ship could find its appropriate level and move from one current to the next at will. Do you know, von Bek, it strikes me we could easily become legitimate merchant-adventurers, the first to adapt modern aerial ships to regular commercial routes and entirely supersede the oceans! We must consider the possibility, my dear, of legally acquired profit—and a place in history!" All this was babbled heedlessly before the unspeaking couple who seemed to have no interest at all in us. St. Odhran's plans became increasingly grandiose the longer we were free of the ground. Soon he was describing vast flying cargo barges. These would be half a mile across. By the time we saw the sky turn a deep and gorgeous red, shading to myriad degrees of purple and blue, the colours reflected in the sleek material of the balloon's envelope and everywhere in silence, he was picturing a ship as big as a town. The beauty impressed him eventually and distracted his attention.

I supposed even Klosterheim must be moved by the awesome grandeur, but when I looked at him he was studying the sunset and frowning, as if recalling a time when all the world was painted the colour of blood—in the days of his Glory. Then, quite shockingly, Klosterheim's companion lifted an arm and with gloved hand pointed:

Rising out of the south, black and jagged, was a massive wall of cloud, so dense it might be a mountain range. Indeed, St. Odhran leaned forward with his telescope, unable to judge for certain what it was we were approaching. When he lowered the glass he was troubled, placing a hand upon his chin. Back he went to consult his charts. We were without fire of any kind, so he turned the maps this way and that to get the last of the light. Klosterheim stepped up behind him and bent to read the unrolled linen. St. Odhran muttered to himself. Another chart was inspected. Then another.

"They cannot be mountains," I said. "There's no range so high."

"They are mountains," said Klosterheim, "but they are not on those charts. Look for them upon your other maps."

St. Odhran glared at him, convinced Klosterheim was quite mad. "Be silent, Sir. It is difficult enough to navigate, without idiots informing me that mountains exist where Vienna should be!"

"You're sailing away from Vienna, Sir," said Klosterheim, perhaps in mild triumph. "Look to your compass."

St. Odhran squinted. Sure enough, we appeared to be travelling due north, when not half an hour since we sailed due south. Yet we would readily have detected so radical a change of wind!

"Klosterheim," said the Scot, newly grim. "Tell me, man. Have ye tampered with the compass? If so, it's devilish foolish of you, for our survival may depend on it!"

"I have tampered with nothing, St. Odhran."

The bloody clouds raced past us now on every side, like the rags of a retreating army. The black mountains came closer. There was no mistaking what they were.

Jagged crags, too sharp to be the contours of clouds, grew by the moment. There were some stars behind them, but I did not immediately recognise the configurations. They seemed, presumably because of the distorting moisture, enlarged almost to the size of the Moon . . .

St. Odhran sprang suddenly for his rip-valve! He meant to take the Air-ship down! It was plain he cared not how quickly we descended—as long as we did descend. But now the other man, in the Turkish costume, threw back his great cloak to reveal quilted clothes designed to guard against the cold. There was a great horse-pistol in his right hand; with his left he cocked the hammer.

The voice was familiar to me. "If flint strikes steel, gentlemen, it will not matter where I shoot. Stand away, Chevalier, if you please! Stand away, Sir!"

"Why," says St. Odhran, suddenly recognising the figure. "You're the young Duke, are you not?"

"Forgive me." Klosterheim's interjection was, as usual, clumsy and inapposite. "Did I not introduce the Duke of Crete?"

But I was looking beyond the domino at those clear, sardonic eyes, so used to obedience.

"It is not the Duke of Crete!" said I. I was firm on that.

The figure holding the pistol began to smile, while the others looked at me in bafflement.

Now I understood the source of all those rumours concerning the Duke, how he liked to dress as a woman and go about the town. I knew, too, why my pursuit of the Duchess came regularly to a dead end, as if she disappeared in smoke (frequently when the Duke was abroad). I gasped with a sensation close to ecstasy.

"An imposter?" says St. Odhran, lifting an eyebrow.

I shook my head. A delicious shudder ran through my entire frame. I bowed low.

"Good evening, my lady," said I, to the laughing Duchess of Crete.

Chapter Ten

Reverses, Advances & Revelations. In which the
Mittelmarch is discussed and described.
The City in the Autumn Stars.

G REY EVENING CAME and we flew amongst the great silent
mountains. The Duchess of Crete, holding her pistol steady,
reached up with her left hand to push back the hood and pull loose
her domino. I watched eagerly for any sign in her handsome, heavy
features that she held me in some kind of affection. "Libussa." We
were never lovers, yet because of her I was everywhere in unmapped
country, both corporeal and spiritual. "Libussa."

No longer laughing, she acknowledged me with a flicker of her
concentrated eye.

"Madam," said St. Odhran in an angry murmur. "There's no
need for this melodrama!"

Carefully, Libussa uncocked the pistol and placed it at her feet.
"The need's past, I agree. For now you've kept your bargain with
me." And she stretched, all of a sudden, and yawned as if only just
awake. "You dealt with me through Hoehenheim the lawyer and
I supplied your aspirant gas!"

St. Odhran was piqued. With disapproval and dismay he
regarded the huge surrounding peaks, then his lips parted. There
was astonishment on his face. He peered towards the west. Following his gaze I saw a line of pink behind the far crags. The line
broadened. Klosterheim and my Duchess showed no surprise at
all. It was less than half an hour since the sun set—now it rose
again! I looked wildly at the compass and remembered it was
reversed, which was a small comfort. We now stared east. The
pink spread into gold and pale yellow and I required no further
evidence that we had truly entered a Magic Kingdom whose real-

ity I had so recently dismissed. I looked out upon those terrific crags with renewed curiosity. Far below were thin silver threads of rivers: ribbons of dark green that were valleys. Did ordinary folk live there or were these the haunts of trolls and hobgoblins? From believing nothing I was now disposed to accept anything!

The sun, when he emerged, brazen and blinding above the peaks, was our same, familiar sun. We observed no dragons or hippogriffs, only a few swallows diving in the air currents below. The morning was considerably warmer; so much so that we were soon removing our outer clothing. St. Odhran was lost in himself, far from reconciled to Libussa's thwarting counterplay with the dragoon pistol, yet evidently excited by the adventure itself. Klosterheim merely leaned upon the edge and noted familiar landmarks to his companion, who paid him scant attention.

Crosswinds pushed us this way and that between the mountains, as if we were steered by Talus's gentle fingers, until we were drifting over high valleys whose meadows were entirely free of snow and which were filled with late Summer flowers. The seasons, too, were mirror-reflections of our own. Otherwise we might be in Switzerland or returned to the Carpathians. The heating air was sweet and lazy; a balm to the troublesome humours which had beset me for so many weeks. My blue devils were all but banished. We saw cottages and little towns, the occasional walled city, its architecture antique and pleasantly familiar, like so many of our German cathedral-towns, save that cannon-fire plainly had never attacked these perpendicular cloisters and castles, these tranquil viaducts and massive, fluted towers, the carved arcades of granite and limestone set upon hills overlooking lovely rivers whose steep banks were thickly forested, all dark shades of green.

"Is this where you told me Hell's army marched?" I asked Klosterheim.

"No," he said. "Not here." He pointed: "Beyond Ireland. Beyond the west."

More relaxed, more the familiar female rogue I had first met on the Lausanne road, Libussa became a kindly tutor. "The

Mittelmarch is not one Realm as you understand it. It weaves in and out of our other world, crossing and intersecting. But you can travel through it without even noticing. If you seek it and know where and when are the Points of Conjunction, the time of certain winds, even, then you can enter as we've entered. We cross a land roughly between Austria and Hungary; yet you could pass through it in the space of moments, though 'tis many thousands of miles square. There again, you might find yourself in some other Mittelmarch kingdom. Time and Geography are not the finite things your Reason demands, von Bek. Your natural philosophy, based upon constants and analysis, is scarcely the keen, pure instrument you insist it is. You narrow the world, Sir, with such logic. We alchemists celebrate complexity and refuse to reduce it. We aim at universal understanding through quite different means."

For some reason I believe she punished me. My groin began to knot. I desired her so strongly it was all I could do to remain where I stood, braced against the basketwork while the great balloon swayed above. In controlled tones I asked her: "What d'ye seek, Madam, in the Mittelmarch? Why did you commandeer our vessel?"

"I seek only what we all seek, von Bek. And since Time is of the essence presently, your Air-ship carries us to our destination faster than horses—and will carry us away, also."

"What do we all seek, Madam?"

She smiled. She seemed to look upon me as if she suspected my innocence to be assumed. "The Grail. My interest is chiefly alchemical. Unity and harmony are two of the most used words in our professional vocabulary. And those are surely what the Grail personifies?" She would answer no more.

"Your ancestor believed, as did Prince Lucifer, that the Grail should bring an easing of the heart, an end to torment . . ." Klosterheim spoke into space.

St. Odhran, still distant and antagonistic, addressed her. "If ye're the adept ye say, Madam, it would have been simple for you to build your own balloon. Why take ours?"

"No time," she said. "My intelligence was recent. Besides, I wanted more than your vessel."

St. Odhran frowned. "A matter of personages, eh?"

Libussa looked away so I could not see her face. I did not fully understand what my Scotch friend said, but he had struck home. "Klosterheim proposed an alliance already," continued St. Odhran, his eyes narrowing. "Which of us is so necessary to your plans, Madam? Von Bek, I'd guess."

She sighed and when she glared at him again she was furiously out of sorts. "Your logic's good, St. Odhran. But 'tis over-complex. This is no maze we explore—merely a simple expedition to the likeliest hiding place of the Grail."

"Which von Bek will recognise, though it's in disguise!" St. Odhran lifted his hat and scratched his head. "Ironically, he might not even know what he finds." My friend now had a calm air of victory. I recognised his stance. His strategy had carried him clearly through to the point he aimed for. And my Libussa was of a certainty displeased, for she stuck out her jaw and her fingers clenched as if she would readily discharge the pistol at him if she still held it. St. Odhran, clearly satisfied, having avenged himself for her outwitting of him earlier, looked across a great valley. "Ain't the scenery pretty," he drawled. "And ain't the weather uncommon warm!"

She stared at me for a moment, brows furrowed, as though I was a dog which might have understood a word or two of their exchange and maybe would become less docile in the handling. But she could not know the depths of my compulsion to serve her and be loved (or at least acknowledged) by her. I was almost singing. It was possible I did possess some small value to her! But then St. Odhran had sprung for the pistol and had it in his hand, straightening. "This will help the balance." He smiled.

Klosterheim looked contemptuously at the weapon. "I've died so often it makes no difference to me should I die again."

"Fire that barker, Sir, and we're all dead," said I, feeling foolishly divided. Sensing me for an unreliable comrade, St. Odhran shrugged and held the pistol aslant his shoulder, as if about to fight a duel.

"You'd do well, Sir," said she amiably, "to accept all this with better grace. Truly, we've no quarrel. Your deceit and our counter-deception's ended. Frankness will serve our interests better and this adventure could bring mutual benefit. Accept me as your commander and you'll find me neither unjust nor ungenerous. By tonight we'll have reached our destination, where the opportunities for enrichment are considerable. And your friend, Sir, is in no danger either from myself or from Klosterheim."

Bored with his own attitude, St. Odhran sighed. "Name your destination, that's all I ask." He had relented. It was not in his nature to bear a grudge nor play a pointless game.

Klosterheim answered, as if there had never been a mystery. "We go towards the Autumn Stars," he said. "We've had a glimpse of them already and they'll be readily visible tonight. You knew this, von Bek . . . The lines of force—"

"Aye." I humoured him, for there was nothing to be gained otherwise. I had begun to believe he was lucid part of the time and given to uttering gibberish for the rest.

St. Odhran picked up his greatcoat and stuffed the dragoon pistol into one of the pockets. He offered me another glance, as if he sought to know which side I was on. I was on both. I was torn. She came up beside me, smiling. She reached out and stroked my face so that I shuddered. "You're tired, von Bek." She spoke intimately, as if we had always been lovers. My legs were weak. Had those dreams been reality? Had she visited me during those nights I thought I merely suffered fever? I was breathing in shallow gasps and recovered as best I could. The woman's strength of character and good looks were obvious to all, but she enjoyed a devilish aptitude for arousing my lust at a touch; and lust was ever the banisher of reason. She was irresistible. Even she, I think, did not fully guess the extent of her power over me. St. Odhran, opening his mouth to warn of her duplicity, saw my face and once more shrugged.

Libussa placed a hand upon my heart. The hand was unusually warm, even hot, as if just withdrawn from hellfire. Her lips were red and kissed my eyes. "You should sleep, von Bek," she whispered. "Sleep, my dear, until you're needed."

My eyelids had closed before I realised it and I sank into slumber, even as I lowered my body to the comfortable, yielding wickerwork. In her presence, I thought ecstatically, I had no will. My will could come between us so therefore must be abolished. My only desire was to be useful to her, to aid her in whatever ambition led her to commit this act of aerial piracy.

I awoke once, hearing Klosterheim's drone. He sat against the gondola's side with one knee drawn up and he described all he understood about the principles of flight, then continued without pausing to discuss his theological theories. "Lucifer could know that God is dying. Thus He bides His time, whereas once He was eager to settle the matter. He made an agreement, I know. And von Bek witnessed it. Has he mentioned nothing? Is that family so thoroughly sworn to secrecy?"

"I told ye, Sir: I'm unfamiliar with the family or its doings! Von Bek's discreet and I'm incurious!"

"God gave Lucifer the Earth to rule—to watch over, at any rate. Where we once brandished swords against Heaven, now we raise arms to conquer Hell. Man must take his Liberty by force, or Liberty will not be valued. It must be won in blood and agony. And the one called Anti-Christ shall lead us. Lucifer destroyed and God exiled, we'll possess their power without their patronage . . ."

St. Odhran scratched his neck. "I'm bored, Sir, to a stone by all this abstraction of yours. If God and Satan are not mere symbols but are personalities, then they'll have things settled between themselves by now. They'd not tell us, eh?"

"Von Bek's ancestor knew what passed between them." He saw I was awake. "And you, von Bek, too, I'd swear! You're the Devil's darlings, all of you!"

"My sole acquaintance with the Devil, Sir, is in Le Sage's excellent *Le Diable boiteux*. That fellow, however, was perhaps less comely than your old master. But he had a monstrous better wit by the sound of it."

"My master was the wisest and most beautiful creature in all Creation," said Klosterheim. This statement, so matter-of-fact and yet so sincere, made me aware of the fragment of life left in his soul. Like Lucifer defying God, Klosterheim had rebelled against the only being he had ever loved. His punishment was to be eternally denied the presence of the master he betrayed. And did not his situation mirror my own, save that I had betrayed an idea and therefore myself? I became disturbed by a subject I lacked the courage or the wisdom to examine. Libussa's hand fell upon my brow, but she spoke to Klosterheim. "Johannes, this dull talk will not do, Sir." The touch of her warm skin sent my blood rushing harum-scarum to my head, so thought was again banished.

Surely, I felt, our passion must soon be consummated. She could not mean to torture me much longer. "Sleep," she said. I returned to my languorous trance. We were fated to be lovers, destined for union, eternal harmony, whether we wished it or not . . .

When next I woke it was at her finger's pressure upon my lips. I heard the Chevalier's voice in the darkness and felt the gondola swaying under me.

"Look ahead! Look ahead!" cried St. Odhran. "Oh, look ahead, all of you!" His grim humour was completely abolished by his wonderment. He was leaning out over the side while Klosterheim stood impassively beside him, black gloves on hands now, hands upon ropes, hat upon his fleshless head, cloak wrapped tight around him. "Oh, von Bek! Look, dear friend!"

My Libussa helped me regain an uncertain footing and led me to stand between Klosterheim and the Chevalier. In silence, she pointed towards the north-east, through a wash of changing light and colour, towards a great, deep valley through which flowed a broad river. We were descending as we drew closer and I was filled with a curious frisson of recognition. Now I could see the outline of a wonderful city, glowing black and white in the light of stars whose formations were unfamiliar, whose size was larger; stars warmer and older than any I had seen. They had faint, but distinctive colours—cinnabar and vermilion, saffron and deep gold—and they illuminated the valley with their hazy radiance. The city seemed to combine every architectural style. She was Mirenburg, of course, but Mirenburg exaggerated, Mirenburg made still more beautiful, larger and inconceivably complicated. Baroque towers were of dark jade; old gabled houses were of worn obsidian and their exposed beams were of milk-white marble, forming a perfect negative to those in the Mirenburg I had known.

The city was silent and still, yet every so often an eddy of subtle yellow light rippled across her rooftops; then it faded, like the valiant last flickerings of a candle. Its source was one or more of those distant, dying suns.

"Duchess," St. Odhran was restored to his habitual grace, "I apologise for my poor manners, and I thank you, no matter what your purpose, for bringing us to this astonishing city. 'Tis a kind of mirror, I know, to the one we've lately departed, but 'tis also an idea of what a perfect city could be. Blood, Madam, but 'tis the personification of every architect's dream down the centuries; of every mason who ever took chisel to stone." He drew in his breath. It seemed to me that he was near weeping.

Klosterheim made a flat interjection. "The City in the Autumn Stars," he said.

"Where all our destinies shall be decided," said she.

St. Odhran looked enquiringly at her. She nodded. He lifted his hand to his valve and began gently to let out gas from the envelope.

Scents rose up to us: spices, sweet-smelling trees, shrubs and night-perfumed flowers; coffee, delicate meats and vegetables; cheeses, cakes, pastries; sausages and preserves; aromatic oils, old parchment, leather, mildew, wine, sulphur, wood-smoke, dust, hot metal, sewage, lye, human juices: that combination (defeating all true analysis) which was the individual signature of every great city. Yet I had never smelled anything so exotic (not even Constantinople, nor yet Alexandria, nor any of those other cities which I passed on my way from Samarkand) as this Mirenburg. There was a little of them all in her; something of London's boisterous eclecticism, of Rome's unconcerned antiquity, of Prague's ornament and Paris's labyrinthine vitality, of Venice's haughty stink and Dresden's fragile granite. As a city she was the sum of mankind's ages: Chaldea, Memphis, Jerusalem, Athens, Berlin, St. Petersburg. She was timeless in her jet-black marble, her clear, white alabaster.

Her geometry, her angles, planes and curves, formed a subtle language. This rhetoric of masonry and mortar described a multiplicity of stresses and tensions, of mutual dependency and irreconcilable contradictions, of deep-rooted permanence and constant change. She spoke, too, of sorrow, of agony, and of joyous celebration.

Klosterheim turned his expressionless eyes to look at me. Clumsily he stretched his hand to show me the city, as he had once tried to show me a snowflake. His voice possessed no resonance. He merely repeated his statement, as if to a simpleton:

"The City in the Autumn Stars."

Chapter Eleven

In which we experience something rarer than we know.
Prince Miroslav Mihailovitch Coromcko. Alchemical
Recollections. Patience rewarded.
Union without Harmony.

A T LAST OUR ship was landed. St. Odhran and I tethered her just beyond the high, tapering walls of that quintessential Mirenburg. We approached the city, the four of us, just before dawn, as the light of old stars gave way to the sun. Smoke began to rise, plume upon plume, as Mirenburg's fires were lit; a cock began his relentless morning gasconade. At the gate of massive, deep blue obsidian a single guard, his bucolic features stiff with sleep, yawned, buttoned the neck of his grey-and-yellow tunic and waved us through with a lazy salute. But St. Odhran, worried lest our gold should be stolen, approached him, begging him to keep at least half an eye upon the balloon, still visible in the meadow where we had anchored her by rope to an oak tree. The man explained he was not on duty to quiz who came and went, but to be of use to any baffled stranger. He promised, however, to watch, though he frowned. "Shall it remain that shape, your excellency, or will it change? I've a natural wariness of all wizardry."

St. Odhran opened his mouth to explain, then thought better of it. "There's nothing to fear from our vessel." We were in the Mittelmarch, where our rationalism might not be entirely adequate.

Klosterheim alone appeared to know his way. The city did not exactly mirror the one we'd left, though there were many familiarities in the configuration of outlines and streets. The architecture, generally on a larger scale, was more featureless, lacking the baroque flair one expected: it was more severe, more classical, more imitative of Greece.

The streets were waking up as the four of us passed across an enormous plaza. At the centre a fountain shaped like a horse poured water into a large pool in which fish could be seen, dark reds and golds, dark blues and ochres, almost reflecting the colours of the near-vanished stars. From here four great avenues marched away into the distance, exactly on the Compass's main points. Their pavements were reflective black marble, veined with grey. The flanking buildings were fashioned of milkstone, onyx and quartz; excessively grandiose in my opinion. They were reminiscent of the monumental coldness of St. Petersburg, that city designed to suit a notion of what cities should be, rather than one which grew naturally from the changing needs of her inhabitants. But a minute out of the plaza and we were in cobbled backstreets full of fruit- and vegetable-barrows, vaulted alleys busy with ordinary people calling to one another. Their colloquial German would not have been out of place in Munich or Cologne.

Up went windows and blinds, out sprang shutters and awnings; behind them were human heads blinking into the morning. Cats were recalled, dogs exercised, slops emptied, husbands awakened, children assembled, domestics rallied. Dignified tradesmen in suits of clothes a little out of date by common European fashion, but not incongruous to me, raised billycock hats to crinolined ladies and remarked on the heat of the day. "'Twill be a scorcher, Marm, by noon!" All of which contributed to my sense of dreaming. It was usual in dreams to find such banalities in the midst of the fantastic. Looking up I saw a steeple some two hundred feet high, of mahogany-coloured stone, sharp against blue Summer sky—there was a statue almost as big: of a weeping child contemplating a broken plate which it held in a chubby hand. And over to my left was a tavern, five storeys of it, with balconies and a wild garden on its roof; a playhouse which could seat, perhaps, sixty people; a Mausoleum, striking in its pale blue polished granite, and then a street of tumbledown houses full of brawling, cheerful children: an alley winding up a hill. There was a little secluded square, mainly sandstone, with a coffee shop, a large elm tree and a well in the middle. Four or five plump middle-aged men sat at the outside tables, reading journals and chatting. They were served by a waiter who wore an animal mask, shaggy and tawny, on his head, and walked as if on Pan-hoofs.

We crossed a bridge over a canal to rival Venice's. Green water, the colour of emeralds, gilded barges—and a man in shirtsleeves using a wooden pole to move a boat so intricately carved with Neptunes, mermaids, dolphins and the like it was hard to believe the cargo it carried: cabbages and onions. What seemed a twin to that boat was sunk some twenty yards back, prow pointing out of the water, moss growing on the exposed wood. A donkey came swimming past and stopped, treading water, to sniff the wreck before paddling to the towpath where he shook himself in a shaft of sunlight. Window upon window rose up, and washing dried on every balcony. Behind us now the donkey let out a bray, like a rusty door forced after a century of neglect. Cowled men came in single file towards us. As they went by they lifted their fingers in an unfamiliar sign, to which Klosterheim automatically responded. We turned a corner and at the end of the short street, whose grassy verges sloped up towards dark, scarlet cottages, was a huge bronze mask, similar to the Greek dramatic kind, with down-turned lips and an expression of tormented ferocity, serving no clear function.

We crossed two more streets displaying the same head and then we were on a quiet little lane with an arch at each end. All varieties of roses climbed around intermediate trellises and archways. There were pretty vines on the whitewashed walls, the terraces of houses were reddish brown, presumably of brick, their beams painted white or yellow, their gables decorated with fretwork fruits and flowers. Each house had a tiny, railed yard outside and in these grew all manner of blooms, sweetening the air. It could have been a village in New England. The bustle of the city was muted there. Klosterheim marched up to the third house on the left, pulled on a bell rope and stepped back until a maid opened the door and curtseyed. We followed him into a cool hallway, wider than I expected. There were several looking-glasses on the wall, a vase of chrysanthemums on a small, polished table. The servant took what outer clothing we could give her. She showed us into a drawing room, also reminiscent of a rural merchant's, with some low chairs and an Oriental table. On the table were sherbet, water, glasses. It strongly brought to mind the quarters of some ascetic Mussulman. I half expected to see a hookah in the corner, the kind the Tatar sultans smoked, but there was only a stove of green enamel decorated with white flowers, a jar of country grasses on top of it.

Klosterheim removed his hat and passed a finger round the inside band, gathering his own sweat and staring at it without enthusiasm. He had told us nothing of the person we visited and only the Duchess appeared to know a little more. We sat down in the chairs. "A pleasant room," observed St. Odhran, to break our silence. "When were you in this city last, your grace?"

"Some years since," she replied. "The travelling is not as easy as it might have seemed to you." She shrugged. "But at least once here I can remain a woman, without the irritation of mannish disguise."

A footman in wig and tails bent to pour us glasses of iced lemon water. "My master offers apologies. He is delayed downstairs." His accent was heavy and foreign, perhaps a Pomeranian's. He had coarse, youthful features, a heavy brow and large hands. He seemed only recently from a farm, but his livery suited his muscular body and he was well trained. Libussa looked questioningly at Klosterheim and made a little gesture of impatience. Klosterheim patted the air with his fingers, as though he hoped to calm her. I crossed to the plain white wall on which a triptych ikon was displayed, two candles burning below. Evidently it was Byzantine, but of a design I did not recognise. On one side was a youth holding, left-handed, a golden goblet; on the other a maiden lifted a sword in her right hand. Both looked inward to the centre panel where the youth's head was set upon the woman's shoulders, cup and sword flourished in each hand as the subject rode astride a gigantic, wolflike beast with blazing golden eyes and scarlet fangs. In the background to this panel, either side, were shown two citadels on identical hills. One citadel was gold and the other black, and in the sky a red sun blazed beside a white. In the left panel the same red sun also shone and in the right the white was prominent. I was puzzled by the ikon. It struck a chord in me, though I could not recall the holy legend it must surely have represented. I was still studying it when a deep voice cried:

"Forgive me for my tardiness, dear friends. Will you take some tea with me?"

I turned to see a huge, fair-haired man, wearing a loose, embroidered shirt of the kind Ukrainians make. He had red silk trousers tucked into red leather boots, a bent-stemmed meerschaum in his left hand. His full beard was greying at the edges and his hair was long, flowing to his shoulders. His blue eyes, apparently frank and amiable, had the smallest touch of that same cold light which filled Klosterheim's. It was the cadaverous ex-priest this man first approached, with "So you were successful. Thank you for your message, old friend." His voice dropped just a little, as if in sympathy. Then he was introduced to Libussa, St. Odhran and myself. He made a deep bow over my Duchess's hand. "Your grace. My house is greatly honoured. The meeting you desired has been called. My own experiments are ready for your approval."

His large, warm hand next grabbed mine. I was kissed on both cheeks. "I am glad you are here." He spoke as if I had been expected by him. He performed the same ritual with St. Odhran, with: "I trust, Sir, you'll explain the principles of aerial navigation to me while we dine."

"Charmed, Sir," said St. Odhran. "Delighted, Sir. You're a scientist yourself, then, Sir?"

"Of sorts, Sir. I'm the despair of respectable society. My name, which Klosterheim's forgotten, is Prince Miroslav Mihailovitch Coromcko."

"From South Russia, Sir?" said I.

"My cousin was Catherine's Zaporizhian hetman. An honour he thought. The other Zaporizhians were divided on the subject!" His laughter was spontaneous and open. "You know Russia, Sir?"

"St. Petersburg. Moscow, a little. And Siberia and Tatary are both familiar. But those regions of your land which lie in the Mittelmarch, are, I regret, completely unknown to me."

"Me, also, Sir. I've never been there. I'm not a native of this Realm, but crossed the border years ago in pursuit of my art, for alchemy is better practised here, or so I thought."

"And you never returned?" asked St. Odhran, already collecting information which might aid his early escape.

"I've never been permitted, Sir." Miroslav Mihailovitch dropped his gaze and rounded on Klosterheim. He patted the puny chest and arms, making the thin man wince and withdraw without actually moving, like a cat. "Here's the rogue who can rove at will, gay and easy as a bird." He winked at me, yet he plainly had real affection for Lucifer's ex-captain. "I paid my passage but once. Klosterheim, unclaimed by Heaven or Hell, is perhaps the only one of us to whom both worlds are thoroughly familiar. But they shall be reunited soon, eh, Herr Johannes? Soon, if all our plans are fulfilled?"

"What?" said St. Odhran in astonishment. "Is that what you all plan? To bring down the barriers? Shall the Mittelmarch melt into the mundane world? Shall Earth suddenly have twice her volume? What must befall the other spheres?"

"All that's accounted for," replied the Russian. "Indeed this blending of the two's a mere conjuring trick compared to our ultimate goal."

"Is that so, Sir?"

"Prince Miroslav," said Libussa lightly, and laughing, "you have known all the freedoms for so long you're in danger of indiscretion here!"

He subsided suddenly. "Forgive me, Sir," he said to St. Odhran. He took a taper to his pipe from one of the Greek candles beneath the triptych. He puffed steadily for several minutes until the meerschaum was drawing to his satisfaction. "Well," he said easily, "old differences are settled now."

"They'll not be fully reconciled," she said, "until the final unity's established. Have you seen any more in your glass, Sir?"

"Klosterheim told you, eh? My discovery was quite accidental while we reduced Saharan sand, sulphur and agatium to a molten elixir. As the liquid solidified it cracked the vessel containing it, spilling across my bench. Dee was with me then, as you know. He saw it all (and spent the remainder of his short life attempting to make his own). The substance formed a small pool and was almost immediately hard. It had become a kind of glass. The incantations had been those used in our prayer to the Future. In a distorted, murky scene I saw Dee. He was in England and being cruelly set upon by the commons, his house and library fired. I've since debated the morality of my decision to say nothing to him. But as it was, of course, the mirror had foretold the future. Events in my own life were accurately predicted—small, domestic matters. Yet the mirror's an unreliable instrument and cannot always be trusted. 'Twas a happy accident. There's no other like it and all my efforts to make one, or a better one, have failed."

"You have lived long, Sir," said I, "if you were a contemporary of Dee's."

Prince Miroslav shook his head, smiling. "Tsar Fedor was my Emperor. The parvenu Romanoffs are too greedy and materialistic for my taste."

"Yet I understood you to say you have an older relative who served Catherine?"

"He was not the snob that I am, Sir."

"Sedenko was your bastard," said Klosterheim, flatly as usual. This seemed to have meaning to Prince Miroslav. "Indeed he was. He'd have been legitimate were it left to me. But I was already hounded. He knew your ancestor, I believe—the Graf Ulrich."

Disguising my impatience I said: "I must tell you, Sir, I know nothing of my forebears, beyond understanding them to be worthy men and women who, if they had vices, leant towards over-education."

"Just so," said Prince Miroslav. "Klosterheim perceives the world as one of those children's fretwork puzzles, each piece needing to be pressed carefully into place—the result, a clear and simple design. Eh, friend Johannes? Well, Sedenko rode into the Mittelmarch with your ancestor. He almost saw the Grail, I understand. I'm not much of a military man myself." He patted his belly. "Exercise ruins the figure and excites the arterial vapours. These vapours, exhausted through the pores of the skin, carry off half one's creative resources. Besides, I sweat too much already, with my retorts and globes in that basement. You, Sir, are clearly of the military persuasion. The set of your shoulders alone would reveal your German birth. Yours is a nation, Sir, rich in great practitioners of that Art. But then, 'twas plain by the way you sat your horse . . ." And he paused.

Libussa was testy. "I've said nothing of all that, Sir. I must soon address Captain von Bek in private."

But I was alert. "You predicted my coming? You saw me in your mirror?"

Prince Miroslav seemed now to be embarrassed. He re-lit his pipe, shrugged, glanced at me as if in apology. "One cannot always be sure." He subsided. It was always strange to see a large man display the discomfort most of us know. He looked for a moment like a bear which had danced the wrong measure. St. Odhran, on the other hand, was grinning in triumph. He wore the self-satisfied air of one whose suspicions had been confirmed. When I looked searchingly at my Duchess all she could do was murmur a line or two from Goethe (*Ist Gehorsam in dem Gemüt, Wird nicht fern, die Liebe sein*) and promise me, with an inconspicuous movement of her head, further revelation in due course.

Klosterheim got up, unsettled by this exchange. "Our duty," he said, "is to proceed with as much honesty as possible."

"And frankness," said St. Odhran sardonically. "Eh, Madam?"

"A lie is like an impurity in an element," agreed Prince Miroslav. "It makes useless any elixir, no matter how carefully mixed or in what auspicious circumstances. The lie will always cloud, distort, damage."

But Libussa had an answer. "Sometimes the impurity proves to be the most important ingredient, however. And leads to discovery, puts us a little further along our path. Your mirror for instance."

Prince Miroslav spoke with quiet reluctance. "The Art and its principles have changed a great deal since I first put on the adept's gown." His attitude towards her was strange, slightly mistrustful yet very respectful, an old master in the presence of a young genius; one who was enthusiastic and clever but still had much to learn.

"Now," said Libussa, anxious not to lose his good graces, "I was promised admission to your laboratory."

"The promise will be kept." His voice lifted. "Now?"

"I'm eager, Sir." She was a winning coquette and I winced to see her adopt the part, but my Libussa would use any role to obtain what she desired, that I already knew.

"What's the mystery, I wonder," said the Scot to me when the others had gone. "Are they making gold down there, d'ye think, von Bek?"

His presumption amused me. "Aye! Twenty ingots a day from rusty nails and old knives. St. Odhran, these are adepts of the so-called 'exotic' faith. They disdain experiments in metallic transmutation."

"I lack your familiarity with the Rosey Cross," he said sourly. "I'll wager, though, there's gold to be found a-plenty round this business. But what of you, von Bek. Does none of this alarm you?"

"Because a magic glass predicted my arrival?" I shook my head. Libussa's influence had banished my previous terrors; my mood was one of faint elation. I was certain Libussa promised love to me, if only to ensure my help. Therefore, contrary-wise, I was somewhat unsuspicious of her. I was glad to be in this city and reunited with my goddess; glad to be free of the Old World's horror. St. Odhran, of course, saw my euphoria as sheer folly and my manner towards him one of unwelcome condescension. I rose and walked to where he sat. I placed a hand upon his arm. "Dear friend, I accept your instinct's warning. We must be careful. We must recall by what trickery we were brought here. But that's no reason for discrediting everything or everyone!"

"I merely recall that Klosterheim commanded the brute who slew our Landgräfin," said St. Odhran grimly. "We were given no

413

choice in this affair. We were made to cross the borders at pistol-point. An action lacking finesse. These people will do anything they must to ensure our involvement in their schemes. That lady has a power which unnerves me, von Bek."

"Would you claim a woman has no right to power?"

"If she were of the masculine race I'd still fear her."

"She's clearly a disciple of Wollstonecraft and works towards the equality of women!" I was still disposed to justify the behaviour of others by interpreting their actions according to my own beliefs.

"She works for herself alone!" St. Odhran was all scepticism. "If she be a supporter of the Common Woman's Rights, von Bek, she's put a great many people to a deal of trouble without advancing that cause any further. Strange to me that what you see as plain in Robespierre you cannot recognise at all in Milady!"

"You accuse her of self-interest? What's wrong with that?" I defended her, yet I did not altogether care whether she was noble or degenerate, for her character was not what I loved. It was her sense and her sensuality I admired. No night with her could be without its fresh discovery. I felt as if an entire creature were about to inhabit my body. That creature would be feminine while the creature she explored would be masculine. And the sum of the two of us would be godlike, a culmination of human passion and wisdom, with masculine and feminine undivided. As in my dream. She had spoken of Unity. My family had educated me to believe harmony all-important. *Do you the Devil's work* took clearer meaning now!

"She's a witch," he said, very serious. "You're mesmerised."

"I'm trapped, St. Odhran," said I very quickly to him, as if the truth would only stay with me for a little while. "By my fascination for her. I feel that I am discovering myself."

"Those are the words of a lovesick convent-novice, Sir!"

"Believe me, my dear friend, this is profound. Even should it prove destructive to me, the exploration will still be justified. I'm her slave."

He shook his head, looking at me askance. "My poor von Bek! Och, I'll do my best to see you cured when this is over, but I'll not encourage you further." He fell silent for a while, thinking deeply. Then he added: "Don't let them take anything from you save what you want to give. And try to remember you possess something of great value to them. How you bargain with them could mean at some point if you live or if you die . . ."

I was puzzling over this when the others returned, babbling in alchemical argot. My Libussa's face was flushed with enthusiasm while Klosterheim's chin was tucked down into his horrible neck as he mulled over what he had seen.

"It will be ready at the Concordance," said Prince Miroslav.

"Your price is too high." Klosterheim's voice was somewhat outraged, almost emotional.

"Not to me," said the Duchess of Crete.

Klosterheim stopped in his tracks, but Libussa, radiant on Coromcko's huge arm, carried on into the room, smiling at me, her eyes narrowing a little as she acknowledged St. Odhran. Perhaps she saw him as a rival. She had nothing to fear from him, however. He was a friend and a good one.

"Today," said Prince Miroslav, "is the last of the sun. Tomorrow, when the Stars begin their long rule, you must present yourselves to the Sebastocrator, for he'll have awakened to reign through the coming Seasons. It will be in his time the Concordance shall occur."

Libussa now crossed to me, taking my hand naturally, as a child might. My body sprang to life again. It had been almost without sensation since I parted from her. My mind was bereft of thought. Klosterheim looked at her quickly, showing consternation. She smiled at him.

"You must not . . ." he began. Then he regretted speaking. With a sudden step he went to St. Odhran. "What of you?"

"I, Sir?" The Scot was baffled.

Klosterheim frowned, as if trying to recall the reason for his question. "What of you, Sir?"

Guarded, St. Odhran stared back at Klosterheim and the rest of the company from his disarming, sleeping eyes. "I've no specific engagements at present, Sir."

"Good," said Klosterheim. "I'd talk with you. I . . ." Again he had difficulty recollecting words. He looked down at the floor. "You'll permit me to show you more of this Mirenburg?" His poor, gaunt features were oddly innocent.

"Much obliged, Sir. Thanks." St. Odhran's tone was light and casual, though his gaze was anything but: virtually his entire attention was concentrated upon me. "Ye'll join us too, won't ye, von Bek?"

"Well?" she asked me. There was pressure from her fingers on my hand.

"Gladly," I said. "But later." She commanded me, like an expert rider, with tone and touch. I had no choice but to gallop whichever way her whim dictated. "I must debate with her grace."

St. Odhran was disgusted. He turned his back on us and walked towards the door. He bowed to Prince Miroslav. "Sir. Most grateful. Your servant."

"You'll dine with us, Sir?" said the Prince.

"At what time, Sir? At seven? Very well, Sir." St. Odhran and Klosterheim, unlikely comrades, strolled out to the warmth of the street. Prince Miroslav left to attend to his tubes and crucibles. My lady led me up a flight of stairs. A long passage cut the house on the next floor, running the length of it. She took me to a door halfway down on the right. Hot sunshine filled the room as we entered. There were shrubs and flowers growing everywhere in pots and baskets. I would swear I heard bees hum. It was a country garden, and at its centre was a bed spread with sheets of golden silk: a bower enclosed by climbing roses, ivy and honeysuckle. She took me there without preliminaries. She told me to stand at the end of the bed while I undressed. I removed my boots, my stockings. I removed my breeches, my under-breeches. I took off coat, waistcoat, shirt and linen. There was blood on them. I noted I had cut myself slightly on the thumb. She smiled. Now I was fully naked. She looked at me, praising my physical virtues, stroking my body lightly but sending fire into me so that I gasped, then gasped again.

She touched me here and there with her lips. I was close to

swooning. She stripped off her bodice and crinoline, her shift, her underclothing, and she too was naked. I looked greedily at the curves of her thighs and breasts. I sank to my knees to bury my lips in her sex, as she desired. My words were incoherent when next I looked up: Nothing I could ever say in the world I had departed. *I am yours. I am your lover, your woman and your man. I belong to you as no-one has ever belonged. Command me to anything and I swear I shall obey.* These are words from my earlier dreams. Her hands grip hard in my hair. Her face is copper fire, glowing, fierce. She groans. She shudders and looks down at me. *Then all that is yours is mine?* she says. I reply ecstatically: *All.* She sighs with contentment. *There is time.* She takes her satisfaction and therefore gives me mine.

An hour later we were cross-legged on the bed and I had been telling her how much I loved her, how lessened life was since she took the road to Mirenburg without me. Her body was soft yet, as always, seemed to absorb and retain heat: a heat which somehow was never dampened, was her natural temperature, as if great furnaces permanently burned within. Perhaps she did, indeed, serve Satan. I was already half convinced she was immortal. "We must find the Grail soon," she said. "For me. Not for Klosterheim."

She flung her body into the direct path of the sun's rays. "Klosterheim has no good will for you, Manfred. He would kill you if it gave him the smallest advantage. He has no conscience. Merely an appetite for power which has for too long remained unsatisfied."

"I thought him your ally?"

"Not so. I'm in debt to him, that's all."

"Borrowed money?"

She smiled and rolled over on her back. "We're rich, the Cartagena y Mendoza-Chilperics. We've accumulated wealth for centuries, wherever we've been. Even those of us killed by the Church left fortunes to the others."

"So the debt's a moral one. Dismiss it."

"I'm bound to him by my alchemical oath. It was the only way

I could gain his knowledge—that part which was useful to our purposes." (When she speaks of us as mutual I'm elated.) "It's taken years to gather all I need. The Grail alone is of no use to me. 'Tis what I place within it that's crucial to our destiny. And there are significant rituals. All my learning leads towards that . . ." She was speaking for the first time with unguarded frankness and I was, of course, flattered, though scarcely comprehending what she said. "Klosterheim would pervert all that, calling on arts and rituals so discordant they'd threaten the very fabric of matter. And all for his own barren ends. He has no other ambition but to make himself in Satan's image so his old master shall recognise him and take him back into Hell's bosom."

"You've known of this for long?"

"I was on my way to France to seek you out when we met at that inn. See how destiny takes its inevitable course? I knew of your family and of you. But I was not fully intelligent of my own fate until Prague. I have had to pose as a man for too long. Only by that means could I achieve what I needed. But now that's all to be forgotten and I can do what I must do without subterfuge." She grew almost melancholy. Starting up in her wonderful nakedness she waded through the mellow light, between the hanging baskets of flowers, and she continued to speak. "So we two, the Grail, my own tincture, are almost ready to combine. When the Concordance comes, then the upheavals shall begin and I—you and I—shall merge in triumph to claim our ultimate destiny!"

I had heard such apocalyptic prediction more than once in my revolutionary past, though without the mystical ingredient. My scepticism fought my will to believe her. With an effort I found my voice. "This is Robespierre's logic, Libussa!"

Her dark green eyes burned with outrage as she turned. She advanced upon me. "Oh, there's a difference, little one."

Her words vibrated with the force of her violent emotion. "A singular difference. For I am not Robespierre and he is mere Rhetoric, Hope, Greed. There's no argument against what I tell you now. Believe me. There is no argument! The world you'll see shall be so transformed—so perfect in its balance—you would weep if

418

you beheld it now. And 'tis your destiny, as it is mine, to create it!"
She was astride me, my head in her hands, and her breath upon
my lips, fit to scald me. "That's what you must understand, Manfred. You are as helpless in what you are as am I. A great destiny
binds us together. Linked by more than the Grail we must follow
our destiny or wait again through an entire cycle before we, in
fresh mortal guise, can begin again! Our moment is here. We are
reborn, come together. We have been one and loved as one since
the beginning of Time!"

I was gasping. She gripped my head and threatened to squeeze
it to pulp, so powerful was her grasp. I cried out. "What is my
fate? What is it, Libussa?"

She dropped me, looking blankly at me, opening her red lips,
she then began to stroke my cheek. There were tears in her eyes
now. She moved against me. "You cannot be told until the
moment. That much is clear from the Book of Ritual. There all
was revealed to me. It is the same as the last. The same as the last."

"Why not reveal it to me as well?"

She laughed, at once bitter and proud. "Because I'm the Active
Force and you're the Passive. As it must be if the alchemy is to
work. Ask no further questions! Do as I instruct and you'll enjoy
such ecstasy, such fulfilment, you'll come to know what it is to be
a truly sentient, sensuous living creature! We drive towards the
ultimate! We drive towards the Greater Harmony! You'll see!"
And laughing still she seized me again and turned me this way
and that so it seemed I was tossed in the maelstrom of sensation
and meaning. "The Elixir and the Grail," she crooned, taking her
pleasure, drawing from me all I had to give her. "Oh, little one,
you are privileged among men. Trust me, von Bek, and you shall
have every desire, be anything you have ever, in your profoundest
dreams, wanted to be."

"It is you I want, Libussa, no more or less."

"You shall never leave me. We shall be together for Eternity,
you and I. I swear it. There's no deception, but I must demand
your trust—and your aid in defeating our enemies."

"I love you, Libussa."

"Of course. You must." She lapped at my body like a thirsty lioness. "The Elixir and the Grail, little one. And the two of us. The old ritual of death and rebirth. The end of all struggle, the end of hatred and disharmony. It will herald the destruction of Heaven and the abolition of Hell!" She sucked in her breasts, she flung back her head. I am the Beast she has conquered. I am the Beast she rides. And I hear the bellowing from the Labyrinth, smell the stink of the Minotaur. And Ariadne is laughing. She holds a sword and a shield. Ariadne is riding. She wars against all Mystery. She cries out in a voice that is neither human, demon, nor animal. The cry is sharp and then it fragments into sobs.

It was as if molten mercury dropped from her forehead to my face, streaming down her breasts, the strong sinews of her torso and groin, scattering across the flexing muscles of her thighs and calves. Her white teeth were clenched, her hair flying back from a face which, no longer controlled, no longer able to deceive, no longer set with a mask, was a burning, molten thing of bronze! A monument to the power of sexuality, to what our chemistry would achieve!

"Von Bek!" she shrieked, the teeth parting at last as all was shrugged away—all false pride, all resentment and all unnatural humility. Is that what lured Eve to Adam's seduction? "Von Bek!" And was the service of Heaven anything to rival it? God could not have known, when He created us, half-beast, half-angel, or He would not have imposed such meaningless conditions upon our entering His Kingdom. Yet neither was this Satan's sphere. It was—whether accident or no—mankind's own! And mankind was now bound to provide its own rules, its own principles, for its own Salvation!

Beyond the windows day slowly gave itself up to a long pollen-coloured twilight. Shadows grew huge and faint, as though the fabric of the world were spreading outwards, threadbare, as insubstantial as smoke on the wind. The colours of the flowers and foliage grew darker and richer and the white of the room's walls turned to a dusty pink. I never saw such a sunset, never knew one last so long. Scarcely able to walk I pushed myself upright and went to the window. The light itself seemed to possess the quality of old parchment, of tallow candle-flame, though stable and diffused. And when I held out my hand into it, it seemed to settle upon my skin like gold dust, gilding me, preserving me. I heard the tired hoofs of a tradesman's dray echo through the streets; musky scents filled my nostrils; my flesh was alive and seemed to emit its own radiance. I heard birds calling, heard citizens speaking their conventional goodnights, coming home in ones and twos. A few sluggish bees staggered up from half-shut roses and made their uncertain way back to their hives. "It's a perfect dreamy evening," I told my Libussa. But her mind was still on destiny and grand designs. "Can there be many evenings like this in one's life, even in Mirenburg?"

For some unguessable reason I had amused her enough for her to forget her reverie and smile spontaneously, sweetly. She asked me to bring her a goblet of water and took a passing interest in the fading light. "Enjoy it, dear little von Bek. It's doubtless the only Mirenburg sunset you'll ever see!"

"What?" I was innocently smiling back at her, though the joke was beyond me. "Is my destiny to die, then? A sacrifice on alchemy's altar?"

She wallowed in the last of the warmth. "Life's ever at risk in such a quest as ours. But that's not why I smile. This is the City in the Autumn Stars. She will maintain herself as that, whatever passes in our other world. Her seasons are predictable to the minute. What you're witnessing, Manfred, is not the end of a perfect summer's day. 'Tis an entire summer's ending. Look."

The leaves, from being green an hour ago, were growing russet before my eyes. "The Sebastocrator will be stirring now," she said. "In eight hours he'll be fully awake and ready to resume his reign. He rules only in the night and will soon be upon his throne. He'll stay there for the rest of the year. The Autumn Stars have peculiar properties and one shadows another to produce this phenomenon. Such complicated eclipses ensure Mirenburg's long night. Not fifty miles hence it's day and night, morning, noon and evening, just as we're used to. But this is the Mittelmarch where many unusual things are to be found and for most of her lifetime

Mirenburg is lit only by those dying stars, millions of miles distant."

"It defies logic."

"Then rejoice," she said, "since a defiance of Nature, or at least her transmutation, is what we strive for, you and I."

The gold slowly faded to silver. She rose and lit lamps. Her body was crusted with sweat. I looked up into the firmament where the old stars burned. "Let us bathe," she said, "then dine. We celebrate the return of a familiar darkness and the true city. This dark and fundamental Mirenburg shall soon grow to full life again."

Later, washed and perfumed, decently dressed, we went downstairs. I heard St. Odhran's lazy tones, Klosterheim's frigid murmur, Prince Miroslav's hearty bellow. Libussa put her arm in mine. I asked for no more. Yet as we reached the bottom of the stairs it came to me that I had learned nothing of substance. Had she sought merely to confuse me, so that she should not be thwarted in whatever it was she really schemed?

The evening passed in casual, easy converse. That night I followed her towards her room but she paused, stopping me, showing me to my own chamber. "From now until the Concordance we must save such vitality. Then we shall be utterly fulfilled!"

Baffled, once again full of conflict, I obeyed her. It scarcely mattered what my brain said. I had renounced my own will to become her puppet. This knowledge amused me and I smiled as I disrobed, crawling into the clean sheets of my narrow bed.

Then, as I drifted towards sleep, I began to weep.

Chapter Twelve

An interview with the Sebastocrator. Of Byzantium
and the Holy Grail. A pact and a plan. Emissaries
for Lord Renyard. Discourse with a beast
who mourns the Golden Age.

IT WAS NOT a dream, for the actions we take in dreams need not affect our waking lives; but it resembled a dream.

The light which shone on this other Mirenburg was the light of a thousand senile suns; old light, dark gold and dull red, amber and ochre; the light of Autumn Stars diffused by a twinkling haze which was the fabric of some earlier universe, rotted and turned to dust. Shreds of weary starlight fell intermittently upon the bulk of the great town, making black marble gleam, reflecting a misty sepia before again becoming one with the massive silhouette above us. It was a unique illumination which set the city to moving like a slow ocean, creating shadows, sudden detail, so that not only buildings but faces were forever revealing a different aspect, displaying a character which, because of that inconstant definition, possibly only existed in one's imagination. One's senses had constantly to be re-examined beneath the Autumn Stars.

Yet, taking Prince Miroslav's carriage to the Sebastocrator's palace, I was surprised to find streets and squares still filled with ordinary business, men and women opening up their shops and stalls, children tumbling and laughing, dogs barking, wagons of produce moving too slowly for impatient coachmen, self-satisfied merchants singing their songs of success and importance behind the sheets of the morning press as they filled the familiar coffee-house benches. Apprentices and school children trudged the routes to unwelcome learning; young women put before the world the results of their two-hour toilets; bucks perambulated with such

423

practised posture they might have been the chorus in some vast performance of the Ballet. Save for the light, that ancient light, the jet and obsidian of the oversized architecture, we could have been in Weimar or Leipzig. Yet I seemed the only one to notice. Libussa leaned back across from me, lost in her own reveries of some gigantic destiny. St. Odhran asked Klosterheim if Satan's ex-general was familiar with the works of D'Holbach.

"There was an Allbach," said Klosterheim, "in Bavaria." He tried to recall what he knew. "I believe he was nicknamed the Butcher of Nuremberg. But that was two or three centuries ago. Did he hang living women on hooks?"

"I refer to the French philosopher, Sir. *Système de la Nature?*"

But Klosterheim dwelt in the glory of his memories when his Allbach had doubtless been a recruit in the hosts of Hell and St. Odhran had to raise his voice. "D'Holbach has written lucidly, Sir, about such things as these strange stars. Suns, he says—and forgive me if I render this poorly into German—are extinguished or become corrupted, planets scatter across the wastes of the sky; other suns are kindled, new planets formed to make their revolutions and describe new orbits, and Man, an infinitely minute part of a globe which itself is only an imperceptible point in the immense whole, believes the universe made for himself! Eh, Sir?"

My lady stirred and glowered. "One expects such stuff from Voltaire! These men invent cosmologies to avoid responsibility for their moral crimes. By reducing all to universal movement one may cheerfully continue to maintain one's behaviour, no matter how unjust. I sometimes believe Galileo invented the Cosmos to avoid his wife's misery."

St. Odhran answered mildly. "Maybe so, Madam. I was merely impressed by D'Holbach's observation."

The coach advanced now across a mighty ceremonial square in which, lost in darkness, were tall columns bearing statues. A fountain of black water flumed at the centre; a pool of mercury swirled and reformed under the action of the cascade. And out of that agitated mixture of incompatible elements occasionally leapt glittering red shapes, elongated, fishlike, fanged, some five yards long. We were the only vehicle upon the black marble pavement and our horses' hoofs set up a distant echo. I leaned from the window. Ahead was a great three-winged palace on some six or seven floors, of white and black stone with complicated multi-coloured mosaics laid into it, with gilded domes and steeples reminding me of my days in Samarkand; they were more Oriental than European, yet not wholly eastern. The palace was surrounded by rails of silver and dark jade. Behind these was a wide courtyard and then the arched entrance to the palace. Guards were present, formal and dignified. They wore a uniform of feathered helmet, short sleeveless jacket over embroidered shirt, baggy silk trousers and boots. But for their features they might almost have been Cossacks. They were armed with pikes and short, curved swords. Reaching them, the coach stopped.

Prince Miroslav's coachman handed down a sealed sheet which the guard captain opened and read, becoming clearly impressed. He folded up the paper, saluted and bowed to us. "My Lady. Your Excellencies." The coach entered the gate and crossed a courtyard, passing under an arch hung with heavily embroidered banners, many showing scenes and portraits reminiscent of the ikon at Miroslav's house. Then we were within the central bailey, lit with huge lanterns suspended from posts and brackets all the way to the top on four sides. The coach drew up at the bottom of a flight of steps down which more soldiers now marched. A tall man in a robe of green and white, wearing over this a chequered cloak and with a soft, velvet cap upon his grey head, descended from behind the guards.

St. Odhran climbed out first, helping Libussa to the ground. Then Klosterheim, moving awkwardly, joined them. I was the last and the man in check was already hailing us with: "Welcome honoured strangers. The Sebastocrator greets you. I represent him as he represents our Emperor and our Despot. I am called the Pankypersebastos Andreas." He took a rolled parchment which Klosterheim handed him. This merely contained our names and part of our purpose there. He read slowly, rolled it up again and ushered us forward. The palace was so brightly illuminated it might have been day. The walls were massive mosaics from roof to floor, depicting scenes of battle, courtship, love and trade. The pillars were all marble, also set with gold mosaics. From time to time we passed decorated alcoves containing benches or cushions. The interior reminded me somewhat of Catherine's Kremlin Court. This Mirenburg seemingly retained more of her Slavic character than her counterpart. Yet nowhere did I see the Christian cross, though I had been told the Mittelmarch had her share of Jesus' followers.

Turning sharply, then turning again, we reached the beaten brass-and-gold doors to what proved to be the Throne Room (described by the Pankypersebastos as the Receiving Chamber). There, without guards or courtiers, reading a book as he sat with legs crossed in his enormous chair of granite and silver, was the Prince of Mirenburg—her "Sebastocrator" (but not, we'd been warned, her Emperor or Despot). He was a heavily bearded man and on his head was a wooden crown set with rubies. His eyes were small, well-spaced, clever; his rosebud mouth made him seem at first a popinjay; he was fleshy, in need of exercise and open air, but when he spoke in rich, musical tones, rising from his throne, laying his book carefully on his seat, he was evidently a man of substance. He descended the steps to greet us. "In the name of the Despot and the Emperor, I welcome you to New Constantinople, capital of the world-to-be."

Klosterheim was our spokesman for that occasion. "We thank Emperor and Despot both for their hospitality and we thank you, also, Lord Sebastocrator. My name is Johannes Klosterheim, known sometimes in the Mittelmarch as Wandering Johannes."

"Aha! The same whose soul was put back in him after the battle at the Edge of Heaven!"

"The same, lord."

The Prince looked searchingly at Klosterheim, then relaxed to listen as the man continued. "May I introduce Libussa, Countess Cartagena y Mendoza-Chilperic, Duchess of Crete."

The bearded ruler brightened. "Of Crete? Are you free of our conquerors at last!"

She bowed deeply, kissing his extended hand. "Sadly not, my lord. Yet that's my title. My ancestors were born there."

"Von Bek," said Klosterheim next.

The Sebastocrator raised his brow. "The same as slew you?"

"A descendant, lord."

I was privileged to kiss the royal rings as he said, graciously, "Greetings, my dear Count." I made no effort to explain that my father still lived and was the present Graf. St. Odhran was last, approaching the fingers with a flourish, as if his lips graced the hand of a Gainsborough belle. "Honoured, Sir. Your servant. I've no old blood, I fear. No inherited Quest. No special destiny. No history of resurrection. I'm merely the boatman who ferried this trio across whatever divides my world from yours."

"Ah, the balloonist! They informed me as soon as I awoke. I should like to see your machine, Sir."

"I'll be delighted, your honour, to demonstrate her powers."

"It shall be included on our Calendar." The Sebastocrator rubbed one half-shut eye, yawning. "Forgive me. I am as yet not fully awake. This hibernating has much to recommend it, but 'tis devilish hard to rouse from."

"Has your honour always slept through Mirenburg's Summer?"

"Always, Sir. I took the vow, you see, not to look upon the sun until Emperor and Despot are both restored to us."

"Are they prisoners, your honour?"

The Sebastocrator was disbelieving. "Know you nothing of our history or our doom?"

St. Odhran made a repentant gesture. "'Tis my first voyage here."

The Sebastocrator laughed in apparent delight at my friend's ignorance. "Of course! Yet in your world lies the source of my vow. In 1453 our Emperor Constantine died at Byzantium's St. Romanus Gate. He defended his city and his religion against Mohammed the Second, Lord of the Osmanli Turks. When the Emperor fell, so did the city, and the Turkish Sultans have ruled there for over three hundred years. Constantine's successors and the remnants of our legions marched through Thessaly and Macedonia, seeking a citadel to command which they might dedicate

427

to those they worshipped. When they entered the mountains east of here they suffered starvation, exposure, hopelessness. Then it was that Stephen Palaeologus, our newly elected Emperor, opened his heart to any being who would listen, promising his own soul, his own life, if the others could be granted a sanctuary from Turks, Bulgars and Serbians. He received a vision. The Byzantines would be granted the boon he craved but, until their capital was restored to them or their descendants, they must cease to practise their religion (though they need not deny it), whereupon they should find the sanctuary. After much debate the Byzantines agreed, believing they should easily, in a year or two, find new allies and restore their city to her former beliefs.

"Next day they made their way from Summer to Winter. They had entered the Mittelmarch. Another day and they discovered this settlement, already a rich trading city, cosmopolitan and tolerant, but under threat from a daemonic tribe, half-beasts, who had wandered into the valley in search of game and loot. In return for their hospitality, Stephen, his Despot Andreius Caractoulos and their soldiers destroyed the demons, sparing only a few for slaves. The grateful city invited my ancestors to rule them. This we have done ever since, until the day comes when we must leave Mirenburg to fight against the Turk."

"You are not yet strong enough for that?"

"Another important matter holds us here. Since we settled it became clear God had either been imprisoned or exiled. Special emissaries, descendants of our old priesthood, search all Realms for news of God. As yet we receive no satisfactory answer. So meanwhile we rule without benefit of Church, without consolation. We cannot demand consolation while God Himself has none. Also we rule without Emperor or Despot until we come again to Byzantium."

All this was given so flat and directly to St. Odhran that I could make no response. Klosterheim seemed the only one of us not confounded. Either he was familiar with their beliefs or had heard such a multitude of heresies in the course of his long existence he was unimpressed.

"This city has not been threatened," continued Mirenburg's

lord, "for two hundred years. The past hundred and fifty have been singularly tranquil. I regret I take little interest in Mirenburg's daily affairs, however. I have my books, my drumsticks, my toads. But you must tell me how I can be of service."

There came a pause. I looked from Klosterheim's frozen skull to my Libussa, who displayed cool self-control. Klosterheim spoke suddenly: "We're come to seek the Holy Grail, lord. We know it's here."

The Sebastocrator was sceptical. "The Grail is in the hands of Satan. Your ancestor, Count von Bek, delivered it himself. It's as much one of Satan's spoils as the Hagia Sophia or the Great Treasure of Jerusalem!"

"But where's Satan?" said St. Odhran with mocking levity. "Is he not exiled, too?"

"We have no dealings with Him. I understand Lord Renyard of the Moldavia accepts Satan as his liege. 'Twas from Renyard I heard the story of the Grail. He rules the Lesser City."

"Did he not speak of Satan's desire to be reconciled with God?" asked Klosterheim in disbelief.

The Sebastocrator was dismissive. "We become used to resisting the attraction of rumours. We remain faithful to our vow."

"But Satan rules on Earth now," said Klosterheim in a furious murmur. "God's charged Him with Man's salvation!"

The Sebastocrator heard nothing. For him, God was either exiled or Satan's prisoner. If He was not, there was no meaning to the Prince's exile and imprisonment. He laughed. "Well, Johannes the Wanderer, perhaps you know your own master best . . ."

"He's no longer my master."

"Then finding the Grail will not be easy, eh? You may search in Mirenburg if it pleases you, of course. Amongst all our citizens with their multiplicity of interests you'll maybe discover a clue to its hiding place." He became vague, to ease away any of Klosterheim's meaning. "While you remain in the city, be ever assured of our hospitality." His voice faded. He studied his throne, its cushions, the book resting upon them. "Can we provide anything?" He looked absently over our heads.

The interview was finished. The Pankypersebastos took a step forward, held a hand towards the exit and bowed. Libussa made as if to ask a further question, then sighed, took my arm and turned to move forward with fierce acceleration. She plainly thought her time wasted. We were ahead of Lord Andreas. "The man's a fool," she said. "The Grail is here."

"You cannot be certain," I said.

"My dear little Bek, I've researched for years. I married my findings with those of the world's greatest alchemists, and with Klosterheim's. A thousand reliable witnesses—seeresses, oracles, demons, men and women raised from the dead, astrologers, necromancers—all agree! The Grail's here. Everything is to be achieved in Mirenburg. All signs proclaim it; all logic insists upon it." Her voice rising, she checked it, slowed us down, waited for a politely frowning Lord Andreas (followed by St. Odhran and Klosterheim) and offered him an insincere apology.

Lord Andreas said gently: "You must see how my master cannot accept what you claim. You'd do best to seek out Lord Renyard."

"Where's he, Sir?"

"The Lesser City—chiefly the Moldavia quarter—is the thieves' city, so-called. 'Tis dangerous. Lord Renyard lacks the desperation of Byzantium's exiles. Though in a way I suppose he's also exiled . . ."

"I thank you, Sir," said she. We were outside the palace and standing beside our carriage. Almost hastily Lord Andreas offered us a "good fortune" and hurried back to his unhappy Prince.

Klosterheim grumbled. "Moldavia's the second most dangerous quarter in the city."

"Why so dangerous?" asked St. Odhran, who knew the thieves' kitchens of half Europe.

"It's ruled as a separate kingdom—like several of Mirenburg's districts. You've seen how little that prince cared for his responsibilities. Lord Renyard's absolute monarch of the Lesser City. He's descendant of the race the Byzantines crushed when they first came here. He has no love for them or those resembling them."

"So he'll not readily grant us an interview?" said Libussa. We were back in the carriage. The coachman set us in motion.

"If we had something worthwhile to offer him, perhaps . . ." Klosterheim licked his lips with a white tongue. "What have we of value? The Air-ship?"

"Not yours to dispose of," said St. Odhran pointedly. "I find it strange you came empty-handed on this mission." He made no mention of our stolen gold.

"How many Talers could buy the Grail?" She was contemptuous. "We must go directly to the Moldavia. If Renyard has the Grail he might not value it. A little clay cup, you said?"

Klosterheim nodded. "Made by Lilith, for the eventual triumph of humanity over its own nature, over the dictates of God and Satan. A little clay cup. Cure for the World's Pain. With it we can challenge Lucifer. Or bargain with Him."

"We've heard all this before, Sir."

He still believed she aided him in his particular schemes. "Lilith she was called. I saw it, long ago, and did not recognise it. Next time, von Bek held the Grail in his hands. Satan took back my soul." He turned to stare out at the city. "Then banished me again to this body! The Grail could release me." He frowned deeply. "I did not recognise her." At that moment I saw all the cold horror of Purgatory personified. I was at once repelled and sympathetic. Libussa, however, remained merely impatient. She barely restrained herself from slapping Klosterheim. She hissed under her breath. She looked from me to St. Odhran, back to the Wanderer.

"I had expected the Grail to be the city's greatest treasure," she said. "Displayed for all to see. Now we must search the haunts of knaves and billy-pickers. Has anyone a notion of their brand of *Rotwelsch*?" She had gone abroad in such places often enough to know that each had its own secret language and one survived by being able to speak at least a little of it. In Spain the argot was called *Germania*. In Naples it was known as *Gergo* and in London *Cant*.

"I speak most dialects," said I. "And St. Odhran, also."

She was satisfied. "Then we'll go at once. I planned to have the thing by now. Time grows short."

St. Odhran was all mockery. "When metaphysics become the

chief concern, practicalities are inclined to be forgotten, your grace."

She darted him a terrible glare. He subsided, unrepentant, smiling to himself as if all his views of the world were at once confirmed. She turned her head away so as not to see him, clearly displeased with herself, for she set great store by her superiority over a fallible and untrustworthy world. I, too, was amused, though I dared not show it. Klosterheim was dogged, far more used to struggle and defeat. Her career had been, in the main, one of implacable success. She felt almost betrayed, yet could find no-one to blame.

"Diplomacy also is needed with Lord Renyard," said Klosterheim.

"We'll employ it, Sir," said she. She looked at me: "I understood you had some sense enabling you to sniff out the Grail. Is there nothing in you telling you where to find it?"

"Not a murmur, Madam. D'ye take me for some sort of occult bloodhound?"

My lady softened. "A unique and superior bloodhound, my dear."

"I've no special affinity with this cup," I insisted again.

Klosterheim unclasped his hands from his lap, leaning forward. "You're simply unaware of your birthright and your powers."

"I'm neither compass nor sextant in any Realm. My sense of direction, indeed, was never very good. Believe me!"

"Klosterheim means you'll recognise it when we're in its presence," she said placatingly. "Does it not change shape? Disguise itself?"

"A chameleon amongst chalices. A sentient ale-pot!" I scoffed at this. Though it were proof of my lady's gullibility it did nothing to cool my ardour for her. But it provided some relief from the weight of it all. "Oh, Madam, there's nothing worse than a faulty chart and useless instruments when one journeys into *terra incognita!*"

Klosterheim it was who leaned from the window and shouted up to the driver to change direction for the Moldavia. And the driver cried back: "I've no instructions from Prince Miroslav. I can only take you to the Obelisk, Sir. It marks the edge of the district. But I cannot take my master's property into the Lesser City!"

"Very well, the Obelisk." Klosterheim flung himself back in his seat. "Well, friends, have we a pact? A plan to follow through?"

St. Odhran was disgusted. "I've not volunteered for this. I'll return with the carriage and inform our host of your decisions. Should help be needed at least he might send it to you."

"We need you for the translating," she said, as if that was an end to it.

"You've no power over me, Madam."

"I can catch the drift of any mumper's tongue," said I.

"Very well," said she. "As you please, St. Odhran." She glared at him in suspicion so that St. Odhran laughed aloud. "Fear not, my lady. I shan't fly free while you keep my companion with you. Unless, of course, I hear he's dead or no longer desires a comrade."

The carriage moved through dark canyons. Here and there candle-flames flickered and lanterns gleamed in the steep walls. After some while we stopped in a noisy market square packed with hucksters and customers haggling at their loudest. The square was lit with a mixture of flambeaux, oil lamps, bull's-eyes, candles and braziers. It stank of fried fish and sausages and sauer-kraut, was awash with cheap ale and penny gin. Vagabonds in patched frock-coats gathered to bicker over the value of stolen rags. Upright men in tall beaver hats, their shillelaghs under their arms, strode in aristocratic glory, looking with disdain at the mere pudding snammers and pavement screevers who darted about them. I recognised the market for what it was—not merely a place where thieves congregated, but neutral territory, the border where crime met honest capital and arrived at compromise. Such places flourished on the edges of the true thieves' quarters of all great cities and sometimes were even termed "Rendezvous" as a fair description of their function. Here were the dolly shops and translation-men, dealing in stolen goods. The gutter bloods in tat-tered finery, often arm in arm with their rum morts (she as covered in stained ribbon and torn lace as he), brought their goods to market, as did the govey burners, pocket nippers and a generality of rapscallions living off the scraps and leavings of the ruffler's trade. The base of the Obelisk—a hundred feet of black granite carved with worn, almost indistinguishable bas-reliefs and mysterious alphabets—was surrounded by wicker baskets, horse tackle, handcarts, sacks, panniers and the general paraphernalia of a busy market. We stepped down—Klosterheim carelessly, myself boldly and Libussa with some caution—leaving St. Odhran in the carriage. He would present our apologies to Prince Miroslav. He seemed concerned for me and I did my best, by my demeanour, to quell his fears.

With Klosterheim leading we threaded our way through to the backstreets lying close to the Lesser City. Here were the lodgings of the honest poor, and little shops; decent people at their domestic concerns, a few rowdy alehouses on street corners. But it was as we progressed further that we began to draw antagonistic attention from the populace. Increasingly they took on the familiar appearance of harlots, loungers and petty cribbers. Doubtless Klosterheim's cadaverous features halted more than a few in mid-catcall and the fact we walked side by side, an unusual trio, gave others pause. My plan was to pose as visiting "High Pickaroons"— the cream of roguish society. I trusted that the cant was the same as I'd used during my own time upon the road.

When at last we were approached direct, it was by six or seven vagabonds, all hung with pistols and poignards like an iron-merchant's window, their wide hats shading already dark faces, their black eyes glittering beneath. The leading jocko, a near chinless youth with a beard clinging from his jowls like thrice-used meatstrings, challenged us with: *"Cast yer daylights on der kinchin cove and the jack-o-legs, me abrams. Shall us crash der culls and jock der mort?"*

To my relief I understood every word (not hard to guess, since he proposed killing us and carrying off Libussa), so I replied: *"Dowse yer crow, ya cork-brain'd cunny wangler and lift yer golgotha ter the finest high toby mort in any cheese!"*

He was impressed enough to put his fingers to his hat's brim and stand back, grinning. *"Dimber dambers! We near mulled our rig and filched yer!"* And he asked if he could be of service. I told him we were seeking Lord Renyard, to present our compliments before we began work. We were stiver-cramped, so anxious to start quickly. The pickaroons fell in with us and I invented a tale for them, borrowed more from paper than from memory, but they would always take the brightest bait, those fish. And now they hailed another group of sword-sporting ragged bravos standing outside a tavern and debating if that or The Nun and Turtle sold the best beer. We were introduced as eminent knights of the road, and three of the youths, flattered by our pretence that we were already acquainted with the Lord of Moldavia, promised to escort us. *"The Fox stalls new rogues this darkmans at Raspazian's in Oropskaya. Yer in rum purl if yer not dry bobbing."*

So with our swaggering gutter beaux clearing the way for us, we pressed deeper into that tangle of twittens which formed the knotted core of the rookery. At last we reached a railed square upon which, momentarily, a beam of ochre starlight fell, revealing half-ruined walls, thick climbing lichens and ivies, empty windows, fallen roofs. At the centre were the remains of a formal garden, thoroughly overgrown but still following the outlines of its original geometry. A path through this chaos of fading cowslips and rosebay willowherb led us to the far side. Here was a large, ramshackle building, part wood, part brick, apparently derelict in its upper floors and bearing a painted unkempt sign in the Cyrillic fashion (the first we'd seen in Mirenburg) reading RASPAZIAN'S: HIGH CLASS BEVERAGES & LIGHT SUPPERS. There were two rush torches stuck up on the gateposts leading to the basement stairs and these were the only hint of occupation. Our bravos stood hesitantly beneath the sputtering flames, hands on sword hilts, skittishly awkward, eyes everywhere, attempting an insouciance and succeeding only in comicality; evidence they lived in terror of their vagabond king.

"Odd," murmured Libussa to me, "that such a prince should hold his noonday Court in a run-down chopshop!"

"He interviews rogues and passes sentence on transgressors," I told her. We stepped forward, but one of the youths, in a greasy billycock hat, put his hand upon my arm. Another ran down the slippery stone steps and rapped a complicated tattoo at the basement door, then ran halfway back to stand, half in defiance, half in apology, waiting. Almost immediately the door was flung open and there stood a barrel-chested buckaroon in the stained and rusted armour of a Selmuk Turk, a half-caste Oriental giant, strutting aggressively to the bottom of the steps and glaring. *"Frölich. The word's nix under upright men! The high cull chive yer?"*

"Yan maund off," replied the youth, all placation now, and jerked his thumb at me. *"Yon tawno spells he's gentry cover. Toby men all. Yond'd varda our Vulpino."*

The giant was cautious, strutting out another yard, while Frölich fell back bit by bit until he was behind me. *"Here's the nipperkin nagpad, Erjizh. Clack'um onsel!"* And he had turned, was almost running with his two companions close behind, and was gone.

Erjizh scowled and ascended another step or two. I told him again we were first-rate highwaymen seeking his lord's permission to work the territory beyond the Lesser City and to use the Quarter as our bolt-hole. He pointed out my sword and pistols. *"Yon'll statch yer pricker and yer poppers aft mayne."*

So we handed over our weaponry, whereupon the door was shut firmly in our faces and we waited in some anxiety until it was opened again. Glaring at us from habit rather than any specific animosity, the Turk admitted us. He led us down a short passage and into a large, dark room crowded with tables, many of them empty and dusty save for those at the front. Here, upon a low dais which normally might have presented entertainment to diners, sat a figure in the feathers and lace of a century previous, one of the Sun King's cavaliers. Yet he was oddly proportioned, his face in darkness.

On either side of their High Cull were rascals in every manner of extravagant costume, lounging in postures of studied boredom and inspecting us with bold, challenging eyes. These were not the streetbloods we had met outside, but the top ranks of the thieves' castes: the Rufflers and Upright Men, barons to Lord Renyard's king. Seated in armchairs at the foot of the dais and looking almost as bold as their men were the autem morts and dells, giving off a near-visible cloud of perfume and powder which blended with lace and silks and brought back a memory of the flash nunneries of Stamboul and Barcelona. The tables contained petitioners and prisoners, some bound and under guard. The hall was lit by huge church candles stuck into massive gold holders, so it seemed the place was on fire.

Lord Renyard's imperious lace summoned us forward. He was still in shadow, knowing its effect. He stood up very tall, with eyes glittering suddenly in the light, and they were penetrating, wise. At first I thought he wore a mask and that he was in some way crippled. But he was neither. When he spoke, his muzzle curled back from sharp, white teeth. He was a fox: a huge, red-haired beast on hind legs, taller than me, and sufficiently manlike to grasp the pommel of his sword and stand in pantaloons and polished, buckled pumps, in long, embroidered waistcoat, fine lace flowing over everything, like foam down a tankard, silk dress-coat near as red as his fur, ribbons here and there and a heavy dandy pole in his other hand, which doubtless he used to help him stand steady. His expression was curious but not a whit friendly. His strange voice was close to a bark and his whiskers twitched. The ostrich plumes of his great hat wobbled fit to fall off but it was impossible for that creature to look ridiculous.

"Ain't yer just a pair o' notch-nuzzlin flashmen and their Mab Laycock playing the noddy? On the pad, yon chive? And where, with no nags?" said he.

"Lord Renyard," said I at once, "though I've some claim to be what I told your men, we're here from the Seitenmarches to see you and beg a boon." I knew it would not be possible for all three of us to pose as highway thieves and it seemed better to announce the truth (if slightly coloured and flattering to himself) before Lord Renyard guessed it.

It seemed I'd sworn foul in church, for the rufflers were close to being outright shocked at my use of conventional German, but

Lord Renyard stilled his followers with a gesture of his red hand. He put his long, cunning head to one side, staring at us for a full minute or more. Either, I thought, we would be torn to pieces or we'd be held in the hope of a ransom. There was the faintest chance, however, he would hear us out. I had expected a less clever Prince of Thieves, and a commoner one.

"*Yon'll be scholards, nek?*" He seemed to muse for a moment.

"Aye, sire." I was exhausted of any wit.

Then he sat down suddenly with a thump in his great chair, crying: "Well, let's hope, damn me, that at least one of you is familiar with the works of Diderot. For if you're not, there's little point to your admission here and, being diddycoy nabblers, ye'll not be allowed back to Swellonia alive. Not unless you prove yourselves somehow." He turned his muzzle, grinning. "The Fox, as you may appreciate, I hope, is bored."

I was stunned by all this and found myself babbling. "I've read the *Supplément aux voyages de Bougainville*, Sir. And other things."

"*Rêve de d'Alembert*," said Libussa, a schoolgirl. "Little else."

"I do not know the gentleman," said Klosterheim in hollow, disapproving tones reminiscent of his Lutheran origins.

Lord Renyard pointed up his snout and laughed, a series of short, high yaps. "I shall not quibble with that. Good enough. Who d'ye read, Sir?"

"I'm not in the habit, Sir." Klosterheim spoke like a Quaker invited to the Balum Rancum as Guest of Honour. "Nor have I been for the past two hundred years."

This further amused the fox. "A fellow more full of ennui than myself. What a novelty! What a mismatched trio of otherworldly travellers you are! A spider-shanked cadaver, a foppish minikin and a doxy looking like a rome mort who's just pissed on a nettle!" This won the laughter of his crew and put us all more at ease. "Where are ye from and how did you come here?"

"We're Germans, Sir," said I. "Come here by air."

"So! Your ship's moored out there, eh? Your credentials are perfect!" He turned to his gaudy ruffians. "*Nix on the crash, nor fleecing, nor lumping, nor fuddling, ban out wen starats!*" And they had his orders we should not be harmed. I was certain he would be obeyed. He said in more conventional language to them: "Have ye listened, ye stains, you whoremongers?"

"On record, your worship," said one, fingers to forelock, single calculating eye on us.

"What names d'ye want?" asked another, his mouth red in his blue-black beard. He opened a dog-eared ledger and licked a quill.

For my own part I could not resist giving: "Tom Rakehell!" which would be, in London at any rate, an acceptable alias. But Libussa went the whole hog, with all family names and qualifications: "Alchemical adept, member of the Council of Prague, Elder of the Brothers of the Sacred Triangle, First of the Triumvirate." She paused. "I have degrees from several Universities. And my blood is the blood of Ariadne, older than Time."

Lord Renyard was pleased (she had read him right) and said: "We've that in common, at least, Duchess. I trust you're not here in quest of some other poor manbeast to murder? Or is a mere fox unworthy of Ariadne's cunning and Theseus's bludgeon?"

"No violence at all is intended, my lord. We're in the Lesser City for your help. If necessary to trade."

"Trading rarities? I'm devilish partial to rarities."

"Knowledge," said she.

"Rare enough." He re-sat himself, evidently never comfortable in that chair. "Give me half an hour for my duties, and we'll talk."

"Klosterheim," said the ex–Captain of Hell, and the brigand noted it in his ledger.

We arranged ourselves beside a table at the back and watched as the plaintiffs came and went. Lord Renyard allowed this cutpurse a licence, while that one was sentenced to "the top" (which was hanging) for some mysterious transgression of the Vagabond Code. Half the proceedings were conducted in the canting tongue, half in such refined language it went over the heads of most of us. For all his graces, he was a fox: high-pitched, staccato—but a fox whose authority was unquestioned, even by those he sent to their deaths. When the Court was over we were summoned forward once more. His followers fell back, most of them looking at us with wariness and disguised dislike, as if somehow we threatened them by parleying so with their master.

"So you've read *D'Alembert's Dream*?" said he to me. "And the *Encyclopaedia*?"

"Not every word, Sir."

"I've read all seventeen volumes, Tom Rakehell. Thus I know all there is to know of your world. I long to visit it. But it would be foolish, eh? Here, I am already a sport. There I'd be a Monster! You're familiar with current theories of spontaneous creation, are you?"

"Not exactly current, Sir, those notions. Fifty years ago . . ."

"A Golden Age, Sir," said our Fox, "a better age than this, Sir. Voltaire, Rousseau, Buffon, Daubenton, Montesquieu, d'Alembert! How I should have loved to have conversed with them!"

"I've known several who did, Sir. I served at Catherine's Court where, as you know, Diderot and Voltaire spent much time."

"You knew Diderot?"

"Only slightly, Lord Renyard. He was leaving for France as I arrived."

"Your date of '74," said the Fox with a knowing nod.

"Just so. I was very young."

"But he impressed you?"

"As a lively, sweet-natured, curious man."

"So I've heard." The fox eased his strange body in its chair once more. "He alone reached through intellect what the rest of us know by experience. In *Bougainville*, for instance, he asks us 'Who knows the early History of our Globe? How many stretches of land, now cut off from each other, were once joined?' A mind as lively as Voltaire's, Sir, but more humane, eh?"

"Quite," said I.

The fox stood up. "This way." He pointed to the steps leading to the dais. We mounted obediently. His men surrounded us, all sweat and woman's perfumes, and we were escorted off along a passage, down a flight of steps, to a great underground kitchen where servants roasted meat and prepared vegetables over trembling open fires. Running the length of this chamber was a great

oaken table and benches, like a monastery's. "We'll feast," said the
fox, his red mask enlivened by the fire, "and we'll converse. To ape
Catherine's banquets, eh?"

We were set with me on his right, Libussa and Klosterheim on
his left. Then his delicate muzzle sniffed at beef bones, though he
was hard put to lift them in his strange paws and his lacy sleeves fell
always in the juices. The meat was unremarkably cooked, a little on
the raw side. The vegetables were short of salt. But the conversation was one of the strangest I'd attended. He was a thorough
student of our Enlightenment. He knew them all by heart! He
quoted Voltaire: "Destroyed or degenerate Suns make a graveyard
of the Sky!" It was, said the fox, as if Voltaire had actually journeyed
to this Mirenburg and seen the firmament for himself. Did we know
that "Autem Star" in the local argot meant "Church Prison" or
"God's Enclosure"? He wondered if it was a name coming from the
fate of the Sebastocrator, waiting in his palace for a signal which
would never come and believing, therefore, that it was God, not
himself, who was trapped? Libussa was barely interested in that.
Her own obsessions filled most of her mind. Klosterheim, too, listened without much attention. Libussa was hard put, in her pride,
to show patience with philosophers who did not share her somewhat more romantic views. Rousseau was now touched upon:

"Did he suffer the pox, d'ye think, or d'ye believe what he
wrote on the subject in his Confessions?" The fox ate daintily
while all around was such a snorting and snuffling, such a clatter
of knives on plates, sucking, burping, guzzling, such a gabble of
coarse jests and observations, it was sometimes hard to hear or be
heard. Lord Renyard seemed sublimely oblivious of his lieuten-
ants' bestial manners.

Klosterheim, though a twice-damned ex–servant of Lucifer,
still disapproved in his way of all those non-churchmen and their
Godless notions. He would have no part of it. But Libussa aired
her considerable knowledge. When she allowed it in herself she
displayed a greater taste for metaphysics than I, and was soon in
her element. Yet always she steered a course relentlessly towards
the Grail, cheerfully inventing references to it by every name the

fox revered until she'd arrived in this port: "And didn't Diderot, Sir, consider the Holy Grail's scientific properties in one of those lately published posthumous works?"

"I do not recall that, Madam." He was apologetic. "It takes many years, sometimes, to receive books from your world."

"Yes, Sir—an essay on sentience, Sir, and its manifestations, active and latent. He wonders if an inanimate object is capable of volition. The legendary Grail's his example—its tendency to come and go apparently at its own will, to exercise a healing property, to impose peace and order within its influence, to guide, maybe, the affairs of men or choose to remain dormant. He suggests such an object exerts a change upon its environment for its own survival and is thus the chief instrument of harmony: perhaps the very pivot of our universe. This Grail (if there be only one) maintains the Rhythm of the Spheres, yet also aids mankind to act in concert. If God created Unity, Diderot suggests, perhaps He also created something to preserve that Unity. Another school says that Grail and God are one, possessing power and sentience, but not moral intellect."

"God, Madam, has abandoned this planet," said the fox, matter-of-fact. "Is the news so late in reaching you?"

"Most refuse belief," murmured Klosterheim.

"So," continued Lord Renyard, "maybe another force than Satan seeks to fill God's place. Reputedly, Satan's no pursuer of Order . . ."

"Satan renounced the easy means to Order," said Klosterheim. "By His will and His severity, He could rule now. But He refuses. He seeks unity with the very being He once defied, and thus abandons all His followers."

The fox looked startled, licking his snout before opening his mouth to speak, but Klosterheim interrupted with: "Satan alone rules our planet." He was oblivious of the effect he had. His white face bore the marks of strange tensions within him. "The war when it comes shall be against Him. With the Grail in my hands, Sir, I'd soon have Hell in full rebellion. Then mankind would be sole master of its destiny!"

(More "destiny," thought I. Why had I heard so many differing descriptions as to the exact nature of this inevitable destiny? How could they all be inevitable? Destiny was apparently a word describing an individual's desperate need for certainty.)

"You'd lead this rebellion?" The fox was deeply curious. "In the name of Enlightened science?"

"In the name of Man," said Klosterheim. "That is our intention." He was unaware of the fox's ironic glint at the word "Man." "Sir, if you possess the Grail, your advantage would be served as well as ours!"

Libussa almost winced. Klosterheim had cut across her pretty seductive tune with a flat horn. But the fox was amused as he answered Satan's ex-captain: "How can that be? What rational world would permit the existence of such monsters as myself?"

"It *would* be a rational world, Sir," said Libussa quickly. "A world setting high store on liberty and self-direction. A world based firmly on the belief that equality's the bedrock of happiness."

"But France's revolution argued the same." The fox put paw to muzzle, frowning down into gravy-stained lace. "And now unreason is observed at every turn! Intolerance and tyranny . . ." His lips curled back again from pointed teeth, a vulpine smile. "Worse than mine!"

"Von Bek here was a Deputy in France, Sir." Libussa hardly knew which tack to take, she was so discomfited. "He'll tell you why the Revolution did not succeed."

"Von Bek?" Lord Renyard was delighted. "Follower of Cloots?"

"Tom Rakehell, Sir, if ye don't mind." I prayed he would respect the Rogue's Code and not make enquiries of me.

"Forgive me, Tom. You were saying, Madam?"

Libussa was baffled. Then, grimly, she said: "He'll confirm they lack wisdom." She took a breath, furious with both Klosterheim and myself. "And, Sir, they lack the Grail! 'Tis insufficient that a few lawyers form a parliament and make fresh laws. If mankind would change, great upheavals are in order; a new age born from the destruction of the old. One tiny nation's floundering revolution, in which only half the population's represented (if that), is useless. Of course it must collapse! We must have fundamental change, Sir! Out of Chaos shall come Order—that order based upon a harmony hitherto unguessed at, whose great symbol is Hermaphrodite: the Woman-Man! Theseus and Ariadne combined against the Beast. Not a Beast like yourself, Sir. The Beast is all that's stupid, brutal, unthinking, greedy in Man. The Beast is selfish, unjust, cruel. It's swaggering posturing and the simple pleasures of war! It's harem-keeping. It's using the female sex to maintain the vanity of the male, at women's great expense. Today the Beast speaks in the accents of civilised democracy—but he is still the Beast!" (Klosterheim grew puzzled, as if unsure she'd understood what he required of her when the Grail was theirs.) "Hermaphrodite, Sir, is more terrifying to the Male race than ever you could be!"

"I'm flattered, Madam."

"Hermaphrodite shall be the leader of this true revolution. A leader as strong, as eloquent, as divine as Jesus. Hermaphrodite must take the same terrible path as Christ, for that is the price paid if one's to influence the course of history. A leader who no longer spreads the word of God, but spreads the word of humanity! This being shall incorporate the experience, the hopes and idealism of our *whole* race: the sum of male and female experience, the sum of all we've learned. The Grail's our true salvation, Sir!"

The fox picked up a chicken and lifted it to his sardonic mouth. "No room for monsters."

"No room for those who'd fear singularity, Sir!" She was glib. "Any reasoning world would reckon itself rich with Lord Renyard in it!"

The fox looked hard at me. I would support her, but I knew not how. He gave Klosterheim a stare. The skull-faced ex-priest attempted to absorb the meaning of Libussa's rhetoric. "Good flattery, Madam," said Renyard, chewing, "but poor observation. We all know how one species will destroy another, by whatever logic the times require. As for those hybrids like me, we're lucky if we're merely isolated. And isolation produces a kind of inescapable madness, though it adopts a guise, like mine, of rationality and breeding. Your sexes are not equal, as you say. Your colours war against one another. The Arab race, calling itself the white race, despises red and black; the red race, calling itself the white race, despises brown, black and yellow. The yellow race, calling itself the favoured race, makes war upon another yellow race, also calling itself the favoured race. Can all that be banished by your Grail?"

She was sincere. "Aye, Sir."

He put down the torn chicken, "I can't believe you, Madam. This new messiah would not do for me. I'm better off upon the edge of Chaos, in my criminality and my kingship over thieves and whores. My rufflers are easily understood. Those who fear the singular also fear the sword." His glance towards his gorging captains and their doxies was meaningful and tolerant.

"You support your vanity, Sir, by consorting only with inferiors," she said. "That's your argument, I think!"

"Madam, I have no equals."

"The Grail shall change the world, Sir, so all stupidity is banished and we'd begin as equals."

"Your case remains unproved, Madam. It does not attract me."

"'Twould put an end to your boredom, Sir."

He placed both paws before him on the table and laughed again, as field foxes laugh, with a little bark and head half lifted. His tail would have fanned if he'd had one (I wondered if he'd docked it to fit his fancy breeks). "I'd fear your price, Madam," he added softly.

She had a puzzled smile upon her own lips and seemed not entirely sure of him. "But you'd take a risk, Sir, if offered?"

His head came forward bearing its huge, scarlet hat and a host of ostrich plumes, so his face was hidden again. He spoke from beneath the brim. "I owe you something, to be sure, for this entertainment." Raising his head again he reached for damask and wiped his greasy muzzle. Then, unconsciously, he licked his nose. "I do not possess your mystic cup." He smiled and his freshened whiskers fluttered. "Otherwise I might well barter it for some of those recent volumes you've mentioned. Indeed I hope there's still room for trade between us. But if you'll make me a promise I'll be glad to help you towards your goal. It seems we are, if not of mutual interests, at least of mutual intellect . . ."

He now reached under his buttons and pulled a small, leather-bound sextodecimo from the back of his pantaloons. His paws fumbled a little. They were hardly fitted even for turning the pages and I guessed his forelegs shook with the strain of seeming easy. His brain was not at odds with what he read, though his body was indeed at odds with his brain's commands. I began to understand his claims of isolation.

"The promise, Sir?" I felt considerable respect for this mysterious creature. He showed me the book. I opened it. It was wonderfully printed in sharp black type on pure white paper, with red decorative capitals and so forth. It was called, in German, *A New Understanding of the Universe*, and I did not recognise the author at all. It was an impressive mouthful, more associated with the seventeenth century than the eighteenth: Philarchus Grosses von Trommenheim. I wondered where he had obtained such an unusual book in that condition. "I don't know it, Sir." I saw it was printed in Mirenburg and dated AB 339 (meaningless to me). The prose was exquisite, perhaps a little stiff; some sort of essay on perception. "I'm surprised I've never come across it, Sir. It's not the usual dull stuff."

"Keep it, Sir." Lord Renyard gestured. "'Tis by myself. A single copy was printed and there's only me to read it here. My real name's on it. And my real vocation, I suspect, is displayed. You'll keep the promise?"

"Of course, my lord." Libussa was eager as she leaned forward. Perhaps she thought there were secrets in those pages. Lord Renyard waved his paw at me again and I slipped the little book into my shirt lining. "What must we swear?" she asked.

His bright eyes still regarded mine. "To remember me," he said. There was unusual pain in his expression. Next he was looking at Libussa, his chin up, sly and charming. "I'd want you to send books you think would interest me. Goethe's work whets my palate for more. And certain Englishmen: Burke, for instance, and the North Briton Hume. Though my reading in their language is inadequate."

"It will be impossible, Sir, not to remember you!" Momentarily Libussa forgot diplomacy and could not flatter.

"Without remarking my appearance?" He took a pewter chalice of wine in both paws, drinking deep. "Is a gigantic fox a scholar first or a freak? And a speaking fox at that! Make him a fox dressed in foppish flounces and commanding a nation of rogues in a city which scarcely ever sees 'lightmans' (as day's known here)—why, how could you resist retailing this wonder? A marvel, a sensation! Oh, I'll live on as a performer in some distant Circus of the Imagination, and 'twill become impossible to tell if I was ever really fact or fiction. This Upright Fox, they shall announce in voices loud enough to drown out already shrieking dinner guests, was, moreover, *an enthusiast for the Encyclopaedists!*" He paused, then: "A man in a mask, surely? they'll say next. A hoax. Some poor creature with a hideous deformity? Well, perhaps one's memory is not all it might be. Perhaps Lord Renyard was merely a cripple using his disfiguration to control the brigands. He could become quite human before the century's out. Remember me!" He drank again. He smiled at Libussa, he winked at Klosterheim. An ear twitched and his hat fell slightly to one side, giving him a still more rakish look.

"Well," he said, "if we're to believe Voltaire— 'A taste for Marvels engenders Systems; but Nature seems to take pleasure in Uniformity and Constancy, just as our own Imagination likes great changes!'" This seemed mockery of Libussa's heartcry. "So Renyard's an aberration. Yet Diderot celebrates Change and Difference. Perhaps that's why I love him. Do you love him too, Madam?" He grinned, drank, again wiped the muzzle on fresh linen. "I'll need no more of M'sieu Voltaire. But if you could see I'm sent Maupertuis I'd perhaps enjoy him better."

"Sir," said the Duchess of Crete, "if it's within my power you shall have the entire Bibliotheca!"

"You're extravagant, Madam. You shall have all I can tell you of any substance. Everything else you must discover for yourself. I recall a meeting some time past, when I learned the story of von Bek, Klosterheim and the Grail. This is slim reward for having been bored by an under-educated, not to say *vulpine*, Jackthief, and at such length, but here it is." He considered what he had to say, lifting his red snout towards the shadowy beams and staring at flickering tallow. His words were measured, significant, yet almost whispered: *"You must find the Red O'Dowd."*

He slumped a little in his chair. Evidently this statement cost him something of value and moreover had exhausted him. Kitchen fires danced and crackled. Lord Renyard looked sadly across the table at Tom Rakehell, already protecting himself from despair should Tom fail him. His followers guzzled obliviously, and he grew tender as he regarded them. He was a humane monster ruling bestial men.

I could almost smell the Minotaur's foetid breath pouring from his flaring nostrils and hear that angry stamping of hoofs upon hard earth. A massive club beat against strong walls. The ground shook. The Bull screamed his challenge. Theseus advanced through the Labyrinth and reason took up sword against brute ignorance.

Libussa dropped her eyes and spread her wide hands on the table, as if in shame.

Chapter Thirteen

*In which begins the search for the Red O'Dowd. We leave
the second most dangerous quarter of the city and enter
the first. Several conjunctions and a hint of the reasons.
A sword, a lamb & a Prince of Hell.*

IN TRUTH WE had rather more than "the Red O'Dowd" from
Lord Renyard: we had a map and intelligence of the map's terrain. We moved amongst narrow walls, beneath the slow, unsettled
light of those senescent stars. The alleys were at the city's very
centre which was the Oldest district of all, enclosed by its own
walls and called Amalorm, perhaps after those Amarian tribes
existing there before the Svitavians came to kill and enslave them.
We descended.

Our route took us steadily downhill, by sloping streets and
flights of dark, winding steps. Sometimes a gap in the buildings
showed fires and lanterns twinkling below. It seemed the centre
had grown around an enormous spiralling crevasse, a valley
whose floor could not be seen. In Amalorm the Rätt ran underground. Building had been placed on building, some ten or fifteen
ramshackle storeys high, all leaning at unstable angles. I was half
afraid some great pile of bricks, stones and timbers would fall on
us at any moment. I refused to raise my voice, remembering the
landslide I'd caused.

Typically the natives of Amalorm were squat, taciturn and
dark, counting their social position (they set, we were informed,
strong score by such things) according to the height they lived
above ground. Thus, because we moved at the lowest level, we
encountered only the miserable poor, most of them sleeping on
some form of opium. This drug, Lord Renyard had told us, was
the real currency of the Deeper City.

Somewhere here, we were assured, we'd find the Red O'Dowd, if he still lived. Lord Renyard had not been able to speak for that, nor could his men, in spite of all their conscientious head-scratchings, tell us much. Lord Renyard and the Red O'Dowd were rivals. The Lesser City enclosed the Deeper City; and the Deeper's existence meant all Renyard's vagabonds had to circum-navigate walls, so could not directly cross their domain at any quarter of the compass. There had been attempts to reach com-promise, but all had failed. They said the Red O'Dowd was not, like the fox, ruled by reason. Moreover the territory of Amalorm was coveted, for it was the greatest stronghold in the Mittelmarch and not difficult to rule since the richer inhabitants did not care what happened in the gulleys and valley floors of the lowest streets; they had no loyalty to their own kind.

It was as if we moved through a natural limestone cave system; the walls were wet with pale lichen and semi-luminous grey moss growing upon them. There were echoes, the greatly magnified sound of drops of water striking a deep pool. We had been told that the Red O'Dowd had arrived twenty years ago with a merce-nary band. He had fought those who ruled and in the end his control of the centre had no longer been disputed. His purpose in seizing that territory by force of arms (and at hideous loss of life) was unclear. He would only claim that he "guarded his property." The fox had been of the opinion that the Red O'Dowd guarded an idea, for any negotiations over territorial matters had always become enigmatic and fallen down. Lord Renyard had told us that he had no inkling what that idea might be.

The buildings swayed and creaked in the Autumn Starlight. It was as if an earth tremor constantly shook the Deeper City. "It is like a ship," said Libussa wonderingly. "Or the giant in Gulliver. They've surely built this place upon the back of a living beast." She was now as volatile as ever. She had only temporarily been daunted and was freshly convinced that she had only to meet the Red O'Dowd for him to hand her over the Grail. Lord Renyard had allowed no such reassurance. She laughingly clung to my arm and Klosterheim's. "Or could this settlement, d'ye think, be one single organism?"

Klosterheim was disapproving of her Fancy. "It's merely age," he murmured.

"It is more than that," said I soberly. Every lynchpin, brick and slate and bit of guttering cannot already have crashed. Why should what was left retain its peculiar stability?

We entered a steep-dropping lane. From above came a distant booming, a faraway clamour of metal and the sound of masonry tumbling into a street. We received a glimpse of burning points in the valley; the smell of dank smoke. Then there were yellow torches bursting round the corner and dancing up the cobbles towards us; now we saw black, martial figures, their swords already drawn. They were confident bodies, well-armed and steel-cruel. Our own weapons had been left at Lord Renyard's, thanks to Libussa's flaring impatience, but it would have made little difference. We looked back, guessing the presence of the half-dozen who crept behind and who now stopped and straightened when they were seen, hands on hips, their faces hidden. Klosterheim (maintaining against all experience a somewhat legalistic turn of mind) cried pompously: "What comes?" and "Be warned, we are on important business."

A tall bicorne hat with a cockade in it, atop a face with a thin, handsome mouth, upon a lean, well-muscled figure, broke from the general crowd. Montsorbier wore a smile of considerable satisfaction, as if the pike had caught the trout at last! Had I dreamed all that time? Was I in actuality upon some Parisian spiral, near Mont Martre? Or had Renyard sent me into this bristle of greedy ferrara cutlery? Did the fox give me up as Montsorbier's reward for services rendered? No, I thought, some other treachery was afoot, for I had a book in my shirt with the name Philarchus Grosses upon it. Or perhaps there was no treachery at all, save Fate's. Every adept spoke of concordance and certainly conjunction at any rate was evident at every step, no matter how hard I tried to break the pattern. Then Montsorbier recognised me with genuine astonishment and laughed in sheer joy. "Oh, ha, ha, ha! Von Bek, is it thou? This is better than anything!"

I was still not so much alarmed by the danger as mystified by the coincidence. Libussa's earlier words made unacceptable sense. Too much that happened now suggested a unifying design superior to my ordinary cognisance. This thought greatly unsettled me. I had no liking for the idea I might be a pawn in some game of Olympian chess. I would have fought then, had I my blade upon me, not because I hoped to win, but to free myself from the sticky net which gathered us beneath the Autumn Stars. I was a fool, I thought, to have left my Samarkand scimitar and Georgian flintlocks at Raspazian's, but I supposed I too had been dazzled by the golden prospect of the Grail.

Now it seemed Montsorbier also hesitated. Maybe he was equally uneasy. His thirst for vengeance surely dominated him. I could see him trembling with anticipated satisfaction, like a stork in courtship. And I, weaponless, was reduced to putting arms akimbo, legs wide, stomach out, and smiling at him like a forward village maid. He stood and licked his lips, looking from face to face, still twitching—a terrier to my impudent rat—still forcing himself to control his admirably capacious passion. "You were called here also, then?" he suggested. It was as if he longed for a printed questionnaire to flourish and thus contain his terrible emotions by means of bureaucratic formality. There was no Public Safety to be protected here. It was his lust for my life that was naked now, more than when we had stood in the inn and arranged to acknowledge his honour. I prayed he would recall the appointment was unkept through accident and that he would offer me a sword and thus a chance at least at life. But it was his holding off that puzzled me. He plainly did not know if he should kill me or shake my hand. Someone had instructed him, but not on every eventuality. I decided therefore to play direct with my instinct and went forward at an easy pace. "Fool," said I easily, "we're no longer enemies. Where go you now?"

"The Lamb," he said. "And you?"

There was nothing for it but to nod. "The same," I said, believing he described a tavern.

Libussa and Klosterheim, who had also been anticipating their imminent slaughter, greeted Montsorbier with uneasy smiles.

Our elegant duke-catcher, sliding his sabre back into its heavy leather scabbard, took a breath or two and regained control of himself. He scratched his neck. "By Lucifer, von Bek, this is a paradox indeed! If we're all comrades now, what's to become of our individual ambition?"

I had grown so light-headed I clapped him on the back. I was devilish jovial. "D'ye really believe there's no point to struggle if all it achieves is reconciliation and equality?"

"Compromise, you mean," he said, teeth gritted. "I was promised leadership."

"By whom?"

"Don't jest, von Bek. All adepts know we journey to the Centre of Time, to the Concordance, there to receive supernatural intelligence and consequently ultimate power." He bowed to Klosterheim. "We expected you sooner, Sir. When you failed the rendezvous, we continued on our own initiative."

Klosterheim was discomforted, believing himself privileged to a better kept secret. Now, it seemed, he was merely one of a score or more. I guessed he experienced the terrible confusion of a true solipsist when the outer world impinges. "Who made this bargain with you?" Of course, he suspected Satan, the arch-betrayer.

"'Tis implicit to our search." Montsorbier looked askance at Klosterheim. "You know that, Sir." Then, to me: "How were you called here?"

"I followed impulse," said I, taking advantage of the family reputation.

"You von Beks are lucky." He was clearly envious, and gave me a further clue to his hatred of me. "Could we be brought together in order to settle all scores at once? A final fight?"

"Any fight shall follow the Concordance, not precede it," said Libussa. But she was not sure of herself. She, too, had believed herself destiny's only candidate for command and considered this man a mere follower. Now she found too many rivals. I, it appeared, was the only one present not believing himself an alchemical adept!

"Well," Montsorbier was surly, as if for the first time aware of her true ambition, "we had best continue."

We had no choice but to fall in with his party. Quarter of an hour later he was knocking his pistol butt upon a blackened door which was swiftly opened by a young girl with white-gold hair and a pale but healthy complexion: innocence personified (save for a suggestion of lewdness about the eyes) in blue-and-yellow gown, its sleeves flowing and medieval.

"Welcome, my nobles," said she, curtseying as we entered.

Filing in, the men removing their hats like Sunday parishioners, we eventually found ourselves in a stone chamber which, in its severity, greatly resembled a Low Church chapel, with narrow pews and a plain altar. There was no crude Satanism in evidence, no inverted cross, merely a triangle of gold hanging above the altar. By movements of her hands the girl showed we were expected to kneel, so down we went. Libussa, aware as I of danger in any unconscious disobedience, looked right and left for potential escape. Klosterheim simply folded his hands under his long nose in gloomy surrender. Here was something neither of my companions had planned for!

The chapel was entirely lit by massive yellow candles, their melted wax making strange traceries, their restless smoke writhing like damned souls. Montsorbier, one stall forward of me, settled his sword at his back for comfort, pushing long hair away from his pale face, glancing at a man in a wine-red, high-collared coat, already deep in his devotions in the opposite pew. When the man turned his head I saw it was the coward, von Bresnvorts, offering us all a shifty, conspiratorial grin. I was half out of my seat, ready to kill, when Libussa's firm hand stayed me. My heart pounded, but I obeyed.

From both sides now emerged a group of figures in purple, gold, white, black and yellow robes festooned with tassels. They wore great peaked cowls (like some *auto-da-fé*) and lace, and embroidered motifs in obscure parody of Christianity's. Some wretched collection of Masonic officiates with supernatural leanings, I thought, all grunting and hobbling and sweating, their visible flesh so coarse they might have been farmyard creatures. They led a pretty, bleating lamb, bucking in its halter of woven gold. Next came our flaxen-haired maiden to take it in her soft arms, stroking it, murmuring, letting her tresses fall over its shivering body like a curtain. It bleated uncertainly and tried to suckle one of her pink fingers. She smiled and crooned. She was a head taller than her cowled companions, who now swayed in a semicircle before her as she mounted to the altar.

Behind us more men and women filed in to take their places. It was evident that Libussa recognised some of them, though Klosterheim saw nobody, remaining with his eyes downcast.

In sweet, high tones, like crystal ringing, the maiden spoke: "The demand has come at last and the price asked. Shall you pay readily?"

"We shall pay readily," was the response.

"By this means," she continued, "shall ye ensure the gathering of suns and witness the great moment when all worlds conjoin. Ye shall become free to pass amongst those worlds at will. And each shall possess the power to change whatever they wish changed. A million realms in concordance! A million suns! So shall we determine mankind's fate for the next great revolution of the Cosmic Wheel. The Balance steadies. The change is inevitable."

"The change is inevitable."

"Its nature shall be determined."

"Its nature shall be determined."

"Its nature shall be determined. By the privileged, by the adepts, by those seekers of the Centre who are gathered here now. Decisions will be taken and new debts incurred. But first the old debts must be settled."

"The old debts must be settled."

"The Time of the Lamb was a time of failure. The Lamb promised hope but brought only despair."

"Only despair."

"Now we are permitted to create if we can the Time of the Lion!"

"The Time of the Lion."

"The Time of the Lion shall be the triumph of mankind's ambition. A time of power. A time of fire. A time of destruction."

"A time of destruction."

"A time of destruction when we shall be the leaders of Man. Our dreams shall become the unquestioned realities of the coming Millennium. None shall dare deny us."

"None shall deny us."

She paused. "Who speaks for the Lamb?" The little animal no longer struggled but looked at her with wide eyes. She held it out before her. "Who would save the Lamb?"

Her silent congregation merely swayed and stared in silence.

Then the girl lowered her head as if to kiss the cradled beast. She buried her mouth in the little creature's neck. There came one strangled bleat. She twisted her head and her hair swung in an aura of gold. She lifted her face to the congregation: blood was smeared across her lips while the lamb jerked and pumped more blood over her gown, over the altar, over the officiates who giggled and chanted, who pranced around her, beginning to cry: *"The Time of the Lamb is gone. The Time of the Lion must come. The Time of the Lamb is gone. The Time of the Lion must come."*

Save for we three, all the rest, including Montsorbier and von Bresnvorts, were up and swaying, like a methody flock at its monotonous hymns. Men and women, looking ordinary enough to me, of all ages, some with children, lifted up their voices in that chant. I could not bring myself to conform. Then, as the glaring eye of their golden-haired priestess fell upon us, I flung myself suddenly over the pews, reaching for Montsorbier's sabre still tucked at the small of his back, and pulling it clear shouted to Klosterheim and Libussa to find the exit. That bestial ritual in no way accorded with what few beliefs I still professed. By taking action, however doomed, I felt I was damaging a small part of the design drawing us all together.

The bloody-lipped girl became a shrike. "THIS THREATENS ALL!"

I struggled backward over the bench, cutting at Montsorbier's arm as he brought up his pistol which flew high into the air and was wonderfully caught by my Duchess who pressed it against the throat of the man behind her while she slipped his dirk and rapier from his hips, taking the whole belt.

Only Klosterheim held back, staring at the golden maiden like a monk at a vision of Our Lady. He was useless to us. I had another pistol now. The men were dazed cattle, only gradually waking, and I was harvesting their weapons willy-nilly! I aimed a barker. With a flash and a roar its ball struck a little cowled officiate who went rolling and squealing to the feet of his baffled mistress. Another pistol took one of Montsorbier's military pack. Libussa also pulled triggers, downing two of von Bresnvorts' pox-polluted coven.

Now every lip snarled and all I could see were angry teeth, glaring eyes. My own throat was no safer than the lamb's. Libussa discharged a further brace of sticks, almost simultaneously downing two more. The chapel had taken on a charnel-house look, with blood all over it, with bits of bone and brain spattering walls and pews. The congregation milled in panic and Libussa and I were almost at the door. Another flash—a great roar. She might have touched off a cannon, the sound was so amplified. It missed the golden-tressed vein-biter but took down one of the great candles which fell in a rush against the tapestries and fired them. Our advantage temporarily increased, we opened the door. Air fanned the flames. We fled out into darkness and cold. But nothing would hold those hounds for long. We dropped our emptied barkers and ran hand in hand down a slippery alley, up a street so steep it had rails set in its walls, pushed through a few languorous opium-eaters who interfered with our progress only because they could not see us, and we were fully lost!

Behind us was the chase. Klosterheim had carried our map. Libussa was confounded. We leant beneath a bridge which crossed above the lane and she whispered: "What happens here? Why do they sacrifice and chant? Bestial nonsense! For what? I gave no such instructions."

"Plainly more than you and Klosterheim believe this Concordance will provide an antidote to their frustration," said I. My observation was unwelcome to her. I went on. "'Tis a veritable epidemic, my lady. Familiar enough to me. So frequently we believe ourselves unique, only to find our ideas are shared by half the world . . ."

"Oh, be silent, you fool." She was brooding, considering fresh strategy.

My peril, however, made me babble. "Surely they waste their time if Satan's already master of our world?"

"He must be ousted. The father must make way for the child." She spoke severely. "Mankind must rule itself."

"With your encouragement?" My levity was also a condition of my fear.

"Von Bek, it is your destiny as well as mine. You forget." Her fingers squeezed my arm. "We need allies in this. But who? I thought Montsorbier was in my following— Ah, I am betrayed!"

"Sense calls for retreat to Prince Miroslav's. A fresh battle plan."

"We lose important hours."

"In the circumstances—" Then we were running again as beast noises, torches, footfalls, Montsorbier's and von Bresnvorts' recognisable voices, turned in our direction. We were in utter darkness for a moment, passing through a tunnel. We slowed to catch our breath as the sounds of pursuit faded once more. I leaned back against the slippery wall, reaching for her hand. Our fingers touched.

Then, with a gasp, she had fallen away from me. To the ground? I was on my knees, stretching out. Not there. An alcove? I felt along the wall's base. Nothing. "Libussa!" I whispered. "Libussa?" My foot touched a step, an empty doorway. I heard something flutter, as if a bird were trapped. But she had gone entirely. Surely she had not been netted by our enemies. I was horrified. I could not exist without her! I plunged against the doorway and my face struck stone. I turned—stone again—and more stone. "Libussa!"

She had vanished. *Oh, Satan, take my soul, but give me back Libussa!* There was a terrible silence. No Montsorbier or gibbering von Bresnvorts—no torches—no animal cries. I stumbled to the other side of the tunnel, hoping to find her there. The street was empty. The red-gold radiance of the Autumn Stars was fitful in the far-off vault of blackness. "Libussa!" Someone had ripped my heart from my breast. My bowels were torn loose of my body.

She was *myself*! In furious misery I hammered with my sword hilt on stone so thick it had no resonance. How I yearned for a brand, even a tinderbox. The long buildings rustled and swayed like trees in a wind. They groaned and ached. They cried out. The Autumn Stars seemed to grow dimmer.

This was horrid confirmation of my every secret terror. The Black Host was coming! The Beast, the Anti-Christ, was coming! Chaos and the Day of Judgement followed . . . This was hideous nonsense to me. I was still at heart a rationalist and a democrat. The rule of Common Consent remained the only reasonable goal of mankind. It would be sheer madness for me to follow demagogues even greater than Robespierre! In speaking of the Rule of Man, Libussa and the others meant the rule of an élite, themselves. And like Robespierre they now claimed dominion by right of the common people. Better wicked Lucifer for a master, thought I, than a pious Tyrant!

Yet she was more deeply informed than I. Perhaps I did misunderstand, as she insisted? My love for her overruled my logic. Could it overrule my morality? I ran like a frightened cur, up alley, down steps, in and out of archways, doorways, even, once, an open window. Love, love, love! She possessed me. No ecstasy had ever been more intense. I was a pigeon pecking at the place where the barley used to be. I scuttled in circles. My sense had deserted me.

Tripping suddenly I fell upon a bundle. It was warm and sweet-smelling; a sleeping girl, little more than twelve. I turned her face to the faded starlight. Her eyes rolled and she snored faintly. Opium doubtless poisoned her. The lips parted and from them came a song which seemed to fill the alley, the whole quarter. It was a song so lovely in its complex melody, so accurate in its rendering, so subtle in its cadences, I think my obsession was momentarily abated.

At first the language of her song was new to me—perhaps the ancient speech of the Deeper City. Her chest rose and fell in perfect control. Gradually the song's words changed to Slavonic, telling of ship's sails against a coppery sky, a burnished ocean, a creature that had no home save the deepest grottoes of the sea and even those were lost to it, while women waved upon a cliff, looking back: the village was empty. One fire burned in the square. The sun was banished. On its worn mast a flapping flag was revived by a powerful wind and then was set on fire so it blazed even as it fluttered. But the cup could neither be filled nor drained. Thor drank from such a cup, as did Hercules. Yet both were lost.

Both were lost, she sang. A black beast with red eyes stalked into the square. He had a club in one paw and in the other the severed head of a child. He lifted his muzzle and uttered a red roar. Chaos was come upon the world! The cup was drained. The cup was lost. Where were the men and women who had promised victory and tranquillity? Were they captured or dead?

In her song a black sun rose. Huge riders came from each horizon. Their helmets were black and their eyes were red. They had wings at their shoulders. They were the angels of the final fight, the sworn enemies of mankind. Now they were closer, she sang. Now they were nigh upon us. And the cup was lost!

I was still on my knees, peering into her sleeping face. "You sing of the Grail?" I spoke Russian. She did not hear. She sang on. The ancient people of Britain had such a cup and let it go. The Persians knew of it. It had been in India and in China, and all Christendom's lands. What was it that could bring life so easily and let men perish in its pursuit? There were horsemen riding slowly on big stallions. When the tapestry was woven, they could go free. But the tapestry was not complete. None could know the future, not even God. The future they pretended to see was only the past repeated. The true future, by definition, could never be revealed. There were ship's sails in a coppery sky, a burnished ocean, a creature that had no home . . .

I kissed her full on the lips and she sang no more. This was an oracle of an accuracy not to be endured. She returned to her laudanum stupor. Around us the buildings grew restless again. They tilted and rasped as stone shifted on stone. I panted like a hunted dog. I sat down beside the girl, attempting to recover myself.

She spoke suddenly in an ordinary voice, though her eyes were blank. "Every native of Amalorm is psychic by disposition. It is neither a choice, nor yet an outstanding gift. My intuition says you should seek the Goat Queen in the forest."

"Forest, girl? There's none hereabouts!"

"Yonder."

She sat upright and pointed, her eyes still sightless, at a hole in the wall from which issued a faint lamp glow. It was a window, but on a level with the ground. No place for a forest.

"Yonder," insisted the blind child.

Then I was crawling towards the window, staring in, seeing nothing. I squeezed under the arch to drop down into a small room full of damp books and mildewed vellum. The door was of thick glass and it was from this the lamplight issued. Opening a rusted catch I followed the source down a short passage. It grew brighter. Grey stone shone. A large lantern swung on chains from the roof. Beyond this was a pool of clear water and on the other side of the pool an enormous oak tree, smelling of fresh Arcadian woods in full leaf.

There was no Voltairean fixedness to the nature of the Mittelmarch, especially at the centre. I approached this single tree, the blind girl's forest. But where was the Goat Queen? I cast an eye about for Nanny Regina, expecting nothing. I sniffed. Not a perfume or a neigh.

My sword still comforting my fist, I pressed on, skirting the pool. Again I was convinced of some kind of preordainment. What was it which pushed me? I could not even tell if it were benign or malevolent. I remained, however, offended by whatever it was interfered in my own volition. I rounded the oak and there was a rustic bench. On it sat a frail old lady wearing a silver coronet. She looked up at me with mild, reddish, purblind eyes. She had a little white beard, folded ears, but (unlike Lord Renyard) there was no telling if she were beast, human or hybrid. Her thick lips parted in a toothless smile. "The girl sent you to me?" Her voice was high and quavering.

"She did, Madam."

"What were you offered?"

"It's hard to say, Madam." I felt awkward with the sword in my hand. I placed it beside the tree. She noted my gesture. "If you've information, I'd be grateful for it, Madam. Perhaps I was promised sanctuary. I'm fleeing enemies and seeking a lady who disappeared but an hour or so gone. Others tell me I'm upon a quest for the Holy Grail." I grinned at this last.

"The girl pities me," said the white crone. "She sends anyone to me who'll go. She's a well-meaning, dreamy child. If you've been distracted from more important matters, Sir, I apologise. I'll not regard your leaving as impolite."

"Pardon my curiosity, Madam, but what keeps you here alone?"

"Habit, I suppose, Sir. And my apes, of course. They sleep at present. And my tree. Have you seen such a tree in any city?"

"I have not, Madam. But I can't understand, still, why you lack courtiers or emissaries from other monarchs."

"We are," she said, raising red eyes to look directly into mine, "no longer fashionable." There was a trace of a smile on her lips.

"I hope you're soon in vogue again. Would you have a notion, Madam, as to the whereabouts of a gentleman called the Red O'Dowd?"

"The Red O'Dowd is a ruffian, Sir. He brought wild war to the Deeper City and for no good reason. My guard—only four of them to be sure—all died in battle against that Hunnish oaf. Yet, when he'd won, he asked for nothing, took no spoils, claimed no authority. That's insensible, Sir. He's a wolverine! What do you want with him? Some revenge?"

"I'm told, Madam, he knows where the Grail is to be found."

"I've heard that, too, Sir." With arthritic, knotted hands she stroked at her little beard. "I know not where he dwells. He neither visits nor receives. He issues no edicts. It is not kingly, eh, Sir? Nor seemly. He keeps all in suspense and has done these twenty years. He does not rule us and he announces no abdication. He demands no tribute. What's that, if not the uncouth action of a mere Hun, Sir?"

"I hope to discover the answer, Madam."

She lifted a sleeve to point. "Go that way, Sir." A low door. "Since you say you're pursued, likely it will be safer for you."

"I'm obliged, Madam."

"I'm obliged to you, Sir. Take one of my flambeaux."

"If there's any service, Madam, I can perform for you . . ."

"Thank you, Sir, no. The girl brings food."

I bowed, trying to kiss her hand, but she would not let me. Laughing at herself, she drew back her arthritic hoof, then she shrugged. "Good luck to you, Sir."

I saluted her with my sabre.

Approaching the exit she had recommended I became again sensible of the chase close by. It was still possible to detect Montsorbier and von Bresnvorts baying on different notes. Suddenly, at my back, the Goat Queen spoke: "Were Theseus more constant to his Ariadne, mayhap she would have wept less. But would the world have known such mighty wars?"

I could not place her quotation, but there was Theseus again! Crete, it seemed, was everywhere. It was mighty disquieting to a rational man who had failed even to approve the Classical pretensions of the French parliament and whose Latin and Greek were ever weak. As for that Hero, all I recollected was that he habitually carried off maidens, with unpleasant consequences (or considerable inconvenience at very least) for a great many Attic Greeks and through absent-mindedness killed his own father, whereupon he was made King of Athens. Then there were the other tales, of his killing the last of Earth's old monsters and bringing to an end the reign of the gods. Was that what the Goat Queen meant?

Beyond the doors were spirals of stone: I moved without any real goal, merely relying on the constrictions of the Deeper City and the prejudices of Providence to see me safe. I would give myself so much time, then try to return to Prince Miroslav's for aid.

Libussa! I love you!

My brain scarcely ruled me at all as I blundered on through passages and flights of steps leading me lower at every pace. My brand gave off sufficient light to mark my way, but it scarcely heated me against the chill. I heartily wished for a cloak. My teeth were chattering when at length I paused to rest, having come to a flagged landing between two flights of stairs. Then I found myself staring down into a golden haze which was surely the natural dawn!

This alarmed me. I was thoroughly underground, but here was air so clear and warm it might have belonged to a spring day in Saxony! My bodily need for comfort defeated suspicion and I continued down. The stairway led into a massive hall with a per-pendicular, richly decorated ceiling and the light came through huge Gothick windows. It was as though I had entered a Cathe-dral transept. The windows were stained with simple, rural scenes, the work of a genius, so it was impossible to see beyond them. At the far end of the hall, which was furnished only with white flagstones, benches of dark onyx, a carved wooden chair and table, sat a figure beckoning me forward.

"Welcome at last, von Bek. You are without doubt most dis-similar to my old friend, your ancestor. I am glad you have found me." I could not tell if man or woman spoke. The face was obscured by a shaft of light from the far window. The same light half blinded me. Blinking, I lifted a protecting hand. "Friend, you have the advantage."

"So I'm frequently informed, Sir."

I still held up my flickering brand. It had no function, but nei-ther could I see anywhere to put it down. This time I tried to shield my eyes with the flat of my sword. The light was not unusually bright yet it possessed an odd, unstable effect which continued to dazzle me.

The figure rose to its feet. There was a kind of aura around its silhouette which made it difficult for me to distinguish details, yet it was tall and well proportioned and I received the impression of great beauty.

"Sir, would you be so good as to tell me where this is and to whom I'm speaking."

"Not at all, Sir. You are intermediary, at present, for this room lies half in earth while the other half's in Hell. And though I'm called by many fanciful names, I prefer Lucifer. The same as bargained with Graf Ulrich, Sir."

I held my ground. There had been so much deception already I refused to be easily convinced by such claims. "Hard to believe you, Sir."

"But true, Sir, nonetheless." The voice was melodious, the bearing graceful. Lucifer strolled towards me. He was two and a half yards high, if an inch! "I cannot bargain with you, Ritter von Bek. Neither can I offer to reward you. I have my own contracts, you see, which I must honour. But I have a gift for you."

I grew still more nervous. The creature was powerful, even if he were not the Devil. Again fear made me attempt levity. "Dem' me, Sir, but I'd be inclined to mistrust any gift of Satan's. Ain't they meant to have unpleasant consequences for the recipient?"

"I'll not make an effort to persuade you, Sir. I've agreed to forgo that means of gaining my ends. Your ancestor, the *Krieghund*, did me a great service in finding the Grail. He it was who set in motion a course of events which led to our present meeting. Could you remind me, Sir, of your family's secret motto?"

"*Do you the Devil's work.*"

"Just so, Sir. And what's that work, do you suppose?" His voice, so gentle and beautiful, lulled me, yet by an effort I maintained my reason.

"I've never quite guessed, Sir."

"It is to help bring harmony to mankind. To seek a Cure for the World's Pain. But lately you've seen for yourself how certain political experiments do nothing to ease that pain. And now comes what the alchemists term 'the Concordance'. Do you understand their eagerness, Sir?"

"I'd be devilish pleased—" I paused in some embarrassment. "I'd be mighty pleased for some illumination on that, Sir."

"They have a chance to alter history's course. To change the principles on which humankind bases its actions. Whoever gains ascendancy at the time of the Concordance shall choose the *method* by which Man seeks salvation."

"But no path is certain, surely, Sir?"

"No path is certain. But it is not my place to show bias."

"Surely you've shown that already, Sir, by bringing me here? If you are indeed Lucifer!"

"But what shall *you* choose, von Bek? I cannot know that. I gather you ally yourself with the Duchess of Crete."

"It seems so, yes. If she still lives."

"I know her family well. Questing and questioning minds, all of them. They've had an eye on the Grail before. And you also seek that cup again, eh? The Grail scents von Bek blood, perhaps, and awaits its trusted friend. Or shall it find its own way to you? What do you think, Sir?"

"Nothing, Sir. Not about the Grail. Those are riddles you are better equipped to answer than myself."

The creature seemed pleased with my obstinacy and laughed softly. "I cannot tell you where the Grail is, nor indeed which guise it presently prefers. Neither could I say if you would benefit from finding it or harm us both! But I'm Lucifer, you see, Child of the Dawn. 'Tis in my nature to take a risk. I'll gamble on you, Sir, as I did on your ancestor, and trust you'll act to our mutual benefit!"

"Gamble, Sir? I've been told God gave you whole charge of these Earthly realms."

"So He did, Sir."

"Then your power must be considerable. Enough to determine any issue! Any fate!"

"My bargain with God included the undertaking that I should play no direct part, merely supervise mankind's self-redemption. Like yourself, my agents are those whose independence of thought is already well-established."

"This sounds close to Satan's famous flattery, Sir." I was honestly amused. "Do you speak of Klosterheim? Montsorbier? Von Bresnvorts? The coven that pursues me even now?"

"Not one of them serves me, von Bek. Those who make free with my name would as easily make free with God's if they believed it helped their interest. They identify me with their own corrupt desire for domination of mankind. Klosterheim will bring war to Heaven and Hell if he can. His relation to me is quite different. Oh, I'll not deny the perverse and bestial aspect's in me; but while I despise and tame it, they celebrate it. Those depraved creatures, I repeat, are no more my servants than Klosterheim is God's."

"Sir, I'll take your word ye're Satan, and sincere. But I must know where Libussa and myself feature in this grand scheme."

"She believes you're two halves of the same apple."

"She does not serve you?"

The golden shoulders shrugged. "Who can say? If her will's strong enough she could well prove every claim she makes for you both and determine what is real and what is mere abstraction. Now's her chance, along with the rest, to make dreams actual. I would guess she is the strongest of them. But she could destroy you ultimately, Sir, and thus do damage to my own hopes, too. The choice, I suppose, shall come to rest with you . . ."

"I fail to understand how fresh realities can be *created*."

"Only at the Time of the Concordance. And by the exercise of monstrous will. Redefine the terms by which Man views the world, and thus eventually you redefine the world itself. So you see, Sir, the stakes are very high in this adventure."

The prospect weighed heavily on my mind. "So why, Sir, did you bring me here?"

"I did not. You do me great credit if you think I engineered your movements! Since Switzerland I've attempted to place myself somewhere along your route. In Prague, in the Carpathians . . . You were never long enough alone! Well, Sir, here's my reason for wishing to see you—you've heard of Paracelsus? He's said to be the originator of most ideas in your modern natural philosophy."

"Aye, I've heard Klosterheim speak of him quite recently. A respected alchemist, thought to be the base of the Faust story. Others call him a charlatan, I know. All agree he drank too much and was an unpopular employee."

"He was everything they claim, possessed of considerable intellect and gross appetites, an innovator of the most accurate instincts. His logic and character were sometimes flawed, but perhaps it took a self-indulgent, self-loving creature like him to map the crooked paths to fresh understanding . . ."

"It's a view commonly held these days, Sir. Klosterheim mentioned a sword."

"Exactly, Sir!" The demon seemed delighted. "That sword protected him against his enemies. No matter what his excesses, or whom he offended, or what danger threatened, his sword always saved him. One drunken Summer evening, here in Mirenburg, on his way back to Prague, Paracelsus embarked upon a programme of wenching and guzzling so thorough that even he became fascinated by the range and duration of his own capacities. At last he traded his sword for the favours of (in his own words) a common pox-box and two bottles of inferior Moldavian wine. Soon after, as you'd guess Sir, he died in mysterious circumstances. Whereupon his legend continued to grow unabated. The sword was already too powerful and strange an object for his terrified debtor, who relieved himself of it to a Moroccan conjuror who in turn, when he understood what he owned, also became uneasy. The blade had unusual properties." Lucifer's great frame began to move across the room. It was as if the sunlight followed His outline. I caught a glimpse of perfect features and was entranced. "He buried it. The gentleman who eventually unearthed the sword traded it, so he believed, for the return of his immortal soul. Well, you must know I claim nothing of that sort now. Souls, as well as living people, await the outcome of my Guardianship. My agent was, perhaps, a little vague in the matter. Nonetheless, he obtained the Sword of Paracelsus and I have kept it until now."

I had the impression Lucifer was smiling. This was my mother, Libussa, my father, my dreams of Man's salvation—all I had ever loved! My impulse was to fall on my knees before Him!

"It is over there, von Bek." The gestures were delicate, tender. I reminded myself He was, after all, an angel, albeit a fallen one, and it was not surprising I should be thus impressed. In the furthest corner of the hall, beyond the sunbeam, something flickered; something glowed. It could be a volatile mineral or even flesh. I moved one slow step at a time until I stopped, the shaft of sunlight still between me and a long, flat-hilted, round-pommelled sword leaning against the wall, as if casually abandoned.

"Put down your torch, Sir," said Lucifer. "It's of little use presently. Put it on the floor, Sir. No harm will come to you."

I lowered the flambeau to the floor and my sabre, too. I crossed into the sunlight and again was blinded. Yet I could see it. I put out my hand towards it. A magic blade. It could be nothing else but a magic blade! My fingers touched it and a shock ran through my arm!

"Be just a little wary of it, Sir," said Lucifer as I drew back. "But you or any part of you shall be the sword's master from now on. Its properties are at your disposal the moment you lift it."

My palm went to the worn blue velvet of the hilt. I curved my fingers upon it. I had it. I gripped. It seemed monstrous heavy.

Then I had lifted up the Sword of Paracelsus. The pommel was a ruby globe, but within that globe I saw a bird. A captive eagle, its coppery wings beating, beating at the sky. It circled, perpetually restless. Its beak opened in a great shriek. Its claws were extended, as if for the kill. Its eyes were quite mad. A wonderful eagle, held in thrall by the blade's power. At last I felt equipped to stand against those who threatened me!

"*The Grail goes its own way and has gone from Hell already. Perhaps only the Grail decides our destinies, von Bek. Pray you, Sir, use that sword for our mutual benefit. It is all I can give you . . .*"

I turned to thank the infernal monarch, but only Lucifer's voice remained in the hall. "*Remember, I cannot hold you in any way. No bargain is made by your receiving that blade. I trust you simply to remember your family crest—the secret one—and what is written upon it . . .*"

"*Do you the Devil's work!*" I raised my new sword higher, feeling its perfect balance. I knew something of the elation which came when I lay with Libussa. I laughed in delight. All fear was lifted from me at that moment, all anxiety for the future, all morbid terror at my fate.

"*Should you choose to do my work, von Bek, I pray you, for all our sakes—DO IT WELL . . .*"

The sunlight faded from the windows. A huge, cold darkness

began to flood through the chamber as Lucifer withdrew into Hell. I stopped to pick up my guttering brand. Shadows fell on rotting granite.

His voice became a distant echo, a whisper, a memory. *"It is all I can give you . . . The rest depends entirely upon you . . ."*

Suddenly I was grinning. I seemed to grow until I was larger than the universe itself. I contained the universe as the universe contained me! We were One. I was all mankind!

And I held a magic sword.

Chapter Fourteen

An equaliser of considerable comfort. Fancy and
Actuality confused. Apes, an idiot and a fresh corpse.
Does a coincidence of men prefigure a coincidence of suns?
Further traps and tangles. To Salzkuchengasse
in pursuit of a lady!

I RETRACED MY way to the surface wondering if any man had ever so casually entered Hell or so easily left it. I had Montsorbier's sabre in one hand, the near-spent torch in the other, and in my belt was the scabbarded Paracelsian blade with its writhing red pommel and its constantly agitated eagle.

By now I was almost laughing at myself. Since leaving Paris I had gradually fallen in league with the supernatural, against all my rationalism! Now I was told that the world's future could depend on me. Even if that were likely, I would have had little relish for the responsibility. Perhaps at some point in those mysterious proceedings, assuming I was given the power, I could hand it over to one who would honestly relish it: my Duchess?

I was in an alley now, amongst the shivering buildings and the bitter air. The sky was almost brilliant in comparison to the warrens I emerged from and I was able to see the great circle of unsteady towers which surrounded me. They formed an horizon, faintly red, shading up into purple and blue, behind and above those monstrous stars. It struck me that if Mirenburg truly lay at the exact centre of the Mittelmarch (or of the Astral Concordance, or both) then the Deeper City was dead centre to Mirenburg, the whole built around a great pit. The whole city, then, protected a hollow, a kind of emptiness—almost an *Absence*. The notion so disturbed me I discarded it.

There was no way to tell the time. I was near faint with weariness and assumed it was morning. I had relinquished my few remaining ambitions and was ready to return to Prince Miroslav's to enlist his and the Chevalier St. Odhran's aid. Libussa might have been spirited back by some Russian alchemy, so it was possible I wasted my time seeking her in the Deeper City. Yet returning was not simple, for I could not tell left from right or north from south. All I could do was trudge onwards, trying to gain height and hoping eventually I would find a landmark amongst the dancing tenements.

My eyes were blurred and my senses distorted, so I heard and saw too much that was Fancy, not enough that was actual. I felt I should sleep before I resumed my search. The buildings were like mourners round a coffin, swaying and wailing. I traversed a few more yards before I stopped in my tracks in a little square surrounding an old stone well. The houses there were relatively stable. There was a sense of seclusion about the place. It seemed safe enough. I sat myself down with my back to the well's mossy granite and attempted to reason out my situation. I was lost . . .

My reasoning lasted perhaps two seconds before I was fast asleep with my head on my chest, having no notion how much time had passed when I lifted my head again. My shoulders, back and posterior were aching mightily. I had an urgent need to relieve my bladder.

I rose to my feet, stiff as a parson in a brothel, when to my astonishment from all sides there rolled a tide of white fur and I was surrounded by apes, each one the colour of snow but with red eyes and black muzzles: a kind of large baboon. They were capering and gibbering and grinning at me, pulling at my clothing.

"Gentlemen," I begged, "spare me a moment alone, I beg you!" But they could not understand and I was dragged across the square, clinging to my two swords, through an archway and into a courtyard. From there I was hauled down a hall panelled in beaten gold which reflected the firelight while at its centre grew an old oak tree. From this came the fresh scents of a forest. It was where I spoke with the Goat Queen. But the old woman was gone, her rustic bench empty.

On the far side of the pool stood the idiot girl whose song I had listened to as she lay drugged outside. Now she sang in the language of Mirenburg, sang what she had to say in the same pure, crystal voice. "She is dead. She is dead. The Goat Queen is dead."

The white apes fell back against the walls as if in respect. They squatted and watched us.

"She did not seem sickly when I saw her a few hours since." I tried to attract the girl's attention, but her eyes remained blank.

"She was not sickly. She was well, Sir, and lively. She was lively. But it was men who killed her, Sir." Her face moved a little, to seek me out. Then, very gradually, her eyes began to focus on me.

I was finding it hard to take so much horror and wonderment. I became banal. "She was murdered?"

"Murdered, Sir, by those who pursue you. By the one who led them."

Sleep and misery thickened my tongue. "By Montsorbier?"

"The pale one, Sir. Is that Montsorbier?"

I shook my head. "He's pale enough, but I think you speak of Klosterheim. Why should he kill your mistress?"

"Because she helped you where she would not help them."

"How, child? How killed?"

"With teeth, Sir, and with a sword." Her eyes were aswim with terror.

I was aghast. "They had no reason!" And Klosterheim led them. He had always been their leader! Could Libussa, too, have conspired with them?

The apes came forward on all fours. They surrounded the idiot child. They lifted her up in their hairy arms and she pointed into the branches of the oak. Something was cradled there. A little, frail corpse. It was the Goat Queen, all bloodied from half a score of wounds, the worst in her throat.

"She offered threat to no-one!" I was weeping as I moved towards the tree. "Oh, Madam, their crimes are ever against the innocent. Why do they kill so?"

"They are envious," sang the girl. "They think all we strive to earn is free and given us by Fate. And your Klosterheim, he hated

473

my queen. He called her Mother of Satan. It had been a million years, he said, but now she would pay for her crime. He thought, Sir, that she'd conceived the Devil! She did not protest. She was eighty-two years, so she told me. Now I have no-one to comfort."

In my rage and grief I felt little sympathy then for that bereaved child. "Do you think she served Lucifer, girl?"

"We all serve Him now, Sir. Those few of us who are not in conflict with Him." She stood beside the bench, touching the wood. The apes looked on. "I saw who you were, Sir. I warned her you carried death with you. Yet I did not know you when you held me and I sang. I did not recognise you, Sir, as the shadow I'd fore-told. Is it man or woman? she asked me. I cannot see, I said. This time I cannot see. One part of a single creature. Yet there are both sexes mingled in it. I did not recognise you, Sir. And I sent you to her."

"Damn you, girl," said I. "You're an uncomfortable Oracle. Did you really see all of this?"

Her eyes drifted out of focus and she pointed her head up, fac-ing the little corpse above. "I see nothing, Sir, for I'm blind. I am a singer who feels and has language. But the languages are earned. Only the words are crude, Sir. Still, I could not tell your sex, though I now call you 'Sir' and you address me as a man would and are garbed as a man would be. Are you a woman, too, Sir?"

At that instant I could not in honesty answer her. Even my phy-sique was in doubt. I made some poor joke, saying she should ask that question of another, the one I sought. I touched my body and recalled it easily enough. I said roughly: "I'm in a devilish need of a piss, girl. Wait one moment and I'll demonstrate." And with that it was down with the flap of my breeches and drawers and let loose with great pleasure and force into the pool. "I appear to be male, child." My sabre tucked under my arm I completed my business. I looked down at the Sword of Paracelsus in my belt. The ruby pulsed.

"Then the female half must be close by," she sang.

At which, without reason, I shuddered.

The apes crept to the pool. They had been watching me. Now half of them began pissing, too. The vault was full of our common stench. The girl's song became wordless. In the branches of the oak the little white Goat Queen slept, wrapped in the blood she'd once protected. I was unbalanced by contrasts and paradoxes. This symmetry was too complex for my worldly brain. Yet even I could tell that it was indeed true symmetry; not Chaos in disguise. Chaos, which precedes the Final War. Besides, I thought vaguely, how could the Final War be waged when one party had abdicated and the other had turned pacifist?

"Perhaps the world shall be at her weakest when the Concordance comes," continued that unnerving child, "when the individual will is stronger than the mass. So reality can be changed. Is that why they all struggle with such desperate violence, Sir? So that each imagination shall not be opposed? Does that make the nonsense into sense again, good Sir? Would that be why all rival dreams must be extinguished, so that one—or those, at least, of one accord—shall dominate?"

"Girl, I've no desire to hear further puzzles," I shouted. "Ask no more, I beg you! I am grieved your lady's dead. I'll avenge her if I can. But your Higher Wisdom's beyond my understanding and merely confuses me. With respect, child, therefore—confine your occult visions!"

"You could be resisting truth, Sir."

"Aye. Resisting it mightily, if that's what I do. You know more than Prince Lucifer Himself! Or"—I was struck by a sudden idea—"does Lucifer speak through you? Are you Satan, girl? Were you not forbidden natural form under the terms of your compact?"

"I shall sing of these things no more, Sir." It was a descending note. "I'll sing no more the unwelcome songs . . ." The note decayed. She was silent.

I began to pant. The apes moved in single file around the pool which no longer steamed with their waste nor mine. That forest could not be corrupted, even after the death of its queen. The oak prevailed. The leaves breathed their wonderful scent. The apes

squatted in little groups beneath the oak. They grunted, they gib-
bered, they wailed. They were mourners again.

Tears dazzled my eyes and were bright on the cheeks of the
child. The funeral dance of the apes was slow and dignified. They
rose on their hind legs, they extended their long arms. The white
fur moved with a thousand little shadows. Down on their knuck-
les again, swaying beneath the tree. The blind girl began to sing
again, a wordless agony.

Then it was done.

The brands were taken from the wall and thrown on a heap at
the oak's base. Slowly the wood charred. The smell of the sap was
stronger than ever as it was driven, hissing, to the outer air. Yet,
though flames jumped into its top branches, touched the little
corpse, ran along the trunk, the tree was invulnerable. Even as it
burned it revived itself. I watched in further wonderment, and I
was still weeping.

The girl's song changed, then. It became a wail of warning. Her
head turned and her blind eyes stared beyond me. Montsorbier was at
the door, perhaps attracted by the sounds, or possibly the light. There
was a fresh sword in his hand. His face was no longer handsome. It
was twisted with some horrid, unnameable greed. Klosterheim came
pacing slowly from another arch, von Bresnvorts from a third. I
guessed they had been moving in ambush for some minutes. Behind
them, brought into relief by the pyre's flames, were the faces of their
followers, their expressions more bestial than any honest beast's. How
strongly those men and women contrasted with the baffled apes,
who turned their heads this way and that to look.

I did not see Libussa and I was grateful. "Oh, Klosterheim, why
have you descended to cowardly murder?" I asked him. "You
wished to be my ally."

"The opportunity remains." He was cold. His teeth were
so tight in his head his voice emerged as a tortured whisper. It
made me believe he regretted his impulse yet must now pursue its
consequences. "You can join us, von Bek. We must all be bonded
now, as one, if we're to fulfil the common cause. If we refuse to do
so, then we should be cut swiftly down, as a cancer on our body."

"No room for compromise, von Bek," cried Montsorbier. And, sickeningly, he giggled at me.

"We must wrest this globe from He who rules," said Klosterheim. "We're all agreed on that now, von Bek. You agreed with us. There's no need to die."

"I've nought in common with those who kill old women." The flames hid her in their glare. The flames absorbed her blood. The flames were all part of the same entity—queen, oak, pool. The presence of those degenerate cut-throats there was a blasphemy. "I am your enemy, Klosterheim. I humoured you once, felt pity for you. No longer. You are a creature doomed to commit acts of foolish evil. Doomed to wanton and inevitable self-destruction. And it is, I note, a well-deserved fate!"

Klosterheim shrugged.

"You have but one chance, Sir," said Montsorbier, momentarily recovering from whatever madness possessed him. He was loud and imperious, as of old. Then his voice grew insinuating and sly again. "All others you've rejected. But we are merciful. Come in with us."

"Those not within our compact shall inevitably be destroyed." Von Bresnvorts parroted as usual. I doubted he even knew the meaning of his words. He had been rehearsed.

"Where's the inevitability? Where's any proof?" My disgust and my fury gave me courage. I had my sabre in my right fist. The other sword was held in reserve. I still had scant taste for magic. "You all speak of destiny when you mean 'despair'. You're frightened as donkeys braying in a storm. Not one of you—not even Klosterheim—has the bottom for this. So now you huddle together, calling it a Compact. You're hypocrites. You've lied to yourselves and now pay the price." I took three long paces so that my back was to the blazing oak. And I laughed in their wicked faces. My own self-deception at least promised some kind of pleasure. Theirs offered nothing but terror and guilt.

They had become too hungry to rise immediately to my challenge. Even Montsorbier, who was the best of them, was irresolute. Only Klosterheim was consistent. "Forget this false sentiment, von

Bek. Lucifer betrays the world. He'll betray you. He refuses power. Ousting Him will be effortless after the Concordance."

"You lie, Sir. You want sweet reunion with the only creature you've ever loved. If He called you back to Hell now, you'd crawl to join Him. He is your master, whether He chooses to use you or not!"

"Not so, foul-mouthed heretic."

I had angered him. I had not expected to affect him so readily. He was pulling free his long, slender steel from his belt and he moved forward to kill me, a farmer stalking a chicken, as if he failed to consider my retaliation.

Montsorbier cried out, "Johannes Klosterheim, we agreed a plan. Von Bek must join us, otherwise the scheme will founder. And there's the woman to convince!"

My heart lifted. I felt a thrill of pleasure. I would not perish yet, thought I, while she remained opposed to that rabble. Thus my faith was kept glimmering. But where was she? Had she already found the Grail and was that why they were so viciously desperate?

The apes were restless around the blazing oak. The blind girl crooned as if to soothe them. Firelight made animate the features of that horrid sodality. Perhaps they maintained a semblance of sanity by anticipating early triumph. But Libussa and I, in interrupting their gathering, had thrown them too dramatically out of balance. What with apes swaying behind me and the bloodthirsty officiates lurking before me, many of them still in pointed cowls, I became frozen. I was unwilling to move lest the flicker became a signal for ferocious bloodletting. The blind girl sang on, swaying as the apes swayed. I would not wish her harmed, as the old lady was harmed.

"Von Bek," said Montsorbier, "will you answer me a question?" His handsome face was etched in lines which had not been there yesterday. He had grown much older and there was a slackness about his mouth, a fear in his eyes. He had joined the jackals completely. "Please, von Bek, as a civilised man, rally to us. Does O'Dowd really guard the Cup? Have you sniffed it out yet?"

"I seek O'Dowd as you do."

"But you ally with Satan," said Klosterheim. "It was always likely. You did it before. As I understand, only the pure and perfect can handle the Grail."

I laughed again. "Then there's little point to any of us here seeking it!" The branches crackled. The apes grew more restless. The girl raised her voice, still singing to them.

"The ritual," said Klosterheim soberly, "will purify us. Those who join the Lion against the Lamb. Montsorbier—tell him. The same as you told me. Tell him how the ritual he interrupted would have made him pure."

"It is a wiping away of all past sins," said Montsorbier. "Including the sin of following Christ. There is still time for the ritual to be re-enacted. Christ has to be exiled, do you see, before the Lion can be summoned."

It was purest nonsense to my ear. "Then why aren't you at your ritual now, Sir?"

"She—" Montsorbier hesitated.

"She demands blood, eh? Me and Libussa, eh? Are you fearful that your destiny gets more distant every passing hour? Your cunning is transparent, Montsorbier. As for you, Klosterheim, you made a stupid mistake. You were impatient once and paid your price for it. Now you've made a similar error. I must believe you doomed to eternal life, but also to eternal repetition! Your true doom is simple to me. You lack brains, Sir."

I had struck deep again, better than any blade. His eyes went wild, his mouth opened to reply. But he could not. He was trawling his memory for proof or denial of my hideous suggestion!

Montsorbier, fearful that I had made a comrade of the excommunicated Captain of Hell, now called urgently on a note of reconciliation: "Von Bek. We plan no treachery against you. We need you for the Grail. The woman must die. All the omens say the same. But you will survive and join us and become one of the Earth's remakers. We once sought, together with Cloots, Marat and Robespierre, to create Paradise. But too many tried, you see. The Revolution failed. I realised that in Vaud. Whereupon I at once reconciled myself with my old Brotherhood. Now just five or six shall have the ultimate power. We'll build a world where Order shall prevail. A few more deaths are inconsequential, surely, if they guarantee us eternal life and absolute fulfilment?"

"Perhaps you are also sentenced to the Doom of Repetition," I said to him. "Your words are over-familiar, Sir. Your ambition's greater and your hold on sanity's looser, that's all. Well, I pray for the sake of good manners at least that I'll avoid that particular doom."

"You're a coward, Sir!" Von Bresnvorts spoke thickly and he was leering. "There are those of us who welcome the responsibility of power. We're not afraid to take the action demanded of us!"

"What's morally right about accepting such responsibility?" I asked. "It is precisely what I do not require. Be silent, von Bresnvorts. At least your two comrades retain the vestiges of passable intellects. You began with nothing, save appetite and malice."

He snarled. Montsorbier again restrained him. "Von Bek, I of all people have reason to wish you dead. You have humiliated me. You have insulted me and attacked my most cherished ambitions. However, it is not a crime to defend one's interests." Now Froggy was a Sophist. "We should all be prepared to understand and be tolerant. Are you aware we anticipate the Apocalypse, von Bek?"

"The obsession's common enough, Montsorbier, amongst ignorant folk."

Klosterheim's sword was coming up again and he resumed his stalking towards me.

Montsorbier was beside himself, fearing for the destruction of that brittle alliance. "Gentlemen!" Behind me the oak whistled in the wild flame. I glanced back. The little Goat Queen was consumed.

"Liars and cowards!" I shouted in outrage. "All of you are corrupt murderers! I'll not join you. I would delay my own corruption for as long as possible! Can't you see what you've become? This unsettled ambiance has found each weakness and amplified it in you. Montsorbier, you're no better now than the creature beside you! You are no better than von Bresnvorts, who killed his aunt for a fragment of a fortune! Look into those waters, Sir!" I pointed with my blade. "Look, Sir, into the pool—and see what you've become!"

Montsorbier's features twitched and shifted. He snarled. "I renounce diplomacy. Alive you're too great a danger to us!"

"I thank you for that, Sir," said I with a sudden lift of spirits. "There's now an incentive for me to survive!" Then I ran at him with my sabre. He brought up a near-identical blade and parried. He had lost none of his quickness.

As we fought we turned until I could see his watching followers, the intense, uncertain frown on Klosterheim, and von Bresnvorts' wet mouth opening and closing like a praying Turk's arse. They began to stir, all of them, to crowd towards me. Montsorbier no longer cared for his honour.

But a white tide was moving, a foam of apes, all scampering and leaping at me and Montsorbier until I was knocked off my feet and they were carrying me, struggling and cursing, out of the room and back to the cold little square where they had found me. Was it that they refused to tolerate violence while the oak burned?

I heard confused shouts from within, the crystal song of the blind child. Then the apes were a pyramid, passing me up furry backs like tumblers. Soon I was high above the square, looking down at Montsorbier, Klosterheim and the others as they burst into the square, shrieking with frustrated rage. They realised I'd escaped them. I was lifted clean out of their grasp. I rose higher and higher still, with apparently an infinity of apes to accomplish my ascent. I was set down upon a balcony. The pyramid tumbled back and dispersed out of the square as those furious enemies of Satan struck savagely about them. And the girl was still singing, but her song was distant, fading. I stared down from my safe perch!

Suddenly there was silence. I heard Klosterheim panting, almost detected Montsorbier's grinding teeth. The two men separated themselves from the press and came to stand looking up at me: one gaunt and pale (Death personified in a Holbein print) and the other red with rage and weariness, his cold eyes given life by his hatred.

"That circus trick shan't save you, Sir," said Montsorbier.

"You'll be cast out," said Klosterheim. "Ostracised by your peers, eternity shall be lonely for you!"

"If you're the peers, gentlemen, it's a devilish petty threat," I countered. I watched for a trick. Corrupt they might be, but they were dangerous enemies. I would lose more than life if they succeeded in their ambitions. A world where that triumvirate ruled would be a ghastly, bloody place indeed! Since the prospect was by no means impossible I felt I would need powerful aid if I were to overwhelm them. Who could I trust? Anyone? Libussa, even, could decide to join them, letting some other pawn stand and be sacrificed. It came to me that she had already found the Red O'Dowd. If the Grail was in her keeping, she no longer needed me. Thus she could already have traded me off for some other advantage!

From the far side of the square the blind girl began to sing again. Klosterheim and Montsorbier glanced this way and that, ready to kill her. The language was the same she had used the previous night. She was calling to me. I strained to catch the words.

To the tavern, to the tavern, she sang, *To the older tavern in Salzkuchengasse. To the tavern called* The Friend Indeed, *of the son of the ancient king. To the defender of the spring, to the place of the four apostles. To the meeting place of all tales. To the tavern, to the tavern. To the tavern of conjoining realms!*

At first the song sounded mere rhetoric. *To Salzkuchengasse!* That was a street I knew in my own Mirenburg, so doubtless it existed in the Mittelmarch city, too. I shouted in Russian: "Is that where she is? Is that where I'll find my lady?"

To Salzkuchengasse . . .

"Where is my Libussa?"

She is not lost, but a decision is due. To Salzkuchengasse . . .

I took her to mean Libussa awaited me at The Friend Indeed. Now I feared Klosterheim or one of that crew knew Slavonic, or had picked out the street from the song. In which case, every rogue in the square would soon be en route for the same tavern. I turned away from the balcony and pushed through doors to find myself in a luxury of furs and silks: a bedroom. A sleepy, naked youth tried to show anger at my intrusion but was too uncertain. I crossed his floor to the next door and, as I unlocked it, thought to ask: "Beg pardon, Sir. Is there a hostelry nearby called The Friend Indeed?"

He yawned and rubbed sticky eyes. "That would be . . ." He pointed unsurely, changed his mind and pointed again in another direction. "East, I think. Salzkuchengasse. It's a little twisting alley, widening to a cobbled square, eh, Sir? And the tavern's there. A quarter mile, I'd say. Where Nachtigall's monument to God's memory was erected." He grew more confident. "Aye! It is that way. Off Korkzie—no, off Papensgasse, I think. No. Königstrasse, that's it. Off Königstrasse, Sir." He scratched at tangled black hair. "Now, Sir, while I am not an inhospitable person, I must ask you your reason for calling upon a man by means of his balcony."

I bowed to him. "Much obliged to you, Sir. My regrets, also, Sir. And my apologies for disturbing you. I'm in urgent pursuit of a lady, Sir."

He brightened. "Then good luck to you, Sir." He winked. "And *bonne chance!*"

"Thank you, Sir." I was out of the bedroom swiftly, down a long passage, and opening a door onto a wide landing. Stone steps wound down and I took them several at a time. A long gallery was at the end of them, swaying like a ship at anchor, with windows which overlooked the distant street. I had little fear of direct pursuit. But they could be making their own way to the tavern even now.

Through a wide, white passage set with little market stalls, not yet open, I made my way, enquiring of a tall, red-headed woman in some sort of Graecian evening gown, strolling her spaniel, if I was right for Salzkuchengasse. She pointed and I darted down more steps, along another passage, to emerge again into the gloomy lanes of the Deeper City. This was Königstrasse, however. Now I had to find Salzkuchengasse.

The street turned into a bridge, as ornamental as any in Venice, over an exceptionally straight and rather narrow canal. There were two boats upon the black glass of the water. Both were filled with misshapen men and women scarcely different from the ones I had escaped. It seemed all the world's lunatics and monstrosities were flocking to Mirenburg and I was the only one anxious to leave.

I looked behind me. I was not followed. I could not hear the baying of Montsorbier's pack, but that was not to say they were losing the race. So anxious was I to see potential pursuers I almost dashed past the covered stone arch bearing the somewhat faded sign of *Salzkuchengasse.* The entrance to the street was barely three feet wide. It had old flagstones which were misshapen and broken and lay at peculiar angles, one to the other, so that I tripped several times as I stumbled forward in the dark. Eventually the alley widened and the roof was first higher, then vanished altogether. Once again I was in the Autumn Starlight.

Salzkuchengasse fell away very steep again and at one point became worn steps with a central banister. I paused on the first step, noting the open space between the buildings, looking up at the hazy, twinkling firmament. It seemed I was equidistant from all points of the horizon. I was at the very middle of the Deeper City. Beneath my feet the Rätt purred underground.

I became suddenly nervous and was almost on the point of turning back to see Prince Miroslav. I felt a great need to hear St. Odhran's common sense. The reason for my hesitation was the unwelcome suspicion that I was guided by a powerful, invisible force. If that were true, I had received no direct sense of it and could not tell if the force were benign or malevolent. Did I act in my own interest or the interest of others? I put an extra turn on my sash to hold Paracelsus's sword. The ruby hilt was hidden by my coat. The other blade was back in my hand. I began to tread wearily forward. As I reached the bottom of the steps I saw the narrow street went on only another few yards, then widened into a cobbled square.

Thought left me again! I began sniffing the wind like a wolf on the seek. Libussa was close by, I would have sworn. The pain of separation from her increased even as I arrived in the square. I was yearning for her again.

I love you, Libussa.

My boots struck cobbles. Salzkuchengasse opened wider still. There were leafless plane trees growing at regular intervals on both sides. There was a costermonger's and a chandler's shop open for trade, though I saw nobody in them. Yet it was the most ordinary scene I had come across in the Deeper City. And across the road from the costermonger's was a cheerfully lit inn, four storeys high. Its signboard, recently painted, went well with the homely, pleasant atmosphere of the place. The tavern was called The Friend Indeed and the sign showed one youth stretching out his hand to another, who had fallen down. The only unusual feature of that picture was that it was painted in exactly the same style, with the same rich colours, the same precision, as the ikon I had seen at Prince Miroslav's. But then, I said to myself, it could be a common mark of all Mirenburg artists, deriving from painters who came from Byzantium.

I heard laughter from within The Friend Indeed. It occurred to me that all the struggling, mystification, supernatural twiddle-twaddle, lunatic cults and high-sounding metaphysical predictions might be over for me. The tavern was ordinary enough, after all. I looked forward to calling for a stein of ale and perhaps a pie.

I paused at the door to admire the handiwork of the sign. Above the picture was the lettering of the name, and below it, in small, neater letters, picked out in white, was another commonplace line of words, found on such publicans' boards the world over. It was the name of the proprietor, an unusual one for these parts:

C.M. O'Dowd.

Chapter Fifteen

*In which I take a tankard of porter at the centre of the
world. An ordinary taverner speaks his mind.
An old friend is restored. A question of
dreams and reality. Rules of the house.*

T HIS IS DEVILISH queer, thought I, hesitating with one hand
playing upon my pommel, the other taking a firmer grip on
my sabre's hilt. I could see through the windows there was nothing
overtly sinister about the place. It was full of plainly dressed fellows
in honest homespun, in broad-skirted brown riding coats, moleskin
breeches and jackboots, bewigged, like most Mirenburgers, after
the fashion of a generation earlier than mine, with slouch hats or
tricornes and rather more ribbons and buckles than was thought
good taste by the demi-monde. But none was armed. None waited,
with leering eye, for the Ritter Manfred von Bek to come strolling
in. Indeed, all the people there, including the serving maids, were
the healthiest I had seen in the whole city. The tavern had the air of
a sanctuary rather than a trap. Yet all had agreed that the Red
O'Dowd came there a score of years since, with bloody steel to carve
a ruthless path to kingship of the Deeper City. A Hun, the Goat
Queen had said, who killed for pleasure or merely to command the
Centre. Were tavern licences so rarely granted in this Mirenburg?

I bent to pull up the flaps of my boots until they rose towards
my thighs, pulled back my hair and tidied it in a fresh knot, adjusting my neck-cloth and dusting down the rest of me. I was not
wholly satisfied by my outlook, but it was the best I could produce. Without further ado I pushed open the doors of The Friend
Indeed and, with a "good evening to ye, gentlemen," strode up to
the counter and ordered from the barman a tankard of their best,
black porter.

It was when I felt in my pockets for coin I sensed the worst danger thus far—the threat of ignominious dismissal from the premises! But luckily I at last discovered a few schillings—more than enough for a whole evening's swilling—and was at my ease again, with the pot in my fist, going to sit in an empty booth furthest from the door and nearest the stair. It was not so warm there, and the spot was unpopular, but I felt comforted with my face to the whole assembly.

The only peculiarity about those men was that they were all of about my own age; there were no youths and few above forty. They were at dice or played cards or grew animated around the dominoes. While none evidently bore arms, I began to gain an impression of soldiers (or possibly thief-takers) off duty. Taverns everywhere were patronised by their like, so I saw no special significance in that, save that I appeared to be the only stranger. The Friend Indeed possessed some of the character of an informal garrison. From what I could tell, there were no casual customers.

I was not, however, quizzed or threatened, nor given anything more than the most cursory attention. In return I showed little curiosity towards them. I was hoping Libussa was on her way, that she would soon burst through the door and greet me. My divine compulsion remained as strong as ever. I loved her.

An hour or two went by. The gaming and drinking around me was unabated, yet the atmosphere remained moderate. I took another pint of porter, which was of excellent quality, like that brewed by monks in the Low Countries and a fair match to our best German beers. I instructed a red-cheeked, buxom maid to bring me a plate of grouse pie and Muchwurst, the same as was advertised upon a board overhead. She complied. I enquired after beds. She told me she would ask the proprietor if any were available. Then, as I was eating, there came a heavy tread on the unseen stairs behind me and a second later a huge bulk filled the entrance to my booth. I put down my pie and stood as best I could between bench and board, giving a slight and unbalanced bow, for this was evidently mine host. His beard flared wildly about his great face like Jupiter's aura, red and unkempt and curly as his locks. From all this redness—for his skin, also, had something of the brewer's flush—glared two pale blue eyes. It was as if twin nuggets of ice were the core of flames.

"You'd be wanting a bed," said he. He wore a heavy leathern apron from neck to knee, and was in shirtsleeves. His arms were brawny and muscles stood out upon his entire physique, pushing against the simple linen and wool of his attire.

"I desired, Sir, to stay the night here," I said.

Looking carefully at me, he grunted. "Night? A Mirenburg night?"

"Maybe ten hours at most. Do you rent chambers, Sir?"

"We have 'em, aye." He frowned. "Most here are residents. Where are ye from, Sir?"

"From the Upper City, just lately. I'm a few days at most in the Mittelmarch. I've seen no clocks and if it's possible to tell time from those stars, I've not yet learned the trick, Sir."

"Fair enough." He seated himself on a corner of my bench. He was twice my size. A surly giant, thought I, and one best placated. "Then would ye know I'm the Red O'Dowd?"

"I saw your name upon the board outside, Sir."

He frowned again. "Ye've been travelling long, by the look of ye. And sleeping rough, eh?"

"Perforce, Sir."

"So ye'll not know much of the hostelries hereabouts?"

"This is the first I've seen, Sir."

"'Tis the only one, really, in the Deeper City. The only true tavern, at any rate. And I'm the only ordinary taverner. I give clean beds, simple food and good ale at a fair price."

"I'll vouch for the food and ale, Sir. I'm sure the bed, too, will be excellent."

He cocked his head on one side. "Most folk are feared of coming here. They think the Red O'Dowd a monster . . .

"You're large, Sir. And have a temper, if offended, eh?"

"I've an Irish temper," said he soberly. "For I am an Irishman, you know. From Kerry. But raised in Cork. The temper brought me here in the first place, on account of the Great Rebellion."

"I know it, Sir. I fought with Lafayette."

This puzzled the Red O'Dowd. "I don't remember a Froggy."

"One of Washington's greatest generals, Sir." I began to think him a kisser of the Blarney-stone.

"Ah, Sir, we're at cross purposes. Ye refer to America while I speak of Ireland. Of Cork to be precise. Or rather, to be entirely precise, of Clonakiltey and the Great Rebellion there."

"I'm unfamiliar with it, Sir."

"I forgive you, Sir. A great deal of English plotting goes to abolish the memory of Ireland's history. We took on the British and we were betrayed, Sir. That was in 1762, before ever I arrived in this accursed Limbo. Betrayed by a woman, Sir, before we could as much as raise the money for the weapons. Which caused my God-fearing father to send me for a soldier so as to escape scandal. From which, after two years of it, I deserted."

"To the French?"

"To the British, Sir, as it happens. On account of already serving with the French at the time, my father being a good Catholic man. 'Twas a troublesome and confusing period for us. It had become my ambition, even then, to settle somewhere after I'd raised the money for the purchase of an inn. One thing leading to another, and finding the British army no more congenial than the French, I resigned from that during an expedition to Wiltshire to put down the riots there. For a while after, Sir, I'll not mince words, I worked Hampstead Heath and the Great North Road as a gentleman of the toby. Whence circumstances led me abroad again and service with various Balkan peoples against the Turks, then with the Turks and Poles against the Russians. It was during one of these campaigns I became lost in the Pripet Marshes, near Pinsk. When at last I found my way out I was somewhere in this Mittelmarch. Having little hope of salvation I joined forces with a group of Ukrainians in similar circumstances to myself. For a while I lived as a rural bandit. Eventually we came to Mirenburg. Learning that the Deeper City had no decent tavern of its own, I decided to provide one. This, as you see, I eventually did."

"What, Sir? You conquered this whole district simply to establish your inn?"

"It's a well-situated inn, Sir. And it is what I wanted for myself all along. 'Tis built upon a sweetwater spring, forever fresh."

And so a mystery was explained. Certainly, it was the most mundane of solutions, yet welcome to me. I had become too used to claims of high destiny and supernatural ambition. "Well, Mr. O'Dowd," said I, "I'm mighty glad to have found you."

"I hope you'll be very comfortable, Sir," said he, "and recommend us, should you have the opportunity. There were, I discovered, certain drawbacks to the site."

"What would they be, Sir?"

"Well, Sir, save for my men and a few others like yourself, there's no trade to speak of. What's more, until recently we were subject to raids, from bandits of one kind or another, who presumably wish to take over my property. It's been troublesome for us, Sir."

"How have you maintained yourself?"

"The tavern's subsidised by our shops across the street, and by means of a small levy on local persons, whereby we guarantee to protect 'em against thieves. In that we've been successful and many hard cases have been brought to justice." The Red O'Dowd now had a melancholy air as he retailed his problems and their solutions. "I suppose you could say Fate's not been wholly unkind to me, Sir. I had hopes of finding a wife, too, and raising a sizeable family, but so far nothing's come of that ambition. There's been much talk lately, Sir, of some great gathering of stars in the heavens, which will change the fortunes of many. I live in some optimism there. Perhaps when that occurs I'll find more customers, more cash and more chance to go courting."

"You can hope, Sir. All must suffer some frustration in this world. At least you've achieved much of what you most desired."

"I don't complain, Sir, though with so many anxious to lay hands on my property 'tis not always possible to rest easy at night. I have to quiz strangers, you understand."

"I understand, Sir."

"They try every means of taking my tavern from me. Security's maintained by a force of bravos I'd rather have dismissed years since. Lord Renyard, who otherwise always seemed a decent enough feller for a fox, casts his eye on the place. He's tried to take it off me once or twice. But I've heard he's sick, possibly dead, so maybe I'll see no more trouble from that quarter. It's been quiet for some while."

"But you'll not relax your guard just yet, eh, Sir?"

"We're defended excellently, in all aspects."

"You've supernatural aid in this?"

"With God vanished from our Realm, Sir? How could you think so? I have the fish, of course. But she's not as young as she was. And the helmet's been of use, since the local people seem afraid of it. But otherwise what we've done has been done by our own efforts!"

I was now reconvinced the Grail did not exist. It was either a phantasm or it was anything a believer (even Lucifer) wished it to be. I could as easily call the tankard I was supping from a "grail." This led me to ask after Libussa. "Has a young woman called at your tavern recently, Mr. O'Dowd?" I described her and her clothing.

He shook his head. "I'd have noticed if she had, Sir, for I'm still on the lookout for a wife. Indeed, our only customer aside from yourself is a young man who'll becoming for his supper any minute, I shouldn't doubt. A Herr Foltz, I understand, from Nuremberg. A scholar interested in our old architecture. Have you heard of him, Sir?"

"The name has a familiar sound. It's some years since I was last in Germany, however."

"Just so. Well, Sir . . ." He rose ponderously. "I trust ye'll accept a pint of porter on the house."

"No doubt of it, Mr. O'Dowd. I thank you!"

He was on his feet. "And ye'll recommend my inn?"

"Enthusiastically, Sir. I find it very acceptable."

He was pleased by this and beamed. "I'm flattered by your condescension, Sir." He looked up. There was another footfall on the stairs. "Ah, here's the scholar gentleman now, Sir."

And round the corner of the booth into my line of vision, between the great bulk of the Red O'Dowd and the table, stepped a spry young fellow in a suit of deep red silk, white linen and a wig powdered the faintest of pinks. He grinned at me as he made a leg. "Enchanted, Sir."

"Delighted, Sir," said I, almost laughing aloud with my joy, for it was my Libussa, back in mannish attire in her role as Duke of Crete, and full of good cheer.

"Mind if I join you, Sir?"

"Not at all, Sir. Most welcome."

The Red O'Dowd, pleased that his guests were compatible, went to see the preparation of supper. Libussa sat herself across from me and in a low voice explained how there was no occult mystery to her disappearance. "A loose paving stone, a chute, and I was fifty foot underground. The moving flagstone was doubtless part of some antique defence. A trap for attackers. Emerging from the tunnels I simply asked directions to this inn, and here I am."

"But how did you change your costume?"

She put a finger to her lips. "My clothes were filthy after the fall, stinking of animal dung, I think, so I was anxious to change them. By luck I bumped into an old rake from the High Floors, as they call 'em. I accepted his invitation for a tête-à-tête, ate a good meal, drank some excellent wine, bumped him on the head, took some clothes and a portmanteau, borrowed his carriage and left him trussed for his wife to find. She was visiting relatives in the Lesser City. Due back tomorrow. Do you know what the time is, von Bek?"

"You should have stolen your patron's watch."

"He didn't carry one. Few do, it seems, in the Deeper City. You found your way here easily enough, eh?"

"With no difficulty, after my conversation with Lucifer."

She began to laugh and I derived considerable satisfaction in telling her the whole tale of my adventures and finished by slyly showing her the pommel of my sword. She was mightily impressed and looked at me, I thought, in a fresh light, more admiring. I doubted if I had ever been so happy. Libussa was in fine spirits. As we ate our supper she spoke lasciviously of the pleasures we should know in an hour or two. I did not question her earlier remarks concerning a period of celibacy. I felt buoyed upon scented clouds. "We'll stay here tonight," she said, "and as soon as we have the Grail, we'll be on our way. We must begin again . . ."

"The Grail isn't here, Libussa."

She pushed her plate aside. She was amused. "Of course it is."

"You've had confirmation from the Red O'Dowd?" I asked.

"He knows nothing. He's a good-hearted simpleton."

"He'd know the Grail, Libussa. He told me he has no super-natural objects here. I believe him."

"He may think he does not have it, but he is wrong!"

"Libussa, how can you know?"

"It cannot be anywhere else," she said.

Having no wish to argue with her and thus threaten the prospects of our night, I said nothing. I could only hope that in the morning, when she could not find the Grail, she would agree to return with me to Prince Miroslav's, giving up the pursuit which had already ruined the sanity of Montsorbier and Klosterheim.

A little later, having told our landlord we had become such good friends we would share a room together, to carry on our conversation there, we ascended to the top of the house. The room was large and a great window let in the light of Mirenburg's stars. They seemed clearer there than anywhere else. I stared at the huge, old suns, at the beautiful smoky colours, until Libussa seized me by the shoulders and turned me to face her. She kissed me gently upon the lips; the signal for another long celebration.

I was her lover, her son, her wife and brother. The Corinthian columns were falling. The ruins of Athens and Minos were eroded by the long wind. Roofs and walls crumbled into the sea. The fortresses of reason were besieged. Mercury cried out, face burning, body contorting, writhing as he was pulled into the sun's gravity and there consumed. *Io is drowned. Europa's hacked into rotting fragments. The Gods are withering, fading; some scream in their death throes; and Theseus grins with contemptuous bloodlust, believing he alone dismisses them. Theseus, the slayer of monsters, betrayer of women.*

I am drugged on this. If it is only dreaming, it remains more intense and pleasurable than any reality. I would dream for ever rather than return to that world of injustice and disease I've left. I become he/she and Libussa is she/he. We are one sex, one creature. We have found the path to true, mutual harmony.

If the Grail were indeed Harmony, I thought, then I had found it, after all, in this tavern at the centre of the world, where all dimensions of the multiverse (as Libussa called it) intersected, in the city called Amalorm, timeless city of the pit. Amalorm was all cities and all cities were the sum of mankind's ambition, its wisdom and its failings. Amalorm, whispered Libussa, could never be destroyed, even if her very foundations turned to dust. Amalorm could not die. *And soon, when the Concordance is here, we shall become immortal, also. We shall be immortal, you and I, von Bek. And we shall be one for ever.*

I screamed, somewhere beyond Time, as her lips and fingers touched the instrument of my body. I was burning. I was Mercury. I was Io. I was Zeus himself, dying in flames upon Mount Olympus, yet laughing at the foolishness of those who had allowed him to rule them for so long. She anointed my body. Oh, Lucifer, she anointed my body with creams and oils which bore the scents of all that was beautiful. We were a million shadows, multicoloured, faceted, of a million living men and women, plunging through the multiverse, through the richness, the densely populated spaces, the timeless places that were all times, the infinity which was the multiverse. She anointed my body with creams and oils. She anointed her own. And we flew as the witches and the warlocks of our Gothick past flew. We flew at night under the Autumn Stars and were laughing at the world. Oh, Libussa, crucible of ancient, fiery blood, inheritor of a thousand martyrdoms, pray we shall not be martyred again. In our divine frenzy we flew. Shall Daphnis be born again?

Here was Achilles brought before Lycomedes; Simplicissimus delivered of all affliction. Oh, I thought, let her prophecy be a true one so we shall see an end to lances, muskets, flags and drums, an end to the ruin which lets flow so much blood. And the blood turns to poison spreading over the whole map, destroying the roots of the Tree. Let the Tree be saved! Torquemada, enemy of flight, wrote it down in his Hexameron. Let them call it what they like. Let them say it was the Witch's Gallop and speak of hellish vengeance, but I knew it was no sin. We would be purified and become one. It was there in the parchments and the vellums of certain libraries; always there, waiting to be understood. But understanding came only through experience. *We were flying beyond the world. And the furious beast with blazing eyes and red fangs beat his club upon the Earth in a madness of frustration. Hermaphrodite steals the power, then scatters it to the winds of limbo. None shall have it! All shall have it. Within us, she is our salvation. We are whole.*

Yet beating through this triumphant wonderment of molten brass and fiery gold, of mercurial silver, was the dark temptation, the greedy Beast which lurked still in the Labyrinth, which threatened when it was confident, which scuttled and hid when challenged (so that once we thought him banished for ever) and which could destroy all we valued when we least expected it. I tried to speak of the Beast to Libussa, but she would not hear me. *We must be careful,* I said. *We must not succumb.* She laughed. *Von Bek, we shall be invulnerable, inviolable, omniscient!* I said: *But not omnipotent.*

Oh, yes, she said, *omnipotent, too . . .*

I told her I did not want such power. She was amused and stroked my head with her tender fingers. We were dreaming together. We were the same thing. We explored eternity without urgency. This was the time of our flying, glistening naked; burning like the sun; across the dark, musty heavens where the old stars gathered to die. After Daedalus helped Theseus, the engineer was imprisoned in the very Labyrinth he had built to contain the Minotaur. With his son Icarus he escaped on wings of his own invention, reaching Sicily, though Icarus perished. Pursuing Daedalus to Sicily, Minos was slain by the daughters of Cocalus. It did not matter how close to the stars we flew, but I wished she would not speak of the future, for it made me fearful. We were gliding towards a gigantic tower. It was white, a tower carved from a single, massive femur. The Bone Tower, she said. We slipped through one of the windows, like a fracture in the paleness, and here were all the kings and queens, emperors and empresses, even some gods and goddesses, who had inhabited

Earth's history, all gathered in one place. It was a Ball, held upon a vast, irregular, circular floor. They danced stiffly, constricted by their responsibility and their desire to will their dreams upon the world. The music was distant, hollow; perhaps it was the Bone Tower itself which provided the sound. They danced. I would not join them. Libussa separated from me and drifted down towards the floor. I cried out for her to return to me. I would not go down to that terrible minuet.

Was I drugged? I was in a fever of lust and monstrous images, all mingled. Libussa/Lucius, Duke/Duchess, last of a line of tormented sorcerers tracing its ancestry to Ariadne. I peered at her heavy beauty. Ariadne, or perhaps the Minotaur? Did Theseus slay from jealousy? Was there an incestuous union between Minos's son and daughter? There remained, in spite of my obsession, the sense that she was somehow flawed, as Lucifer Himself claimed to be flawed. I heard the Beast roaring. The thump of his club echoed in the Labyrinth. Those dark corridors were unknown to me. I had neither chart nor compass. I had only the Sword of Paracelsus which for so many years had protected the Father of modern science from cuckolded husbands and cheated innkeepers. Perhaps the flaw was in us all? Without it we should be angels of the first rank, or God.

She danced alone in the Bone Tower, amongst the dignified prancing of all those powerful monarchs, weaving her way amongst them, smiling up at me. She beckoned. I was foolish if I refused to follow her. Or, she seemed to say, did I lack courage, loyalty, generosity? She had brought me to life, given me more than the world. She was my Pygmalion. Where was my gratitude?

I wished to please her, to join the dance, but I could not. I reached out my hand to her and reluctantly she returned. We were one creature again. We flew away from the Bone Tower. We flew over Mirenburg and were tempted by the luring cries from below. We descended. There, in a brightly lit brothel, dead harlots beckoned. Dead harlots whispered of necrophiliac delights and again she paused, her curiosity stronger than her outrage. We entered that

Versailles of brothels. The harlots were gaming. They stood about a great wheel, marked with numbers, red and black, and within that wheel was a wretched human creature, flung like a puppet from one numbered section to the next until at last the wheel stopped. If the person on the wheel remained alive, they could claim whatever prize had been set upon their number, or could elect to take another turn, risking death against the prospect of a greater reward. The harlots described the enormity of the potential winnings. Their bones peeped through rags of flesh. They pressed us to join the game. They pushed us towards the wheel. Again Libussa would readily have taken the chance but I was the one to pull back. She would see what degradation there was in the experience, but she could not go without me. She was contemptuous of me in my refusal to take the risk. I lacked ambition, she said. It was enough, I said, that I flew. So we returned to the centre of Time and Space, to tranquillity and ecstasy at The Friend Indeed.

In the morning I found my breeches and shirt freshly washed and ironed by O'Dowd's own laundress. The Sword of Paracelsus throbbed in the cupboard where I had placed it. Libussa did not touch it. Evidently she had already felt the shock from the blade. She crouched in front of the opened cupboard, staring at the eagle as it flew round and round, glaring at us and voicing his silent shriek, so full of insane rage he would kill whatever came within reach of his poised claws. "Whoever it was gave you this," she said, "and perhaps it was Lucifer as you say, not only trusted you to fulfil your destiny, but was also a true friend to us. All we require now is the Cup. Miroslav's tincture is prepared. The Concordance is a matter of hours away."

"You've heard, then, from Prince Miroslav, Madam?"

She pretended vagueness. "Did I say aught of it?"

"How have you seen him? I thought he refused to enter the Lesser City, let alone the Deeper."

She frowned. Her expression suggested she thought me stupid and coarse, or maybe my own self-doubt supplied the interpretation. "We must breakfast," she said. As she strode for the door of our room I attempted to stop her (perhaps because I was unwilling to end the spell of the previous night). "Madam, you'll go mad if you do not relent in this matter!"

"We must have the Grail," she said. "Do you really think O'Dowd maintains this peace by the employment of a handful of pickaroons? The Grail makes its own harmony. Now, use your nose. Sniff it out. You must try!"

"Madam, I repeat to you—I'm not bred as a Grailhound, and I suppose I lack your terrier's instinct. I desire no more than to be what we become when we're together. 'Tis more than any human creature could fairly expect!"

She glared at me. "You speak of the means, not the end. The horse, Sir, is not the destination. Far more is promised."

"And feared by me, Madam. You know how to recognise the Beast, and you've shown me how to recognise Him also, but you're reluctant, it seems, to renounce Him!"

"Is that what you fear?" She was honestly curious.

"Aye, Madam."

"You have a strange perspective on this, little von Bek." She paused, her hand upon the door latch. She frowned down at me, studying me. "The power I see is for the commonality. But much must be undertaken and something sacrificed before it can pass to us—and from us to the world at large. That is not the ambition of the Beast."

I was reassured. "I apologise, Madam. Let's to breakfast."

I left both my swords in our room and stepped out onto the gallery. From this a stair led down to the public saloon where the Red O'Dowd's men were already at their beef and small ale. Beyond the windows was a blackness made more intense by the cheery lights which burned within. As we stepped down, the Red O'Dowd came out of his back rooms with a plate of bread and butter. He no longer wore his apron but had on a good coat of black broadcloth, black breeches, white stockings and front-tied shoes. Were it not for his great size and flaring red beard and hair, he would have resembled a respectable parson. He said that he hoped we had slept well. He was jovial. Business, he said, was improving. He looked forward to a better season. He pointed into one of the booths. We could not see who was there.

"A third customer!" said O'Dowd. "Good luck comes in threes!"

Now we had moved so that the new visitor was visible to us. Sitting on the bench, picking with his knife at the fat of a small ham, was Klosterheim. He looked up at me. He might as well have been the Spectre of Death himself with his hollow eyes and sunken cheeks. "Good morning to thee, von Bek," said he formally.

I was too furious to contain myself. I raised my voice and my fist. "You killed a harmless creature, Klosterheim, when you killed the Goat Queen. I'll not forgive you. Neither can I forget what you've become or whom you've allied yourself with. By God, Sir, you had better leave this tavern or risk my steel in your heart."

Klosterheim shrugged. "As for the latter, I'm used to it. You have no right, Sir, to order me from a public ordinary."

The Red O'Dowd loomed up behind. "Watch your tongue, Sir, if you please," he said to me. "There are rules to this house. The first is that O'Dowd says who stays and who leaves. The second's that all are welcome who behave themselves here, gentlemen or ladies. The third is—anyone who starts a brawl shall be at once ejected." He paused, picking me up in the most insulting manner, by the back of my shirt, and turning me so that I was staring directly into his beard. "So do not make me eject you, Sir."

He lowered me gently and again I was standing, on my own feet. "Sir, this man's a murderer. He slew the Goat Queen."

"The little white lady who made such a fuss? Well, if that's true, Sir, it would not be a pleasant thing to have done at all. But we have only your word for it, Sir. And it's the essence of Law (as I well know, having been tried by it more than once) to need material substantiation, Sir, in the way of evidence."

"He tore her throat out with his teeth. The blind girl saw it."

O'Dowd pursed his lips and looked thoughtfully at me. "Did she indeed, Sir?"

Klosterheim uttered a terrible laugh.

Chapter Sixteen

In which house rules are broken. An infestation and a
visitation. Vermin destroyed. The Red O'Dowd's fish.
Some useful attributes of a Magic Sword.

CLEARLY THE RED O'Dowd misliked Klosterheim's expression of humour as much as I did, but the Irishman intended
to maintain his principle. He glared severely at the gaunt man. "I
welcome good customers, but I'm dreadful weary of conflict, so
I'll thank ye all to remember your breeding in my house."

Klosterheim snapped shut his mouth and glowered, sulking.
Libussa and myself, watched by O'Dowd's men, went to occupy a
booth nearer the door. The men's expressions were mild and neutral, more from a habit of composure, I would guess, than from
natural disposition. They returned their attention with apparent
casualness to their beef and eel pies. We took a light meal, of
bread, cheese and bones, with port and water for our drink. We
ate sparingly, sensing tension. When the Red O'Dowd returned
he displayed disappointment on his great face as if he were revis-
ing his expectations of increased business. He looked hard at
his front door, then came towards us. "Are your weapons still in
your room, gentlemen?" When we nodded he continued: "I'm
re-introducing an old rule of mine, given the situation between
you three. If you'll be so kind as to hand all weapons into the
house, I promise their return when ye leave."

Though reluctant to relinquish the Paracelsian sword, I con-
curred. At that moment the door opened and in came a man and
woman, their heavy travelling cloaks giving the impression they
had just stepped off the Dresden diligence, though we had heard
neither coach nor horses outside. They made a great display of
dusting themselves while the woman called in a high voice for the

landlord. O'Dowd, frowning still, strode forward. "I'm he. Welcome to The Friend Indeed."

I was trying for a glimpse of a face within one of those hoods, but without success. I chewed the meat from my last bone and placed it on the trencher with the others.

"Have you rooms, my man?" asked the woman.

"Aye, me lady." He looked them up and down. "Do you bear weapons under them cloaks?"

The hood went back at this and the shortest figure was revealed as von Bresnvorts (certainly no lady) bringing up a carbine and levelling it at the O'Dowd.

The landlord's men were suddenly no longer at the benches but arranged, almost in military ranks, behind the tables. Each had a pistol and we were all targets. The O'Dowd grumbled to himself. "I've grown too damned lazy. Are ye all together?"

"I think so," said I, "given the circumstances." I stood up in the booth. Von Bresnvorts darted a grin of triumph.

"You'll run with the winning side, after all, eh, von Bek?" said he. "Well, maybe our offer is no longer open to you!" The pistol trembled in his hand, in anticipation of murderous fulfilment, I suspected, rather than fear.

"Von Bek?" said the O'Dowd in surprise. "Same as in the story?"

"It depends, Sir, what story you mean." I stepped boldly up, as if I meant to search him. One of his men cried: "Touch him and you'll have a ball through your head, no matter who dies after!" I lowered my hands with a shrug.

"I'm surprised that a von Bek's descended to mere tavern swaddling. We've little gold here, man." The Red O'Dowd sighed.

"You've something far more valuable, eh, Sir?" Klosterheim rose and began to saunter towards us. Meanwhile von Bresnvorts' companion stripped back his hood. It was one of Montsorbier's men. "And that's what we're here for, Sir."

The O'Dowd seemed genuinely puzzled. "More valuable? And you'll leave if ye have it?"

"Just so." Von Bresnvorts motioned with his popper. "Thus we'll all save the expenditure of powder and shot."

"Then ye'd better tell me what it is, man." The Irishman's voice dropped and grew dangerous.

"The Grail, of course!" Klosterheim grew impatient. "The Holy Grail. It's here at the Centre, where the lines converge. The maps all agree. It's here in your tavern, Sir, as you must know! Give it over and we'll end the matter."

The Red O'Dowd had begun to grin; his eyes remaining wary. "You're all fooled, if ye think that! Ask him"—a thumb in my direction—"his family's supposed to protect it. In turn the Grail protects them. If it's here, von Bek brought it with him. What madness makes ye think I possess a holy relic of that magnitude? Should I risk such damnation?"

"God has abandoned you! You risk nothing!" Von Bresnvorts' weak face was suddenly afraid, his eyes shifting everywhere, from Klosterheim, to O'Dowd's men, to me and to Libussa. She stood with one foot on her bench, still in the booth, sipping port, her eyes narrowed. "We'll fetch the chalice for ourselves. All you need do is tell us where it is. Will that relieve your anxiety?"

"I have none," said the O'Dowd heavily. He grew slowly angry. "What manner of vermin are ye?" He glanced at Klosterheim's skeletal figure, at von Bresnvorts' decrepit flesh, at the soldier's unhealthy features. "Methodists, are ye? Baptists? Or worse? What d'ye want with the Grail?"

"That need not be your business, landlord." Klosterheim took the dragoon pistol from the militiaman and pointed it up, under the O'Dowd's beard. "We'll take responsibility for it. When we leave you'll be none the worse off. There'll have been no violence."

"You'd be wise, Sir, to follow his instructions, Sir," said I to our host. "Klosterheim's killed just lately and you know what rats become when the blood's in their saliva. They like to strike again."

"If, von Bek, we're to be allies," von Bresnvorts gestured with his own heavy handpiece, "I'll thank you to be less insulting."

Klosterheim did not care. He quivered. He had a greed for the Grail beyond anyone's.

I had knocked Klosterheim with my shoulder and was diving

for von Bresnvorts' barker in the moment while Lucifer's ex-captain was still between the gun and the Irishman! Grabbing it from his soft hand, I brought the butt down heavily on von Bresnvorts' neck and then his nose. He screamed and nursed his face. Klosterheim foolishly turned the dragoon pistol at me, rather than keeping it on O'Dowd—and the Check was over. There was movement from one side of the great taproom to the other. The O'Dowd ran for the gallery. His men barred the doors and slammed shutters tight against windows. Libussa was now atop the table, smacking her pot hard on Klosterheim's skull, and the pistol went off in my hand with a deafening bang! The militia-man was flung back across the tables, a great hole blossoming in his chest. He screamed.

As if to answer that scream there was suddenly a monstrous heavy thump against the whole outside wall of the tavern. Another. Everything shook. And another—as if a cannonade were loosed against us, or gunpowder exploded by the keg-full. Thump! A pistol in one huge red hand and an old-fashioned spontoon in the other, O'Dowd went to peer through the window. Libussa had Klosterheim's sword. His pistol was on the floor.

"May we assume, Sir," said the O'Dowd in some exasperation to me, "that both you gentlemen are with us, and that the other three represent our enemies outside?"

"You may, Sir."

The dying militiaman screamed on. "Save me, master! Save me!" It was unclear whom he called for.

Von Bresnvorts, white with anger, resembled an ancient, petu-lant schoolboy. Klosterheim, half dazed, sat down suddenly upon the table, Libussa still above him. Clutching his head he brought his eyes up to look at her.

Weapons appeared from trunks, hidden panels, under floors. The whole place, it was now clear, was a bristling arsenal. The hard-faced pickaroons took familiar positions here and there about the tavern. O'Dowd himself continued to peer out, a pistol in his right hand, the spontoon under his arm. "How many d'ye think?"

"Hard to say," I told him. "Maybe fifty. More. They'll have been gathering recruits for some while, I'll be bound. It's in the nature of such creatures."

"What creatures, Sir?"

"You described them yourself, Sir. Vermin, Sir. Devil worshippers of the lowest kind. Cruel murderers, every one. Blood ritual and torture's their sport."

"I take your meaning, Sir." The Red O'Dowd wiped a finger almost delicately across his lips, as if to clean them. "That sort's always come to Amalorm. Yet they never learn. 'Tis—though ye'd not think it—the last place they should be." He called instructions to his men. The tavern became a fortress within moments. He himself was freshly animated. I suspected his vocation was more soldier than innkeeper, though he might have wished it otherwise. He was pretty cheerful as he positioned his men here and there, sending some to the upper floors. Most lights were dimmed. While Libussa presented a newly borrowed pistol at Klosterheim and von Bresnvorts, I joined the O'Dowd at the window.

There were figures scuttling everywhere across the square. The shops were shuttered. "I've more men there," said the O'Dowd. "We'll catch 'em in a crossfire as soon as we want to." Our enemies did indeed have the appearance of vermin, perhaps because of their numbers. There seemed a couple of hundred at least. The pack moved forward in concert suddenly and I had an impression of ruined faces, bestial hands, twisted bodies, ragged clothes—men and women both. But Montsorbier was not with them.

Another *thump* as the pack collided with the inn. The Red O'Dowd shivered. "A disgusting assembly, Sir. The worst I've seen. They've recruited every degenerate in the Deeper City." His face showed his contemptuous hatred as their squealing began. We could even smell them, a scent like long-neglected wounds.

I glanced back. Libussa wrinkled her nose, not so used to that battlefield stink as I. She put a hand to her face, looking as if she might vomit. The gesture made von Bresnvorts confident (he was fool enough to ignore the fact he was trapped with us) and he lunged for her pistol, which went off. Von Bresnvorts was struck in the stomach and doubled up, croaking like a frog. Blood and bile streamed from his lips. Libussa looked down in almost uncomprehending dismay. Klosterheim shifted his foot so that the stuff should not strike his boot, but otherwise he made no move. He was aware his position was dangerous. Von Bresnvorts tried to speak through the filth in his mouth. His eyes rolled up into his head. His features writhed.

"See if he carried powder and shot on him," said I to her. "Then reload your pistol."

This rallied her as I'd seen no woman rally before. I was not surprised, for I trusted her courage. She conquered her horror and even as von Bresnvorts fell to the boards she had ripped back his cloak to find the horn at his belt. She pulled that and the pouch free, setting foot against his still-living body so that she could tug the harder.

"For the love of God!" he croaked. "Spare me a moment, Madam, to die in!"

One last eruption and he was quiescent—not dead, for that would take a while longer, but in a death faint preserving him from the worst of his agonies. Expertly, Libussa began to reload the dragoon pistol.

Another great *THUMP*.

"Discharge!" merrily shouted the Red O'Dowd, and off went the muskets from every aperture and back fell the mob, holed and bloody, but still squeaking. I had seen nothing like it before, even amongst the crazed Indians of the Americas who chewed some kind of root prior to battle, thus becoming unaware of pain or fear, uncomprehending even of their own deaths.

Another volley. More fell into the cobbled street around the horse trough. Then, from the opposite side, came a further rattling of musketry. Down went some more. They turned as a mass and began to run at the source of this fresh annoyance. And there came a second wave of leaden balls to smash them to the ground. At that rate, thought I, there would be no real work left to do. Montsorbier was a fool to think he could succeed with such an attack. Those people were almost all unarmed, save for a few butcher's knives, flenchers and clubs.

"Discharge!" cried the grinning O'Dowd. "They shall not deceive an old soldier so easy, Sir," he said to me. He chuckled. "I've been at this for twenty years and learned every weakness of my own defences and covered 'em. They'll be on the roof no doubt—and this simply a diversion. Well, I've plenty to greet 'em when they've made the climb!"

Off went the muskets again and down went the vermin. And soon I heard terrible cries from above. In ones and twos, then in threes and fours, flaming figures dropped into the street. The Red O'Dowd regarded them with an expression of deep satisfaction, much as a craftsman might look upon a finished artefact.

But then there came a sound from underfoot. Still, the Red O'Dowd was unperturbed. Klosterheim glanced down, his expression mysteriously knowing. Had they mined their way in? Were there tunnels?

"Sewers, Sir," said the O'Dowd. "A warren of 'em. There is a junction of some kind here, because of our spring and the Rätt I'd guess. So they all think they can strike from there. I'm surprised they got so far. There must be scores of them!"

"You had men waiting?"

"Not men, Sir. Oh, no!" He winked at me, turning his head to look once more out of the window. He pursed his lips, stroking his red beard, half-smiling as corpses piled one upon the other and blazing bodies, arms still waving, plummeted on top of those. It was grisly. It was essentially a massacre. But it was of their own doing. The O'Dowd sighed. "This reminds me of Culloden, Sir. Were you ever there?"

"You mistake me for an older man, Sir. That was in forty-five. I cannot believe you witnessed the battle either!"

"I heard it from my father. His brother joined what he saw as the Catholic cause, the Stuart cause. He was with Bonnie Prince Charlie when all those poor boys were mown down. He did not run at the guns as they did. There was no point to it, he said. Charlie was drunk. Insensible, my father said. Half the time he looked the wrong way. He had to be propped back on his horse, wig all askew, fingers seeking the brandy kept in a great flask on his pommel. Well, Sir, me uncle went back to Kinsale. He said he would rather starve in the Famine than be harvested like corn." The O'Dowd chatted easily, as if relaxed with a pot of ale at his own board. Then he was alert suddenly, cocking his ear.

He grew uneasy. "They should not be up this far." He called across the room. "Grigorief—take three of the lads to check all's well in the cellars!"

Musket in hand, the Ukrainian ran to obey.

Libussa, casually directing her pistol at Klosterheim, since our former ally now sat at the bench, sipping an abandoned glass of wine, crossed to where I was still positioned at the window. "What's afoot down there?" she asked.

"Attack from the sewers, Sir," said the O'Dowd, who still believed her a youth. "I was telling Herr von Bek—they always think I haven't defended that point. But 'tis the best defended of all!"

The violence of the frontal attack was subsiding under the steady musketry. Fewer bodies slumped, blazing, onto those below. The storm was apparently subsiding.

Then Grigorief came bursting up, face wild with astonishment. "They've breached the alestore! The wall's giving way!"

"Impossible!" cried the Red O'Dowd. "Oh, I'm an idiot for being so complacent. This is what brings down good men and empires both!" He ran for the stairs to the cellars and I ran with him. But he was ahead of me by a good few yards and had turned in the torchlight, coming back, face grim and pale, to bellow for reinforcements. "Send half the lads to me here!"

"Is it bad?" asked I.

"Bad as can be, Sir. They've killed or drugged my fish."

I had no time to ask him to explain that fish. Either it was a nickname or an unfamiliar piece of cant. There were yells from further into the cellars. A ragged musketade, more shouts, metal against metal. Down the steps, precise as Hessians, came more of the O'Dowd's men. He directed them forward. I was an obstruction so I started back up again. "I'll fetch my weapon."

Libussa was there as I came up. "I'll bring you a sword," I said. "I have two."

Up I went to the gallery where pickaroons were calling out for more shot and powder. The serving maids brought this as readily as they hauled ale. I entered our room and from the closet drew Lucifer's gift to me. The pommel was duller and the eagle could not be seen (it appeared to have seasons, that pommel) but yet it pulsed faintly. I picked up my sabre for Libussa. Back down the stairs, where Klosterheim glanced at me. He ate nothing as a rule, yet now he was folding his mouth upon a pork bone, as if he could only take nourishment when enough were dying around him. I had the impulse to run him through at that moment. He sensed my hatred. For a second time, he laughed.

This sound was drowned by a scream.

A window at the front was bulging. The scream came from several throats. Half a dozen creatures had hurled themselves forward at once and were through the glass, almost into the tavern. The O'Dowd soldiers sent concentrated fire into those unsavoury bodies. The mass fell back. Shutters were slammed and secured. Into the fresh silence, Klosterheim continued to laugh.

I ran on, back down the cellar stairs. Down into a stink of gunpowder and sewage, of rush torches, fermenting hops and sour wine. In the darkness ahead I saw the flicker of lights, the flash of guns. Libussa made herself visible and I handed her the sabre. "Hard to say if Montsorbier's goal is the Grail or us."

"Both," she said. "I'm certain. Everything must combine. And he must get hold of the tincture, too. Though it's possible he has his own concoction. Or the girl has it. But the tincture's useless without the Cup to put it in. The Sword"—she glanced down at my blade—"will give additional power. 'Tis perfection if the ritual's performed accurately. That is why I grow so impatient! Von Bek, I've half a mind to let Montsorbier through—simply in the hope he'll lead us to the Grail. Or must we torture Klosterheim?"

"I doubt it's possible," I said, "to torture Klosterheim. What's more, I doubt he knows more than we do."

The Red O'Dowd came by cursing. "Where's my damned fish?"

The musketeers had fallen back by a yard or two. They still fired, but the fire was now returned. Here were all Montsorbier's men. He had put his best troops into that branch of the attack, and with good reason, it seemed. The O'Dowd's men were going down, one or two at a time. Soon there would not be enough to defend the whole tavern against a major breach.

We were grouped in a beer cellar now, with great casks stacked on all sides of us, some against the walls, some on free-standing racks. I felt colder, ill-smelling air and could just see ahead to the far wall, where it had been burst in as if by a gigantic fist. Through the gap leapt armed men, covered by fire from behind.

O'Dowd was muttering to himself. "Maybe our only real chance is to blow up the whole damned cellar. What a terrible waste of ale. I never thought it could come to this. Who leads 'em, von Bek?"

"One of France's best captains," I told him. "A seasoned veteran of both battle and revolution. Montsorbier."

"He's a good soldier." The Irishman lifted his loaded horse-pistol to scratch his red nose. "Especially since he's found a way to overwhelm my fish."

"The fish, is it some sort of war machine?" I asked.

The O'Dowd laughed as if I'd told a deliberate joke. "Of course, Sir! Of course it is! Oh, ho, ho, ho!" And tears started in his eyes and rolled down his red cheeks like marbles on plush. "Ye've a keen wit, Sir!"

I could only wish the jest were intentional. I was still none the wiser on the matter of his fish. More muskets barked; more accurate retaliation came. They had stalemate, it seemed. Then a voice called out from within and I saw a great white kerchief waving on a sword. "Parley!" cried Montsorbier. "Parley, Sir!"

"What the devil have ye done with my fish, Sir?" called back the Red O'Dowd.

"He'll furnish the victory feast now, Sir!" Montsorbier was elated. That storming and breaching was as much to his taste as it was to the O'Dowd's. I saw him now in the torchlight, his black coat buttoned across his chest, his bicorne side-on, a tricolour cockade freshly sported, a Revolutionary sash about his waist. He seemed to have restored himself as Klosterheim had not. He lifted a sabre to his smiling face in salute and the white flag was waved again. "Parley with us, Sir, I beg you. All we ask is your Cup!"

"Cup?" exclaimed O'Dowd in some annoyance. "That damned Cup again. Von Bek, will you tell him I have no damned Cup!"

"The Red O'Dowd has no damned Cup!" cried I.

"Apart from the pots and tankards in my taproom!" added the Irishman, shouting louder than myself.

Montsorbier was remorseless. "Give it up, Sir, and we'll retire. Let von Bek and his companion bring it to us. They'll be hostages for the rest of you."

"He wants you now, von Bek!" The Red O'Dowd winked. "They must feel they have a strong position. Don't they think I'd know if I had charge of the Holy Grail? Eh, von Bek? Your family guards it, not mine . . ."

"And searches for it when it's lost, I'm told. Ironic it should fall to me, an atheist and a sinner, to fulfil that search!" I was contemptuous of them all.

"Well, Sir, God chooses us for strange tasks. And hides His greatest treasures in queer places, so the priests used to tell me."

"Make haste, gentlemen," called Montsorbier. "Do you give us the Grail or must we fight on?"

"What have ye done to my fish, Sir?" cried the Red O'Dowd. "Where is she?"

"Ready for cooking, Sir!" Still under the white flag, Montsorbier began retreating. I wanted to take another potshot at him and was about to borrow a gun when suddenly, from a corner of the cellar, there sparked a candle brighter than the rest. The flame grew suddenly stronger, dazzling us. Libussa cursed and put both hands to her eyes.

The Red O'Dowd was jubilant, on his feet and grinning. A shot went off and a bullet almost caught him. I pulled him down. "What is it, O'Dowd?"

"Why, Sir, 'tis our old helmet," he said, "though I'm not sure it can achieve much against a seasoned warrior like Mr. Montsorbier."

The light shaded from gold to silver, spreading until it entirely filled our cellar. The Red O'Dowd beamed, as if at a friend.

"Who does it belong to?" I asked in astonishment.

"It's the property of us all, I suppose, Sir. I don't rightly know. 'Tis just our old helmet . . . Does it not make ye feel peaceful, Sir, and full of joy?"

I could now just detect the source of the light, from a high shelf above the barrels. It was apparently, as O'Dowd had said, no more than a simple helmet, of the sort the French called *chapelle-de-fer*; this one of steel studded with brass; an ordinary enough war-hat, like an upturned porringer.

Now Libussa started forward, her eyes shining. "Surely you recognise it, von Bek? Surely you know the true nature of your helmet, O'Dowd?"

All at once the Irishman began to laugh at himself. "Aye, Sir! Of course! Is it the Holy Grail?"

"Aye," she said sardonically, "that is what it is."

"There's the reason," continued the O'Dowd, "why 'tis so elusive. But what's it doing in a common tavern?" He put his hand on her shoulder as she reached towards it. "Don't try to handle it, Herr Foltz. 'Tis inclined to bite anyone who tries."

Frustrated, she turned to me. "You could take it, von Bek."

"But I don't choose to," I told her. "I might well be the only one of us who can handle the Grail—I'd believe it now, I suppose—but I'm also the only one who has no interest in it. Why not let it remain where it is, undisturbed to the end of Time?"

She fumed and was grim. "If you love me, von Bek, you will take that Cup down now!"

I was about to go forward at her bidding when, with a great roar, Montsorbier's men pushed another yard or two into the cellars and were forced back. Montsorbier knew the significance of that light! I could not see him, but I could hear him, cheering his men on. There was more musket-fire, then silence. Both defenders and attackers were so blinded they could no longer see to fight. The entire warren of cellars was one shimmering mass of intense pale gold and silver. The silence was such it almost formed a sound of its own; perhaps a sound from within ourselves. There were no human voices; nobody moved.

Then, suddenly, the light was gone. The Red O'Dowd, quick to take his advantage, for he alone knew the properties of his "helmet," cried: "Forward!" and our own people charged as they fired. I saw Montsorbier's white face. I saw him fall back from the pile of rubble he had been standing on. His militiamen were running. I could hear their boots striking the water of the sewers, heard them splashing and wading and Montsorbier's angry shout. "It cannot harm you! 'Tis what we came for!"

Uttering some kind of hideous war-shout from the back of his throat, the O'Dowd let off his pistol in the general direction of Montsorbier. Then I heard someone screaming in the distant tunnels. It was a ghastly sound.

"At last," said the O'Dowd in tones of deep satisfaction. "My fish!"

We were into the sewers ourselves now, chasing them back. Libussa and myself remained close to the O'Dowd, who had the lamp. We heard echoes. Montsorbier was close to weeping as he begged his men to resume the attack. A couple of twists and turns and we were in a high vaulted sewer with about four inches of water coursing around our legs. The screaming continued, though it was not from the same gallery. It was persistent and horrible.

The Red O'Dowd waved on his men. "Follow 'em to the surface and find how they entered. I must deal with my fish."

The three of us took a tunnel to the left. The gallery grew wider and taller—ten men could have stood shoulder to shoulder across it—and ahead was one of Montsorbier's men, caught in our lamp's light, flopping and screaming still. Then he was up out of the water, as if wrenched into the dark air by a great hand, and flung forcefully against the wall. His body crashed into the filthy water. He still lived, still sobbed, but almost every bone was broken.

Something made a sucking noise.

Eyes waved on stalks overhead, peering at us with no more, it seemed, than mild curiosity. The Red O'Dowd grinned in relief. "Are you unharmed, my darling? What did they do to ye?"

"Oh, Mother of God!" said Libussa. "'Tis a gigantic crayfish!"

It was nothing else. Up came the Sword of Paracelsus in my hand. Instinct urged me to hack at the thing, but it seemed docile when it heard the Red O'Dowd's voice. Slowly, with almost delicate movements of its claws, it began to eat its victim until at length the man's cries ceased.

"They must have drugged her," said O'Dowd. "Or lured her off. She looks fine now. What d'ye think, Sir?"

"I've never seen a healthier fish, Sir," said I.

"Your Mr. Montsorbier's a cunning strategist." The O'Dowd was admiring. "He's the first to get past her."

"He'll not forget this campaign." Libussa was amused.

The crayfish clacked her claws against the sides of the tunnel and the Red O'Dowd made a sound with his tongue which seemed to imitate her. In this way they conversed for a minute or two.

The O'Dowd sighed deeply. "She's not harmed. They doubtless sent one of their number in ahead. They'd have packed him so full of opium it made the fish drowsy. A good scheme, eh? He's a clever man. Poison your advance guard and in turn poison the fish. Ha!" The Irish giant rubbed at his beard. "Well now, there's not much to be doing here. The cellar wall shall have to be built up and strengthened, but otherwise we shall simply wait and see. I cannot stop your Montsorbier from poisoning my fish, but I can be better prepared for him in future."

"Did you never realise it could only be the Grail giving off such a light?" asked Libussa.

"Sir, there were piles of old armour and weapons, at least a hundred years out of date, when we arrived." The Red O'Dowd continued to be puzzled. "I suppose I should feel honoured . . ."

There came a keening shout and several of Montsorbier's party, cut off from the rest, were rushing at us from a side tunnel, blades raised to strike. To defend myself I raised the Sword of Paracelsus, hearing the battering of the eagle's wings within the globe. I parried and thrust two-handed, so fast it seemed to me the sword itself did the lion's share of the work, and when it was done there was more fresh meat for the crayfish. As I sheathed the sword, the Red O'Dowd looked at me in some wonderment and Libussa, too, wore a strange expression. "There were five of them," she said.

"I learned my fighting techniques with the Tatars," I boasted.

"You quartered 'em all in the space of ten or fifteen seconds," said the Red O'Dowd. "I've fought Tatars, Sir. Even they take longer than that, with all their skill. You're a master swordsman, Sir!"

"I assure you I'm no such thing." I scarcely remembered the encounter. The evidence of it, however, was grisly.

"Then 'tis a master *sword*," said she very softly.

I was in no doubt on that score. We waded slowly back along the sewers until we climbed through the breached wall. The Red O'Dowd's men already worked to shore it up.

"The fish was a little drowsy," he told them, "but she's fine now."

Libussa looked at the shelf where we had seen the helmet. In the darkness it was impossible to tell if it was still there. The Red O'Dowd chuckled. "I told you that helm's elusive. You never know where she'll reveal herself. Or when."

He lived so casually with his marvels I was forced to wonder if it was my idea of reality that was lacking.

Until now, I thought, it had been far too moderate.

Chapter Seventeen

In which madness is apparent in more than one of us.
"The Grail draws all threads together." An attempt
at amnesty. Klosterheim's fury. A fresh attack.
Intervention from the heavens.
Imitation of Lucifer.

K LOSTERHEIM HAD COMPLETED his meal in the taproom; his
plate was piled high with clean bones. "Montsorbier was
sure he'd succeed," he said casually. "He recruited every creature
in Mirenburg which Hell had abandoned; every wretched laudanum swallower, every low pickaroon who resisted Lord Renyard's
rule. Enough scum, he thought, to flow over everything and
drown you in filth." He looked upon von Bresnvorts' contorted
corpse. "This one lacked character. He was bound to fail." Klosterheim nodded to himself. His body rocked for a few moments,
then he took himself in charge and glanced up at me, still
chewing.

"Did Montsorbier have a further plan?" I asked. "You must see
it's now in your interest to reveal it."

Klosterheim sighed. "I am abandoned by all! Even human allies
desert me!"

"'Tis you, Sir, who turned traitor, when you thought your
ambitions better served elsewhere. You were never a real rival to
your master Satan." Libussa bristled with angry contempt.
"You've played every side now. And every card you've put on the
table has been too low! All you held were Pride and Foolish
Dreams, when you thought you had Aces and Queens. Is that not
plain to you?"

"He fully expected to win." I presumed Klosterheim spoke of
Montsorbier. "He had the whole collection bottled up, he said,

and the bottle perfectly positioned. Aesthetical, he said, as well as supernatural, a perfection and symmetry. But as for myself . . ."

"The Grail draws all threads together." Libussa spoke under her breath.

"I have great power," said Klosterheim dreamily. "Power I've not yet deigned to use. I did my best to be like the rest of you, but in doing so I lost my way. My main fear's that I lack a core. My soul's been in and out of this body so many times it might have grown threadbare. I thought it might regenerate if I joined the commonality . . ."

"What, Klosterheim? You sought to emulate Everyman." I laughed.

Klosterheim pursed his lips. "I should not have let von Bresnvorts kill his aunt. It put everything out of kilter . . ."

"Your mistake was to slay the Goat Queen, Sir. You indulged your hellish bloodlust at the very moment you might have saved yourself! You let the Beast overwhelm you. In that sense you emulate Lucifer. He knew what it meant to be both more and less than human." I was grim. By slaughtering the old woman he had lost the sympathy I once felt.

"I have the flaw," said Klosterheim seriously.

"We all have it, Sir." Libussa looked towards the cellar, whence came a great banging and scraping as the men shored our defences.

The Red O'Dowd, dusty and soaked to the knees, came up the stairs and into the taproom. He wiped his face with a cloth, calling to us. "Can we expect 'em back soon, gentlemen?"

"While the Grail's here." Klosterheim offered him a corrupt grin. Perhaps because all initiative was now taken from him, Klosterheim had gone quite mad. He pulled more cold bones towards him. He had gathered them off every table.

The Red O'Dowd was impatient. "Well, I cannot give 'em what's not mine. 'Twas here before I came—that and the fish and the spring. 'Tis an implicit feature of the tavern."

"Eh?" mocked Libussa. "Is this inn a shrine? A chapel on the site of a Christian miracle?"

"I would remind ye, Sir," the O'Dowd spoke with dignity, "that you give offence to some of us here, who remain good Christians, even though we lack the benefit of priest or Church."

"God's gone from this world, Sir," she said.

"That appears to be the case, aye," he agreed. "Yet I was brought up in a certain religion and see no reason to abandon it, for the virtues remain. And, besides, 'twas Christ taught us, not His Father."

"So you remain a good Catholic, O'Dowd!" Klosterheim selected the largest bone. Half-cooked meat hung from it. He nibbled. "Well, we all button ourselves into roles, eh? We're both anachronisms, Sir."

The Red O'Dowd misliked any affiliation suggested by that ex-servant of Hell. He glowered at Klosterheim. "You may be abandoned by Satan, Sir, and I abandoned by God, but that does not put us in the same cart, nor even upon the same road."

"There's only one road now, Sir." Klosterheim grinned around his bone. "Or shall be in a day hence. And it's my road, O'Dowd, not yours."

The great Irishman was dismissive. "Your Time's past, Sir. And I'm not pleased with you. You helped bring disturbance to my house and I'll see you tried and punished when this business is settled!"

Klosterheim fixed insouciant eyes upon his feast. "I'll kill you first," he muttered.

There was another shock against the tavern's front. Lamps and candles danced on every wall. "Muskets to positions!" yelled the O'Dowd. There came a weird wailing from the street, and brighter light. O'Dowd turned his furious face from the window. "They've fired the chandler's!"

Musketry still sounded from the various positions and wretched leprous creatures still collapsed one on the other. It was as if every prison, plague hospital and grave in the world had been opened and its contents disgorged upon us. That they were living men and women and not undead ghouls was both a comfort and a dismay. Montsorbier recruited the hopeless, the powerless, the weak. What could he be promising them? The same as Robespierre? A heaven on earth? It made me wonder if, without dreams, mankind would continue at all! What ancient genius invented the myth of the improving future?

They rushed mindlessly now upon our walls. They screamed, they giggled and they wailed. O'Dowd leapt from taproom to gallery to roof, half mad with horror. His tavern had never been attacked thus. He had thought his wars over. Now he realised peace had been merely a lull.

Libussa and I took up muskets and went to the shutters, firing into the Mass. Montsorbier was nowhere in evidence. This attack lacked a sense of strategy and seemed merely a vengeful display of power. Montsorbier had doubtless decided to destroy us if he could not capture what he thought we guarded. Klosterheim within had grown increasingly amused. With every wave, with every shaking of our walls, he laughed as if he had some secret denied the rest.

Then, of a sudden, there was stillness again. Peering out, we saw only the dead and the dying. Ragged, pale creatures, many with ghastly wounds, dragged themselves over the piled corpses of their comrades. Framed against the flaming chandler's Montsorbier appeared with three or four of his men. He was obscenely elegant, the dandified sans-culotte. Hand on hip, he paced back and forth, back and forth, studying our tavern.

The Red O'Dowd was grimmer than ever, all his elation gone. He growled: "We're forced to parley now. Soon our shot and powder will be low and I've lost more men than I ever reckoned reasonable. I'll not die or let any more of my people die in defence of a public ordinary with a declining trade. I'll find another hostelry for my old age."

"You've changed your tune mighty quick, Sir," said Libussa.

"I've always done so, Sir, in the face of fact." He replied without shame. "One of us must parley."

"I'll go out," volunteered Klosterheim from behind us. "I've nought to lose by it."

"That's why ye'll stay, Sir." The Red O'Dowd was savage, sincere in his plan to bring Klosterheim to justice. "Let Herr Foltz go. He's most neutral, I think."

Libussa nodded. "Very well, Mr. O'Dowd."

I was amused by his mistaken assumption yet feared, too, for her safety. However, I would not argue, since I had every respect for her cunning, her ability to strike the best bargain with Montsorbier. She would keep her head better than I could, I felt sure.

Klosterheim left the table and came up near the door where we stood. "Everyone conspires against me now," he confided, "yet you forget, 'twas my plan from the outset. You're here, all of you, to aid *me* in the fulfilment of *my* destiny." He resumed his chewing.

"You never had a destiny, Sir," said Libussa, "save what you concocted in your soul's poverty. You're self-described as an anachronism and that's what you are. You've served your turn, Sir. You're as worthless as one of that decrepit mob. Lucifer has rejected you. Now mankind rejects you. Have the good taste, Sir, to accept a fact!" As she spoke she seized a white scarf from the O'Dowd's hand and tied it to the spontoon he gave her. "I'll make Montsorbier call his mongrels off. You, Sir, will keep your place and hold your tongue!"

Klosterheim's fleshless skull went a shade whiter. His dead eyes revealed a flicker, faint and swift, as when damp coals promise to ignite. "You cannot treat me thus, Madam, for 'tis I inspired your ambition!"

"My blood inspired me, Sir. While you proved useful I let you think what you wished." She seemed almost as mad as Klosterheim at that moment, ready to reject any debt, moral or otherwise, which by her own admission she had owed him.

"You'll never be the Anti-Christ!" He grimaced. "Not now. I renounce you!"

Her smile was cruel triumph. "Can the Baptist renounce the Messiah? You continue to add folly to your pride, Klosterheim. You've betrayed too much. In us and in yourself. Find some other Salome to make, at least, a dramatic ending to your tale!" Then she had opened the tavern door and was crying: "Truce! Truce! We'll parley now, Montsorbier!"

I watched her move between the mounds of corpses, clambering over near-dead bodies, holding up the scarf like a victor's banner. She could never know defeat, thought I. Montsorbier gave the order to stay his men and hooked his thumbs in his sash, calmly awaiting her.

When Klosterheim uttered a strange noise I turned. He made a kind of choked keening. He was shuddering with impossible emotions. It was almost grief! "All conspire," he grunted. He stumbled back. His dark eyes were fully on fire at last. "All betray me. Everyone I sought to serve! Why?"

The Red O'Dowd flung back his great head and shouted with laughter. "You sought to serve mankind? Faith! 'Tis a claim I've often heard, Mr. Klosterheim, but none more ludicrous than yours!"

Satan's ex-captain rounded on the Irishman. "What can you know of it, Sir? What?"

The O'Dowd looked down on that furious skull. "Only the little I need to know, Sir. I'm a common man. I've listened to them: the Whigs, the Tories, the Jacobites and the Jacobins, the ranting ministers and the masons and those that call themselves the Children of God. And each of them, Sir, when they fail in their attempt to gain power, claim to have been betrayed by those they would 'save.' Well, Sir, I'll tell ye direct—I'd rather be saved by one of those cancerous creatures out there than I'd entrust my fate to your kind!"

Klosterheim appeared to resume his old composure. His body ceased, gradually, to shake. His colour returned to its normal grey. He shrugged and went back to the table. He began to eat again, if anything even more voraciously.

Our attention was drawn to the street. Above the circle of swaying towers and tenements which rimmed the district, the stars glowed the colour of rust and worn velvet; meanwhile Libussa continued to talk to Montsorbier. Both were bargaining. Both were determined.

Then, as we watched, they appeared to reach agreement. Libussa nodded. Montsorbier removed his hat and settled it upon his head again. The Duchess of Crete turned, holding high the spontoon, and approached the tavern. Behind her, Montsorbier began to instruct his men, pointing this way and that.

She came through the door frowning. "His terms are simple: we vacate the inn, taking nothing with us of value."

"There's nought of value to take," said the O'Dowd.

"He means the Grail," I said.

"If that's done," she continued, "we may go away free. And no attack shall be made on us."

"That sounds like an Englishman's bargain," said the O'Dowd with a frown. "The same as was made at Munster, where the garrison marched out in good faith only to be butchered by the king's army."

"Well, Sir," said Libussa, "this could indeed be English honesty, but it looks to me as if it's the best we have."

"You'll give up your desire for the Grail?" I was astonished.

"That search can begin afresh," said she, "once we're clear."

"No time," said Klosterheim sniggering, "for a new beginning."

She ignored him, addressing our host. "Well, Mr. O'Dowd? How does it strike you?"

"Not well, Sir. I think there are insufficient guarantees. How long do we have for discussing the bargain?"

She shrugged impatiently, as if she had already decided her strategy and was irritated by the O'Dowd's understandable hesitation. "Five minutes."

"Oh, that is not enough! Go out again, Sir, I beg you, and get us half an hour!"

Klosterheim had moved subtly, picking up an emptied musket from the floor. There was a bayonet fixed to the end. With frothing lips and unstable eyes he charged directly at the O'Dowd. *All betray me! All conspire!* It was like a battle-cry.

The O'Dowd arched his back, pushing out his pelvis towards us, shoulders in the opposite direction, and a little tip of steel emerged just above the bottom button of his waistcoat. "Oh, Jesus Christ!" he cried, aghast. "Sirs, I am buggered!"

Grinning like a jackal, Klosterheim had bayoneted his anus.

There was no way a person could die with dignity from such a cowardly wound. I had seen it before, amongst Washington's men in particular, when they punished Indian renegades. The musket was still dragging behind him, like a wooden tail, as he moved on tiptoe, trying to escape the pain, trying to ensure the metal moved no further into his vitals. "Stand man!" I shouted. "Bend forward!"

"Oh, Mother of God!" A little blood came from his mouth now. I pulled the musket free and more blood followed it, gushing. There was no saving him. His men hardly realised what had happened. I pointed at Klosterheim, who stood, crazy-eyed, upon the stairs, then ran up past the gallery and beyond, to the upper floors. Two men left in pursuit.

The O'Dowd was weeping, lying on his stomach at last, upon one of his own trestles. "This is an unseemly, un-Christian death. An unmanly death, Sirs. Would ye hear my confession?"

"You'd best have a co-religionist," said I, signing for one of the Ukrainians to come over.

"That's what ye get, Sir, for turning your back on the Devil." The Red O'Dowd offered us a small smile. There was so much blood around his mouth that the smile was almost obscured. Then he changed his responses and received his consolation.

Libussa slung a pouch of shot and powder over her shoulder and retrieved another musket. "The cellar," she cried, racing down the steps. I was torn between following her and staying with the dying Irishman. Then she was back again, shaking her head. "I thought it was a fresh attack on us. Come, von Bek, we'll defend the roof. Montsorbier's interlude is over!"

And sure enough the horrid mob was on the move again. The walls rattled, the whole tavern threatened to fall, everything was shaking loose. The O'Dowd's men fired back in concert—it was discipline battling disorder. I handed the spontoon with the white flag on it to the square-faced Ukrainian who took O'Dowd's confession. "I'll leave you with this, to use at your discretion." O'Dowd's eyes were closed. His great red beard stuck up around his poor, pallid face as he continued to murmur the appropriate catch-phrases which he hoped would lead him through the Gates of Heaven, or at least to wait patiently outside them until Lucifer and God came to a decision. It was a terrible, vicious action of

Klosterheim's. He struck at any vital creature which possessed what he had been denied. Libussa had been right, moreover. It was that following of murderous impulse which denied him unification either with his master or with mankind.

We were rushing up the stairs now, in pursuit of Klosterheim. Up the narrow servants' stepway, up a spiral, then a final ladder of polished wood which pointed towards the open skylight. It was obvious he must have climbed to the roof but there was no sign of him. Some of the O'Dowd's bravos were still positioned there, with Greek fire burning and ready to be projected, and the two who followed after Klosterheim were there, too, looking very baffled. We searched across the slopes and chimneys. He had gone. We peered over the knee-high battlements, but there was no sign of him on the ledges below, no sign of his body in the street. The Mass was like writhing, maggoty meat from that perspective. I drew back.

"I'll keep watch here," she said, "you search downstairs again."

I returned, flight by flight, to the taproom without seeing any sign of Klosterheim and I began to believe he had magical powers as he had claimed. O'Dowd was breathing his last and wanted me near him. I approached and placed my ear close to his mouth, to hear what he so urgently wished to tell me. "Don't, Sir, I beg ye, retail to anyone the manner of my dying . . ."

"I see no dishonour in your death, Sir. The dishonour was all Klosterheim's." I made no promise.

His eyes closed and his laboured breathing was over. But there was smoke curling under our doors and windows. "They're firing us as they fired the chandler's!" shouted the Ukrainian. Dropping his master's dead hand he reached for his musket again. "Oh, Christ, they're using petroleum!" The stench could have been nought else. At the same time I heard Libussa screaming from the gallery: "Von Bek! Up here! Hurry, man!"

Certain that she had found Klosterheim, I took the stairs in twos, but she led me upward, all the way back to the cold air of the roof. She was shouting to the soldiers. "Down there. Quickly lads, you're needed!" Wearily they abandoned their positions and, one by one, lowered themselves through the skylight. Libussa looked oddly gratified. I was not sure we should risk leaving the roof unprotected and said so. She glared at me as if I were the victim of a March moon. "We've no further need to stay," she told me, and pointed upward. "Look, fool!"

There was a great shadow crossing the Autumn Stars, but it was not a bird, nor yet a witch. It was St. Odhran's aerial ship, with its little sails and paddles, its monstrous round canopy and its body the form of a flying Gryphon. There were peculiar muttering noises issuing from it now. Every so often a small explosion, like a gunshot, cracked out, but no-one was firing from there. I saw sparks and feared lest they catch the inflammable gas and take the whole thing, a roaring ball of fire, to the ground.

The thing jerked, quivered and dropped lower. St. Odhran seemed to have better than usual luck in steering the craft. He shouted to us now, through a great brass megaphone: "Stand clear! Stand clear! We'll throw you down a ladder!"

The whole tavern rocked as the Mass collided with it once more. The musket-fire grew more ragged. I prayed the defenders would leave before they were overrun. Would they leave their dead leader and escape through the sewers? I was tempted to return, to order them to leave, and then, out of nowhere, I heard a voice at once strange and familiar. It called out softly to the Mass. There were no words to the song but it lulled them. As one the mob began gradually to calm, like a sea after the storm. The voice crooned on, gentling that filthy tide until it had subsided completely. Next the Mass began to sway, moaning in concert. I was scarcely able to accept the change, wondering if I were victim of an illusion. Then a rope ladder had struck the roof and Libussa began to climb, dropping her musket but keeping shot and powder. I could now see, peering from the side of the gondola, Prince Miroslav's face. The Russian was grinning down at us, plainly delighted with the adventure.

I did not pause to wonder for long how they had found us, but thankfully put foot to ladder, starting my own climb, which was hampered somewhat by the unwieldy sword in my sash. I reached the gondola at last and was pulled to safety by a chuckling St. Odhran. Libussa was already being wrapped in a great woollen cloak by Prince Miroslav. The balloon swayed and jerked in the air. It seemed heavier and differently weighted. "Good morrow, St. Odhran," said I. "I'm glad to see your steering's improved!" I, too, was slightly crazed on account of our experiences, but remembered to ask: "How did you know we were at the tavern?"

"Don't credit me with the steering, Sir," said St. Odhran. "You can blame Prince Miroslav for that! And surely you know your lady arranged this rendezvous, when she came from here to Prince Miroslav's in that stolen carriage!"

I looked across at her, but she was hidden in the cloak. Now both her movements and her costume were explained. But I could not guess why she had not told me the truth. Why had she lied to me on so many issues? It suggested that she sought to manipulate us all by the best means: confusion and deceit.

When in the next moment the gondola jerked violently, St. Odhran was mystified. "What's this now?" He went to peer over the side, then whistled in surprise. "By God, man, I didn't know ye were with us! Hold on for pity's sake! I'll drop the ladder to ye!"

"Who is it?" Libussa broke free of Miroslav's comfort. She and I went to join St. Odhran at the gondola's side. "Ah!" She was furious.

We were high above the tavern now, with the roof at least a hundred feet below us, but there was a creature holding on to our trailing rope, swinging and kicking like a monkey. I heard his thin, desperate voice screaming: *Traitors! Traitors!*

Libussa put a restraining hand on St. Odhran as he stooped to gather up the ladder piled at his feet. "No."

St. Odhran was disbelieving. "It's your ally, Madam. Kloster-heim! What? You think it more prudent to lower the balloon. If he slips he's done for, eh? Very well—" He reached for the valve cord but Libussa shook her head. "No."

St. Odhran glared at her in outrage. "Madam, I've made it plain that I do not serve ye! Would ye have me do murder for ye now?" He released gas from the valve. Slowly we dropped back towards the tavern roof and it became apparent that Klosterheim, with daemonic tenacity, had succeeded in climbing a few more feet up the rope. I could hear him panting, see his black eyes glowing in that terrible skull.

"By God!" said St. Odhran in admiration. "He'll do it without the ladder. He's still stronger than Hercules!"

Soon Klosterheim was little more than twenty feet from us. His expression was fixed—a silver mask of hatred which bordered on lust. He climbed steadily. He would be revenged on us all if he could and was entirely without reason. St. Odhran held the descent steady, his gaze on Klosterheim almost as intense as Klosterheim's on us. Prince Miroslav crossed the gondola to busy himself with a new piece of machinery blowing and throbbing there. Then the balloon stopped altogether, hanging as if frozen in the air. There was the sound of wind in the rigging, some mutterings from Miroslav's machine, our own breath, and we looked down.

Far below, the tavern was shaking violently, seemingly torn asunder by the swaying and chanting of the mob. Flames rose everywhere in Salzkuchengasse. It was as if we stared into Hell itself.

Klosterheim clambered another few feet. His gasps became the sound of bone scraping bone. His ghastly face glowed in the hot light from the fires below. I shuddered, for it seemed that Death itself climbed implacably up through Old Night to claim our souls for damnation.

Then Libussa had unsheathed her sabre and, before St. Odhran understood her intention, had made a single expert passage and the rope was sliced!

Klosterheim screamed, but it was not a scream of terror. He was screaming pure outrage, a predator thwarted of his victims!

He screamed, even as he flailed towards the distant surface, towards the greedy fires and that swaying, unwholesome chorus of the damned. It seemed there was a moment when, screaming still, he clawed at the very air for support and found purchase—he was *refusing* to fall! During that moment I truly believed he would arrest himself in mid-descent and continue his climb. His hating eyes met mine and I shuddered.

But those clutching, skeletal fingers found no purchase in the cold emptiness.

Down dropped Klosterheim in noisy imitation of his old commander: Lucifer flung out from Heaven. With one last bellow of angry impotence, with one shrieking curse upon his lips, he plunged, twisting, into the flames and was consumed.

Libussa smiled her satisfaction and sheathed the sabre, careless of St. Odhran's horror. "He must have been hiding in the flues," she said. "Did you notice how dusty his coat was?"

Chapter Eighteen

An intimation of the Nineteenth Century. Libussa displays
an acquisition. An informal proposal. More Omens and
Portents. Theft in the night. Our desperate pursuit.

NOW RELATIONS ABOARD the *Donan* were, to say the least,
somewhat strained. My lady at once began murmuring to
Prince Miroslav, who leaned over her, his hair and beard blowing
in the wind, listening like an old Russian boyar doing courtesy to
his liege. St. Odhran would not speak to her at all and, since his
opinion was of no special value to her, she ignored him. Thus it
was left to me to explain why Klosterheim's killing was justified.
My friend shrugged and accepted what I said. "But there's been so
much double-dealing in this business, von Bek, it's impossible to
guess who's now friend and who's foe!"

He softened enough to explain to me, with growing enthusiasm,
how Prince Miroslav had improved the Air-ship by furnishing her
with an engine turning a screw. We went aft to admire the screw, a
great four-bladed affair, whirling on an axle. The alchemist had also
provided a new gas of his own discovery, not nearly as combustible
as the Hydrogen and which he called Vodorodium. The Engine was
worked, St. Odhran said, by firing off tiny gunpowder charges in a
series of cylinders, and while not wholly reliable it allowed him to
steer against a fairly strong wind. This was not unlike the steam
experiments, he told me, of the new school of British engineers,
but far less bulky. The contraption was all pops, wheezes and sudden shudders: a collection of rods, cylinders and cogs whose logic
defeated me. The Russian was proud of it and was pleased to
explain its principles to me, but while his enthusiasm was inspir-
ing, his language was meaningless. I was almost grateful when he
returned his attention to the Duchess of Crete.

"It's ready," he said to her, "and tested as best I could."

"And all astrologers agree?" she asked. They spoke in tones just above a whisper.

"All. The Concordance will be complete in a little over twenty-four hours."

"Then we have only to consider the ritual." She was aglow with excitement, her smile a grimace of anticipation. But Prince Miroslav was disturbed. "If the transmutation could be achieved without the ritual, Madam, I believe our chances of success would actually improve . . ."

"Nonsense!" Angrily she turned away from him.

"I still hold that it's a perversion of our idea!"

"Hold what you like, Sir!"

The Air-ship crossed from Deeper City to Outer in a matter of a quarter-hour. Soon we were dropping down to the grassy street where Miroslav had his simple residence. The haze which filtered the old starlight parted for a moment: it was almost like early dawn as we descended. Barely conscious of what went on around me, I could scarcely believe we were rescued. The horror of all that death was paramount in my mind and I had entered a kind of shocked daze.

The Air-ship was tethered to Prince Miroslav's tall chimney, then it was but a step to his roof and through the skylight to his upper landing, where servants were ready with rum toddy and bricklings, blankets and towels, as if we were survivors from a shipwreck. We sat ourselves in Prince Miroslav's parlour, where an open fire cosily danced, and soon it was possible to believe the whole episode at the tavern a terrible nightmare from which we had just awakened . . .

Were it not for Libussa's overbright eye and flushed cheeks, I would have been happy enough to sink into the contentment of that pleasant domesticity, at least for a few hours, but I could tell she was a primed cannon waiting for a target. She could not keep still. In a corner, she spread charts and diagrams over Prince Miroslav's tables. She asked obscure questions of him and received cryptic replies: they spoke the argot of alchemy and natural philosophy, and half of it was mathematical while the rest concerned wombs and the binding of elements, with references to the Philosopher's Stone, the Male Element (sulphur) and the Female Element (mercury), to incantations, tinctures, elixirs, furnaces and the final marrying. I had heard much of it before, but never understood a great deal, for it had always sounded as if one discipline were confused with another—the cracks in the logic filled in with gaudy abstraction—and the result, while sounding devilish convincing, was always a useless Hybrid when put to the test.

I dozed in the chair next to St. Odhran and from time to time instructed him in what had befallen us since we had left him at the Obelisk. Each new tale astonished him more. I said nothing of Lucifer or how I had acquired the sword my friend admired. "The image of the eagle is almost real, von Bek! One might believe the poor bird actually shrieked to be released." He laughed. "But I would not risk setting it free, would you? It could rip out your liver in a flash!"

"Perhaps Paracelsus used it to carry off his creditors," said I. We were enjoying this speculation when Libussa crossed the room to put a hand on my shoulder. "We should get to our beds, Sir," said she. "I should like tomorrow to be our wedding day."

"Wedding?" I turned in some surprise. She had said nothing so direct before, and I was used to such things being announced months, sometimes years, in advance. "What? Married at the barrel?"

"Sir, I've no burden awaiting legitimate entry to the world, but the auguries are good. There's no question, by all the signs, that we should not become one."

I became inane with joy. "I should have welcomed, Madam, the chance to order a new suit of clothes! Is the parson picked?"

She smiled. "And the choir and congregation, too."

"The Church?"

"All arranged."

St. Odhran did his best to note this exchange with good grace, but it was plain he liked it not at all. Could men be jealous of other men in such matters? Did St. Odhran love her himself? Was that why he hated seeing her kill Klosterheim?

"And here's what shall join us in our matrimony," said she, striding across the floor and picking up the sack she had carried with her from the tavern. It was still heavy, presumably full of shot and powder. She loosened the top and drew forth an old metal helmet, a battered iron-and-brass *chapelle-de-fer*, with a simple half-sphere for the head and a flat brim all around. This she put upon the sideboard. St. Odhran looked at it and made no comment at all. I knew she believed herself to be in possession of the Grail. She had gone back to the cellar on the pretext of anticipated attack and grabbed the first old helmet she had seen. "It's not hard to withstand the discomfort of handling it," she said. I could hardly keep a sober face and nodded very slowly in the hope that my response would satisfy her. Yet I did not give a fig for her peculiarities and aberrations. I loved her and she intended to marry me! And if I must balance an antique salade upon my head while the ceremony took place, or indeed wear it forever cemented to my skull, I would do it to please her!

"What's that, Madam?" asked St. Odhran innocently enough. "A relic of your family's wars?"

"'Tis more a relic of von Bek's family's struggles," she said.

"It looks the same as sheltered the Welsh archers' heads at Agincourt," said he. "It must be two hundred years old at least, eh?" He attempted joviality. "Is there some ceremony attached to it? Some antique tradition, like the riding round the oak tree or the spinning of the bridal fleece?"

"Some ceremony's involved, aye, Sir." She was pleased by his amiable ignorance and delighting in what she thought her secret knowledge, but I remained convinced the thing was just an old war-hat dug out of O'Dowd's untidy cellars. What had made the supernatural light could have been the Holy Cup—but not that helmet.

So much, thought I, for any so-called affinity with the Grail we von Beks were supposed to possess. Neither it nor whatever I had seen in the cellar produced a twinge of recognition. But I would not spoil her moment, particularly if I risked her changing her mind as to our nuptials. I would humour her in every way, concur in any fantasy, join any club, coven, clique, canting sect or secret society to please her. I was hers. Now, she'd be mine! Joy for ever! I had grown used to her volatility. Her decisions it seemed were always made suddenly. It did not surprise me she had chosen this unconventional means of announcing her desire to wed me. The fact that she had announced it was enough to overwhelm any other consideration. I grew drowsy, I thought, with delight.

"Which church did ye say, Madam?" I heard St. Odhran politely enquire. "Presumably it's picked."

"It shall take place within the crucible," she said.

"Aha!" He raised his toddy in a toast. "A civil marriage, eh? Ain't they the rage in France at present?"

I was more than half-drunk as I stumbled towards her. She grinned. "Are you sure you'll welcome our becoming one flesh?"

"Madam, I can think of nothing more fulfilling, though I lived through eternity!"

"'Tis that possibility I presently investigate." She winked.

Did I understand her? I had grown so weary. Did I speak plain words which she interpreted as profound? Or did she love me so much she thought anything I said of magnificent eloquence? Could it be? Befuddled as I was I still doubted that! I could make a good leg and my brain was normally sharper than most. I could display a decent suit of clothes and was less short of courage than of inches, yet it did not seem to me enough. What was it then that had struck the crucial chord? Then it came to me she saw all in terms of alchemy: she believed we were *elementally* compatible— my sulphur to her mercury, an Adam to her Eve!

Or was it, I thought, that she was attracted to an opposite? Was she attracted to the notion of my line of honest, decent Saxon freeholders combining with hers of questing, darkling, intellectual Mediterraneans? I thought I heard the Beast roaring but it was only Prince Miroslav clearing his throat.

"Twenty hours," said she gently. "Can you wait, Sir?"

"I think so, Madam."

She looked at me with repressed glee, with a crazy, near-disbelieving glitter, her lips just parted a fraction, signifying lust: but it was lust for more than physical joy. It was lust for the wisdom carried on the blood. A wisdom fresh-born, like the Earth in *Genesis*, that was ancient as the dust of the former universe whose remains obscured the light of the Autumn Stars; a wisdom that was the body's rapture and the mind's delight. For this her lips were parting and her breath gasped while she assessed me from the depths of her darkening, heated eyes. "Oh, it will be the ultimate marriage," she said.

St. Odhran, either missing all our intensity or ignoring what he could not approve, said: "If it's a Best Man ye need, von Bek, I'll cheerfully volunteer."

"Thank you," said I sincerely, "dear friend."

Libussa swayed like a snake captive under the fakir's flute. Prince Miroslav came forward to touch her. "Madam."

She blinked. The spell was not dismissed, but set aside. I returned to my normal stance, though still confoundedly muzzy. St. Odhran's face was slightly shadowed. "Marriage is an adventure for only the bravest," said he. "'Twould not do for me. I lack the bottom for it. But I wish ye well." He turned, as if he hid his expression.

Libussa swiftly ended their whispered conference by glaring at Prince Miroslav. "*It has to be!*" She almost shouted. Did he object to our splicing? Was he perhaps her guardian or mentor, whose permission she must seek? No, it was inconceivable my Libussa should ever require blessing from anyone! She would command God Himself if He came down to Earth. She was His senior in divinity, that goddess who had ruled before the Hebrew Jove cast His first thunderbolt! The Beast roared from the centre of the Labyrinth, but he was tamed. She ruled him, contained him, and he was her ultimate power to release only at the final moment. But I prayed that moment would never come. Was it not bad faith to let the Beast live on? I realised my lids had fallen over my eyes and I rose, bidding them all good night. A servant led me to my bed.

I went to sleep still within my ecstatic fantasy. She would come for me, she had promised, to carry me to our wedding. I should be garlanded in white and red flowers, dressed in samite. I should be one with my destiny, with my Duchess of Crete. Was it not cowardice, I insisted as I dreamed, to let the Beast live? Surely he should have been left to die, where Theseus left him, groaning, with slowing heart, with flooding lungs, with gushing jugular; dying in his own hairy stink. I could not believe the Beast would be allowed to remain. She said he was only a threat, that he need never be released, but why lead him, even on a golden rope fixed to a golden ring which tugged at the flesh of his red, flaring nostrils, into our paradise? I thought she claimed in that dream to protect paradise? Did Jehovah employ the Serpent to protect the Garden of Eden?

This was beyond my understanding. I was perturbed. Yet I would follow her like the Beast, even if my nose were pierced and my ankles chained and all my strength shivering to break those massive links. As the Baptist to Salome, as Samson to Delilah . . . no madness was stronger, none more worthwhile, whether it end in death or triumph!

Alone in my bed I anticipated resolution and ultimate fulfilment. It would be no ordinary marriage. Perhaps a pagan ceremony or a Byzantine one. Who would witness our unique, our universal union? All? Or would it be secret? I cared not. O, Madam, I murmured to myself, so much in me is changed through your alchemy. Your powerful femininity turns all to quicksilver. How shall we be when the transmutation's complete? 'Tis absolute malleability we look forward to, absolute chaos . . . *Are we truly set to accomplish nothing less than the re-creation of the world? 'Tis logical, if things are to be properly improved. 'Tis all we wish: and no unworthy ambition, surely? Did not God make His first human creature androgynous? And only later did it divide, male and female. Then later still came the Snake, which is also named the Beast. Who welcomed the apocalypse? God? Satan? Humanity?*

The Beast strained on an iron harness. Mad, crimson eyes were glaring. His breath was a great stink infecting our Earth and poisoning Paradise. The tree was dying. It had a foulness in its roots.

We were only flesh and could be nothing else.

But now it was cold in my room. I opened my eyes. Through the uncurtained window I saw the Autumn Stars and it seemed their light faded rapidly. As the light faded, so did the cold increase. I was shivering. She is gone. Von Bek, man . . .

St. Odhran stood there in a white nightshirt, a candle in his hand. The linen fell away from his strongly muscled arm. He was breathing heavily, brushing unbound hair from his face. He was drawn and pale. "Von Bek! For the love of God, rouse yourself man! Are ye drugged?"

She had fallen away from me. We could never truly be parted. I closed my eyes to sleep.

"Von Bek, 'tis murder! And they've taken your damned betrothed!"

It was hard to lift my head. It rolled on my shoulders. I heaved with arms and buttocks until I was sitting. All the adventuring, I supposed, had tired me. Now there was fresh murder and I scarcely cared. And what else?

"Libussa," said my friend harshly, "is kidnapped."

I did not believe him. Libussa could be neither stolen nor threatened. She had too much power and intellect. She controlled her own destiny more thoroughly than any mortal before her. She was Libussa Urganda Cressida Cartagena y Mendoza-Chilperic, descendant of the world's most antique races, daughter of the Merovingian kings, who claimed direct lineage (and could prove it) from Jesus Christ, who in turn was of the direct blood of Solomon, Scourge of the Genii. In her our wisdom was crystallised; she was the rightful bearer of the Cup and the Sword, the Lion, first alchemical adept . . . this was no dream. St. Odhran was shaking me. His face was terror-struck in the faded light. The dust of that long-decayed universe became a fog obscuring all hope...

"She's gone, man! And Miroslav murdered!"

"It's not possible," I told him reasonably.

"Sir, I assure you—Miroslav's downstairs, breathing his last on his own damned carpet, with a sabre cut that's chopped him near in two! And he says 'twas Montsorbier did it!"

"He's still alive, of course. The last of the Beast's captains. And the most determined." I put bare feet to floorboards while St. Odhran helped me dress. I insisted on the proper attire, for I still had it in mind I was to be married that morning. Linen, stockings, breeches, waistcoat, front-laced shoes, a fresh neck-cloth. And my friend continued to call to me, slapping and swearing at me. "For pity's sake, man, rouse yourself from this rum reverie. Was there opium in your drink last night?" Frock-coat, a wig, now to the mirror. The suit was good, though the man within had a sleepy, silly look about him and the man behind was almost leaving the ground in rage at his friend's slowness.

"I must look my best, St. Odhran, for my wedding." The sword had a ceremonial look; it was an old one with a great scarlet pommel in a blue velvet scabbard. Now there was a figure, not quite in the fashion, yet you could not call him absolutely unmodish. It would do. The face was so gaunt. Was that von Bek or Klosterheim? Did we merge? Klosterheim screamed and clawed at the air . . .

"By God, von Bek. D'ye not care if she lives or dies?"

I shook my head to clear it. What folly had seized me? Some spell of Montsorbier's discovery? Was I to be subject to witchcraft on top of all else? And St. Odhran hobbled with me, having got himself half dressed between his shouting and his slapping at me, his breeches not quite buttoned, followed me as I went stumbling down the stairs to the hallway where huddled, frightened servants waited.

Prince Miroslav had been cloven right through, shoulder to waist. He was holding on to the sabre which had killed him, as if the sword was life itself. His pink face was wonderingly boyish but his blue eyes were round with agony. "It was one she knew," said he carefully, perhaps afraid his speaking would rob him of a few moments. He loved life too much to leave it carelessly. "A Frenchie. Polished boots. Tricolour."

"Montsorbier," supplied St. Odhran. "Have you a potion, Sir, to cure you of that cut?"

Miroslav said in a small, even voice: "No." He smiled.

I had an urge to embrace that kindly bear but knew any

movement would kill him sooner. Though he would dearly have loved the comfort of another human body, he held me off with a look. "This is wrong," he said. "She does not need to make the sacrifice. It is the old, black thinking somehow got into her. She has summoned up the Beast." He paused to draw a slow shivering breath. "Well, it was in the blood. But she had such genius. I did not expect her, out of all of them, to succumb. I'll take that brandy now, St. Odhran. Can you remember the principle of my engine?"

"I think so, Sir." My friend's gentle hand extended a glass to those full, bearded lips. The adept sipped almost sensually.

"My lord," I said urgently, "what is she doing?"

"We alchemists have a tendency to merge the symbol with the actuality. It gives us our path, of course, but it can create the most abominable perversions. She's fallen back on the old, debased methods and nothing will, it seems, inhibit her. She's convinced it is the only way. You might have persuaded her otherwise, von Bek. You might still." He drew another careful breath, clinging to life by the force of his will alone.

"She went willingly with Montsorbier?"

"I think not. Originally, I gather, there were secret bargains, long since broken. The ritual is not intrinsic to the marriage, but you, of course, are. You have only yourself as collateral. Could you refuse the ritual, von Bek? Refuse her?"

"No," I told him.

"At least pretend." He swayed where he sat and his hand grew limp upon the sword. "They will have returned to the Centre. They took everything—cup, tincture—and she knows by heart the incantation. Worse—they have my crucible . . ."

His body began to slump, but St. Odhran and I moved forward to support him. He thanked us with a smile and died.

"St. Odhran," said I, straightening, "they've returned to that tavern. We must follow."

"If she wished to go," said he heavily, "then it's her decision and I'll not interfere. Von Bek, I mislike all mysteries and all magics. These are waters I'll not swim in, Sir. Let Montsorbier substitute for you. Don't he plan to be the groom?"

"I can save her. Prince Miroslav said so." The sluggish wine still hampered my movements and distorted my speech.

"Let us simply leave this place, my friend," said St. Odhran, "and return to our own Mirenburg. I'd rather face their whole militia than continue with this black magic. Miroslav told me that conditions were now perfect for crossing the realms. He gave me all the information necessary for the journey . . ."

"But you're my Best Man, Sir," said I. "And on your honour to escort me to my wedding!"

With the shrug of one who had volunteered to ascend the scaffold with good grace, St. Odhran led the way back up the stairs and out to the roof where his great Air-ship swayed like a pendulum overhead.

Soon we sailed again beneath the Autumn Stars, while rooftops, dark and glistening with rain, passed slowly down below. The engine had constantly to be tended and failed four times. I grew agitated with each pause as St. Odhran tinkered. Montsorbier was probably already in the Deeper City. I began to long for a horse, but the Air-ship was all we had. As the strong wind sprang up, our *Donan* was hard put to fight it. We were blown this way, towards the wide, transformed Falfnersallee; we were blown that, towards the palace and the ornamental lake. We dropped too low and horses reared not twenty feet from our gondola's keel, while citizens gaped and pointed. Then we were up again. The new gas was more responsive than St. Odhran was used to, he told me.

The Air-ship's screw laboured and our bulk pushed hard against the wind which seemed to conspire to keep us ever from the Centre. Our hair and clothes were blown every which way. Then all at once there came a lull and our machine gained sudden momentum, a sort of grip upon the air, and we were above that strange spiral of streets and swaying buildings which creaked still more energetically around the central pit, the core of the Deeper City. It seemed their agitation had increased and I was reminded of mourning Indians I had once seen, not far from Brandywine Creek one December morning, wailing as they watched their dead chief's body, on its high bier of birch saplings, pecked clean by carrion birds. We began to drop down. Those mourning terraces rose to surround us. We were directly above the embers of what had once been Salzkuchengasse. The Friend Indeed was entirely gone, was smoke and charred timber, flattened. In a vast circle, some two thousand supplicants, all in pale robes, in the high pointed hoods of the *auto-da-fé*, stood looking inward at the Centre. Their silence was the silence of creatures who had renounced humanity in favour of that horrible semblance of power.

They had raised a black cross, some twelve feet high and five wide. Upon it, hands nailed and bloody, feet impaled likewise, clothing stripped and rags fluttering, a halo of pink briar roses twisted about the lifted, agonised head, bruised naked body, still strong and proud, bearing many thin cuts, still oozing, was the woman I would wed.

And beneath that cross, like some centurion transported by deep emotion, hand upon the sword at his hip, stood Montsorbier. His other hand was gauntleted and held an upturned helmet of antique form in which he caught, drop by drop, her blood.

I believed I witnessed the ritual Prince Miroslav had hoped so passionately to forestall. Here, indeed, was tragic perversity.

Chapter Nineteen

In which I confront the incredible and accept the impossible.
The Alchemical Goal. A Marriage of all elements. Galliard
of the Old Stars. Concerning the properties of certain
magical objects. The flaw in the formula.

T HEY HAD RAISED a black cross amongst the ruins and hanged
my betrothed upon it. I had heard her speak of Christ and
the necessity of the ritual of repetition, but I had not once guessed
her full intention. She was dying, I was convinced. Overhead the
sky swam with turbulent dust and the light from the old stars
faded, flickered and expired. Exhausted rays fell upon her body.
Then her eyes lifted up to the heavens and met mine. I was horrified by her sweet smile. "Hermes to my Aphrodite!" she called.
"My husband comes!"

Montsorbier saw us descending now and although he could
not move the vessel in which he caught her drops of blood, he
grew greatly agitated. He was inspired, I knew then, by profound
jealousy. He shouted: "Ha! Here comes Citizen Cockerel flapping
to the slaughter. Fly away little rooster. You are not needed here.
Your hens call you back to your coop!"

Though she could only be in inconceivable pain, Libussa carried
her familiar authority: "Beware, Montsorbier. You are commissioned to perform certain tasks. Perform those and no others!"

He sulked. Her blood dripped, bead by precious bead, into the
upturned helm. From amongst the mumbling crowd now stepped
the golden girl, the same as sacrificed the lamb, and she was singing in Latin, much garbled, with some Greek and, I guessed,
Hebrew. The entire ensemble joined in that hymn and Montsorbier's reply, if any, was drowned.

Pale St. Odhran trembled in disgusted terror. "There's nought to do here, von Bek. She conspires in her own blasphemous martyr-dom! If we linger, we'll be drawn in for certain and destroyed."

I was calm; reconciled now. "Do you not understand, dear friend, that it is my destiny as well as hers?"

"I feared you would grow mad as she," he said soberly. "Will you try to listen to reason, von Bek? For love of what you were?"

"I have no love, St. Odhran, for what I was. I have changed beyond redemption and must fulfil what Fate demands." I smiled at him. He drew back, gasping as if I were leprous, and my stretched hand could not touch him.

"You're Satan's creature now, von Bek!"

"Always, it seems." I was tranquil. "There's no sinister meaning . . ."

"Sir, until but lately you were a human soul! A good heart. Now you are possessed. I'll wait a day for you. No longer!"

As I threw the ladder groundwards I shook my head, pitying his ignorance. "I must away now, my friend, to the wedding. I'm much disappointed you do not see your way clear to keeping your word."

He took a step or two across the gondola, as if to stop me, but I had swung over and was climbing towards the smouldering wasteland and an oblivious congregation of Witnesses whose eyes were entirely held by that dark crucifixion, the manifestation of what prophets had called "Anti-Christ'"; the new messiah. Rejecting God, this messiah claimed the Earth in the name of mankind! As part of that destiny I would be second only to she, whose wisdom had reorganised my blood and illuminated my soul. Clinging to the ladder I looked down on all her Witnesses. The wind drummed against the balloon's canopy like a tremen-dous heartbeat; the surrounding silhouettes of buildings waved like agitated wheat; the dust formed shapes in a huge sky and behind it still glowed the Autumn Stars.

I jumped the last few feet into the hot ashes of The Friend Indeed. Embers flew about my legs, smoke attacked my eyes, yet I waded unconcerned through the red-hot débris until I reached the congregation. Most there were taller than I and I could see nothing of the cross. I pushed against bodies as cold as corpses, but they did not resist, and at last I stood to the left of the golden priestess. Montsorbier turned, lifting the bowl, crying out until the hymn gradually died and they waited again in silence.

My lady hung upon the great cross, her head limp against her left shoulder, her body white, as if every drop of blood was drained. I could not see her breathing.

I record these events to the best of my memory. While much is vivid some is vague and one image blends with another. Some was doubtless illusion, much definitely was not. In my daze I had decided all was preordained. To play my part in it was effortless for I merely followed my own desires. No prayer was ever more fervent than my prayer to her (for to whom else should I pray?) that she complete her ritual and be resurrected. Now I knew why Prince Miroslav had been so afraid, for like so many of his genera-tion he reverenced God and believed that blasphemy must surely be punished.

Montsorbier's voice lifted like a bishop's: "Here is the Grail! Here is the blood of the Anti-Christ mixed with the divine tinc-ture. Here is sulphur, mercury, salt and cinnabar; here is gold and silver and an essence of rubies. Here is the stone made liquid." And he displayed that battered helmet as if it were the crown of Zeus. "So sayeth Marduk: *I shall maketh my blood solid. I shall maketh bones therefrom. I shall raise up Man from mine own dismem-bered flesh. So sayeth Marduk!*"

"*So sayeth Marduk!*" They gave chorus again, as they had at the sacrifice of the lamb.

"When the Holy One, blessed be, created the first of our race they were called Androgynous," intoned the priestess. "So sayeth the Holy One."

"*So sayeth the Holy One!*"

"Behold," she cried, "the truth hath been revealed to thee! The seed hath been sown."

"*The seed hath been sown.*"

"Whomsoever sows the holy chryosperm shall know rebirth for eternity. They shall know the secret of holy metals, the alchemical tree, the seven waters and the thirteen vapours. The tree is cut down! The tree is reborn."

And while she chanted, Montsorbier, reluctantly, yet helpless as anyone to do otherwise, came slowly towards me, offering me the helm in outstretched hands.

"Behold!" shouted the priestess. "The male that is female shall be wedded to the female that is male. Brother to sister, mother to son, daughter to father! Here is the old king dying and the young king being born. Here is Kibrit come to Al-baida, his sister, to be swallowed in her womb. From darkness there shall come light."

"From darkness shall come light."

"So shall Hermaphroditus come to the fountain of Salmacis and the two become one. Animate and inanimate shall be called *Rebis*, which is our stone. Immortal, it shall be whole, self-reproducing with the sum of all our wisdom!"

"Thus at last," chimed in Montsorbier, "is Christ recrucified; Christ made complete; Christ who is man and woman and the child of man and woman! Thus the plural is abolished." And he handed me the upturned helm which I took in my palms. Swirling gold, dark red and green, the elixir within gave off a gentle, delicious vapour, that tincture which in the alchemical belief was the essence of divine wisdom, as it was the essence of my Libussa.

"Drink!" cried the priestess. "The ritual must be completed and we shall witness the crucifixion and resurrection of the female Christ; the marriage of opposites, the final reconciliation. Then shall Harmony come upon the Earth. Drink!"

I drank. It was salty, sweet, heady. My stomach attempted to reject it, but if I was to be married I knew I had to consume every drop. I took another sip. The Witnesses had now disrobed. Their limbs were pale in the light of the Autumn Stars. The black dust swirled around them. The coals glowed red. They watched as I drained the cup. They moaned with ecstatic approval.

Montsorbier took the Grail from my hands. The priestess reached out to me. I feared her. I was suspicious of her. She was ally to the Beast. I believed it wrong she should officiate at the ritual. Neither should Montsorbier have been there. But few others were now alive. The priestess came towards me again and I could not draw back. She and Montsorbier removed my clothing until I stood naked before the black cross, my sword raised before me in my two fists.

They withdrew. I was alone before my mistress, her face serene in its power, even though life had left her lacerated body and swept through my own like a tremendous tide, through every channel of my being. It was as if I were the universe and was populated by elementals. Never had I known such strength.

From behind me the priestess declaimed. "So shall ye be the second of the two, the whole, the creature some call Anti-Christ but which is called in the secret lore *Krystous Androgynous: The Lord that is both Man and Woman.*"

Stiffly upright I was lifted upon the backs of the Witnesses, and used my sword to prise loose the nails, then catch her in my arms as she fell. She was my sweet love. She was my Libussa, who taught me the meaning of lust. Her cold body hung in my arms.

"First comes the resurrection, then the marriage, then begins your eternal rule, when justice and equality shall be the same as harmony and all shall be whole. We shall have achieved the End of the World's Pain!"

The Sword of Paracelsus, my gift from Satan, was slung over my naked back. Bearing her limp remains I stood ankle deep in the black ashes beneath that great cross. They surrounded us again, the Witnesses, chanting with uplifted hands. Montsorbier and the golden girl, priest and priestess of this rite, were the leading voices. I scarcely saw them as I looked upon the face of my tutoress; I looked upon undaunted Faith.

"The winged one with two heads shall stand upon the pyre of old hope; here is the Cup and here the Sword. Where is the Beast?"

Now it seemed a great lion stalked through the ruins, in his jaws the body of a pelican, round his neck a snake, and he was crowned with yellow lilies. The Witnesses fell back before him. He stood upon a spur of fallen masonry and, dropping the pelican from his mouth, lifted his head to utter a great, triumphal roar.

The roar echoed amongst the swaying towers of the Deeper City, amongst the Autumn Stars, at once a lament and a victory shout. Then, from beneath his feet there suddenly burst a huge fount of silvery water which washed away the ash and the coals.

The Lion vanished but the fountain remained. It was the same O'Dowd had spoken of, the old spring upon which the inn was founded. It was gushing mightily now as I carried my Libussa into its centre. The water was so powerful it appeared to dissolve us as our bodies were washed and grew white. Moaning, Libussa stirred in my arms and a tracery of blood sprang from her wounds and was at once washed away. *Libussa! Libussa! Mistress of my desire. Wake, I beg you!* She opened her astonishing eyes and smiled at me. "It is as it should be," she said softly. Still holding her in my arms I reached down my head and kissed her lips.

"I knew you would follow." She was still weak as she lowered herself to the ground, the water pouring down her face, pressing her hair flat against her skull. Holding my hand she peered through the silvery curtain of water. "Where's the crucible?"

She led me from beneath the fountain. Blood no longer issued from her hands and feet. She was purified. The bulk of the Witnesses lay face down in the wet ash, still maintaining a muffled chant, and from across the square came a score of naked men and women pulling a wooden tumbril upon which stood upright a thing of copper and brass: a great cylinder with a domed top. From the dome issued tubes and vents. I had never seen one so large, but I knew it was an alchemist's crucible: the Chemical Womb where the elements were blended and fresh elements created.

"You have done well," said Libussa to them. "Now you must prepare the *Catinus Uteri*. There is little time. *Nec temere; nec timide.*"

Her blood was now my own. It was fire in me. I was a god. They placed the crucible beneath the black cross and began the work of bringing it to life. Great bellows heaved, charcoal blossomed red, steam and sparks poured into the darkling air. Montsorbier and the priestess supervised this work while Libussa embraced me, smiling more tenderly than ever before. "It is all as it should be, my darling. Every ingredient, every equation, every formula. At the moment of the Concordance we shall be joined. Do you fear this, little one?"

"I fear nothing, Madam. I am yours."

She stroked my body. The combination of the tincture and her touch upon me made me gasp. And if that were ecstasy, what could the ultimate ecstasy she promised be? I trembled as we approached the crucible. Montsorbier lifted up the helm, still glowing from the remains of its contents. The red light from the furnace fell upon all our faces. The heat was terrific.

Montsorbier and the golden girl grinned in their mystical glee. Libussa's arm was around my shoulders. She stood gracefully, staring up at the hazy sky. It grew darker. I placed my own arm about her waist and for a moment it was as if we were rustic lovers taking the air in the evening fields. I had no intimation of what was to come, but it was enough for me that we were to be married. It did not matter what future she sought to create. I would serve her however she wished. This thought was enough to thrill my blood, her blood.

"The Time of the Lion," whispered the golden girl, "shall be upon us. The Time of the Lamb is past." I recalled her lovely, innocent lips rimmed with the blood of the sacrificial creature. I recalled Montsorbier's cruel carelessness, his lust for revenge. These were poor servants for my mistress, I thought. "The Beast shall be set free," murmured Montsorbier. "All who refuse his worship shall be destroyed, so shall cowardice be cleansed from the world." I looked to Libussa, who said nothing to contradict him.

"But the Beast must be banished," I said. "He is part of the Old Time. There can be no real justice or harmony if he comes over with us!"

Libussa pursed her lips, frowning at me, demanding silence. Montsorbier flashed a glance from her, to me, to the priestess who said: "We combine our forces, Sir, and so ensure success. It was agreed that if we helped you two in this transmutation, you would help us in our ambition."

"But they are at odds!" I felt wounded, fearing fresh betrayal. "There is no reconciliation between Reason and the Beast!"

Libussa wished me to say nothing. I could only suppose she intended to settle the matter later, when the power was fully hers. "They are reconciled," she said. "We have found a satisfactory formula."

This talk was too familiar from my Commune days. By such compromises we had lost all we hoped to achieve. Yet my silence was assured. I loved Libussa. If she wished me to say nothing of our mutual principles, nothing would be said. Nonetheless I remained perturbed. Both Montsorbier and the priestess had shown they would use any bestial means to achieve their ends. Surely Libussa found them as degenerate as did I? She drew me closer to her. In spite of the unnatural strength in my veins I yet grew weak at her touch. I smiled into her face, from which some of the pallor had gone, driven out perhaps by the flames from the crucible which grew hotter by the moment. She returned my attention to the sky. "Do you detect any alteration, little one?"

The dust was swirling faster while the Autumn Stars continued to emit their faded light. I believed that she detected a change in the configuration of the heavens, but I could see no difference. My betrothed looked again upon her crucible. She stretched out her resurrected limbs to feel the heat upon her flesh. She uttered a lazy yawn and she might have been the Lion herself. Her tawny skin glowed with its old vitality. Her breathing was more rapid. She pointed to the upper chamber of the machine. "'Tis in there we'll be united for ever. Within that metal womb there is space for our bodies. We shall enter it at the exact moment of the full Concordance."

It seemed to me we would hardly both fit into the little room and would be mighty hot if we did. She noted my uncertainty. "The Grail shall go with us, von Bek, to provide spiritual fire as the crucible provides our temporal. I shall eat what I must eat. Now you have the blood and the tincture mixed within you. Next I must take that blood and tincture within me. This shall occur at the moment of maximum power. It is in all the grammars. For sixteen hundred and forty-seven years, seven months, thirteen weeks and nine days have the alchemical adepts worked to achieve this specific moment. True, we have worked in different ways and sometimes, as Montsorbier and I have done, towards different ends, but between us we have accumulated wisdom enough to predict the exact moment when the stars conjoin and the new era begins. This knowledge shall give us control of the fate of the world! We have waited long, little von Bek. Great men and women have lived entire lives, accepted torture and death, to bring about this moment. John Dee said we shall be called *Monas*, the One. He devoted every moment in his search for a formula enabling us to create the One. Before him came the great Paracelsus. And Cleopatra, of course, who searched for Balance and Harmony, the two paramount goals of the alchemical life. Are you aware, Sir, of the numbers who searched and experimented, writing their learned works so that you and I could be joined on this day?" She returned her frowning concentration to the sky.

I shuddered and grew suddenly cold. "We shall be united," said she in a whisper, "with all this!" And her hands went out to encompass the universe. "Two great concordances have occurred since the adepts began their work. Both times we failed to take our advantage. We were not sufficiently ruthless. Henry Cornelius Agrippa exhorted us to dedication in the *Three Books*, and Basil Valentine was urgent that we take advantage of this Concordance for it could be our last chance. Our master, Hermes Trismegistus, even Cagliostro . . . Every one of them, living and dead, shall be vindicated, for the Occult Reign shall soon begin. All will be in balance! All, male and female, shall be equal. All injustices shall be abolished! Can you not see that whatever I choose to do now is right, so long as it achieves that harmony?"

"The Beast is not harmony. He should die . . ." But I was entranced by her enthusiasm and could only accept it. My arguments seemed dull and pointless in my own ears.

Sweat shone on our bodies as the crucible's heat turned from red to white. The darkness wavered in that radiance and again I imagined the Lion, stalking back and forth, as Montsorbier had stalked before The Friend Indeed, with lashing tail, waiting as impatiently as Libussa for the *Moment*.

The Sword of Paracelsus was like an icicle against my back and recalled Lucifer's urgent pleading that I use the sword to win the greatest possible advantage. Libussa, too, had said she had a use for the sword . . .

There was now a distinct flickering in the sky; a shift, as if one thin plate of glass slid across another. The Autumn Stars seemed unchanged, but behind them were now fresh points of light. Libussa grew alert. "'Tis coming." She shivered. "Oh, 'tis coming!"

The priestess and Montsorbier also peered out into the stars. "Aye," said my old enemy with grim satisfaction. "And we are ready."

The Earth lurched, it seemed, and became unstable, perhaps an illusion caused by what took place in the sky. There was still no sign of the spectacular conjunction Libussa had promised and I became uneasy. If all her calculations had been wrong, then what would she do? Would I be of no further use to her?

"More heat!" she demanded of the acolytes, who set to with their bellows until the crucible must surely explode. Another slight flickering above caused her to turn her eager, burning face to the top chamber of the *Catinus Uteri*.

"Oh, Madam, we shall be consumed," said I.

She shook her head. "Fear not. The chamber shall hold us for as long as is needed. The Grail will protect us."

Now I had to call upon a faith near as great as her own. Yet I knew I should possess the necessary courage while the tincture and her own brave blood flowed in me. I believed we were inviolable and that we should become one flesh, as she promised, and would emerge to rule the world in the name of Reason. My scepticism was in abeyance. As long as we were together I cared for nothing else. I was ready to step as willingly as any Shadrach into that fiery womb and feel no pain. My body was already blossoming with a delicious numbness, together with a sensation of joyous ecstasy, all from within! My flesh was armour which nothing could pierce, no weapon, no heat, no cold . . .

As the Autumn Stars subtly flickered for the third time Libussa whispered very quiet in my ear. "You must be ready to use your sword as I direct. When that task's done, you'll hand me the blade."

Obedient, I nodded to show I had understood her instruction.

There came a rapid, noisy shuddering in the Earth. Distantly, all around, here and there, the Deeper City's older buildings fell as if shaken by a Tatary tremor. Slowly the shuddering ceased and there came another movement in the sky, sudden, flickering streaks of colour, new patterns appearing behind the old. When I studied them under Libussa's guidance I made out familiar constellations, from my own Earthly realm. "They all come together, you see," she murmured. "A million spheres in conjunction—more! The Mittelmarch and our world combining, and as they combine, so do they marry with all the other planes of existence. And as they congregate, von Bek, so do they turn!"

"Soon," the priestess stood beside us as if to utter an invocation. "Soon the Old Stars shall begin their Dance!"

"And when the Dance is finished," said Montsorbier in a calm, matter-of-fact voice, as if he issued orders from a Tribune's desk, "the new positions shall be fixed. The new order shall be established."

Their voices continued but became distant to my ears. I seemed divorced from them, from everything save Libussa. She squeezed my arm and led me closer to the crucible. The acolytes grew so hot it seemed their skin bubbled on hands and faces, yet crazily they continued to pump, to feed the noisy furnace. "It should be hotter still," she demanded. I had seen these creatures attack and kill, yet nonetheless I pitied their condition, though doubtless they felt little pain, as I felt none at all.

"There!" The golden priestess pointed. At last a single Autumn Star had begun to move, describing a shallow arc across the blackness. The huge pink-and-yellow disc was surrounded by a halo of dusty lilac. "*Astra Sultant*," murmured the girl, relishing the Latin words as another might roll wine on their tongue.

Montsorbier's face now seemed clear of all corruption. The

depravity and cruelty fell away from him in an instant as he wondered at that marvel, his lips parting like a schoolboy's. He craned his head back to follow the star progressing with stately majesty across the cluttered heavens.

Another moved, as if it must surely crash into its fellow. It was smaller, faint ochre in colour.

"The stars are dancing," said Montsorbier. "Oh, it is beautiful."

The crucible began to tremble and groan on its base. Strange, small whining noises escaped it. "It can be heated no higher, mistress!" cried an attendant.

She said softly to me, "Prepare your sword, my love."

I slung the scabbard from my back. I drew forth that superb blade. The polished steel reflected every light, almost as if the universe in miniature lived in my sword. The pommel was vibrant, but misty, providing only a glimpse of the still-screaming eagle. His mad eyes glared urgently at me for a moment before they vanished. For all its weight the sword had uncanny balance, resting lightly in my palm. My love for Libussa informed my love, at that moment, for the blade. I looked upon it in joyful wonderment.

All my life has been led in order to achieve this moment!

Two more great stars moved in unison across the sky and the Dance began in earnest. From a more distant point came a dark yellow sun, moving forward, yet seeming to fade as it grew to twice its size, then it danced to the north, held steady for a moment, then to the south. Other stars swirled around it, first in small groups, then in scores, then seemingly in thousands, sweeping and swirling, describing exact geometrical figures, moving in concert as they had always moved, but at incredible speeds. It could have been the course of their original progression through the heavens, but what had taken millions of years now came about in the space of minutes.

The sky was alive with the mellow colours of those Dancing Stars as they performed the measures of their cosmic galliard. Still precise, still majestic, there seemed a simple joy in the nature of their movement, like dignified old men and women determined to relish the life remaining to them. Sometimes they created mysterious pictures, with features shifting and transmogrifying and colours changing. The shades became subtler now, as the great stars drew closer together.

The Witnesses moaned in awe and moved in awkward imitation of those mighty suns. The Deeper City lost its appearance of nocturnal gloom and instead promised dawn. Her buildings still swayed and tilted, whispered and creaked, but they were no longer mere black silhouettes; their brick and stone was washed with warm light revealing individual features. They lost their menace and their mystery as they were displayed in their decrepitude. Great cracks were visible in their walls, pieces of masonry flaked and fell, chimneys twisted and crumbled, windows were distorted, as were doors, while shutters hung at unlikely angles. The spiral streets were undulating, rippling like flood water down the steep hills towards the Centre where we stood upon the O'Dowd's demolished dream. Meanwhile, beside me, the instigator of that ruin, the arch-arsonist Montsorbier whistled through his teeth as he observed the ever-moving firmament.

Our crucible now threw off vapour from its trembling metal as if it must soon melt. Libussa turned to Montsorbier. "Give me the Grail."

He turned, abstractedly, as if he could not remember who she was.

"Last night, when we made our bargain, you said you had captured something in the depths. You said I would recognise it."

"Aye." Casually he handed her the upturned helm, his main attention still upon the dancing stars.

"Well, Sir, I demand you reveal it to me before the Concordance."

Dreamily he shook his head. "No, Madam. After."

Then, to my utter surprise, Libussa said to me: "Kill them both, von Bek. Kill them, quickly!"

I was obedient. I could be little else. I was hers. The sword, light as ever, jumped in my grasp, almost anticipating my action. And I had sliced off Montsorbier's wide-eyed head and I had cut down the golden priestess in an instant and the sword had done what it did before, in the O'Dowd's sewers.

It had quartered them, all in the space of a second, precise as any experienced butcher. The limbs were neatly sliced from the torso and lay so that only by careful inspection could it be seen that they were not all of a piece. Yet this was certainly no trick instinctively learned from the Tatars. This, I was convinced, was the chief property of the sword itself. It was no wonder the enemies of Paracelsus had feared It.

If I said I had assassinated Montsorbier and the priestess I should scarcely describe the true sense of the event. That they deserved death was not in question, but I had acted as little on my own volition as the sword had acted on mine. I had merely been Libussa's instrument. I felt no pang of conscience, no self-disgust. Not then, though I had performed an action at odds with all I held honourable and humane.

Slowly, a certain distress filled me as I watched Libussa stooping as cheerfully as any farm lass gathering sticks to pick up the severed limbs and fling them into the furnace. In went an arm and in a golden head. In went Montsorbier's mildly astonished face. Would all of us soon be reduced to miscellaneous rubbish tossed into a stove? Was this the future Libussa sought to create!

"Madam, I would not wish to do such a thing again," I said to her, fearing lest my disgust angered her, for my love was as fierce as ever, my loyalty to her as complete. "This was no part of the prescription you offered me. You spoke, as did I, against blatant treachery, immoral life-taking. And this is as bad as anything I've been called upon to perform in France."

"Montsorbier, Sir, was evil and ruthless. Nor was his priestess less guilty of crime."

"That's a reason to shun them, Madam, not to kill them."

"You slew them, Sir."

Their blood continued to stain my steel and until it was off I had no wish to sheathe the weapon. "True," said I sadly.

Libussa frowned. "It is a question of Time, von Bek. There is so little now."

"You had made a compact with that pair and you never intended to keep it." I did not wish to persevere with the argument. I dropped my gaze to the black ash at my feet. I could tell that her anger grew.

"What, Sir?" she challenged me. "Shall you betray me, also? Like Klosterheim? At this crucial hour?"

"No, Madam, I shall not. But I cannot be dumb. By these actions we remain in league with the Beast. We succumb to fear, however subtly. No New Age can ever be truly that if it be founded upon the methods and the follies of the old. I learned as much in France. It is how I came to leave Paris and meet you."

"You were destined to leave and come here for your marriage."

"Aye, Madam."

This acquiescence satisfied her. She did not give a whit for my opinions or my sensibilities, so long as I continued to maintain the course I had committed myself to, body and soul. I would rather die than be separated from her. Yet I would have given a great deal for St. Odhran's reassuring vulgarity at that moment. I had murdered in cold blood and without a thought, there was no escaping that grim fact.

The colours flooded over us. The monstrous stars continued their elaborate dance. The Deeper City shook and swayed and all those naked Witnesses to our coming marriage huddled back from us, perhaps convinced now that they, too, should soon be slaughtered by my surgeon's cutlass. I had a sickening notion that they were right to be afraid of me.

Montsorbier's elegant bicorne, still with its tricolour cockade, lay at my feet. I picked it up and used it to clean the blade. The sword's pommel reflected the light above, all turbulent, misty colour, but then cleared to show the eagle, flinging himself against the crystal, his coppery wings beating harder than ever, his furious claws extending and contracting.

Libussa and I moved towards the fuming crucible. All the ashes stirred around us, reheated and smoking. Her tone was kind again. "Come, Sir, this is a marriage requiring no officiate.

Together we already possess more authority than any living creature and soon we shall enjoy omnipotence."

But, though I could do nothing save obey her, the joy was gone from it. There remained the thrilling anticipation of pleasure, the satisfaction that the union was to come about, the curiosity as to what we might expect as the resolution of all that ritual, but she had refused to banish the Beast and the purity was lost for me.

"We stand at the Tangential Core," she said. "No other sentient creature occupies this space. He who holds it shall impose all his dreams upon the generality affecting every future moment in mankind's history. We shall describe those terms, von Bek. Could God Himself ask for more? We shall set down the terms of the human condition!"

There was a roaring from above, as if an ocean were bursting through the skies to engulf us, but it was the tidal movement of the stars themselves as they began the concluding measure of their dance. Every colour there had ever been was now represented in the sky, points of hard light, swirls of soft; like watching eyes behind great war-banners blowing in the wind. But already the dance was slower.

She began to talk with rapid intensity so that my blood and brain quickened, my memories slid away. She was so awesomely confident. "You've not hesitated thus far, Sir, and you've proven my sense in choosing you. You have great courage for a man, great willingness to see the world afresh, great imagination. Now, Sir, tell me you are ready for the last stages of our marriage ritual!"

"I have always been ready, Libussa."

She stroked my flesh. "We shall be combined soon, sweet love. One flesh, one mind, one soul. The greatest prophecy shall be fulfilled and the yearning of all those mighty adepts shall find resolution at last. The golden work has always led to this moment, for thousands of years, since my people first began their search." She held up the battered helmet. "And here's the key, without which we might never have succeeded. With it, we cannot fail. Is it not the very essence of harmony?"

"You must let me slay the Beast," I said.

She either did not hear me or refused to listen. The colours were breaking and merging again. The massive stars grew threadbare. It was possible to see through them to new constellations, hard and sharp, upon the misty black. A vast disc dropped below the horizon and as it fell its very substance shredded away, like breath on a winter's evening. Another great body simply faded into invisibility. Yet still the dance continued, slower and slower, with fewer suns at every moment. It seemed the remnants of our Autumn Stars were staggering now, shivering with the fatigue of simply maintaining their existence. They had squandered their last few thousand years of life upon that single, splendid galliard.

"It is coming," she murmured and held my hand tight. "When this finishes, von Bek, it is the Concordance. Are you still loyal?"

"To perform the marriage?"

"Aye, to your destiny."

We were very close to the crucible. I understood now that she meant to consign us to those flames. It was her madness, yet at that moment I was no more free of it than she. If she intended to die, then I would die with her, for that was better than living without her.

In the shadows behind the crucible the Lion was prowling. I saw light fall intermittently upon his tawny skin. I heard him give a sound, half questioning whine, half threatening growl. Was he afraid he would lose his mistress? Or was she his sister? I remembered my dream of the Minotaur.

Star by noble star the great orbs faded and were gone. Again the sky appeared to shift while at the same time it grew deeper to reveal layer upon layer of points of light and shining swirls that were galaxies, still moving but now apparently close to their ultimate positions. It appeared that the point of space upon which we stood was the only fixed matter in the whole universe, as if the Earth, or our part of it, refused rotation. Perhaps that was why the tall buildings of the Deeper City had still not ceased their swaying; they resisted the general gravity.

The Lion made a low, unsettled noise. The crucible, groaning and whispering, was still white hot. Libussa herself bent to heave upon the bellows. There was a rush and flame flowered. It achieved a steady roar. She smiled as she moved closer to the crucible. She reached her hand towards me. "Quickly. We must become one at the very moment of Concordance. Quickly, von Bek." Her red lips opened as if she were swallowing fire. Her powerful body vibrated with anticipated lust—or was it merely greed? "Come!"

"Libussa," said I, "I love you for who you are. I love you as a human creature."

"I know that."

"You are the perfect woman. Your femininity is positive and potent. Your spirit is the bravest, your mind the keenest, your body the most beautiful. I love you, Libussa of Crete, and I offer myself to you in matrimony."

"Come, then, Sir. Come. Let's get on with it." Her back was almost against the fiery metal of the crucible. I looked at her wonderful, naked body and I almost wept. She held the helm in her left hand and beckoned to me with her right. She was smiling. Her lips were soft. She cajoled me. "Come, Sir . . ."

"This is no casual decision of mine, Libussa."

She smiled. "Your pride remains with you, my dear. Very well, if you wish it, I acknowledge your masculine generosity."

"I give myself up to you." I moved slowly towards her. Her lips were parted again, her red lips. Her teeth gleamed and her eyes were cloudy with desire. "Come, little one."

The crucible sputtered and the charcoal hissed. I saw a blackened hand twisting in the furnace as if Montsorbier waved a sardonic farewell. Libussa threw open the crucible's door and she was careless of its heat. Within I saw white fire glaring. "In here, little one. For the final blending. We shall be a single body. The Two shall become the One. Do you understand, little von Bek?"

I was now standing close to her, my naked flesh touching hers. The heat was terrific, but I could feel it no more than she. We were truly invulnerable, it seemed. She bent her head to kiss me upon the lips. She took a long, delicious kiss, as if she savoured me for the first time. And she sighed. "Ah, Sir, you cannot know what joy your courage purchases. But it will not be long before you are rewarded. Give me your sword, little one."

I made to pass her the blade but, in spite of me, my hand refused to move.

"Give me your sword!" In her eyes was the suggestion of a frown.

I forced my arm to move, to offer up the scabbarded steel. She stared languorously at me, her breath loud in her throat. "Oh, my beauty," she purred. "Promises shall be kept by us both, I swear." Her fingers touched the hilt and she gasped in pain. "Ah! What's this? I had forgotten. It is worse than any Grail!"

"It is *my* sword," I said, "but therefore I am sure it would not do you harm, Libussa, since we are almost One even now."

With the Grail still in her left hand she reached determinedly for the sword's hilt, plainly controlling great agony as, deliberately, she drew forth the blade from its scabbard. She smiled again at me and I knew fear.

For the first time I understood that she meant to slice me up as I had sliced Montsorbier. Perhaps she truly believed she would resurrect me when the deed was done, by placing my remains within the crucible. Or did she intend to *eat* me? I knew enough of a chemical notions of how adepts believed they could confer immortality on themselves and others by the process of dismemberment. The quartered corpse was duly resurrected, they hoped, in water, or sometimes fire. Or both. I looked into Libussa's eyes and saw the truth.

"Oh, Madam! Is it my execution?"

She was smiling still. "It shall be true immortality, von Bek. We shall soon become a single, hermaphroditic creature. Hermaphroditus Rex shall rule upon the Earth. It is all true, little one. Have faith, as I had faith upon the cross, and we shall be assured of eternal life. It is so. You must believe me now. Come. Waste no more time. The Astral Concordance is here . . ."

The scabbard dropped free, into the ash at her feet. She stood, with lips drawn back and teeth gritted, framed against the glowing copper and brass of her Chemical Womb, the Cup in one hand, the Sword in the other. Her tawny skin had always held its own radiance but now she herself seemed made of metal as she reflected the glare from the crucible. And she continued to smile.

Her body was enough to draw me close to her. Her sex, her beauty, her power. She required no logic to coax me. Her hand holding the sword shook as if every nerve knew excruciating pain. "Come . . ."

I was reminded of the ikon I had seen at Prince Miroslav's, then of Miroslav himself, split by a sword and clinging so hard to life, of the warnings he had given first her and then me. Momentarily alarmed, I stepped back.

Her smile vanished. Her expression was agony and disbelief mingled. "Little one! Come. Quickly."

I could not speak, though I opened my mouth. I was frozen.

"Little one!" She was close to weeping. She was incredulous. "You gave me your oath!"

I forced myself again to move forward. Relieved, she stood with arms outstretched, almost as if she still hung upon that cross. "Come!"

Slowly, panting, I tried to push my body towards her. I felt that my own agony echoed hers. I grunted. I gasped.

"What is it, little one? Why can't you come to me?"

"The Beast . . ." my breath was noisy in my throat. "Leave him behind. Slay him first. We have no need of him."

She laughed. "He shall be our imprisoned power. There is no need to discard such power if it is truly contained. I have tamed the Beast, von Bek. Come to me, von Bek. Come."

"Dismiss the Beast, Libussa. Kill him, I beg you. Let our harmony be won with nothing but our love and faith! Kill the Beast and I promise I shall let you do what you wish. Your risk, Libussa, must be as great as mine!"

"What?" In her obsession she was all but uncomprehending. "Would you betray me now?"

"You betray yourself. You betray us both. Reject the Beast."

"The Grail must be defended. The Beast defends it. Fool! Is this all mere excuse for cowardice?"

I stood still again. My eyes were fixed upon her body. I was a few feet from her. If I was to be executed I would rather it were there. "Slay the Beast. Then you may slay me. Let the Minotaur be abolished for ever from our world! Libussa, it is the only way!"

"I offer you resurrection, von Bek, and eternal life!"

The furnace, fuelled still by flesh and blood, began to howl and scream as if demanding further sacrifice. I was weeping helplessly. Still my feet would not move. In the shadows I was sure the Lion still prowled, ready to kill me if she did not. I wished so much to go to her, no matter what she promised or I threatened, but my body was immobile with terror. An enormous effort brought me another step nearer.

Above us, in that smoking sky, the last of the Autumn Stars went out.

In that black stillness now remained only a myriad of cold, white points, hard as the angry eyes of God. Their movement had stopped entirely. The Earth became utterly silent. A hushed tension infected the universe. It was as if everything in Creation awaited the outcome of my decision. The Concordance was upon us.

The Concordance of every sphere, of every occult and natural realm, was upon us. Lines of light began to pass now from star to star until soon the entire firmament was an infinitely complex web of gold and silver threads. It was astonishingly beautiful. And those threads shot down to touch us. Yet the darkness remained. Now I grew aware that the darkness was filling with the scream, the fiery glow of our Chemical Womb, as if the flames of Hell combined and were concentrated therein.

"There is still time," she whispered. She was an imploring statue with the Cup and Sword. "I mean you only good, von Bek. I offer life, power and union. I offer harmony, a Cure for the World's Pain. You have drunk my tincture and my blood. Does that mean nought to you, my own betrothed? Please do not betray my faith in you."

"Madam, if you embrace the Beast, you betray me." Those threads of light curled about us as if curious to inspect the upturned helm, that Grail.

My betrayal, it seemed, was not of any great importance to her scheme. I swayed. I dragged at my muscles until I was moving again.

"Ah!" Her hair was a blazing crown as she swung her head to glance into her furnace. She was still shaking with the pain of keeping hold of my sword. "Quickly! Quickly!" She stepped back to the Crucible's open door. "Quickly." She roared: "'Tis almost too late!"

Behind and above us was the cool light of the new stars; ahead was the glowing furnace. All these things were to be married at once, as we were married. I was to become part of that wholeness. This thought helped me revive my legs until I walked a few further steps, aware that the enormous heat from the Crucible did not burn me. Neither did the white radiance from within blind me. At last I stood beside her again. Though unharmed by the flames I could still feel the warmth and wonder of her flesh. I touched her and leaned up to kiss her lips, but her eyes no longer looked at me. Those eyes had turned to molten brass! "Not yet." She was a whispering volcano.

I shall never be able to explain the next sequence of happenings. I no longer hesitated. No matter what my argument, I was drawn to her, passing fluidly into that hissing Chemical Womb, my body alive with a terrible coldness and a terrible heat. They were consuming me. I was melting.

"Libussa!"

Within it was as though a silver universe heated and cooled then heated again all around me. I was trembling and weak but my faith (since I was as yet unhurt) was improving rapidly. By now I should have been dead; instead there was liquid metal in my veins; my eyes were steel, tempered and re-tempered a thousand times. My brain lost all indistinct thoughts. Every impression, every idea, had the clarity of a perfect diamond. I held up my arm. My skin flowed like quicksilver. I looked up and saw the Grail.

She held it above my head.

"We shall be the New Messiah!" Her voice rang like a golden bell. "We shall begin our ministry on Earth. Let them call us Anti-Christ, or Daemon, or anything they wish, but we shall define them and that will be inescapable. The Concordance encompasses us. Kneel!"

I obeyed her.

"We begin the Marriage of Sulphur and Mercury; that each may feed upon the other's flesh and blood. Thus shall our conjoining echo the conjoining of the Million Realms and lead us towards our Resolution and our Magistery. Behold! The fulfilment of our Art. The joining together of the Bride and Groom and their becoming One!"

I looked up into her incandescent beauty as she raised the sword. My lips opened and I cried out my love for her; all my divine love for her! There was metal in me. There was metal in my Womb. I was fully alive!

Now I give her my blood and my flesh. O, Libussa! I give you all my life. And you are drinking from the Cup and you are smiling down on me while our Crucible rocks and wails. You plunge the point of the Sword into the Cup and fresh fire blossoms. Your features are my features and seem to fuse; then become molten again, and writhe and smoke. But you are frowning, your eyes are suddenly puzzled . . .

The Crucible begins to shake. A different light fills our Womb. I try to rise but my limbs seem truly severed. The light comes from the Grail and is a cold light, like the starlight outside, and it opposes that which melts and marries us! The Grail begins to utter a sound, like the muffled tolling of a gigantic bell. It contains anger. It protests!

Throw away the Sword, my sister. My bride, I beg thee to banish the Beast! Renounce him and we shall be truly wed!

"Throw away the Sword. Renounce the Beast!"

She raged and she screamed in her agony but she would not discard the sword. Her flaming hair erupted about her head. Brazen lips screamed their furious pain and burning copper eyes became of themselves a terrible holocaust.

"NO!"

She would not be ruled. Neither would she be controlled in any way, not by me, not by any supernatural agency, not even by herself! Not at that moment, the greatest moment of her power.

"NO!"

Our Crucible, our cradle, our womb, creaks and sways. The Grail-light gradually fills it, banishing that other, more hectic, incandescence. You fling it from you, but it does not fall. Instead it hangs directly overhead, continuing to give full voice to its distress and anger. It tells us clearly how we produce a mere parody of Harmony, in direct conflict with its own. It will not go in alliance with the Sword or the Beast.

Yet you will not give up the Sword. Instead, taking it in your two hands you bring the blade, blow upon terrible blow, against the dented metal of the helm and you are shrieking with anguish. But all you achieve is a deeper tolling, beating more rapidly now and seeming to grow. Golden tears start from your eyes. Your mouth is unstable brass and silver saliva streams unchecked into the surrounding aura. The blade begins to buckle. You cry out in your frustration and now I understand how peaceful is the Grail, how more profound a destiny has been contained in me than ever any of us believed—for you have reversed the ruined Sword and you are bringing the pommel hard against the Cup. Down again! And the Cup is as unmoving, as fixed in its position, as those stars outside. You attack bedrock! Deeper comes the note of the bell, faster until it vibrates the entire Chemical Womb. You smash the Sword's pommel for the third time against the lip of the Grail. Your voice defies it. NO!

"NO!" she cried. She would not be cheated. It was unjust to cheat her. My blood, my flesh, the steel in my womb, all were unstable now. A dozen metals, swirling and shrieking, were in conflict therein. Drops of silver and gold fell upon me.

Drops of silver and gold fall upon my severed limbs and now here is pain at last. Yet my body heals. Every wound heals the moment it is made. But it is such agony. The marriage is not complete. I struggle towards you. Your face is the face of Medusa. Throw away the Sword, Libussa. I reach towards her. Her agony is without reward!

"Libussa! Throw away the Sword and we shall be united!"

"NO!"

The ruby pommel has touched the rim of the Grail for the third time.

The Messiah is still-born . . .

The ruby crystal burst with such deafening loudness it seemed to shatter my ears and drowned the booming voice of the Grail. Libussa paused. She was startled. Her mouth opened but she did not speak. The Grail grew silent. Slowly its light withdrew into it, then faded until it was just an ordinary, antique battle-hat again. Libussa plucked it from the air. She stared abstractedly from it to me. I began to climb to my feet. My body was so sore, so lacerated, so reddened by strange wounds about the throat, shoulders and thighs that I groaned in my distress and my despair.

She raised the ruined Sword again, turning towards me. Her eyes had lost their heat and her lovely breasts lifted and fell even more rapidly than mine. I moved towards her, to embrace her or be slain, I did not care.

"You were coward too long," she said. "You allowed the moment to pass."

"No, Libussa. You should have slain the Beast. Is that what Montsorbier brought up from the depths?"

"I saw nothing. I knew not what he brought."

"You did not see the lion?"

She shook her head.

"It was the Beast," I said. "The Grail protested." It had grown very cold. "Those who would harness the power of the Beast to rule their fellows shall be destroyed by it. Maria the Jewess gave the warning in all her writings. You must remember."

She stiffened like steel plunged in ice. She drew her wonderful brows together, looking down to the shattered ruby at her feet. Something moved there. It was a tiny, fluttering creature, a Phoenix . . .

No, it was the eagle, released at last from his captivity. It was the Beast within the Sword! Now I understood the pattern and I was afraid. I reached out to her but she ignored me. I believed I had no importance for her since I had failed to keep my bargain. She grinned as she dropped the sword and stooped to cup her hands around the bird. It screeched. It resisted. It was all noisy anger. She imprisoned it within her palms, looking at it through a chink in her fingers, then placing this cage to her ear, she listened.

"Libussa!"

Could I be of so little worth to her? Would she discard me so completely? I saw no reason why she should not. In her eyes I had failed to accept the greatest challenge offered to humankind.

The Crucible had grown cold. I stepped out into warmer darkness, cheered by an ordinary heat, the heat from the furnace and the ashes. That fire was almost spent.

Overhead traceries of light formed a pure and rational geometry. In wonderment I looked upon perfection. All we had sought to achieve was shown to be rude savagery in comparison.

"Libussa!" I wanted her to see so that she would know and be heartened. "Libussa!" But she remained within the Crucible, speaking in a low voice to her miniature king of birds.

I looked up into the mighty tranquillity of a fully ordered universe. I began to weep.

Then suddenly she was shouting.

"There is still time!"

Bursting from the Crucible she rushed through billowing ash towards the black cross. The vile gibbet still stood where we left it. Out of the drifting dust figures began to rise, the last of her congregation. Dust clung to her naked body. I called to her, but she did not hear. She would not hear me. I had ceased to exist. "Libussa! Stop!" I still loved her.

Her followers began slowly to stumble or crawl in the direction of the cross. Their filthy bodies, their wretched faces, their horrible, weakling eyes, caused me to wonder if I resembled them now. Had that been my true destiny?

She turned with her back to the cross. What could she be planning? To begin the ritual over. It was too late. The Concordance was here. She called out.

"Come!"

From behind me I heard an echoing shriek; a shriek which displayed a fierce thirst for revenge. How long had that bird been locked within the sword? Had Paracelsus harnessed the Beast or had the Sword been forged during an earlier Concordance? It shrieked again, reminding me of Klosterheim's scream as he fell towards this very spot. Had my old enemy been reincarnated so quickly?

I turned towards the Crucible. The metal had cooled and the horrid fire was out, but from within the sphere, his great body framed for a moment against the fading luminosity within, his eyes as mad and wounded as Libussa's, the spines of his feathers rattling as he shook his huge wings, strutted a massive golden eagle. Without pausing he took to the air. He was the shining one now. He it was who seemed made all of copper and brass as he beat his way up into that brilliant night. He had been born and reached maturity thanks to the last shreds of our Crucible's magic!

Libussa's body was flat against the black, charred wood of the cross. Her gaze followed the eagle's flight. Up he went towards the orderly web of starlight. Higher and higher he flew until he had vanished. I sighed in relief, unable to guess why I feared him more than I had feared anything else.

"Libussa, I love you. Come from this place. There is yet hope . . ." I wanted her so much. Still, I would have died for her. "There is work you and I can do, Libussa. The Grail would aid us, if we obeyed its rules . . ."

"I shall make the only rules, von Bek! You hesitated. You failed us both."

"I warned you against the Beast. Come away from here, Libussa. I beg you. Accept my love . . ."

"What does that mean, von Bek?" She shivered, her whole body blue with cold. She stretched up and tried to touch the horizontal timber with her finger-tips. She turned back. "If you would serve me still, you must re-crucify me! Will you prove your love by doing that?"

Helplessly, I said, "I will do anything, Libussa. You still cannot understand."

"Good. Then help me up, man!"

"There's even less meaning to this ritual," I told her softly. "The moment's gone. You said so. It is true."

All her old authority returned to her voice. "If you love me as you say, von Bek, you will do as I ask."

I obey you. I shall always obey you. Upon your instructions your servants replace the Crucible upon its tumbril and roll it until it stands at the base of the cross. Climbing on this we help you back to your original position. The nails are in my hand. You display your stigmata. The holes go clean through you, but they do not bleed. It is not difficult to replace the nails so that you hang, almost in contentment, breathing with difficulty, your head upon your shoulder, your eyes looking up at the myriad intersecting streams of light. "Thank you, von Bek," you say. "You may leave me now."

But I am disobedient in this one thing. I kiss you upon your cheek, your lips, your breasts, your stomach and your sex. Your flesh is so cold. I would warm it with my own breath.

You begin to laugh, but it is a terrible mockery of laughter, containing so much torment it is possible to believe your pain might indeed be half the world's! I fall back, blocking my ears. This is the least bearable of all the hideous sounds which lately came to me. I cry out, unable to stop my own pathetic pleading. I roll from the roof of the Crucible into the ashy filth below.

I got slowly to my feet. Her laughter continued. She stared directly at me. Her pain and her cynicism were torment for me. I threw my weight against the Crucible, scattering her Witnesses, and I pushed at it, rocking it until it crashed over. As soon as it fell the metal sphere cracked, steaming; I searched amongst pieces of ruptured metal, looking for the helmet. The Grail would save her, I was convinced. The Grail would heal us both, for it cured all pain. As I searched, I heard her laughter cease. There fell a dreadful silence, a silence of expectation. What more could happen? Frantically, I continued to search.

Then, from the darkness above, I heard the beating of huge wings. I looked up. The eagle was rushing back, as if that had been his purpose all along. His curved beak opened in a ghastly croak; his monstrous claws were extended. He fell towards us, striking as if we were prey, his mad, betrayed eyes fixed upon the cross. Unconsciously I fell back, certain I was his victim.

But I was wrong. He had marked the crucified woman! In a hideous confusion of flapping wings and feinting talons, his claws were raking her and his croaking was muffled as his beak rent her flesh.

"Libussa! Oh, Libussa, my love!"

She had begun to laugh again, that same chilling laugh. She jerked upon the cross but could not get free. Every movement added ruin to her body. She did not wish to die in this way but was yet amused by the irony!

Desperately I searched now for a weapon.

Here is the twisted remains of my Paracelsian dissector. Picking up the shard I fling myself towards the cross. Still the eagle feeds, and still the woman laughs, alive though already half-eaten. Clambering upwards, I am weeping as I stab wildly at the gigantic bird. It is my own body he kills. He screams; his movements growing more agitated. I am inflicting monstrous wounds on him, Libussa, but he refuses to turn on me. He is possessed. He will feed only off your living flesh. You are blood from head to foot and now at last your laughter ebbs. I stab at his throat, at his eyes. Your laughter is almost inaudible now . . .

His talons are ripping through your breast. Screaming some profoundly obscure victory shout, the eagle holds up one dripping claw, displaying to me your living heart! Your beating, human heart!

Libussa! I love you!

A final burst of laughter. Blood pumps. The eagle glares at me almost benevolently. Then his ragged flesh and gory feathers rise into the air and fly up, up towards the fresh Conjunction, the blinding heavens. His last scream fills the sky, blending with the fading echoes of Libussa's humour. Libussa, you hang dead upon your black cross, without hope of resurrection. You are Anti-Christ betrayed. How complete was the ritual of reversal which you borrowed from Montsorbier! You did not realise, Libussa, how complete it was.

Frantically, I stood upon the remains of the Crucible, trying to prise out the nails once more, but I could not get purchase and my fingers slipped in her blood. I was wailing in my own unbearable grief. I found that I was licking her corpse, licking it clean as an animal would. I had it in mind to make a fire under the Crucible again, to fling her remains into her Alchemical Womb and somehow bring her back to life. I searched for the spring which had gushed there not long since and restored her to me. Rubble had collected over it. As we performed our abortive wedding in her furnace, the buildings of the Deeper City had continued to subside. Many were still standing, still swaying and groaning, still tumbling majestically into the pit, falling towards the tangent where I stood, my face in her belly, my arms about the cross of charred oak. Here there was no history. We were on the very edge of time.

"Oh, Libussa, tell me what I must do! Tell me your desire! I serve you. It is all I wish to do."

More of the tired tenements of Amalorm made a final spastic jig before toppling from the highest rim. Others fell from her many terraces. They flung stone and brick and slate at my feet. There were clouds of dust. The noisy crashing of stone upon stone seemed designed to drive all living creatures out, so there should be no witnesses to their indignity. Only I was left. Up those damaged spirals ran the Witnesses and all the other survivors. Everyone fled to the Lesser City's dubious sanctuary.

Oh, Libussa, you were never a villain. You did no wrong which had not already been practised on you. You are martyred, as woman is ever martyred, particularly if she seeks her own power.

Is it true, Libussa, that I lacked courage at the last? When I willingly knelt before you and offered blood and flesh in that celebratory wedding feast? I understand now that you meant me no harm and that all I experienced was probably no more than your inspired insanity, the power of your will over mine, my lust for your person. I think you truly believed you could make of us one creature, one physical hermaphroditic immortal. It was not I that slew you, remember? You do understand as much, I am certain. Neither did you slay yourself or engineer self-destruction. It was an inheritance from the past which brought about our ruin. You would not relinquish the past any more than I. And you were destroyed by that, as it will always destroy you, that captured Beast of Paracelsus, that creature of magic and animal rapacity.

Or were we all among the victims of cunning Lucifer?

The power of the Beast cannot be controlled. It must be abolished. The Grail protested because you sought to pervert its function. In your anger you released the Beast and in return the Beast ripped out your heart and flew with it into the stars. Are you fated, Libussa, in some other universe, to suffer for ever that Promethean martyrdom? Or does your heart beat for ever in Hell?

"You cannot hesitate now!" you cried as the stars conjoined. You commanded me to enter the Chemical Womb. "I trust you with my future, with my spirit. Do not fail me, von Bek."

Thus woman trusts in man down all the years and so, as always, is betrayed.

Chapter Twenty

In which I witness the end of an age and meet old
acquaintances. Some speculation concerning
the aspirations of mankind.

I SAT AMONGST the cold ruins of Libussa's crucible and kept vigil at her feet, occasionally staring up at the fresh constellations and patterns of light which crossed from star to star. All was frozen; lines and spheres. I wondered if it would stay fixed thus for ever. When might they begin to move again? I asked Libussa, but she was in no condition to reply.

I had waited there patiently in the hope that magically she would heal. I did not know, even if she did heal, if the eagle would not return to rip out her heart again. I remembered reading in some old grammar about the dangers of the rituals of repetition. I tried to recall how Prometheus had escaped his similar fate.

The Deeper City was now almost fully down, although a few houses remained upright, defying all the laws of nature, before they too went shuddering into dust with a weary roar.

The Lion was lost to us. I suspect he vanished when her spirit left her body. Yet the longer I waited at her feet the more I believed I could hear, from somewhere beneath the débris, the snorting and panting of a beast. I was certain I had detected, at least once, the angry pounding of some enormous club.

I still did not know the exact nature of Montsorbier's secret discovery in the depths. Could it have been Libussa's Minoan ancestor? And mine. (*Libussa, your blood is my blood. It remains vibrant, wonderful blood. I need nothing else. I am yours, Libussa, still. And you belong for ever to me.*)

It grew increasingly cold in those ruins. The young stars lacked warmth. I breathed too much soot. Could the pair of us have succeeded, at least partially, in changing history's course? Had we perhaps defined just one of the terms by which humankind would live and struggle to seek its cure from pain? Or had we opened the gates of the world to Chaos?

Her ragged corpse was limp upon its cross. She had been an extraordinary woman who had believed she could remake the world in a saner mould. She was no martyr. She died because she longed for power, but she wanted power because she recognised that there was inequality in the world. And that, perhaps, is ever a contradiction.

As I considered this, a thin pallor began to spread across the Deeper City's broken horizon; a grey strip of light established itself. This gave me to hope that Libussa and I might be astonished by some fresh Mirenburg miracle. If we could only have retreated in time to happier days and retained our experience of the future . . . We had harmed no-one, changed nothing, save ourselves. The miracle, however, was not for us.

Old Mirenburg's unique night was coming to an end for ever, with the abolition of the Autumn Stars. Her particular wonder was disappearing from the city. No longer timeless, she would come to know the rule of stricter princes than the Sebastocrator, for it seems that Chronos must inevitably gather power.

I witnessed Mirenburg's first ordinary dawn. It revealed strange shadows dissipating amongst the broken stones of Amalorm. Little beasts and larger bugs scampered through the fading gloom and wriggled into cracks between the toppled slabs, many doubtless beginning an exodus for lost starlight. The sun shimmered with dissipated radiance which fell upon Libussa's body. I hoped for a moment it would bring her to life. I watched intensely to see if those new rays would affect her. I hoped to see her lift her head and smile; to tell me simply that she had played a game, that she had sought only to demonstrate a lesson. But there was a raw, red wound in her breast, where her heart used to be, and from it dropped the occasional bead of blood which fell upon her shattered metal womb. The only movement was when the breeze made strips of flesh or hair flutter.

The sun was up in earnest now. For a while I was blinded by golden light. I could not leave her. I had nowhere to go. I loved her.

The light remained bright and the surrounding ruins became misty. Some time later I had the impression of a tall figure wading through the ashes, stopping now and again to pick amongst the rubble. Eventually the figure paused nearby and turned to me. Still dazzled, I could not determine any details of its features, could not see if it were a man or a woman. But then I recognised its outline.

"Can you save her?" I asked. "Can you restore her to me, Sir? Or tell me how I may command the Grail to do so?" I realised to my surprise that I had been weeping all the time.

The figure shook its head and gestured sadly. "I'm no longer permitted such power, von Bek. Not here on Earth, at any rate. And neither you nor I, nor any living thing, natural or supernatural, can command the Grail. The Grail, as I told you once before, is itself. It brings all to balance. But it will not be manipulated. It is Harmony personified!"

"Is that why you gave me that terrible sword?"

"My gift, you recall, was unconditional. You were told as such. It was yours to use as you saw fit. I had no special intent for it . . ."

"You are still the old Lucifer, then? Still devious, still mystifying, still obfuscating?"

"You do me wrong, Sir, if you think so."

"Oh, Lucifer, what is it you want from us? Pity? Forgiveness? What?"

"Victorious triumph!" said Hell's monarch frankly. "That alone shall restore all to Grace."

"And what shall restore Libussa to me?"

"She is within you."

"I do not appreciate your comedy, Sir."

"It is for you to determine, Sir." Was he hinting at a bargain?

"I do not serve you, Lucifer." I was shivering in the cool air but noted that my body was coming to life again as my anger grew. "I would have served her, Sir. I wished to serve her. It was through no lack of desire that I failed . . ."

"Not a moral scruple?"

"For her sake. I did not wish to see her destroying what she valued so highly. I lacked courage. I feared the Beast. Together we would have beaten you, Sir. Where did the eagle carry her heart?"

The figure came to sharper focus for a second. The face was gloriously, androgynously beautiful and very gentle in its concern. "Well," said Lucifer, "at least you serve the truth, still. And I can thank you for that. And you judge, still . . ."

"Sir, I do not judge! I cannot judge!"

"Sir, you judge others and you judge yourself." He smiled. "As for your question," his expression changed, "I can only answer that there are certain realities less pleasant than Hell."

Lucifer had positioned himself where the crucible had burned that night. He stooped very suddenly and bent down. He lifted the battered antique helm into the air. I had no liking for the Grail, for it had destroyed the woman I loved. I considered its guardianship not as a family duty but as my family's curse.

Lucifer held it up to the sky, almost in celebration, and for a moment a million coloured rays sprang from it, fanning upwards and seeking the bodies of those new constellations.

"This was in its place?" he asked. "During the Concordance?"

"Aye."

"Then there may be more than a little hope for us, von Bek, after all."

I wanted no further intercourse with Lucifer, nor any further mysteries. "Take the thing back to Hell with you, Sir. That is where it deserves to dwell."

"I shall try to hold on to it," said Lucifer.

Again the Grail caught the sun and blinded me. When I next could use my eyes both it and Lucifer had vanished.

I spent that morning pulling her corpse from the cross and lighting a pyre on which I placed all surviving relics of her ruined dream, then, gently, I laid her on top of that ramshackle heap. A few coals remained to set the thing afire. It burned well enough. Again I had half a hope it would revive her, that primitive imitation of the night's rituals, but the corpse burst and roast and stank like Christmas pork and became one with the rest of the ashes. Yet Lucifer had been right. I had her within me.

I walked away from the cooling pyre, with some intention, I recall, of taking my own life, when I heard overhead a familiar collection of coughs and bangs and stutterings. It was the sound of the gunpowder engine.

Flying very low through the noon mist, its peculiar machinery giving off brown smoke, came St. Odhran's battered *Donan*. The green-and-gold Gryphon had a faintly ridiculous air to it, hanging so soberly, so dramatically, beneath the bulbous canopy of his weather-stained scarlet-and-white balloon. I found that I was weeping again, and waving. I had never guessed how much I should welcome that contraption and her master, or how sweet his friendship would prove to be.

My dandy Scotchman was peering over the side of the basket, a telescope in one long and elegant hand, his finger and thumb upon his valve cord. "Halloo, the ground! Come aboard, Sir. We leave the Mittelmarch this day!"

Then St. Odhran narrowed his eyes and looked aghast, as if he had just noticed something freshly peculiar about my person.

Then he offered me a devilish broad grin. "By God, Sir, ye're stark naked!"

I looked down at my own resurrected body.

"By God, Sir," said I, "so I am!"

Epilogue

THAT SAME DAY we sailed from the Mittelmarch, with the intention of never visiting those regions again. Prince Miroslav's maps and instructions were invaluable, as was his gunpowder engine. We were able to steer a direct course into our own world.

At my insistence we returned to Mirenburg. There I planned to give up all the money we had raised on our Air-ship swindle. We were received as heroes by the populace and invited to attend the Prince himself. He had not, we discovered, put a pfennig into the scheme but in her will the Landgräfin had left large sums to us both (the reason, it was revealed, for her nephew's fury), while much of the rest of the gold had come from the estate of the Duchess of Crete and was judged to be rightfully ours. Suddenly, we were legitimately rich!

If I say that St. Odhran was almost suspicious of his own luck, while I had mixed feelings in the matter, the reader will understand. I would have given up everything to have had Libussa restored to me.

Only my old friend and comrade Sergeant Schuster (who, it appeared, had entertained more than an inkling of our original plan) was unambiguous in his joy at our good fortune. He insisted upon giving us a celebratory dinner in the main hall of The Martyred Priest. The atmosphere of good will and jolly fellowship which infected the occasion did something to relieve my grief and remind me of the world's ordinary pleasures. Shortly thereafter I began the journey back to Bek, leaving St. Odhran in Mirenburg where he and several local people of a scientific persuasion intended to discover the secrets of Miroslav's gunpowder engine and build the aerial boat which until then had only existed in his imagination.

In Bek I was soon enjoying the pleasant comforts and familiar love of my mother and father. Both were delighted to welcome me, though they remarked me much changed (and chiefly for the good, they thought) and my father, who was by that time ailing, began to speak of giving me gradually increasing responsibility in the running of the estate I would inherit, since my older brother was not expected to live much longer.

There was no denying the appeal of that peaceful and ordered life, that rural harmony, that habit of rigorous reasoning and moral investigation which is our family tradition. The Library at Bek is known to be the finest in Germany, and I soon discovered, once I had learned what to search for, that it gave me a wealth of reading upon those subjects dominating my thoughts. Yet in spite of the tranquillity, the profusion of learned works, the benign affection of my dear family, and the leisure, in which to trace almost the whole romantic history of the Cartagenas, the Mendozas, the Chilperics and that specific line which brought the three together, I slowly concluded I did not have the appropriate character nor, indeed, vocation to become Bek's next Lord.

In truth, I was fitted to be nobody's Lord; and my mother's hopeful references to matrimony, though well meant, became offensive to my ears. Libussa remained my betrothed, in life or death, and in case the reader should conclude I fostered a morbid affectation within my breast, such as the heroines of the modern romances exhibit in the new breed of English novel and its progeny, I should make it plain I neither despaired nor was unusually subject to fits of Melancholy, wild frenzy or mysterious terrors. Libussa lived within me, as she lives now, and I was easy in that knowledge. Unlike the heroines of, say, *The Castle of Wolfenbach* or *The Orphan of the Rhine*, I, as Libussa, had scant capacity for languid terror and continued to be of an active disposition. What I most desired was the easy, unselfconscious, trusting comradeship of women, whose sensibilities often nowadays seemed so much closer to my own.

Whatever worked that alchemy, whether it be the mixed tincture and blood of that terrible ritual, or simply my ordinary experiences as Libussa's lover, there was no question that it had transformed me irredeemably. My interests remained the same (I had never had much taste for heroical warfare, hunting or the like) but they gradually broadened to include those which Society tells us belong to the Woman's Sphere but which are not simply occupations; they suggest a certain way of observing the world. My energies were devoted increasingly to gardening, it is true, and to music.

Perhaps this change in me is best explained by my mother's references to my "affectionate and devoted nature," my honest willingness, considered unusual in a man, to attend my poor brother when, in the last stages of his Consumption, he was permanently bedridden. Yet I continued to love late nights, talking of the most outrageous and unlikely subjects at extravagant length with my father's friends or my youngest brother (soon summoned home in expectation of Ulrich's demise). Also the frequent visits of Baron Karsovin, whose wife I found both charming and intelligent, though much in awe of her raconteur husband, were always anticipated with considerable pleasure. What greatly frustrated me was the segregation of the sexes, so that I was unable, much of the time, to choose the company I momentarily desired, and the deep-set assumptions expressed (as frequently by women as by men) on the matter of what did and what did not constitute either Man's or Woman's estate. Increasingly, after my brother's death, I began to make trips abroad, to ease my boredom and restore my wits. The frequency of these trips at length began to distress my parents and I knew that I must resolve the matter sooner than I had planned.

I arranged an interview in my father's study. This lay upon the ground floor in the east wing of the house. It looked out upon the ornamental hedges and flower beds I myself had created only the previous year and which were pleasing to my father, who enjoyed beauty but always swore he had "no cleverness for making it." My father welcomed the interview. I suppose he believed he was to learn what I had been doing on my trips abroad.

At the agreed time he seated himself in his usual chair, patiently lighting his old churchwarden, looking out into the late Summer garden; it was a Monday afternoon in the year of 1797 (the second year of the Directory, following that in which Bonaparte became General of the Army in Italy and won victories at Lodi and Arcola). We discussed the news from France, as we often did, and he expressed some pleasure in his sense of things "settling down again." I seized, as we say, the deer by the antlers. Hesitantly at first I explained why I felt I was unsuitable for the responsibilities of the next Graf von Bek and that I believed my younger brother Rickhardt was the better choice. Moreover he would be sure to provide Bek with an heir. My father frowned at this last and enquired delicately if there were any "difficulties" in that area— perhaps a wound, he suggested—but I assured him that my life had been dissolute enough in France and America; my tendency at present was towards celibacy.

I reassured him hurriedly that I was not ready to become a Jesuit. I believed thoroughly, I told him, in the old family tale concerning God's commission to Lucifer, therefore I did not see much to be gained from a directly religious life. However, my tendency, I said, was to join some lay group dedicated to good works—some arm, I had thought, of the Moravians.

After some discussion he gave me his blessing and there was a tear or two in his eyes which he wished me to ignore.

"This running of land," he said a few moments later, as we walked together in the garden, "is a difficult business. It imposes duties upon one, and sometimes pointless disciplines. It imposes a role, too. I do not believe I was much cut out to be a patriarch, Manfred, yet here I am—a good, old typical Saxon *Vaterstädter*, indistinguishable, no doubt, from a hundred others. 'Tis my choice and I don't much regret it. But I must let you know, my son, that I have sympathy with your decision. And Rickhardt, doubtless, will be only too happy to step into my shoes, since he never had hopes of that!"

We walked out of the garden and across the meadows, towards the old, ruined Abbey which had stood there since the eighth century. There was little of it left and most of that was covered with vines. It lay amongst trees, on the other side of a rustic bridge.

My father paused on the bridge, looking down into the slow, weed-strewn stream and the minnows darting just beneath the surface. "What constitutes a man's duties and what are a woman's is ordained by God, they say. Yet, if 'tis true God's abandoned us (and our family motto says that's so), then why should we not refuse His reasoning as He refuses us the comfort of Certainty?"

As good parents will he had somehow found the crux of my problem without, for a second, guessing the superficial truth.

"I am not sure I know, Father."

"It's money, it seems," he said with a smile. "All a question of inheritance, and power, of course, since that comes with it—with Land." He looked about his fields. "You are certain you wish to give up this easy, comfortable power, my boy?"

"Fervently," I said with a smile which set him to chuckling. We continued on across the bridge and into the shade of the old Abbey. Midges clustered there and my father blew smoke from his pipe to drive them away.

"We enter an Age which values all this far more than I ever did," he said, "and at the same time conspires to destroy it. Was the world always full of so many paradoxes, Manfred?"

"I think so," I told him. "Always."

"I believe you're right, my boy."

St. Odhran was due to visit us. He had written to say that not only had he failed to understand Miroslav's design, he had spent half his fortune on a scheme to manufacture the gas called Vodo-rodium and met with complete lack of success in that direction. He had, however, met a wonderful English woman who showed intelligent and original interest in scientific enquiry, and he wished me to meet her. Her name was Lady Susan Vernon. In his letter he could not resist adding that he had certainly gone up a notch or two in Society since his early beginnings running "close to the gallows" in the Scottish slums. I looked forward to their visit and arranged with my father that I would leave with them when they returned to Mirenburg.

Lady Susan Vernon was everything St. Odhran described and moreover she was a great beauty, with curly black hair and brilliant blue eyes, a wonderful match. We became excellent friends almost at once.

St. Odhran said he was tiring of Mirenburg, that all countries were backward now, even the new France, compared to England. "It's a land of engineers, old friend," said he when, in stripes and flounces and tilted beaver, he brought the latest mode to Bek. "It may lack even a moderately good cuisine, or comfort, or decent weather. It is a land, in the main, of drunken brutes and condescending Philistines, of hypocrites and complacent know-nothings, but it has the raw materials of my trade. Moreover, of course, it is Susan's home. Her family has met me. Her father's something of an amateur experimenter. She's a genius. I'm thought a suitable groom. And you must be my Best Man."

Doing my best to disguise any sudden sadness at his words, I accepted with what I hope was good grace. Then I made a joke. "And what are those raw materials? I always thought them a pack of playing-cards and a brace of barkers!" I would never let him forget our less respectable past. It always amused him. He was proud of it and had kept no secrets from his fiancée.

"Odd's blood, me dear," said he in that new limp manner of the English dandy, "but ye'd dem' near have a sense of humour if ye wasn't a German!"

He continued in great enthusiasm about the experiments with steam, the new metals and the machines which would soon make England one vast manufactory. After Mirenburg, where he was arranging his affairs and transferring his funds, he would go first to Glasgow then join Susan Vernon in London. He meant to do great things, he said, but would have to begin in the North. And, he told me privately, if anyone recognised him for a Newgate-absentee, it would not present much of a problem for him now. "Lud, it'd cost me a hundred guineas! For the Prince himself would have to be sweetened!"

I told him of my decision and what had happened to me. He thought the matter over, then nodded and embraced me. "She still inhabits you, then?"

"Aye. 'Tis part of it." We stood upon Bek's remaining battlements (all that was left of the old, dark Schloss) and looked out over lovely Autumn fields, where placid cattle cropped amongst the fallen, over-grown trees, beside the winding stream. There were oaks and lichen-covered elms, meadows of wild flowers. In the distance was the smoke of our village's hearths, for we were feeling the first hint of Winter. It was almost sunset.

He put a long arm about my shoulders. "Courage is never con-stant, dear friend. It comes and goes, according to circumstances. Like water in a well. And 'tis as hard to keep steady as mercury."

The morrow brought a very sober morning, the sun making only very few efforts to appear; yet I augured from it everything most favourable to my wishes. We were upon our way. St. Odhran, Lady Susan and I boarded the diligence for Mirenburg, and all my bags were packed up on it. My mother kissed me farewell while my father hugged me with sudden strength. I told them I could be reached in care of Sergeant Schuster at The Martyred Priest. St. Odhran lifted his hat to all and amiably said "Good day" in English, to the delight of my youngest sister's children who thought him fine amusement. Then we were off on the Prague Express, squawking tantivies and rattling harness, as the six-horse team galloped against the clock to ensure its record.

After some time in Mirenburg, where I found my memories and dreams mingling too painfully for my taste, I accepted St. Odhran's request to return with him to Glasgow. In that pretty city he found himself part of a new élite. They were called by the press in England "Kettleheads" and had a common interest in the uses of the improved steam-engines, some of which were already driving carriages at over five miles per hour! In St. Odhran's shadow, I became fairly famous in my own right, since I shared his enthusiasms and saw all that machinery as a means of ultimately liberating mankind from bestial toil. He planned to launch a new steam-powered Air-ship. In the meantime he invested in engines for the driving of ships and weaving-mills, and that type of machine proved so popular he could scarcely find sufficient follies on which to squander his profits. I, too, benefited from the enter-prises and began to consider the possibility of founding a model village, a tiny universe, as it were, where at least a few of those new labouring men and women could find equality and tranquillity. St. Odhran entertained hopes for a Steam Carriage Roadway which would carry several vehicles at a time, perhaps utilising the Canal towpaths.

St. Odhran, in Lady Susan's laughing presence, confided that it was difficult for him to believe, after so many years a Swindler, that people possessed dreams which actually, by dint of experiment and careful investigation of Nature, could be made reality. He continued to speak as someone who had hit upon a perfect Fraud for which the Law could not reach him. "I've decided that I have not changed by a hair, neither have those people's dreams changed—what has changed, I would guess, is Reality itself!" They both laughed at this and I joined in, but I wondered if perhaps Libussa had achieved something, after all.

Occasionally I wonder if both of us had been allowed to go only so far—to accomplish the Devil's work. We had nothing but Lucifer's word he did not control us. Yet it is also true that my failure of courage and her failure to banish the Beast would inevitably have conspired to ruin any large success for her alchemical schemes. Yet perhaps we both viewed matters too simply.

Alchemy, in a few brief years, has become the material for low comedy: it is no longer feared for its occult powers, as it was in my day. The engineers like St. Odhran are suddenly ascendant, when not long since the public had decided that those same men were the buffoons and crackpots. So there, too, it is possible to say Libussa failed. She threw her entire fate upon a single card. Her stake was not merely her own. She risked the fortunes and lives of dozens. And she lost. The Day of the Lion failed to dawn. Today is the Day of the Steam Engine. Perhaps she was after all a martyr: a martyr to changing times. But her death might also have been valuable in bringing those times about.

I am still in London, though I have paid visits to Bek and to Mirenburg (where, by a mysterious personage, I exchanged letters with and send books to a certain Philarchus Grosses, whose little singular volume I still possess). I stay always at The Martyred

Priest. Old Schuster still maintains a share in the hostelry run by his daughter. We talk for hours, the same stories in the main, about our days as Revolutionaries in America, the fate of France, the fortunes of young Krasny (who writes to Ulrica) after his considerable achievements with Bolivar in South America. Less frequently I delay my journey in Prague when I am on my way to Bek. I go in my carriage to a certain house near the Château-le-Blanc, where a group of old men meet to discuss the days of their former power and plan for a time when they will again startle the world. We discuss the old wisdoms, the arcane lore of alchemy, the Chemical Marriage, the Great Conjunction and so forth. I am honoured by them as their High Magister and enjoy considerable respect. If they are disappointed in me it is only because I refuse to support them in their dreams of a revival of what they term "the Golden Work." There are some amongst them who would flatter me. They say I have scarcely aged at all, I am still the same Duke of Crete, last possessor of the pure Tauran blood, older than the human race itself; the same they knew a quarter-century since. And if I smile and make light of all that, it is not to mock them. These days it is wise to keep perspective. Unless we do so, can we ever hope to see true Harmony: a Cure for the World's Pain?

"That secret lies in the Grail," they tell me. "And the Grail is locked up in Hell. Lucifer has charge of it." Thus they explain their failures, the decline of their power. On that subject I would not display my scepticism.

We all continue to grow rich in England on the profits of our former idealism. I have described to St. Odhran my feelings of ambiguity on the matter but he tells me I have no need to agonise over the morality of it. The New Age will come, he tells me, but it will be a messy and sometimes painful birth, too complex for any single being to understand. "The danger will lie in attempting to simplify it," he says.

On the insistence of Lady Susan, I began in the Summer of 1817 to set down this account of my story. She insisted that my experience should not go unrecorded. Thus I complied and the manuscript, as agreed, shall be put in her safe-keeping to do with as she pleases after my death (she being a few years younger than myself and in better health). Should she die, the manuscript is willed to her nearest female relative. Of my further adventures and discoveries, I have said nothing. They belong, I believe, to another account, which, if ever I am able, I shall also retail. It is my intention soon to return to Mirenburg, where I have bought a small house in Rosenstrasse. I believe I would rather live with what remains of my pain in a place which we once shared.

I look forward to taking an open carriage and driving beside the Rätt during the month of October, when Mirenburg grows mild and sleepy. My coachman shall take me out just before dawn, when the stars are still visible. Later I shall ask him to stop upon the Mladota Bridge. The air is always clear there, bearing the smell of wood-smoke, Autumn leaves and late Summer flowers. A few barges move slowly through the mist of the Rätt; early-risen boatmen call mutual greetings from a distance.

Then there's the sun! A golden Mirenburg dawn flooding into the pale blue of the sky, washing across the river, illuminating glittering domes and silver spires on either side, and the doves which nest nearby flutter up through the morning, a cloud of white enlivened by the light.

When Mirenburg begins to come fully awake, opening cafés and shops, trundling produce through her streets, setting off to school, I shall begin the drive back to Rosenstrasse. Mirenburg is an extraordinary city, more peaceful and beautiful than most, but the people who live in her are no different; they conduct their lives and business pretty much as others do. It is a warm, old city, with a traditional tolerance of strangers.

She is within me always, my Libussa. If her alchemy failed radically to change the world, it achieved permanent transformations elsewhere, through those she influenced. But I prefer to remember the earlier times, when it seemed our love must result in a more conventional marriage. I love to imagine she rides with me in the carriage, enjoying those simpler pleasures I now relish.

We shall be happy, shall we not Libussa, in our decaying Autumn days?

MICHAEL MOORCOCK (1939–) is one of the most important figures in British SF and Fantasy literature. The author of many literary novels and stories in practically every genre, he has won and been shortlisted for numerous awards including the Hugo, Nebula, World Fantasy, Whitbread and Guardian Fiction Prize. He is also a musician who performed in the seventies with his own band, the Deep Fix; and, as a member of the space-rock band, Hawkwind, won a platinum disc. His tenure as editor of NEW WORLDS magazine in the sixties and seventies is seen as the high watermark of SF editorship in the UK, and was crucial in the development of the SF New Wave. Michael Moorcock's literary creations include Hawkmoon, Corum, Von Bek, Jerry Cornelius and, of course, his most famous character, Elric. He has been compared to, among others, Balzac, Dumas, Dickens, James Joyce, Ian Fleming, J. R. R. Tolkien and Robert E. Howard. Although born in London, he now splits his time between homes in Texas and Paris.

For a more detailed biography, please see Michael Moorcock's entry in *The Encyclopedia of Science Fiction* at: http://www.sf-encyclopedia.com/.

For further information about Michael Moorcock and his work, please visit www.multiverse.org, or send S.A.E. to The Nomads Of The Time Streams, Mo Dhachaidh, Loch Awe, Dalmally, Argyll, PA33 1AQ, Scotland, or P.O. Box 385716, Waikoloa, HI 96738, USA.

MDCCXCIV

Vos Facere ☙ *Diaboli Opus*

A PRECISE MAP OF

EUROPA

AS IT WAS ON THE
Winter of 1794 AD

IN THE DAYS OF
Manfred, Ritter von Bek of Saxony

The City in the
Autumn Stars

ONGOING CONFLICTS

FRENCH REVOLUTIONARY WARS
1792 - Ongoing (2 years)
French Republic vs European Powers
Location: Europe

WAR OF THE FIRST COALITION
1792 - Ongoing (2 years)
First Coalition vs French Republic
Location: France

WAR IN THE VENDÉE
1793 - Ongoing (1 year)
French Republic vs Vendean Royalists
Location: Western France

(Red lines represent current boundaries
of the Holy Roman Empire)

SHETLAND ISLANDS

ORKNEY ISLANDS

SCOTLAND

EDINBURGH

Newcastle

THE NORTH SEA

IRELAND

ISLE OF MAN

York

DUBLIN

THE UNITED KINGDOM
OF GREAT BRITAIN AND IRELAND

Bath

LONDON

Winchester

Plymouth

ENGLISH CHANNEL

THE UNITED PROVINCES

AUSTRIAN NETHERLANDS

Rouen

PARIS

Caen

St-Malo

Nantes

Île de Ré Belle

FIRST REPUBLIC OF FRANCE

BAY OF BISCAY

Bordeaux

Cahors

Toulouse

Montpellier

ANDORRA

Coruña

San Sebastian

León

Zaragoza

Barcelona

Salamanca

MADRID

THE ATLANTIC OCEAN

KINGDOM OF PORTUGAL

Porto

LISBON

THE SPANISH EMPIRE

Valencia

IBIZA

Seville

Cadiz

Ceuta

REGENCY OF ALGIERS

ALAOUITE SULTANATE